Gordon's Hodgepodge

Gordon Offin-Amaniampong

Gordon's Hodgepodge
Copyright © 2018 by *Gordon Offin-Amaniampong.*

ISBN: 978-1-947825-47-5

All rights reserved.

No part of this publication may be reproduced, distributed, or transmitted in any form or by any means, including photocopying, recording, or other electronic or mechanical methods, without the prior written permission of the publisher, except in the case of brief quotations embodied in critical reviews and certain other noncommercial uses permitted by copyright law.

For permission requests, write to the publisher at the address below.

Yorkshire Publishing
3207 South Norwood Avenue
Tulsa, Oklahoma 74135
www.YorkshirePublishing.com
918.394.2665

Introduction

'Gordon's Hodgepodge': it's a mega basket with all kinds of fruit put together. They include, feature articles, wise sayings, riddles, satirical write-ups and short stories. It's like shopping from one store to another at a mini plaza— crisscrossing aisle by aisle, checking out the goodies at the same time doing people watching.

The stories are beautifully synchronised in a way to capture the readers' attention.

Hodgepodge is also woven like 'Kente' a signature cloth by the people of Ghana in the West Africa region. It opens the first chapter like a store, as a door greeter holds a placard with a question scrawled on its face: **Where was John**?

It follows it up with an article about one of the world's best football/soccer coaches. And that merges into a political lane, to energy, to riddles, galamsey operation, alleged scandal in Ghana's Parliament and on and on and on…

The book hooks the reader up right from the get go. And one can't drop it until one gets it all tasted and feel mesmerized!

It's a must-read Book.

Where was John?

The tyre prints were visible at his driveway. They'd been enhanced by the sludge that resulted from the rainstorm last night. He could tell a pickup truck left those marks behind. But it wasn't just a pickup truck. There were semi-trucks too.

Back of his mind remained several unanswered questions though.
What happened to the guards at the main gate?
Where were those who usually stood next to his front door?
Where were the wild dogs?
Why didn't they bark to alert him?
Were they sleeping or dreaming? What happened to all the guns he kept in his room?
Did he find those on his rooftop? And how about the military-styled –assault rifles he stashed beneath his bed?
Incredibly all was gone, nothing was left behind!
John Bull had always trusted his money, his dogs, his guns and his guards. Friends meant nothing to him. He looked down upon the people in his community—threw food away when folks were going to sleep on empty stomachs...
"I walk alone, "he said. That was his mantra.
So, where was John?
Indeed John thought he'd it all covered –all wrapped at his finger. But that was a big joke. His waterloo was shaping up. By midnight that fateful night John and everything including everybody that dwelt in his household were strangely put to sleep. Nature had lulled them into deep sleep!
With the way cleared it was time for pillaging. And the bad guys made sure not a pin was left. The big trucks left the scene so full of booty. Their huge footprints debased the face of Mother Earth. In fact he woke up the next morning and found himself naked: Butt-naked!

That means the robbers had enough time to undress the 350-pound rich man, whilst he was still snoring in his cozy bed.

But guess who came to John's rescue –the 'broke' that lived across him. The one he'd always despised. The man he'd always scorned and vilified. The man came running when he heard John howled. He put cloth on John's back, gave him food to eat and last of all consoled him for his huge loss.

"I thank God for your life," said the man to John.

Stunned by the words John asked:

"What did God do? Where was He, when the robbers robbed everything from me?

Why didn't he stop them? Was he sleeping too?"

"All that mattered was your life. You aren't dead, you're still alive in the midst of all this," the man simply replied.

It was thereafter that John understood it wasn't his wealth, not his dogs, not his guns neither his guards. The man told him he was always happy, always at peace and was always kind to others.

"See John, you know me as broke, that's an open secret. But what you probably don't know about me is this—I'm spiritually and knowledgeably rich. Besides I'm always grateful to Him that causes the sun to shine, the rain to fall, the wind to blow and the birds to sing for me when I feel lonely.

You may not like the rains or the sun or the wind but somebody likes them. Someone needs them. So, don't blame God for what you've no control over. Why chase the wind?

What do you hope to catch or achieve? How far can you pursue her? Where would that end you?

You fortified your doors fearing you'd be robbed, yet you got robed!

Why Mourihno's troubles still tail him.

Several years ago, when Cameroonian footballer Roger Miller was asked by the media whether the Indomitable Lions were the best African team: His response was (to paraphrase) the world hadn't seen the best from Africa yet.

The football legend who had helped his side to reach a quarter-final belt in the 1990 FIFA World Cup tourney staged in Italy, added they should wait and see the Brazilians of Africa. He was referring to the Black Stars of Ghana—four-time African champions in 1963, 1965, 1978, and 1982.

Mr. Miller was right. The Stars had the name, they had the players and of course they were the best at the time. They taught most African football nations how to play the most beautiful game—the Green Eagles of Nigeria can't be left out as the beneficiaries. In December 1965 the Stars humiliated Kenya national team, Harambee Stars by a whopping 13-2. It was Kenya's independence celebration!

Ironically they (the Stars) never made it to the global football fiesta. Not only that they'd been denied any trophies at the continental level much as urine has denied the fowl. That glory was fading!

Its enviable record has since been equaled and even surpassed by nations such as Egypt. In fact the Stars didn't qualify for FIFA World Cup until 2006.

What went wrong with the Stars then appears to be a similar bug that's troubling Manchester United's newly—hired Coach Jose Mourinho (former manager of Chelsea Football Club). To understand clearly why things seem not to work out for the celebrated coach one has to look at the Stars' performance back in the day.

Without a doubt the Stars wanted to end the trophy drought. They wanted to retain their past glory and put smiles back on the faces of Ghanaians. But tried as they did it turned out there was a deep-seated schism .And that division would cost the team for over a decade.

This is what cost them. The Black Stars had two most powerful players—Abedi Pele (captain) and Tony Yeboah aka Yegoala (who once captained Frankfurt, German club) '.Rumor had it that the two weren't in good terms and they'd cliques in the team. Though both denied the allegation, there was a shred of truth in that rumor or perception.

Bottom line you can't win a football match with a divided team, with no clear understanding and purposefulness. The cliques played to the tune of their idols and the end result was always abysmal and distasteful.

Lesson for Mourinho

He's one of only five coaches to have won the European Cup with two different teams. In 2009-10 he led Inter Milan to become the first Italian club to win the treble of Serie A, Coppa Italia and the UEFA Champions league. His successes in Chelsea FC were equally outstanding. He won the premier league title with a record 95 points, the club's first league title in 50 years.

And his second spell with the club in 2013 saw Chelsea winning another league championship .But he was sacked in 2015 after a poor run of results. Yes the special one as he calls himself lost favour in the eyes of his teaming supporters.

Part of the problem had to do with his leadership style. His critics see him as controversial, brusque and not playing good football. The Hazard, Costa and the Eva controversy could be seen as another factor that spurred his fall in Chelsea.

In August this year Jose Mourinho got booed by Man-United fans after substituting Spain midfielder Juan Mata just 29 minutes after introducing him from bench in United's 2-1 Community Shield win over Leister City.

On Sunday September 18 Man United were beaten by Watford 3-1, their third defeat in eight days. He said his team was low on confidence after Watford loss. Certainly confidence is one of the problems bedeviling the Red Lions. But I'm pretty sure it goes beyond that.

In association football every team has what I describe as their 'Demigods'. They are often the senior players with long term service in the club who wield power and influence. They can help make the team and they can break it too.

Zlatan Ibrahimović, Wayne Rooney, Bastian Schweinsteiger, Phil Jones, these are players with influence, hence benching anyone of them for weeks has the potential to spark indifference in the whole team regardless. Remember, I mentioned the cliques. And I'm afraid that's what Mourinho is reaping now.

Last but not least, United's world-record signing fee of 119 million pounds for France midfielder Paul Pogba could be a factor too, if for example the player in question can't find the net. He will soon become a pariah in the team. A classic example was Fernando Torres from Liverpool who joined Chelsea 2011 for a British record transfer fee of 50 million pounds.

MMDCEs Meet at Ogbojo

Did The President's Message Sink?

The setting was like a classroom or lecture hall with a teacher or a lecturer with her students prepping them up for their final year exams. It mirrored a dressing or locker room get-together where a football coach and his players often gather before a crucial match. Usually, they're psyched up and given pep talks by their head coach or manager in anticipation of the crunch match-up.

It was also like a baptismal ceremony or an induction service. The good old shepherd in frock waits on his flock and one by one he dips their bodies wrapped in sheets into a pool of water. It's a symbol of newness and spiritual up-liftment. Indeed every exercise worth its sort requires a refresher or orientation course. And it wasn't out of order that about 10 kilometres away from the Flagstaff House, Ghana's seat of government Ogbojo — a small town off Accra's outskirts on the Accra-Dodowa road (East) hosted a number of dignitaries.

On Wednesday July 5, 2017 the Ministry of Local Government & Rural Development organised an orientation programme at the Institute of Local Government Studies at Ogbojo, Accra for about 199 metropolitan, municipal and district chief executives (MMDCEs) who were recently endorsed by their respective assemblies.

And there was the President of the Republic of Ghana Akufo-Addo!

At the great hall some of them for the first time got the opportunity to meet the man who hired them and also has the power to fire them. President Akufo-Addo travelled to Ogbojo to meet with the men and women he'd appointed to steer the affairs of the metropolises, municipalities, and districts of the nation.

Like a football coach he knew the stakes couldn't be higher and his legacy is astake. His new appointees must live up to expectation and they must give a good account of themselves. Of course the message to them was as clear as a bell. And you know why the bell is significant in this context. This simile alludes to the bell's clarity.

So before he would even offer any advice to the officials the president dropped what seemed like a warning: "You all have up till Monday, July 24 to declare your assets."

All the names of the appointees would be submitted to the Attorney General's Office on Monday, July 10 after which they would have two weeks to file their assets declaration forms. Mr. Akufo-Addo said this to the MMDCEs: "That exercise will be monitored."

Also the president reminded the officials that their duties as public office holders begins with the declaration of their assets as demanded by the Public Office Holders (Declaration of Assets and Disqualification) Act, 1998, (Act 550), (Schedule 1 (V).

"It is important that the Ghanaian people understand that, for us, public service is exactly that, public service, not personal gain. The people in your districts, municipalities and metropolises are not looking for a different set of people from the last set to lord it over them, he advised. They are not looking for a new set of people to jump the red lights and traffic queues, instead of working to find solutions to the traffic jams for all of us," he told them.

Mr. Akufo-Addo asked the MMDCEs to be humble and kind towards their people as they represent central government. "You, like all of us in central and regional government, have to live up to that expectation."

And I think they really needed that. The president has prescribed the right medication. No doubt about that, yesterday's meeting was an opportune time for every appointee to make a new resolution, that's serving Mother Ghana with a true heart and refrain from serving their greedy stomachs. But that remains to be seen whether these public office holders will use these tablets and capsules or pills in the execution of their respective duties. It's ironic how most of them quickly forget their status before the new appointments.

As a people let's remember our rights to vote is very powerful. It's that single thumb that makes change happen. Your one vote gives the president the power to appoint these men and women. Nobody's vote is bigger than yours. And absolutely no one has Octopus hands that in effect make him cast more votes than the other.

See every Football coach wants victory for his team. They aren't ignorant of the fact that sometimes what they crave for don't materialise. Yet, they're constantly pursuing victory. But you have to work towards that. Victory doesn't come on a silver platter.

Interestingly, even teams that find themselves at the bottom of the league tables aren't without hopes. They always pump their hopes up. The hope that one day or someday the sky will be bright and they too can see the glowing light.

Governing a nation mimics a football game, though the former is tougher than the latter in terms of scope and size. However I think every coach when a game is on goes through what I describe as the Trauma Cycle... And I think Arsenal's head coach Arsene Wenger is a classic example. When supporters expect a win for their adorable team they lose.

And who would they blame for the loss?

It's none other than the manager, when it's even obvious that the players have failed to give a good account of themselves or live up to expectation. Charity begins at home so they say. That might probably explain why the president decided to meet with his new appointees before they get onto the pitch.

Mr. Akufo-Addo charged the new local authorities to abide by a strict code of conduct.

"Chief Executives, change will be measured in better sanitation and a more wholesome environment; people will know there is change when the quality of local schools improve; they will know there is change when there are jobs for young people; and they will know there is change when officials come to work on time," he said.

The president also assured them of his trust and emphasised that "the people of Ghana have put their hopes in us. We dare not betray their trust. This is a sacred opportunity. Join me to make this nation the happy and prosperous place it should be."

Well the coach has spoken, would the players live up to his expectation?

Tired of Politicians?

Then beware of Wednesday. Do not throw caution in the wind. Be wise and act wisely—it isn't dice throwing. You better wise up because politics is an idiotic beast. Politics divides, politics is fuzzy, and politics is too greedy.

Aren't you aware of the cliché 'winner takes all'?

I bet you are. Therefore, beware, for the stakes are beyond high, the turf is beyond rough and the campaign is beyond ugly. Matter of fact they'd get uglier and perhaps nastier as we get closer to the furnace.

What's about Wednesday one may ask?

Ghanaians will go to the polls (to elect the 5th president since the inception of the fourth republic in 1992) exactly 82 days from today, amid ridiculous promises from the presidential candidates, particularly NDC/NPP: Promises that even tick the cat off and make her wink repeatedly. Outrageous promises that spread their wings from Axim in the south to Zanzugutatale in northern Ghana.

To begin with, if they couldn't put money into your pockets, failed to increase your allowances and the promise to help every teacher own two cars or build his/her own houses in 2012, what makes you think that the 2016 promises will be fulfilled.

Don't we get it folks?

American theologian and author James Freeman Clark wrote this: 'The difference between a politician and a statesman is that a politician thinks about the next election while the statesman thinks about the next generation."

"I have a deep and profound mistrust of all politicians," says television host and a stand-up comedian Craig Ferguson (Scottish-American).

Indeed it's common knowledge that not every village or community in Ghana has electricity or connected to the national power grid. First graders know this. Head porters are aware and the unschooled need not to be schooled about this.

So why promise to provide every house in Ghana with a meter when undying 'Dumsor' stands like an Egyptian mummy over heads? It's like putting a cart before the horse.

And did I hear someone mention one factory to a village? Wait a minute...

Is this feasible? I mean is this realistic?

What happened to all the GIHOC factories President Nkrumah built in the 60's?

They were left to rot right?

Oh guess who is calling the kettle black!

"The NPP are saying free education system, this is not doable," said president Mahama in 2012. It is doable Mr. President. This scheme was first introduced by the first president Dr. Nkrumah. It was piloted in the northern region and it worked successfully.

He continued: "We can't develop our country education without paying teachers full salaries and other benefits. When I am voted into power, I promise you Ghanaian teachers that arrears, back pay, promotions and increments will not be a problem at all."

Are you really sure about that Mr. President?

And the promises continue to flow unfettered——from one sea one town, one bank one community to providing tablets to all Ghanaian school pupils and building stadia across the three northern regions to the Brong Ahafo region.

Warwick Leslie Smith, an Australian politician once said: 'Politicians must choose either stand up for what they believe or maximize their vote. To put it bluntly they either lie or they lose"

Warwick a liberal member of the Australian House of Representatives from December 1984 to March1993 representing the Division of Bass, Tasmania noted that few people expect politicians to tell the truth and few are particularly surprised or affected when lies are exposed."

The question is do politicians care about lying?

They don't. Warwick is right—their aim is to 'maximize votes', capture power, line their pockets with state funds and consolidate power. In developing democracies where incumbent governments make desperate attempts to retain power tension often hits apogee before, during and after elections.

I ain't a clairvoyant but I can assure you it won't be an ordinary Wednesday. The temperature will soar, the players will be up to the game and observers as usual will be worried. But peace will triumph over anarchy and chaos.

BAD GOVERNANCE
The Cause of NDC Defeat in 2016 Elections

The National Democratic Congress (NDC) lost the battle for the Flagstaff House on Wednesday 7, December 2016. It was the party's third defeat in 25 years since the inception of the Fourth Republic in 1992. The first and the second losses happened on the 7th of December 2000 and December 7 2004 respectively with late President John Atta Mills then as the party's nominee.

It was a comeback victory for the former tax master and a law professor in December 2008. On the 7th of January 2009, and the 7th of January 2013 the NDC took the reins of power again under presidents John Mills and John Mahama respectively. And then the biggest defeat many dread to talk about or hear—the 2016 general elections. It was a humiliation for the NDC They lost sorely to their arch rival the NPP, the New Patriotic Party.

From the woods the Elephant came like a beast gone wild and mauled its prey. 88 days on, it seems the umbrella family hasn't recovered yet. The shock was too strong too deep— warranting an investigation, if you like a post-mortem to find out the cause of defeat.

· On Monday 4 April, 2017 before noon Pacific Time, I chanced upon what seemed like a dossier on a business tycoon who'd passed on, amid controversy over his debts, his will, his estates, his wealth and what caused his death. I rubbed my eyes to make sure if I was seeing things right and whether the coroner's report had indeed captured the sentiments of the people.

He did. Cause of death was terrible. It's a contagious disease called 'Polimyelitics', as deadly as bubonic plague. It's dreadful—something no one would want to face or contract it. However, the coroner was raw in his delivery. He didn't cover up anything that would perhaps resurrect to haunt them tomorrow.

Instead he'd catalogued all his findings in bullet points or highlighted them in asterisk. And point after points he pointedly spelt out what went wrong. What caused the astronomic debts, what brought about the apathy, what produced the resentment, the disillusionment and how things got to where they landed?

The tycoon led a self-centred or egoistic life, according to the report. He was extravagant and beyond that he mismanaged not only his wealth but also state resources, recommending that all monies lost must be refunded. Here is one of the quotes I lifted from the 13-member ad hoc committee's preliminary report.

"John Dramani Mahama's intolerance and desire to enrich himself overnight was a factor. The President was too divisive. He never respected the leadership of the party which resulted in the running of a parallel campaign."

If you didn't catch the first line well, it implied that 'intolerance and desire for wealth were among the factors that caused NDC's defeat in the 2016 general polls.

And I think I can sum it all up in two words 'Bad Governance'.

Also I am tempted to give readers a few of the findings plus a recommendation: The report noted that "The arrogance of some members of the party was also a factor. Especially, Kwaku Boahen, Kofi Adams, Solomon Nkansah, Felix Kwakye Ofosu, Stan Dogbe, Omane Boamah etc. They never respected the Ghanaian voter and thought they could use propaganda to win an election."

Among others the committee recommended: "JM should not be allowed to lead the party in the future. A new face will save the party from further embarrassment."

Up to a point I had to pause and catch my snort. How could one man be responsible for all that I wondered? Then I reminded myself with this old maxim: "Uneasy lies the head that wears the crown'. Indeed, you will never know how it feels like until you wear it. Until you walk the talk you will miss what I call the life line or the safe line.

The Elephant had walked here before. And time will tell if they would be able to avoid all the trappings. You can walk the fine line, give fine promises, wear fine clothes, commission fine projects –like the Kwame Nkrumah Circle Interchange in Accra (what's the other name they gave it—'Dubai') but if you miss the life line– the one that connects you to the people (the ruler and the ruled) then it's over. Frenchman would say 'Ce'st fini'.

Those that plod on Jupiter's surface can afford to walk naked on Earth without a flinch. Why? The reason, we cannot see them even though we have eyes. Our ears are as large as a barge and they're wide awake yet they can't hear. I'm being sarcastic right?

Yes, governments in Africa and for that matter Ghana often don't have the listening ears. Tell them you need schools and roads, they would provide you I-Pads and I-Phones. Ask for jobs and higher remunerations they would give you V8's and meters when there's no power in the first place. Tell them to decrease high spending (cut cost) they would rather increase it. Ask for energy they would tell you, you don't need that. They'd provide you a footbridge and outboard motors instead. And when you ask for health facilities they would be branding buses.

Does that make sense?

No it doesn't but it shows you how insensitive our politicians can be. They appear to be caught up in their own bubbles. And it seems to be a never-ending rendition: Government after governments repeat it as though they aren't familiar with what goes on in Ghana. They tend to forget that democracy is government for the people and not for the government. It's by the people and not by the government. Supreme power is vested in the people and exercise by them and it's my hope that one day things would change for the better. And one day our leaders will see the bright light.

That said, I should commend the NDC's ad hoc committee chaired by Dr. Kwesi Botchway for coming out with this report. Not every NDC member may like it because it stepped toes and ruffled feathers.

But that's how democracy is all about. The report might not be a perfect one, but it seemed to me it's a step in the right direction. I think its move to prevent recurrence of such defeat is timely and appropriate. .They say once bitten twice shy. And you don't throw caution out of the window when you see a neighbour's beard is on fire.

Lavish Tombstone

Is this Opunis way to unveil his Opulence?

Bibianiha has gone viral on the Social Media. The small town has become a cynosure. Until probably the past Monday June 19, 2017 about 99.9 per cent of Ghana's population knew nothing about her. It's archetypal farming community—peaceful and perhaps quiet during night times.

Over the weekend the small town which is located in the middle belt of Ghana, precisely in the Brong Ahafo region caught the intrepid eyes of the Paparazzi and many from far and near because of what one funeral expert described as a 'lavish' tombstone built by the Opuni family to memorialise their departed mother.

The deceased woman was said to be a successful cocoa farmer and had businesses throughout the region and even beyond.

It is understood the Upright tombstone, which stands like a self-contained house was jointly financed by the former Ghana COCOBOD Boss Dr. Stephen Opuni and his siblings (an aristocratic family sort of). According to the local media the edifice 'shocked 'and 'surprised' many that attended the funeral or saw it on the Social Media.

The cost of the headstone is not known. But given the backlash Dr. Opuni had received in recent times regarding his alleged involvement in some financial impropriety at the COCOBOD, I wondered whether the former CEO made the good judgement.

It's reported Dr. Opuni's siblings had expressed similar concern.

"But for the political consequences our brother might suffer considering our polarised political environment and the associated mischiefs, we would have constructed something more elegant than what has become a public issue," his siblings said.

Tombstone or Headstone

Traditionally, materials like marble, granite, and field stone are used to make headstones to venerate the dead. Some manufacturers choose or prefer to use concrete, wood, bronze, sandstone, limestone, iron and other similar materials too. In the United States, an upright headstone shall cost up to $10,000. Nonetheless one can get simple upright tombstones in the range of $1,000 to $3,000. So the average cost of gravestone is$1,500 to $2,000. However companion headstones are priced higher than the ones made for individuals.

Now let's put Dr. Opuni mother's tombstone into perspective vis-à-vis the wall and the land space. Given its sheer size I think it was built probably for the family. It fits into a companion headstone category, which possibly can accommodate more than four people. Thus the cost of the project could be put in the region of $20,000 about GHc 60,000.

Without a doubt the edifice has generated lots of argument. Dr. Andrews Prempeh a neurosurgeon based in Canada reacted to it via his twitter handle and facebook wall. He described the criticism as 'primitive', adding the practice is a common one and nearly everyone who loses the mother feels bereft."

He however advised the public not to build such tombstones. I" think such tombs shouldn't be constructed in the cities because of scarcity of lands."

Political Consequences

I certainly don't think the storm has the wall as its main target, things happen and they happen for a reason. As matter of fact before walls were built there were storms. They've been there since creation. However, the conflict between the two began when walls strayed into storms' pathway.

And this is why many are talking about this issue. Yes it's their own money and they can choose to do whatever they decide on. But, did he Dr. Opuni consider the political ramifications? Is this Opunis way to unveil his Opulence? Couldn't he and his siblings have perhaps set up a foundation to help the poor and needy in society?

Be reminded, beforehand, Dr. Opuni and his brothers knew that constructing such a monument in a tiny town, where probably the satellite villages aren't connected to the national power grid, probably his neighbour's children cannot afford three square meal in a day, possibly there are dropouts because most parents can't afford their children's school fees etc. In fact, it truly begs the question.

Indeed Ghanaians revere the dead so much so that funerals have become the heartbeat of Ghanaians' social life. Profligate spending on funerals has no doubt sparked criticism from political and religious leaders.

Charles Gabriel Palmer-Buckle, the Archbishop of Accra, said this sometime ago: "We are investing in the dead rather than the living ... and that is bad. The surest way to remember the dead is not the type of coffins used to bury them nor is not the type of cloth or T-shirt won during their funerals, but doing something positive for the dead which would benefit the living."

To say funerals in Ghana cost fortune is an understatement. An average funeral should cost between $15, 000 to $20,000' Burial $689.00 and the installation of a headstone. Compared to the United States, today the average North American traditional funeral costs between $7,000 and $10,000. This price range includes the services at the funeral home, burial in a cemetery.

Cremation

In the US Cremation starts at $489-$589. But that practice isn't popular in my native land. The first public figure in Ghana who opted that he be cremated after his death was Vice president of the 4th Republic Kow Nkensen Arkaah who died in April 2001. The next distinguished Ghanaian whose name quickly comes to mind is a couture designer Kofi Ansah.

Kofi Annan Has Spoken

Would The Leaders Listen?

A leader must listen...A good leader must be a good follower—Busumuru Kofi Annan

'Stop, Look and Listen" used to be railroad warning sign for motorists and pedestrians until flashing lights and gates were installed. The message was single and simple: Beware of approaching trains. There comes a time that we need to do self-inventory. To see how far we've come and strike a balance so that we don't get caught up in the drudgeries of life. As humans we need advice, we need to be talked to and we need to change our ways of doing things.

Apostle Paul had such engagement with the Church of Corinth (1 Corinthians 3:2). It was a speech meant for the people he'd once mentored. The Corinthians had metaphorically become accustomed to feeding on milk and there was the need for them to gravitate from milk to bones—signifying maturity but it seemed they weren't ready hence Paul's speech.

On Thursday August 10, 2017 at Mfanstipim College a former old student, an illustrious Ghanaian, a diplomat extraordinaire was welcomed by his college and class mates. There were also other special dignitaries at the event. The second President of the Fourth Republic John Kufuor— a Prempeh old student was present. The former UN Secretary General Kofi Annan was once here at this prestigious Methodist school and he completed his education here in 1957 the same year Ghana then Gold Coast had independence.

Like Apostle Paul he'd been invited by the Old Students Association to come and share his invaluable experience with them and the world. Though a mate he's seen as a mentor, though once a student he's seen as a trail blazer, a teacher and a prime mover.

His speech was pregnant with hopes, advices and encouragements. Not only that it was so uplifting so assuring and so inspiring. But it wasn't also devoid of admonishment. Mr. Annan called on African leaders to listen to their people and invest in the youth of their countries.

The renowned diplomat who was speaking in a lecture dubbed "An afternoon with Kofi Annan," in the Central regional capital Cape Coast said: "The only path towards growth and development on the African continent is to invest in the youth."

The lecture themed "leadership and public service" was organised by the old students of Mfanstipim College to fashion out a new path to leadership and public service. Indeed most African leaders have lost touch with the people, a problem he's very familiar with. The former UN Boss said: "A leader must listen...A good leader must be a good follower. When leaders fail to lead, the people lead the leader follows," he emphasised.

Mr. Annan believes leaders of Africa must do and can do more to help their teeming youth, noting that for a continent whose youth are challenged with poverty, lack of education and jobs, it was time for the leaders to invest in them.

Still on the youth Mr. Annan made reference to former Afriican leaders who were themselves youth when they assumed the reins of power. "We must remember the youth of our past leader Dr. Kwame Nkrumah and Abdul Nasser both were presidents of Ghana and Egypt at ages 48 and 38 respectively."

According to him African leaders must be preoccupied with "enhancing the welfare of their people" and "invest in a democratic Africa. We must offer growing population the opportunity for employment," he said.

Indeed this is what Apostle Paul did when he realised that the Church he helped to nurture and mentor was backsliding and everything seemed to be going wayward.

Certainly, the Corinthians faced several challenges. They were dealing with lawsuits among believers, case of incest, sexual immorality, idolatry etc. This happened in the Apostolic Age—people didn't have much, the brethren broke bread together, lived together and shared together.

Today, we are in an advanced world. We live in an age dubbed 'Technological Age—the age of science and technology. We've been able to put man on the Moon, built I-phones, I-pads and robots. We've been able to reduce the size of the globe through internet connectivity. The age has come up with drones and other stunning devices. And it seems everything is now on a fast-lane and at high-speed.

Yet, like the people of Corinth we in Africa are dealing with several if not many problems—poverty, hunger, diseases, wars, droughts, unemployment and many more. Africa is facing huge problems which require not just solutions but immediate solutions that would transform the lives of the youth.

And once again Mr. Annan couldn't state it better. He hit the nail right on the head:

"Africa is at a crossroads, counting on its leaders to make good decisions that will change the destinies of the countries on the continent. The decisions we take today can determine whether we can ride the waves ahead, more than ever our future is in our hands. We ride the wave that began long ago at independence," he said.

Who is Mr. Kofi Annan?

He's a career diplomat born to Ghanaian parents in Kumasi on the April 8, 1938. Mr. Annan became the 7th UN Secretary General from January 1997 to December 2006, and has since presided over a number of challenging global issues including the threat of terrorism. The former UN Boss and the UN were the co-recipients of the 2001 Nobel-Peace Prize. And he's also the chairman and founder of the Kofi Annan Foundation in Accra Ghana.

Currently resident in his native home Ghana, Annan said leaders "cannot pretend to have all the answers." Therefore there was the need for them to demand better engagement with civil society groups on the continent.

"We must look beyond the state and build a strong civil society which is just as important. The continent's development cannot come from a single leader. We each have a role to play," he concluded.

Was it Mother of all Lectures?

Dr. Bawumia's breathtaking lecture on the state of Ghana's economy:

Old wounds appeared revived and caused wide-eyed in Ghana's capital city-Accra: The National Theatre the-last-minute-venue for the NPP vice presidential nominee's public lecture didn't disappoint its august guests. It lived up to expectation.

It was themed: "The State of Ghana's Economy—A foundation of Concrete or Straw?"

And it mimicked a town-hall-styled debate attended by dignitaries, journalists and diplomats from across Ghana. Since that surreal public discourse on Thursday, I'm yet to observe anyone or group of persons from the other side of the aisle thrust a double-edged sword or a knife into Dr. Mahamudu Bawumia's 'toasted bread'.

The profound delivery and repeated applauds that greeted the address emphasised its veracity. There'd however, been a few criticisms from the civil society among them economic Think Tank—IMANI, with regard to the dollar rates. It points out that there were inconsistencies in the rates he uses for his analysis.

With a 'broad brush' the architect of the lecture meticulously painted the state of the nation's economy in a way that wowed the crowd. It resonated… amid emotional appeals to register their displeasure as if to say– 'never again shall we go to sleep this long'.

But what did he (Dr. Bawumia) do differently, that made most Ghanaians act as though it was the first time they learned about the sordid state of the economy or Ghana's woes?

Sydney Casely -Hayford a member of OccupyGhana crafted it so beautifully: "The dexterity with which the former second deputy governor of the Bank of Ghana uses data and figures to his advantage always gets the governing party flummoxed."

The question is how long would this well-delivered message stay with the Ghanaian voting public as they head to the general elections in December 2016?

And as this writer points out, generally Ghanaians seem to be suffering from a mundane disease called 'forgetfulness' (it isn't dementia)

—which tend to favour politicians very often but to the disadvantage of the citizenry.

It is ironic a voter would forget all the troubles he's been going through for years. Just drop him a bag of rice, GHc50, cooking oil and sardine. That's all it takes—problem solved. A major reason why politicians have taken us for granted.

Meanwhile, 'Dumsor' is undying, unemployment still lurks around, inflation bouncing year-in-year-out, public debt ballooning, fiscal deficit peaking, minimum wage thinning, exchange rate fluctuating, GDP per capital tanking and GDP growth relapsing.

Thankfully, the lecture which could be described as Bawumia's campaign speech kicked off in a different style. This kind of style seldom happens. Very rare to see African leaders debate on issues or engage in political/social discourse without maligning or hurling abusive epithets at each other or one another . It seems to be a norm we've charitably embraced.

But the astute economist broke the gremlin during the public lecture and shed more light on the state of Ghana's economy. All it took was power-point presentation, illustration, facts and figures, imageries and metaphor to wake up many Ghanaians from their slumber. And he kept going on and on—cataloguing, comparing and contrasting.

"Virtually every single economic indicator proves that while the eight years under the NPP 2001 and 2009 were better than these last eight years under the NDC, NDC's first four years under late president Mills were even far better than these last four years under John Mahama," he said.

He went on to say that: "Under the eight years of NPP government, from 2001 to 2009, taxes and loans amounted to GHC20 billion. In contrast, taxes, oil revenues and loans alone under the eight-year period of 2009-2016 would amount to some GHC 248billion. The Mills-Mahama government would have had in eight years more than 12 times the nominal resources that the NPP had."

I still maintain, I haven't read or heard from the ruling party's side any compelling article(s) that attempted to perforate the facts and figures presented by Dr. Bawumia.

Would that cut be deeper than what the renowned economist showcased?

Is there one?

Mr. Okudzeto Ablakwa, a deputy minister of education has taken Dr. Bawumia on. His criticism bordered on the education sector and the claims by Dr. Bawumia that the NPP established University of Mines and Technology UMaT at Tarkwa in the western region. He described the largest opposition party nominee's lecture as 'intellectually dishonest.'

He said: "It was intellectually dishonest for him to claim that it was the NNP that established UMaT which had existed under various forms since 1952."

The minister also mentioned two polytechnics in the Upper west and east regions: "Bolgatanga and Wa polytechnics were established in 1999 and had enrolled students long before the NPP came to power: His claims that the NPP established both polytechnics are untrue," Mr. Ablakwa noted.

'In any case Dr. Bawumia should be telling Ghanaians why they failed in eight years to fulfil their promise of establishing polytechnic in every district as contained on page 29 of the NPP's 2000 manifesto."

So let's assume both parties failed to deliver. Both reneged on the promises they gave and couldn't go by their own blueprint. However, let's do some kind of assessment: Assessment not based on the abovementioned factors either macro or micro economic indicators. Let's be honest though and ask ourselves this question— which of the two parties (NDC OR NPP) took Ghana into HIPC (heavily indebted poor country)?

Was it NDC OR NPP? It was the NDC.

Which party took Ghana out from HIPC? Was it NPP or the NDC? The answer is NPP

How did Ghana's economy fare at the time? Fairly robust, the country witnessed major influx of foreign investors and there was business and economic boom.

When did Ghana lift its first oil? March 2011.

It earned a whopping $112,271, 187 from 995,259 barrels of crude oil lifted from the Ghana Jubilee Fields at Cape Three Points in the western region, according to official figures.

And under which party's administration did this windfall happen? The answer is the NDC.

Is the economy better today than it was in the HIPC era, given all the problems that confront the country?

Where is all the oil money?

The proof is truly in the pudding.

The Fight Against Land Grabbing Has Begun

Is this battle Winnable?

Ghana's lands are fast dwindling and we cannot afford to lose them. The forest cover has changed and the threat to wildlife, water bodies etc. are imminent, according to its forest data. Between 1990 and 2000 the country lost an average of 135, 400 hectares of forest per year. That amounts to an average annual deforestation rate of 1.82 per cent.

Overall, between 1990 and 2005 Ghana lost 25.9 % of its forest cover or around 1, 932,000 hectares. Indeed the above numbers tell it all but it could be worse. Yes, I'm pretty sure today's (2005-2017) data wouldn't be pleasant, given the rate at which our lands are being sold indiscriminately and the wanton destruction of the ecology by Galamsey operators over the last decade.

Thus, I couldn't agree more with the Lands and Natural Resources Minister on his clarion call that's seeking to stop the sale of state lands. Mr. Peter John Amewu has warned officials of Lands Commission across the nation to halt the sale of state lands with immediate effect.

The sector minister, who was inaugurating a newly constituted 30-member Volta Regional Lands Commission in Ho, also issued this fiat: "The practice where a few politicians, political parties, people who consider themselves rich, fight and grab government lands shall no longer continue under President Nana Akufo-Addo. The past is gone and we are in a new era where democratic practices will need to direct the citizens that we are really taking good care of their resources"

"Yeate Abre." Someone said that to me in Ghanaian Twi Language: Meaning we've heard these kinds of threat from government officials many times. We've seen the chest beaters and those that pound the tables, yet with no fruitful results. They've failed to back their threats with action, according to the concerned citizen.

So, Mr. Amewu I put this to you.

Art thou he that should come, or do we look for another? (Matthew 11: 3 KJV).

See, ants aren't elephants but they've giant plans. They don't procrastinate. They attach eagerness to their work and they always ensure that they've enough food in the barn to feed not only for themselves but also their not yet born. And I shudder to say we haven't proven to be good custodians with regard to our lands. The ants have stockpiled their barn while ours is tanking by the day.

Our forebears bequeathed to us fat lands: Lands that stretched from Accra to Zagreb and beyond. They left us lands that had abundant resources stored up to take care of tomorrow. We used to have picturesque landscapes. We used to have greenbelts that mirrored the Amazon in Brazil. Backyard gardens took care of households and families.

Do we still have them today?

Before we lived here they'd lived here. But they didn't rob the lands of their resources. The forest maintained her virginity. Even though they farmed a lot they preserved their sanctity. How about the streams and rivulets? Tiny as they were they still maintained their status regardless.

The endangered species were protected. When was the last time you sighted a four-legged (I am not referring to domestic animals) in the thicket near you? The threat level of their very existence has crescendoed. And that steady increase is a warning to humanity. Just like the trees. Back in the day, gold, diamond and other mineral resources had a sanctuary. They weren't bastardised as we've done to them today.

Today all of them are facing extinction. God forbid if we continue this way we would have nothing to show posterity. It appears every pocket of land today in our big cities has a property on it. For example, lands earmarked for schools, clinics, roads, malls and stores or amusement parks have often been encroached by either squatters or land guards. Unfortunately, we've painstakingly, fought to deface, deplete and destroy the lands.

The Lands Minister says the indiscriminate and aggressive disposal of state and government lands for private use across the country will no longer be tolerated. According to him, the country depends heavily on land to execute projects to ensure socio-economic development. He emphasised government's resolve to eradicate poverty and unemployment through the 'One District One Factory' and the Planting for Food and Jobs,' adding that the projects would be executed on lands, and that adequate steps would therefore be taken to protect all government lands across the country.

Compensations

One problem that has often dogged lands sale in Ghana is the issue of compensation. Fair play is jettisoned and in most occasions land owners are unjustifiably treated. Mr. Amewu said the issue must be addressed without any recourse. He therefore charged the Commission to ensure due diligence to address the concerns of aggrieved land owners, who have not been paid compensation after the State acquired the lands.

"In addressing these concerns, the Regional Lands Commission, is expected to take strong measures to curb the activities of quack surveyors in the region, whose work encourages conflicts over land ownership resulting in delays in the payment of compensations," he added.

Dr. Archibald Letsa, the Volta Regional Minister, who is championing the fight against indiscriminate disposal of government lands to private individuals in the region has tasked the Commission to take hard steps to address challenges facing land administration in the area.

Meanwhile, the chairperson of the newly-constituted Volta Regional Lands Commission, Mama Dzidoasi, has charged the members of the Commission to be truthful and fearless in the discharge of their duties to protect the integrity of the Commission.

She also pledged to work in partnership with the various Municipal and District Assemblies to carry out an inventory of State acquired and occupied lands to ensure the execution of government's infrastructural projects.

Finally, to Mr. Amewu, I wish you good luck in your fight against land grabbing in Ghana. I've chosen to call it World War II. Galamsey, illegal mining is the First World War, which is still ongoing. As you're well aware none of the battles is going to be easy. To win these battles, you'll need the unwavering support of the government. And I think anything short of that would backfire. Nevertheless, I think you've demonstrated commitment and eagerness so far. Remember, you've today picked up a fight not with your enemies but your cohorts, friends, kinsmen, politicians. But do I need to remind you of this biblical line: 'How can Satan fight against Satan," remarked Jesus.

Who's to Blame: The Weather or the Ghanaian?

If the weather could impersonate mankind he would probably not survive a day. He could get harassed, threatened or lynched by some angry folks or mobsters. If he's lucky to survive that, the litigants amongst us would pursue him. He could be sued and if he refuses to go to court he might be subpoenaed and possibly end up imprisoned for life. Why?

I may be wrong but I think the weather get blamed for almost everything under the sun that goes wrong. It's the weather that causes allergies—the runny nose, coughs, watery eyes and the sneezes. It's the weather that causes drought, erosions or runoffs. It's certainly the weather that causes the thunderstorms, the rainstorms, the squalls, the cyclones, the tornadoes, the blizzards, the twisters, the typhoons and the monsoons.

In apropos, the weather is like the policeman in Nigeria or the politician in Ghana. He's like the pastor in South Africa, the teacher in Kenya or the footballer in Brazil. The weather is like the immigrant or Muslim in the US, the doctor in Cuba or the surgeon in Venezuela. The weather is like the carpenter's Son in Jerusalem or the bride in India.

Indeed these guys get blamed for everything that goes wrong. The rest of us are holy and we can never be faulted.

When farmers get low yields they blame it on the weather. When intoxicators run into ditches and get stiches they say it's the weather. I get it. At times the weather could be blamed for accidents and incidents that occur on our roads. However, we cannot blame the weather for everything. I'm inclined to believe that pretty soon our school children would blame the weather for poor academic performance because that's what we're teaching them.

Initially my architect had suggested I cited Satan because the bad guy is blamed more than the weather. But Satan is on sabbatical leave. Beside the master designer told me this: Never give Satan credit. When things go wrong or when everything is tumbling look into yourself first before you start to blame someone else.

Yeah, Satan is on vacation. On the eve of his departure I overhead my neighbour pray like this: "I bind you Satan, I paralyse you and I cast you into the bottomless pit." That was Sunday night. On midnight Monday it was 'Aluta Continua'.

May I ask: Is the weather responsible for the Tamale Teaching Hospital incident that happened yesterday?

Are we supposed to blame the weather for unemployment or the poor state of Ghana's economy?

Can we blame the weather for ghost names in our payroll systems/?

Is the weather the cause of fire outbreaks in our petrol stations?

How about using petrol stations as lorry terminals?

Let's remember, if we don't flee we would get fleeced.

Fact is we cannot run away from ourselves. And we cannot blame others all the time for our troubles... How can you steal the textbooks at your school and turn around to blame the politician in Accra.

Paradoxically, in Ghana the politician is the 'All Sinner'. Yes the Ghanaian politician is like the weather. He represents the Almighty Weather and it's his fault that the tap isn't running and not the Water Company. Dumsor is all governments fault too. How about those illegal power connectors? How about ECG or GRIDCO or PURC? If the cookies don't turn out well it's the politician and not the baker or the chef. . The politician causes examination malpractices and poor exams results and not the pupil, the teacher or the parent.

Traffic isn't moving, who's to blame? It's the politician. The traditional rulers are selling stool lands, town lands and community lands to illegal small-scale miners (Galamsey Operators) regardless. The water bodies are being destroyed, the lands are being degraded, the forests are being demolished, and the soils are desecrated. Yet the blame is on the politician.

I think it's about time we did self-inventory and stop the blame game. The rot in Ghana isn't peculiar to the politician. It isn't capsid disease (Kum Akate) which is probably limited to cocoa. It's a widespread disease. Journalists are corrupt, civil servants, teachers, judges, nurses, doctors, pastors, queens and kings, bankers, and the list goes on.

How do you deal with Phantoms?

We have a problem, let's admit. It's a huge problem because in Ghana he who fights the ghosts fights the living too. And the ghosts are still in town drawing huge sums of salaries at the expense of the Ghanaian taxpayer. You might be aware of the rot the Youth Employment Agency (YEA) discovered recently. *Isn't that stunning?*

The Agency says it has transferred some members of staff to various regions across the country as a measure to stem corruption.

A statement from YEA explained that the transfer was part of an "ongoing restructuring exercise to reposition the Agency for higher productivity."

The move followed days after a payroll fraud was discovered at the Agency. And internal audit carried out by agency exposed a huge financial malfeasance believed to have cost the country GH $50 million.

The amount is believed to be a sum of unearned salaries paid to unposted beneficiaries, funds for official use which were paid into personal accounts, and procurement without adherence to due process. Earlier this year, YEA suspended the payment of allowances to over 60,000 beneficiaries on suspicion of discrepancies in the report handed to it by the managers under the previous administration.

The full-scale audit revealed that many people who did not deserve to receive money from the Agency were doing so fraudulently. So far, the Agency under the new managers has deleted some 16,839 names from the payroll, which it says has saved the country Ghc20 million.

And as YEA is fighting the ghosts in Accra, residents in Tamale in the northern region are dealing with the Kandahar Boys a vigilante group affiliated to the governing New Patriotic Party. The group was said to have stormed a news conference and vandalised properties. It's also understood one person sustained injury.

Reports said the press conference was been held to mobilise residents to demonstrate against one Dr. Daniel Akobila who allegedly stormed the Tamale Teaching Hospital to take over as the new CEO.

According to media reports there was a standoff at the hospital after the CEO Dr. Prosper Akambong refused to hand over the post claiming he hadn't received any letter from any higher authority to stand down from his post.

Why should this happen? Where did justice go? And can we blame Satan for this?

ASHAIMAN: The Eye of the NDC

How Did The Party Conduct Herself?

And they began to see…

The Mandela Park at Ashaiman in the Greater Accra region played host to the opposition National Democratic Congress (NDC's) 25th anniversary rally on Saturday 10, June 2017. The sprawling town known to be the bastion of the NDC is nestled between the twin cities in the region —Tema, the port city and Accra, Ghana's capital.

Basically, it was time for sober reflection and time to see how best the party could stage a comeback in 2020. Unity was a common strand that ran through speech after speeches given by its speakers. But the rally lacked electricity and the usual crowd-storm. Truly, the Saturday's crowd didn't compare or come close to the multitude that attended then NDC's parliamentary candidate Ernest Norgbey's campaign launch in October 2016.

However, one could argue that perhaps crowd wasn't the centrality of the rally. It had more nuggets on its bowl to digest. The rank and file was asked to eschew bickering, back-biting and back stabbing as well as reposition itself to face the governing NPP in the next general elections. They believed this was the way to go if the party meant business.

After all who likes to remain in hibernation or stay in opposition?

The last December's election defeat was the party's third. It lost the 2000, 2004 and 2016. One of its main speakers admonished the Umbrella family not to 'fight over spilt milk' but look beyond the fall. Fact is it hurts so badly to lose power especially in Africa and for that matter Ghana, where being in opposition can be equated to being in Siberia. What it does is it makes one see things clearer and bolder. Thus the NDC wouldn't like to see another humiliation, another defeat and another Siberia. What do they say: "Once bitten twice shy" or thrice beaten quadruple shy. Not again, they seem to be echoing that now as the ashes in Ashaiman begin to rise.

Following the party's defeat in the 2016 elections there have been some rancorous and unhealthy development. And members of the largest opposition party in Ghana have resorted to the proverbial blame game.

How did the party conduct itself during the rally?

Yes, the rally lacked the proverbial pomp but it wasn't denied with the big-wigs—those that dug the trenches and got their hands dirty. The founder and former President Jerry John Rawlings was at the rally to sell unity to the party. He also used the occasion to resell his signature products –probity, accountability and honesty.

He gave this admonition: "How many times have we not gone through this stage? I say if we are serious, we are genuine, we are sincere, and that unity can work. Power corrupts us too quickly, too easily. We need to re-examine ourselves. We need some serious education," he admonished the party.

Mr. Rawlings told the gathering, the ball was in their court to prevent the process of unity from being hijacked. He also touched on the theme of unity that echoed through the statements made at the rally. To him, "... unity is a beautiful thing but it comes at a price - truthfulness, sincerity etc." He agreed with the sentiments that the party stands a chance of returning to power in 2020 if they do their homework well.

Another big-wig that graced the Ashaiman NDC 25th anniversary rally was former President John Mahama. He took a course this writer describes as a 'safe route'. Possibly he did so to put himself firmly at the driver's seat (as the putative candidate) in the NDC 2020 presidential race. Already there are names mushrooming to contest the former president.

Speaking at the rally Mr. Mahama didn't blame the party's foot soldiers or the surrogates. He didn't blame the campaign strategists or those with sharp teeth for the party's defeat. Instead, he literally claimed responsibility. "I have accepted all blame as a leader of the party. And I am confident and I pray that after the re-organisation we shall win as party," he said.

According to Mr. Mahama, what matters in life is not how many times one falls but "...how you survive and make new impact". He appealed to party members to "...stop crying over spilt milk and instead think of how to get new milk to enjoy". He further expressed confidence that with appropriate re-organisation, the party shall win.

Also in attendance were the General Secretary of the NDC Asiedu Nketiah, and his deputy Koku Anyidoho, the Chairman Kofi Portuphy, former ministers of state and parliamentarians both sitting and former.

There was also time for a few jabs to be thrown at the governing NPP. And guess who spearheaded that Former Vice President Kwesi Amissah-Arthur. He seized the occasion to challenge the ruling NPP to answer all the 170 promises the party made to Ghanaians ahead of the 2016 elections.

"I have been told that they have made 170 promises. They have to ensure that all those 170 promises are fulfilled so the people of Ghana can also benefit from the work that they came to do. "

The NPP during the electioneering campaign made a number of promises which include, free education, free health care, building 216 factories across the country, building an irrigation dam in each farming community in northern Ghana, and disbursing $1 million dollars each to the 275 constituencies across the country.

Mr. Amissah-Arthur pointed out that it was important for the NDC as a party to hold the Akufo-Addo government accountable. He also urged the NDC to continue to champion the agenda of the people. "This agenda is simple: we have to protect the interest of our people. We have to ensure that the NPP government meets all the promises that they made," the former Vice President said.

Like the previous speakers Mr. Amissah-Arthur called for unity in the NDC, saying it was time the party closed its ranks after the December defeat. "The 2016 election is over and it is important for us to move on because the agenda of the Ghanaian people is important. We must unite our people so that we can work together combining all strengths and attributes of the people in the NDC so that we can work for the good of this country."

The NDC was formed on Tuesday 28, July 1992, more or less as a lateral branch of the then ruling Provisional National Defence Council (PNDC) under the chairmanship of Jerry John Rawlings. Ghana at the time was transitioning into multi-party system of democracy after eleven years of the military ruler.

The party went on to win the first two elections of the fourth republic under the leadership of Mr. Rawlings .It must be noted that the 1992 parliamentary elections was boycotted by then main opposition party the NPP. NDC won 189 out of the 200 seats.

The Tribute: A Widow Pours Her Heart Out

O' woman where didst thou get thy strength?
Where didst thou get thy love?
Thou unshakable love
Thou make thy story seem like a painless one
Restless thy heart yearns. She longs for her King
O' king why didst disappear from thy bosom friend?
Did thou know that thy light has hit the twilight?
Didst thou Maker tell you about this flight?

The no return flight!
O' woman thou art strong...
Monday night was tough. Monday night was rough. Jaws dropped and eyes popped.
A heart ripped apart. A peaceful home wrought by fate.
Every paragraph of thou tribute evokes love. And every line of thou story induces resilience
Altogether 66 lines in a 20-paragraph tribute
I wonder where thou get thy strength from.
In the midst of grief thou lace humor into thy tribute as though thy heart isn't pained from the jab
Didst thy heart compensate you?
And didst thy mind ponder o'er the unspeakable
Part of thy flesh is gone and part of thy heart has been stabbed.
Yet thou managed to tell the whole world thy story.
If thou breakfast could tame hunger, I wonder what thou lunch and supper did to the hungry
Yes, no soldier has ever gone this way. Not even in the annals of the Kaya Maaghans of the Old Ghana Empire
The cameras capture thy lifeless body. The Paparazzi comb around like a drunken hippie
Cell phones flit like drones. Our soldiers fall not by stones and blocks not by sticks and bats.
They fall by guns and swords:: Guns that ring from the RPG's and katyusha rockets.
O' history tell me if my pen is twisting that which is factual?
And I will compensate thee with an unqualified apology.
But is that what thou want when we're mourning our fallen hero?
O' woman thou art a true daughter of the ever powerful, most faithful and ever merciful God
The strength thou exhibit every day since the passing of thy 'king' belies the grief that hangs o'er thou head like dark clouds.
Thou beloved children are still clueless as to what has befallen their quintessential home.
They're unaware that their loving father and a hero is gone forever.

A mother and father shattered by the distasteful death of their child.
Certainly, a family mourns a husband, a father, son, an uncle a brother, a nephew and a cousin.
And a courageous soldier leaves his comrades without a hint, while friends bewail a good friend.
This is a tribute from a poet to a broken-hearted.
This is a poet's token— to show thou that even from afar— a million miles away thy story pulls heavy strings
This day, this time, this hour is our time to show thou our love.
Our thoughts and prayers are with you. And our hearts will forever cherish thee and thy family.
May thy Maker continue to give thee an immeasurable strength.
Woman, Be steadfast. Woman, Be strong, Woman be blessed for thy King is asleep with Jesus
Damirifa Due!!!

Is The Military Covering Up Its Footprints?

You probably didn't think that we would get here. That there would come a time, the Military High Command would stand accused by its own men. The Command would be accused of covering up or withholding some information about its slain army officer which occurred 10 days ago. Indeed that seemed unlikely to happen and it also challenged conventional wisdom.

But here we are, standing in a crossroad, smack bogged by new details of information arising out of that unspeakable incident.

The men are said to be livid about the way the Command has been handling the whole tragic event. And they fear what happened to their comrade could happen to them if serious measures aren't taken. The upset soldiers who spoke to a journalist in Accra have also vowed to go public if the command refuses to release information that precipitated the fall of the hero.

In an audio trending on the Social Media this week, the journalist said the angry soldiers are many. "It isn't just a handful of men or a few individuals that are saying this, they're many," he said.

Today marks ten days of Major Mahama's tragic death. Was he really on a 20-kilometre walk or jogging?

Or he was attending a scheduled meeting with the Galamsey operators at Denkyira Obuasi? If true why didn't he use a military vehicle? Ghanaians are pleading with the Military High Command to let us know what really transpired prior to the officer's tragic end.

Be mindful the schemer schemes but the binocular eyes of the owl prowls scrupulously. Untroubled by the turn of events, it vows to unmask the masked beast. You know the longer it takes the murkier it becomes but it all works for good inasmuch as investigators and intelligence officers keep their fingers on the tabs and their eyes on the ball.

In the midst of all this the stories don't add up. Something isn't right but who knows what. Major Mahama had been replaced by a lieutenant officer (name still withheld) to enable him travel to Accra to write his promotional exams. It is understood; while he was gone a sting operation against Galamsey operators at Denkyira Obuasi in the Upper Denkyira West District in the Central region had been carried out and a number of equipment seized by the said officer and his men.

Following that a meeting was scheduled between the officer and the Galamsey operators, ostensibly to release the equipment back to the operators. But the officer either failed or refused to attend the said meeting. Instead he commissioned four noncommissioned officers –two of them WO'1s and the other WO'2s. The four according to reports were nearly lynched by the operators.

But what happened to them upon their return to base would raise your eyebrows. Reports have it that they were sent back to Accra interrogated and subsequently put in a guardroom. It's believed the men were not released until the murder of Major Mahama.

Why did the military do that? I have no idea.

I can however, speculate that perhaps the operation was either not sanctioned by an authority or they realised it was uncalled for.

Remember a few weeks before the murder of the army officer, the Minister of Lands and Natural Resources John Peter Amewu had said illegal small-scale miners in some areas in the Ashanti region were using the military as shield to protect them.

"The law enforcement agencies, especially the military are protecting an illegality and I think that this is time the truth be told. Most of the sites we visited today were heavily manned by the military command," Mr. Amewu said.

However the deputy minister of defence Derek Oduro (Rtd) debunked the allegation that military personnel were protecting illegal miners. "The Ghana Armed Forces hasn't sanctioned such an operation. But any military officer involved in such an act may be doing so by himself and if found culpable would be punished," he pointed out.

So where was I?

Major Mahama is back to base and the commander that relieved him returns to Accra. And I assume he was briefed about the happenings while he was gone. Was he to continue where the lieutenant left off, given the fact that four of his men came under attack?

If yes, then he wasn't supposed to travel by himself to meet with the illegal gold miners as we're made to believe. If no that would suggest that Major Mahama embarked on the trip without informing or notifying any of his subordinates. But that doesn't make sense.

Standard operation in the military requires that an officer must have a runner or body guard whenever he's going anywhere. However in a volatile place such as Denkyira Obuasi he ought to even have more men unless he was oblivious of the situation in the area which also begs the question.

The military has what they call Standard Operative Procedure (SOP), a former army officer told me. "The procedure simply requires soldiers to move in pairs. So granted major Mahama was scheduled to attend a meeting with the supposed galamsey operators whose equipment had been seized by the lieutenant he was to have a runner with him," the officer said.

According to him, the same standard requires the individual to contact for example the District Chief Executive, the Traditional Ruler as well as opinion leaders in the area. He suggested a forensic intelligence was needed to help get to the bottom of the case. This he noted is in the best interest of the soldier.

"Even though you're there to protect the people, your security and safety is equally important. So the procedure must be followed to the letter. We have lost a soldier who had sworn to protect our national sovereignty and the people. Thus I think it's prudent for the military high command to come clean with any exhibits that would assist investigators to unravel any mystery that surrounds the murder."

On Monday President Akufo-Addo posthumously honoured Captain Maxwell Mahama the distinguished soldier who was murdered in cold blood by blood thirsty mobsters. He's now Major Maxwell Adam Mahama, may his gentle soul continue to rest in peace.

Yes, we all pray the fallen hero will have a peaceful rest but that won't happen until all the pieces that led to his murder are pieced together. So far about 41 people in connection with the killing of the army officer have been arrested.

Captain Mahama's Murder

Eyewitnesses Account to avoid or not to avoid?

What happened on Monday morning to Captain Maxwell Adam Mahama a platoon commander deployed to a tiny mining town called Denkyira Obuasi in the central region of Ghana would give police and investigators a heck of time to get to the bottom. Good news is we already know how it happened, when it happened, and where it happened.

Indeed we've seen the heart wrenching images—the stone-faced crowd, the baton/machete wielders, the stone/block throwers, the fire-setters/ burners, the videographers, the onlookers/bystanders including those that hurled insults and added salt to injury. We've heard and listened to the horrid and outrageous accounts, some of them as bizarre as the word itself. We've seen the bylines and read the screaming headlines. And the tributes continue to pour from daylight to twilight. . .

But that's not enough. We still have a puzzle that hangs around our necks like an albatross. What precipitated the devastating event on that fateful Monday morning remains unknown. And it appears to be a jigsaw that would linger for months to come.

That doesn't sound pleasant but here's why. Intelligence gathering is mosaic. Connecting the dots is time consuming plus it demands huge resources and energy. Also given the murkiness of this murder case I am afraid things might not move as fast as we envisage.

And that concern or fear has been confirmed by the District Police Commander at that hotspot. Yesterday, ASP Osei-Adu Agyemang told Joy News an Accra-based radio station that the huge presence of the military personnel at the community in the wake of the incident had forced the residents to flee the town.

"The presence of the military has forced the residents to flee their home, which is thwarting police efforts at getting witnesses to give them credible information and to what led to the death of the officer. Our fear now is the soldiers storming Denkyira Obuasi and most of the people leaving town. It will take time for police to take the possible witnesses to help us speed up investigations," he said.

The Police have called for the withdrawal of the military from the town and also accused them of hindering investigations into the incident.

In the meantime, Defence Minister Dominic Nitiwul has described the incident as 'weird' promising that government will investigate the murder thoroughly.

"The circumstance under which this officer was murdered callously has not yet been established so I will urge that we don't draw conclusions until a thorough investigation has taken place".

According to him the circumstance surrounding the killing is eerie because the deceased was armed.

"If it was the normal Ghanaian way of shouting 'jolour' [thief] then straight away the officer would have wasted some people if he knew they would kill him. It is clear the way he was murdered, the villagers might not have raised the thief syndrome of shouting. They may have hit him without him knowing what their intentions were," the Minister said.

In fact at its fluid stage and even 48 hours later many had questions like these:

Why did he put himself in a harm's way, a place notoriously known for lynching?

Well, it's been established that wasn't the first time he was undertaken such exercise. He knew the terrain. And I think he knew where he was going. Therefore, the account that he stopped by on the way to make an enquiry from some women, to me was an afterthought. I think the supposed women knew who Maxwell was. And knowing where he was heading to they quickly informed the Assemblyman who in turn mobilised the mob to carry out the dastardly act. So I think he was sort of ambushed. But as agile as he was and given the fact that he was armed he quickly fired warning shots when he sensed danger.

That move, I believe gave him a little leeway to run for his life but as fate would have it the wolves outran him. Did they have a gun or guns at the time?

No, I don't think so, even though one eyewitness claimed they fired multiple gunshots. I bet they would have killed him instantly the moment he pulled his trigger. Be reminded their mission was to kill and not to spare or pamper him.

Did he have an ID to prove he was a soldier? Yes he did have an ID and also had a cell phone on him. The irony is his attackers didn't mind his identity card. They saw him as enemy, someone who was denying them their livelihood. Their lifeline is Galamsey and he who is against it is viewed as enemy # 1.

Danger was all around him. The atmosphere was unfriendly and mercy had petered out. He was between the sea and hard rock. And he'd to withdraw all the stamina, faith and hope he'd put at the bank as the mob pursued him.

Sometimes Good Samaritans are difficult to come by when danger looms. There was one on a motorbike who could have rescued Captain Mahama but he wasn't a Good Samaritan. Maybe he was used as a decoy or maybe not. The account by the Okada rider that he feared for his life and couldn't move the bike after several pleas by Maxwell (as he recounted) must not be bought. That account smacks foul to say the least.

From his account, Captain Maxwell had outrun the irate crowd and they'd to use a car to get him. Was he coming from behind him or at the opposite direction? Or was it stationed? If it came from the same direction then it could be that they'd asked him to pretend he was given him a ride.

"I told him I could not move the motorbike because I was afraid the people might attack me too looking at the way they were coming at him. So he moved from my bike and started running but they chased him with a vehicle. Before they got to him, he was shooting to scare the people away and the bullet hit me in the process".

So why did he stop in the first place?

Why didn't he move? I believe Maxwell would have shown him his ID.

Here this is me; I am a military officer not a rogue, not a criminal, not an armed robber as they're chanting. I could hear him say that repeatedly.

Beware of Eyewitness Account

Many high profile cases have either gone unsolved or become cold due in part to eyewitnesses' accounts. Around May/June 1999 a cab driver was killed by his passenger at Roman Ridge near PAWA House in Accra. The incident happened on Saturday morning between 7:30-8:00. It had been witnessed by several passengers onboard a tro-tro vehicle that tailed the taxi.

I got a phone call while preparing the major news bulletin at 8 am. I rushed from the newsroom to the scene which was less than a block away to Choice FM premises. The killer had bolted with the taxi. The victim laid in a puddle of blood. And eyewitnesses told their varied accounts. To cut a long story short the suspect had managed to drive the taxi to Kumasi (a 4-hour journey) without been apprehended.

Some eyewitnesses had given the police wrong information— the car make, colour, registration number all didn't match the one the suspect had taken away. See, in a well-planned or premeditated murder cases investigations take longer than expected And I am pretty sure things would not be easy in this case.

In a related development security analyst, Dr. Emmanuel Kwesi Aning has expressed anxiety about the general acceptance and glorification of violence and mob justice among Ghanaians.

Dr. Aning is worried about the general belief by a section of Ghanaians that they will not be punished when they offend the laws.

His comments followed the widespread condemnation that had greeted a mob action by the youth in Denkyira-Obuasi, who lynched the commander of a military detachment to the area claiming he was an armed robber.

Like many Dr. Anning does not see a clear pathway to correcting this way of the Ghanaian thinking anytime soon.

"If we cannot use the law to serve as deterrence…this is what we see. There is absolutely no clear pathway because, as a nation, we don't see [violence] as an existential threat to us at all and therefore, we need to do something about it. And that is why we have allowed all these threats against our institutions to go on," he said.

So the embers of Captain Mahama's death might be fading but there remain many unanswered questions.

Going Wind: Not a done deal yet while hopes of five communities in Ghana ejaculate and expectations get high and higher.

The announcement by Volta River Authority (VRA) that a yet-to-be-built wind power plant in Ghana will create more jobs and attract tourists from far and near upon the project completion has left peoples of the five communities in the Keta municipality and Ada West district in the Volta and Greater Accra regions respectively salivating.

VRA is in talks with prospective investors to build Ghana's first wind power plant. The 150 megawatts wind power plant will shore up power generation in the country and it will be the first of its kind, reports local media. The project is in two phases—75MW at each stage.

Wind power is a vital renewable energy source and an alternative to burning fossil fuels. It's widely distributed due to its no greenhouse emissions during operation, no water consumption and it uses little farm lands.

Is the authority ready to fly on the wings of wind power?

Does it find itself in a pole position to finally achieve its renewable energy ambitions?

And would it receive government backing and huge investment from domestic and multinationals to make this dream a reality?

What is VRA's anticipation in the next five to ten years in this renewable energy programme to enable Ghana become the main hub in the sub region and not play a second fiddle role?

Energy experts say developing nations of Africa are popular locations for the application of renewable energy technology. Currently many nations already have small-scaled solar, wind and geothermal devices in operation providing energy to urban and rural populations.

Meanwhile, the authority has identified five locations in two regions in the country as aforementioned. Notably the Volta and Greater Accra regions to site its farm wind plants. But three key features of the project remain unknown at least for now.

Who are the key stakeholders? What is the project investment deal?

What is the project initiation date and an estimated project completion date?

Experts believe there is much to be done in order to get the deal sealed. They estimate VRA will need at least a loan scheme in the region of us$ 5billion to get the project actualised.

Speaking to journalists in Accra early on in the week, the Principal Engineer for Renewable Integrated Resources Development of VRA Mr. Ebenezer Antwi said the company hasn't secured loan or funding yet. "We are discussing with two partners for loan acquisition".

It is also not known whether all the plants will be sited onshore and some offshore.

Offshore wind is steadier and stronger than on-land and offshore farms. They have less visual impact but construction and maintenance costs are considerably high.

Bigger they say is better. And I think stronger and steadier is equally better.

How many of these plants will be sited off shore if any?

As a country our culture of maintenance leaves much to be desired notwithstanding the fact that the economic life span of wind power is 25 years. If we do not routinely maintain the blades and turbines (as needed) running the facility could go rusty and obsolete even before its scheduled life span.

It won't be bad to tap or source ideas from elsewhere. Egypt is attracting major investment plans from some of the world's largest multinational companies—such as Siemens and General Electric to develop wind energy component manufacturing capabilities and training facilities in the country.

Siemens alone has signed power generation agreements with Egypt worth almost US$9billion including propositions of up to 12 wind farms in Egypt along with a rotor blade manufacturing facility. Wind power is booming in Egypt because of firm government support which is fueling investors' interest and confidence in the country's renewable energy future.

Other things that Egypt is doing: The Egyptian government plans to invest over US$10 billion in renewable energy projects over the next decade. It has encouraged international investment in the sector by offering developers the opportunity to secure long-term profits through the Build-Own-Operate (BOO) and feed-in Tariff (FIT) schemes.

Is the VRA abandoning its plan to build coal power plant?

The plan to construct the country's first wind power plant has left some energy experts to speculate that the country's number 1 energy producer is perhaps abandoning its plan to build a 700MW coal plant in the country by first quarter of 2017.

In May this year VRA said it planned to site the plant in the coastal town of Aboano in the central region of Ghana (about 60 kilometers from Accra)

Ghana's total installed electricity generation capacity is 2,546.5 MW of which 52 percent is produced from hydropower, while 47.9 per cent is thermal power generated from light crude oil, distillate fuel oil and gas. About 0.1 per cent of the country's electricity comes from solar."

At least 83 countries are using wind power to supply their electricity grids. In 2014 global wind power capacity expanded 16% to 369,553 MW. Yearly wind energy production is also growing rapidly and has reached around 4% of worldwide electricity usage.

Denmark generates 40 per cent of its electricity from wind, according to 2015 energy reports. The first windmill use for the production of electricity was built in Scotland in July 1887 by Professor James Blyth of Anderson's college of Glasgow university.

Why do voters sell their votes?

What would a peacock have to show if it loses her striking feathers. She would be like an automobile without fuel. Or like a bike running on a deflated tyre. Its value becomes insignificant the moment it loses its luster and beauty.

One of the critical ways by which individuals can influence governmental decision-making is through voting. It is the fundamental human right of every individual. In 1948, the United Nations General Assembly unanimously adopted the Universal Declaration of Human Rights (UDHR), which recognises the integral role that transparent and open elections play in ensuring the fundamental right to participatory government.

In fact Article 21 of the UDHR in part states: Everyone has the right to take part in the government of his/her country, directly or through chosen representatives. Everyone has the right of equal access to public service in his/her country.

And that the will of the people shall be the basis of the authority of government: This will, shall be expressed in periodic and genuine elections which shall be by universal and equal suffrage and shall be held by secret ballot or by equivalent free voting procedures.

Indeed as a registered voter you've the power to influence any election, be it mayoral, legislative or parliamentary and presidential. Not only that but also the voter's one vote counts immensely and it surely can make a difference in a grand scheme of things.

So, if voters have this right and power to impact on governmental decision making, why do they choose to sell such bona fide or genuine right?

The answer may seem simple but it's so convoluted. It can be attributed to two major reasons —abject poverty and ignorance. The third but perhaps more troubling cause of this problem is the undue pressure politicians bring to bear on voters before and during elections.

Vote-buying and vote-selling is a common phenomenon in most developing countries. My country of origin Ghana like many African countries where vote-selling and vote-buying is prevalent there have been series of campaigns and educational programmes by National Commission for Civic Education (NCCE) to sensitise the voting public.

The NCCE is a government agency responsible for the education of Ghanaians on civic matters. It was established by Act 452 of the Parliament of Ghana in 1993. And since its establishment it has been working vigorously in the midst of financial and logistic limitations.

Another body that strives to ensure there's sanity in all public elections held— are free, fair and transparent is the Electoral Commission of Ghana (EC). It's a seven –member panel and its independence is guaranteed by the 1992 constitution. The current commission was established by the Electoral Commission Act (Act 451) 1993.

However, the problem rather seems to be getting more traction during electioneering season. The reason, politicians like foxes will go anywhere they can hunt for votes. But as this writer notes what has fueled the enigma is perhaps monetisation by politicians. They entice voters with money and other incentives, which range from buckets to pans, cooking utensils and roofing sheets/bags of cement, machetes, foods (rice and edible oils), sardines and mackerels to working gears like boots and many more.

They target typically deprived communities, slum kingdoms and battleground areas viewed as the hotbed for the trade. Consequently, the seller faced with these goodies time and again forgets about the future and the power he/she possesses. And as money being doled out left and right by politicians it's often the ones with higher bids that win.

For instance, Accra the capital city which is in the Greater Accra region— suburban areas such as Sodom and Gomorrah, Nima, Maamobi, Chorkor, Madina, Sakaman, Ayikai Doblo, Ashaiman etc. the trade becomes intense during parliamentary and presidential elections. The situation even wells up in district assembly elections (though less competitive) where voters elect local assembly members known as Assemblymen/women.

Nowadays politicians appear to have widened the scope of operation to include even areas considered their bastion. They will do it in Alavanyo in the Volta Region. And they will do it in Bantama, Kumasi in the Ashanti region regardless. The former is the stronghold of the National Democratic Congress (NDC) and the latter is the New Patriotic Party's (NPP) fortress.

Apparently they aren't taking anything for granted. The two major political parties the ruling-NDC and the NPP which is the largest opposition party are the chieftains in this unholy trade.

It used to be like batter trade done behind closed doors but not anymore. At political campaigns and rallies party leaders including presidents are seen engaging in the practice. That suggests how fast and how far we've gone with this canker.

Barely four months ahead of the general polls which comes off in December 7– are images of these items being flaunted at every quarter and gown.

Where is the beauty of the peacock?

The voter has power but he's been rendered powerless by way of vote-selling.

A few years ago, Researchers asked voters in the Philippines to make a 'simple unenforceable' promise not to accept money from politicians or to promise to vote according to their conscience even if they do accept money. The purpose of the study was to test the impact of promises on voters' behaviour,

It turned out a majority of respondents made promises not to sell their votes. Again, the researchers found out that the promise significantly reduced vote-selling, cutting the number of people who sold their votes by 11 percentage points in the smallest points in the smallest-stakes election, but was not effective in the mayoral election with higher pay-outs.

So the study concluded that simply asking voters to promise not to sell votes can help reduce vote-selling in elections where vote-buying payments are typically small.

Interestingly the menace isn't peculiar to developing nations. It happens even in developed countries such as the United States and United Kingdom.

A Washington Post writer David A. Fahrenthold in an article titled: 'Selling votes is common type of election fraud' which featured in October 2012, wrote that the practice seem to be widespread in the US Mr. Fahrenthold noted: "It may still be possible to steal an American election, if you know the right way to go about it."

Making reference to the 2012 election he said court cases from Appalachia to the Miami suburbs had revealed the tricks of an underground trade. Conspirators allegedly bought off absentee voters, faked absentee ballots and bribed people heading to the polls to vote one way or another.

He added that in West Virginia over the past decade the cost was as low as $10, whereas in West Memphis, Ark, a statehouse candidate used $2 half-pint of vodka to buy vote.

In Ghana C.I. 91 (Constitutional Instrument 91) passed by parliament and legislation makes electoral fraud a serious issue. And like many other democracies elsewhere, electoral fraud such as vote-buying, vote-selling, faked ballots and buying of absentee voters are considered election offences.

Fact is anytime a voter sells his/her vote it basically means one's pursuit of happiness has been mortgaged for four years, it means perpetuity of mediocrity, it means assassination of one's conscience, it means blatant endorsement of systemic corruption and it's a mutiny against democracy.

In summation, an act of vote-selling and vote-buying has the potential to paralyse free and fair democratic process. Nonetheless they still remain unescapable in many developing democracies. And it appears to be a bane that has left many rural Africa impoverished.

HERO's DEATH

Amid the encircling gloom you're remembered and immortalised.
May your path be smooth and may your family and descendants never see this again:
Captain_ Maxwell _Adam _Mahama.
My heart bleeds and my head spins. My heart bleeds for a fallen hero. It bleeds for a husband. It bleeds for a father. It bleeds for a son. It bleeds for an uncle, a brother and a patriot.
A soldier dies not at his backyard a soldier falls whiles at war.

xxxxxxxx

Peace be still. I beckon you to stay still for I am on the hill, till I see violence flee. But if I die let no man cry or wail. O' don't sail away, for I see a whale advancing, angry and poised to kill me.
How many times must my people be told this?
How many, how many times must we not use violence to settle scores?
Instant justice is needless act!
Instant justice is heartless act!
Peace be still. Please don't sail away for they may nail me down on my way. They're merciless, they're heartless. O vampire while spill fire on my way. Blood everywhere, Mother Earth loathes it yet you spill my blood.
Did I curse you?
Did I taunt you?
Did I abuse you?
Did I rob you of your gold and ornaments?
So, why take my life?
Why humiliate me?
Knew ye not that not everyone that walks on the streets is a rogue?

Knew ye not that not everyone that treads the lonely alley is a thug?
And knew ye not that not everyone on the highway is on your way?
Peace be still. I beckon you to stay for there's no bailiff.
My saviour is asleep.
Did he sanction this?
Did he see this?
Why did he not intervene on my behalf?
Was I fated to go this path? This path littered with grief, disbelief, sorrow and tears.
I didn't say goodbye to my wife. I didn't say goodbye to my lovely kids and I didn't say goodbye to my friends and comrades. My freedom has been hijacked. My troubles have been compounded and violence pursues me for no apparent reason.
I curse not. I rant not. I swear not yet violence aims at me.
My wife and children mourn. The horn of the ambulance churns fear.
They didn't expect this yet undying death announces his presence.
Peace snail on your path and let me dovetail you.
Peace be still let me ride with you .Carry me gently, gently to my father's house and let me Rest In Peace!!!

Do what we wear to Church matter?

'Clothes make the man. Naked people have little or no influence on society'—**Mark Twain**

"Our clothing is one of our most elemental forms of communication, "says Duane Litfin an American Evangelist and the former seventh president of Wheaton College in Wheaton, Illinois.

According to Mr. Litfin what we wear tell people about us i.e who we are even before we get the opportunity to be heard.

"Long before our voice is heard, our clothes are transmitting multiple messages. From our attire, others immediately read not only such things as sex, age, national, social economic status, and social position but also our mood our attitudes, our personality, our interests and our values," Duane said.

That is so true. Our society is wrought by gossip when it comes to the issues above-mentioned. We unleash instant justice, make hasty generaliisation and draw our own conclusions to suit our whims.

So think about that for a second. Why would you let some people prosecute you with their thoughts, crucify you with their tongues and write your obituary when you're naturally not dead yet?

Why would you put yourself in that situation or give someone who doesn't know you from Adam the licence to draw an inaccurate impression about you, badmouth you or judge you, just because of what you wear?

The irony is you wouldn't even have the same platform to tell your own story let alone validate it.

And you'd think that would douse the flame. No, there are people who have developed a thick skin and don't really care what people say about them. They believe that what they wear to social functions, be it Church, funeral, movie theatre, tavern etc. is nobody's business.

After all, they argue, God does not look outward he looks inside. He doesn't care about what one wears and how one looks. What he cares about is our faith/trust in Him, showing love to our neighbour, being merciful, being compassionate and caring for one another.

The Bible says it eloquently: "There is nothing from without a man, that entering into him defile him, but the things which come out of him, those are they that defile the man," Mark 7:15 (KJV).

I'm personally not a Bible-thumb Christian. I don't look at what people wear to form an opinion or make a judgement. I've always asked myself this-: *who am I?*

Who am I to judge or pass judgment or question ones moral behaviour? Had it not be His grace and mercies who am I? We are all not perfect and can never be perfect. Yes, I know I am right. We live not because of our supposedly pious deeds but we live because of his amazing grace and unbending love.

The parable of the 'Good Samaritan' is a didactic story Jesus told in Luke's book. It speaks about a traveler (believed to be a Jew) who was attacked by some thugs and left half dead. A Jew supposedly passed by and a priest walked by too. Both of them didn't care about the condition of the traveler. But the Samaritan attended to the man. And I think you know how the whole story ended. Therefore, it's needless to ask who showed love to the traveler. But why did the Jew fail to take care of his fellow Jew? And I guess the priest with his long cassock and the scroll tucked under his armpit was racing to the pulpit to preach about love, mercy, caring for our neighbour and paying tithe.

Jesus concluded that it took the unchurched or the least —the 'Good Samaritan' to save the troubled-soul.

So often, it is not who we say we are that truly defines us. It isn't by our status or nationality or profession and not by our religion but by doing God's will. By following the things Apostle Paul mentioned in the book of Galatians.

"But the fruit of the Spirit is love, joy, peace, forbearance, kindness, gentleness and self-control," Gal 5:22).

The Samaritan showed mercy, he showed compassion and gave love. Obviously, that is more important than showing up at Church with flashy clothes every Sunday. It is more important being in tarps with pure heart and good conscience than paying lip-service.

Thing is those who are lashing out at you might have nice clothes and drive the best cars to Church but they might be wearing uncircumcised hearts. We don't see it but God sees it. God sees us and knows us all!

That said let's now put this into perspective. Let's ponder on a couple of questions first. Would you show up in an interview dressed in tattered clothes if you had good clothes? Would you do the same when you're meeting your first date or visit your in-laws?

I agree it isn't what we wear that wholly defines us but first impression counts and you'd always like to put your best foot forward. So, I don't think you'd like to appear scruffy for an interview when you're desperate looking for a job. Your clothes could be old and dirty, yet you'd wash them with some sweet-scented detergent and have them well-ironed. All set ready to kick it.

Indeed I don't think you'd go to the house of your in-laws-to-be looking unkempt and broke, because you fear you might lose your suitor. That's right you'd surely fall out of the perking order.

"There is a moral and spiritual dimension to human clothing. Our clothes serve a variety of practical, social and cultural functions. Protection and modesty spring first to mind, but our clothes do far more," notes Duane.

We witnessed loads of that at the just ended an historic funeral of the Asantehemaa in Kumasi. The public was informed about the dress codes—what to wear and what not to wear. For instance, attendees were not supposed to wear necklaces and jewelry. And I don't think anybody that showed up there dared.

I don't think churches make dress codes a big deal. Most Churches are more flexible, there might be some that are deep in bed with the Mosaic Law. However the majority is tolerant as to what the congregants wear.

But for Christ sake, why would you put on a flip-flop (Chalewate), or a dress that barely covers your front gate or torso to go to worship the Holy One. Why would you wear a T-shirt that has the words 'I'm Satan's Agent,' or has the F-world scrawled at its back to the church house?

If you and I agree that we serve an awesome and all-powerful God, the Lord of Lords, the Conqueror of the universe, the Master Designer, the Alpha and Omega why would you go to worship or praise Him dressed in something that speaks evil, smells evil and highlights evil?

So get this, much as God doesn't care about what we wear he is also not oblivious of what our motives are. More often than not our intents are what cause us to sin. Remember what Jesus said in Mark, it is not what goes into our mouths that makes us sin. Rather what comes from within us? He knows what's in our hearts.

Perhaps it is this new trend of dressing creeping into the Ghanaian clothing arena that has prompted a renowned Ghanaian priest to sound a note of caution to the Christendom particularly the youth of the country.

On Sunday 23 January 2017 the Metropolitan Archbishop of Accra, Most Reverend Charles Gabriel Palmer Buckle couldn't hide his disappointment at what he described as the 'bad dress code' of the Ghanaian youth. The nobler was worried that the youth are losing their relationship with God because of their appearance in church.

Speaking at the chapel rededication of the St. Theresa's Catholic Church in Accra, the clergyman charged parents to correct their children's dress code at home.

"Take control of your sons and let them know what they can wear, where they wear it and where they cannot wear it period."

They come to church with T-shirts written in front 'kick me' and at the back is written '37', adding some of the inscriptions are obscene with writings such as "kiss me."

He wants the youth to be told that such clothes are not entertained in the church.

"You don't even go anywhere decent with it how much more the presence of God,"

He explained that the human body is a 'temple of the holy spirit, for which reason it must be kept clean with appropriate lifestyle pleasing to God.

Most Reverend Buckle also cautioned about what he called 'overdressing', urging ladies to ensure that their dresses are befitting for whatever occasion they are dressed for.

ZONGO TO GET FACELIFT

Are We For It?

It takes two to tango so the adage goes. But it takes a visionary to develop Zongo. Zongo is a Hausa name or word for a slum or ghetto. Over the years Zongos have been left and forgotten. Viewed by many as a no go area, gem-infested, dirty and filthy, unsanitary and unhygienic. It's crime prone and overpopulated.

Ghana like many countries in the world has its slums too that spread across most of its big cities. Popular amongst them are, Nima, Sodom and Gomorrah, Maamobi, Agbobloshie, Suame Magazine, New Takoradi, Ashaiman, Fadama and Kojokrom.

Rising population begets slum dwellers. It's estimated that 1 billion people worldwide live in slums and the figure is projected to grow to two billion by 2030, according to the United Nations.

The UN agency for habitation UN-HABIATAT defines slum as a rundown area of a city characterised by standard housing, squalor, and lacking in tenure security. The UN said, the percentage of urban dwellers living in slums decreased from 47 percent to 37 percent in the developing world between 1990 and 2004

But rising population, the UN notes has caused the number of slum dwellers to rise significantly. The UN further says the number of slum dwellers in developing countries statistically increased from 689 million in 1990 to 880 million in 2014.

Perhaps it's this rising populations coupled with other factors that informed Ghana's President Akufo-Addo to create the Ministry of Inner City and Zongo Development. The new ministry, first of its kind is to handle Zongo affairs. It also intends to give slums across the country face-lifts, according to the sector minister Boniface Abubakar Saddique.

Mr. Saddique told a journalist in an interview that the ministry is mandated to undertake some special programmes including; infrastructure and sanitation enhancement; economic empowerment, social development, cultural promotion and security and crime control.

"One of the critical areas of concern for the social cohesion in the country is the developments taking place in the inner cities and the zongos, hence the need for its establishment," Mr. Saddique noted. Another area he spoke about was infrastructure.

He said infrastructure in these communities is poor and government would take steps to improve upon them through the Ministry, adding the money that would be allocated for the Ministry will not be used for on social and traditional engagements.

"Development over years had been discriminatory with residents in the Zongo communities neglected. And I think in my view the president has to be commended for establishing the ministry," he pointed out.

How would this work without resistance from the dwellers?

Over the years, attempts by many governments to develop slum areas across the world have faced resistance from slum dwellers. A classic example is the Kibera slum in Kenya. Residents have gone to court to stop the government for building road through the community, bulldozing schools and clinics and thousands of homes. Kibera, which is home for 700, 000 people, is Africa's biggest slum.

Governments in India have also faced resistance from residents of the Dharavi slum time and again. Residents have opposed attempts to develop the area. According to reports business in Dharavi thrives like an oil town. The community has an informal economy with an estimated $1 billion annual turnover.

In the 1960's Ghana's first president Kwame Nkrumah attempted to develop Nima but that dream got botched even though the residents had been paid off. I'm told Nkrumah even adopted Nima as his constituency all aimed at developing and beautifying the place. It's believed residents in the community refused to be resettled in Madina –an area close to Ghana's premier university- University of Ghana, not too far from the Airport City and also close to East Legon– Ghana's most affluent community and absolutely not too far from famous Tetteh Quarshie Roundabout—the biggest in West Africa.

Nima, for example, until about mid 90's had no clinic, no streets, no playgrounds, and lacked other basic social amenities. The Kanda Highway built by President Rawlings during the period had a number of homes in the community grazed down. Back then we used to joke that when in Nima tread cautiously else you might end up walking straight into one's room. And I almost did that one hush afternoon when the path I was on led me to someone's door. It's my hope that the new wind of change will affect the communities in a more positive way.

But unlike Nima and Kibera in Kenya where residents resisted governments' infrastructure development, residents of Orang Town in Pakistan wanted it but their governments neglected them. This is how a journalist put it in one of UN reports. "Fed up with living without proper sanitation, residents of Orang Town gave up waiting for government to install sewer and built them by hand themselves."

Orang Town now has nearly 8, 000 streets and lanes have sewage pipes—all put in by residents.

Ciudad Neza in Mexico City (with a population of 1.2 million) was rated as the world's largest mega-slum in 2006. I don't know her current status in terms of ratings. But the story in that community is also a positive one. Today, Cuidad has become more like suburb courtesy of the great efforts by the residents to build a community and deliver public services.

The world has five biggest slums. They are Khayelitsha, Cape Town in South Africa, with 400, 000 population, Dharavi Mumbai India with 1 million people, Cuidad Neza Mexico city populated by 1.2 million people and Orang Town in Pakistan, Asia's largest slum has a population of 2.4 million.

Botchwey Clears The Way

Who or What Killed NDC?

The NDC autopsy report is finally out. And the disease that killed Madam ZUZU or ZAZA is now in the public domain. This writer believes the release of the Botchwey Committee Report would culminate all speculations that had dogged the umbrella family since its 13-member committee tasked itself to find out what caused NDC's defeat in the 2016 December general elections.

Thankfully, we now know it wasn't pneumonia that killed Ghana's largest opposition party as many had thought. And it wasn't asphyxia either. The report also didn't cite 'Bad Governance' as the cause of its fall.

In April this year yours truly speculated (based on what's now known to be fake news) that the cause of death was a contagious disease called 'Polimyelitics'. Well, that also turned out not to be true.
So what is it that killed the mighty umbrella?
The answer to that question rests in the bosom of Prof. Kwesi Botchwey the chairman of the 13-member committee. The former finance minister under the Rawlings PNDC regime had managed to keep the cards close to his chest for a considerable time. But it was finally time for him to produce what he'd conceived for months.

At the party's headquarters in Accra on Monday Prof Botchwey disclosed that the National Democratic Congress (NDC) has a 'Weak Intellectual and Research Base', noting that this played a key role in the party's defeat in the 2016 elections.
What does that mean?
It sounds like the generic name for 'incompetence.' But the eminent professor's explanation didn't seem to suggest that. Instead he said the NDC ought to take steps to 'crowd the party with critical thinkers' in order to make her a better party.

I still think that explanation failed to undercut my perspective, because of the operative words there 'Critical Thinkers'.

Who are critical thinkers? Does that suggest NDC don't have the manpower or lack governance ability?

Also the committee's report recommended what it calls a "peacemaking and healing tour" which should be led by some eminent personalities of the party. Again let's look at the two words in parenthesis: 'Peacemaking and 'Healing'.

Readers may recall, in that April 27 article: BAD Governance ': The Cause of NDC Defeat in 2016 Election defeat 'a supposedly preliminary report by the committee catalogued in bullet points some findings it claimed spelt out what went wrong.

Notably, what caused the astronomic debts, what brought about the apathy, what produced the resentment, the disillusionment and how things got to where they landed?

That alleged report accused former President John Mahama of leading self-centred or egoistic life, according to the report. He was extravagant and beyond that he mismanaged not only his wealth but also state resources, recommending that all monies lost must be refunded.

Additionally, it said: "The arrogance of some members of the party was a factor. Especially, Kwaku Boahen, Kofi Adams, Solomon Nkansah, Felix Kwakye Ofosu, Stan Dogbe, Omane Boamah etc. They never respected the Ghanaian voter and thought they could use propaganda to win an election."

There seem to be some parallelism in the two reports, which gives the April report some sort of credibility.

In the Monday's report subtitled "listening to the voice of the grassroots", Prof.

Botchwey advised the NDC leadership to consider the peace-making and healing tour as "extremely important".

So if there's no smoking gun why would the report recommend a peaceful and healing tour?

What is there to heal if there's no wrong doing?

Is that a tacit admission that its leadership and members disrespected the electorate, the very people who wield power and gave them power in 2012?

Prof Botchwey underscored that it was imperative for them to embark on the tour: "This is because it will create the "necessary conditions for any serious work that needs to be done" in restructuring the party, he said.

The Committee also touched on the big issue of the party's biometric register which become a source of discontent within the grassroots. There were claims the register had been infiltrated by non-NDC members while recognisable party figures at the branch level could not find their names on the list.

Prof Botchwey's committee further recommended, the party must work to "restore the integrity of the biometric register" The report mentioned the expansion of the party's Electoral College in its recommendations.

In 2014, the NDC announced an expansion of its electoral college from 4,000 to about 250,000. The NDC General Secretary explained "our intention is to scrap the Electoral College system and then allow every party member to vote when it comes to our primaries for the selection of parliamentary candidates and then for the selection of the presidential candidates."

The 13-committee suggested the expansion of the Electoral College to include ordinary party members needs to be re-examined to restore confidence in the democratic novelty.

Another major recommendation was that the party needed to reconnect to its social democratic roots. Other recommendations included restoring the capacity and effectiveness of party organs believed to have been sidelined in the run-up to the 2016 elections.

Professor Botchwey summed it all up with this: "My job is done…it is up to you to implement recommendations".

The NDC lost the battle for the Flagstaff House on Wednesday 7, December 2016. it was the party's third defeat in 25 years since the inception of the Fourth Republic in 1992. The first loss happened on the 7th of December 2000 and 2004 with Late President John Atta Mills then as the party's nominee.

It was a comeback victory for the former tax master and a law professor in December 2008. On the 7th of January 2009, and the 7th of January 2013 the NDC took the reins of power again under presidents John Mills and John Mahama respectively. And then the biggest defeat many dread to talk about or hear—the 2016 general elections. It was a humiliation for the NDC They lost sorely to their arch rival the NPP, the New Patriotic Party.

The Elephant's candidate Akufo-Addo won a decisive victory by polling 53.85% of total valid votes cast against incumbent NDC Presidential candidate John Dramani Mahama who managed 44.40%. The story wasn't different in the parliamentary election as the NPP increased its seats from 122 to 169 to form the majority, while the NDC saw its representation drop from a majority of 148 to 106.

AKUFO-ADDO'S FIRST 100 DAYS

Did the President Accomplish His Targets?

President Akufo-Addo marks his first 100 days in office today Monday 17, April 2017. But even before he began the 100-metre race or to put it more appropriately the 400x4 Relay race, he'd the odds against him. *How did that happen?*

Well, the team that was handing over the baton to him had run out of steam, gasping for breath. This, coupled with other factors, made it difficult for his then newly-inaugurated team to keep up pace from the onset. In other words he couldn't do much as expected of him during the period under review because the tuff was rough.

Certainly, like a Relay race, the team that ran before him had had almost everything gone wrong. It seemed all had gone amiss! The NDC, National Democratic Congress didn't take the competition very serious. They thought they were competent enough to handle all the players on the field but it turned out to be disaster. What happened was they allowed complacency, apathy and laxity to outplay them resulting the following:

They got swallowed by corruption, overwhelmed by debts, overtaken by inflation and out-smarted by the lootees. What more, there was fraud everywhere. Indeed, everything a champion should be mindful of or observe in a keen competition (in their case) was rejected and relegated to the background. And the upshot was nothing but abysmal performance. Thing is, it's often difficult to do the catch up strategy when situation like that occurs. Obviously it tends to make real champions like Jamaican Usain Bolt (the reigning world champion) even look bad.

So, personally when it comes to reviewing presidents' first 100 days in office I incline to downplay it a little bit. I do so not on the basis that it's insignificant or inconsequential. But against the backdrop, as to whether given the circumstances that present themselves— a particular president could have done either good or bad, better or worse, underperformed or performed well. In that vein, I think pundits and critics must always examine the antecedents when assessing presidents' first 100 days.

It's also worth noting that some presidents are given blank cheques when they're sworn into office while others are handed large surplus. For example, the US President Bill Clinton (42nd) oversaw a very robust economy during his tenure. The country had strong economic growth (around 4% annually and record of job creation (2.7 million). But his successor George W. Bush (43rd) blew all the gains away and left behind colossal debt for the 44th president, Barrack Obama.

Did the President have a good start?

Akufo-Addo the 5th president of the Fourth Republic didn't have a good start. He was denied that luxury right from the blast of the umpire's whistle. He'd unemployment, debts, corruption, inflation, cedi depreciation, Dumsor and Woyome's judgment debt saga all running before him. All had taken the centre stage which gave him little or no room to navigate during his first 100 days.

His predecessor president Mahama (4th John) played his part. However, his best wasn't enough to save the country from slipping into economic quagmire. In fact by the end of his (Mahama's) tenure in January 7, 2017 Ghana's economy was in shambles. And one thing that has since remained as an imprint or indelible mark in the minds of Ghanaians is 'Dumsor.'

For instance, Ghana owed neighbouring Nigeria $ 60 million for gas. But on Good Friday the President disclosed on his twitter page that the gas debt had been paid off. The cedi which had a free fall is now appreciating, showing strong performance against the major currencies— the dollar, pound sterling and the euro.

Besides, the president fulfilled several of his campaign promises a few weeks into his induction in January 7, 20017. On Thursday 2, February this year the Akufo-Addo administration fulfilled some of its campaign promises. He abolished market tolls for the 'Kayayei' (head porter). This was viewed by many as a budget with a human face as it seemingly gave the ordinary Ghanaian a sense of hope and a breather.

Importers were not left out. And like a marked down product the 1 per cent special import levy that hitherto hanged around their necks like albatross had been abolished.

Also abolished was the 17.5%. VAT/NHIL on financial services. Real estate developers had been lucky too they'd the 5% VAT/NHIL abolished. And who else benefitted? The scrap dealers, —duty on imported spare parts has been eliminated. In all about 8 taxes had been abolished by the new administration since Akufo-Addo assumed office.

There were also tax credits, tax incentives and tax replacement for some companies and a certain group of the human resource. Clearly the NPP has demonstrated that it is a pro- market party. During the campaign it promised to reduce corporate tax to 20 per cent. And it kept that promise on Thursday. Akufo-Addo's finance minister Ken Ofori-Atta announced tax incentives for entrepreneurs and also reduced corporate income tax from 25% 20 % in 2018.

In Ghana, the fourth Republic has seen a more stable democratic government and the first transitional government from one administration to another took place in January 7 2001. At the time Ghana's macro and micro economic indicators were not good. The country was heading down the cliff. And so when President Kufour took the reins of power he'd to declare Ghana as Highly Indebted Poor Country (HIPC). Nonetheless, he ran the race well putting the country on a sound economic footing.

This is what Economy Watch in 2010 wrote about the country: "Ghana's economy is growing at a blistering 20.15 per cent."

But the next team would once again shave off all the successes chalked. And it's enough to say that both the Mills and Mahama administration did Ghana a great disservice. Inflation rate remained 18.5% in February 2016 compared to 17.7 in February 2015. By October 2016 it stood at 15.8 per cent. Today, the inflation has fallen for the sixth consecutive month to the lowest since September 2013. The current rate is 12.8 per cent.

Also I think critics and pundits' assessments must take into account whether one president's performance or under-performance was engendered by prudent governance and pragmatic ideas or it was self-inflicted. Were there obstacles from the start to the finish? You'd agree with me that some athletes get jolted by obstacles that are either caused by themselves or others at the start of the race.

This scenario outplayed itself during Akufo-Addo's First 100 Days in Office. Akufo-Addo administration apart from the enormity of the task it faced initially, the activities of vigilante groups such as Invincible and Delta Force and the appointments of 110 ministers was dogged with huge resentment from the public. And I think it was a self-inflicted wound. And those I think were some of the low marks he scored in his first 100 days.

A socio-politico think tank the Centre for Democratic Development, CDD-Ghana, registered its displeasure on Friday three days before the president touched the finish line for his 100 days.

CDD Ghana in a statement released on Wednesday, although commended government for speedily assembling its team in real time, it was not happy with the number of ministers the President appointed.

According to CDD Ghana, the 110 ministers assembled by the President will put pressure on the public purse.

"CDD-Ghana feels badly disappointed by president Akufo-Addo's decision to appoint 110 ministers. It flies in the face of the president's own declared commitment to protect the public purse as well as its longstanding good governance advocates' campaign for meaningful reduction in the size of government and resultant government spending. We believe that the appointments of so many politicians to manage the state bureaucracy will further deepen its politicisation and undermine its authority," statement added.

CDD-Ghana was also not happy with government's seeming silence on attacks perpetrated by some vigilante groups affiliated to the NPP, namely Delta Forces and Invincible forces.

"First, the many instances of NPP-affiliated vigilante groups' forceful takeover of state assets and public facilities (including toilets, toll booths, school feeding programs, etc.) and the unlawful seizure of vehicles of members of the previous administration put a dent on the hitherto smooth transition process. Worse still, the failure of government, and law enforcement agencies to deal decisively with the NPP-affiliated vigilante groups, mainly the Delta and Invincible Forces, that invaded sensitive government installations such as the passport office and Tema Ports and Harbour, appears to have encouraged the recent brazen attacks on the Ashanti Regional Security Coordinator and a Circuit Court in Kumasi, by the so-called Delta Force."

CDD-Ghana further chastised government for hurriedly sacking Metropolitan, Municipal and District Chief Executives as well as heads of some state agencies.

It emphasised that, such practices are inconsistent with good corporate governance performance.

"We are also disturbed by the continuity in practice after electoral turn-overs whereby the chief executive officers and senior managers of public agencies and parastatals are summarily removed or asked to 'proceed on leave,' and to handover to a caretaker officer/acting CEO. Such actions are inconsistent with good corporate governance practices, it fosters politicization of the public service as well as political exclusion, and undermines the fight against winner takes all politics. The centre deems the interpretation of who is a political appointee under Section 14 (6) in the Presidential Transition Act 2012 too broad and badly in need of review informed by best practice," the statement added.

My final take: From the foregoing, I think the president has done well in his first 100 days. He's shown a mark of resilience and determination in the midst of the huge challenges. Indeed the Elephant has proven that 'size matters' sometimes and by virtue of its size it was able to weather through the monstrous storm. Remember, Usain Bolt's world speed record of 9.58 seconds remains unbroken. So Mr. President I appeal to you to maintain the momentum you've under your belt and also consolidate on the gains already made. The administration still has the goodwill of the people. That means he the president can deal with monsters such as Galamsey, Vigilante groups, indiscipline, corruption and many more. But I will like to be put on record here that his (Mr. Akufo-Addo's) fight against Galamsey and corruption won't be easy, especially Galamsey.

Marine Drive Project

Is it a Dream Come True?

The dreamer dreamed building a beautiful skyline in Accra's beachfront 60 years ago. It was part of Ghana's first President Dr. Kwame Nkrumah's dream—putting Ghana at the top rung of the economic, socio-political ladder or as a champion of the African continent.

Unfortunately, the dream (Marine-Drive-Project) was dunked in a pool of abandonment and its revival would since be shaped by time and fate. Hope. Hope remained the only life line for her. Six decades on, indications are that the new NPP-administration plans to commence the Marine-Drive Project two months from now after a sod-cutting ceremony by the President Akufo-Addo.

It reminds me of this story: While on a visit to Johannesburg in South Africa a little boy asked his father if he could move the skyscrapers he saw from that beautiful city to Obuasi, in Ghana. Stunned by the question the father looked at his son and remarked:

"Kojo this is impossible. How can you do that?"

To which his son replied: ""Why is it not possible Dad?"

"Look how tall the buildings are. They're so huge where would you put them– on a boat, a train or an airplane? It's just impossible," the father explained.

"You're right about that Dad," the little boy submitted. "But I didn't mean carrying the structures from here to Ghana. I was just curious. How come the two cities produce gold: Yet one has a charming skyline and the other has nothing to show off?"

"Kojo you never cease to amaze me with your poignant questions. Don't worry, I will tell you more about that when we get back home."

An imposing skyline is like a magnet— she attracts visitors and tourists. She flaunts her glory and tells her story to the world. Her beauty is like a diamond, enhanced by the morning rising sun as its glass windows sparkle. Its towering structures serve as canopy during sweaty sunny weather for its teeming inhabitants...

At sundown she sheds light upon the whole city, inviting revelers to dine wine, dance and prance at her numerous venues across the city. Ghana's yet-to-be-built Marine-Drive project seeks to provide a picturesque skyline at her coastline.

On Wednesday, a ceremony to hand over the 241 acres of Land for Ghana's Marine Drive Project was held at the Arts Centre in Accra. The 60-year-old project, the brain child of Dr. Nkrumah will house about 30 hotels, arts and craft village, conference facilities, fish markets and landing beach sites among others.

This was made known by the Tourism, Arts and Culture minister Mrs. Catherine Abelema Afeku. According to her the development of the project formed part of the New Patriotic Party's election 2016 manifesto pledge.

The sector minister also revealed after clearing the site, President Addo Dankwa Akufo-Addo was expected to officially cut sod for the commencement of the project in two months.

Is it a Dream Come True?

Truly it has been a long wait. And many were those who thought the project would never see the light of day. However what we witnessed yesterday was an indication that probably it was time for serious business. The assurance from the sector minister rekindled hopes and produced a sense of excitement. Certainly it was a hope for the country's youth and a hope for tourism, art and culture in the country. So I am keeping my fingers crossed for the meantime, in the hope that everything will work out as planned. And I believe that's the hope of many Ghanaians. It's all about jobs, jobs and jobs. I don't know the project's workforce projection but whatever the case maybe it would be a feather in the cup for the administration if it's able to execute the project as envisaged.

I can't wait to see that work is in progress with bulldozers, earthmovers and excavators ploughing the site. The scaffolds and the cranes will cease to be a dream but rather a reality. And perhaps this write-up would remind the minister and the government that the whole world is watching them.

Mrs. Afeku told the gathering that the Ministry had received separate Memorandum of Understanding from two traditional houses, adding that, the Ministry would ensure that their demands were met as the project kick started.

Also the project would ensure that the indigenes especially the youth would be offered jobs. Not only that it would propel transformational development and that Ghana would become a beacon of hope in Africa, she said.

'We should endeavor to give the youth of the land priority over job seekers,' she said. That's a good idea too. And I think it would help prevent acrimony and disenchantment which often greet many projects of the sort.

According to her, livelihood that would be affected by the project would not be marginalized and the right compensations offered.

She acknowledged that there had been consultation over the past 18 months with the stakeholders including those at the Arts Centre and debunked the assertion by people at the Centre that they were not informed about the project.

The minister said countries like Kenya, South Africa, and Seychelles have developed their sites and could now boast of Arts and Crafts Village which deals in various wares.

Gbese Mantse of the Ga Traditional Council, Nii Ayibonte II, recounted that the project site was known as Accra Hearts of Oak Park and commended the team for protecting the site over the years.

Nii Ayibonte was excited that finally the project would start and urged all to do away with bickering and litigations that may cause delay of the project.

The call for de-politicization was highlighted by the Gbese Mantse, reiterating that the project should be executed peacefully and must be devoid of politics.

"Ga State also needed to be developed," he said.

There have been calls for government to also consider developing the Korle Lagoon which is close to Old Fadama near the Accra Business District.

Contract Killing

Is it another creeping bug?

Don't say never until you get jinxed. A few decades ago certain crimes and practices seemed alien to the Ghanaian but not anymore. Those were the days one could proudly say we didn't have this or that happen in our backyards. They probably did happen but went unobserved, perhaps not as widespread as we find them today.

Those were the times that you didn't associate a murder with a pastor/priest, a police in a heist, a father and daughter in love affair, a judge involved in a bribery scandal, a teacher cheating in an examination, or a woman involved in arson or assassination etc.

Sometime in March 2000 a man and his brother walked into Choice Newsroom.

"Sir I need your help. My child has been kidnapped," the man told me.

Did you mean kidnap Sir? I enquired.

It was like telling someone that the Pope (a Catholic) has converted into Islam and is now a Moslem. But his response was affirmative. The man's 10-year-old boy had been kidnapped by an unknown assailant, he alleged. When, where, how, why, what were legitimate questions that followed immediately.

Truly it sounded strange to me because the word 'kidnap' at the time was unfamiliar to Ghana. Newspapers and radio stations carried ads of lost and found children. But we didn't hear news about hostage takers and demand for ransoms. I could not imagine that happen in Accra Newtown—a sprawling suburb of Accra, where the man claimed they lived. My instinct told me something wasn't right.

I started to probe the father of the alleged kidnapped boy and lo and behold it turned out to be a fabricated story. I dispatched them immediately, upon discovering that his ex-wife who was resident in London, UK had returned home. The woman had told him she would pick up their son after school. She did exactly that and they went to her family home in Labadi, Accra.

So what motivated him to do that?

I had no idea. From my investigation it appeared he and his ex-wife were in good terms. He even told me they'd been talking since they got divorced. Perhaps he wanted to be heard on radio (an attention seeker). Well I killed that unholy ambition. And barely a week later a man approached me at the Ministries and asked if I remembered him. He was the man's brother. What did he say?

"You really tortured [drilled] my brother .how did you know that his wife was back?"

That was 17 years ago. Things aren't the same. Not everyone that smiles at you is a nice person. You cannot ask an unknown driver for a ride. You cannot take custody of someone's luggage or baggage any longer. That was common then you cannot do that now. Bottom line nothing is alien to Ghana nowadays. *But what went wrong?*

And did you hear the news over the weekend about the contract killer?

Yes, reality has hit home and it seems all of the above have now found a breeding ground. The frequency at which they happen is also mind-boggling. The Ghanaian is left in a profound state of bewilderment. The Ghanaian is amazed at the turn of events as it appears things are falling apart and the centre can barely hold the pieces together. It's like a seismic shock turning and shaking the very socio-cultural foundation.

That raises the question: *Is contract killing another creeping bug?*

Without a doubt Ghana has found herself dealing with all manner of menaces and there appear to be one factor that's fueling all of them. It's the love for money!

Money is driving people into ditches. People are seeing Malams, consulting Oracles, Mediums and Juju men for money. 'Sakawa' the code name for 'Quick Money' seekers is on the rise. Cyber fraud and ponsy schemes which used to be a western fad is growing astronomically at Ghana's backyard. It's all about money, money and money. Life means nothing anymore to humankind. If one could take another's life and become rich overnight so be it. You cannot trust your business partner, a friend or a brother.

Apostle Paul in his first letter to his young disciple Timothy said this: "For the love of money is the root of all evil. Some people eager for money have wandered from the faith and pierced themselves with many griefs," (1 Timothy 6:10).

Over the weekend, a 41-year-old Ghanaian business woman was caught up in the picture painted by Paul. Joyce Antwi a resident in Kumasi in the Ashanti region had barked up the wrong tree, when she thought she'd found the right person to kill her business partner.

In 2015 the suspect received an amount of GHc 99,000 from her partner to expand her (Joyce's) business and pledged to pay back her debt by April 2017. Instead she conceived a wicked plan to make sure that her partner was killed. Unfortunately for Joyce, she got arrested by the police on Saturday following a tip off by the man she'd hired to kill.

What's contract killing?

Contract killing is a kind of murder in which one party hires another to kill an individual or group of persons. It involves an illegal agreement between two or more parties in which one party agrees to kill the target in exchange for some form of payment, monetary or otherwise. In the United States the crime is punishable up to 15 years or life imprisonment.

Between 1989 and 2000 the Australian Institute of Criminology carried out a study of 162 attempted or actual contract murders in Australia. The study showed that the most common reason for murder-for-hire was insurance policies payouts. It also found that the average payment for a hit was $15,000 with variation from $5,000 up to $30,000 and that most commonly used weapons were firearms.

Contract killings accounted for 2% of murders in Australia during that time period. Contract killings also make up a relatively similar percentage of all killings elsewhere For example they made up about 5% of all murders in Scotland from 1995 to 2002

One of the world's most notorious contract killers was an American Glennon Engleman (1927-1999) from St Louis a dentist by profession. Glennon moonlighted as a hitman concocting and carrying out at least seven murders for profit over the course of 30 years. He was already serving ten life sentences in a Missouri jail when he pleaded guilty to the murder of a man and his parents in a separate contract killing. Methods used to kill his victims included shooting, bludgeoning with a sledgehammer and car-bombing. Engleman died in prison of a diabetes related condition in 1999. The exact number of his victims is unknown.

Ashanti Regional Police Commander DCOP Ken Yeboah told the local media that Joyce informed the supposed assassin on the 23rd of May to assassinate the business partner. She paid the purported killer GHc 2,500 out of the total GHc 5,000 contract fee she offered him. But her days had already been numbered. On Saturday the police went to Joyce's residence and she was arrested.

Community on EDGE: As Danger Looms

Their voices are unfamiliar and their faces unknown. But like biblical Zacchaeus they showed up on the national television sets in our homes and offices. Against the odds, they vented their feelings, unveiled their fear and anxiety. For me it was the first time I heard the name of the town they live–Appiah-Junction, which is near Kasoa in the central region not far from Accra Ghana's capital city.

The community is situated along the newly-constructed Kasoa Highway that stretches from the sprawling suburb (Kasoa) to the Liberia Camp. Unfortunately their daily activities have been wrought by terror and apprehension. The voices represent school children, mothers and traders and they're appealing to the government to construct a footbridge on that highway or find a solution to the looming disaster.

Sometimes you just can't help it but let it out. Beat the drums hard, scream your lungs out and challenge the status quo to wake up.: Wake up and see the rot going on under your watch. Ask them to wake up from their seemingly long slumber, if that's what would make things change for better or necessitate the authority to take quick action.

A frustrated young man resident at the town did just that: "Leaders of Ghana don't think about anybody, it's themselves and their children and family. They don't think about other people's children. Who made them who they are today," he rhetorically asked.

"We made them who they are. We placed them where they are."

Certainly, there are times you have to demand answers: Find out why things are in a wrong state when they're supposed to be in the right way?

But it seems to me that we are averse to that which is right- doing the right things or delivering the right goals and projects. And I am not laying the blame squarely at one particular administration; it goes for all governments that had once steered the affairs of this nation in the last three decades nearly.

I've got a few questions on my mind though, just can't let them stay any longer my head is spinning.

Is it possible for one to eat Fufu–the Ghanaian staple food without soup?

Or fly an airplane without a compass (navigation device) and drive a car without wheels: how is that possible?

How do you get goods and services from the opposite or other side of the Offin River?

First and foremost you would consider this if you've the means to do so: Build a bridge across the river. Alternatively, you would use a ferry or pontoon a canoe or boat to cart the goods and services. I can assure you, if everything is done right— that's employing the right engineers to do the right job and the funds are used for the intended purpose we would have everything in its right perspective. Remember you cannot achieve that if the project is fraught with freebies– ministers and project directors slicing their shares of the enchanada. It's normally the 10 or15 per cent cuts that throw us under the bus or screw us up.

No doubt something spooky is shaping up at the south-west corridor, on the Accra –Kasoa road. And if the eyes could speak I don't know how their story would be received. More than one thousand school children cross that stretch every day to and fro. And nearly the same number of women some of them pregnant, some breastfeeding, some with loads on their heads and some aged cross the same road day in day out. More than ten thousand vehicles ply that road and every day hundreds of pedestrians are seen jostling with these machines for space.

There's no zebra crossing (crosswalk), no speed rumps and no footbridge. But there's a midriff concrete wall built in the middle that divides the four-lane highway.

How does that sound?

I don't know when this is going to stop but I know where it's heading to. Disaster looms!

It's a disturbing scene. So scary that one wonders if the planners considered the people who live in the community. I've heard some make this flimsy excuse that oh, they won't even use the bridges, if you build them. Yes, I know my people. Some of them are stubborn– stick in the mud. They won't use them but the majority would. You don't starve your 10 children to death because three of them say they don't like the food. Therefore build the footbridges because it's their money and not yours. You're just a trustee, a custodian of their wallet.

Helloooo!

Did you hear me? Do you know how many lives you would save if you build a bridge on that stretch? I suppose you've no idea of the economic, social and political impact. How do they go to school? How do they go to work? How do they see their doctors at the clinics and hospitals? How do they go to the church or mosque or synagogue? How do they attend a social function? I mean how!

I know all the answers to them. Simply they don't matter. Perhaps all wasn't factored into the grand scheme of things. They aren't considered in the equation. They only count when it's time for their votes. So you expected them to scale over, jump over, walk over and be run over r. Of course they're already doing all that, putting their lives in danger.

Then when they enquired to know if there would be a crossover foot bridge this is the response they get like a slap on the face: : "Go and see the big men at the top."

The question is who made them the big men and big women?

See, I told you in our part of the world government is not for the people it's rather for the government. They call the shot and not the people who gave them the mandate to govern in the first place a cheek of that.

The N1 (National highway 1) had claimed many lives not several and communities that line the highway are still counting the dead—motor accidents. And already the Appiah-Junction highway has registered its first victim—an elderly woman.

We missed the sunrise, we missed the mid-day bus I don't think we can afford to miss the midnight train. That said, I will like to plead with the government and ask the minister in charge of Roads and Highways to look into this Kasoa road expansion project once again. Something isn't right!

Speaker's Life Jacket Saves MP

"Go and sin no more," Ghana's Speaker of Parliament tells a lawmaker.

Is the Speaker a Messiah Mr. Writer? No he is not.

So by what authority does he have to make such pronouncement when he knows, it's impossible for Mahama Ayariga to go without sinning any more or not to repeat what he did to bring shame upon himself and to the august house in general?

Good question honourable Jomo. I think you know better than I do as a Member of Parliament (MP) for Asem mpe Nipa. But let me try if I can answer your double-barrel question. First by which authority does he (the Speaker)…It's by the power vested into him by the executive or the president. And per that authority he oversees and moderates the proceedings and deliberations of the house.

The Speaker used the verse or phrase figuratively, which can be found in John 5:1-18. Jesus told a man to stand up and walk after being crippled for 38 years.

But sin as used in this context is euphemism for misbehaviour. Remember it was his seemingly stubborn disposition that invited all this controversy. That said, the Speaker used the phrase as a note of caution. 'He understands the infallibility of Man. 'Go and sin no more' else something worse will happen to you. It could also imply that this is your last chance—your next offense would be a red card.

Lest I forget, the Speaker has the powers to discipline members who break the procedures of the chamber.

I hope that answered your question.

"Sure, you did."

Well, Hon. Jomo, there will always be crumbs on the dinning or kitchen table, because that's where the foods—breads, grits, sugar, eggs, bacons, rice, vegetables, spaghetti, meat and many more get served. And mind you where there are crumbs insects and rodents are likely to thrive. They do so for the simple fact that we allow it to happen per our negligence and carefree attitudes.

If your house is infested with guys like mice, roaches and rats, then you've a big problem. Trouble is you may need non-toxic foods to lure them into traps or get rodenticide poison baits to kill them. Otherwise you'd become their food. For insects such as black flies and ants you're more than likely to see them once in a while nipping on your fruits etc.

Nonetheless, all it takes to get rid of these little ones is total upkeep or be vigilant. Keep the house clean, disinfect it and vacuum the dining room, kitchen and anywhere you sit to eat after breakfast, lunch or brunch and dinner. Did you miss that?

Well, they say who the cap fits let him wear it. I still haven't mentioned any names right but you already know who I'm talking about here. So stay with me. I wasn't soliloquizing! I needed that dialogue with my architect. Yes, in the writer's mind dwells an architect who makes things happen. And my inspires me, directs me and motivates me. Through him I draw my inspiration day in day out. I'm indebted to him and my gratitude to him will never cease because I owe it all to him.

Seriously I had closed the chapter on the Ayariga's Saga.' After all, the former information minister and a legislator failed to prove to the Ghartey Committee that there was a bribery scandal. No evidence, no testimony except rumours. I knew from day one that it was all meant to draw blood.

Let the sleeping dogs lie, I told myself. "No you aren't done yet," the architect told me. You've got to deal with the crumbs. Until you do that your sunken image and the perception about you as a corrupt institution would linger on. And I heard it loud and clear from the wilderness. It was from Eminent Justice Emil Short, (an authority not a spurious source) the former chairman of Commission on Human Rights and Administrative Justice (CHRAJ).

"The way the bribery allegation made by Mahama Ayariga was handled may not erase the perception in the minds of Ghanaians that the legislature is corrupt,' Justice Short said.

Magnanimity

So, why did Ghana's Parliament fail to disinfect its house?

I didn't mean that. I meant this: Why did Ghana's Parliament fail to purge its house when it realised that one of its members had broken the laws or no law was broken?

Last Friday the House of the Legislature stretched its arm of magnanimity or the mercy arm to a member who'd dragged the image of the noble house into disrepute. Bawku Central MP Mahama Ayariga had found himself neck deep in a sea of shame breathless. But for the Speaker's life jacket tossed to him he'd have gotten drown.

The Joe Ghartey Committee, in its final report, said it found no evidence to support allegations of bribery made by the Bawku Central MP Mahama Ayariga. Presenting the report of the committee to the House, Mr. Joe Ghartey, the Chairman of the Committee, said Mr. Ayariga failed to adduce any evidence to substantiate his claim bribery.

"Everything he said was nothing more than rumours," Mr. Ghartey said, adding: Multiplicity of rumours does not constitute a fact."

Speaker of Parliament Mike Oquaye warned Mr. Ayariga not to peddle falsehood in the legislature after the ad-hoc committee found him in contempt.

The Committee came to the conclusion that the MP (Mr. Ayariga) failed to prove that Mr. Boakye Agyarko, the Energy Minister, gave money to Mr. Joseph Osei-Owusu, Chairman of the Appointments Committee, to be distributed to the committee members with a view to bribing them to approve his nomination (by consensus).

Over the weekend the former CHRAJ Boss Short weighed into the issue.

According to him the probe did little to clean up parliament's image. He wasn't sure if Parliament did enough to allay the corrupt perception people have about the institution: "There are those who may not still be satisfied about the credibility of parliament because of the many previous bribery allegations levelled against the institution," he told Class FM an Accra-based radio station.

The Nation Ghana

Who founded it, was it Nkrumah or a group of founders?

The debate over Founder's Day is becoming a highly charged emotional issue across the nation amid the notion by some politicians that it's nothing but an act of sour grapes on the part of the governing NPP. They hold the view that the ruling party is simply disparaging something desirable, something the founders of the UGCC couldn't achieve. But, that begs the question says this writer.

Throughout history nations and states have had to fight or struggle to gain their freedoms and independents. Men and women that championed such emancipation movements paid heavy price as they often laid their lives for the good and love of their nations. Ghana isn't exception, our pursuit of self-rule was wrought by intense struggle in the pre-colonial era and it wasn't one without bloodshed. In fact its path was littered with grief and sorrow.

The 28th February Road incident in 1948 that took place in Accra near the Christianborg Castle ,Osu is typical example. The rioters were brutalised, several of them arrested and jailed.

But the freedom fighters did not give up. On March 6, 1957 Ghana (then Gold Coast) gained her independence form the British under the presidency of Dr. Kwame Nkrumah. His party the Convention People's Party (CPP) which broke away from the United Gold Coast Convention

(UGCC) of the J.B Danquah group became the first political party to wrestle power from the colonialists.

Three years on July 1, 1960 the country became a Republic. And just as her pre-independence was not without struggles, post–independent Ghana was punctuated by political upheavals, economic meltdowns, unemployment, riots, uprisings etc.

Thankfully, history had been generous to us, if it weren't so we would have plunged ourselves into a sea of misery. Historians both home and abroad over the years took ample time to record events that heralded our freedom. They also chronicled movements, pressure groups, political parties and individuals that had played leading roles in the fight to liberate Gold Coast from the jaws of imperialism.

Of course, the struggle for independence goes beyond 1950's. And one cannot forget the exploits by the Anomabo native John Mensah Sarbah. His Aborigines' Rights Protection Society (ARPS) opposed the Lands Bill of 1897 which threatened land tenure and another layer of the indigenous sovereignty. A little over 20 years after the birth of ARPS in1897, another movement was born called the National Congress of British West Africa (NCBWA). It was founded by Thomas Hutton-Mills Sr. and J.E Casely-Hayford. Other co-confounders of NCBWA were Kobina Sekyi, AB. Quartey-Papafio, Henry Van Hien, Nanka Bruce, Edward Francis Small and A. Sawyer. According to historical records, the idea of creating the NCBWA was first conceived in 1914 during a chat between Casely-Hayford and Dr. Akinwande Savage a Nigerian physician.

In fact the decade leading to the nation's freedom had witnessed powerful resistance against colonial rule. So, 27 years after the founding of NCBWA, in 1947, (over 100 years after the Bond of 1844) J.B. Danquah, George Alfred "Paa" Grant, R.S Blay, William Ofori-Atta, Magnus Sampson, Kwei Lamptey, Kofi-Ayensu-Dadzie, Ako Adjei and others also founded the UGCC to push the agenda for self-rule. Later Dr. Nkrumah would join the UGGC as its General-Secretary. This followed an invitation by the party's leadership. However ideological differences would trigger a break up. Nkrumah founded the CPP on 12

June 1949 —an appendage of the UGCC. His campaign slogan was 'independence now."

And here we are today 60 years after independence. A period that had seen our first, second and third republics which spanned from 1960, 1969-1979 failed due to incessant coup d'**états. However, the country has also made significant gains. We**'ve successfully held 7 democratic elections from 1992 to date. This is no mean a feat and it's an achievement by all Ghanaians. The people of Ghana and their leaders have ensured that the gains of the fourth republic is upheld and safeguarded.

So who founded Ghana?

It's worth noting that resistance against colonial domination pre-dates the period above-mentioned. Indeed our forebears had fought the Dutch, the Danes the English among other Europeans .And as a people we cannot and will not pretend that their contributions are inconsequential. But do such contributions automatically make them founders of the nation?

Perhaps the answer is no. Nonetheless we can ensure that their sacrifices made would not go uncelebrated, unrecognised and unnoticed. This was evident during Nkrumah's time, streets and monuments were named after certain people who helped in the struggle for independence. Indeed some politicians have argued that if the August 4 commemoration is about recognition, 'then certain important national monuments and other things can be done in honour of all those people who played the role'.

Martin Luther King Jr. Day is federal holiday held on the third of January each year....because he's well-known for campaign to end racial segregation on public transport and for racial equality in the United States wasn't recognised by some states. Even though it was officially observed in all 50 states for the first time in 2000 following resistance among some states, I think his life is worth celebrating. So I'm of the view that our nation must honour her unsung heroes and heroines and it must be devoid of partisanship. Let's honour them while they're alive and not when they're dead.

Be reminded commanders don't win war (s) by themselves. Rather it takes collective and sterling efforts by platoons and battalions to do so. Yet, oftentimes it's the commander-in chief that's credited or given honours. His name is more projected than everyone else's. Our traditional rulers once enjoyed such status at the time when they were building empires and kingdoms. Leaders take blame even when they aren't blamable and in like manner they take credit for progress and victory.

Was Ghana Born Twice?

On Friday 4 August government held a memorial and thanksgiving service as well as a lecture to commemorate the birth of UGCC. According to government, the 4th of August is a very significant day in the history of Ghana and as such, the day ought to be celebrated as Ghana marks its 60th anniversary. Why should merely celebrating a day trigger a national debate?

Or there was more to that?

I don't think it's wrong for the NPP party to observe August 4. The NDC has been observing June 4 over the past 38 years. And I don't see why that should also cause heads to spin and jaws to drop. But I think what has generated the controversy is the argument put forward by some Elephant bigwigs including the Speaker of Parliament Rt. Honourable Mike Ocquaye that Nkrumah alone isn't the founder of our nation.

And I think I've made myself clear in the foregoing paragraphs.

Retired diplomat and statesman, K.B Asante had already weighed into the debate. He wasn't enthused about the celebration which is seen as 'Ghana's day of destiny 'had therefore questioned its significance especially in this period. The 93-year-old man had asked government to rather focus on more important matters confronting the nation.

"Ghana was not born twice," he said. Even an ordinary human being are you born twice?. Ghana became Ghana on the 6th of March 1957…I mean I don't understand. "I don't know of any party which is happy with what is happening now, we have not gone far as we all expected and that is what we should be thinking about and not when we were independent and all that," Mr. Asante said.

Earlier this year the issue reared its ugly head, when President Akufo-Addo delivered Ghana's 60th independence anniversary parade. He came under attack over what some said was a cockeyed account of Ghana's history to suit his father, Edward Akufo-Addo and uncle, J.B. Danquah who played critical role s in Ghana's fight for self –rule.

Speaking at the 60th Independence Anniversary Lecture in Accra, the current speaker of parliament lectured under the theme '4th August; Ghana's day of destiny' where he gave a detailed account of how the idea of Ghana's independence was birthed. Prof Mike Ocquaye said he has great respect for Nkrumah; however, he disapproves of anyone suggesting that Dr. Nkrumah was the founding father of Ghana. He described that view as propaganda.

"One of the things we have done very wrong in this country is to turn everything into sheer politicking, To the extent that whiles journalists say facts are sacred and comment is free, we think we can make facts free and comments scandalous. We cannot build a nation on half-truth and propaganda," he said.

I still don't see the die cast here. And my fear is that if we resort to nick picking and attempt to politicise every national issue we would be doing ourselves a great disservice. Former president Kufour rebuilt Flagstaff House and renamed the edifice the Jubilee House. However the citadel was reverted to its previous name when NDC John Mills took the reins of power in January 2009. The argument was that it'd been named by the first president so it couldn't change. Need I remind you that there are number of state monuments or landmarks that had had their names changed after they were reconstructed? For example Ambassador Hotel, which was built during President Nkrumah's time, is now called Movenpick, and I think Star or Continental Hotel is also known as Gold Tulip.

I think, we should remind ourselves that the nation is bigger than our political parties. And if we continue to walk this path on the grounds that this is NDC's and that's NPP's we would soon cease to be one nation, one people, with one destiny.

It's against this backdrop that I think our first president Dr. Kwame Nkrumah should and must remain the founder of our nation. I don't see any historical anachronism here. Did he fight for the liberation of the Gold Coast like his peers Dr. Boakye Danquah, Paa Grant, SK Blay etc.? If so, let's remain united to build our nation.

Delta Strikes Again Like Thunder

The sound Woof whoof, reminds me of this song titled: "Who Let the Dogs Out"? And I guess many of you are much familiar with the song when it hit the airwaves in the Y2K's. Back then I didn't fancy it. But I think it probably caught my attention because of its repetitive dog barks—whoof, whoof, whoof, whoof, whoof.

Today, the song's beguiling title has put ketchup on my French fries. In other words the title is right for this write-up.

Before I get down to business let me quickly give readers a brief history regarding the song. It was performed by Bahamian group Baha Men and released in July 26, 2000 as a single. The song was originally written by composer Anslem Douglas (the original song was titled 'Doggie'). The lyrics are about disrespectful men who hit on women at a party.

xxxxxxxx

'Black Thursday' was how someone described Delta Force's attack on a Circuit Court four days ago in Kumasi the Ashanti regional capital. The vigilante group of the governing New Patriotic Party (NPP) had struck again. This was the militants' second attack in less than three weeks. On Friday 24 March 2017, Delta Force forced itself or invaded the Ashanti Regional Security Council Head Office.

In that attack, there was a forceful removal of a lawfully-appointed public official. Blood was shed and property was destroyed. And just about 17 days, of that bizarre attack another state institution has suffered similar fate—reeling fear and concern amongst the populace in the Garden City and across the country.

Their target was the Kumasi circuit court. Where Again?

I said at the court. The third arm of the government —the judiciary or court(s) has the responsibility to apply the laws to specific cases and settle all disputes. The Judiciary also adjudicates and interprets the laws. This was what the court was doing –performing its required constitutional duty, when it got attacked.

But why would someone or a group choose a court as target? Why would someone dare to degrade, demean and disgrace the very institution we the people have reposed our trust in? Well, given the scenario, it appeared, that thought didn't even cross the minds of the militants, I suppose. It must have been in their rear view mirror. It could be concluded that the group had already made up their minds and they would strike at all cost.

It was on Thursday 6 April, 2017. It's understood 13 of the group's members were standing trial for the March 24 attack.

The trial judge had no idea what was shaping up. He'd no clue whatsoever that his cool chamber would in no time be set ablaze as in action. A shake-up was in the offing. From afar the thunder had roared like a lion. The macho-men were soldiering on to the court as though they were on a warpath. They stormed the court and in what looked like a Hollywood movie-style whisked all 13 members away.

Did their colleagues in court know about the plot?

Maybe they did or maybe not. Remember it happened to former President John Rawlings after his 5th May Uprising. He'd to be freed by his colleague soldiers from a fortified security facility somewhere in Accra.

Local media reports indicated the 13, who were remanded into prison custody and billed to reappear on 20 April, were taken away through the backdoor of the judge's chamber by their supporters.

As earlier pointed out the suspects were standing trial for assaulting Ashanti regional security coordinator George Agyei on March 24 after his appointment. The group contended that Mr. Agyei wasn't their preferred candidate.

The Unknown

There are several things we don't know about this group, regarding its modus operandi. However, the good news is that, all 13 accused persons had since turned themselves in to the police. But there still remain some unknowns. No one knows the group's next target or place to attack. Would its next target be Manhyia— the seat of the Ashanti monarch or would it be the Kumasi Airport?

If they storm the Kumasi Airport they could hijack (let's assume there's a pilot among them) an airplane and fly it to the Flagstaff House in a matter of minutes. Right, but what happens thereafter? Indeed we don't know where and we also have no idea as to when. When would the group strike again? How would they strike? It's an issue that seems to bother many.

Suffice to say, up to this stage, we've all been left in the unknown world but armed with predictions and speculations. We have no knowledge of what's going to happen tomorrow. The group is acting like a wild weather—unpredictable. When you think it's going to rain it rather pours amid thunder storm. Who knows tomorrow, it could be a tornado?

Call for Punishment

Meanwhile the first vice chairman of the party Fredrick Fredua Anto, has said members of the Delta Force who are found guilty of attacking the judiciary should be 'punished', He sees the group's action as an affront to the judiciary as an institution and a dent on our democracy.

Mr. Anto told a local radio station in Accra Class FM that: "the rules are there" and the accused, if found culpable, must face the law.' According to the station he wasn't happy about the action of the vigilante group given what their conduct has brought the party into "disrepute".

The Goodwill

"Ayie yi amma na'afiri Krotwamansa", (Delta Force).

It remains to be observed whether the goodwill the NPP has been enjoying since the party's election victory in last December would be able to stand the test of time. Certainly, much of that would be predicated on the activities of these vigilante groups. Already there'd been signs of romance fatigue. It seems the fangled love between the party and the general public is shaking. People are getting fed-up with the news of Invincible and Delta attacks on innocent citizens. No doubt the majority of Ghanaians like the president, Akufo-Addo but for how long could this wild ride go on?

Readers will recall when the first incident occurred there were varied reactions across the nation. The uproar was huge. Even people deemed pro-NPP couldn't zip-up their mouths. It seemed the attacks were snowballing.

Social Commentator Casely Hayford couldn't hide his frustration. He said this in the wake of the March 24 attack: "People invading political party headquarters with cutlasses and machetes and fighting among themselves and nobody is arrested?

This is where it is all going wrong...Because we think it is politically not going to help us we will not do the right thing. It is too much. I am tired of it," he fumed.

A former minister of state in the Mahama administration Oye Lithur wrote this in a letter addressed to the President, the Interior minister and the national security coordinator:

"The forceful removal of a lawfully appointed public official was violent and blood was shed, with Government property being destroyed. This adds on to the list of forceful seizure and management of state property, that is, the Kintampo Falls tourist facility, seizure of toll booths, seizure of vehicles etc.

There have been numerous reports of extra judicial and unlawful violent acts by these groups. Ghanaians are peace loving and law abiding. We have been sustained as a nation by respect for the rule of law.

We do not want this violence to escalate; neither do we want this situation to degenerate."

The Fallout

In the wake of the Delta Force's attacks there seemed to be a division among the Elephant family as to what to do and how to deal with the group. Some of the stalwarts have expressed their dissatisfaction about the way the group's issue was handled.

Notable among them is the (NPP Member of Parliament for Assin North Kennedy Agyapong. Mr. Agyapong had threatened to bring down the party if Kan Dapaah, the Minister of National Security did not stop his threats.

The Minister in an interview with the local media was alleged to have made some comments that did not sit well with the legislator.

But responding to the Minister, the MP took a swipe at him and questioned his loyalty to the party. He also criticised the Delta Force over their attack on the Kumasi Circuit Court. He underscored that, although he appreciates and supports the efforts of the group, he is unable to back them following their actions on Thursday.

The tough-talking lawmaker described Kan Dapaah as a 'disaster' and further blasted him for poorly handling the Kumasi Security Coordinating Council attack.

In the meantime the National Security Minister, Mr. Kan Dapaah has denied reports suggesting that he insulted the Assin Central MP over the attacks by Delta Force.

According to Mr. Kan Dapaah, the stories making rounds are fabricated and are intended to damage his hard earned reputation.

Mr. Dapaah had been quoted in earlier reports to have asked Mr. Agyapong to "shut up" because he was naïve about matters of national security.

However, the minister in reaction to the report has stated categorically that in as much as many might disagree with his approach to dealing with issues of national security, he never expressed any words of insult: "Because my focus has and remains ensuring that the citizenry abide by the rule of law despite their political affiliations," he gave the assurance.

Auditor General Is Now Armed

The public purse drips by the day, as looters dip their long hands into the kitty.

Is this the real deal? And would the Auditor General be able to crack the whip or live up to expectation?

The Auditor General's Office can now bark and bite courtesy of the powers granted it yesterday by the Supreme Court of Ghana. Bark and bite, what does that mean?

It simply means the office can now retrieve all monies stolen from the state by public officials and also surcharge them. Hitherto, the Auditor General could only document cases of misapplication of public funds. Though that ammunition is in the 1992 constitution, the Auditor General's Office had over the year's failed to test its mettle or apply it.

Article 187 (7) (b) of the 1992 Constitution states that in the performance of his functions under this Constitution or any other law the Auditor-General -

(a) Shall not be subject to the direction or control of any other person or authority;
(b) May disallow any item of expenditure which is contrary to law and surcharge.

It was as though the apex court was telling the Auditor General's Office to wean itself from feeding on the daily milk. It's now time to eat bones and crack the whip. And I will urge the office to let the wild dogs begin to bark and bite. It should also ensure that there will be no more room for fraud, pilfering, thievery and corruption.

Nobody could be happier than Daniel Domelovo the Auditor General, regarding the Wednesday's remarkable ruling by the SC. He told the local media in Accra that he was elated as the decision reinforced his powers of disallowance and surcharge.

"This brings clarity to provisions of the 1992 Constitution which for several years have not been enforced. We have started implementing the constitutional provision," he said.

The ruling as earlier indicated empowers the office to surcharge and retrieve monies embezzled by officials at the Ministries, Departments and Agencies. It seems the old order is gone, the period that the office would hand over its final report to the Public Accounts Committee of Parliament (PAC) to decide on what to do. It is time for the Office to call the shot.

This is what Ghanaians have been expecting, making sure looters account for their loot and not let them off the hook. The citizenry would like to see governments give looters tougher punishments rather than rebuke them or give them a slap on the back of their hands.

Ever wondered what to do when an intruder breaks into your home?

Sometimes we have the guns in our rooms but we lack the courage to shoot. Remember the intruder comes to steal, to destroy and to kill. One would expect the Auditor General to take his gun and do justice to it.

Interestingly the Auditor General knew about this retrieve and surcharge but for several years two powerful guns idled in his room. He couldn't use them and never bothered to enforce them. And probably the result is what we have been reaping over the years. The looters saw the loopholes and they capitalised on them.

However, OccupyGhana a pressure group saw the absurdity in the entire process. The group saw the Auditor General's Office as a toothless bulldog or lame duck. How could the office not bite? Why did it limit its function to only documenting cases of misappropriation of public funds and not put to use the power to retrieve and surcharge?

It was against this backdrop that the group filed a suit at the Supreme Court and asked it to remind the Auditor General of his duties of surcharge and disallowance as stipulated by law and to ensure that all public officers found to have embezzled public funds are surcharged and prosecuted where necessary.

On Wednesday 13, June 2017, the court granted all the reliefs by Occupy Ghana and ordered the Auditor General to issue disallowance and surcharges in respect of all state monies found to have been expended contrary to law. The second relief granted by the Court was that the Auditor-General must take steps to recover all amounts lost to the state, and this covers private persons.

In a related development, the Attorney-General has been ordered to ensure enforcement of the orders including criminal prosecution where necessary.

To that I say kudos to OccupyGhana. Blessed are those who file law suits to stop corruption in Ghana. And now woe unto those who still think they will harvest where they haven't sown, the wild dog has been given new teeth.

Reacting to the ruling a member of Occupy Ghana Ace Ankomah told Joy News in Accra that for once the power given to the Auditor General by the constitution, which has never been exercised will finally be exercised. He was hopeful the new Auditor General appointed in December 2016, as well as the Attorney General appointed in March 2017 will both execute the reliefs granted by the court.

An estimated GHc 5bn of taxpayer's money has been lost through mismanagement by public officers. This was made known by Sydney Casely Hayford another member of the pressure group. According to him the judgement emboldens the Auditor-General to do more 'than document the sins of public officers in his annual reports'.

"OccupyGhana will assist in this effort to identify persons who through mismanagement, negligence or corruption have caused public funds to go waste," he said.

In 2014, the audit report revealed in 152 pages blood-cuddling stories of wastages and corruption. Some 43 district assemblies dissipated GH¢1 billion. And in last April, the Auditor-General submitted 13 reports to Parliament on public accounts for the year ended December 31, 2015. These yearly reports, according to the group are forwarded to Parliament's Public Accounts Committee where indicted public officers and managers are invited to explain themselves.

CUFFED AND DEPORTED

Did the Sojourner know of his fate?

Music legend Kojo Antwi in his 1995 hit song 'Atentrohuo' casts the life of an illegal immigrant like that weightless material from the silk tree. Across the world illegal immigrants live under the shadows amid fears that something untoward might happen to them. They could be arrested, detained by immigration officials and deported back to their countries of origin.

On Wednesday 14, June 2017, that dreaded fate befell 75 Ghanaian illegal immigrants in the United States of America. They'd sought asylum to regularise their stay but it didn't work out as they were all rounded up, handcuffed and deported back to Kotoka.

Were they criminals?

No, none of them was said to have any criminal record. Yet, they arrived in their homeland cuffed, shamed and humiliated. Their stories may vary but they all carried one name— deportees. This isn't the first time and might probably not be the last of its kind. Peoples from Africa and for that matter Ghana get that a lot. And I think it's about time our governments stood up against this appalling treatment.

Also, what many Ghanaians witnessed at the Kotoka International Airport (KIA) last Wednesday wasn't the first. Ghana has had her nationals deported from outside its frontiers before. In 1983 up to 1 million Ghanaians and other African immigrants were deported from Nigeria. This was the period the country faced severe drought and economic meltdown.

Prior to this, Ghana in 1969 deported many Nigerians back to their home country. The exercise which happened to be first in the post-colonial era was carried out by the then Akufo-Addo-Busia regime. Many believed the 1983 repatriation exercise executed by then Shehu Shagari's administration was retaliation.

The West African nation's people are known to be adventurous. They've over the years travelled to Europe, North America, Oceania, and Asia and most recently to the Arab world in search of greener pastures. Life has treated some well, but others haven't been lucky.

Reports say there are currently, about 7,000 Ghanaians living in the US illegally who are being processed by ICE (US Immigration Customs and Enforcement) agents for a possible deportation. That report was disclosed by US Ambassador to Ghana, Robert P Jackson in April this year.

"In fact, about 7,000 of them are currently at different stages of the deportation process. And we are not apologetic about that."

Did the Sojourner Know of his Fate?

Let's read this anecdotal piece:
Kotoka, I never planned it. I didn't plan this home coming. It came like a bombshell. All along I lived my life like 'Atentrohuo' constantly tossed around by storm anyhow at its choosing. Time was ticking and my fate was on edge. Indeed a chicken drank to a stupor is often clueless of her fate. There was no date set for this trip. Not on my own volition!

It was too late to take a flight. The falcon had cornered me (his prey). And I'd found myself in captivity. The captor had been lurking around the corner yet I didn't know. And I couldn't see him. I didn't know my fate had been numbered.

From far away we'd sojourned: Away from home. We left behind our loved ones and friends. We'd been gone for years. Needless to say our departure from home was dictated by necessity and poverty. Yes, abject poverty had driven many of us away from home—young and old, men and women, students, professionals and many more.

Remember, we left our shores unshackled but we've returned today in handcuffs as though we're criminals and didn't deserve our human dignity. But we're proud to be back home. Don't forget our story could be your story, her story and his story and anybody's story.

In case you didn't know there are more Ghanaians who are waiting for their deportation documentation the local media had learned. Like the 75 whose applications had been rejected and deported, 10 other

Ghanaians who had also applied for asylum but their applications were not successful are also expected to face similar or same fate. And it's my hope that the authorities in the US this time won't fly them home cuffed as they did to the 75 deportees earlier.

Narrating his account to the local media in Accra one of the deportees, said he was part of a group of Ghanaians who went to watch the 2014 World Cup in Brazil but managed to stay back after the tournament. He would eventually as many had done it before proceed to the US whereupon he sought an asylum.

"I was detained in California for a period but later moved to Arizona and then to New York before I was arrested and deported," he narrated.

So what's Asylum?

Asylum is the protection granted by a nation to an individual who has left his/her native country as a political refugee. For example, in the United States asylum may be granted to people who are already in the country and 'unable' or 'unwilling' to return to their home countries due to persecution, on account of race, religion or political opinion.

The above definition makes it difficult if not impossible for any Ghanaian immigrant to be granted such reprieve in the United States, either with a lawyer or no lawyer. In the 90's Ghana received refugees from Liberia and Chad. Unlike its neighbours which had been plunged into civil wars and ethnic conflicts over the decades Ghana has been enjoying a relative peaceful atmosphere.

Internationally, everyone knows Ghana to be politically-stable as compared to many of the countries in the sub region. Its thriving democracy has become an envy of the continent. This in part explains why our kinsmen were sent home. Their cases were looked into but they failed to meet the requirements.

One may ask why someone would consider the asylum option.

Unfortunately our brothers and sisters took that route. On that note I will say this to all prospective Ghanaian travelers, don't seek political asylum whether in US, Europe or Asia. Typically political asylum doesn't favour Ghanaians. It tends to favour peoples from Congo, South Sudan, Somalia, Syria, Yemen etc.

The U.S. government spends more on immigration enforcement than all other federal criminal law enforcement agencies combined. From 1986 to 2012, the federal government allocated nearly $187 billion for immigration enforcement. In 2012, it spent almost $18 billion on immigration enforcement—24 percent more than its combined spending on the FBI, Drug Enforcement Administration, Secret Service, Marshals Service, and Bureau of Alcohol, Tobacco, Firearms, and Explosives.

Currently nearly 43.3 million foreign-born people live in the United States. This is broken down as follows by immigration status:–the foreign-born population includes 20.7 million naturalized U.S. citizens and 22.6 million noncitizens. Of the noncitizens, approximately 13.1 million are lawful permanent residents; 11.1 million are unauthorized migrants, and 1.7 million hold temporary visas.

Why Presidents Must Have Media Encounters

If success were to be measured based on the number of rungs one climbs on a ladder, then success would have no meaning and the achiever would have no recognition in the eyes of critics and pundits.

Ghana's 5th president of the Fourth Republic Akufo-Addo yesterday had his day not at the court but with the men and women of the inky fraternity (the paparazzi). Among other things he said "The Ghanaian media has enriched the nation's governance by its persistence, curiosity and its investigative reportage."

It was the president's first media encounter at the Flagstaff House in Accra, since his induction into office on January 7 2017. The meeting sought to highlight two key components. First, the president had the opportunity to give account of himself and his stewardship. And second he gave assurance to the people who gave him the mandate. In effect he said they gave him the chance and he would give them their choice.

Mr. Akufo-Addo touched on some major issues notably, illegal mining, job creation, and the economy. Traditionally journalism is known for its information dissemination. However, the New Age or the New

Media has oiled the wheels of journalism. According to Pew Research Center journalism today 'does more than keep us informed'.

The Center said: "Journalism enables us as citizens to have our voice heard in the chambers of power and allows us to monitor and moderate the sources of power that shape our lives,"

At the media encounter on Tuesday the Q&A segment did exactly what the research team is talking about. It broke the gremlin and it brought home what perhaps most Ghanaians weren't aware of or hadn't been privy to.

Did they vote for a wild guy?

Does he condone or approve of the unruly behaviour of the NPP vigilante group—the Delta Force and the Invisibles?

Also, for the first time the nation heard that the president might not run for the 2020 presidential poll. He affirmed his stance on fighting illegal mining 'Galamsey operation and assured Ghanaians that the sun would soon catch up with businessman and NDC-bankroller Alfred Agbesi Woyome.

And did you know that the most dangerous person in Ghana is not Ataa Ayi? It's former Minister of Lands & Natural Resources, Alhaji Inusah Fuseini. His bugging binge had caught fire. The Q&A also put Assin North MP Kennedy Agyapong on the spotlight regarding his recent outbursts and threat to what he termed (to paraphrase) 'exposing the NPP of their shady dealings. But the president somewhat downplayed the issue: "Kennedy Agyapong's utterance doesn't irritate me," he submitted.

How do you gauge the success of a presidency?

Renowned historian and writer late Elizabeth Brown Pryor asked the above question in her provocative final book titled: 'Six Encounters with Lincoln."

She said: There are standard measures like passing durable legislation and responding well to crisis. Keeping campaign promises and pledges and maintaining popularity through statements and speeches, according Pryor are also good standard measures. Indeed such standard measures are commonly employed in the US and UK democracies. Even though developing democracies often try to imitate these giants but their input don't measure up.

The average Ghanaian doesn't care about the number of legislations passed by Parliament. He or she doesn't think those legislations are something that would translate into say job creation or increase tariffs. How about responding to crisis?

That's a good one. How did the president deal with the issue of Galamsey? Or was the president able to end 'Dumsor' the energy crisis? These are the stuff that scores the high marks and not the legislations even though they're equally as important as the others; the masses don't see them that way.

Some presidents are media-friendly others are not. US President Barack Obama (44) is known to be in the good books of the media. His successor Donald Trump (45) is the opposite of that. His relationship with the American media leaves much to be desired. Political analysts say Mr. Obama's goal seemed to be stability and incremental progress. On the contrary his predecessor President Bush (43) 'disregarded the headlines' content to let history judge his bold actions. Each administration seems to offer a new lens through which to view the office and its occupant.'

Indeed, the acclaimed biographer of Robert E. Lee, Pryor in that book (Six Encounters with Lincoln) discovered six untold, unnoticed and overlooked episodes that revealed Lincoln's, character, his fallibility and the awesome task he confronted, at times with mixed success.

And don't we all as humans tread this path? Don't we all face challenges that tend to make us feel like a blob or a wimp? Don't we show signs of meekness and weakness at times? It's basically this pathway that often shapes us. It defines who we are, our character, our temperament and our persona. On this path your critics would see no good in you. Your success would be overlooked and your person would be subjected to scrutiny. Bottom line when we think we've done so much to be rewarded our critics look at it from a different perspective or negative lens.

Galamsey: Fighting the Undying Witch

What did our governments clamp down in the past and were able to sustain it?

Is it illegal logging by loggers? Is it squatters at Sodom and Gomorrah or those around Kwame Nkrumah Circle in Accra? Is it power cheaters who indulge in illegal power connection? Is it cocoa smuggling in our country's borders by smugglers? Is it vigilante groups who're constantly terrorising people? Is it the activities of land guards? Or is it middle-men who swindle prospective travelers trying to obtain passports?

The irony is that all of them have bounced back—operating vigorously. Their activities seemed emboldened! Inhabitants of Ghana's biggest slum, Sodom and Gomorrah are back: They're back to where city authorities evicted them from, less than two years ago. The squatters and hawkers are also back in the streets.

And the key argument hasn't changed: they must earn their daily bread. The Kwame Nkrumah Interchange Area which not too long ago had a make-over is relapsing —going back to its ugly and insane state. In fact, on Wednesday some hawkers held placards amidst inscriptions like this: "We won't leave this area today or tomorrow."

The stubborn amongst them all is illegal mining operators also known as 'Galamsey 'in Ghana. Their activities in recent times have reached an alarming proportion. No doubt about that, they've stepped up their game. This followed the influx of the Chinese. I recall awhile back government deported a number of Chinese citizens who were in the country illegally.

Today, they're back in their numbers. And together with Ghanaians they're degrading and destroying our ecosystem. They're poisoning and exterminating our water bodies. Our vegetation covers have been laid bare—raped and left naked.

They're creating man-holes, producing sinkholes and setting up deathtraps. They're as dangerous as explosive mines. Over the last 10 years it appears the operators have sworn an oath– basically to launch a deadly onslaught to our very existence.

Is this the land of our birth? Is this the land we swore to protect? Is this the land (the greenbelt) our forebears bequeathed us? Where did our leaders go? Where are they?

And whether it's legal or illegal Galamsey has come to stay. That sounds crude or rather rude. But it's the hard truth. Galamsey isn't going anywhere at least not for now. Maybe not until the lands have run out of those much-sought-after minerals. Until the gourd is down empty or tanked the drunk knows no stop.

Backed by invisible hands they have succeeded in growing not an ordinary roots but giant roots, making it hard for authorities to deal with them.

But what is Illegal mining?

Writer Phillipe Dozolme defines illegal mining as: "The absence of land rights, mining licence, exploration or mineral transportation permit or of any document that could legitimise the on-going operations."

It can be operated on the surface (open cast) or underground. It's illegal because in most countries underground mineral resources belong to the state. The latter applies to Ghana too, but Galamsey has trespassed that. I must note there'd been crack downs on illegal mining in the past but all to no avail.

Question is: Are we at our wit end?

The Minister of Lands and Natural Resources John Peter Amewu announced recently that he'd placed a moratorium on licences for small-scale mining. This is part of activities to halt illegal mining operation in the country. The move, the sector minister also indicated was to help ensure saneness in the environment.

"I have not signed a single small-scale-mining licence, since I assumed office. This is an attempt to sanitise the system," Mr. Amewu told the media in Ghana.

Indeed Ghana is fighting an undying witch. We've picked up a fight which portends to be a lifetime battle. You may not like the way I've put it but that's the reality on the ground. I normally don't say things like that. I am a man full of hope, full of aspiration. I am an optimist and not pessimist.

Obviously, the conditions on the ground leaves one to wonder whether our governments had been waging these fights with kid's gloves or they'd condoned and connived with the operators or they didn't have long-term strategies or plans to do so. It could be that we're at our wit end.

Remember the father who brought his demon-possessed son (Mark 9:14-29) to Jesus' disciples to be healed? They'd no idea what to do and how to fight the demon. They lacked the firepower. Bottom-line they couldn't do it. Jesus rebuked them after healing the boy.

I felt I had been wounded twice or three times this past few days. The images I saw—the photos and the videos on social media platforms grieved my heart. I couldn't understand what's going on. I struggled to make sense out of all that–the degrading state of our ecosystem is so graphic. It looks so atrocious so horrible and so terrible.

The activities of these miners are out of hand. Sad though, we have to come this far to realise that we're losing or have lost something that is so precious. It's so sad our leaders couldn't stop it at its nascent stage. It seems to me it was business as usual and politics at its best. It seems to me they went to sleep whilst the busy bees got busy to degrade, to destroy tad to pillage that which our forebears fought graciously to possess and passed it on. And perhaps what's left now is misery and hopelessness.

World Bank report on Ghana had indicated, by the end of 1995 the total hectares of the land destroyed through the activities of Galamsey were approximately 150,000 hectares. That was then, over 20 years on the acclivities of illegal mining have picked up like never before .Thus your guess could be my best bet.

Between 1994 and 2001 a study discovered that there were five major cyanide spillages and leakages. Five rivers in the Prestea area in the western region of Ghana suffered greatly'.

Last March, Minister of Environment Science and Technology Dr. Frimpong Boateng kind of raised the threat level. Whilst meeting staff of the Environmental Protection Agency (EPA) during a working a visit in Accra Dr. Boateng hinted that our water bodies were under siege. He said the country risk losing the very existence of these precious water bodies if radical steps are not taken to resuscitate their lives.

"We know that our rivers are dead, some of them …Some of the rivers are dead—Offin, Ankobra, Pra, Oda, there's no fish in them, in most part of the rivers. And when you find animals and fish dying from our empty forests and dead rivers it is only a question of time that it will reach the human beings," Dr. Boateng said.

According to the sector minister if we don't change our negative practices we would literally kill these rivers prematurely. "We have to change our attitudes there must be a change like President Akufo-Addo said. We should not be spectators but be active participants."

"If you look at what is happening to the environment, it is something like a self-inflicted injury.

Certainly the danger has become imminent, so disturbing that if stringent measures are not taken we would end up as sore losers. The country that once boasted of its virgin forests, safe water bodies, rich soils, beautiful vegetation, and the picturesque landscape is gradually losing it all by the day. The ecological damage has been great.

Bittersweet

In Africa, Ghana is the second largest gold producer contributing to about 5.7 per cent of the country's GDP. And the activities of illegal mining have tremendously contributed to the growth of the economy. The jobless youth have found jobs, crime rate has gone down. However the environmental impact of their activities is unparalleled. Galamsey depletes environmental resources such as water; soil, landscape, vegetation, the ecosystem among others.

Also lives had been lost over the period and we're still losing lives. In November 2009 a collapsed occurred in an illegal mine in Dompoase in either Ashanti or Western region. At least 18 workers were killed including 13 women who worked as porters for the miners. A similar incident occurred at Kyekyewere near Dunkwa-on-Offin in the Central region.

Solution

Perhaps the solution to this cancerous problem rests in the bosom of the new administration's 'One-District-One-Factory across country mantra. It's a long term project, but if implemented they would go a long way to help bring the activities of illegal mining down. Remember, when there was Aboso Glass Factory, when there was Kumasi Jute Factory there was no galamsey but there was gold. When there was Nsawam Cannery Factory, the Komenda Sugar Factory there was no galamsey gold was there. When there was the Bonsa Tyre Factory, the Bolga Meat Factory and the Tomato Factory at Wenchi there was no galamsey but there was gold.

As a people our problem has always been not providing alternative measures. And not being proactive but reactive. You don't evict the Sodomites and the Gomorrahites if you haven't made any provisions for them. Then when you provide the alternative, ensure the laws are implemented to the letter. That's the way to go…Don't blame me, if you can't make the dogs bark and bite.

'No Where Cool':
Illegal Operators in Oil Palm Industry too?

In recent times those in the mining industry have had to endure the sting from the Aisha virus. The now quarantined germ attacks its victims indiscriminately—deep shaft, open cast or surface including dredging and mining on rivers and streams. And as there appear to be relative calm in that area another industry has begun wailing.

The Oil Palm Development Association of Ghana (OPDAG) is ringing the alarm bell. It seems to be under strong attack and needs government's intervention in a matter of urgency to save its existence as well as end the activities of illegal operators.

The stubborn fact is there are illegal operators in almost every industry across the country. They're in the cocoa industry, mining, logging, quarrying, fishing you name it.

Certainly, nowhere is cool. Like the mining sector OPDAG says illegal operators are threatening the industry's growth with their unholy activities.

This came to light during a press conference in Accra last Wednesday. The association's president Samuel Avaala emphasised that government must set up a supervisory body to check the illegal activities.

Now troubled by the virus OPDAG revealed that the illegal operators indulged in duty/tax evasion as well as tax avoidance. All this happens in the form of under-declaration, under-invoicing, mis declaration, smuggling, removal in-bond, removal in transit and other forms of corruption at entry points, the association pointed out.

In this regard Mr. Avaala has called on government and other stakeholders to urgently check the increasing number of illegal operators in the oil palm industry, stressing that the illegal operators in the industry are the cause of the lack of revenue generation in the business.

"We want the government to perform its supervisory role and ensure adherence to proper duty on import of refined oil products under protective measures or even consider an outright ban on importation of finished packed oils that are currently being produced locally as it pertains in countries like Nigeria and others" he stated.

According to him failure on the part of government to ensure strict compliance and adherence to the rules of the game would go a long to adversely affect the industry.

"If the government fails to do this, local production of oil palm will be stifled and it will have a negative impact on the refining industry and a ripple effect on the value chain including the farmers and all the suppliers," he added.

Regulating Imports & Exports

Mr. Avaala also bemoaned the negative effects of importing finished packaged oil into the country, noting that it robs the state of money. He noted that the Association was pursuing the formation of the Palm Oil Regulatory Authority to regulate the importation and exportation of palm oil. He said the oil palm industry in Ghana risks a total collapse if strict prohibitive measures are not taken by policy makers.

I couldn't agree with him more on the issue of importation. I think it's a huge problem that's facing farmers, agric industries and the nation as a whole. In fact Ghana spends close to US1 billion annually to import sugar, tomatoes, vegetable cooking oil, frozen fish, poultry including wheat.

And you probably didn't know that she now imports plantain from neighbouring Cote d'Ivoire (the Ivory Coast).

It might sound ridiculous but that's the reality on the ground. Ghana imports onions from Niger, tomatoes from Burkina Faso, garlic from China, cabbage from Togo, carrots from Holland and oranges from Egypt.

Former president John Mahama told BBC this: "We must look at the basic structure of our economy which is heavily imported dependent and also dependent on the export of a narrow band of primary products. Until we change the structure of our economy in order to address the trade imbalance that we have between exports and imports, we'll continue to have the pressure on the economy."

Well that dream never got realised during Mr. Mahama's presidency. And I pray the Akufo-Addo administration would address this issue as early as practicable.

Gangadhar Shetty, Chief Commercial Officer of GOPDC in his presentation as lead facilitator maintained that the country's palm oil industry has the capacity to meet local demand. He explained that the existing oil palm refineries in Ghana have a combined capacity of approximately 626,400 metric tonnes per annum against a market requirement of 228,000 metric tonnes per annum.

"This is a clear indication that the local manufacturing companies have the ability to cater not only for local demand but also the ECOWAS markets through exports of international quality packed oils thus bringing in the much needed foreign exchange earnings," he stressed.

Great strides

Despite the problems the association enumerated ,its performance over the years has been remarkable –producing more than double each year of the global market requirement. Across the world the demand for palm oil is increasing, putting pressure on rainforest. It is understood that large scale plantations log and burn to make space for oil palm production.

It is estimated that 17 million acres of rainforest are lost each year to industrial agriculture, including palm oil production. And with galamsey operators mining indiscriminately the fear is that Ghana like Malaysia and Indonesia could soon face what's known to be the 'Palm Oil' problem.

Research has shown that rainforests absorb and store huge quantities of carbon from human-caused dioxide emissions. Therefore rampant logging could speed up climate change which causes increasingly erratic weather patterns around the world. This huge threat oil palm production poses to human existence has led to calls for an alternative crop production.

Soy and canola have been suggested to take palm oil's place. However, it's been established, that would also require more land to produce the same amount. So it looks like we're stuck with palm oil because the crop provides a huge employment for millions especially countries such as Indonesia and Malaysia. That said I think what we need to do is to protect our rainforests, intensify reforestation projects and regulate excessive logging as a way to conserve our forest reserves.

The Battle of Mojabiyedum

Does Sergeant Bukari have the credibility to lead?

Rot in Mojabiyedum (Mogya-bi-ye-dom) has sent the people on the streets. A former 'mutineer' is leading the crusade. It's a war that has never been won. And it's unclear whether crusaders of today would be able to get the mission accomplished. Amid the public outcry sergeant Bukari and his anti-graft marchers have hit the streets.

His mission is simple—to free the people from economic bondage. The people are economically burdened not because they don't have the manpower and natural resources. Mojabiyedum is endowed with gold, manganese, bauxite, timber, cocoa, oil and many more.

By many standards, it is not a nation that should resort to panhandling. Ironically she's doing exactly that. Mojabiyedum has been dwarfed by debt, haunted by Dumsor, overwhelmed by unemployment and paralysed by corruption. In many years they that pledged to fight the canker got themselves embroiled in the mess. Unless you're strong and have the will power to do so, you'd lose focus and grip.

For many years the leaders have been stealing, looting and plundering her. It seems nobody is bothered and if they did the thought that their efforts would come to naught often put that idea at the back burner.

Something ought to be done to end corruption. But who will lead the fight against the graft?

In the meantime sergeant Bukari has been gauging the terrain, carrying out investigations, conducting interviews, collecting facts and data. Bukari has in his possession a dossier as fat as Goliath's head. And he concludes that the time is ripe to storm the streets. It's time that all monies stolen from the state must be retrieved as early as practicable.

The people have bought into his idea. They're bent on retrieving all the monies that public officials have looted.

The story reminds me of English author George Orwell's Animal Farm novella, published in England 72 years ago in 1945. The animals had won the battle at Cowshed against their master and renamed the farmland Animal Farm and that led to the writing of the seven commandments.

Indeed the commandments had been hailed by all the animals after their revolt. But I think what probably made it more popular was the seventh commandment which said. "All animals are equal." However, the leaders among the animals soon wound up amending the very tenets they'd set in the first place during the revolt. Power is a treasure. Therefore, they would do everything animally possible to consolidate it. And they came up with this: "All animals are equal but some animals are more than others."

This isn't different from what we often hear during electioneering campaigns. Politicians speak like that when they're looking for power. We witnessed some braiding hairs and sewing dresses in the last general elections. Some of them had become culinary experts overnight. Corruption must be defeated they pledged.

Doesn't that resonate or give you a clue as to what our country is going through?

xxxxx

Perhaps this is just a tip of the iceberg. A whopping GH¢112 billion is believed to have landed in the pockets and hands of some corrupt public officials in Ghana last year alone (2016). The ironic twist is, Ghana's public debt from the time of the country's independence to date is in the region of GH¢127 billion.

Think about it for a second. How did they do that?

This startling revelation was contained in a 310-page document compiled by journalists at Adom FM –a local radio station based in Tema in the Greater Accra region. Yes, the hawks stepped out of the proverbial 'Mad House' (Newsroom) to rake the muck in the system. On Friday Captain Smart led thousands of people on a demonstration in Accra to present the said report to the Economic and Organised Crime Office (EOCO) an anti-graft agency.

"We are giving EOCO three months within which they must work and investigate persons engaged in acts of corruption who are in the documents we have presented to them. If the agency failed to heed our request, we would stage another protest in Kumasi, the Ashanti Regional capital," Captain Smart stated.

The protestors carried placards with messages, including "Stealers need psychiatric evaluation, Ghana Must Work, We need our gargantuan money," "Pass RTI Bill", "Simpa Panyin hates corruption," "#Yegyeyensika."

Does Captain Smart have the credibility to lead?

Even though many have commended Captain Smart for leading the fight against corruption in the country, it seems not everyone is happy about what the Adom FM presenter is doing. Former Communications Director of the National Democratic Party (NDP), Ernest Owusu Bempah is the latest person to raise bribery issue against him.

Mr. Bempah has alleged that former President John Mahama gave Captain Smart a Toyota land cruiser Prado ,whiles his brother Ibrahim Mahama also gave him 1.2 million cedis two weeks before elections to do dirty work on radio for the then ruling government .

"The persona of the character who is championing the course is himself fraught of corruption allegations and I am wondering how he can get the moral fiber to demand accountability from persons who are also alleged to have dipped their hands into the purse of the state," he stated on his Facebook page.

I think this is a serious allegation and needs to be investigated too. In recent times there had been unsubstantiated accusations of bribery scandals. It's either someone is receiving or someone is giving but the accusers have often failed to provide evidence to back their claims. So the question is: How true is this allegation against Captain Smart?

Can Mr. Bempah prove this in a court of law if he's asked to do so?

Or better still, I will per this write up urge the former communication director to report the presenter to any of the anti-graft agencies in Ghana. And I think if he cannot do this as suggested herewith, then he must equally not pigeonhole the good work Captain Smart is embarking on. We want our stolen monies back.

Again my question is why now?

Are you sceptical about Akufo-Addo's pledge to fight Corruption?

Back in March 2015 Ghana's Catholic Bishops described bribery and corruption as the 'two evils' that are wrecking every fabric of the Ghanaian society. No doubt about that bribery and corruption if you like are defining us as a people—good or bad, developed or developing, successful or a failed state.

At the time former President John Mahama who'd been elected into office two years following the demise of president Mills (the second term of the NDC) said he was the key to defeating corruption in Ghana but his fight against the canker came to zilch.

In fact the Fourth Republic had already seen four pledges gone a begging. The fifth and the latest one was made by President Akufo-Addo on Monday at the Chief Executives Officers' Summit in Accra. His predecessors–presidents Rawlings, Kufuor, Mills and Mahama had all made pledges during their respective tenures to bring corruption onto her knees. All of them identified bribery and corruption as the bane of Ghana's progress. And all of them fought it.

I remember the term willfully causing financial loss to the state was applied in the 2000's during Kufour's regime which saw former ministers of state in the NDC previous government imprisoned. That clause had since been criticised and viewed as biased by a section of the Ghanaian populace. Somewhere in December 2016 a former head of the Ghana National Petroleum Corporation (GNPC) Tsatsu Tsikata said the term was skewed.

"In my view willfully causing financial loss to the state has always been applied for political gains as against the national interest. If this persists it will tend to discourage and frighten officials from giving out their best while in office, with the fear of being persecuted," he said.

Has Ghana been able to exorcise the two demons yet?

No they're still with us, possibly more than emboldened–tormenting the nation.

The question is why are we at the same spot or retrogressing?

To many Ghanaians fighting corruption is like flogging a dead horse. What do you get apparently no result (s). However most people hold the view that the canker can be dealt with if a more concerted effort is injected into the crusade, allow transparency and making the two glamorised evils unattractive.

Can we do that?

Well, it seems there's going to be a new or an exciting anti-corruption initiative here. But before we touch on the juicy part of the president's novelty idea let's look at two or three of the statements attributed to him (in quotes) by the local media.

Mr. Akufo-Addo said: "The scale and level of tolerated corruption" under the fourth republic and especially in recent times needs to be arrested immediately."

There's no newness about that statement, I can state emphatically. As matter of fact each of the former presidents preached same or similar sermon (The 4 Johns invoked GH chapter 4: 192 through to 2016). Also they recognised the enormity of the problem but they couldn't kill the bull.

As president he said: "I will not sing the chorus of the problem without addressing it."

Equally the former presidents addressed the problem. They talked about the problem but they diddled Ghanaians out of that pledge to fight corruption.

"I'm not naïve about the enormity of the problem and how that continues to undermine efforts of development. We need to fight corruption collectively and the joint efforts of the captains of business will be most welcome," adding: "We need all hands on deck to fight corruption because corruption fundamentally is the giver and the taker – both are guilty."

That paragraph is beautifully crafted. However it isn't different from the rest. Truth of the matter is Ghanaians have heard those expressions such as 'all hands on deck' time and again. Indeed we've heard some say corruption will be a thing of the past. Ironically, you and I know that we're living it. We lived with it yesterday and we might live with it tomorrow, if we don't change the mindset.

But here's the nugget. This is what I consider to be first of its kind– the creation of a bureau at the presidency to deal with bribery and corruption.

In a speech read on his behalf by Senior Minister Yaw Osafo Maafo, the president said he would create an office at the presidency where business people can directly report corrupt state officials whose names will, in turn, be published in the dailies along with whatever punitive actions were being taken against them. That's a novelty. I haven't heard it anywhere in the past regimes.

"I will establish a Business Reporting Bureau at which corrupt activities of staff and officers of State Owned Enterprises, regulatory institutions, revenue agencies and the public and civil service will be reported to. We need to go about this in a very transparent manner with time so that together we can fight corruption," Mr. Akufo-Addo said.

Seriously I think we need this of bullet to kill the two demons. The good results might take long but we will get there.

That leads me to my next question: *Who will police the police?*

Again it seems the president has an answer for me. According to him complaints received will not be swept under the carpet. "To ensure that action is taken against persons reported and that heads of these institutions are held accountable, I'll cause it to be published, on quarterly basis or in certain periods, all complaints and steps that are being taken in respect of these persons."

The President said his office is open to suggestions from the business community with regard to the establishment of the Business Reporting Bureau so as to uproot corruption. "I encourage ideas on making this proposal more feasible and effective being submitted to my office through an avenue to be announced by the middle of June, latest by July."

Across the world corruption has forced many investors to quit doing business. Reuters, an international news agency headquartered in London England reported on Monday 15 March 2010 that 'extortion by corrupt officials in Russia has got so bad that some western multinationals are considering pulling out altogether.'

Corruption isn't an African disease or problem. But African governments lack the political will to fight the canker. That explains why we are where we are. Corruption is in the West, the Far East and Oceania. Corruption can be found in South America, the Caribbean and the Middle East.

SPECIAL PROSECUTOR's BILL

Did the Majority Err?

When you hear this: 'The Special Prosecutor is coming,' you get the sense that there's a potential 'waterloo 'shaping up at the political arena. Sounds also like a roaring lion pursuing its prey viciously. Literally it means individuals deemed to have willfully caused financial loss to the state, involved in financial impropriety, scandals, looting, thievery, corruption, bribery, larceny, fraud, embezzlement, misappropriation etc. will be investigated by the special prosecutor to be appointed by the president Akufo-Addo.

Well that alarm bell was sounded by Senior Minister Yaw Osafo Marfo and it's already creating uneasiness and discomfort in/around the political domain.

Some politicians (mainly from the Minority NDC) have criticised the creation of such an Office, citing conflict of interest and other factors. A former deputy Interior minister James Agalga said: "The new political experiment to fight corruption could be nothing more than old witch-hunting repackaged."

However, most Ghanaians hold different view. They seem to be very enthusiastic about it. According to them they can't wait to see the special investigator investigate, probe and prosecute corrupt public officials as well as deal with corruption which is a major problem facing the nation.

"We want the Special Prosecutor Bill get passed as early as practicable," one political analyst told me.

"At times our politicians make a fool out of us. They tell us blanket lies and make us to believe that they hold the plumb line. Like it or not it seems they almost always have their way. And I think if we fail as citizens to hold them to account of what they say or tell us, what they do or how they do it we would be fooled again and again and again," the analyst said.

What's happened to the Bill?

The Special Prosecutor's Bill which was introduced on the floor of the Parliament House last week didn't have a smooth ride as expected. And it appears the momentum it gathered from the onset had been jolted. It seemed like a ditch on a highway but as this writer notes it rather tends to deepen our fledgling democracy.

On Friday 21 July, 2017 Parliament announced that it will no longer consider the Office of the Special Prosecutor Bill, 2017, under Certificate of Urgency. The move followed a report by the Select Committee on Constitutional, Legal and Parliamentary Affairs to the plenary recommending that the Bill be allowed to go through the normal legislative procedure since they do not see the urgency of such Bill.

The Bill 2017 was laid in Parliament under certificate of urgency on Tuesday 18, by the deputy minister of Justice and Attorney-general Joseph Dintiok Kpemka on behalf of the Attorney General and minister of Justice in accordance with Article 106 of the Constitution.

Criticisms swirled following its introduction and its quest for 'Certificate of Urgency'.

Dominic Ayine, a former deputy Attorney General, said even though the Minority supports the Majority and government on the issue of fighting corruption, the group maintains that due process must be adhered to.

"What we are saying is that the procedural requirement of the Constitution and the standing orders must be complied with. If this is an important government Bill, if we have to enact it, we have to enact it in accordance with law. Our fight is about due process of the law," Dominic Ayine

The Bolgatanga East legislator who is also a member of the Constitutional, Legal and Parliamentary Affairs Committee contended for such a Bill to be laid, it had to be gazetted 14 days before it will be brought to the Parliament but that was not done.

Article 88 of the 1992 Constitution puts the responsibility of prosecution under the ambit of the Attorney General and any attempt to hand over that responsibility to another agency or person must be done in accordance with law, Mr. Ayine stressed.

But his argument was undercut by the Majority Leader Osei Kyei Mensah Bonsu. According to Mr. Mensah Bonsu who doubles as the Minister in charge of Parliamentary Affairs, the Office of the Prosecutor's Bill came to Parliament under a certificate of urgency for which reason it did not require a 14-day maturity period.

Did the Majority Err?

Sascha Mueller a Lecturer in Law at the University of Canterbury, Australia writing under the topic: Where's the Fire: 'The Use and abuse of urgency in the legislative process,' said: "In some circumstances speed may be desirable, but rushing legislation comes with downsides. The different stages of the legislative process have an important purpose: they are designed to *improve the quality of the bill*. The committee stages are meant to scrutinise the bill as to its ability and efficiency."

According to the law professor the regular use of urgency in New Zealand for example is by no means a new Phenomenon. He thinks it may rather be viewed as tradition, noting that even though the term has its demerits, it also has many advantages..

'Since the late nineteenth century, the ability to accord urgency has allowed the New Zealand Parliament to prioritise certain business, and thus accelerate its completion. This is done primarily by extending the House's sitting hours until the urgent business has been completed. Normally, the House sits for six and a half hours on Tuesdays and Wednesdays and for four hours on Thursday. However, under Standard Order (SO) 55 urgent sittings can be extended to last from 9 am to midnight on any day apart from Sunday," professor Mueller submitted.

The Office of the Special Prosecutor Bill, 2017, was laid in Parliament under a certificate of urgency on Tuesday, July 18, 2017, by the Deputy Minister of Justice and Attorney-General, Joseph Dindiok Kpemka on behalf of the Attorney-General and Minister for Justice in accordance with Article 106 of the Constitution.

The Bill was then referred by the Rt. Hon. Speaker, Prof. Aaron Michael Oquaye, to the Committee on Constitutional, Legal and Parliamentary Affairs for consideration and report pursuant to Article 106 of the Constitution and Order 179 of the Standing Orders of the House.

Following the debate as to whether the Bill should be treated under a certificate of urgency, the Rt. Hon. Speaker asked the Committee to determine the urgency or otherwise of the Bill in accordance with Article 106 (13) of the Constitution and Order 119 of the Standing Orders of the House.

However, at a sitting on Friday, July 21, 2017, Chairman of the Constitutional, Legal and Parliamentary Affairs Committee, Ben Abdallah Banda, told the House that the Committee had considered the Bill as directed by the Rt. Hon. Speaker came to the conclusion that due to the nature of the Bill and the interest it has generated in the public domain, there was the need for time to allow for broader consultations on the subject matter in order to avoid any chaos it may cause.

"The Office of the Special Prosecutor as envisaged in the Bill will transcend different political regimes, hence, the need for the Committee to engage in broader consultations with Civil Society Groups and other key stakeholders to solicit their inputs," Mr. Banda said.

"The Committee acknowledges that the Attorney-General's Office is overburdened in the discharge of its duties and therefore the need to carve out some of its investigative and prosecutorial duties to the proposed Office of the Special Prosecutor. The Committee, however, does not see any vacuum created by the absence of the Office of a Special Prosecutor to warrant the Bill to be treated as urgent," he noted.

The Microphone, Armchair Journalists & Newsmakers

Is the Honeymoon Over?

Tempt not. Try not but flee if you can't see them in your rearview mirrors. They're like sharpened razors. Microphones are as deadly as the sting of a cobra, shrewd as a politician, innocent as a dove and dangerous as fire. They can put Man into Moon or the outer space. And they can also send Man to Lucifer's kingdom, Hell. But they don't act on their own. They aren't their own bosses. Without their architects they're like Egyptian mummies. They're as lazy as a lazy creek and as dumb as a rock. I didn't say cock. So don't put words into my mouth. They're remote-controlled by journalists.

'They're controlled by who?'

    I hate it when you let me repeat myself. I bet you don't want me to subject you into a drill? Fill it you spill it. Kill it and you stand still. Pay the bills and you pretend to be ill. Now what? Are you sure you didn't hear me say they're remote-controlled by journalists?
    'Massa', (Master) I think you like that. Don't you?
    I know what you want. Your doubts are just demands for more.
    And I promise to spoil you today, make sure you keep your fingers on the tabs though. Meanwhile I like you to focus on the car's number plate. I can't believe you missed it at the first shot. Don't forget precision is our watch word. We shoot to kill. So go ahead and retake it. *Voila!*
    That was good old President Mr. Dr. Jerry John Rawlings posing a photograph by a car that looked like a Mercedes Benz CLS Coupe 2017. And the eyes beheld him!
    Mr. President I still owe you a cow, a car, a cigar, a cat, and a camera on the occasion of your 70th birthday anniversary which fell on Thursday 22 June 2017. God bless you Mr. President. By the

way, what happened to my invitation it didn't show up as promised? You made me wait in vain and got my pen slain.

Did I tell you this: It pleases me sometimes when people act like the biblical Thomas .Until they see the wounds forget it. That means cross check and double check. It's key ingredient in journalism profession. If you can't do that you must equally forget it because citizens today, are doing just that in bathrooms, bedrooms, boardrooms, dining rooms and in their living rooms.

I now understand why Jesus spanked the guys (the money changers) at the temple. And it also appeared he was frustrated by Thomas' behaviour. How could he not recognise the man (Jesus) he'd worked with for nearly three years?

Was the thought of Jesus as a ghost made him blackout?

Or he was just been himself as a doubter?

'Hey Thomas this is me Christ the Saviour,' Jesus told the doubting Jew. Thomas replied: 'But you were crucified yesterday my Lord. How could I explain this to the brethren? Here, look into my hands, my midriff and my feet, Jesus told Thomas. I believe you now my Lord.

Well that isn't the end of the game. Therefore brace yourself for another bout.

Did he come incognito? I guess he did.

And what's his name? Benito Bio.

Oh he has a middle name too. What is it? He's Owusu.

What does that mean?

I may have to explain this by telling a short story. 'You can't come to Africa and not hear a story,' apologies to Finance Minister Ken Ofori Atta who was in Germany a few weeks ago to showcase/market Ghana. He brought home $100 million from our great friends.

And here's the story: A man had been laid in state after his sudden death two days earlier. As the mourners mourned him they saw tears coming from his eyes. They were awestruck. It was the first time the people had seen this happen. His wife was pregnant. And a month later she'd a baby boy and they named him Owu-su, because his father cried in his death. Massa, now you know that's a brief bio on Mr. Bio, the deputy Minister of Lands and Natural *Resources.*

Arm chair Journalists

In October 1 2009 journalist Brenda Norrel wrote an article headlined: 'Lazy Journalists are the darlings of the corporations."

According to the News Reporter lazy journalists are great friends of the corporations. They are known as 'armchair journalists,' because they sit in comfort and rewrite press releases from politicians and corporations. To spice it up a bit they dial a few numbers, get a few comments and call it a news story,"

They're the darlings of the energy companies'. She was quoting Buffy Sainte Marie a Canadian singer-songwriter.

Is the honeymoon over?

Last Friday some radio presenters and journalists at FOX FM a Kumasi-based radio station in Ghana incurred the wrath of Mr. Bio. It appeared he'd had enough from those he described as 'armchair journalists' and he unambiguously stated his mind.

Perhaps the deputy minister's ranting comes as no surprise to many. Nowadays most newsmakers in Ghana tend to think or feel that journalists are not working hard enough to get behind the news. And it seems they're fed up with journalists when they sit in their offices and interview or literally cross examine public office holders. Indeed it seems the honeymoon is over.

"Stop your usual arm chair journalism and go round to seek solutions and answers for the galamsey menace." His comments followed an illegal mine that collapsed at Nsuta near Tarkwa in the Western region and claimed about 20 lives.

According to FOX F M Mr. Bio also took a swipe at the station's presenter, Kwaku Kyeremanteng Nkansah.

"Journalists from BBC are the first to take their cameras reporting that people have been trapped in a galamsey pit at Nsuta-Prestea while journalists in this country are making calls to me. Now you are sitting in your studio and calling me for the number of people alive and dead. ...this is lazy journalism. I cannot talk to lazy journalists on phone. ...I am tired of the numerous telephone calls from journalists in Ghana. ...I can't even open my mouth anymore."

You should go out to dig for your own information. I am not obliged to speak to you. I have very important meetings with some white men now," Mr. Bio snapped.

"And then he dropped the call," the station reported.

Yes you know who 'dropped the call', the minister.

And after all that this is what the station reported: "It is not clear if the minister had been infuriated by an unknown person prior to his answering the call for the live interview, but as soon as he was brought on air he started attacking journalists urging members of the inky fraternity to step out for first-hand information rather than to sit in the comfort of their studios and grant interviews."

Really, what is not clear about the minister's action?

He didn't mince any words. He called spade a spade and not a tool for digging.

The minister may be right at some point. I agree with him that some journalists sometimes don't want to get up, stand up and walk to the news. They want it all cooked, all baked, all grilled, all roasted and put in their plates–that kind of journalism is now trending on the social media—Facebook, WhatsApp, Twitter etc. However, calling a public office holder and engaging him on a civil discourse isn't armchair journalism that I think the minister overstated it and also he was too harsh. I will end here with this: 'Remember the Sabbath and keep it holy'

THE WHINING FUSE: What Did Lindsay Say?

Hodgepodge isn't born yet that's the title of my fourth book. But its innards can be tied to this story. In August 21 2016 I posted on my Facebook Page an article titled—'Hopeful & Doubtful: The Saga of Two Brothers". And I'm sure excerpts from that write-up would probably help unlock the barricaded doors of 'Whine City'.

First of all, don't get carried away. There's no city in the world called Whine City. I made it up. It's an abstract city and it doesn't exist. It fits into the popular idiomatic expression, 'building castles in the air'. Whine City is designed and constructed by rumor mongers and naysayers.

To understand this discourse we must remind ourselves that:

'...People are people and will remain as such. They talk they gossip they whine and they gripe. They will tell you—nothing works down here. Everything is bad and everybody's corrupt.

They'll tell you about the giants. About how powerful that man is. They'll fill your ears with the story of the untouchables and how everybody in town fears them. About how they tried it and failed miserably. When they say things can't be done here. Tell them my father taught me better than that. And everything is doable."

Be reminded positivity is what it takes to make things work. Conversely, negativity kills passion and it beclouds hope and optimism. Don't let the world scare you. Do when you can and if you can. Don't blame everyone for your woes. And never say nobody can do it if you cannot. Do your best and leave the rest. Before long there will be a new crop of generation which can pass the test that you failed..." End of quote.

Sometimes right messages don't fall at the right place or get good landing. Instead they fall on hard rocks and thorns like the Parable of the Sower in the Holy Bible. Invariably, when that happens the messenger is ostracised and labeled as arrogant, idiot, narcissist, bootlicker mudslinger etc.

Reggae legend Robert Nesta Marley in his 'Who the Cap Fit', hit song, wrote this moving line: 'Man to Man is so unjust...".

And indeed if it weren't so how did a 14-minute speech given at the recently held Ghana Diaspora summit in Accra by Deputy Minister of Trade and Industry, Robert Ahomka-Lindsay wound up in an about 3 minutes video that sought to portray him as one with his nose in the air?

But I think Mr. Ahomka-Lindsay meant well and he was right. However, his speech got twisted by unknown twisters. It was taken out of context and the ripple effects had since bled onto the Social media platforms.

Is it abnormal? No I don't think so. In my view it's human nature. Give a man GHc99.00 or $99.00 and in between the cash insert fake $1:00 bill. I can guarantee you within minutes the whole world would hear about the fake money and your good deed would be insignificant. God forbid, if Jesus doesn't stay in Bethlehem but go to Gethsemane then you'll be in trouble. Expect mob attack and your crime— you're a money launderer or an armed robber.

"Nobody likes whiners, people that spend all the time whining all the time really get on people's nerves so stop whining," the Deputy Minister said.

And is that not the truth? Truth hurts but I think he couldn't put it any better than the way he crafted it.

I think he stated what's obvious. Who doesn't know that it's frustrating to get business started or done in Ghana? The reason, one has to see the minister of Sea, the minister of Fisheries, the minister of Salt and all that. And who doesn't know, one has to bribe his/her way through? Does that portray a business-friendly environment and are we happy about that? Absolutely no, and I think the Thursday meeting basically sought to discuss and address issues like that.

He was also right about the examples he gave concerning renting apartments or buying homes abroad. You don't get it by a snap of a finger it takes time. But the good thing about that long wait in the UK or anywhere abroad is that you'd not pay a bribe to the Sea Minister or middle man.

The participant who used the wealthy constituency analogy was right to the extent that you'd certainly put the money where one's mouth is. However, we cannot allow ourselves to be battered by the usual blame game and also to conclude that nothing works in Ghana.. In fact a step in a wrong direction is better than making no move and which is why I agree with the deputy minister. Let's make a move and prove to them that we're ready.

Please find below Mr. Ahomka-Liindsay's statement which was issued on Thursday 13 July 2017:

I refer to recent discussions on a 2 to 3-minute clip from my 14-minute speech given at the Ghana Diaspora meeting in Accra. The clip is a complete misrepresentation of the speech and taken completely out of context.

I was asked to give my candid opinion on my experience as a Diaspora returnee and how I would advise others who intend to make a similar journey. My speech was in 5 parts: 1. Your approach to trying to get results in Ghana 2. What you should expect when you make the move to Ghana 3.

The opportunities available for you in Ghana and the rewards for perseverance. The next steps.

The clip being shown referred to section 1 of the speech. Listening to it independent of the other three sections gives a completely different meaning to the speech I would implore all that want to get a true picture of my speech to look at it on You Tube: https://youtu.be/YbkQCoNgSBc

None of my comments were meant to cast aspersions. They were an expression of my personal experience. I wish to assure the people of Ghana and all those who have been offended by my comments that I did not in any way intend to sound offensive in my presentation. I hold all Ghanaians in the greatest respect and would not in any way do or say anything that would impugn their integrity.

LITTERERS JAILED IN GHANA?

Was that a crow I saw last time in a video picking up after litterers?

Yes I'm sure it was a crow. The black-feathered bird was seen undertaking the task as though she'd been hired by a city mayor. Back and forth, to and fro, she picked up and dropped off the mess created by humans into a trash can or bin. Wondering how we got here? Simply, we're gradually shirking our social responsibilities as citizens of the world and now our reckless activities have caught the attention of the lesser creatures.

Tinkers don't fix automobiles and computers. They mend pots, kettles and pans.

So what went wrong? What caused us to be careless and indifferent?

I'm inclined to believe that those who litter are probably filthy-blind. That means they either don't realise the negative effect of their actions to the environment and society. Or they just like to be deviant —not conforming to accepted norm. They would prefer to stay in filth rather than live in a more hygienic environment. And I won't hesitate to describe them as anti-social group. They don't bother whether society will grow or will tumble. A Lagosian will say it in pidgin like this: 'Country broke or no broke we dey.'

Town Council

Back in the day filth had no place in the streets of our villages, towns and cities. Sight of the guy (the sanitary inspector) in a short/long sleeve shirt tucked in a khaki shorts, socks pulled to knee with black polished shoes and a hat to match was more than enough to warn residents to keep the surroundings clean as well as healthy. Sorry, the story is different today.

In Ghana during the 60's and up to early or mid-70, those town council officers or inspectors were outstanding in their duties. Basically, they ensured litter laws, enforcement efforts, and court prosecutions (delegated to them by the central government) were used to help restrain littering. *Where did the laws go?* The laws are still sitting in the books. But they've become white elephants. Bribery, pilfering and extortion have been cited as some of the factors that have caused the breakdown of the hitherto vibrant town council or the statutory body. Overpopulation, cultural attitudes, deviancy and lack of proper sanitation facilities are also to blame. There are other factors too.

Madina Judge

Thankfully, there's now a 'Big Brother' watching litterers and there's also a judge that's ready to hand down punishment. So next time you decide to litter or dump refuse in the streets be mindful else you might end up at the court to face not Judge Judy Sheindlin (the American television court star born Judith Susan Blum) but Judge Efua Tordimah of Madina district court in Madina, Accra.

On Friday 7 July 2017, the no nonsense judge convicted 18 persons in the La-Nkwantanang-Madina municipality for dumping of refuse on the main Madina-Aburi road. The court sentenced them on their own pleas to a fine each ranging between GHc120.00 to GHc140.00 or in default serve between two weeks to a month imprisonment.

The sentence, this writer believes would serve as a deterrent to others. But Her Lordship was also magnanimous. She tampered justice with mercy. A minor who'd been sent to dump refuse was acquitted and discharged by the court.

Prosecutor Mr. Lambert Kwara told the court that the litterers were arrested by a joint Police and LaNMMA Sanitation Task force within the La-Nkwantanang-Madina Municipality for illegal dumping of the refuse. He explained that all the accused were busted in a night swoop at various parts of the municipality dumping refuse indiscriminately.

The exercise is aimed at keeping the municipality clean. Mr. Joseph Quacoe the Municipal Environmental Health Officer told the state News Agency: "This swoop is to bring sanity not only into Madina area but the municipality."

Lethargic Approach

Large cities in Ghana such as Accra, Kumasi, Takoradi, Tamale and Tema have been plagued by this menace. Littering is common spectacle. It's uncommon to see people hurling empty cans, bottles, food containers and wrappers from car windows or dumping them in the streets. Aside that I think leniency has played into the picture and our approach to dealing with littering to say the least has been lethargic.

Chairman of Public Hygiene Council in Singapore Liak Teng Lit thinks people are unwilling to litter if there are fines and punishment for example. "We have become reluctant to do the bad thing. I'm referring to enforcement, including fines and Corrective Work Orders (CWOs), and speaking up when one sees others littering," he said.

Enforcement was more thorough in the 1970s to early 1990s, when photos of people queueing up to pay their littering fines were published. When CWOs were introduced in 1992, offenders made to clean public areas did so under the glare of the media. Photos of them carrying out CWOs were splashed in the newspapers. Over the years, we have become more forgiving, with more emphasis now placed on education," said Mr. Liak.

When was the last time you stopped someone from littering?

I did that decades back and I felt good after that. I made a guy picked up his own trash on the Kwame Nkrumah Avenue near Ghana COCOBOD Building and my buddy Nana Boadu who was with me at the time laughed his head off. The guy had dropped banana peels in the middle of the road. *Hey you, would you mind to pick up your mess I told him.*

His response was: "Is this place your home?" I knew right there, he was going to be unruly. I thrust two fingers in my breast pocket in an attempt to fish out my ID card. And before I could say Jack *'Opana'* was already on the ground. He'd picked them up. But he left me with this colloquial phrase: You're too known."

Accra was declared a city on the 28th of June 1961 and became Accra city Council. The Accra City Council was dissolved to become Accra Tema Council in August 1964.. And the AMA was established by the PNDC Law 207 which has been replaced by enabling Local Government Act 1993 (ACT 462)

My question is: If birds know how to keep our environments clean then what are we doing as humans? And I think authorities in Singapore know the answer to the question. 'Complacency is most likely reason for Singapore's litter woes," one environmentalist wrote.

Experts say: 'when people know there will be an army of cleaners to pick up after them, they become too lazy to do the right thing."

The National Environmental Agency (NEA) study also found that about two in 10 people did not think they were littering if their serviettes blew away in the wind. Three out of 10 thought leaving rubbish on a park table after a barbecue was also not littering.

Elsewhere in the United States litter is an environmental issue and littering is often a criminal offense, punishable with a fine as set out by statutes in many places.

Litter laws, enforcement efforts, and court prosecutions are used to help curtail littering. All three are part of a "comprehensive response to environmental violators", write Epstein and Hammett, researchers for the United States Department of Justice.

For example in Washington State, the littering of (especially lit) cigarettes can incur a fine of up to $1025. During the summer months, drought-like conditions and tinder-dry forests, lit or smoldering debris have started many wildfires State litter surveys have shown that an average of 352 pounds of litter is picked up for every mile of highway including about 3,000 cigarette butts.

'Gold Diggers' Resort to Plan B?

There's a popular myth in Ghana that a cat has nine lives. And there's also the expression: 'There are more ways than one to skin a cat. Did the latter expression originate from the former per the belief that the cat has several lives? I am not sure if it did. But perhaps a brief history will give us an insight into its origin.

The term simply means or refers to a task that has a number of ways by which it can be accomplished. For example in a football match you can pack the bus to frustrate your opponent or change the tactical play to outwit the perceived adversary and get the result.

My online search showed that an appearance of the expression is in Way down Easton Portraitures of Yankee Life by Seba Smith of about 1854. And the writer wrote: "This is a money digging world of ours, and as it is said, there are more ways than one to skin a cat, so are there more than one of digging for money."

I was on my way not to Jerusalem but the ministries in Accra this afternoon. The sun was shining but it went unnoticed. Wrong place to display her vital statistics isn't it? She glided the stage unpatronised. The taxis tooted their horns to lure customers. Uber services have penetrated Ghana. Accra the capital city is served first. Kumasi, Takoradi, Tamale and Tema might soon get their bowls full. Tro-tro drivers are unhappy. But taxi drivers seem to be more aggrieved. Uber has landed. She's like the popular Chinese Galamsey queen Aisha Huang.

A little yonder my eyes capture the newly refurbished Accra Regional Hospital formerly Ridge Hospital situated in the Financial District of Accra. She needed the makeover (the plastic surgery) and she now looks more than beautiful. But beneath the façade there appears to be tension brewing –two captains in a ship.

I don't seem to understand what's going on. First there was a sack isn't it? And how did that change or later reversed to a transfer? Apologies to Charles Kwadwo Fosu's (Daddy Lumba) hit song– 'Aye Hunhunhu." This is Ghana, everything is politicised or is politics. The loo is politics, food is politics, and we're even politicising and 'theocratizing' (that's my word) the traditional ban on drumming, which is done once in a year in the Greater Accra region.

Anyway, that isn't the subject to be discussed. So take it easy. Thing is whichever way I will have touched, someone would cry foul, someone would say, I stepped on his toes or poked his nose.

Ever heard the chant choooboi? "Ohinahin, oboa bi reba o gyata bi reba..."

It literally means one must brace him/herself.

Come on board my people. Let's go down to Apremmodo, Gonda, Kamina, and Arakan barracks. They all fall under Ghana Armed Forces. The barracks are in different regions—Apremmodo is in Takoradi, W/R, Kamina in Tamale N/R, Gonda and Arakan are both in Accra.

See sometimes we get stuck or stopped in our tracks for a good reason. I saw a video on Facebook on Monday. It was shared by my good friend Samuel Kyei Manu. A lowly duck had taken her time in rail tracks—walking at her own pace while a passenger train slowly dovetailed her. The unperturbed duck on two occasions lay down, the clip revealed. The train stopped too and waited on her. And I could tell at that stage the impatience of the passengers was growing increasingly, but the train driver had time for his/her innocent risk taker. She couldn't even be baited to leave the rail tracks..

Again, this isn't the subject for discussion. As aforesaid I was on my way to the ministries, but something cropped up. Something I had no wind of. I'd read, that as part of measures to provide market for tonnes of food expected from the Planting for Food and Jobs programme, the Ministry of Food and Agriculture was to sign a Memorandum of Understanding (MoU) with the ministries of Education, Health and Gender, Children and Social Protection.

The MoU will enable the government to use its procurement power to supply foodstuffs to health and educational institutions and the School Feeding Programme. That's a laudable idea, I said to myself.

Why don't you catch up with them I soliloquised?

Geographically I 'd found myself on the south side of Accra close to the Independence Square, by the Atlantic Ocean near Osu and not far from Accra Sports Stadium. Also not far from the National Theatre and in proximity wise I was closer to the Accra Court Building than Kempiski hotel in Gold Coast city.

How did that sneak my radar screen?

I'm sorry this isn't the subject either. I don't seem to get my bearings right. I can't wrap my head around what I have stumbled upon. Everything, I mean my schedule appears so tight. I can't think far. Don't blame me. But finally, I think the buck stops here. Where? I said here at the Ministry of Defence.

Sure, I had no idea that all the barracks in our military establishment are to be investigated. Was there a coup or rumors of coup? Days of military coups are gone, they're in Ghana's rearview mirror. However, at times their uninvited services cause the eyes to blink and the nose to shake.

Certainly there is more than one way to skin a cat. The Galamsey operators have discovered a new strategy. They've got plan B to enable them continue to mine despite government's six months moratorium. It is understood, they've employed the services of the military to restart where they left off.

The Minister of Lands and Natural Resources John Peter Amewu made this known on Tuesday. He said illegal small-scale miners in some areas in the Ashanti region are using the military as shield to protect them.

"The law enforcement agencies, especially the military are protecting an illegality and I think that this is time the truth be told. Most of the sites we visited today were heavily manned by the military command," Mr. Amewu said.

"We tried finding out from the Minerals Commission and the Minerals Commission has established beyond all reasonable doubt that they have never under any occasion established any contract with those military personnel and so whoever authorised those military personnel to be protecting the Russian and Armenian sites."

If this is true then Ghana is in trouble. Under whose command were they deployed? I don't think it would be difficult for the military High Command to find those involved. All roasters must be checked and double-checked. . Who were on duty or off duty on the said date and day? Where did they come from, Kumasi, Sunyani, Tamale, Takoradi? The ministry of defence must look into this with extra pair of eyes.

The story reminds me of this line: 'Choose this day who you shall serve?

Meanwhile deputy minister of defence Derek Oduro (Rtd) has debunked the allegations that military personnel are protecting illegal miners. He emphasised that the Ghana Armed Forces hasn't sanctioned such an operation. However, Mr. Oduro pointed out that any military officer involved in such an act may be doing so by himself and if found culpable would be punished.

And I welcome the investigation ordered by the Minister of Defence Dominic Nitiwul. I hope they will get to the bottom of the matter and it wouldn't be a slapdash one.

DELTA EIGHT CASE: DEAD OR ALIVE?

The attack on Kumasi Circuit Court on Thursday 6, April 2017 became an increasingly important subject across country .And it appears to be rearing its ugly head once again. It's been dominating the airwaves and grabbing the headlines in the broadsheets now—probably more than it did over one month ago.

It was masterminded and executed by a crowd of eight brawny members of a vigilante group, called the Delta Force. During the onslaught, the militants were said to have aided the escape of 13 of their members who'd been arraigned before the Kumasi Metropolitan Assembly (KMA) Circuit Court.

It didn't make sense then and it truly doesn't make sense now. The style and everything about it smacks indiscipline at its highest apogee. The question is: Who does that? Who in is his right mind would dare invade a sitting court and free suspects standing trial. But it happened!

There was public outcry. There were calls for their rearrests. And pressure was brought to bear on the authority. Eventually the eight were rearrested. They'd been in custody. The streets in the Garden City were quite quiet. Until Wednesday!

Is the arm of the Judiciary broken?

Who can break the arm of the law one may ask?

Well you might think the judiciary is untouchable. However it seems the third arm of the executive has come close to that crucial moment. The powerful Lady's arm appeared to have been twisted or near to be broken. Did anyone see that coming?

No I don't think so. It seemed unlikely following the infamous 'Montie Trio' saga that generated a huge debate after the Mahama administration granted them clemency. The three media men are said to be NDC apologists.

The Discharge

On Wednesday 17 May Senior State Attorney Marie Louise Simmons advised prosecutors to drop charges against the accused persons because of what she called 'the lack of evidence against them'.

And consequent upon that advice the Kumasi circuit court not only discharged but also struck out the case.

The eight had been charged with causing disturbance in court, resisting arrest and rescuing persons in lawful custody when they aided the escape of 13 Delta Force members arrested for assaulting the Ashanti Regional Security Liaison Officer. The seemingly bizarre case has since drawn the ire of a number of institutions and eminent individuals. Notable among them is the Ghana Bar Association (GBA).

So how could there be no evidence based on what their dockets say?

Weighing into the subject the GBA in a statement said justice would not be served if the discharge of the said accused persons ends the matter.

Mr. Benson Ntsukpu National President of GBA said: "the GBA has noted with disquiet the discharge of eight persons by the circuit court in Kumasi on 7 May 2017 supposedly on the advice of the Attorney General's Department."

The statement co-signed by the GBA president and the National Secretary Justin A. Amewuvor stated, the association was 'disturbed 'by the turn of events and hoped that the discharge of the accused persons would not signify an end of the matter. "It is the view of the GBA that justice will not be served if the discharge of the accused persons ends the matter."

In the meantime the GBA has asked the Ghana Police Service to scrupulously investigate the matter in its entirety. "We call upon the police to interview the court officials, lawyers and litigants who were in court on the day in order to bring the perpetrators to justice," it said.

In a related development, the Editor-in-Chief of the New Crusading Guide newspaper, Abdul Malik Kweku Baako has stated that the decision to free the eight is 'politically unwise.'

Mr. Baako who claimed the Attorney General, Gloria Akufo and her two deputies did not advice the prosecutor in the Delta 8 trial to discontinue the case described the decision as 'politically imprudent'. The advice may be legally sustainable (based on the contents of the duplicate docket) but politically imprudent! A case of this nature should have been allowed to run its full course in court," he said.

The Denial

The discharge of the eight has ignited hot discussion and debate in the West African nation, compelling government to react. It has however, denied the allegation that it sanctioned the decision to drop charges against pro-NPP vigilante group,

Mustapha Abdul-Hamid, Minister of Information in a statement made available to the local media said the Principal State Attorney in the case did not consult the Attorney General before dropping the charges against the accused. The statement added the ministry, had since launched an investigation into the circumstances that led to the prosecutor declaring that the AG did not have sufficient evidence against the accused persons.

"The action by the State Attorney may amount to "a breach of internal procedures on matters of this nature," the statement emphasised.

It further revealed that it would deal with persons whose actions in the matter "bring the work and commitment of the department into disrepute" and gave the assurance that it would take the necessary measures to remedy the situation in the interest of the Republic.

Meanwhile, the Attorney General's department has also begun investigations into the matter.

According to the department preliminary investigations suggest that the decision was taken without recourse even to the Director of Public Prosecution and may amount to a breach of internal procedures on matters of this nature. It reiterated: "We are committed to ensure that the rule of law is applied at all times and persons found culpable of any breaches that bring the work and commitment of the department into disrepute will be sanctioned and the appropriate remedies adopted in the interest of the Republic."

Also reacting to the case is the Minority group in Parliament. The group said they found it bizarre that the AG released the culprits on basis of lack of evidence. It has therefore urged President Akufo-Addo to immediately order the re-arrest and prosecution of the eight members of the Delta Force.

The Minority made this known at a press conference held in Accra after the court freed the eight accused persons. Speaking at the impromptu meeting Minority Leader in Parliament Haruna Iddrisu said: "We demand, therefore, that the cancerous discretion that has just been exercised will be reversed immediately and the accused re-arrested and re-arraigned before court. We also do demand that justice must be done and justice must be secured and justice must be seen being done."

And this is my final take: I hope the matter isn't dead yet. I hope the two-prong investigations currently underway will yield good results and I hope the demands by GBA and the Minority in Parliament will be met. Finally I hope Rule of Law will rule and indiscipline will be silenced.

Ghana's Economy

Do We Need Knee-Jerk Fixing?

Highways and urban roads have speed limit signs. The signs determine the rate and pace at which road users can go. Same can be said about an ailing economy or one universally-known to be broken or collapsed. Meltdown economies take longer time to recover and they vary too. This isn't peculiar to Ghana it's a global trend. If the injury is severe it would need time and resources. In other words, a badly injured economy needs time and resources for its recovery.

That's a fact no one can deny. Even critics and non-critics of the Akufo-Addo-led government, be they the opposition NDC surrogates, serial callers or the impatient ones in the NPP know that as an inescapable fact.

However, I think what we may disagree on is probably the calls on the administration by some section of the populace or individuals 'to quick fix' the economy. To say the least, it's an unnecessary pressure.

Not everything in our lives needs a quick-fix or can be fixed at a breakneck speed. There are some things that can be fixed within or at a shortest possible time, which in itself is relative, depending on the severity or otherwise of the thing or person.

And I can emphatically state, it doesn't take 130 or 131 days to fix a collapsed economy. What does (131) that translate into? That's four months and 10 days, it's incredibly impossible. I think we need to remind ourselves that fixing a bedridden economy isn't like fixing a hot plate pancake for a morning breakfast. It's equally not same as re-roofing a house that's been taken down by a rainstorm.

Moreover, I think we need to be honest to ourselves rather than engage in or resort to gladiator politics. Mind you we're all in it together. Who goes to the Intensive Care Unit (ICU) with a heart attack and expects to be discharged same day? I hate to remind people that Ghana's economy is under pressure and has heart attack.

Yet, there's been this pressure-storm mounting almost every day. Fact is putting unnecessary pressure on the surgeon won't solve the problem. He needs time, energy and resources to work on our patient, your patient, my patient and his/her patient.

Have you in your widest dream thought about Professional footballers? They've no patience when they sit at the bench (as a result of injuries) but truth is they cannot go back onto the pitch half—fit or with half-treated injury. The problem will worsen. It's like borrowing millions of dollars from the IMF and throwing it back into their pockets.

What's the healing time of a knee ligament injury?

Studies show that treatment of a ligament injury varies depending on its location and severity. For example Grade 1 sprains usually heal within a few weeks. I discovered that during my research into the subject. Maximal ligament strength will occur after six weeks when the collagen fibres have matured according to medical studies.

For a torn ligament studies have shown that it takes six weeks to 3 months before ligament healing occurred. However, at 6 weeks to 1 year after injury, a large percentage of participants still had objective mechanical laxity and subjective ankle instability.

I think it's too early to make a fair assessment or judgement. Thing is if we all agree that the government inherited a broken economy then let's give them ample time to fix it. And I have no doubt that it's fixable and they can do it with dedication, commitment and modicum effort.

Years ago McKinsey & Company– a global management consulting firm that serves leading businesses, governments and non-governmental organisations did a report on the country's troubling economy. The report noted that from the 1948 recession through the recession in 1981, the US economy typically recovered to pre-recession levels in six months.

However, in the 1991 recession the trend changed. According to the report it took the economy, 15 months to recover. The 2001 and the 2007/8 recessions were much different. In the case of the2001 recession, it took 39 months to recover. And the 2007/8 which President Obama inherited from Bush 43, economists expected full recovery in over 60 months period.

So let's give the government time to fix the broken economy.

Did I say 'the broken' economy'? Yes I did. Who else said that a while back? It was the Member of Parliament (MP) for Assin North Kennedy Agyapong. He jabbed the Vice President with this line: "Dr. Bawumia, if the NDC has collapsed the economy, fix it....we don't want more complaints..."

Without a doubt, I think it's prudent for anyone to call on the government to fix the economy because we need the jobs and the monies in our pockets. In that vein I support Mr. Agyepong, he has challenged Dr. Mahamudu Bawumia to fix the country's economy for the masses, who are unemployed to find jobs.

According to him, the NPP is now eating back its words after the party led by then flagbearer, Nana Akufo-Addo, told then NDC government to fix the economy, if it's broken.

But I tend to disagree on the argument that the NPP criticised the NDC to fix the economy so they must also fix. Yes NPP must fix it but at which time frame? What's the speed limit here? Remember you cannot go 60 mph in/at school zone.

That said the best way to get a handle on what is happening with the economy is to look at the economic indicators—Inflation, Gross Domestic Product (GDP) and the Labour Market. For now I can say they don't look good, especially the labour market, unemployment is increasing .And with the recent government anti-galamsey operation I expect the numbers to skyrocket.

But at least every one knows what's going on. Everyone knows that we have a patient at the ICU who needs special treatment and experts who can get the job done. That implies pooling resources and demonstrating commitment and dedication. We don't need arguments, we don't need partisan politics and we don't need any bickering whatsoever.

Inflation is a significant indicator for securities markets because it determines how much of the real value of an investment is being lost and the rate of return one needs to compensate for that loss.

So far Bank of Ghana's report on current inflation isn't bad. It shows improvement. The cedi is also appreciating which is a good sign too.

Inflation inched up to 13 per cent in April from two and a half year low of 12.8 per cent reported in March. Cost of transportation surged 24.9 per cent due to rise in transport fares, according the Banks' report. Food inflation slowed to 6.7 per cent which was the lowest since November 2014. Inflation Rate in Ghana averaged 17.07 per cent from 1998 until 2017 reaching an all-time high of 63 per cent in March of 2001 and a record low of 0.40 per cent in May of 1999. Government has targeted 8+/-2%.

It had earlier eased to 15.4 per cent in December of 2016 from 15.5 per cent in the previous month. The performance was the lowest inflation rate since July of 2014 as non-food cost increased at a slower pace.

Why Newsmakers Are Vulnerable: Ghana in Perspective

A silhouette doesn't stay long on a stage even though he exudes a bigger image than the one that carries him. He hobbles away like a whirlwind, his destination unknown. The memories of him die quick after his exit. Sometimes he resurfaces if luck smiles back on him. But most of the time, his glory disappears forever.

In fact his existence is dependent on one's sweat if you like. So when the body dies he dies with him. Yet, he never ceases to plunge himself in a sea of delusion, where confusion holds the mind captive and the upshot is often a disaster.

What a lesson right!

Yet, Newsmakers—politicians, celebrities and the influential in our societies pay little or no heed to the obvious fact. That no condition is permanent and when it blooms it falls. So why are newsmakers vulnerable? It's because they forget quickly where they came from, how they started the labyrinth journey. Plus they forget what to do and how to do it when they get the call-up onto the public stage.

The Managing Editor of Insight Newspaper, Kwesi Pratt Jr. yesterday made a benign statement about Ursula Owusu-Ekuffo Ghana's minister of communication. And how's that newsworthy or important to highlight here, because Mr. Pratt is an avid or a known critic of this government. Also he's viewed by many as anti-NPP the New Patriotic Party.

He says he's shocked by the minister's behaviour. Well, many of the Elephant's supporters too, are perhaps surprised that the statement came from him—a notorious criticiser of the administration. But Mr. Pratt is right.

"Ursula has shocked me and many others. I thought she was going to be a hard nut to crack and also give Nana Addo lots of problem but she has so far behaved in an admirable way," Mr. Pratt said.

The veteran journalist went on to commend the minister and also asked other public figures to emulate her shining example, adding though Ursula was noted for being 'harsh' and a 'sharp' critic of the Mahama administration, she'd now turned a new leaf.

"Ursula Owusu is now a role model for many…they have to learn from her as well," Kwesi Pratt Jnr recommended.

Generally, News makers make the news, notwithstanding the fact that media personnel are called newsmen. But the media or journalists write the news and digest the views. They (Newsmakers) may have the bragging rights as the source and champion of the news. The irony is they've no control over what they produce.

I have warned Newsmakers time and again to stay away from the communication device called 'Microphone'. The tool is like fire, a good servant but bad master.

When you cough it magnifies it, when you sneeze it amplifies it and when you boom it electrifies it. So why stay close or poke your nose to that seductive tool? Once again here's my pesewa advice: If you don't know what to say and can't filter what you're going to say. It's as simple as eX whY Zet.

Isn't that a sign of magnanimity?

I gave you all that for a token—pesewa. And I still have a dime to give away. Henceforth, please Mr. and Madam Ministers, MP's etc. show some respect to the party members on the ground. For courtesy sake let your regional chairpersons know you're in town or coming to town. It doesn't demote one's status for example as minister in charge of the Ocean or minister of the Desert. It rather enhances your image.

See I thought they knew this, how quickly did they forget that as they lead they'll bleed. It seems the poor Ghanaian cocoa farmer even stands a good or better chance than the newsmaker when it comes to 'pricing'. Of course the cocoa farmer's price is determined by the international market ('Enye koraa entese' payday). That's an open secret. He loathes it but he's to deal with it.

Lest I forget, as newsmaker always remember not to throw your toys out of the pram.

The unknown that gawks the newsmaker is huge. He has no idea how far his story would go, who would receive it (his spouse, mother-in-law, mum or dad), what impact it would create (negative or positive) out there? It's all wrapped in mystery. It seems to be worse in this day and age– in the advent of the social media. News goes viral— good or bad. But the bad news travels farther and wider.

Without a doubt the fate of the newsmaker's product rest in one's hand and the price of the commodity is often determined by its status.

The chief culprit in this affair is the politician. He casts himself as invincible and untouchable. He thinks the mandate given him is immutable and he will always have the political capital. But that's untrue, the people wield the mandate and whenever the time is right they will make the right decision by striping him of the power.

Some or most of them tend to believe that the whole world belongs to them and they can do whatever they intend to do. Yes newsmakers sometimes act as though they've been pimped or they aren't aware of the dangers they face per their actions and inactions.

Remorse & Apology

"I am sorry," says Otiko Afisa Djaba. .And ...I'm truly sorry," states Bugri Naabu.

I'm not going to revisit the 'Otiko-Bugri brouhaha' that turned the wheels of decorum upside down over the weekend. In the meantime, it appears the sky that got saturated with toxic is clearing. Visibility is still poor though. Nevertheless, forecasters will tell us the status of the weather but time tells it better. Time will tell whether going forward it would be a rebuke or fire when it recurs. I talked about it on Monday 8 May and I think the listening ears heard me.

Thank God the speeding locomotive finally got stopped. It was flagged down at the Flagstaff House. It's understood the patience of the first Gentleman of the nation was thinning. How could he sit and watch his children go wayward, or run their mouths like 'NIKA-NIKA', to pollute the atmosphere with invectives and wreak shame upon the party?

And I could hear him like a father rebuking his brat kid. Stop it or you get spanked. You understand what spank implies when you get summoned before the father of the nation.

Was this expected?

The Wednesday cargo ship docked Ghana's coast with two heavy loads–apologies. First is the Gender Minister's apology:

"It was totally out of order and I apologise to Ghanaians for what happened. I want to use this opportunity to apologise to all Ghanaians, but it is a lesson to each other and we need to respect each other and we need to respect women," Otiko Afisa Djaba.

"I went to see the president and apologised to him and told him it was not in the interest of Ghana...I think that we need to respect women in this country 60 years on in Ghana. I felt disrespected by him and if it were a man he wouldn't have done that."

Next, the Northern Region NPP chairman Bugri Naabu. His was contained in a letter sent to counsel for the Upper East regional minister (Rockson Bukari) Mr. Samson Lardy Anyenini. "I write to sincerely and unreservedly retract wholly my comment about your client in an interview with Accra-based radio XYZ. I don't have any facts beyond what we know about the police investigations on the matter and I am truly sorry to the Minister's family and all those I have hurt by those comment," Mr. Bugri Naabu stated.

And I am not going to examine or comment on the apologies rendered by the two kinsmen. But I am glad they did. Indeed time will tell, time alone will tell it better. A word to the wise is 'not enough' but it's in the North.

Yamoah Ponkor Makes Bribery Confession

Or is it an allegation?

Has it always been like this or it's a new phenomenon that's shaping up our political landscape?

Suffice to say the entire political playground looks messy, dirty and filthy. It appears to be a triangulation or manipulation tactic involving the very people we gave mandate to take care of our nation. I really don't know what is it and I don't understand why there have been series of accusations of bribery scandal lately.

The latest one is coming from Afrifa Yamoah Ponkor the former Municipal Chief Executive (MCE) for Ejuisu/Juaben. The outspoken MCE claims he gave the Assembly GHc 300.000 as bribe to tilt the assembly's election to his favour but it didn't work out.

Speaking on a local radio station in Kumasi Mr. Yamoah Ponkor accused the former Ashanti Regional Minister of the Mahama-administration Alexander John Ackon and Regional chairman of the New Patriotic Party (NPP), Bernard Antwi Bosiakoh of working against his second term bid in 2014.

There must surely be a cause to this entire political row. But as I alluded to I can't pinpoint it.

It kicked off from the Parliament House late January this year. They say if gold can rust what would iron do. The eggs were incubated from the chamber of the nobles. That's right you'd think it's the last place one would associate them with scandal but the lawmakers got bitten by the bug. In fact what changed the game there, was the person behind the so-called bribery scandal. The accuser was one of their own (a sitting MP) and a former minister of state.

Wasn't that repulsive enough?

He stoked the fire. Then energy minister designate was purported to have given money to the chairman of the Parliamentary Appointment Committee and he in turn gave the money to then minority leader of the house and it snowballed from there to the 10-memebrer committee that was vetting the nominee to influence the outcome of the exercise.

And like a can in the road it was kicked from left to right, centre to the middle back to the flanks and anywhere it landed. As the cancer spread Parliament instituted investigation into the allegation. The Joe Ghartey Committee, in its final report, said it found no evidence to support allegations of bribery made by the said MP.

Presenting the report of the committee to the House, Mr. Ghartey, the Chairman of the Committee, said the accuser failed to adduce any evidence to substantiate his claim of bribery.

"Everything he said was nothing more than rumours," Mr. Ghartey said, adding: Multiplicity of rumours does not constitute a fact."

Thus, the accuser was told by the House Speaker Mike Ocquaye to go and sin no more. Bottom line the image of the august house was bruised. It's unclear whether the respected Legislature had recovered from that deadly storm.

If one thought that melodrama would deter others, perhaps the red tide was about to rear its head. The Otiko-Bugri feud would raise the bar to another level. Theirs seemed unmatched, unbeaten and unrivaled. Invectives rained. The cows mooed. And the sheep /goats bleated. There was even an allegation of murder. There appeared to be power struggle between the two Elephant bigwigs. But none could substantiate his or her allegation. It took the intervention of the President to calm the troubled waters.

The gunpowder still hangs in the air—not settled yet: But when a crocodile comes out of the Paga Lake and says it is very cold down there you need no validation. Many across the world especially Catholics do confess their sins in Churches. However, he chose a different route. Was it the right route and the right time? That I don't know...

Sure, he didn't do it before the Pontiff neither did he do it before the priest clad in cassock. Indeed, millions of dollars had been embezzled by our politicians and trustees and they're looting more on a day to day basis.

Throughout my career as a journalist I've never heard any public official either retired or still in active service come out to say for example: I paid bribe or received bribe or I looted the state or caused financial loss to the state.

They've always been defensive, always belligerent and an unapologetic. Our hands are clean we never took money from the state, they would tell you. Simply ask them: Did you ever take a bribe? And the response will tickle you to death. You'd rather get a counter question like: "Me as a mayor or legislator or you mean I as John Doe? Just throw back the statement to him: You as John Doe. And the comedy and parody start to develop right there.

Often you hear them say or play the big V-card. "We're the victims'. 'We're being witch-hunted'.

So what prompted Yamoah Ponkor to make his confession now?

According to Mr. Yamoah Ponkor he knew this opportunity would come and so he kept mute over it till this day. And there we go again... a pattern of wrong accusations. Or is it not? Like we've been witnessing lately he fingered two notable persons in Ashanti region.

Former Ashanti Regional Minister in the immediate past National Democratic Congress (NDC), Alexander John Ackon and Regional chairman of New Patriotic Party (NPP), Bernard Antwi Bosiako have been accused of working against the second term bid of a former Municipal Chief Executive (MCE) for Ejuisu/Juaben.

The outspoken former MCE, Afrifa Yamoah Ponkor had given account as to the reasons surrounding his failure to get a second term in office despite being adjudged as the best MCE in 2014.

"Chairman Antwi Bosiako, Kofi Senya and NPP fraternity thronged to Ejuisu to work against my endorsement as MCE. They even managed to influence some government appointees who are members of NDC to vote against me", Yamoah Ponkor alleged.

He said Mr. Ackon as then regional minister also contributed in a way which he believes went against his confirmation.

"Then Regional Minister Alexander Ackon refused to tell the Electoral Commission to organise another election because after first round, I needed only eight votes to sail through. But for reasons best known to him he and other NDC members, they did not ensure second round be organised. I kept mute over all these issues because I know a time like this will come for me. You know me I cannot just be pushed over on issues like this," he said this on Nyira FM's 'Kroyemu Nsem' programme.

Komenda Sugar Factory: Is it a sleeping giant?

Komendans dreamed it was raining last night but in reality it was very warm and dry. Their expectations had been hyped. Their once melting pot—Komenda Sugar Factory was coming back live, the Mahama administration had told them months before the 2016 general elections. And they saw the building and they saw the giant plant and they also saw its inauguration all in a grandiose style but the multi-million dollar facility is idling like a sloth.

Yes, that's one piece of the puzzle and I'm sure the chiefs and people of the area are getting worried by the day. Whose report must they believe now? How long must they have to wait to see the Sugar Factory start its full operation?

And you probably didn't know that it has other challenges thwarting its full scale operation. For the first time since its inauguration last year May 30 2016, the status of the company that was estimated to employ 7,300 people had been made known to the public. And it isn't a pleasant one!

Deputy Minister of Trade and Industry Ahomka-Lindsay in plain language said Komenda Sugar Factory hasn't produced any sugar since its revamp. He told the Public Accounts Committee (PAC) of Parliament on Friday, August 11, 2017 when he appeared before them.

Does anybody remember this phrase?

"Read my lips: no new taxes:" It became the most prominent sound bite in 1988. Then-American presidential candidate George H.W Bush evoked that phrase on August 18 1988, while accepting the Republican nomination as its presidential candidate at the National Convention. He'd promised Americans that there would be no new taxes under his administration but it turned out to be the opposite.

Indeed, shortly after the Factory's inauguration its plant was shut down. Of course that report was initially denied. But later Parliament in November 2016 approved a $24.5 million Exim Bank loan facility for a sugar cane and irrigation project to feed the Factory. There was also report that Komenda had started to produce sugar. Well, we're finding out the truth now.

Was it fake news? Or was it for political expedience?

Semi-processed sugar

Today the rooster has come home to roost. And what seemed like a jig-saw in the past was unpacked last Friday. The sages are right, you cannot fool all the all the time. It might take time but the day of reckon will come in due course.

According to Mr. Ahomka-Lindsay contrary to claims by the previous government that the factory produced some bags of sugar; the said sugar which was exhibited to Ghanaians was derived from semi-finished products which the government purchased for showcase.

"Here's the current reality of Komenda factory," he said.

"The sugar you tasted at that time the government of Ghana bought semi-processed sugar, part of it was used to process and that is part of what you tasted. We have never put cane sugar through the full system of the Komenda Sugar Factory. That is the first thing you've to note."

So why did they lie to the whole nation that Komenda had produced sugar? Well how would you understand that's the name of the game? Politics has different clothes and it wears them as needed. No doubt it was for political convenience. And it isn't an NDC disease. So don't run away with it and blow it up.

Mr. Ahomka-Lindsay also went on to explain why he thinks Komenda's operation might take a little longer despite its potential and viability. So, what are the other challenges?

Land Issue

"The second thing you've to note: Is that the total land area of that Komenda Sugar of about 200,000 doesn't' have the capacity to produce the cane sugar so we have to look at places around Winneba. I understand those are the areas where we've a bit more land…to make sure that we've the appropriate acreage we estimate between 15-18,000 acres... is what's needed to make sure that whatever cane we produce is available for the actual factory to process."

Aside that he said the Indian company that undertook the project brought in a little bit of a variety from India that they grow...but the process of a proper nursery to identify the actual variety was never done. Currently, he said there were 125,000 acres set aside for nursery, noting that 25 of that were ready to be transplanted to the 200,000.

Issue of Quality and commercial

I think one key thing that stood out in the deputy minister's encounter with the Public Accounts Committee was perhaps the issue of ensuring that Komenda Sugar factory embarks on a large scale commercial production when it restarts operation.

He believes the factory could fail to realise its desired potential if proper measures aren't put in place. Mr. Ahomka-Lindsay explained the NPP government was working hard to get the factory operational because the variety of sugarcane which was procured for the nursery did not contain adequate amounts of sugar for commercial production.

"The problem we have is that if we transplant those 25 to 2000," Mr. Lindsay said. "It's basically a waste of money. Because the sugar content of that variety as we know, is not to the level needed to make the commercial operation of Komenda. This is something we're very very keen on looking at. Komenda will operate but we want to make sure when it operates it operates on a commercial footing to ensure that it will keep going we want to bring to the local farmers involved," he said.

In the meantime Komenda Sugar Factory is saddled with some debts running into several millions of dollars, according to the deputy trade minister. PAC was told that government currently owes the contractors who worked on the factory to the tune of US$ 7million.

The Ghosts: And the Apology That Followed

He who fights the ghosts in Ghana fights the living too, says this writer.

"I'm not sure the labour unions are trying to support that type of action, so we do apologise for those who should not have been in but I think we should all resolve that we are going to clean up so that individuals do not privatise this business."

Finance Minister Ken Ofori-Atta made the above statement at the ongoing National Policy Summit in Accra yesterday. The sector minister also called on labour groups to exercise restraint as the ministry resolves the challenge.

"With wage issues we have to stay within appropriation and control of wages. We did an exercise recently in which quite a number of people were taken out of the payroll. We've had some remarks from some unions, but the real question for all of us in the country is that we know that there is some rot in there, we know we need to take some action and in the process of taking the action a few wrong eggs will be broken and we should apologise for that," he stated.

'There's some rot in there'…And indeed it was the ROT that necessitated the excise aimed at plugging the loopholes in the payroll system. This issue reminds me of two stories—one biblical the other a fairy-tale. Thanks to Apostle Matthew who painstakingly penned down the Parable of the Tares also known as the Parable of the Weeds. The account can be found in Matthew Chapter 13:24-30.

A farmer sowed wheat but later his servants found out there were weeds among them. They were perplexed and asked their master the question below:

"Sir did you not Sow good seed in your Field? How then does it have tares?"

He said to them: "An enemy has done this."

Indeed there are enemies in Ghana. They're averse to growth, hostile against progress and selfish. They are the reason the ghosts live amongst us and as long as their names continue to be in the payroll system the nation's kitty would remain empty.

And here's the second story:

There was a town called Apolonia (not the charming city in Ghana) which had been invaded by a pack of wolves. That summer hush afternoon had been disturbed by the beasts. Apolonia had become a ghost town. Men had remained mum, women and children in doored. Not even whispers. Whistleblowers feared they might be heard, sighted or get mauled. The wolves had run amok terrorising the inhabitants.

And the community was losing it all—its livestock and business was dipping.

Life had become unbearable and so one day the people approached the chief of the town and suggested to him they hired a hunter that lived at the backcountry about 50 kilometres north east of the country to help bring peace and sanity back to their loving township.

"This is a great idea," said the chief. Let's go ahead and hire Kuntunkunuku."

He was a well-known hunter, astute and experienced. He rarely misfired. He barely got it wrong. He never missed his target and even in occasions that he missed they were negligible or insignificant.

But would the people forgive him if he misfires?

The great hunter was brought to Apolonia. And within days after assessing the terrain he got the job done but in the process of smoking out the wolves a few of the domestic animals were hit by strayed bullets and died. This was greeted with hue and cry from amongst the people. The livestock Association of Apolonia (a unionized group) threatened to take the hunter to court and the anger was palpable. They'd become so enraged that Kuntunkunuku was forced to apologise.

How quickly did they forget the wrath of the wolves?

Was he the one who brought the wolves into town?

No he wasn't? But they blamed him for it.

The blame game was played in Accra on Monday 15 May. Mr. Ofori Atta had to apologise to the country's civil servants for the inconveniency his recent action to purge Ghana's payroll system caused. The system over the years had been wrought by ghosts' names.

Yes the ghosts labour not yet they get paid every month. Their habitation no one knows yet they receive salaries. No one has ever sighted them—not in the alleys or the streets of the national capital but they still draw monies from government's coffers.

The Ministry of Finance had ordered the removal of 26,589 names of public workers from government payroll. Those affected had not been registered on the new SSNIT biometric system, despite several directives to do so.

"Quite a number of persons were taken off the payroll and we've had remarks from some unions. We know that there's some rot in there we have to take an action and in the process of taking an action a few wrong eggs would be broken and we should apologise for that," Mr. Ofori-Atta noted.

He further disclosed that some of the affected persons are staff of his own ministry.

"Going through the numbers I actually found one or two of the directors at Ministry of Finance have been included in that list they don't exist. So there are mistakes..."

But his primary targets are/were the wolves in sheep clothes and not the hard working civil servants. Unfortunately some of the good ones got hit by strayed bullets. Mr. Ofori-Atta has said the move, was to protect the public purse by plugging all leakages in the system. However, some genuine public sector workers were mistakenly deleted from the payroll, angering some labour unions.

He continued: "But in terms of principally understanding and appreciating and working towards a solution, I think that should be the spirit of which our labour partners talk to us. I don't know the labour partners who we may have wronged, but going through the numbers I actually found one or two of the directors of finance being included in the list that they don't exist.

"So there are mistakes, which are OK, but truly we are talking about six, seven hundred or even a billion cedis of potential savings. I think it's incumbent on all of us to work in that spirit because we at the Ministry have no personal interest in individual names but in making it efficient because if we also pursue the investigation I think it will be very embarrassing to realise that your young friend Kojo or Kwame in

Elubo is actually able to continue to pay three other people and put that money in his pocket," he underscored.

Prez Akufo-Addo Nominates Sophia Akuffo as Next CJ

What does this mean to women lawyers in the judicial service & Ghanaian women in general?

Here they come. They're here to rub shoulders with the topnotch in society. But not just that to send a message to the world that they aren't who the popular myth describes them —as 'pushovers' or kitchen queens. They're women who have it, live it and can do it regardless. They aren't here or there because they are beautiful women, or share the same name or per their political leanings.

They're here or there as partners in development not subservient, as managers that have what it takes to make things happen. They're result-oriented and have proven it over the period.

You might've already heard or read the news. Yes another distinguished Ghanaian woman is on her way to ascend the top rung of the judicial ladder as another illustrious, dedicated and tenacious woman coasts to the end of her tenure in office with 40 good years in active judicial service.

The news didn't surprise many in view of the pedigree of the nominee. However, it points to one inevitable fact-the renaissance of women supremacy in Ghana's political landscape, since Ejisuhemaa Nana Yaa Asantewaa led the Ashantis to the 1900-01 War against the British, says this writer.

This followed the announcement on Friday 12 May by President Akufo-Addo that he had nominated Sophia Akuffo a Supreme Court Judge as the next Chief Justice of Ghana. She will replace Mrs. Theodora Georgina Wood who retires on the 8th of June 2017.

"I expect discipline, fairness, integrity and the continuing modernisation of judicial activities to be the hallmarks of her tenure as Chief

Justice if she is so endorsed by the constitutional bodies," President Akufo-Add said.

Early on, the Council of State ((a small body of prominent citizens that counsel the president) had approved Mrs. Akuffo's selection whereupon she received her letter of appointment to become head of the judiciary in the country.

In the meantime observers are keeping their fingers crossed as they await the Legislature to return from recess by the end of May. Her nomination will then be advanced to Parliament for approval. And if she's endorsed it will be the first time in the history of Ghana since independence that two women have ascended the throne of the Chief Justiceship in succession.

Indeed if she receives the nod it will also signify that perhaps the old order is gradually giving way. And what was long viewed as the preserved of men as evidenced in the pre-colonial era (the Gold Coast) and four decades into post-independence Ghana is clearly on a knife edge. In the Gold Coast period all 13 of the Supreme Court Justices including Sir Korbina Arku Korsah (the only black) who became Ghana's first chief Justice 1956 - 5 March 1957 and 1957-'63 were men in wigs.

But that strand didn't change even after the departure of the colonialists; male lawyers continue to dominate the legal terrain until the new millennium. In 2007 Ghana had her first woman Chief Justice Mrs. Theodora Georgina Wood.

Today, Ghana is on her way once again to have another renowned lawyer as Chief Justice and the fourth most powerful individual in the country. Mrs. Akuffo will also be the country's fifth Chief Justice under the fourth republic since the Supreme Court Ordinance of 1876 ended the 10-year absence of a Supreme Court, which ultimately established the Supreme Court of Judicature for the Gold Coast Colony.

Partisan Battles

As expected there have been a few partisan battles mainly from the opposition National Democratic Congress (NDC). Critics believe there's a possible conflict of interest situation because the President and the nominee had known each other for decades. Moreover they contend the judiciary will not be able to affirm its independence as enshrined in the Constitution.

But the criticisms had been mixed as well. The Minority Leader in Parliament Haruna Iddrisu had earlier congratulated Mrs. Akuffo's nomination. According to Mr. Iddrisu Justice Akuffo is a capable hand because she has distinguished herself as an independent-minded person. However, he has also questioned the rationale behind what he describes as the 'hasty appointment' of successor to the outgoing Chief Justice.

"My disappointment is that there's no Judicial Council (now) even though the requirement for this is maybe in consultation with the approval of Parliament," the minority leader said.

Meantime a member of the NDC legal team Abraham Amaliba has expressed misgivings concerning the president's selection. He said the President was biased in his settlement on Justice Sophia Akuffo. Mr. Amaliba who spoke to the local media criticised the president's nomination and characterised it as biased.

"Humans as we are, much as you are a professional in what you are doing, the likelihood of you exhibiting some bias towards a person whom you have worked with, who you are related to in terms of where you come from… it [increases] the fear of ordinary citizens," Mr. Amaliba told a local radio station in Accra.

That claim by the NDC lawyer attracted a reaction from Nana Damoah a government communication expert who thought Mr. Amaliba's argument was flawed. He said: "Those that have advanced that argument of relationship, I don't think it holds. I do not think that this president would just make a decision on the whims of it that he would just get up and make a decision."

What I want all of us to focus this discussion on is: will she be able to do what we expect of a Chief Justice of the Republic of Ghana to ensure that all of us are served Justice?" he said.

What does this mean to women lawyers and women in general?

Already goodwill and congratulatory messages are pouring in from some influential women across the country. It's an indication that they relish Mrs. Akuffo's appointment as the next Chief Justice. And more importantly they view it as a catalyst to speed up women's involvement and participation in any discipline, especially in politics in the country.

In a letter to congratulate Mrs. Akuffo a former minister of Gender Nana Oye Lithur, has backed the choice of Justice Sophia Akuffo as Ghana's next Chief Justice. According to Nana Oye Lithur, Justice Akuffo has the requisite experience and track record to deliver as the head of the country's judiciary.

"You were strict, efficient, hardworking, no nonsense and compassionate as head of chambers. One of the few female senior lawyers heading a law firm in those days. You had left Mobil Ghana as their solicitor and set up the law firm Akuffo &Co. You groomed us all in your law firm to become sharp lawyers."

Another came from former Attorney General Betty Mould-Iddrisu. She has also congratulated Mrs. Sophia Akuffo on her selection as Ghana's next Chief Justice. Mrs. Mould-Iddrisu said the new Chief Justice has "excellent credentials," she said this on Class FM an Accra-based radio station on Friday.

"I'm truly delighted by the choice of Sophia Akuffo as the next Chief Justice of Ghana. Ghana has led the way and stayed the course. She has excellent credentials and has impeccable gender credentials all her working life. Her Ladyship Chief Justice, my senior in the law and most respected woman on the bench, I welcome you as I welcomed Her Ladyship Georgina Wood some few years ago to this prestigious and high leadership position," Mrs. Iddrisu said.

The Chairperson of the Electoral Commission (EC), Mrs. Charlotte Osei, also congratulated the newly nominated Chief Justice, describing her knowledge in law as "solid".

"I am totally thrilled at the nomination of Her Ladyship Sophia Akuffo JSC as our next Chief Justice. I first met Her Ladyship in 1992 as a young law student at her office at Mobil House where she was General Counsel at the time. Her knowledge of the law is solid. She's an extremely brilliant woman, with solid credentials and solid integrity. I believe she will lead our judiciary with wisdom and purpose. We pray that God grants her strength, courage, and wisdom. Congratulations, Her Ladyship," Mrs. Osei said in a short statement.

Indeed, women constitute 51 per cent of Ghana's population yet not many of them are seen in the limelight. So in effect this is a wakeup call for women across the country to let Mrs. Akuffo's nomination revive and inspire them to strive to go higher and increase their numbers in top positions.

Since Independence Ghana has had 12 chief justices 10 of them were men. Ours like many judicial systems across the globe whenever the Chief Justice's position becomes vacant selection or nomination of a substantive one strikes the inner cord. For example in the United States since the passage of the Judiciary Act of 1886 the court has consisted of chief justice and eight associate justices. US have a life time appointment.

Elsewhere, in the United Kingdom Judges of the Supreme Court are appointed by The Queen by the issue of letters patent on the advice of the Prime Minister to who a name is recommended by a special selection commission. The Prime Minister is required by the Constitutional Reform Act to recommend this name to the Queen and not permitted to nominate anyone else.

Article 144(1) of the 1992 Constitution provides that the Chief Justice shall be appointed by the president acting on the advice of Judicial Council in consultation with the Council of State and with the approval of Parliament.

Alex Nartey president of the Judicial Service Staff Association of Ghana (JUSSAG) says the association is unhappy because President Akufo-Addo failed to consult it before choosing the new Chief Justice, although that is not a constitutional prerequisite. He stressed that the Association's input in the matter is not to be taken for granted, given the role of judicial staff in the work of the Chief Justice. Again, JUSSAG's appeal comes despite the absence of any constitutional precedent necessitating that the judicial staff be consulted ahead of the nomination of a Chief Justice.

Gordon Offin-Amaniampong

Watch Out For The Bugs

Ghana's ministries might be prone to or infected with bugs says this writer.

How would you feel if you learned that your office or home has secretly been bugged?

Certainly you could snug as a bug in a rug. But you cannot snug in a furtively bugged home or office. Ghana's current Lands and Natural Resources Minister who's been leading a sting operation against illegal mining (also known as Galamsey) in the West African nation has had his office bugged.

The spying gadget which was discovered on Monday by the National Security includes a camera, a storage unit plus another device suspected to be a transmitter. It is thought to be able to pick a whisper 35 feet away. The audio-visual recorder was covertly planted in a huge Coat of Arms plaque that hangs in the minister's office.

This writer says the incident is already causing controversy and debate among the officialdom. And it comes seven months or so, since the minister moved into that office at the Ministries enclave in Accra. Speculations are rife that there might be more bugs planted in the ministries, departments and agencies in the enclave.

The history of wire-tapping or bugging is legendary. But perhaps the most unforgettable is the one that involved former 38th American President Richard Nixon in 19972 (Watergate Scandal). Some employees of President Nixon's re-election committee had been caught when they broke into the Democratic National Committee (DNC's) headquarters to plant a bug. The incident led to Nixon's resignation and it's believed it would have possibly led to his felony prosecution had he not been pardoned by his successor, Gerald Ford.

Mr. John Peter Amewu the Minister in the centre of the bizarre event says he feels he's been unclothed: "I Feel Naked," he told the local media.

In the early stage of the discovery the media reported that the sector minister had no idea whatsoever as to who planted the device when it was put there and why it was placed there. But on Tuesday a former minister of the Mahama-administration Alhaji Inusah Fuseini who once occupied the Lands and Natural Resources ministry claimed responsibility, saying the bugging device discovered and retrieved from the office of the current Minister, Mr. Amewu belonged to him.

The former minister said a private citizen who works with a private security company presented the equipment to him at a time concerns were raised about his personal security in the wake of his fight against illegal mining.

"I thought to all intents and purposes that it was a white elephant and had nothing to monitor my successor. "Let me take the opportunity to apologise to my successor as it was never intended and nobody speed or prowled on the office when I left office," Mr. Fuseini apologised"

He's also reported to have said that the anxiety that welcomed the development was 'unwarranted' because in his own words 'the device was not fully installed'.

"It was not working. The installation was not completed," he remarked.

Alhaji Fuseini has since rendered an apology to Mr. Amewu:

"Let me take the opportunity to apologise to my successor as it was never intended and nobody speed or prowled on the office when I left office."

"The device was not working", he explained. That was why security agencies that went to 'sweep' the office the first time they did not get any transmission signals. The office was 'swept twice which he emphasised goes to show there was nothing untoward done."

Did his revelation calm nerves?

Not at all, it's perhaps heightened anxiety and caused red-eyed as I pointed out earlier. According to Mr. Amewu, it would have been prudent for Alhaji Fuseini to divulge such information to the security agencies rather than go public with it.

"I would have preferred maybe if he had remained quiet and just inform the security that he is the one behind it and they can handle it at that level," Mr. Amewu stated.

Asked whether the device was working he said: "I am not in a position to say whether it's working. It is a feeling made worse by the confession by my predecessor, Inusah Fuseini that he planted the device while he occupied the office."

The Majority Leader and Minister of Parliamentary Affairs, Osei Kyei Mensah-Bonsu waded into the debate. He'd said that member of a group which met with Mr. Amewu received signals on his phone which prompted him to alert the Minister.

He said the incident could happen to any Minister of the state adding he has taken caution by inviting security experts to 'sweep' his offices for bugs.

So if the device wasn't installed as claimed by Alhaji Fuseini how then could it pick up signal (s)?

Also a former Lands and Natural Resources Minister Nii Osah Mills who took over from Inusah Fuseini and spent two and half years in that office have expressed disappointment following the revelations.

"I can't believe all my days and nights in the office were under the watch of a secret camera, "he bemoaned.

Mr. Amewu told the media that the he'd been shocked by the whole development following the disclosure by his predecessor. "It is a feeling made worse by the confession of my predecessor, Inusah Fuseini that he planted the device while he occupied the office .I feel naked."

However, he was hopeful that the Minister of National Security who is in charge of ensuring that there are no bugs in the offices of Ministers of the state is taking steps to do that.

So what's been said or unsaid on that wire-tapping machine isn't going to go away now. It has brought in its wake, apprehensions and anxieties. It also could prove to be a red tide not only for the minister in question but to all public office holders. And I strongly believe it's a wakeup call for public office holders and big corporations as it reminds them to be careful and act diligently in their day-to-day activities.

GHANA PEACEKEEPERS: WE Salute You!!!

On Wednesday 3 May 2017 the United Nations Mission in South Sudan (UNMISS) extolled Ghanaian peacekeepers in that country for preventing what could have been a deadly attack at a United Nations' (UN) protection site in Leer town of former Unity State.

The heroic soldiers put their lives on the line and foiled the attack. The enemies ran away with their tails in between their legs. And the soldiers stood guard, guns drawn, combat-ready, psychologically and emotionally prepared to face whatever onslaught that could come their way.

They rose up to the occasion and acted 'swiftly' to prevent the attackers from unleashing their venomous assaults.

Their display of heroism in Sudan last week reminds me of a famous 19th-century English hymn 'Onward Christian Soldiers', which had been adopted by the Salvation Army as its favoured professional. The hymn was originally written by Sabine Barring Gould in 1865. Six years later (in 1871) another British, Arthur Sullivan composed the hit song.

Arthur Sullivan described as a versatile musician from the British Isles perhaps who'd never been to war or was never conscripted into the imperialist armed forces fell in love with the song. He would later make the hymn become one of the world's greatest.

I must add, back in the day in primary or elementary school this song was one of our school's marching songs. Onward Christian Soldiers marching on to war....And we marched on into our respective classrooms. Hands and legs swayed back and forth as the school band played along.

Why did the Salvation Army adopt the hymn?

Indeed like Arthur Sullivan, the Army couldn't resist its flavor. There was simply something good about it: Something irresistible something worth to be praised. Sure, praise must be given to whom praise is due. And I make reference to this ancient hymn not because of its antiquity but for its morality.

Soldiers all over the world stand for something—the principle of 'do before complain'. It's high principle that enjoins them and binds them to give their all in the midst of firestorm. Soldiers risk their lives to defend our lives. They lose their limbs so that we can keep our limbs and they bear our cross when they're overburdened. In a nutshell they're a remarkable people.

Permission to greet or salute you all– you brave men and women out there. That's how they (the military) say it. After quarter guard they ask for permission too. 'Permission to fall out Sir'…and the sergeant major will 'respond permission granted'.

Bravo!!!

A press statement issued by the mission on Wednesday said: "The base came under small arms attack around 11 pm and midnight (at the Mission's Temporary Operating Base) from the direction of the nearby Government-held town but the Ghanaian peacekeepers at the base swiftly responded to the attackers and repulsed them."

The attack had since been condemned by the head of the UN Mission in South Sudan (UNMISS), David Shearer, as being carried out with callous disregard for the lives for civilians as well as UN and humanitarian workers.

Mr. Shearer lauded the quick response of the Ghanaian forces for successfully repelling the attack and remaining on high alert throughout the night.

"They reacted in the best possible manner, according to the true spirit of peacekeeping. Their quick defensive action secured the safety of all of the internally displaced people who had sought UN protection adjacent to the base," he said.

"We strongly condemn the attack, and call on all parties to the conflict to respect the sanctity of UN premises. We are here to protect and support the people of South Sudan. The base is located at Leer for that reason. The people are hungry and deprived as the result of the famine. However, it is clear the attackers have no consideration for their plight, given those who most desperately need help will suffer more because of a likely resulting delay of humanitarian aid," said David Shearer.

The statement added that there were no UNMISS or other casualties within the base from the attack.

Ghana's Contributions

Ghana's contribution to UN peace keeping service goes as far back as in the early 1960's. She is among the list of 126 nations with a total of 2.973 peace keepers contributed to UN operations based on the organisation's report as of 31 July2016. And she comes as number 10 in that long list. Countries with least contributors in terms of numbers are –Guinea Bissau, Mozambique, Latvia and Jamaica with one personnel each. East African nation Ethiopia (in the horn of Africa) tops the list with 8,333 peace keepers.

Indeed Ghana's peace keepers have served in a number of countries such as Lebanon, Haiti, Liberia, Sierra Leone, the Ivory Coast, Sudan to mention but a few. And the service members comprise personnel of the Ghana Armed Forces (GAF) and Ghana Police Service (GPS).

Records gleaned from the Kofi Annan International Peacekeeping Training Centre in Accra, says since Ghana's first participation in the UN Operation in the Congo (ONUC), over 80,000 Ghanaian military, police and civilian personnel have served in various capacities in more than 30 UN missions.

As pointed out earlier, the country has been a top ten contributor for more than two decades, the records note. As at 30 September 2015, Ghana ranked eighth, with a total number of 3,247 peacekeepers, comprising 353 police officers, 2,820 troops and 74 military experts.

According to the records, at the 28 September peacekeeping summit in New York, Ghana pledged to provide a helicopter unit, an infantry battalion, a signals/communication company, two naval patrol boats, a riverine unit, a level-II hospital, and two formed police units (FPUs).

"Currently, there is no confirmation of which party to the conflict carried out the attack. UNMISS is continuing to investigate the incident and will examine whether the TOB (Temporary Operating Base) needs to be further strengthened," the statement said.

Letter to My Kinsmen

Greetings my kinsmen,
"We greet you back our brother."
Surprise to see me isn't it?
Sure, your facial expression highlights that. But I am here. The Savanna knows his brother. Did I fly? Did I drive? Did I gallop on a horse back or did I ride on a bike? I think all isn't important. What matters most is my presence. When you see me in Battakari (smock), remember something isn't right. I seldom chew cola, (don't want dyed-teeth) but I'm doing it today.

I don't think we have forgotten where we came from. How hard we had to fight to get here. The Ya Naas and the Na Bas fought for our freedom. They taught us how to unite and live in harmony. And they reminded us always that we're one people regardless of our ethnicity, dialect, culture and many more.

The Chinese have this saying: "If you must play, decide on three things at the start: the rules of the game, the stakes, and the quitting time." Certainly if you can't quench the fire then you better don't set it in the first place. Otherwise you'd burn your own house and that of your neighbour's.

Of course you know what you'll get if it is horseplay ('Agrobone'). Don't forget you might leave the playground either with a broken nose or a twisted jaw.

Last night just a minute past midnight I'd an urgent phone call. I was getting ready to snuggle myself under my Duve. And in three words the caller intoned: "Come down now." It sounded like there was fire in Soweto. What's amiss, I enquired. He told me there's apparent fire in the north.

How could that be and which part in the north?
In a fraction of second one could hear a pin drop. The caller was gone!

Two elephant babies had locked horns in the jungle—stubbornly trying to prove who's tough or tougher. But their battleground wasn't far from the lion's den... Where's my pen? Yes, it was too close to the enemy's camp. Their frustrated mother looked on helplessly. She knew it wouldn't take the predator long to strike, if they lose guard.

Alas she yelled at the two calves: "Idiots knew ye not that our enemy is watching in delight and will attack soon?"

Bolga hasn't been burglarized yet. No don't panic, There's also no war in Wa. I can assure you Bolga and her western neighbour are in good shape. There's relative calm in the Upper East and Upper West regional capitals. Good news is business is booming and no one has boomed yet. The master boomer hasn't been there yet. And all the guinea fowls that made the pilgrimage (brain drain) to Burkina Faso have returned home. I am yet to take stock though...

There's rather a seeming feud brewing down south not south as in southern Ghana. The northern region is witnessing a kind of political vendetta between two of her kinsmen.

"If you want trouble, I'll give you one," Otiko Afisa Djaba, Minister for Gender, Children and Social Protection warns Bugri Naabu.

At the moment Tamale the northern regional capital isn't enjoying the air of camaraderie that's blowing across Bolga and Wa. Two of her royals are butting like goats. They say goats but to bully others to establish their place in the herd .And how long can that be allowed to endure. We can certainly not become spectators— watch our kinsmen throw acrobatic war words. That isn't right.

I don't think the threats and tantrums being exchanged here and there would help the parties involved. It would rather hurt them and hurt the party in general, hence this letter and my appeal to Ms. Otiko and Mr. Bugri to cease fire immediately.

Yesterday we stood together, we fought together and we won together. How cool is that! Why can't we exercise restraint and think about the bigger picture—the party. We have tons of fight to engage notably unemployment, corruption, sanitation, inflation, depreciation, Dumsor and 'Pressor' and many more. This 'Wahala' will take us nowhere. Instead it will distract and derail our forward march, our quest to build a stronger economy.

Ms. Otiko has warned the Northern regional chairman of the NPP Mr. Bugri to stop peddling "lies" about her if he does not want trouble. Who wants trouble my sister?

She says Mr. Daniel Bugri Naabu is a bribe-taking politician who goes around extorting money, cows and goats from people with the promise to secure them appointments in the Akufo-Addo government.

Ms. Djaba, whose meeting with some women in the Northern Region on Friday was stymied by Mr. Naabu and some, agitated women, told a local radio station in an interview that if Mr. Naabu wants trouble, she will gladly oblige.

Apart from accusing Ms. Djaba of failing to inform him of the meeting since she was in his territory, Mr. Naabu also claim the gender minister was plotting to thwart the President's appointment of the regional head of the School Feeding Programme.

He described the meeting as "illegal" and "unconstitutional", saying even President Akufo-Addo would not venture into the region to hold such a meeting without informing the regional executives.

Look here my people, power sweet, but power belongs to the people and not those who beat their chests like a gorilla. So let's think through what we're doing now because the opposition NDC are watching us. And the more we bleed the better for them.

In her reaction, Ms. Djaba said: "Mr. Naabu came there to throw his weight about. ...As we speak nobody has appointed anybody for school feeding. ... I understand that Chairman Bugri wants to give this position to a woman Dakora Bama or something, and then he also tried to cover up about issues concerning the DCE. I have nothing to do with the DCE. ... I don't know why Chairman Bugri wants to lie and use me as a cover up for his problems."

"He cannot appoint School Feeding people, he's not the only one in the region, he wants to be the one to appoint DCEs, council of state elders, who and who, ...all the things he collects from the people before assuring them [of posts], he should go and give the things back to them. ..." she threatened.

One local media wrote: "The dirty linen of the New Patriotic Party in the Northern Region appears to have been flown high in the open by the Minister for Gender, Women and Children Affairs, Otiko Djaba, as she launched a scathing attack on the Party's Northern Regional Chairman, Daniel Bugri Naabu with a slew of allegations."

Is this what we want? I don't think so. Let's bury the hatchet.

KATH BUILDING ABANDONED

What was the KATH (Komfo Anokye Teaching Hospital) building for?

Supposedly a maternity block meant to save souls but time had passed her by. She hadn't been lucky and would probably never live to see her dream fulfilled. Its abandonment had seen many deaths recorded in the Ashanti regional capital Kumasi (the Garden City). So would it ever get completed, given her current status? That remains to be observed.

A 1,000-capacity- bed facility that was begun in 1974 stands depressed, uncompleted and abandoned while deaths occur almost by the day. Months have come and gone, years have turned and decades are rolling on like a rolling stone. Goodness only knows if it would survive another decade. It's been left to decay.

It was begun in 1974 abandoned sometime in 1974 and had been left to rot since 1974. The project must have been initiated and started by the Kutu Acheampong National Redemption Council (NRC) government in 1974.

Today it stands like a bronze wall riddled with bullet holes–defamed: Like the two iconic buildings I saw in Heidelberg, Germany. The Ottoman War didn't spare the beautiful city, they set it on fire but the two relics survived the brunt of the evil. On the street to the famous Heidelberg University (the oldest in Germany) they stand.

On the contrary the KATH building had been left at the mercy of the weather–drenched by rainstorms dried by scorching sun. Apparently, regime after regimes had failed to rescue her or continue the project that could have saved thousands of lives.

I've got a thought. If comparison would help change our mindsets, let's do it without any hesitation. In fact per this very project I am tempted to believe that there are perhaps more of its kind abandoned somewhere in the country. Some may date back in the precolonial and postcolonial era.

On Wednesday 23, October 1974 Her Majesty the Queen of England Queen Elizabeth officially opened Ninewells Hospital in Dundee, Scotland. The hospital is internationally renowned for introducing laparoscopic surgery (assistance of a video camera and several thin instruments) also called minimally invasive surgery to the UK.

Construction of the huge project began in August 1964 (10 years before the KATH project began), which presupposes that it was a protracted development but with an estimated final cost of 25 million pounds Ninewells saw the light of day. In other words the project was completed.

Since its opening in 1974 Ninewells has had major impact not only upon Dundee residents and UK citizens but also millions of people across the world. It was reported that apart from the health services it provided its clientele the hospital in 1986 employed over 5,000 people.

Forty-three years on, the KATH project is sitting uncompleted and abandoned!

Imagine how many people Ghana would have saved. Imagine the number of people the facility would have employed. Unemployment is swallowing us today—breeding galamsey operators and crime. Imagine how many homes had been broken and how many more had been left broken-hearted. And I bet you've an idea where your leaders run to when they're sick. They go to the Cromwells in London, the Ninewells in Dundee and other first-rate or state-of-the-act hospitals abroad. Those are places they seek medical care and not Korle Bu or GEE.

Still on Ninewells, at the opening ceremony an elated Queen Elizabeth said this: "Nothing that science can devise, nor money provides will be lacking for the treatment of the patients."

Also in 1974, elsewhere in the United States of America a giant project was born. The Oregon Health & Science University (OHSU) a public university in Oregon with a main campus, including hospitals in Portland was established.

What am I up to? Well change doesn't happen until it happens. Change requires willingness, alacrity, determination, patriotism and devotion. It requires killing selfishness, purging corruption, apathy, and being honest and dying for your nation and not lining your pockets with state funds or stifling progress.

Glad we've made it here but some people couldn't. Glad we survived the turbulence; we weathered the storm and kept our heads up from sinking to the depths of the sea. But they couldn't. They saw death approaching –pacing like a murderer with a scalpel but they couldn't avoid its onslaught. Thing is we could have helped them live longer but we failed them.

Let's remember that we are not an island so let's learn from others. Let's imbibe good work habits, can- do-spirit, continuity and good maintenance culture. Yes, let's replicate the good values and let's jettison the vices.

Joy News documentary

Thanks to the Multi Media Group of companies. Thanks to Joy FM an Accra-based radio station that put KATH on the spotlight. The radio station is reported to have aired a documentary titled 'Next to die' that showed the overflowing maternity wards where one baby cot accommodates as many as eight newborn babies.

According to the station the situation at the hospital is awful. Expectant mothers are left to lie on benches with some sat on chairs as they waited for their turn to use delivery beds. It reports an account about troubled parent: Mr. Owusu Ansah who lost two of his babies at KATH broke down in tears after he revealed the incident to Joy News. "So who will be the next to die?" he asked.

Ironically the station reports, "Whilst the deaths occurred, a 1,000-bed facility that was begun in 1974 was left uncompleted for decades."

It says the situation at the largest hospital in the Ashanti Region feeds into UNICEF's 2015 report on Ghana that showed newborn mortality rate is at 32 out of 1,000 babies. This means the country losses these babies before they get to one month.

First Lady's Intervention

Already, the KATH documentary by JoyNews has touched the hearts, minds and souls of many in the country and abroad. Ghana's First Lady, Rebecca Akufo-Addo on Thursday kicked off an event to raise an amount of GHS10 million to finance a new Mother and Baby Care Unit at KATH. The ceremony which was held at her Ridge office in Accra attracted massive support.

She said the drive to put up a new Mother and Baby Care Unit at KATH will bring relief to mothers and their newborn babies. The new Unit, will have about 20 incubators and have well-fitted ventilation, according to her.

Speaking at the joint Multimedia Group and Rebecca Akufo-Addo Foundation Fundraising event the wife of the President said she was troubled after watching the station's documentary about avoidable deaths at the Komfo Anokye Teaching Hospital, adding she was committed to rewriting the story at the hospital.

Mrs. Akufo-Addo noted that: "the disturbing story of mothers losing either their lives or their newborn babies at the hospital should prick the conscience of every Ghanaian and jolt them to take action to reverse the situation."

Importers & Freight Forwarders

Is this their time 'Paperless Ports Clearing System'?

I've always been intrigued by what goes on in our nation's sea ports particularly at the Tema Harbour. What keeps the undue delay in freight clearance at the port? What causes the rampant stealing and loss of goods? Why do custom officers demand bribes and kickbacks when freight forwarders and importers have duly paid all taxes and monies required of them? Why importers end up paying penalties to customs?

There is incredibly lots of paperwork (at the point of clearance) which adds up to the stress. The daily shuttling from point A to point B in a bid to get the consignment cleared. How could I forget the anxiety and the unknown that build up right from the bedroom or living room. Perhaps the early morning phone call from the custom officer that suggested that the goods are stuck somewhere. Where's somewhere? Is it somewhere in Tema or somewhere on the high seas?

But it never stops there. There's also palpable tension that swathes the atmosphere. That sets the two—the importer and custom officer on a seemingly collision course. There, arguments swirl, common ground is hard to find—often jettisoned in the deep blue Ocean amid insults, curses and retributions.

This and many more put a lot of complexities on the pathway of the Ghanaian importer. And whenever you're able to get the goods cleared after that long hustle and bustle you wonder: when is this going to end? Would there be a time or day when the Ghanaian importer can heap a deep sigh of relief?

Thankfully there appears to be a solution on the way. There's a man called 'Paperless Ports Clearing' system. And much has already been spoken about him. The question is: *Could this be the real deal to end the age-old port clearance problems?*

Ghana's Vice President Mahamudu Bawumia has announced that from September 1 2017 – which is probably less than two days away the NPP government is going to commence a policy called 'Paperless Ports Clearing' system.

"It's a robust system that enables customs clearance to be carried out in four hours," he said.

But wait the package was more than that. He also made it known that the administration was introducing what he called 'First Port Rule' in Ghana. *What does that mean?*

Basically, it's a rule which will provide the avenue for the duty on goods destined for countries such as Burkina Faso, Mali and Niger to be paid here in Ghana. According to the vice president this should provide a check on the dumping of goods destined for Ghana's neighbouring countries on us (Ghana).

It's understood that the yet-to-be introduced initiative, which is already being practised in many advanced countries where importers often enjoy quality and efficient services; has the potential to open the Ghanaian economy up and also to ensure rapid growth.

There's currently a test trial of the project towards the September commencement, journalists were told.

"Under this new policy, Customs officials, Ministries Departments and Agencies (MDAs), agents, shipping lines, the Ghana Ports and Harbours Authority (GPHA), Ghana Institute of Freight Forwarders, Meridian Ports Services (MPS), Tema Container Terminal, other terminal operators, courier providers, and scan operators in the value chain are mandated to work together to generate instant results at the ports."

In the meantime, there have been agitations from some freight forwarders and clearing agents, but government is urging them to exercise some level of restraint and allow the system to work for the benefit of their clients and the country as a whole.

That notwithstanding government has stated that as a people we should not forget that the public over the years had been dissatisfied because of the overall procedures, inexplicable charges, delays, lack of transparency and the complexity in port operations.

Also, the general public particularly importers were reminded that the paperless initiative doesn't eliminate the middle-men i.e. agents and freight forwarders out of the system. Their presence and activity will still be visible on the ground.

"The current system replacing the lethargic one, we understand, is going to reduce the number of hands mandated to inspect imported goods. The joint mandatory inspection will become the order of the day. The fact that it is going to be paperless, in our humble opinion, does not suggest that it is going to weed out the important work of agents and freight forwarders from the system. In fact, it is rather going to enhance the value of all those who are in the business of clearing goods on behalf of their clients as a senior customs official remarked last week. The paperless transaction will instead speed up the clearing processes at the ports and increase the revenue to the State," government gave the assurance.

Meanwhile speculations are rife that when the new paperless system is in full operation it would result downsizing or job-cuts at the port. But government has quickly debunked the suppositions. In effect, saying there's no such thing in the pipeline.

"It's clear that the target of this noble initiative is not job-cuts, but to make clearing of goods at the ports easier and more comfortable. The joy of bringing in more goods and the fact that it will help freight forwarders and clearing agents to be clearing goods within a couple of hours – some say four hours – should be good news to everybody."

It has further prompted Ghanaians that by adopting the e-clearance system, the much-talked-about issue of corruption was going to be reduced drastically as the processes that lead to payments at every stage were going to be centralised.

"We are moving from a system of applying sub-standard and unnecessary complex procedures at the port to a system which meets international standards. We need value for money as a nation and we are going to insist on that."

Is everything going to be cool and smooth as we go paperless?

Not really, I think we should expect some bumps on the road which is normal for every innovation. Nevertheless, going paperless has huge advantage over its counterpart and I can't wait to see what I call Ghana's' New Dawn' roll out. But some businesses across the world haven't performed well under this environmentally friendly option.

The reason, they've been facing challenges such as cost of hardware and software. For example, the need to updating hard wares and soft wares often come with huge cost. If this is not factored into the equation the paperless idea might suffer eventually. Another challenge is the cost of keeping IT specialists. First of all, you have to consider the size of the office, so for a place like Tema Harbour you will need more IT specialists to keep your soft wares and hard wares work effectively and efficiently.

Remember also that we're changing lanes if you like moving from the outer lane to the express lane. It's obvious that we cannot switch to a paperless office overnight without giving our employees formal training or orientation. It means cost and resources. Be reminded also that not all the employees would want the new norm. They simply hate to adapt.

What do you do in that scenario fire and hire a new hand?

We also have to think about hard ware failure, this could result loss of data which is a major threat to the business. Mind you, business can be down for days if proactive measures aren't put in place. The question is: Are we prepared to deal with all that? And last but not least, is the issue regarding security failure. Can we protect our system from being hacked by hackers? That said, I'm all for the paperless project, I think it's even long overdue.

Clock Watchers

Can We Work Against the Clock?

The Chinese worked against the clock, to build the robot (580 ton monster machine) that can lay bridges over pillars in a fraction of the time possible. The Japanese worked against the clock to come up with the new wearable chair—a gadget that eases the stress of long hours spent on foot.

The Koreans worked against the clock to build the automobiles—KIA Sorrento, KIA Forte, KIA Cadenza, KIA Optima, KIA Rio etc. And these nations afore mentioned haven't stopped working hard. In fact I think they look hungrier than nations that have nothing to display as they remain as ambitious as Lucifer working against the clock to come up with yet more inventions as the years roll on.

But, it seems the story is much different in our part of the world. The paradox is that it appears the hungry man is unprepared and is not poised to make his presence count. Instead of being productive, it looks as if the famished is working against the clock to kill man hours.

At Ogyakrom working hours are used for chatting, Facebooking, whatsApping, tweeting, texting, instagramming etc. The end result is under development. It's this kind of work attitude that got Ghana's President Akufo-Addo to call on Ghanaian workers to eschew tardiness, slackness and carefree attitudes at workplaces.

"I have said it at another forum but I think it bears repeating. We arrive at work late and then spend the first hour in prayer. We are clock watchers and leave in the middle of critical work because it is the official closing time. Everything comes to a stop when it rains and we seem to expect the rest of the world also to stop," Mr. Akufo-Addo lamented.

On Monday 1, May Day President Akufo-Addo called time on idlers, timewasters, slackers, malingerers and lazybones. He said Ghanaian workers seemed to be stuck in a mundane attitude and wasting time when the rest of the world is busy working or making good use of man hours.

The president who made this observation in Accra while addressing the workers at the Independent Square said: "We have no respect for the hours set aside for work. We pray, we eat, and we visit, during working hours. We spend hours chatting on the telephone when customers are waiting to be served, thereby increasing our labour costs. We take a week off for every funeral. And then we wonder why we are not competitive.'

Can We Work Against the Clock?

Yes we can. Ghanaians are known for their hard work and they excel at any field they find themselves. But somehow that demand-driven spirit often deserts them when they work at public services— government ministries and departments, schools and hospitals. In fact anything that's state-owned is more than likely to face the enemies of hard work. I know what I am talking about.

I did my one year national service at one of the departments at the ministries in Accra. Most of the workers would show up between the hours of 10am and noon. Surprisingly by 3pm those faces (the late-commers) that turned up at noon or before noon in the first place would be long gone. You can't even trace the dust behind them. There was another group that would basically show up to use the land lines (phones) to make international phone calls.

This practice went on till the end of my service. And I am pretty sure the saints that joined them later had already been corrupted while the practice is ongoing.. It's baptism by blood tonic once you ingest it, it gets into your DNA and it's incurable. Fact is even if you're a workaholic and you stay there longer you'd most likely become a slacker. My chief executive had asked me to stay on after service. But I respectfully declined the offer from my Boss. I told her: "No thanks Mum.".

That said Ghanaians by nature are hardworking and industrious. And they've proven that beyond all reasonable doubt that when they're placed at the private sectors they give their all and they excel. Just take a look around you—from the telecoms, airline industry, banking, aqua –fishery, commerce, & trade, technology, farming, agro-business, estate development and many more, they've performed excellently. The likes of Nduom, Sam Jonah, Kwadwo Sarfo, Kasapreko, Despite, Nkulenu, Abena Amoah (Baobab Advisors), Adelaide Awhireng (Fio Enterprise Ltd.) have made immense contributions towards the growth of the nation's economy.

Meanwhile, the General Secretary of the Industrial and Commercial Workers Union (ICU) Solomon Kotei has commended President Akufo-Addo, noting that everything that the president said was right. Mr. Akufo-Addo had charged public sector workers to change their attitude towards work if they wanted Ghana to progress.

Mr. Kotei also asked the government to pay public workers well and urged supervisors to begin to allow the systems to work because the conditions of service are there. "The agreements are there, so we should allow them to work and make sure that people are brought to conduct themselves according to conditions that are set up," he said.

We also have to look at the conditions under which they work. Some of the offices you go there and the kind of chairs and tables they sit on, the infrastructure and the building itself, the environment, you'll find all kinds of traders hawking around. So they don't help the place to become operational," he pointed out.

Are Ghanaian workers ready to change their attitude?

I think the president's call must be taken seriously and should rekindle all and sundry to give their all. Let's develop the habit of working hard to break deadlines. Be reminded: Time is money. A stich in time saves nine. Time and tide wait for no man. Time lost can never be regained. It's time for change so let's make good use of our time. By so doing we will be able to realise our dreams, we will be able to meet our aspirations and we will be able to build the Ghana we envisage.

Time has always beaten us as a people it appears. We've never managed to beat the clock. We rather get beaten by the clock almost every single day. The clock beats us at state functions, meetings, fora, conferences, assignments, ceremonies you name it. It seems we're late to everywhere at every time. Let's make it a thing of the past.

Last but not least, I believe our race against time, for instance to save our degraded and devastated rainforest, water bodies, landscape, ecology will come to naught if we continue with this attitude. Our race against corruption, indiscipline, dishonesty, apathy and exploitation will yield no positive results if we don't shun this attitude. I also think our quest to put the ailing economy back on track will be fruitless, if we continue to kill man hours and be unproductive.

Not only that but also we will lose the race against our neighbours in the sub region and our pursuit of making Ghana the hub of the ECOWAS community will be a mirage. Thus, it's high time we got crazy busy to nip this laid-back attitude in the bud. And it's about time we found our bearings right so that we can navigate well and excel.

What's Kwame Benjamin's Crime?

Was he the one who sold his brother Joseph?

I suppose they were awakened by his chime. They weren't expecting the 'Big Ben' to ring that early—not in that wee hour of the morning when even the early bird was still snoozing in her nest. Indeed when the Rooster (cockerel) forgot to crow at 3:00am Big Ben chimed.

Yes, Kwame Ataapem would have no time to waste, no time for the snoozers. The hour had come. Time was in labour. His bell was ready to toll. And the deafening noise would cause the slough to wake up from its slumber.

Evidently they'd been stung but as expected they turned their anger on the ringer—blaming him for doing what's right. To them what's right isn't right. They see it as their right to perpetuate what's wrong and I think the right word in this context is not wrong it is fraud. My caution though, we must all look before we leap-frog because there must be a Benjamin spying on us with his binocular eyes.

He's shrewd and smart, vocal and affable. He likes association football and his team is West ham United. Hate him or like him Jon Benjamin is becoming a household name in Ghana. He's UK's High Commissioner to Ghana who tells it as it is. He flows with the flow, flows with the crowd. He does not only pry into Ghanaian politics but also in sports, entertainment and social discourse.

Sometime in April 2015, I sighted one of his shared postings on the social media—Facebook to be precise. It was about a former TV3 news anchor (a devout Man-United fan) who claimed to have watched a football match between Sunderland and the Red Devils at Old Trafford Stadium in the UK but it turned out to be hoax. The other one, which is most recent, is about a popular Ghanaian actor who's alleged to have stolen a state vehicle.

That's Kwame he's not shy to speak his mind. He loves Ghana and loves its people.

But he wouldn't behave like biblical devoted High Priest Eli. Eli loved his two scoundrel sons—Hophini and Phinehas. And even though the rogues treated the Lord's offering with contempt their father Eli failed to discipline them. "Why do you scorn my sacrifice and offering?"

Both sons died same day as it had been prophesied. And Eli's household would come under curse.

What's Benjamin's crime now?

Has he done anything unthinkable?

Is he the one who sold his brother Joseph?

No, I can tell you emphatically that the High Commissioner has done no wrong. He hasn't acted disrespectfully to Ghana's Parliament as it had been reported by the local media in Ghana. His critics are just chasing a fly in the jungle when the big elephant is roaming around. He seemed to have hit the nerve of the third arm of the government. Truth hurts isn't it?

Mr. Benjamin stated what's obvious he can't act like Eli: He must do his master's will as a diplomat –commissioned by the UK government. The alleged visa fraud involving three MP's has changed the dynamics of the game. It ought to be looked at with extra pair of eyes. The rules must be stream lined and the bar must be raised. Ouch!

"Given what has transpired the British High Commission would request the Ghanaian parliament to be aware of the following," Mr. Benjamin stressed in a letter to the Speaker of Ghana's Parliament.

1) We will henceforth only entertain and prioritise request for visas from MP's if they are made through the parliamentary protocol office who should verify that there is an official parliament reason for the proposed visit.

2) However MP's wishing to make private visits to the UK or to be accompanied on official visits by non-official relatives must apply on-line and through our Visa Application Centre at the Movempick Hotel like any other applicant.

Abraham Lincoln once said: "You can fool some people sometime but you cannot fool all the people all the time." You may be able to harvest fraud at the passport office, at Tema Habour, or reap it at the nation's international airport KIA but you cannot harvest it at Benjamin's backyard. He won't allow fraud to sprout.

By the way Ben's bell is till tolling.

Isn't it worrying to wake up on Monday, or Tuesday, or Wednesday or Friday and you hear this: MP has accused Parliament of taken bribe? Or Parliament is embroiled in a bribery scandal? Or a legislator has been arrested at JFK for carrying narcotics with a street value of say $30million?

Doesn't that bother you as a proud citizen, a lawmaker, a judge, a public office holder?

For how long must we allow some few bad apples to spoil the good ones or drag the hard earned reputation of Parliament in the sludge?

I doubt if the nation has forgotten Eric Amoateng or Mahama Ayariga's saga? Image building is hard to do but it takes a second to tarnish it. So let's jealously guard that which we have toiled to build and let's uphold it firmly.

Jon Benjamin isn't the problem. The guys who purportedly sold Joseph are there, the blame must therefore be channeled to those who set the fire, stoke the fire and attempted to burn down the august House.

The blame must not have his eyes focus on the one who's trying to put his house in order but to those who knew better but failed to do so. And I hope once again Parliament will look at the case with wide-eyed.

So, I will appeal to the critics and the attackers of the High Commissioner to leave him alone, for beads don't rattle until they're touched. Leave Benjamin alone and deal with the guys that set the fire, stoke the fire and attempted to burn the House, meaning to bring shame upon Parliament. And for those of you who still think you've an axe to grind, there isn't one to grind. No, you can't burn the Big Ben he's insulated.

xxxxxxx

The Background

A former Member of Parliament (MP) for Asunafo South in the Brong Ahafo Region, Mr. George Boakye, who is alleged to have engaged in visa fraud by the British High Commission e r has threatened to sue the commission if a 10-year travel ban imposed on him is not reversed.

The High Commission, in a letter addressed to the Speaker of Parliament, Professor Mike Oquaye, had accused the former legislator of engaging in visa racketeering, using his diplomatic passport. According to the High Commission, Mr. Boakye used his diplomatic passport to apply for a United Kingdom (UK) visa for himself and his 37-year-old daughter to visit London for 17 days.

The visa, the High Commission said, was granted on September 14, 2012, and the MP and his daughter travelled on September 17, 2013, but instead of the 17 days, the daughter ended up staying in the UK for three years. However, Mr. Boakye, in a letter signed by his lawyer, Mr. Kwabena Asare Atuah, and addressed to the British High Commission, said he travelled with a normal passport on September 17, 2013, and not a diplomatic passport as claimed by the High Commission.

"My client travelled with a normal Ghanaian passport with passport number H1050729 and not a diplomatic passport. My client was granted a two-year visa from 14/9/12 to 14/9/14 with visa number 011164422," the letter said.

Daughter travelled alone

The letter also claimed that although he travelled together with his daughter she had applied for a separate visa which was independent of his own.

"The purpose of the visit to the UK by my client and his 37-year-old daughter was a private one. My client returned as scheduled. His daughter who is an adult failed to return as scheduled. My client cannot in any way be blamed because his adult daughter overstayed her entry permit into the UK.

"My client has not engaged in any form of visa fraud. All documents presented by my client were genuine and he made the application directly to the UK Commission and not through any supposed third party. He has not abused the privileges and responsibilities as a Diplomatic Passport holder," the letter said.

Reverse ban

The letter, therefore, called on the UK High Commission to reverse the travel ban imposed on the former MP or "my client will use all legal means to appeal against the decision to impose a travel ban on him to the UK and also clear his name".

The letter was copied to President Nana Addo Dankwa Akufo-Addo, Professor Oquaye, the Majority Leader, Mr. Osei-Kyei-Mensah Bonsu, and the Minister of Foreign Affairs, Ms. Shirley Ayorkor Botchway.

Other MPs

Three sitting MPs: Mr. Richard Acheampong, Bia East in the Western Region; Mr. Joseph Benhazin Dahah, Asutifi North in the Brong Ahafo Region; Mr. Johnson Kwaku Adu, Ahafo Ano South West in the Ashanti Region, were also alleged by the High Commission to have used their diplomatic passports to secure visas for some family members to travel to the United Kingdom (UK) but they did not return per their visa conditions. Three other MPs whose names are yet to be disclosed are also under investigation for similar offences.

Superstition: Africa's Scarecrow

Like a caricature or mannequin he stands hunched. He looks down at the dawn's rising sun that mirrors the pond at the eastside of downtown Ashong Valley. She's tucked deep in the valley surrounded by the rivers and rivulets that shine light upon her beauty and allure.

The sound of the Greyhound echoes beyond the walls. They're walls of superstitions: The walls that stand between science and myth, religion and agnostics, tradition and modernity, facts and rumours. They're rumours of war, rumours of tragedy. They're walls that evoke calamity, walls that scare humanity, walls that drive investors away and stifle progress.

The indigenes are scared away like sparrows and crows. Fore finger firmly placed on mouth to remain mute—signifying they're on a sacred place. Be silent. Absolute silent is required. You can't do this here you can't do that!

They've their own interpretation about the sun, the moon and the stars. The Heavens and the Earth exude powers beyond their comprehension. Amid the apprehensions, they pay homage, libation is poured, sacrifices and pacifications are ritually made. You can't let go what the forebears had passed down. And the tradition goes on.

Did I mention the forefinger? Yes, the finger that has several names. It's called index finger, pointer finger, trigger finger or the first finger. Among the Akans in Ghana one does not point the forefinger to the father's house, according to folklore. It connotes disrespect and contempt. This practice or belief is still held among some section of the populace.

What is superstition?

This write-up will have a look at three dictionary definitions of the subject.

Merriam-Webster dictionary defines superstition as a belief or practice resulting from ignorance, fear of the unknown, trust in magic or chance or a false conception of causation. For example it's a superstition that the number 13 is unlucky. It's also a common superstition that a black cat crossing one's path signifies bad luck.

Oxford dictionary simply defines it as "unfounded belief, credulity". It's a widely held but irrational belief in supernatural influences, especially as leading to good or bad luck or a practice based on such a belief.

Last but not least is the definition by Wikipedia. According to the online dictionary superstition is the belief in supernatural causality—that one event causes another without any natural process linking the two events—such as astrology and religions, like omens, witchcraft, and prophecies, that contradict natural science.

It further explains that the word superstition is generally used to refer to the religion not practised by the majority of a given society regardless of whether the prevailing religion contains superstitions. It is also commonly applied to beliefs and practices surrounding luck, prophecy, and certain spiritual beings, particularly the belief that future events can be foretold by specific unrelated prior events.

Indeed superstition is legendary, passed down from generation to generations. And to this day the myth has been perpetuated somehow in some places in our beloved continent and across the world. Centuries have seen the practice grow and glow. For instance it's taboo to go to farm or fishing on certain days in Ghana. Taboo to sing in the nights. It's taboo to pound fufu in the twilights —all amounts to abomination, curse and disaster.

The consequence, you may lose your mother or relation. Lands are left to fallow. Lands earmarked for development—schools and colleges, hospitals and clinics, roads and bridges industrial parks and amusement centres etc. But for modernity and civilisation most parts of the world today, would still be living in darkness.

Opposition to Superstition

Records have it that ancient Greece was the first place where superstition was challenged. The opposition was ably put up by Philosophers such as Protagoras and the Epicureans. Pluto is said to be one of the early fighters who showed his aversion to religion and myths. His work Allegory of the Cave played a leading role disproving superstitions. Also, history has it that philosophers–Pluto and Aristotle both present their work as parts of a search for truth.

Historians say in the classical era, the existence of gods was keenly debated both among philosophers and theologians. And consequent upon that opposition to superstition emerged. And this would in effect change the dynamics of superstitious belief. The Middle Age period saw the idea of God's influence on the world's events mostly undisputed.

According to records the rediscovery of lost classical works (The Renaissance) and scientific advancement led to a steadily increasing disbelief in religions. This led to studies of biblical exegesis, pioneered by Spinoza and to a more skeptical view about superstition.

But that couldn't purge superstition from our social-cultural milieu. Enough to say, despite technological advancement, the 21st century Man seems to be married to superstition. It isn't as deadly as Slave Trade, not as dangerous as colonialism or imperialism, yet like a scarecrow superstition has somewhat put impediments into Africa's progress or forward march, probably more than any country across the globe.

Mr. Kwamina Dadzie, a respondent writes: "A certain day is taboo to go to farm on Tuesdays because it's believed to be the day of the Earth Goddess 'Asaase Yaa'. When this taboo is broken there can be calamities in the community. This applies to fishing communities too, but that one is not linked to the earth goddess but a sea god."

Another of such superstitious beliefs is ancestral worship, he says.

"Ancestral worship which is based on the belief in life after death. In Ghana, especially among the Akans and other ethnic groupings it's believed that life doesn't end at death but continues in another world as elaborate funeral practices are held to usher the dead to the next world. Messages are sent and gifts are placed in the coffin. It's believed that those who lived good and exemplary lives are believed to watch over the living and protect them and so forth. So prayers are offered to them through pouring libation. Also, there should be no whistling in the nights."

Peoples have hated the idea of being free, free from the chains of superstitions. They hate the idea of bringing development and progress. You can't touch them, they're simply untouchable. And their names aren't supposed to be mentioned, they're purely unmentionable.

Yes, the indigenes fear them. A smell of them gives one a sense of palpitations, a taste of them sends one away at the throes of calamity and a sight of them smacks evil or phantom. If they aren't evils then they're obviously saints, the saints of our gods. And if they're not dangerous then they're courageous.

Dr. Dan Koroma a Sierra Leonean based in the United States shares his native country's belief in the power of what he calls the 'Witch Gun.'

"The belief in the power of the witch gun to kill people …it's a very popular belief in Sierra Leon," he states.

Dr. Koroma argues that this belief has to be viewed in the context of the lack or the non-existence of the white man's gun in addition to probably the cost of owning one including all the legal minutiae involved. "So it makes sense they would argue, to hire Juju man to do the dirty job."

But superstition (s) isn't a thing of African. In other words it's not peculiar to Africa. Across Europe, the Far East, North and South America, the Oceania and the Middle East peoples' belief in superstitions vary.

Madam Michelle Tillman an American has this to say: "For example knock on wood when you say something presumptuous so it doesn't happen. Also saying bless you when someone sneezes is said to ward off evil spirits. And don't walk under a ladder (common sense) because it forms a triangle representing the trinity and if you walk under it you're in essence breaking the trinity and that's bad."

Why do people still believe in these? Here's Michelle's response: 'It's probably because it's been passed down from generation to generations, however, I don't know why others feel or think the way they do.'

For example the Germans have this superstitious belief: Do not answer a witch's question, or else she can take something from you. It is not good if one goes out in the morning and encounters an old woman. And another interesting one–he who walks between two old women early in the morning shall have only bad luck the rest of the day.

This is a belief shared by the English too. On the eve of St. Valentine's Day it is an old custom to pin bay leaves to your pillow, one at each corner and one in the middle. You will then dream of your future lover, or the man you are to marry. And it's also believed that a woman may not draw water from any well for six weeks following the birth of her child, or the well will dry up for seven years. If a dog runs between a woman's legs, her husband will beat her.

Are the Walls of Galamsey Tumbling Down?

Politics is about power. It's about control, influence and supremacy. Politicians all over the world have a winning mentality. They've a never-give-up mindset. But don't misconstrue them. They aren't oblivious of the fact that the big game has its limitations. It can only produce two babies—victory and defeat. However, in most instances politicians have inclined to downplay defeat even when the giant is up in their face. To them victory must come at all cost—by any means necessary. They hate defeat they can't stand it and wouldn't want to lose power whenever they seize power.

So, is this man different?

It seems Ghana's president Akufo-Addo is daring the devil—defeat. His administration which assumed power four months ago is already up in arms with illegal mining operators also known as 'Galamsey'. And it portends to be a marathon battle. So far, days of persistent crackdowns by a combined team of the police, military and task force after

Gordon's Hodgepodge

government's ultimatum elapsed are reported to be making significant gains in its determined fight against the Undying Witch.

The signs look positive says this writer as local media reports suggest, the operators had been running helter skelter leaving their excavators, water pumping machines and other mining tools behind. Also the reports have it that over 500 excavators had been seized since the Ministry of Lands & Natural Resources launched its sting operation.

At Dunkwa-on-Offin alone, it had been reported that a total of 69 galamsey mining machines had been confiscated and 19 destroyed by the anti-galamsey task force. The operators were using the machines to mine on River Offin which serves as a major source of water for the communities in the Upper Denkyira East District.

However, the ultimate concern is whether the administration would be able to sustain the on-going exercise. To me the centrality of this operation must be sustainability and total elimination of galamsey, plus finding alternative skilled and unskilled jobs for the teeming unemployed youth that basically depend on this business... That said I like to commend the government for instituting the Multilateral Mining Integration Project (MMIP). The project seeks to absorb the people who will be affected by the crackdown. It's also expected to provide an alternative means of livelihood for the people.

My earlier point was about sustainability. I believe the pursuit of national environmental sustainability or ecological development by governments must be holistic and uncompromising. Fact is I know my leaders and you know them too –they don't seem to be good at it. The 'convenience disease 'appears to have attacked all of them as a result of bowing to pressures.

In Ghana there are certain things politicians don't do or are afraid to do because of political expediency. They're in two layers like croissant— the pastry that's made of layered yeast (leavened dough) and butter. For example, it might be convenient today to evict hawkers and traders from our cities' streets...But not so for tomorrow. We saw that played out in the last electioneering campaign season and the seasons that preluded it.

Yes it was convenient for the AMA or KMA authorities to drive the hawkers away from the streets in January 2009 (after the '08 general elections) but it was taboo or declared a no-go-zone around January 2016 (before the 7th December elections) . And I'm sure it won't be convenient for any politicians to do so around January 2019. It'd been so with galamsey operation in the past and other acts of indiscipline.

By the way, have you wondered why residents of Sodom and Gomorrah are still where they are? Or seem to comeback season after seasons?

Interestingly, whenever the authorities seemed to have held the bull by the horn and challenged the norm you see a situation like this: If NPP taskforce evict the squatters today, an NDC taskforce will show up tomorrow to welcome them and vice versa. That explains why the Accra Business District and Kwame Nkrumah Circle Area are in the state we find them. Sanity becomes insanity and it's business as usual. It's nothing but fear of retribution—the people might not vote for them (politicians) if they dare to evict them. It might be convenient today but it may be inconvenient tomorrow and the cycle moves on.

Remember this saying: "Don't send us to opposition..."' Koku Anyidoho NDC deputy general secretary told Seth Tekper former finance minister in the Mahama-NDC government. The minister was doing what was seen to be right but the season called for absurdity. Where are they now?

The people are gradually seeing the moonlight.

On Wednesday Mr. Akufo-Addo called the bluff of the illegal miners in the country who have threatened to vote his government out of power. Reacting to their recent threats and protests the president said "The 2020 election threats will not stop my anti-galamsey fight,"

I could hear him literally say to them: You guys can go to hell. Simply put he cared less about their threats.

He made this known at the commissioning of an ICT Centre at Suabe in the Eastern Regional town of Akyem Wenchi. According to him he wouldn't allow some citizens to endanger the lives of the entire population with their unlawful activities.

That sounds like a politician whose tenure is coming to an end. Isn't it? And if it were so would that even be justifiable given the fact that his party would still be keen on consolidating power rather than giving it to their opponents on a silver platter. So where did he get this big trumpet from or how did he find this voice?

And the trumpet blared like those that brought down the biblical Jericho walls. Indeed the trumpet had its unique target. It was against the 'Walls of Galamsey', ensuring that there would be no remnants left to haunt the citizenry tomorrow.

The Akufo Addo government has vowed to clamp down the illegal mining (which has immensely destroyed the country's ecology) by end of his tenure. Already it appears the battle lines had been drawn amid threat and counter threats. The Galamsey operators say they will vote the NPP government out of office in the 2020 general election. The president on the other hand has called the bluff of the miners, as if to say bring it on, I am ready for you.

Mr. Akufo-Addo said threats to vote him out in the 2020 election will not stop his government's anti-galamsey fight. He said he would carry through his government's plan to save the country's environment and water bodies that are being destroyed by illegal miners.

"Mining along the water bodies cannot continue if we want to preserve nature and our water. It cannot continue," he said.

His comments followed days after some illegal miners in Akwatia in the Eastern Region threatened to vote against him if he didn't halt his anti-galamsey fight. The galamsey operators told Joy News an Accra-based radio station that government's clampdown on their activities would make them poor. According to them they depend on the mining to provide for their families.

They questioned: "Does the Lands Minister [John Peter Amewu] want us to sit home? Now that our government is in power we want to make money but they want to stop us," he said. Another aggrieved miner questioned the rationale behind the anti-galamsey fight especially when the President has promised to create jobs for the teeming unemployed youth.

In a related development the Small Scale Miners Association in Kumasi had said it intended to petition the Asantehene Otumfuo Osei Tutu II to talk to government to reconsider the galamsey crackdown.

At a meeting in Kumasi on Tuesday the Association said the government was unfairly magnifying the effects of the activities of its members as though it was the biggest threat in the country.

It appealed to the government to help its members find an environmentally friendly ways to conduct their activities rather than stopping them.

Elsewhere in the central region, Dunkwa-on –Offin to be specific, some of the galamsey equipment had been seized and destroyed .The Stop Galamsey Operation Taskforce in Dunkwa in the Central Region had destroyed 19 machines used by galamsey operators. The Taskforce was set up by the chief of Dunkwa Offin, Okofrobuor Obeng Nuako III with representations from the Bureau of National Investigations (BNI), Minerals Commission, police, Environmental Protection Agency (EPA) and Dunkwa Traditional Council.

The chief is reported to have hinted during an interview with a local radio station in Accra on Wednesday that government's effort to stamp out on galamsey would be better fought if traditional leaders and small-scale mining operators got involved.

"I have supported Lands Minister, John Peter Amewu's roadmap to ending activities of illegal miners blamed for the pollution of the country's water bodies. I support him 100 percent [because] of the death traps the galamsey operators are creating in the community," he said.

Why Did GES Expunge History from Its Syllabus?

Maybe it was an oversight. It happens! We focus either too or so much on what our neighbours are doing only to realise that our children don't even know how their beloved nation was founded, who founded it and when it was founded. Most of the things we learn are un-Ghanaian. And often we've been made to believe that our culture is primitive and anything Ghanaian or African is backward or sub-standard. It's called 'Suatra' in Akan Twi language.

Maybe we were over ambitious or overzealous and the idea wasn't properly thought through at the time. Or maybe we forgot the intriguing message reggae legend Bob Marley planted in his Buffalo Soldier album for the black race. The singer, teacher and the Rastafarian said this: "if you know your history then you would know where you're coming from. Then you wouldn't have to ask me who the heck do I think I am."

Did you know the song didn't appear on record until the 1983 posthumous release of Confrontation? That's what history teaches. It reminds you of the past and sets you on a right path. The title and lyrics refer to the black US Calvary regiments known as Buffalo Soldiers that fought in the Indian Wars after 1866. The legend compared the Buffalos fight to a fight for survival and recasts it as a symbol of black resistance.

It appears we're treading the path of forgetfulness. Glad someone reminded me two days ago to look yonder and peer back as well. Someone who identified herself as a great admirer of my write-ups contacted me via WhatsApp.

".. I took my two young boys to the Kwame Nkrumah Mausoleum and I was so fascinated. But to my horror I was told they don't teach History in the curriculum. I was very alarmed to say the least. History as a subject both national and world History is so vital for our generations to learn of great things, like the industrial revolution, our fight for Independence but also learn not to repeat mistakes like genocide, apartheid, slavery, holocaust etc." said Gladys Prempeh.

Indeed it was this reader's appeal or concern that informed me to wade into the aforementioned subject.

Ghana has a rich history. It has history about its beautiful people, history about its dynamic arts/culture, history about its picturesque landscapes, history about its undying heritage, language, values and many more. Centuries ago, history used to be passed down (oral tradition) unto us by our forebears until formal education was introduced. And history would become part and parcel of our socio-cultural and political development until Ghana Education Service (GES) cut the subject into pieces with its switchblade.

Why? We will find out.

History used to be one of the major subjects taught in elementary (primary/middle), secondary schools including universities in Ghana. Its inclusion in the schools' curriculum or syllabus no doubt gave many Ghanaian pupils and students the opportunity to learn both national and world history.

I'm a beneficiary, an Apostle of history. I loved history then and I still love it. But I wonder if our school children today know anything about the battles of Adaamanso, Feyiase or the Nsamanko War. How about the bond of 1844, the Fante Confederation, the Anglo-Ashanti War in 1900's, the capital of the Denkyira's? I wonder if our children today have any knowledge of these kings—Gbewaa, Agokoli, Ansa Sasraku, Asamani, Ntim Gyakari, Boahen Anantuo, Togbui Sri, Tweneboa Kodua etc.

Sad to note, today, history has no stake in Ghana's socio-cultural and political platforms.

Absolutely, it's been expunged from the GES syllabus. And if my memory serves me right I think it's been gone for decades now. Like me you probably never took notice of its demise and the effect it may have on this generation and the generations yet unborn.

But what did GES replace it with?

History was replaced by Social Studies. However, I am informed some expatriate schools also known as International schools like GIS, Lincoln and others do still have History in their curricula?

If true, does it make sense why the expatriates' children are learning our history while the Ghanaian child is denied what s/he is supposed to know?

Are we not missing the point here?

Be reminded apples and oranges aren't the same. In like manner, water and wine are both liquid substance but you cannot replace water with wine and vice versa. Each of them is unique and plays significant role in our socio-cultural milieu.

Social Studies is the study of the problems of society. The subject prepares the individual to fit into society by equipping him/her with knowledge about the culture and ways of life of their society, its problems, its values and its hopes for the future. GES holds the view that the subject is multi-disciplinary. And on the backdrop that it takes its sources from history, sociology, psychology, economics, geography and civic education.

Yes, that's been the argument put forward by GES over the years. Are we seriously producing the right pegs to fit into the right holes? I dare to ask.

"Essential elements of the knowledge and principles from these disciplines are integrated into a subject that stands on its own. As a subject, Social Studies helps pupils to understand their society better; helps them to investigate how their society functions and hence assists them to develop that critical and at the same time developmental kind of mind that transforms societies," GES notes at its website.

Let me emphasise that my piece isn't purposed to pigeonhole GES structured programme. Far from that, it rather seeks to crave the indulgence of the service to reconsider its stance. GES argues that Social Studies helps students to make informed decisions, understand better and what else... Investigate how their society functions. On paper that's true but in practice I don't think the nation has realised that objective. Maybe it's yet to do that. But how long ago was it introduced or incorporated into the schools' syllabus?

Also, how has that translated into the development of our country since its introduction visa vis the period History and subjects like Geography stood on their own before integration or when they were supplanted?

GES makes another case as to why it replaced Social studies with history: It says: "Our society has been a slow moving society. It is hoped that as pupils understand the Ghanaian society better, and are able to examine the society's institutions and ways of life with a critical and constructive mind, the country will surely be on the path to better and faster growth in development."

With regard to pace, I think it's needless to remind GES that we're still in a 'Go Slow' traffic. Maybe the service has lost track of the pace of the period when History was studied or taught at our schools. That presupposes, History had no correlation to our slow growth. It could be other variables. So, I will implore GES to figure that out. And let's also remind ourselves that the two subjects aren't the same. Even though the latter has its bases from History and others, one cannot use that as a case to justify History's relegation to the background.

My final question (s) before I draw the curtain down: Whose idea or decision was it to expunge History from our schools curricula? Is too late to reintroduce it? I don't think so. I therefore per this write-up wish to appeal to GES to reconsider incorporating History back into its syllabus.

The Giant & Petite

Theirs is a shared love. Theirs is mutual and reciprocal. And theirs seem like it's without blemish. They aren't selfish. They love themselves to pieces. Like a couple they're inseparable. Their names rhyme. They call them Bella and Tara .I call them The Giant and Petite.

They aren't humans. They're animals—two living creatures—an Elephant and a Dog living the world as though they're born twins. Bella the dog is always seen tailing her super-sized friend Tara, the elephant. They swing together as if they're birthed by same parents and stroll together as though they've known each other from Adam. Their habitats are different. One is domestic the other lives in the wilds. Yet, they've become bonded friends.

Who would have thought or imagined to see such incompatible friendship grow to an unimaginable height? It's surreal story that challenges humanity to do soul searching.

First of all, I like to put this into perspective. According to National Geographic the average African elephant weighs between 2.5 and 7 tons compared to 2.5 to 5.5 of its counterpart in Asia. Then come the superlatives—given its sheer size—the African elephant is the largest living land mammal on Earth. In addition to their enormous weight,

African elephants stand anywhere from 8.2 feet to over 13 feet at the shoulder.

Wildlife scientists say elephants maintain their spectacular weight by consuming up to 300 pounds of food in a day. That's right!

On the other hand, an average American Water Spaniel adult male dog weighs 30-45 pounds while the female adult weighs 25-40 ponds. An Australian Sheperd female dog weighs 40-55 pounds. The Association for Pet Obesity Prevention suggests a weight range from breed to breeds. For example, Labrador Retrievers weigh between 65 to 80 pounds adding that figure can vary.

So now you can see the difference(s) between the two friends.

Thanks to the social media I couldn't miss Tara's majestic walk in a short video which has gone viral. Neither her wolf-looking friend's diminutive size could sneak my hawkish eyes. Their daily activities which start from the sunrise to sundown are just breath taking. It's like a walk with Jesus. Petite Bella sees nothing to be concerned about. She's a buxom friend not just a friend but a great friend she could count on when need be. When she's weak and when everything seems to be going wrong Tara will be there and likewise her.

Call them soulmates. Side by side they stroll every day– down the valley, up the hills in the wilderness. Both of them now live in a sanctuary. They walk the talk and amaze the world every day. They do everything in common. The two are absolutely inseparable.

'When it's time to eat; they both eat together, they drink together, they sleep together, and they play together," a woman and co-founder of the sanctuary said of the two buddies.

A narrator in the video said: "The two had been close for years but no one really knew how close they were until recently. A few months ago Bella suffered a spinal cord injury, she couldn't move the legs, couldn't even wag the tail. For three weeks the dog laid motionless up in the sanctuary office.

And for three weeks the elephant held the jaw. 27 hundred acres to roam free and Tara just stood the corner."

Tara showed love throughout her friends' ailment. She never gave up on Bella Once again the woman in the video is heard: "To me it really meant she was concerned about her friend."

According to the narrator, "then one day co-founder Scott Blake carried Bella on the balcony so she and Tara can at least see each other. And they visited like this till Bella could walk. Today, their love and trust is stronger than ever. Bella even let TARA pet her tummy with her foot."

They Habour no fears, no secrets no prejudices... Just two living creatures which somehow manage to look pass their immense difference. Take a good look America take a good look the world. If they can do it what's our excuse."

So how come humanity is struggling to make this work?

Several months ago there was a video of a duck that took care of a group of fish. The clip was shared on the social media platforms that also went viral. There was another one which had a little dog that almost took responsibility of a household whilst its owner was in bed. The little one checked the mails, brewed the coffees and woke her owner up from sleep. Certainly there are several if not many of such videos out there.

But there seems to be a missing link. Truly, something's gone wrong. This writer who also authored 'Crows Go Wild' says: The eyes of genuine love see nothin' but love. Until our eyes see no colour, see no race, see no sex, see no class and remain unbiased, our quest for peace, unity and love will be nothin' but illusion.

The narrator of Bella and Tara story put it eloquently: "If they can do it what's our excuse."

What's our problem one may ask? Why can't we make it work as political parties in our countries with the objective of building a stronger and viable economy, building a peaceful country and building stable democratic government?

Why can't we make it work as ethnic groups? Remember we're same people but speak different dialects and perhaps different values. But that should never tear us apart given the fact that animals can make it work despite the immense differences.

Must we all belong to one political party? The obvious answer is no. So why can't we tolerate one another, see them not as our enemies but rather partners in development. Parties today are tearing families apart, creating enmity among ethnic groups and dividing people of all backgrounds. Siblings are nick picking, while parents have become haters of their own kids all in the name of party politics.

And nations are probably doing worse. Powerful nations are bullying the less-powerful. They've turned institutions and agencies as gladiators or alligators —looking for prey to kill. Woe unto nations that are branded 'rogue' failed' or 'axis of evil'.

Remember what Jesus said over two thousand years ago? Our Lord said this: "It's easier for a camel to enter through the eye of a needle, than for a rich person to get into the kingdom of God," Mark 10:25 (KJV).

I'm a messenger of hope, my message stings but it cures...

'YAHOO BOYS' IN POLICE GRIP

Are Our Neighbours 'Noisy'?
When hyenas go rogue only the hunters can stop them, only the men with guts. Their booty spread all around them. Their greedy eyes search for more victims. Unbeknownst to them, the hunters have taken cover and would soon close in on them.

zzzzzzzzzzzzzzzz

On Saturday 26 August, 2017 the Madina Police Command in Accra Ghana arrested 26 suspected cyber fraudsters known as 'Yahoo Boys' all believed to be Nigeria nationals. Twenty-six (26) mobile or cellphones and 33 computer laptops including an unspecified number of flash or pen drives were retrieved at the crime scene.

The police command say all the gadgets have since been handed over to the Cyber Crime Unit of the Ghana Police Service for further investigation.

A tipster's piece of information to the police led the arrest of the 'Bad Boys' around 1pm GMT in that hush afternoon, according to Divisional Crime Officer, Superintended Joseph Oppong. He told the local media that the operation would be sustained until the menace was drastically reduced. All the suspects were busted in a single large room, the media learned.

"They're well versed in this cybercrime. And because of their activity in Ghana the whole world now thinks that cybercrime is a Ghanaian disease. This is why we need to fight it ruthlessly until it's reduced if not eliminated," said Mr. Oppong.

The police chief also appealed to the general public to volunteer information, adding it could be helpful to the community and the nation at large.

What is Cyber Crime?

Cybercrime also known as Internet fraud has manifested in diverse ways in recent times. But not only that its rise has also reached an alarming proportion causing great concern around the world. Cybercrime consists of different types. They include Identity theft, hacking, stolen bank accounts, and stolen online passwords. There's also phishing and cyber stalking. Yes you heard it right. You can be stalked like Mary and her little lamb... Internets are used for terrorists' attacks and bully students and school pupils.

In fact the statistics on cyber bullying and suicide are disturbing... "15 per cent of high school students (grades 9-12) were electronically bullied in the past year. Suicide is the third leading cause of death among young people resulting about 4,400 deaths per year, at least 100 young people attempt suicide and 14 per cent of high school students considered suicide and 7 per cent have attempted it."

Studies have also shown that 'the younger they are the more likely they will attempt suicide.'

With regard to cyber financial crime possibly billions have been lost over the years from individuals, multinational corporations, institutions to governments. In 2016 US retail giant Target lost over US$40 million when hackers hacked into their system.

Where are cybercriminals based?

Cyber fraud is now widespread. The fraudsters are like chickens and can be incubated everywhere. They're like brats found every parts of the world. They're born in cities and born in hamlets. They're in China, Russia, the United States, India, Nigeria, Saudi Arabia you name it.

Indeed Ghana is faced with the conundrum of trying to woo many Nigerian investors as much as possible to inject heavy capital into its economy. But she's also not oblivious of the fact that the 'freight doesn't always come as expected. There are bad nuts that fall through the cracks and it's often difficult to crackdown on such miscreants. And of course you can't put the blame solely on Nigerians. There are also Ghanaians who indulge in cyber fraud.

The West African nation is notoriously known for cybercrime .And I'm pretty sure Nigerians either resident in Ghana or anywhere around the world more often than not cringe at the mention of cyber fraud also known as 419 in that country. .

As I earlier noted internet fraud is widespread—it pervades both in the advanced and developing world. In 2009 Time reporter Randy James reported that President Obama was searching for 'yet another White House czar to tackle a pressing public concern. ..." And so on May 29 2009 the president announced a high-level initiative to address the growing problem of computer attacks—against the government, corporations and Individuals—by coordinating the various efforts to fight hackers and other computer criminals under the direction of a coordinator already dubbed the 'cyber czar,". Randy reported.

"I know how it feels to have privacy violated because it has happened to me and the people around me," Mr. Obama said in the announcement.

Around the same time then Defence Secretary Robert Gates told CBS News that: "The country is under cyberattack virtually all the time, every day." He said Pentagon at the time planned to quadruple the ranks of its cyber security experts due to the insurgence.

Methods employed by cybercriminals

They rummage and rampage websites. One method used to commit such crimes is sending emails with a 'seemingly legitimate link, but once clicked, the link installs a virus on the victims' computer that records keystrokes to enable the acquisition of passwords, account numbers, and emails sent to others', internet specialists have observed.

Cybersecurity experts say most times all of the information obtained from these types of attack are collected by the criminal and put up for sale. This kind of attack which is commonly referred to as phishing is frequently used by the scammers according to HSNO a forensic firm based in the United States.

Are our neighbours 'noisy' if so, how do you deal with them without straining the cordial relationship that exists between the two nations'?

The Nigeria community in Ghana is growing exponentially. The population is not only concentrated in Accra the capital city. Today, Nigerians are settling in cities like Kumasi, Takoradi, Tamale, Cape Coast, Bolga, Ho, Koforidua, Sunyani and various towns across the nation. They're in banking, mining, farming, fishing, quarrying, aviation, telecommunication and many sectors. More and more Nigerians are today educating their children and wards in Ghana.

Sometime in 2010, the Nigerian population in Ghana was said to be hovering around 4 million. Seven years on, it's most likely, that figure could double as the influx continues. Indeed they're neighbours we cannot sever ties with. We need them much as they need us. Therefore let's work together to smoke out the moles from the holes.

Ghana's Ready For Concrete: Why did it take her so long?

At least it's taken Ghana 52 years to figure out, asphalt concrete or concrete road is the way to go. The nation opened its first concrete highway to traffic in November 1965 to connect the Harbour City Tema to Accra Ghana's capital city. The landmark highway also known as Tema Motorway (which is 19 km or 12mi) was modeled after the Autobahn in Germany. Since then the country has been stuck with asphalt bitumen, Coal tar as it's commonly known in Ghana.

What do they say: Better late than never, right?

It seems the long wait is now over. And the issue is no more about which one to go for –Concrete roads or Asphalt roads. It's also not about which one lasts longer or is better. Asphalt concrete (commonly called asphalt, blacktop, or pavement in North America, and tarmac or bitumen macadam in the United Kingdom and the Republic of Ireland) is a composite material commonly used to surface roads, parking lots, airports etc.

On Saturday 15 July, Ghana's cabinet approved a proposal to use the latter product instead of asphalt and plans are afoot to pilot the product on Tema Steel Road. The industrial city, this writer says will be first to see Ghana's concrete highway since the Tema motorway built in the early 1960's by Osagyefo Dr. Kwame Nkrumah Ghana's first president..

The Vice President Dr. Mahamudu Bawumia who made the announcement said the Akufo-Addo administration believes constructing concrete roads would save the country from spending more, as compared to the construction of asphalt and bitumen roads.

Well road experts will tell you no roads last forever. This is because in spite of their projections say 20-40 years they'll at some point during usage require either maintenance or repair be it asphalt or concrete roads. Roads are like any other element they have their natural cycles or life span if you like. The problem we have in Ghana and I believe across the continent is perhaps not the asphalt or concrete per se, but the value for money which has often eluded us.

Every year billions of dollars (tax payers' monies) are sunk into road constructions but the results leave much to be desired. The roads simply don't last long. Some last for months, and perhaps the majority of them wouldn't stand a decade without showing signs of failure. Pathetic to state that some even get washed off in weeks as many of them fail prematurely and it is the frequency of their sudden deterioration that get on people's nerves. Indeed some of them might develop potholes and sinkholes that could swallow a fatling cow or Tico car.

So what really accounts for the fast deterioration of our roads?

Climate determines what kind of road one must construct and materials to use. It's understood concrete highways are better suited for tropical regions like Ghana. But they don't work better in snowy or icy areas which probably explain why my home state Washington state is now diverting bitumen or asphalt pavement. It's easy to remove and cheaper as compared to concrete when the roads deteriorate. That notwithstanding, many countries today are going concrete.

Of course, I'm not an engineer but my little research into the field writing this piece has taught me this: There are three common causes of pavement failures. They're Poor Soil, localised Void and poor design and fabrication. Time and space may not allow me to discuss them in detail. But in brief, if the soil is bad no matter the quality of the product it would end up bad.

What's a bad soil? Clayey soils are most unfavourable in road construction. Also, if the soil that lies on top of the pavement has structural issues it's regarded as bad soil. High water table will lead to run off or erosion and will eventually wash the pavement away. And the way to prevent that is building drainage systems.

Localised void on the other hand is basically the sinkholes and the potholes you detect in the course of the construction. They say, a stich in time saves nine. The earlier you fix it the better, it becomes cost effective and you'd get value for money. Last but not least, poor design and fabrication. And as the name suggests if the engineering works are done poorly the pavement will fail woefully and you'll be back to square one.

Doesn't that sound familiar? This is a typical case in Ghana. Step out from your homes and take a look at the roads in your communities. They're just milking us. Inappropriate cost cutting during the initial design and installation either the property owner insisted on cheap options, the engineer didn't know enough to put in the right materials or the construction company cut corners where they shouldn't have.

Ultimately, where the construction requires six inches base course they will put three. Of course, the ministers, the chief directors and quantity surveyors will all take their 15 per cent shares and what would be left could do nothing but poor roads. This in part is the main bane of our poor road networks. Yes, the freebies (10 per cent tips) lead to shoddy works as contractors would not put the required materials to stabilize the foundation.

Asphalt Versus Concrete — Which Is Stronger?

Concrete road's life can range somewhere from 20-40 years. But the annual cost of maintenance for, asphalt road (pavement) for example is about four to seven times higher. This saves one long-term on repair and maintenance.

Over the years road experts have discounted the common belief that concrete pavements are stronger than asphalt pavements (bitumen or blacktop). They say: "the reason for this misconception is that comparisons are not made on equivalent designs. The traffic-carrying ability of asphalt or concrete pavement is approximately the same for each inch of pavement thickness. "

A typical 3,000-psi concrete slab would also be assigned a structural number of 3.0, per inch of thickness. Therefore, a 4-inch concrete pavement and a 4-inch asphalt pavement have the same load-carrying capabilities.

According to engineers asphalt and concrete will provide the same traffic-carrying strength when the same thickness is used. For instance, a pavement with a Structural Numbers (SN) of 10.0 will always be twice as strong as pavement with a SN of 5.0, regardless of the material used.

In April this year (during Easter, it's understood, the Charismatic Bishops' Conference proposed for roads in the country to be constructed using concrete. The Bishops also urged the government to increase road tolls to a flat rate of $1 as an effective measure of raising revenue for various road projects in the country.

The Vice President, Dr. Bawumia, who took a keen interest in the proposal said at the dedication of a Harvest International Ministries temple in Accra that government had had many discussions on the matter and had also involved Parliament for the discussion. In that meeting he added cabinet took a decision to make the country move away from asphalt roads to the construction of concrete roads.

"Why is it that we are not building our roads with concrete and rather doing all this asphalt, bitumen stuff which gets washed away after about 2 seasons. If you look at Tema motorway which was built with concrete, it is lasting almost 50 years. We started that discussion, it is a simple idea but full of wisdom. I checked and realized that in India, they have the policy to build only concrete road and it works out to be cheaper. We have been discussing this as recently as last week in Parliament," the vice president wondered.

We will consider doing this and it will be transformational because as for laying concrete, we can all do it in Ghana. You don't need to get anybody to come and lay concrete for you. Any mason from any village can come and lay the concrete and go on."

Indeed the Tema Motorway built over 50 years ago saw its major rehabilitation works in August 2009. Part of the highway was reconstructed using epoxy cement. And it took engineers and road contractors eight weeks to complete work.

What Can We Share on Social Media Platforms?

I didn't share it because I couldn't share it. It wasn't because I couldn't bear it. But I reminded myself to be mindful and tactful. To be careful and be considerate about what I could share with my colleagues and friends on the Social Media platforms (SMP). Fact is being circumspect in what we do, what we say, what we write and what we share, helps us as individuals or groups to avoid slip-ups and bad consequences.

That notwithstanding, we all falter one way or the other at times. It's common knowledge that as users of the social media sometimes we tend to tilt the positive handle of the clock to the negative side (anti-clockwise), whenever we ignore these guiding principles if you like.

Indeed what we can share or not share on social media platforms has always been an issue or a bone of contention among group members. And if you haven't faced or heard this question then you could pass as the 'Stranger in Jerusalem.' It's a question that rears its head almost every day and users are very familiar with it. Over the weekend a colleague on a platform asked me: "What can I share on the social media platforms?"

My response: I wish I can tell you to share everything. Share anything and everything that you consider to be appropriate, decent, encouraging, motivating, and insightful: Anything that informs educates and entertains. Anything that doesn't offend one's sensibilities, anything that you wouldn't like someone to post on the platform(s) Mind you, what you might find to be offensive, others may see it otherwise. So, I think, making a sound judgement all the time would help a lot to avoid the bumps on the road. But if you're in doubt or indecisive as to what to share consult the Platform's Admin or a friend via inbox.

Groups on social media can also influence what one could share on platforms. The groups vary from class, gender, sex, race, age, faith to professionals. So which one do you belong?

Is it a college year group say 'Class '94?

Is it a group of professionals?

Or is it a platform for the 'Sweet 16ners'?

I have always maintained that we must attach decorum in our postings. By doing so we will afford everyone the opportunity to express his/her views, display photos, videos, post articles and messages etc. Above all, we will be able to achieve the desired goals and objectives. Also it must be noted that unnecessary censorship would stifle interest in participation. Remember, one's treasure is another's trash. But also don't forget the watchword—circumspection.

Besides, the question as to who's doing what and how it's going to be done often remains problematic. You totally have no clue, what you're going to see or read the moment you switch your cell phone back on. Sometimes the goods are good and other times they come in bad tastes. There are absolutely no gatekeepers in this field. You wield the trump card and you decide what's at your disposal. Someone wrote: "If you can't watch them just ignore or delete them and stop whining."

It could be a prank message about the death of a loved one or a video made up to create panic and fear. There was a disturbing video shared on a certain platform a couple of days ago. It had a huge snake (python I suppose) swallowing a young lady believed to be a student. in an upscale hotel in Nigeria. The clip raised eyebrows. The poster graciously deleted it without crying foul.

There'd also been rumour of deaths churned out by the social media regarding Her Majesty the Queen of England, boxing legend Mike Tyson, African billionaire Aliko Dangote and Ghana's football maestro Abedi Ayew Pele and many more. Suffice to say every hour generates something new, something eerie.

Can governments control SM contents?

By far the New Media today have done or are doing incredible and unimaginable things. They've made our world so tiny, shone mega lights on our secrets, traditions and mores. Privacy has found herself at the eastern window of course. And what more we can tweet, we can whatsapp and we can facebook whilst in bed and even driving.

Despite its marked advantages governments, institutions, agencies etc. across the world have raised concerns about contents put out by the social media. The concerns have to do with indecent materials, vicious attacks, defamatory messages, scary and gory images and many more.

On Thursday 20 April 2017 Ghana President Akufo-Addo made known his government's plan to regulate contents of the social media. He said: "My government will institute regulations to guide and control indecent social media content."

According to him regulating indecent communication was essential and could help control contents posted on social media which would also avoid denigrating Ghanaian societal norms and values.

It is not clear when this regulatory plan will take off. In the run-up to the 2016 general elections then Inspector General of Police threatened to shut down internet services across the country. He said the move was to install sanity in the atmosphere and also ensure users of social media did not put out unsubstantiated information.

Around January this year the U S President Donald Trump also disclosed his government's plan to shut down its own social media accounts in an effort to combat what they saw as politicisation at some government agencies. Already the administration had barred the Environmental Protection Agency (EPA) from using its social media accounts and from issuing press releases an unnamed staffer for the agency told Fox News.

"Not the most inspiring time at EPA right now but we're fighters,' the staffer said.

Elsewhere in Turkey in 2016 the government shut down social media and also detained elected legislators from leftist pro-Kurdish party.

Would the social media be able to withstand governments' shutdowns or regulations?

That remains to be observed going forward. Users of the social media myself included spend hours on varied platforms as if we are at the stores and malls looking for different merchandise. Through google search engine I looked into what's called in the industry as 'Infographic.'

I found out the amount of time people spend on social media is increasing. The most users are teens. Teens are reported to spend nearly or up to nine hours a day on social media platforms, while 30 per cent of all time spent online is now allocated to social media interaction, according to writer, Evans Asano.

Amazingly, Mr. Asano reported that the average person would spend nearly two hours (approximately. 116 minutes) on social media every day, which translates to a total of 5 years and 4 months spent over a lifetime.

It's understood that the total time spent on social media beats time spent on eating and drinking, socializing and grooming. As to how much each media's share in the time constitute or translate into: The beak down are as follows, YouTube comes first, consuming over minutes of a person's day (i.e. 1 year and 10 months in a life time.

Facebook users, the report says, will spend an average of 35 minutes a day totaling 1 year and 7 months in a lifetime. Snapchart and Instagram come in next with 25 minutes and 15 minutes spent per day, respectively. Lastly, users will spend 1 minute on Twitter, spanning 18 days of usage in a lifetime, the report concluded.

Are Ghana Police on Warpath?

The Ghana Police have bared their teeth amid warning to flush out armed robbers in the West African country. *But do they have the logistics to deal with the rogues?*

xxxxxx

Dogs don't bark for nothing. They do so when they sense danger or feel threatened. Ghana Police Service have issued a stern warning to the country's notorious armed robbers as they prepare to engage them in what the service calls 'Fire for Fire," operation. The Police are seemingly under threat following the rampant killings of its officers by armed robbers in recent times.

On Thursday 13 July 2017, two of its officers were shot in the line of duty by armed robbers at Lapaz, Accra... One officer died at the scene while the other was believed to be in critical condition. The Director General in charge of Police Operations, COP Christian Tetteh Yohuno who issued the threat asked the notorious guys to desist from shooting and killing personnel of the police service.

He said the service was more than combat-ready and would do everything within its power to engage the goons in a brutal battle: "The security services are very much prepared for a "fire for fire" battle, therefore, any criminal who tries to joke with officers, does that at his or her own risk."

We will descend heavily on armed robbers. We have sensitized our men to deal with armed robbers. We have charged our men to deal with any armed robber who tries their patience …..We are prepared for fire for fire", Mr. Tetteh Yohuno cautioned.

According to the Police Chief the continuous murderous attacks on police officers by the gangsters are 'unacceptable' and should be 'discouraged'.

So what's the plan and do the police have the logistics to battle them?

I think they will need the firepower, vehicles and other important communication gadgets to be able to win this battle. And COP Yohuno revealed that going forward it would be necessary for all police personnel on community patrols be allowed to carry side arms so as to gun down robbers who threaten their lives.

Also he hinted that a proposal had been sent to government by the Inspector General of Police (IGP) to procure more logistics so that every policeman will have a protective gadget.

If the number and frequency of police officers killed in the last four years in our country don't send wrong signal then what else would? In 2013, 13 police officers died in the line of duty. The affected officers died in several circumstances, including exchange of fire with armed robbers, motor accidents and stabbing.

According to police reports the ranks of the officers ranged from Constable to Chief Inspector.

Six of the officers died in motor accidents: two died on their way to effect arrest; while one died during escort duties. It said another died during traffic control duties; and two others in unspecified motor accidents.

The year 2014 saw little reduction in terms of numbers of officers killed. A total of 11 Ghanaian police officers lost their lives in the line of duty across the country in 2014. This is perhaps more than half of the number of officers killed in the whole of the United States same year if you juxtapose that state by state. The National Law Enforcement Officers Memorial Fund, a pro-police nonprofit, released its preliminary 2014 report on officer deaths, which listed the total number of fatalities at 126.

Ghana is about the size of Oregon in the Northwest region. The state ended 2014 without a single law enforcement fatality in the line of duty — the first time since 2012, according to reports.

Most remarkable noted NBC was 'the number of firearms-related deaths in 2014 (50), which was a 56 percent jump from 2013 (32)'. Traffic-related fatalities (49) was the second-leading cause of death for police an increase from last year (44), when it was the year's leading cause, according to the group's data. NBC added that, despite the increase, 2014's total of 126 is well below the average of 151 for the past decade.

According to preliminary data compiled by the National Law Enforcement Officers Memorial Fund, as of June 30, 2017, 65 federal, state, and local law enforcement officers have died in the line of duty this year, increasing 30 percent over the 50 officers killed during the same period last year.

So the numbers speak for themselves, the police in Ghana aren't safe. It therefore, behooves on all of us as law abiding citizens to help safeguard and maintain the peace and safety in our communities. We should bear in mind that Police officers are not enemies but they're partners in development. And same goes to the law enforcement agents: Treat civilians with much respect and avoid using brutal force on them. Police brutalities have become common in our societies nowadays, and it's about time they viewed civilians as friends and not enemies either. Furthermore, citizens must volunteer information to help make policing less cumbersome. Police alone cannot win the battle against the criminals. Obviously this is not a 'Batman' show—the fictional superhero that appears in American comic books. Let's work together to protect one another. We need the police and they also need us.

What Would NDC Do Without Rawlings?

Would they be better off and could that translate into victory in election 2020 or it would retire them into perpetual opposition?

xxxxxxxxx

Peppers are spicy but we still eat them. Their flavor is unique and indispensable. Arguably, their taste and smell are the elements that determine the impression of foods.

Former President, Jerry John Rawlings' name is ringing everywhere this week. It's ringing in Axim (down southwestern part of Ghana) and it's ringing in Zabzugutatale in the north. Over 38 years ago, the Rawlings' ring tone was much-sought after and it seems it is loud today too.

So what's in that name that's keeping its influence and prominence still in Ghana's political landscape?

Is he the only one with clout in the NDC?

The answer perhaps, is no. However, it appears his influence and undying prominence can be compared to the peppers' sensory characteristics. And with that 'golden belt' still hanging at his corner, I would advise his sworn critics to tone down the rhetoric. You stop a sinking boat from sinking you don't help it to sink because you might all end up perishing.

During the week someone sneezed in her room little did she know that probably many would catch the contagion and it would trend on the social media. A member of the opposition National Democratic Congress (NDC), Alhaji Iddrisu Bature was possibly the first to catch the cold. The editor of the Alhaji and Alhaji newspaper had called on the NDC to sack its founder, Jerry John Rawlings.

What's the reason? According to Alhaji Bature some comments made by Mr. Rawlings before and after the 2016 general elections have brought the party into 'disrepute'. Disrepute! What does that mean, is it euphemism for defeat or shame?

"..Nobody is beyond sanctions in the NDC, not Jerry Rawlings, not Martin Amidu. And if any founder of the party including Jerry Rawlings and Martin Amidu is bringing the name of the party into public ridicule and disrepute, they deserve to be hauled before the party and sanctioned accordingly," he stated.

His comments on Tuesday during a radio discussion programme followed an article written by former Deputy Chief of Staff, Dr. Valarie Sawyer who served under the presidencies of Mills and Mahama. Dr. Sawyer had taken a swipe at Messrs Rawlings and Martin Amidu former Attorney General.

Commenting on the issue Alhaji Bature said: "President Akufo-Addo and the NPP have demonstrated that nobody is beyond discipline in any political party. They took disciplinary action against high ranking members of their party and yet convincingly won the election. NDC can do the same,"

And what did Dr. Sawyer's article say?

In part her write-up stated that Mr. Rawlings was still 'flogging a dead horse' [NDC] although they are in opposition and further criticised him for praising President Akufo-Addo despite some scandals that had rocked the government.

"They say he booms ... I say he buzzes ... like an agitated mosquito ... looking for his next victim. Again, he heads for other Heads of State ... describing their governance as riddled with corruption. Is he trying to say that his reign was unblemished or that his twin brother's (President Akufo-Addo) reign is unsullied?" she rhetorically asked.

So can NDC sack Rawlings?

Article 41 of NDC Constitution under the headline: COMPLAINTS AND APPEALS PROCEDURE states among others that:

1. Any member who has reasonable grounds to believe that another member or other members of the Party are in breach of the provisions under clause 8 of Article 38 may lodge a petition in writing to an appropriate Executive Committee for redress.
2. a. Where the grievance is against the leadership of the Party at any particular level the petition may be lodged with the Executive Committee of the next higher level.
3. a. All members of the Party are enjoined to exhaust the complaints procedure contained in this Constitution before recourse to legal proceedings or adverse publications in the media against the Party at any level.

Alhaji Bature makes a case to the effect that before the December 7 general polls NPP sacked some of its leaders and therefore NDC can do the same. "They took disciplinary action against high ranking members of their party and yet convincingly won the election."

That sounds like a false analogy or comparison fallacy (also known as the look-elsewhere effect). There's always a chance that the conclusion might be false despite the truth of the premise. Yes, it's true the NPP took punitive action against some of its leaders but was that the reason why NPP won the 2016 election?

Perhaps there were factors other than the suspension of its top ranking officials that contributed to the party's victory. It could be its campaign message that there was high corruption in the NDC, which President Rawlings also alluded to time and time again before the general election. Maybe it was also its message that labeled NDC as 'incompetent' party. It was possibly 'Dumsor' and the perceived arrogance and disrespect which many people blamed the NDC for.

That said, I think the Botchwey Committee Report— post 2016 election prognosis dossier will be of great interest to those who still have no clue as to why NDC sorely lost the last election. The reasons for NDC's fall have been captured in black and white in that report.

Above all, I think the comparison between the NPP and NDC is unsound. Probably, Alhaji Bature should have focused on an internal case. For example, he should have made reference to Dr. Josiah Aryeh's case— the former General Secretary of the party (May his soul rest in peace). The former NDC scribe was sacked over an allegation that he'd been bribed by the then opposition NPP.

For the records the NPP didn't just wake up one eerie morning when the Monsoon winds were drubbing the Gulf of Guinea coast and decided to suspend or sack its Chairman and General Secretary. They followed the due process and exhausted the entire process.

Also, Alhaji Bature on the Eyewitness News claimed that Mr. Rawlings' clout in the NDC has dwindled drastically following his consistent critique of the party and any attempt to believe that he still has grip on the party is only an "illusion."

"He [Jerry Rawlings] has forfeited any legitimate right to remain the founder of the party. When the party ahead of 2012 election advertised that it was going to hold a rally at Mantse Agbona and he was the special guest, he issued a statement he is not going to be a part of it because he has not been invited. Rawlings has forfeited his right to remain the founder of the NDC. Nobody is above discipline in any party," he added.

I think his comments rather tend to create sharp schism. It also fuels the notion that some clique are trying to hijack the party and make the former president a back seat observer. Must we always rant on radio programmes to make our cases heard, especially if or when it involves party stalwarts such as Rawlings? Wouldn't it have been better if they'd called him to order through closed door meetings?

If he wouldn't shut up his mouth, what do you expect us to do? I could hear his avowed critics make such remark. But was the right approach used to resolve the issue if there was ever the attempt? Sometimes it's the approachability that gets the result. At times, it's the people involved in the negotiation that make things happen. Fire for fire might backfire.

So what would NDC do without Rawlings?

Would they be singing Hosanna, Hosanna or they'd be singing 'Dabi dabi ebeye yie'? Would Volta region remain its bastion or the 'World Bank' as it's commonly known in terms of votes? How would Rawlings' exit generally impact on the electoral map in relation to NDC's performance? Would there be divisions more than what's already perceived in the party? Would the former president go without taking down the party he helped to found? And would the NDC be able to win an election without him campaigning for the party? I think the 2016 election was a testament, though debatable, when he was virtually sidelined. There are certainly more questions than answers.

Is Amale in Bed With AMERI?

My trip from Lagos (the commercial capital of Nigeria) to Accra had been littered with stress and complications. But I'd know idea that ahead of me laid a more convoluted case. I'd learned that confusion and complexity are not blood-related but whenever the two words cross path they spark fire and create controversy.

Yet, that won't stop me from looking into this inevitable question: Is Amale in bed with AMERI? Amale's name has been trending everywhere. When you go there they say Amale, when come here they say Amale. Amale is at the coffee shop, Amale is in Makola Market Mr. Writer tell me who at all is this Amale girl, is she the most beautiful in this romantic city?

Oh Olusegun, the name is not Amale it's rather AMERI so get over it, come out of the state of confusion. Be reminded we're back in Accra, Ghana. And even though Manna has ceased to fall there are still some people who're lusting after the heavenly bread. In apropos, AMERI is an acronym for –Africa & Middle East Resources Investment Group LLC (Ameri Energy), a Turkish power giant.

Indeed AMERI has generated controversy across the nation but beyond that it's caused individuals and institutions to lock horns amid scathing words. Here is one example: "You are confused about aspects of Ameri deal," said IMANI a policy think tank to a former deputy Attorney General in the \Mahama-administration.

So if the chief attorneys are purported to be 'confused' what would the traders in Makola do? It certainly begs the question. Thank Goodness the ink hasn't dried yet. This AMERII case seems like the biblical Sabbath story to me. Isn't the son of Man Lord over the Sabbath?

My question is: Why are we shooting ouselves in the foot? Who would throw $150 million into the drain for the sake of conflict of interest when it's been established that value for money had been compromised or you got duped for a purchased product?

Who wouldn't accept boarding and lodging fees from the person who supposedly acted in bad faith over transaction, if that's the only way to redeem your lost money/? Why would you sell your cash-cow for a lame-duck? In other words, would you spend more money to redeem that which is lost—flying a team to Dubai and spending days in the oil-rich Arabian city? At whose expense the nation that's already been robbed and bleeding?

Who refuses this, when the one who allegedly duped you says he's now open for renegotiation (come let's talk), not only that he would also foot your bills as you pursue justice and value for money?

The argument in support of conflict of interest is tenable no doubt about that. But ultimately you'd break the Sabbath's ordinance which forbids you to go to the corn farm when your children are dying of starvation.

"Ordinary speaking, when a committee is going to investigate a matter, it is true that the person or institution that is going to be investigated should not be seen to be giving benefits or providing facilities for the committee investigating the matter, but in the peculiar situation of this case there is a twist," said a former commissioner for Commission For Human Rights & Administrative Justice (CHRAJ) Justice Emile Short.

"..But in the peculiar situation of this case there is a twist.' I like that line. Indeed there is a twist. But where is the twist, the twist is embedded in the Sabbath story.

The legal luminary said the Addison committee's Ameri-sponsored trip to Dubai would require a thorough investigation since the situation is complex. According to Mr. Short although the incident appeared to be conflict of interest, the context in which it occurred makes it peculiar and complicated.

He further explained that the situation looked rather complex and it required some thoughtfulness before conclusions can be made. "We have to look at the special circumstances of this case. The provision of government especially with regards to this Ameri deal and the fact that the company was the one that insisted the committee should travel abroad. So these are the parameters which any institution investigating the matter would take into consideration. It is not your normal situation," Mr. Short stated.

A-17-member committee chaired by Philip Addison was constituted by the government to investigate a $510 million power agreement with Turkish giants –Ameri Energy signed by the previous Mahama government. The committee said it discovered the former administration paid $150million more than they were expected to pay.

Meanwhile the Minority in Parliament says the committee's report was 'biased' and 'compromised' by AMERI's sponsorship of the team's trip to Dubai to meet with the company's executives\. On Tuesday 18 April 2017, Minority Spokesperson on Finance Cassiel Ato Forson told the media in Accra that: "What comes to us as a shock is that a three-day trip was extended to a week for reasons known to members of the committee?"

"Strangely the (Energy) minister's brother who is Member of Parliament for Ayawaso West Wuogon who is not a member of the committee joined the trip on the second day of their visit, also under sponsorship of AMERI. A situation that is embarrassing, unethical and shameful," stated Mr. Forson.

In a sharp rebuttal the Attorney General, Gloria Akuffo says the Addison committee did not compromise itself by allowing AMERI to fund its trip to Dubai.

Elsewhere in the capital a policy think tank IMANI Ghana had locked horns with Mr. Dominic Ayine a former deputy Attorney General of the NDC government over the controversial $510 million power agreement with the Turkish power-giant. IMANI believes that the power agreement signed by the previous administration was a swizz.

And if you thought the confusion was over, it had rather oiled its squeaky gears gathering momentum The IMANI-AMERI team had copied Myjoyonline.com a statement regarding the power deal and had squarely put the blame on the deputy state Attorney General. In part the statement alluded that Mr. Ayine who led the legal transaction of the AMERI deal 'may either have been confused about aspects of the deal or let down by specialists at the Volta River Authority.'

Led by the Vice President of the think tank, Bright Simons, the IMANI AMERI team maintains the power agreement was a rip-off. Here is an abridged form of the statement.

IMANI principals have been locked in a debate over the last week with the former Deputy Attorney General ("ex-DAG") who led the Ghanaian side in the AMERI deal.

Our exchanges with the former Government functionary on Facebook in recent days have however brought us to the sudden realisation that the ex-DAG may be completely confused about certain fundamental aspects of the deal he led.

Aspects so fundamental and elementary as to suggest that he was either woefully let down by his VRA specialist advisors or he failed to heed to their counsel.

Since the best path forward for Ghana is to get him and the former Power Minister to testify on our side, enthusiastically and emphatically, in any mediation or arbitration, to the effect that Ghana was lied to by AMERI regarding the costing of the "balance of plant" work and the derivative calculations for the implied tariff, we are going to add to our list of goals for this our longstanding AMERI advocacy project.

Top of that new list is the need to find more elaborate means to "demonstrate" the deceits this country has endured at the hands of AMERI.

Firstly, let us address the two main defences of the AMERI deal being canvassed by the ex-DAG and his supporters.

1. He is still unwilling to back down from the position that there was some massive extra work done by AMERI on the GE-made TM2500+ power plant-complex supplied by PPL through Metka.

    He believes that AMERI or its subcontractors paid $120 million in order to get the machines ready to start supplying power to the Ghanaian grid despite our very clear explanation of the scope of work using the contract annexes, the GE product manuals, and a bill of quantities approach. So let us try a more vivid approach.
    A. There is no dispute that Ghana secured ten TM2500+ power plants from AMERI. This is confirmed in the contract.
    B. The TM2500+ is a compact, "power plant in a box" and NOT just a gas turbine.

        It is the gas turbine PLUS several components of the "electrical balance of plant" and "mechanical balance of plant", mounted on four mobile trailers, needed to complete the "power plant in a box" concept of the TM2500+
    C. The actual gas turbine inside the TM2500+ is the LM2500, a derivative of the CF6/Tf39 jet engines made by GE.
    D. The LM2500 is sold on the open market for $9.5 million.
    E. Everyone knows that the TM2500+ is also sold on the open market for $22 million.
    F. That means that in addition to the gas turbine, there is at least $12.5 million of additional components added to the LM2500 in order to complete the TM2500+ package.

Well that isn't the end of the IMANI-AMAERI statement and it's certainly not the end of the confusion and the complexities of the whole power deal. But it's an eye-opener and a food for thought. Going forward we have to be guided by the principles of value for money and due diligence.

I Told You So Yahya Jammeh

The ego of a kite or balloon knows no stop until it's brought down by the same squall that gave him an elevation in the first place. So be reminded that a balloon cannot fly on its own until that rubber sac is inflated with air, then sealed at the neck and let loose.

Once upon a time, a little boy had his kite unfastened. Moments later he noticed the object had wandered miles away from him. He cried for help, tried to catch it but the light frame object with thin material continued to soar. It had stretched its pace floating in the wind, meandering courses, diving in the clouds -from east to west, his eyes tailed the kite as he continued to sob.

After a fruitless attempt the little boy stood still and watched his tiny kite flaunt its weight and ego as it flew high up in the skies. There was a moment the boy thought the reunion with his toy was imminent. Indeed he wanted his kite back. But the object had faked its descent only to be seen going higher and higher and it ducked in the clouds.

As hours morphed into days the boy forgot about the kite and minded his own business. But not long afterwards the kite's glory faded. They say, 'whatever goes around comes around'. The kite came down but not the same way it had been seen bouncing around –in midair. It had run out of power, no steam and no vim. Bottom line it had reached its endpoint.

Did you know that five of the current Africa leaders combined have ruled their respective countries for nearly 200 years (168 years to be precise) since 1979?

Here are the five Africa's longest-serving leaders: Teodoro Obiang Nguema, Equatorial Guinea (36yrs), Jose Eduardo dos Santos, Angola (36yrs), Robert Mugabe (Grand Papa) of Zimbabwe 35years, Uganda's Yoweri Museveni 29 years and Paul Biya of Cameroon 32 years.

The longest, Mr. Nguema born June 5, 1942 has been President of the central African nation since 1979. He ousted his own uncle Francisco Marcias Nguema, in an August 1979 military coup.

Without a doubt it is this kind of egocentric attitude by some African heads of state that influenced the likes of Gambian dictator Yahya Jammeh who took his people for a ride for 22 years. And also he thought he could make the Gambia throne his personal asset—and make it father to son one day. Thank goodness Gambians have had a new president. Thank goodness Jammeh had banished himself.

"Agyewodin, wo'agye wani so'. What were you thinking? Did you think I was kidding? I told you the people had had enough of you. I told you, you wouldn't have it easy if you chose the Kabila path. But thank Allah that things didn't go the other way. So go in peace with your stolen booty but I can assure you Gambians will come after you soon. Don't sleep too much.

On Friday 2 December 2016 Jammeh was defeated by Adam Barrow and conceded defeat. But a week later he challenged the election results at the Supreme Court. He also declared a state of emergency ahead of the deadline given to him to leave office on Thursday 19 January 2017.

I don't really know if the action had been triggered by the resignation of some of his key cabinet ministers—i.e. finance, foreign affairs and environment in his government. And it appeared he wasn't going anywhere any longer.

However, pressure had been mounted on him by the Economic Community of West Africa States (ECOWAS), the Africa Union (AU) and the United Nations (UN) to cede power to his challenger in the December polls Mr. Barrow.

Midnight Wednesday 18 January 2017, when ECOWAS realised that Jammeh wasn't ceding power it deployed its troops into the tiny West-African country. The regional group had spent weeks working to convince Jammeh to accept the election results. He still wouldn't budge.

But what perhaps broke the camel's back was when it became obvious that he had lost one of his final allies, Gambia's military.

"I shall not involve my soldiers in a stupid fight," said Gambian army Chief General Ousman Badjie. At press briefing on Saturday morning General Badjie said he recognised Mr. Barrow as his commander-in-chief and not Jammeh.

And courtesy of Guinean President Alpha Conde, Jammeh had sought temporal exile in Guinea. O' ye coward who warned you to flee from the wrath to come, I thought you'd hard balls and would choose to stay on just as Muamar Gadhafi in Libya did.

You thought you could fool your people forever and ever. Well the same Allah who you claim gave you the power to rule had spoken through the Gambian people. And I don't know who you were addressing —bragging 'as a Muslim and a patriot I believe it is not necessary that a single drop of blood is shed."

Have you forgotten many had perished under your regime? Brace yourself to face the International Court of Justice tomorrow, for crime against humanity. I can assure you that will also happen live. It's all a matter of time.

In the early hours on Saturday Jammeh went on television telling Gambians how he served the nation and loved its people.

"I have decided to relinquish in good conscience, the mantle of leadership of this great nation."

Who takes you serious again Jammeh?

Wall Street Journal reports that: "Until his plane left the tarmac at Banjul airport on Saturday evening many Gambians were still questioning whether his rule was over."

Also, reports have it that the deal that was reached on Saturday shields Jammeh his family and supporters from prosecution and protects his assets from being seized. He also will be allowed to return to Gambia 'at any time of his choosing," according to a statement from ECOWAS the African Union and the United Nations.

But incoming Barrow's administration says it is not satisfied with the terms secured by Jammeh and even cast doubt on whether it intended to respect them."

"That is the perspective from that side," Hallifa Sallah, a spokesman for Mr. Barrow's coalition.

Post-Election Trauma Talk (PETT)

Who says he will put the feet of the NPP to fire?

Thirteen days after the election blues NDC Deputy General Secretary Koku Anyidoho says his party can't wait to drill the yet-to-be inaugurated Akufo-Addo government.

"We intend to be a very responsible opposition but we are not going to sleep on issues from day one, we are going to put the feet of the NPP to the fire and the candle," he said.

That's right. This is what we need. Let's debate the debate. Let's talk about issues and refrain from hurling abusive epithets on people, stop intimidating and distributing rice and corned beef to the electorate to think that they don't know their left from right.

Koku I can't believe you learnt the lessons so quick whiles many of your comrades are still brooding over the huge loss. .

See candle lights don't stay long in the wind. The paradox is that the people who lit the candle think it would last forever or be able to stand the test of time. But soon the evil storm (tsunami) shows up and the light disappears.

What a way to learn Koku. It's my hope that the majority of your people would see the light and not confine themselves to politics as usual (the woods). Remember, it's only the light that can lead you to the pinnacle. Politics is a great teacher but his students are stubborn. They want to grow feathers overnight, develop talons 'asap' and start teething from the get go says this author.

Tell your guys to slow down. The speed limit says 20kph. You know what that means?

Good for you. Well done my brother!

Remind me though to get you 'Akple and Fetri-Detsi' before I take leave of you. I'm heading down to Aflao the border town. Actually I'm going to Adafianu. I've got some family and friends there to visit. The last time I visited there– good old Christophe and Davi (May their Souls Rest in Peace) hosted me like a king. I had the best Akple ever with duck meat and almighty fetri-detsi.

"It is not 'Aflawo' Massa. It's pronounced Aplao— you say the letter P as if you're blowing a kiss to Asiedu Nketiah (the General Mosquito himself)."

Thanks for the correction. And look at you—you're teasing your Boss. Talking about your Boss how's he coping?

When is he going to Canada?

And tell me I hear some of them have had the blues for almost two weeks now.

"I think he's recovering now. He'll finally get over it. I'm not sure when he wants to go, maybe after the inauguration of the President-elect.

We're still mopping up the tears. I must confess to you. And this is for your ears alone. Generally, everyone in the family was shocked to the marrow."

You mean the NDC family right?

"Yeah, but mind you it's for ears alone."

Gotcha! Koku, remember walls have ears. So don't blame me if you hear it at the bar or elsewhere.

Hey bar man, please give me one tot to check my how far, trying to quit. But I think I need that right now to be able to read in between the lines. The lines look blurry.

"Say you don't have the money to buy…"

Koku don't bring yourself this morning ok. I don't have the money. Do you live in my pocket?

Listen I've important things to discuss with you so let's set the ball rolling before I miss the bus to Aflao.

"I said it is not Aflawo La."

Stop your diversionary tactics Koku. Time isn't on my side so don't drag this into another thing.

Did you really say this and can I quote you?

"We intend to be a very responsible opposition but we are not going to sleep on issues from day one, we are going to put the feet of the NPP to the fire and the candle."

I also want to find out if the other guys are in the same page with you. And is this the new way to go?

I couldn't agree with you Koku. It's all about issues. Trick number one is issues. Trick number two is issues and trick number three is issues. Issues win power they don't insult. Issues win hearts and minds of the people they don't attack and issues calm tempers they don't incite hatred and animosity.

I told you Politics is a great teacher, but his students are stiff-necked.

How quickly did they forget that power belongs to the people and not the rulers?

The ruled, the majority, the people exercise power. They call the shot…However, politicians in our world have tinkered that fundamental human right clock. And they've 'whimsically', (apologies to Dr. Omane Boamah) turn the tables upside down.

They say, no condition is permanent but more often than not when people find themselves at the political echelon they forget the lifespan at that stratum is just like the candle in the wind. It doesn't last long.

So on that note I think the NPP stands ready for the opposition's challenge. But it remains to be observed whether going forward the NDC would keep to its statement of not sleeping on issues but rather act 'very responsibly.'

"Let them provide the dams, the factories, let them restore the allowances, let them reduce the tariffs drastically; let them not go in for loans. Those are the things we will be putting to them so we need peace," Mr. Anyidoho said.

Well I need to remind the NPP of a famous line from Amedzope Secondary school's 'Jama' song: "We shall show them we shall put pepper in their eyes."

Just remember, if you fail to deliver Koku will put 'pepe' in your eyes.

The Shadows

Our shadows stay with us; we cannot run away from them. When we run they run, when we walk they walk and when we talk they talk even though we don't hear them make the sound. What is striking though is their ability to prove to humanity that they exist because we exist. And when we resist our ability to act, they seize to act.

They lived yesterday with us. Today, we stomped together and we gathered together but they know not what the future has in store for them. They're like us and we're like them.

Till death do us part because the driver won't be driving any more. The dancer won't be dancing. The sculptor won't be sculpturing and the farmer won't be farming any longer. Till the celestial bodies stop to function our shadows will forever be our secret agents. They will follow us wherever we go. And until we understand the game plan, until we keep pace with them and until we act in sync the synchronisation will become an illusion.

They are characters with no titles, they are champions without belts, and they're kings without crowns. Shadows have secrets. They understand Job's famous line: "Naked I came and naked I shall return." A fact Man has struggled since creation to come to terms with or comprehend.

O' shadows, you cannot tame them, you cannot gag them, and you cannot catch them. They mimic us and sometimes they think we are stubborn. Because we are born to believe that we can run away from ourselves.

What the eyes behold the ears snub. And what the ears withhold the eyes refuse. Have you ever seen the spider's web catch an elephant? Have you?

If you do not like your own shadow who and what else would you? That which cracks them up makes you frown. And that which tickles them irritates you. Thou shalt not harness darkness if you cannot wear a smile to lighten up the world.

UT & Capital Banks Closed Down

A takeover deal has already been sealed. Forensic audit is likely to kick in soon, according to Bank of Ghana (BoG).

Would this open a can of worms? Or we would see no more banks' collapse?

If you didn't believe the banks had collapsed did you also not see men with ladders tearing down signs and inscriptions of UT& Capital Banks from atop of the buildings?

Yes they're gone. They were suffocated and couldn't stand the test of time.

xxxxxxxxxx

The collapse of Capital Bank Limited (CAL) and UT Bank limited on Monday 14 August 2017 must not be viewed as a disaster for Ghana's banking industry says this writer. This is nowhere near a typical financial crisis. Rather, it must be seen as a blessing in disguise or reawakening as it would ginger the ones already in the system to remain vibrant, vigilant as well as take pro- growth measures to prevent such recurrence in the future.

Also, I believe this isn't an investor- threatening development that should trigger alarm in the business world. The reason, banks rise and banks fall like governments and empires if they fail to take the right measures to consolidate their gains and fortunes. Certainly, this wouldn't be the last and not the first. We've seen banks and other financial institutions collapse across the world. Perhaps the most recent and catastrophic one was the financial crisis that hit the United States in 2008.

In fact by 2010 more than 30 banks had collapsed including mortgage institutions.

Nevertheless, we must be reminded that the collapse of the two commercial banks didn't happen overnight. What the world witnessed on Monday, I believe, might have started first as some challenges or like teething problems which generally many banks face but the managers failed to address them properly and then they morphed into crisis.

Would this open a can of worms?

Well the Apex Bank has given the hint that it would begin a forensic audit into the operations of the acquired banks. The findings of such investigation would inform or give the public a sense of what is to come or not to come. Of course we will know whether there are still some ailing banks that need resuscitation or complete takeover as it did happen to Capital and UT banks.

But that seems unlikely to happen, referring to bail-out. In the meantime, the Central Bank has given the public assurance and an insight as to what actually triggered the collapse of the banks. At a press conference on Monday the Governor of the Central Bank Dr. Ernest Addison said the two banks, UT Bank Limited and Capital Bank Limited had had their licenses revoked due to what the Apex bank described as "deeply insolvent".

According to the governor the two banks had been supported by the central bank for two years in the hope that they would experience a turnaround, but that never happened necessitating the buyout on Monday.

Couldn't the Central Bank bail out the banks as the US government did in 2008?

The Obama administration provided what it called 'stimulus funds for distressed financial institutions to help them get back on their feet. There was such consideration yours truly learned. That package was an option BOG considered initially, but it refused to have its hands tied at its back after realising the degree of the banks injury. It's understood that would have constrained the Apex Bank and it would also compelled it to manage both banks. Indeed one cannot cry more than the bereaved.

Dr. Addison also used the platform to assure the business community and prospective investors that there were no more banks in distress that would call for the revocation of their license.

"Ladies and Gentlemen, you will recall that after the AQR [Asset Quality Review] exercise, a number of banks were not compliant with the capital adequacy ratio. I am happy to report that most of these banks have put in place credible action plans to restore the capital deficiency, and majority of these banks are already compliant as at today, and the overall banking system remains solid and well capitalized", the Governor said at a press conference organised at the central bank on Monday, August 14.

So what is insolvency?

Insolvency can be defined as the incapability to ones debts. This usually happens for one or two reasons. Basically two reasons have been assigned to this. First, for some reason the bank may end up owing more than it owns or is owed. In accounting terminology this means its assets are worth less than its liabilities. Second a bank may become insolvent if it cannot pay its debts as they fall due, even though its assets may be worth more than its liabilities. This is known as cash flow insolvency, or a lack of liquidity.

Was that the case that befell the two banks?

According to Bank of Ghana (BoG), despite repeated agreements with UT Bank and Capital Bank to put them back on track following their capital and liquidity shortfalls, the two failed to implement action plans agreed on. In effect, the Bank noted that "the owners and managers of UT Bank and Capital Bank were unable to increase the capital of the banks to address the insolvency.

"Consequently, to protect customers, the BOG has decided to revoke the licenses of UT Bank and Capital Bank under a Purchase and Assumption transaction. UT Bank and Capital Bank were heavily deficient in capital and liquidity and their continuous operation could have jeopardized not only their depositors' funds, but also posed a threat to the stability of the financial system", the Governor added.

The Purchase and Assumption transaction model is very common in planning for the exit of banks in distress. With this model, healthy banks take over the running of unhealthy banks, significantly ensuring that the process is smooth so as to avoid any possible industry-wide problems.

The Bank of Ghana has approved a Purchase and Assumption (P&A) transaction involving UT Bank and Capital Bank and the GCB Bank. This action, the governor stressed was taken to protect depositors' funds and strengthen Ghana's financial sector."

GCB Bank Ltd., the largest indigenous bank in the country with an asset base of GHS 6.3 billion, has assumed the businesses of UT Bank Ltd. and Capital Bank in a purchase and assumption transaction by the Bank of Ghana, effective Monday, August 14, 2017. The Bank has assured Customers of UT and Capital Bank of unconstrained access to their funds through their known channels and staff of the assumed banks, working with GCB staff to ensure seamless transactions. Also GCB has in effect assumed the 53 branches of the two banks thereby, growing its network to 214 branches across the country.

Capital Bank (formerly First Bank Capital Plus Bank) was established in July 2009. As of 2013 it had total assets of US$140 million equivalent of GH S 286, 80 million.

On the other hand UT Bank (formerly UT financial Services (LTD)—A medium-sized financial institution in Ghana with total assets of GHS 720, 007 million and customer deposits of GHS 600.288 million as of March 31, 2012. UT Bank commenced business as a finance house in 1997 under the name Unique Trust Financial Services.

What could prevent future banks 'collapse?

There are several preventive measures, but I will leave herewith the following two factors:

The current Bank of Ghana minimum capital requirement is pegged at GHC120 million cedis. This was reviewed from GHC 60 million cedis it set previously. The upward adjustment was to stream line the mushrooming of banks across the country, which currently stands at about 34 even more than neighbouring Nigeria—Africa's most populous nation. This writer believes the current development might compel BoG to raise the bar. And I believe any attempt by the central bank would trigger more mergers, the next factor.

In December 2011, Pan Africa Bank Ecobank Transnational Inc. acquired 100 per cent of Ghana's Trust Bank Limited (also known as The Trust Bank -TTB) in a $ 135 million deal. The merger involved the swap of shares for Ecobank Ghana shares.

Who Can Fix the Tyre (tire)?

In the Free World everything is fixed or fixable. We fix relationships, we fix marriages, we fix automobiles, we fix human beings, we fix meals (breakfast, lunch and supper) and even corruption is fixable. But when things get tough and rough or go haywire you rarely get Mr. Fixer to fix the problems.

The situation becomes more problematic in developing countries because the requisite tools, the manpower and institutions to help fix the problem might just not be available.

If you'd ever had a flat tyre (tire) on a highway or in the midst of a bad weather you'd understand this better. On Wednesday 30 November this year, I experienced that situation. It was cold and breezy accompanied by slight showers. I tried a couple of times to get it fixed after some people I'd called upon failed to show up or ignored me.

But I continued to ask for help. I never stopped until I found someone.

Mr. Brian Moore a fuel tanker driver came to my rescue. Brian jumped out from his double truck and helped me put my car back on the road.

The following day on Thursday December 1, I received this terse message: "Hope you were able to get your tire fixed. And I'm glad I could help you." That was Brian my new friend.

Yes, Brian checked on me the next day. And yes I'd got it fixed.

What an awesome person– an angel without wings. See, we all need help sometimes. There are times we cry for help and it seems that life line isn't available or might never come. There are some battles we cannot fight and win on our own– we would need backup troop or external force to help get it done. Nonetheless, there are some people who have refused to admit they're sick or have a problem. They simply decline to access support because they carry egos.

A professor once asked his students if they could get their tyre fixed whiles they were on a safari.

"Who can change the tyre on the vehicle?" the professor asked.

Trapped in sludge with a deflated tyre the group had an awful experience during their first ever expedition to Kenya in East Africa. Their vehicle wasn't just trapped in that quagmire but they'd found themselves in a serious trouble.

Apparently the group's vehicle had run into a ditch midway causing the tyre to deflate. And within minutes they'd some strange visitors from a village nearby the excursion place surrounded their vehicle.

The macho-looking guys had yellow-gold coats on. They looked strong with compact bodies and powerful forelegs, sharp teeth and wild jaws. The visitors stood guard by the disabled vehicle snuffling and pawing the vehicle's windows. Their impressive manes signified their masculinity and reflected their health.

They'd resolved to keep guard from dawn to dusk until the occupants in the vehicle stepped out. And it appeared all the excitement the group had carried in their pockets and backpacks was fading so fast.

The guys had come to give the travelers a welcome party but none of them was ready to attend. The professor who asked the question had closed his eyes in a way to tame his blood pressure levels. Meanwhile, the guys stood still making sure not a single soul escaped from the trapped vehicle.

"Is there no one amongst you who can fix this problem?" the professor wondered.

Silent had consumed noisiness and even the dare-devils among the group wouldn't dare to utter a word. Everything was done in motion, eyes amazed at what they saw as everyone remained tight-lipped. A few minutes later the professor repeated the question but this time no one would even look him in the eyes let alone make a sound. Nobody appeared ready to do what might be seen as the unthinkable.

It's obvious no one would dare come out to fix or change a flat tyre when you've six hungry lions on guard. Probably there were a handful of them or more who could fix the problem but fear had also joined them. Or was it apathy? I day say it wasn't apathy. I'm told amongst them were, mechanics and automobile engineers.

The question is what do you do when you're faced with such a dire situation?

That's how a country looks like when it's drowned in corruption. Nobody has what it takes to fight it. Nobody seems to know how to get out from the danger zone. Why would the professor (in this case the leader of the group) ask his students if they could fix the problem?

What was he doing himself?

And why was he chosen to lead?

They say to lead is to bleed and uneasy lies the head that wears the crown. Many leaders particularly in our part of the world have failed the peoples because of corruption. It's a disease which is difficult to fight because even the one fighting it is himself corrupt. I mentioned it in one of my write-ups somewhere. Nonetheless, I will go ahead and raise the issue once again here.

A man told his two sons who were leaving their village to the big city: When you hear people say there's corruption here and corruption there: Ask them are you corrupt?

Obviously the response you'll get is no.

So who are those engaged in corruption? Do we know them or do we know ourselves?

Is it too hard to find them and too tough to bring them to face justice?

Or we are acting like the proverbial ostrich?

Corruption resides everywhere in our social milieu and it would be extremely difficult to fight it if in the first place we don't admit we've all been corrupted and are corrupt. It doesn't matter who and where it occurs— it's either you in person or the office you occupy .You're corrupt, it doesn't matter where you take the bribe or receive it. Be it on the streets, in the classrooms, at the offices, at the border posts or at the airports, on the high seas or underground the value is the same. It is still corruption.

Ironically, everyone pretends to be sacrosanct when it comes to dealing with this social canker.

How can we deal with the problem if we've no knowledge of its source or cause?

Or is it because all of us have been corrupted?

Without a doubt we can slaughter corruption if we begin to point the accusing fingers to ourselves rather than someone else.

The students (call them managers) in the trapped vehicle appeared to have no idea, no clue and no clout to find solutions. The CEO or the leader of the group in this the case the professor also seemed to have lost touch with reality. Instead of taking the initiative he was asking his students if there weren't anybody amongst them to fix the problem.

Who can come out to face a hungry lion? Or how can Satan fight against Satan?

It wouldn't work. And it hasn't worked since we ushered into the Fourth Republic. Perhaps they all had egos which made it difficult for them to reach out for help. But this is one way to fight it. Appoint an anti-corruption Czar with an office that can go after the government and anybody deemed to be corruptible.

In neighbouring Nigeria one man was tasked to purge the system when it descended into the corruption quagmire. Renowned anti-corruption chief Mallam Ribadu became the country's first executive chairman to fight corruption.

"With no money and no office, in four years I built that institution into one of the most successful and formidable anti-corruption agency not just in Africa but the world", said Ribadu.

Indeed it takes a courageous leader to step up like biblical David against the Philistine giant Goliath.

And we can even make it work better if we adhere to this simple phrase 'Change begins with attitude' echoed by Reverend John Tello Nelson. The Co-coordinating Minister of the Accra Ridge Church who officiated the New Patriotic Party (NPP's) Victory Thanksgiving Service on Sunday stated:

"Beloved in the Lord the election on December 7, 2016, showed that many voted for change. But the honest truth is that the change can only happen by all of us having changed our attitudes—the corruption, greed, the lazy attitude to work, the I-don't-care attitude, the pilfering in our offices, the lack of maintenance of government property, the nepotism, our tribalistic attitudes and the 'The Ghana Time' mentality."

"These are attitudes that we have to change, because if we have called for a change and we don't eschew all these negative attitudes in our lives, the change can never happen."

Twenty-Two Years in 'PAWA': Jammeh Still Wants More

Now it's my turn to make the most difficult phone call. The call many world leaders dread. I'm calling Gambia President Yahya Abdul-Aziz Jemus Junkung Jammeh.

I don't know where he got Jemus Junkung from. He was born Yahya Abdul-Aziz Jammeh. But anyway, that's beside the point. Well let me start it this way, if we can't get it into the warehouse we would dump it at the junkyard.

Hallo!

"Hallo...Eiish." Are you hearing me?"

I wish you all the best. The country will be in your hands in January and you're assured of my guidance on your transition and I don't mean to ....but afterwards work with me..."

"Who's this?"

Mr. President this is Gordon Offin-Amaniampong (GOA for short).

"Hey, you sounded like me."

GOA: Yeah right, I'm mimicking you if you get it. Doesn't the line sound familiar?

Those were the exact words you spoke barely two weeks ago to congratulate President-elect Adama Barrow following his victory on Friday in the December 2, 2016 presidential election.

Did you really say you aren't relinquishing power because there were irregularities in the election process? And I suppose such irregularities only affected you and not the other candidate right?

Chaiiii, Yahya you've disappointed me. You've disappointed many too, many across the continent and the world at large. Most people thought you meant well in your concession speech. But it didn't last long. You've proved your sceptics right. I was one of them. I knew something wasn't right.

Remember I likened you to a 'Born-Again' Lion?

See what you've done. You've put the whole Gambia on edge.

The ECOWAS nations are worried about what's going to happen should you follow through this wacky plot. I'd barely crossed the border to my homeland when the news came in that you aren't going to hand over power to Mr. Barrow. For a moment I thought I was dreaming. Wasn't he the one I spoke to? So what happened to all the admonitions and the sweet talks you sang to the ears of the world?

Please tell me, what came upon you this time?

I recall the first one you said: "Allah is telling me that my time is up and I hand over graciously with gratitude to the Gambian people and gratitude to the Almighty Allah to you."

You said that right?

YJ: "Yes, I did."

Don't tell me Allah commanded you to continue to stay in office. Allah himself knows Gambians are sick and tired of you. They've had enough of your gimmicks and antics. They've had enough of your despotic rule. They gave you the chance but you blew it away and they've voted for a change. So I'm appealing to you to back down your decision. I guess it isn't that bitter to swallow it now.

Back to my question, you think I'll let you lose.

What necessitated your dramatic U-turn?

Was it Zeinab who influenced your decision?

YJ: "No."

GOA: Did I get that right are you guys still married, I learned you're getting divorce?

Anyway, let's get back to the substantive issue. You don't want us to talk about it. Why?

I called you purposefully for that.

What was that for? You cleared your throat as if to say leave me alone. I ain't leaving you alone. You're hurting the whole continent; you're psychologically and emotionally torturing your people. So let's talk about it.

I bet you saw my president there (and you met all the guys Buhari dems). I'm talking about Ghana's president John Mahama. He's leaving office as the first one-term president in the fourth republic in our nation's political history. And if you think that's cool reconsider your stance.

Mind you, it isn't about you the leaders anymore. It's about the people—the citizenry. It's about us. The young chap in the village who squats or lay on his belly to study at school while you guys line the state funds in your pockets. It's about the unemployed graduates, it's about the teachers and nurses and the judges whose allowances haven't been paid for months or years.

The leaders have come to talk to you. Listen to them as they pump some ideas into your coconut. Have you forgotten what happened to Kabila of DR Congo? How about Sani Abacha of Nigeria? Where are they now?

See how your nose is shaking like that of a mouse caught in a trap. You're laughing Mr. President. Well, this isn't funny. This is a serious matter. Ok go ahead and tell me what made you change your mind not to hand over.

GOA: Are you just power-drunk?

I shouldn't kid myself anymore. You must be intoxicated with some substance.

Did you sniff something?

YJ: "No."

Did you drink something? No.

Did you smoke something? No.

Did you swallow or ingest something? No.

I don't want this to become a telegraphic conversation. So please give some tangible reasons.

What actually made you change your mind?

Let me tell you something quick you probably don't know what's going on around the world. CNN failed to give coverage on the Ghana's general election because of you. We'd a successful, peaceful, free, fair and transparent election yet they spent days talking about you. The good image about us went unnoticed because of you and your ego.

All the cable news networks were taking about you. It was all about you as usual as ambitious as Lucifer. Because of you the west thinks we Africans aren't capable of ruling ourselves. Yes, because of you and some rogues on the continent who've made themselves life patrons in office—resulting economic hardships, youth unemployment and brain drain.

Excuse me, Baffour can I get some pain relief meds (sorry Sir that was my son). I think Paracetamol or Benadryl would be alright. I've lost my deep thought. I just can't think far Yahya. And it's all because of you Yahya. I feel a little better now.

There's one thing though, I seem to agree with you on. It's about the International Criminal Court (ICC) headquartered in The Hague the Netherlands. I think the intergovernmental organisation isn't fair in its approach when it comes to prosecuting individuals deemed to have committed crime against humanity. How can the ICC be targeting only African, Arabian and East European leaders?

By the way, you're aware former Ivorian president Lauren Gbagbo is there. Charles Taylor was also tried there and former Yugoslav and Serbian leader Slobodan Milosevic. I've never heard any western leader (s) hauled before the international court.

But you can't use that as an excuse to put your country on edge or punish your people. You withdrew from it right? And I'm not sure Mr. Barrow intends to send you there for trial. I hear all the conspiracy theories flitting around in the air.

Do you still have the two speed boats on the waters by the State House and what are they for?

And what's your plan now do you still want to stay or hand over to the president-elect?

I would advise you as a brother to take the deal. Leave peacefully and allow Gambians to have some semblance of peace.' Aba' 22 years and you still want more. You will be offered a safe haven in one of the countries in the sub-region.

Oh I think Ghana would be your next destination. We already have two Guantanamo guys with us. Are you wondering how they got here? It was a deal Mr. Mahama struck with the United States government. So I believe we can accommodate you. You aren't a threat at all. Call me and let me know when you soften your stubborn heart. OK.

GHANA'S NEW AMBASSADORS

Before Paul there was Peter and before Paul there were Apostles and disciples. But Paul being Paul he changed the dynamics of Jesus' ministry during the Apostolic Age, hence the phrase in Ghanaian Twi Language: 'Paul amma ntem osene adi kanfo.' To wit, Paul the latter disciple or saint was master of all.

My dear readers, I present to you Ghana's new distinguished ambassadors extraordinaire —Yaa Baby and Kwame Yeboah. The two are immigrants from the United States and Italy respectively. Both have lived in Ghana for more than a decade. And both are into acting.

Do I need to tell you this? Before Ghana there was the Gold Coast—a name given to her by the colonialists. She would wear this garment or (carry the name) for nearly 500 years until March 6, 1957.

You might not know this. There's something unique about Ghana. *What is it?* Ghana's hospitality is second to none and it's legendary. As early as in the 1400's perhaps before, the Gold Coast had opened her doors for the Europeans.

By 1482 the Portuguese had arrived. They settled in a small coastal town called Edina (which was renamed Elmina by the Portuguese) in the central region of post-colonial Ghana. They traded in salt and gold with the indigenes. Barter was the system of trade. Their influence was growing and their culture was becoming infectious. For example, 'pano' (in Fanti) which is bread originated from the Portuguese word pa'oe' (or vida) pronounced almost the same.

The congeniality would trigger influx of multinationals across the world. The Dutch, the Danes, the Swedes the English/British (in 1553) and many more would follow later. From coast to coast they crisscrossed and later penetrated the hinterlands.

Indeed by the turn of the 19th century names such as Anderson, Rockson, Peterson, Johnson, Harrison Addison, Samuelson, had dominated Ghana's coastline .They were popular then and are still popular today. At the time it was uncommon to meet or come across an expatriate carrying a Ghanaian name unless by marriage.

Gordon Offin-Amaniampong

Where did we lay our quilt?

That which was uncommon back then is increasingly becoming common now. Europeans, Americans, Asians, Arabs etc. are adopting Ghanaian names and if that wasn't surprising, how about those who speak our languages so eloquently. They've immersed themselves into the Ghanaian culture and the mores. They speak in parables and speak in proverbs. They use tropes, figures of speech. They use riddles to communicate!

Yaa Baby and Kwame Yeboah are two incredible individuals. The American Chloe Rose is now married to a Ghanaian. She's an actress and a motivational speaker. Kwame Yeboah the Italian is a divorcee. "I ventured into many adventures' he said during an interview in Accra with Ghana's finest comedian KSM also known as sergeant Lasisi.

If you're a doubting Thomas and wants to see things for yourself make a date with me. If you're unsure of whether they're whites and not blacks or Ghanaians and want to see them live, I will entreat you to meet me at Palm Wine Junction in Accra at 3pm sharp. Don't ask me when and how to get there. Mind you I don't worship the so-called Ghanaian Time. So count yourself out if you're full of that. Smile when the Sun smiles at you. Why frown when you're drowning?

If you still cannot figure out where you're standing, what you heard, who was speaking and why you don't seem to get it, meet me at Kokompe. The men who work with the hammers and pliers, bolts& nots are feverishly tightening all the loose ends. And they're greasing all the squeaky wheels. Oh yes I know. I know what's causing your head to spin. It doesn't often happen. And it's that rarity that's creating the uncertainty.

Indeed what you heard was incredible. They laced their statements with humor, sages and metaphors. "Se wohu gyata ewo abonten a eye nwanwa," says Yaa Baby.

And your face lit up with joy and admiration. You were surprised. Weren't you? You did have doubts on your mind. Didn't you?

The two are projecting the Ghanaian culture while you're beating down your own culture and values. The Ghanaian language sucks right?

You think speaking Ga, Twi, Ewe, Hausa, Nzema in public is primitive, uncouth and uncalled for. You think everything Ghanaian or African isn't good. Now tell me who would you blame the European who you didn't meet 800 years ago or you and your leaders who didn't help the situation?

The two are from different continents outside Africa, and if they saw it fitting to speak our languages, eat our foods, wear our clothes, and take our tro-tros then what's your problem?

See even some natives break it when they speak.it. And some torture it in their attempts to speak it. But they do it impeccably. English Language isn't ours yet we taunt, we sneer and we tease when someone makes mistakes. I'm glad to say Kwame Yeboah and Yaa Baby are making mother Ghana proud today. Besides they're helping Ghanaians and for that matter Africans to redeem their bludgeoned image.

I salute you Great Ambassadors. I salute you Kwame and Yaa. You are Paul the latter but master of all. I hope your great works would not be obliterated by the western media or Africans themselves. I don't know if you've heard about this story. Tourists used to visit this nation (they still go) in Africa in their numbers to see the wild cats, the giraffes and the elephants. Millions of dollars were coming in each passing day. Then one day the leader gets up and decides to sell the animals to the tourists.

Why do you cut your nose to spite your face?

This is not an attack on western media or the West. And may I repeat this piece is not anti-west. This is to tell the world that the story told about Africa for centuries by the western media is skewed and stereotypical. Africa is still labeled as a jungle. That's not true. Africans live in trees and in caves, the lions and the bears live with them and the people wear no clothes. That's also not true.

And the visceral attack continues. Africans are unfriendly and cannibals that's not true. Unfortunately, this propaganda and warped narrative has been told time and time again.

But can the western media alone be blamed for Africa's troubles? No I don't think so Africans themselves have doubled their troubles.

Most of their leaders have probably quadrupled Africa's troubles giving the media licence to perpetrate the age long story.

Why must a continent blessed with so much ends up having not much to feed its starving population, especially children?

Why should a continent – endowed with minerals and great human resources after emancipation lack the ability to manage its own resources? Why must African leaders still chase the West for aids and grants? Why do Africans look down upon their own cultures, customs and arts?

It's all because of wanton loots, greed, misplaced priorities, mismanagement of resource, inferiority complex or insecurity etc.

Yes, you can name the wars and name the diseases, hunger, drought and poverty. But these issues do not represent the broad picture of this big continent, which is next to Asia in terms of size.

Which nation in the world can say that it's a perfect nation? Let that nation raise her hand.

Which nation can say that it is disease free, crime free, she has no hunger, no poverty and no slums? I humbly ask that nation to raise her hand. Is there one? Yet, the western media has spared the West of its ills. The West is seen as utopia, everything glitters, and everything is perfect. It's all skyscrapers and high bridges. The roads are golden. An Asian friend told me that many years ago many Asians believed every part of the United Kingdom was cemented—you don't see dirt or muck.

The West is portrayed as heaven on earth, that's great. And it's one of the reasons why millions are dying to travel abroad—either by boats by ferries or by unapproved routes. But the inevitable question is: Why paint Africa with a stained brush?

What did you lose a Nickel or a Broken Pot?

Not all bugs that glow are fire flies. So if you're looking for fireflies take your time, spend time and kill time. It would be worth finding the real deal rather than settling on any bug that glows. Every mole has a hole to hide in but not all holes have moles in them. Our Lord said it best: 'foxes have holes and birds of the air have nests but the Son of Man has no place to lay his head.'

Not everyone has it, but everybody has something—something unique in nature, well-nurtured by the Creator. He owns the nickel and he owns the golden pot. So why cry your eyes out?

Why run amok because of a broken pot?

Why hold your head and cry because of a lost nickel?

Why resort to vandalism and hooliganism?

What would you gain from that?

Absolutely nothing, you'd get nothing!

Don't you know there would come a time the pot would lose its usefulness or better still break?

Don't you know you could lose the nickel somewhere sometime?

And don't you know that we fall to rise if we learn our lessons well and redeem our lost image?

Fall falls from grace to grass. A fall is like a wall –strong and formidable but when it falls it turns into rubbles. A fall is like a mall it gets crowded during daytime– people peopling everywhere but by midnight it's deserted. She becomes a ghost town. She's no friend.

A fall is like a long hall but it has an ending. It can never go beyond its limit. A fall is like a ball (football) when he's high in the sky he forgets someone puts him there and sooner he drops like a meteor oblivious to where he would land. A fall is like Saul, dangerous, treacherous and unkind but if he repents he will be called Paul.

We are all blessed. We access his mercies, his grace, his blessings and his comfort. We find his favour every day and his goodness greets us wherever we pass and wherever we go.

Whatever we do he encourages us and he supports us. He says, he will never leave us nor forsake us. That means he's with us 24/7. It is an assurance from our Lord, the one whose wings are bigger than the universe. The one whose breathe is capable of blowing the earth away.

Be reminded the wings of insects are tiny and fragile yet they're able to fly hours without crashing.

Who told you that?

Who told you that the magician or fetish priest will forever clutch onto to his magic wand when the originator (Mr. Cow) had already lost his?

I met politics at the Town Hall last Wednesday. Not the one that just passed, but the one that appeared to have gone for a sabbatical leave yet showed up audaciously. Everybody was there. It was a hush afternoon. But his presence soon changed the atmosphere. The crowd that hitherto lived in harmony seemed to have smoked something like weed. I suppose something more powerful than Ganja.

Bemused and confused I asked myself what the heck is going on?

What's wrong with you my people are you going to allow this guy to tear us apart, break the solid bonds that we've established for God knows when?

Take a look around you and tell me what you see?

You see women, children and men. You see farmers, carpenters, traders, fisher folks, hairdressers and many more. You see the young and the old but all lived together as one people. Kafui is married to Serwaa, Ajalah is in relationship with Dadzie, Asorbayire is married to Frema, Kaku is my in-law and the list goes on...

In fact this would raise your eyebrow. I saw General Mosquito and Sir John quaffing at a tavern near my house at Tuobodom. *How about that aren't you ashamed of fighting your brother because of politics?*

Aren't you ashamed of making more enemies than friends because of politics?

Aren't you happy that everything went well and cool and life still goes on?

Anyway, so politics was fired up. He appeared so sharp and spoke so eloquently. He'd answers to all questions the public asked him. His Aaron's beard and thick mustache got many ladies stealing glances with him while he was still politicking.

He promised this and he promised that —raising hopes and expectations of the people. And when everything seemed to have fallen apart eyes got red. Anger and frustration were seen on the streets chanting Aluta!

See, we toil, we struggle in our travels to make ends meet and then after all the travail we don't even have a blanket to snuggle ourselves in. It reminds me of a man who lost his nickel on his way to a nickel shop. Looking livid and frustrated he told himself: "I'm not giving up my search until I find this coin. " Besides, that was all he had so he couldn't give up his search even though night was drawing nigh... He spent hours combing the spot where he believed he must have dropped the nickel.

Morning passed by afternoon came and evening passed by too. His search continued hoping to find the nickel. Finally when dusk approached the man could see nothing. There was a silver lining. The fireflies in the growth nearby produced lights which invited a Good Samaritan.

The Samaritan was ready to help the nickel man but he wouldn't let go his lost nickel.

Why can't we get over stuff? Why do we fight over spilt milk when there's an alternative?

Why can't we let go when there's a bigger and powerful hand reaching out?

The owner of the Golden Pot seemed okay when it broke. "I give it all to God," she said. Ironically those that drank from the pot got angry, hit the streets and wanted to lynch the young man who accidentally broke the pot. Really is that how we treat falls, accidents, defeats, failures etc.?

Let's learn to appreciate both because they're bedfellows. Let's move on. And let's remember, when it's over it's over.

BOST BOSS EMBROILED IN ALLEGED OIL FRAUD

When it spills it kills and when it stinks it requires investigation says this writer.

A big test awaits the Akufo-Addo government. I've no idea how far this could go. It appears the president's anti-graft signature message which he's been trumpeting since he took the reins of power in January 7, 2017 hasn't resonated well with some of his new appointees. Certainly some of these newly-appointed public office holders are already exhibiting a character trait that overly contradicts what their Boss stands for.

And analysts believe this kind of behavior by some of his officials could bring the image of the government into disrepute and make his fight against corruption look like one that's bound to fail as many in the past did.

What's going on? The latest headline story in Accra isn't a good one. It isn't one story that we should be proud of as Ghanaians given the signal it sends to the outside world. On Tuesday 26 June, the Minority in Parliament expressed grave concern about the sale of contaminated fuel product to the tune of five million litres to a company known as Movenpiina by the Managing Director of the Bulk Oil Storage and Transportation Limited (BOST) Alfred Obeng Boakye.

It seems everything about the deal smacks what the NDC Minority describes as 'dubious and 'bizarre'. And if you think those two words are hyperbolic and only sought to twist facts, or otherwise, wait till you read the next paragraphs.

First of all how did a company that's believed to have won a competitive bid to purchase oil from BOST, ended up with no telephone number and on top of that had no office? Thus the inevitable question will be: Who's behind the company? It's also very obvious you would ask: How did the person win the bid without a landed property and also managed to purchase t it on 'Open-Credit' sales arrangement?

That big English there 'Open Credit' simply means the company bought the products without paying for it and in turn sold the products to a third-party Company at 30% higher. And lest I forget, the date the company was incorporated to trade as well as transport fuel and its registration at the Registrar Generals Department also don't match.

How could a company that was registered for example on March 19 2017 would be transporting oil two weeks before its registration?

Indeed it's a story that has many twists. It mimics the Akan Twi well-known phrase 'Asem Sebe'. Better translation it looks like a ship when you view it from the left flank but you'd likely see a different image from the right angle. Bottom line it's sleazy and shady deal.

So far it looks like the opposition NDC Minority has shown its readiness to unpack all the myths and lies that seem to surround the BOST deal. At a press conference in Accra yesterday the group made the following demands:

They demanded the immediate interdiction of the BOST MD and a full scale investigation by the regulatory authorities into the company's dealings. It further demanded the immediate withdrawal of the contaminated product from the market to protect consumers and assurances that this will not recur. And last but not least the minority demanded that the financial loss estimated at GHS 14.25 million be retrieved by surcharging the offending officials at BOST in line with the recent Supreme Court decision.

In a desperate move to do what seems like damage control officials at BOST have debunked the allegation that the contaminated oil has ended up onto the market. Media Relations Manager at BOST Nana Akua Adubea Obeng told Joy FM's morning show programme that only 100,000 litres of the contaminated product had been released to Movenpiina and not 5 million as claimed by the minority.

She said the remaining 4.9 million litres is sitting in the tanks at BOST and waiting to be offloaded. Nana Akua Obeng maintained that their tracking system had shown that 100,000 litres released so far to Movenpiina is still within the tanks of the company and has not been released onto the market.

It must be noted, that explanation didn't seem to convince the Minority group.

"The justification by BOST that the contaminated products were sold for use by manufacturing companies is untenable. The norm and practice is that when contamination occurs, corrective treatments of these products are undertaken by TOR through blending," minority ranking member of energy Armah Kofi Buah told the local media.

To BOST the contaminated fuel that had found its way into the public market is a "human error". But energy think tank ACEP sees it differently. According to ACEP the error, has caused the country over $7million in revenue. ACEP's executive director, Ben Boakye claimed to have, unknowingly, bought a contaminated fuel with the potential of damaging his engine.

The five- million litres of oil was said to have been contaminated after diesel was mixed with Petrol.

Read the full statement below:

MINORITY IN PARLIAMENT CALLS FOR FULL SCALE INVESTIGATION INTO BLATANT CORRUPTION AT BOST LTD.

The minority in Parliament has noted with grave concern the sale of contaminated fuel product to the tune of five million litres to a company known as Movenpiina by the MD of the Bulk Oil Storage and Transportation Limited under very dubious and bizarre circumstances in another clear example of escalating corruption in the Akufo-Addo/Bawumia Government.

Even more disturbing is the explanation offered by BOST to justify the sale of this contaminated product as well as the circumstances surrounding the sale which clearly lacks transparency and integrity.

Ladies and Gentlemen of the press, it must be mentioned that under proper regulatory and supervisory protocols, under no circumstance should the BOST Co. Ltd experience such high levels of contamination as we are witnessing.

The question to ask is what led to the contamination of these products in the first instance.

Why was the particular tank in question not properly discharged and cleaned before the intake of the fresh fuel which led to the contamination? Was it due to negligence, lack of supervision or a deliberate plot by some self-seeking individuals to enrich themselves at the expense of the state and the Ghanaian tax payer?

The justification by BOST that the contaminated products were sold for use by manufacturing companies is untenable. The norm and practice is that when such contamination occur, corrective treatment of these products are undertaken by the Tema Oil Refinery through blending.

Why did BOST not arrange with TOR for the treatment of this particular fuel? Available information indicates that BOST failed to exhaust all means to ensure TOR blends this contaminated fuel.

The argument by BOST that the blending couldn't be done at TOR because the CDU is down is most untenable.

These so called off-spec products are not the slops that are usually sold by BOST, we also wish to state that SLOPS are usually in small quantities. SLOPS are sediments of fuels in a Tank and are usually in small quantities and cannot be compared with 5 million liters of contaminated fuel.

Ladies and Gentlemen of the Press, the claim by BOST that this contaminated product was sold at a competitive ex-depot price is false and cannot be justified.

When was the competitive bidding process initiated and who were the companies that participated? Incontrovertible evidence available confirms that Movenpiina Company was the only company BOST dealt with in the sale of this contaminated product in a sole sourced transaction.

It is therefore erroneous to suggest that the sale was done under a competitive process.

Further information available to us indicates that Movenpiina Co. Lt. put in a proposal to purchase the fuel on the 19th of May 2017. Interestingly, checks from the Registrar Generals Department suggest the company was incorporated to trade and transport fuel on the 29th of May 2017.

Kpone Is Prone to Toxic

When will she catch the eyes of the authority?

Maybe not until things go haywire...

It's becoming increasingly risky to live in Kpone, a town which lies in the south-eastern part of the Greater Accra region of Ghana, 15.0

kilometres from Accra the nation's capital. Of late, residents' eyes have been greeted with daily pall of smoke that billows from industries sited in the Free Zone enclave.

Literally, one can no longer sight the blue sky. It's gradually losing its place to air pollution or smoke clouds. Indeed the toxic in the atmosphere is making habitation uncomfortable and intolerable for residents who are already showing early signs of acquiring lung cancer—the disease that starts in the lungs and most often occurs in people who smoke or inhale smoke.

Speaking in an interview with Adom FM a local radio station based in Tema, some residents said they could hardly breathe normal due to the inhalation of the poisonous smoke that has led to the increasing rate of respiratory related diseases.

"The whole atmosphere has been blanketed by smoke. Unfortunately we experience this on a daily basis. And that gives you a sense of what we've been going through every day. It's really disturbing and we have no clue when this would stop," a resident lamented.

According to the residents companies in the area, are not abiding by the air quality guidelines set by Environmental Protection Agency (EPA). This, they believe, had accounted for the insane pollution. They've therefore called on the appropriate authorities to act as quickly as practicable to avoid anything that could be catastrophic. Additionally they're asking the authorities and health institutions to help check the respiratory disease which is on the rise.

Also, it's been observed that the situation has affected productivity in the area. Though there aren't available figures to support that claim. However, residents maintain business activities as well as productivity levels haven't been encouraging.

Rider Steel Limited—one of the companies in the enclave has admitted that pollution is a huge challenge in the area, noting the company's furnaces pose pollution problem to the community.

As part of measures to mitigate the problem, Finance Controller of Rider Steel, Prodeep Dash has revealed, the company had procured chimneys and other air pollution control systems which would help them meet EPA pollution limit.

Meanwhile, Tema EPA boss, Irene Opoku says the agency is enforcing compliance with the pollution limit. But the question is: How come residents at Kpone are facing the current problem, if indeed the agency has been enforcing compliance with the pollution limit?

Could it be that EPA is doing its job but the industries aren't complying as expected of them? And what happens to companies that flout compliance order?

Lung disease

The term lung disease, according to online dictionary refers to many disorders affecting the lungs, such as asthma, COPD, (Chronic Obstructive Pulmonary Disease) infections like influenza, pneumonia, and tuberculosis, lung cancer, and many other breathing problems. Some lung diseases can lead to respiratory failure.

And here are some of the symptoms associated with the disease. Health experts say early stages of lung cancer maybe a slight cough or shortness of breath, depending on which part of the lung is affected. But there could be more symptoms over time, which include shortness of breath or wheezing, body fatigue, loss of appetite, or weakness,. Aside that cough can be chronic, dry with phlegm or with blood. Also common, are hoarseness, swollen nymph, nodes or weight loss.

The experts believe the disease progressions varies from person to person. Some people experience a rapid onset of symptoms due to lung damage caused by the disease. On the contrary others may experience a slower progression. Study has shown 'the exact course of disease progression is difficult to predict; for that reason, doctors cannot be sure how rapidly IPF (Idiopathic Pulmonary Fibrosis) will progress for a given patient'.

"People with lung disease have difficulty breathing. Millions of people in the U.S. have lung disease. If all types of lung disease are lumped together, it is the number three killer in the United States" according to experts reports.

Perhaps what makes Kpone's case seem more serious is the fact that, most or some industries in our part of the region don't observe safety regulations either for their workers or the general public. A classic case is what you read awhile back. Compliance means nothing to them if they can get away with it.

It's pretty ugly fact that companies pay little or no compensations to victims of industrial accidents plus the lack of education. Knowing the cause of the disease is one part of the equation but it's also imperative to know the symptoms that accompany the disease and how to treat it.

Pollution in the world

World Health Organisation (WHO) reports that carbon emissions reach 40 billion metric tonnes high, which presupposes the world faces dangerous climate change. And the worst offenders are China the United States and India. Also the report estimated that the world pumped 39.8 billion metric tons of CO_2 in 2012.

It says more than 80% of people living in urban areas that monitor air pollution are exposed to air quality levels that exceed WHO limits. While all regions of the world are affected, populations in low-income cities are the most impacted.

According to the latest urban air quality database, 98% of cities in low- and middle income countries with more than 100 000 inhabitants do not meet WHO air quality guidelines. However, in high-income countries, that percentage decreases to 56%.

THE IRONY OF IRONIES

Why Bole Roads Have Potholes:

Former President John Dramani Mahama couldn't be forgiven even when he wasn't physically present at Ghana's Parliament House last Friday. Mr. Mahama got booed and jeered by the Majority New Patriotic Party (NPP). The road to his hometown Bole is reported to be in bad shape. They've developed potholes perhaps as deep as bored holes. The Deputy Minister of Roads & Highways Kwabena Owusu-Aduomi had appeared before the august house to brief the lawmakers about his ministry's work plan.

And like a theatrical stage the current Member of Parliament for Bole/Bamboi in the Northern Region, Yusif Sulemana stood on the floor of the Chamber to ask the minister what his ministry was doing about bad roads in his constituency. All eyes at the Minority side had already rolled at his direction. The eyes spoke... 'Don't say anything that would bring us into shame'. But it was too late. The roads at Bole/Bamboi need to be fixed and they must be fixed. And this is where the irony rears its ugly head.

Bole is the hometown of Mr. Mahama who was also the MP for the constituency from 1996 to 2008 on the ticket of the NDC. He served as MP for 12 years, vice president for more than three years president for four years five months. This, in part is what drew catcalls from the Majority. They couldn't understand why the president failed to fix his own hometown roads. What in the world was the Mahama administration doing all these years?

Were they building Ghana's first ever spacecraft to Mars?

Was Friday June 23 2017 the right time to ask about the status of the Bole/Bamboi roads?

As I struggled myself to make sense out of the whole theatrical episode a man who describes himself as Mr. Mahama sympathiser told me the former president had a lot of things to do other than fixing the Bole/Bamboi roads. You're right!

His other argument was that, the former president couldn't do the roads to his home town and the constituency roads because he'd run out of time. Who are you kidding? I broke into laughter.

Mr. Mahama had time to cut sods and commission many projects across the country. From KVIP's, markets, roads, schools to bored holes, hospitals, colleges, super malls, runways, highways, motorways and many more. The question is: Don't the people of his constituency like many others deserve to have their roads paved and upgraded or have their fair share of the national cake?

I know for sure presidents are not road contractors and they don't award road contracts. But they've executive powers. And by such powers they can do and undo, make and unmake anything under their watch. They can grant amnesty and clemency. You know about that.

In fact president Mahama had the political capital and by that clout he could have easily had the roads to Bole, if not the entire constituency' roads paved and upgraded.

And who would have cried foul or criticised him? Are Boleans not citizens of Ghana?

What could have been too difficult for the former president to do given the clout he wielded as the Chief Executive at the time?

At the parliament house the Majority shamed the former president and also heckled MP Sulemana. The NDC Minority wouldn't sit aloof they responded, throwing jabs as well. So is Mr. Mahama to blame for the poor state of the roads in his area?

Don't things happen and don't they happen for a reason?

Former president Kwame Nkrumah built the Tema Township but failed or couldn't develop Nkroful his hometown in the western region. Wouldn't that be viewed as comparing apples and oranges in this scenario? Don't forget it is irony of ironies, no matter how you see it, no matter what you think about it. It is what it is. Some things are created to be like what they are, ugly or beautiful they may appear but they serve a great purpose in a grand scheme of things.

Indeed the Bole/Bamboi story fits into this scenario. After a hard day's work a baker goes to a convenience store to purchase bread. His co-worker sees him and raises an eyebrow. He's lost of words, completely left open-mouthed. The reason, Kofi is the manager at the store and he's basically the one who calls the shot.

What's wrong with this guy? Kofi's friend wonders.

Kofi has been given friends; strangers and neighbours free bread every day and even awhile back. So why would he end up at the store buying bread? It's simply the irony of ironies.

Good news is that the Bole township roads will get done this year. It's about 80 per cent nearing completion. The Bole township roads had been awarded on contract since September 2014. The contactor abandoned the project. I guess it was payment issue.

The Deputy Minister in response to the MP's question said the Dakrupe-Kabilma road, Mandari-Charche road, Mankuma-Kenasibi road and Bole township roads would be completed as planned.

He explained that the Dakrupe-Kabilma, Mandari-Charche and the Bole Town Roads are part of the feeder roads network in the Bole/Bamboi constituency.

According to the minister the Dakrupe-Kabilma feeder road which commenced on May 6, 2016 was expected to be completed on May 5, 2017 but delay in payment for work done had affected the progress of work. The story wasn't different from the Mandari-Charche road which was also awarded on contract on September 14, 2016. It was expected to be completed on September 13, 2017, noting that the project was behind schedule.

He said the upgrading of the Bole Township Roads and the rehabilitation of the Cocoa Research Institute road at Bole was also given on contract on June 30, 2016 and was expected to be completed on June 30, 2017. However, he hinted work had not been completed because of scarcity of quarry products in the area.

Meanwhile, the Majority Chief Whip and NPP MP for Sunyani East, Kwasi Ameyaw-Cheremeh had questioned why most of the road projects in that particular constituency were awarded between May and September 2016 and whether the Deputy Minister knew that there was enough money to execute those projects awarded at a stretch in 2016.

Mr. Owusu Aduomi said he would not be able to tell whether indeed at the time of the award of the contract there was enough money to execute those road projects in the Bole/Bamboi constituency. So, in conclusion it will be safe to say that Bole roads have potholes because the kitty at the time was as dry as Sahara desert.

Does Size Matter?

If our struggles had talons they would have rivaled that of the Eagle's. And if our problems had horns they would have equaled that of the Buffalo's (which stands about 3ft 3 inches on the average). I've heard the Ocean roar like a lion but there are no lions in it. And I've heard the wind howl like a bear but she carries no bears in her wings.

If you think you hold the plumb line that's a figment of your own imagination. And if you think you've got it all wrapped up I advise you to acquaint yourself with King Solomon's incredible biblical story. He thought he'd it all. Solomon believed he had all under his able command, all at his beck and call.

Have you ever questioned why the rolling stone gathers no moss?

And would you believe if I told you that it took one Man to save the world?

Does size really matter?

Indeed it does matter sometimes but not all the time. They say the end justify the means. Take for instance Politics. In politics you would need the size which is basically the numbers to clinch power. To defeat your opponent you'd need the numbers. To retire your opponents to the opposition or better still to 'Siberia' you'd need the numbers.

Also In a game of Association football a large crowd is often preferred. But you would agree with me that you would go to watch a game of fewer spectators (well-behaved) than throw yourself in the midst of a big crowd of hooligans.

"The size of your audience doesn't matter,' wrote an anonymous author.

xxxxxxxx

The glum quietness at Adwen couldn't stop a young boy to play his flute. He'd found himself at an insignificant place. It was a depressed corner. Though known by many they refused to access its seemingly outlandish street. Ironically it was the same corner the young boy lit his little lamp and blew his flute.

The walls resisted its high-pitched sound yet the sound penetrated his thick-layered skin. His dexterous little fingers trafficked across the holes on the wind instrument made from a tube. It'd found a way to reach his solo admirer.

He was focused, he was determined and he was poised. He stepped up his game yet not a single being showed up. But that didn't stop him. That didn't stop his next guest!

From a distance an inquisitive cat had heard the melodious sound. She sat on her paws across the young boy her head tilted up –as she soothed herself with the pleasant music. Interestingly, the cat's presence had inspired her new friend the more. And he let the music played on. The young boy had made her day. Her laughing green eyes beheld an improbable sound: The sound that drowned solitary and ignited joy.

"I have never felt like this in my life time. You're genius," said the cat to the boy.

"Hello Cat," said the boy. "You've also made my day. But beyond that you've taught me something that is incredibly immeasurable. I've learnt today that size doesn't matter."

Was it not mentioned somewhere in the Bible that my father can raise stones to worship Him?

Remember, you can find a friend in a different race: The dog is widely known to be man's best friend and we've seen that character trait exhibited by the cat and other animals too. You would find a true friend who appreciate s your good work, regardless of its size or kind. We saw that in the above narrative, the cat made it count when it mattered most. At times we need the numbers at certain times the numbers don't add value they subtract.

What matters is the delivery –can they get the job done and give value for the money expended on them? Would your audience stay with you till the end of the game? Are they friends who would hail you today and turn around to crucify you tomorrow? No, you don't need them.

Why hire s 50 labourers if 10 can get the job done?

Do you remember Joseph the little boy with coat of many colours? Who would have known or heard about him (Joseph) if he'd slept with Potiphar's beautiful wife? He would have remained in his master's house as a servant or eloped with his wife to an unknown place or ended up killed by the Egyptians for committing adultery.

But it was all God's plan—the Master Designer artistically plotted his (Joseph's) unprecedented rise to stardom and fame. Perhaps his family would have been killed by famine.

"The harvest indeed is plentiful but the workmen are few," Matthew 9:37.

Why did Jesus choose 12 Apostles when he knew the harvest was huge? Biblically the 12 has its significance. It represented the 12 tribes of Israel. But the verse suggests that not many people could stand the drudgery of the mission.

In that case Jesus selected 12 Apostles to embark upon his redemption mission. It took 12 to get the word out of its birthplace. And he charged his men to spread the word to the four corners of the world.

Indeed it's better to have ten committed and dedicated solders than have an army of rogues at the battle field, you would lose the combat even before it commences.

Sometimes we fret for nothing. We think we must get certain things by hook or crook means. We tend to believe that without the huge numbers or following we are losers. We can't get to the top without the majority's endorsement. We can't make it work or count. Without them, we think we are out of the game.

Note, without their inclusion, without their validation, without their approval you can make it. Someone is watching you. Somebody sees your good work. From far away someone is with all ears like the inquisitive cat sucking everything in. So don't give up. Keep up the good work.

Ghana Decides On Wednesday

Good morning Ama...

My father sent me here. He's asked me to come and wish you well. To tell you that everything would hold its sway everything would be fine. Assuredly, Wednesday will come and pass by just like a whirlwind but the people of this great nation will be here. Generations come and generations go and he would call you when it's your turn.

Lest I forget my name is not Amihere (an Nzema name) but I'm here to also ask for a huge favor —to address citizens of this nation. Our nation Ghana needs prayers— our nation needs peace. I observed something on my way here. In my rush here I met somebody camouflaged and hooded. The man was swearing and taunting everyone he met on the street.

Power has sent Trouble. Trouble is in town. And Trouble is apparently looking for trouble.

So, please lend me your ears countrymen and women. Hopefully this message won't be long. And hopefully we will all get along after this bug is gone.

Indeed you've seen many Wednesdays pass by like a passerby. And the majority of them have rolled by like a rolling stone. But nothing is like this Wednesday. This one which falls on the 7th of December (the Election Day) would've passed unnoticed in the land of Utopia.

Understandably, here is not Utopia. This part of our world has many times toyed with peace and the upshot had been despicable. Unfortunately some parts of this world have littered their paths with grief, pain, sicknesses, wars, hunger, influx of refugees, killings, coups, terrorism etc.

"Sir who are you, would you mind tell us your real name before you proceed?"

Not a problem my dear. My name is Peace. I make things happen. Kids love me. Kids cannot play when trouble is brewing. There cannot be education, industrialization, commerce and trade. There cannot be entertainments, sports and infrastructure development when I'm gone. Investments grow because of me. Tourism thrives because I'm here.

Millions yearn to see me when I'm gone. Power labours in vain if he despises me. Power is my brother; we're from the same stock, same parent. If different people can co-exist and live happily, why can't my brother see eye to eye with me?

So, my people here are two major things you must look out for on the voting day.

False Alarm & Trouble

You'll hear a story like this one:

xxxxxxxxxx

People ran to her home when they heard the extreme scream at the midnight. The shrill voice had subdued the peace and silence that at least ruled the community for a couple of hours. The deafening noise was from the night Nurse, Tina Tawiah— a young beautiful lady who worked at the Ridge Hospital in Accra.

She was seen standing at her front porch still screaming still shaking as though the terrible terror had visited her home. Several friends had made it there just in a twinkle of an eye to find out if their friend was okay. Tears dropped like rains from her eyes cowed by Trouble.

At Avenue Lincoln the upscale community, one always had the feeling that s/he was in the 'Garden of Aden' or closer to heaven because of its serenity and picturesque environment. Not far away from down town Accra. Not far away from the iconic 'Job 600' (which accommodates the Lawmakers) and not far away from the Christiansborg Castle and the Arch at the Independence Square.

"But what really could be the problem," a woman wondered as she and her husband closed in on the nurse's residence.

Indeed it was a community that cared for everyone, a community that watched one another's back and a community that showed up when there was a mishap. So, it appeared that night one of their own was in danger, hence the urgency.

"What's going on Tina?" a man asked.

And you won't believe what Tina voiced out. "I came home about 15 minutes ago and saw several ants crawling on my kitchen canter. I've already called 911 for help. But I'm scared to death I fear they'd invade my home. I can't go back in."

"Did you mean little ants?' The man's wife interrupted.

"Yes," She replied.

The shock on their faces was tangible. Some thought Tina was beside herself, she was probably losing her mind. Or she'd been attacked by some strange evil. None of the guesses was right. Tina was sound-minded and wasn't suffering from any kind of disease or sickness. Nonetheless, her behavior that night to her friends was typically unusual.

Some of them laughed it off, while others fumed with anger.

"How dare you disturb our night?" A woman about Tina's age questioned.

Don't forget Tina is a nurse. She worked at the Theatre, where surgeries were carried out almost every day. She'd seen it all at the RH (Ridge Hospital). She'd witnessed and worked on complicated cases: Cases that sometimes humbled the strong and the giants at the hospital. Yet, Tina was fleeing from the little ants. '

Tina's friends would soon leave in droves just with the same urgency and speed at which they ran into her residence. She'd been left alone to deal with her 'little enemies'. Lucky they didn't manhandle her.

Later, to Tina's surprise the 911 team gave her a bill ofGHc650.00 to pay for responding to what the officers called a 'hoax' and 'wasting state resources'.

The Akans say: "Obiara wo, nea o'tume no." Everybody has his/her drill sergeant. Every Goliath has his David as every Samson his Delilah. The lion fears no one in the jungle but he runs away when he senses the hyena. The rat sticks its tale in between her legs when it sees an approaching dog. The fowl fears the falcon and the falcon fears the eagle.

What did the kings do when the aristocrats emerged? They ran away and left their sandals behind.

Kids are kids and they fear no foe because they're innocent!

When the cat shows up the mouse disappears. The moose avoids the company of a tiger or hyena. The worm prays he never strays into the path of the black ant. And the ant dreads the sight of the tortoise or turtle.

Didn't you know that fire consumes all except water?

And rivers, streams as well as puddles tremble when drought sets in. Ironically, it's rain (water) that drives away drought.

So, let's go into the elections with a positive mindset. Be mindful, Trouble is there. Surely, you'll see him lurking around but please don't confront him.

Avoid him as much as possible. If you see something wrong call the police or like-minded agents or special observers. It would better serve you well and the country in general. You'll leave the polling station not with a broken jaw and bloodied nose. That alone makes you a victor or a winner. More so, Ghana will wake up looking stronger, better and greater. And its people will heap a deep sigh of relief.

Hopefully, when the dust is settled by Friday you'll hear from the messenger again.

Good morning Ama!

God Bless our homeland Ghana!

Adehyeman mma me'ma mo tiri nkwa!!

Manhunt for Mr. Greed

Sometimes it isn't about how fast we can run. Rather it's about how fast we can run to catch the finish line. And before you start the gimmicks, I advise you to check and double check, if you have the right tricks to trick the mavericks chances are that they may be more seasoned than you think you are.

Why run to the Sanhedrin Court?

Are they no courts in Ghana?

xxxxxxxxxx

A man sets out on a journey one day to look for Mr. Greed. He's heard a lot about the eccentric figure. Mr. Greed lives by a creek called Seek. Legend has it that Mr. Greed is a Greek and he's a geek. But that assertion has since been debunked by yours truly. Indeed Mr. Greed bears nationality of every nation across the world. His appetite for earthly things especially power and wealth is deep.

Like the voyager, for many years many people have travelled to the small town named after Seek. It is a long journey from home. On his way he meets poverty, hunger and disease. The three friends are also trekking the opposite direction in search of wealth and happiness. They look tired and frustrated. Their whole frame clad with misery, pain and hopelessness.

"These guys must've trekked from afar," the man conjectures.

He's seen different things and has come across different people on his expedition. However, his encounter with the trio was unusual. It would set him thinking. But would that change his mind or lifestyle? He looks at the guys condescendingly, as he struggles to approach them.

What's wrong with these people? He wonders.

It looks like they haven't been eaten for ages. It seems they're sick. It appears they're hippies.

He tries to strike acquaintance with them albeit sceptical. Do you guys know where Mr. Greed lives? "Mr. Greed doesn't live at one place he's all over the world always on the move," they told him. Intrigued by the man's question the three enquired: "Sir what do you need him for?

"I'm appalled by Mr. Greed's behaviour. I've never liked him and I wish I can find him."

But how did he forget that he's the same man pursuing his own self. Greed sees the poor, the needy, the sick yet he doesn't care. Greed sees hunger, he sees poverty, he sees diseases all around him but he doesn't bother. Instead he looks down upon them. He thinks for himself and about himself. Did Jammeh dream he will lose power one day?

I hear he may also end up at the International Court of Justice soon. Yes, soon will come.. Mr. Greed. See there's time for everything. So, don't brag yet till you see that the smokestack has nothing in its belly.

So tell me where else you gonna run to?

Some whispered, you may be considering seeking sanctuary at the Manhyia. Is that a possibility?

Anyway as you may be aware pressure is mounting. And I can assure you the guys have sworn to take you down this time. Already all the people who helped you to loot seem to be running helter skelter. I even heard some of them are now calling you names. Some are swearing that they don't know you. Well, that's how greed ends its journey. Greed knows no stop until shame is brought upon him. Until its seed blossoms greed will continue to feed its ego.

According to Business Dictionary (BD) greed is: "A selfish want for something beyond one's need. Typically, greed is associated with wealth or power. Someone that cannot have enough... The more he or she attains the more he or she wants and never satisfied."

Online dictionary defines greed as having an intense desire for something, especially wealth, power or food.

Erich Seligmann Fromm a German social psychologist, psychoanalyst and sociologist says "greed is a bottomless pit which exhausts the person in an endless effort to satisfy the need without even reaching satisfaction.'

Mr. Greed's story reminds me of the encounter between king David and prophet Nathan. David had amorous relationship with Uriah's wife. And God had asked Nathan to rebuke David. Nathan paints a scenario of two men that live in a little town one rich and the other poor. The poor rears a lamb his only lamb that follows him to everywhere. But the rich has lot of animals. One day he gets a visitor and he decides to kill the poor man's lamb for his visitor. David gets angry upon hearing the story, demanding the man must be punished immediately.

But guess who Mr. Greed is, ironically it's the same man pursuing his own self.

Politics Go Dancing

How the United Ghana Video got the presidents on the dance floor

A satirical video clip featuring four Ghanaian leaders doing freestyle, Azonto (a popular Ghanaian dancing genre) and a seemingly break boogying has generated a huge viewership on the social media arena.

In the video the animated characters —notably former president John Rawlings, former president John Kufuor, sitting President John Mahama and the leader of the largest opposition party in Ghana Mr. Akufo Addo (Edward) called for unity, stability and peace as the country heads to the general elections on Wednesday December 7, 2016.

"This is what we need— **Peace, Unity and Stability**," said Mr. Rawlings.

And he couldn't state it better. Certainly, Ghana needs that to build a stronger nation, build a better economy and build a more stable government. I strongly think nothing should stand between this clarion call made by our statesmen.

Without a doubt if we can humanise politics, inject humor and laughter into the activities associated with it, there surely will be less tension, less acrimony and fewer skirmishes in our political discourse. The acerbic attacks often hurled at political opponents and the launching of incendiary remarks that fly in the airwaves like katyusha rockets would slow down.

There will be less of 'I' and 'Me' semantic—that would fade in the course of time. Instead, we will be talking more about collectivity and inclusivity. Unity would become the nation's watchword and the citizenry would be basking in a sea of peace.

The spoken language could shift—it will be 'We' and 'Ours'. The 'Morning Bell' will chime oneness and togetherness. And in the midst of our differences we will still be a united Ghana—united for a common goal and purpose. Oh what a great nation that would be, if we can stick to that and make it work!

I cracked up when I first saw the less than a minute video. I got drunk in laughter and like Oliver Twist I wished the clip was much longer. It was a virtuoso performance by all standards. The three Johns and Edward showed Ghanaians their dancing prowess. First John in the Fourth Republic said the cool moves reminded him of his days at Achimota College.

The plot or storyline began at an unknown setting (the producers simply named it somewhere) in Ghana.

Sporting their party colours NDC John Mahama in red, white, green and black emerged with the NPP Akufo Addo in blue white and red. The two were seen playing 'Dame' draughts or checkers .It's a strategic board game. Often the individual who seems to be gaining the upper hand taunts or teases the weakling—the one losing the game.

From the onset, Mr. Mahama misfired as he gifted his opponent one marble.

"Ah onua makyew baako m'afa mede3,' says JM as he's affectionately called.

To which Nana Addo remarked: "Ma weda wo dame too mu paao."

In translation: I'm an expert in draughts.' And in a whirlwind they were joined on stage by the two former presidents. Shortly afterwards the Jacks and Eddie were approached by a little girl holding a Unity sign. She called the symbol 'U-TV' and handed it over to Mr. Kufuor.

"Grandpa, gye U-TV, fa'twa wo nan ase. Ah na nipa nso ye de3en," she told the former president.

Earlier on, Mr. Rawlings had enquired: "What station is this?

"TV ben na anim daho clear tes3 Soldier fo march pass," Mr. Rawlings remarked.

They say all work and no play makes Jack a dull boy. Indeed, one would expect nothing but fun galore after the brain exercise game—checkers. Mr. Mahama called on his brothers to hit the dance floor and demonstrate to the world what they've got.

The Akans in Ghana say: 'Agro ene fam.' Better translation, if you think you can dance let's get down on it. And without delay the four gentlemen head to the dance floor amid great swings and contagious moves that earned them huge applause from the backstage. At the venue's' background was Ghana's map showcasing its beautiful Red, Gold and Green colours with the Black Star positioned at the midpoint.

Mr. Kufour was heard saying: "Ghanaman yey3 oman baako." In translation Ghana we're one nation.

Tickled by his own wonderful moves Mr. Rawlings broke into laughter: "I remember my days in Achimota School."

Indeed, humor and laughter have their own way of subduing tension and redeeming themselves. They can make the sadist beast laugh and disarm the armed terror. Pain can cause one to cry and laughter does the same thing when it hits the roof or its elasticity. At that stage you would observe that the tear ducts get activated resulting tear drops.

American author and a computer programmer, Marshall Brain in an article titled: 'How Laughter Works' said 'laughter is not same as humor. Laughter is the physiological response to humor."

Laughter consists of two parts—a set of gestures and the production of a sound. When we laugh heartily, changes occur in many parts of the body, even the arm, leg and trunk muscles, he wrote.

So, even though this wasn't 'Tartan Tempest'—Canadian Armed Forces Reserve infantry Units' exercise that ensures that members meet requisite Battle Task Standards, the brains behind this hilarious contest I believe put smiles on faces of many across the nation and beyond her borders.

In fact I called the Flagstaff House, soon after watching the thriller and congratulated Mr. Mahama. I extended the congratulatory calls to the former presidents, Messrs Rawlings and Kufuor and then to the NPP presidential candidate Nana Akufo Addo. The four gave the assurance that they'd do it again whenever the producers approached them. "We're thankful to the producers and to our people for accepting us into their homes. We are aware that these are difficult times the political contest is getting keener and keener not by the day but by the hour. "

The Anatomy of GHANA Medical Stores Fire: *What Did We Learn From It?*

Perhaps the perpetrators thought no one would ever uncover their terrible act when they torched the Central Medical Stores in Tema, Ghana more than two years ago. But it looks like the chips have started falling.

So, who are behind the loot and the burn?

How did drugs worth more than US$11 million disappear in just 28 days?

Why did the Health Ministry purchase drugs worth US$80, when it knew the medicines were three months old expired prior to their procurement?

Also who diverted the 4million pounds worth of drugs from Tema Harbour to the storage facility?

And can the Akufo-Addo government recover the millions stolen by the lootees?

xxxxxxxxxxx

The UN agency for health (WHO) had its medical supplies at the Central Medical Stores (CMS) of the Ministry of Health (MOH) in

Tema, Ghana. The facility had several drugs worth millions of dollars that were meant to treat, Tuberculosis HIV/AIDS, Malaria including the deadly Ebola disease which had claimed thousands (more than 28,000) of lives in neighbouring Sierra Leone, Liberia and Guinea. But the plot to financially destabilise the nation was pivoting elsewhere in the health ministry headquartered in the Ministries enclave in Accra.

In fact the decay at the sector is as sickening today as it was before, considering the magnitude of the plot, the frequency of the rot and the fire that consumed the drugs' depot in January 2015.Evidently it brings back unpleasant memories and it makes it seem like the incident happened just yesterday. And without a doubt, the incident would remain a blot on the society.

Then sector minister of the erstwhile Mahama-administration Shirley Ayittey had sensed a worrying development and she feared it could cost the nation a fortune if not stopped. However, the plotters outfoxed Madam Ayittey as her efforts to halt the plot yielded no positive result.

Obviously, the master-minders were far advanced in their scheme and had one objective— to wreak havoc on Ghana. They would pillage her as though there was no tomorrow and later set the medical outlet on fire. So, blame it not on natural disaster or human error. It was thought-out. It was an inside job, this writer believes.

How did drugs worth more than US$11 million disappear in just 28 days including other several consignments?

Captain Smart a radio presenter and anti-graft crusader of Adom FM of the multi-media group who's a dossier on the shady deal of the architects said this: "The arson at the Central Medical Stores was master-minded by government officials period."

The report reveals the secret and modus operandi employed by staff of the ministries and its departments as well as agencies across Ghana, how they 'diverted' and 'swapped' consignments, from one destination to another.

According to the dossier in just 28 days drugs worth more than US$11 million had gone missing at the central medical stores in Tema. It further discloses, drugs that were supposed to go to places like Central,

Ashanti or Eastern regions were diverted eerily, not to anywhere in Ghana but they found their way into the shores of our sister next-door, Togo. When the sector minister Shirley Ayittey found out that the consignments had been diverted she asked the staff in the regions to furnish her with all documents pertaining to the drugs. Strangely, the next day all the documents had been gutted by fire.

The news shocked many across the nation. Former US Ambassador to Ghana Robert Jackson whose government had given Ghana drugs worth US$7million lamented when he heard about the CMS fire: "This has dealt a blow to our ability to support public health in Ghana."

Similar reaction came from former United Kingdom Ambassador John Benjamin. The outspoken diplomat said this "UK Parliament is worried over the central medical stores arson." The UK government had also given Ghana 7 pounds worth of drugs. It's believed he'd information that the drugs had been stolen. The dossier notes, when Mr. Benjamin decided to write a letter to the health minister to launch investigation into the criminal act, guess what happened. In less than 24 hours the facility caught fire.

The expose 'which comes over two and half years after the violent fire gutted the CMS on January 13, 2015 also makes other startling findings The report suggests that MOH had even planned to cover up its shady deeds.

Who are behind the loot and the burn?

The dossier names Volta Impex Pvt Limited (Ghana) as one of the perpetrators of the rot that engulfed the Tema-based drug facility. And you won't believe this: Volta Impex was given GHc5 million to print prescriptions forms. It's understood the actual cost price of the project was an estimated one million GHc. What happened to the 4 million cedis balance? They pocketed it without rendering any account. To whom shall we render account they might've asked? Ironically when Volta Impex submitted the work or the prescription forms Ghana Medical Association (GMA) rejected the forms according to the report. The reason, the said printed forms were 'deficient'.

But that wouldn't stop them from carrying out their diabolical plot.

Question is: How did all the papers in Ashanti, Brong Ahafo, Eastern, Western and Greater Accra regions find their way back to the central Medical stores?

Interestingly ministry of health shielded the perpetrators, according to the report.

Captain Smart says the MD of Volta Impex Pvt must be held account. "He must answer how all the documents found their way back to the Central Medical Stores."

Did the nation say enough is enough?

The UK government didn't turn its back on us it further gave Ghana another 4 million pounds worth of drug following the diversion of the previous consignment. And from Tema Harbour to where the freight was designated to be stored, within six hours those drugs also were stolen.

Ghana government continued its profligacy—making more purchases and the crooks would also step up their game plan. Government would again purchase drugs valued at 24.99 million cedis. The following day it established the drugs had been expired for three months before they were purchased. Isn't this absurd? Who does this and for what reasons?

But wait another 12.6million GH cedis worth of drugs were purchased and on January 8, 2015, logged in the log book. And as expected the next day on January 9 the drugs were gone missing. Ghana would wake up on the 13th of January 2015 to the news that the whole facility had been burnt down.

On top of that, a whopping $ 80 million worth of drugs also went waste. Not only that…Malaria, TB Ebola, HIV/AIDS 263 million Ghana cedis. It was also established that all the drugs were expired two months before its arrival…"

Conspiracy theory

In the wake of the fire storm at least three conspiracy theories emerged. The first account was that the medical stores had burnt some pieces of paper in its incinerator. Then on Tuesday a day after, a staff member supposedly burnt another set of papers. At the time it was unclear as to which of the fires caught the numerous of boxes of expired drugs that were packed outside- awaiting clearance before their destruction.

And there was the third theory, which said that the several boxes of the expired drugs had been outside in the open and the severe Hamattan winds triggered excessive heat and therefore the likelihood of some of the drugs exploding and igniting the fire.

Well, we now know that none of the conspiratorial notions regarding the fire storm hold water. And I personally believe it was premeditated. The plot was well choreographed by 'government officials' (as intimated by Captain Smart) to loot and burn.

The unavoidable question is:

Can the Akufo-Addo government recover the millions stolen by the lootees?

Indeed it's a question that many Ghanaians are asking. Of course it's their money and they want it back. But how would the administration do it such that it wouldn't be characterised by the opposition NDC as witch-hunting. And I think the approach will be a key factor. Let's not forget that the opposition also admits and agrees that there's corruption in Ghana and it needs to be tackled head on.

BINGOoooooooo!!!

The Gitmo Guys Are Staying...

Akwaaba my brothers, Mia we zo nustuwo, Maraba yan wuana, Nyemi hii.

I knew it. I knew you guys were staying. I didn't need a soothsayer or palmist to tell me whether you were staying or not. And which is why, if you remember when I met you guys at the KIA airport the very first day you touched down in Accra, Ghana (formerly Gold Coast), I gave you this assurance:

Let not your hearts be troubled because this is it. This could be your home. This is Ghana the land of the kindest and finest people. However, just so you know, do not take that leniency to be weakness on their part else you'd be sorry.

I can't explain it better. But I guess when you push yourself through life and you cannot push it any longer. The theory is you better let go and let push, push himself. Sounds ridiculously ludicrous right? But in reality it works anyhow. In life some people have more and some have nothing. Strangely, the disparity even abounds in the domain of the planetary. Our planet Earth has one Moon while Jupiter and Saturn have 53 apiece. And you want to know which ones have none?

It's Mercury and Venus!

The reason, (first with Mercury) scientists explain that 'Mercury is so close to the Sun and its gravity, it wouldn't be able to hold on its own. They say: "Any moon would most likely crash into Mercury or maybe go into orbit around the sun and eventually get pulled into it."

How about Venus why doesn't she have a moon?

Well, scientists say that's a mystery for them to solve. Ah huh!

See, we're not far from home, looks like it though... But I can assure you we're getting closer to the nugget. Thing is if you don't have it and I mean IT, don't try it. Because in our world it appears those that have it, play it, dance it and use it. Now you're getting it, I hope so.

Anyway, I don't know which path these guys strode. But most likely they overlapped which is euphemism for trespass, I believe. Always remember right to movement isn't comprehensive it has its limitations. When you see 'Beware of Dogs,' on one's steel gate, it means just that. In some places the laws are beautifully crafted but they don't bite. I can cite for you a few examples but time isn't on my side.

Simply, we live in a world full of mysteries. Some people fool around and they get away with it. While some fool around and they get caught up with the laws. Some of us saw what happened last Monday 21 August 2017 when the Moon walked past the Sun or strayed unto its way it was exclusive to the United States but even so not all the 50 states were lucky. I think 14 states saw the solar eclipse.

So, Paul I know, but who are you guys my people have asked me to ask you?

My name is Mahmud Umar Muhammad Bin Atef.

Can you please tell me again where you're from?
"I am from Yemen."
Yemen, you said, in the Arabian region.
"That's right Sir."
And how did you end up here?
'Nsem pii." Wait a minute!
What did you say? And when did you learn the Ghanaian language?
"We've been here since January 2016. I can speak Twi and Ga. My brother and I are trying a couple of other languages too."

That's absolutely incredible. So explain to me (and I will pass it on to my people) our audience out there what does that phrase 'Nsem Pii' mean?

"Well in simple terms, I like to say that the story that surrounds our coming to Ghana is convoluted. "

Convoluted? Which also means?
"It means we didn't come here on our own volition. "
Ok let's rest it there for a moment.

I surely would like to know more about that. And what's your name too. I guess you're also called Muhammad right?

"You're right Sir. My name is Khalid Muhammad Salih Al-Dhuby. And please allow me to take this opportunity to thank the government of Ghana and its people. We love Ghana and we're happy to be here. As you're possibly aware we'd been detained in the US military prison in Guantanamo Bay. And since our arrival on the 7th of January 2016 we've been housed here at this national security compound and I must add that we're grateful to be here."

Can I call you Atef?
"Not a problem Sir."
What's your impression too about Ghana and its people?
"Well I think my brother has said it all. But I must tell you initially we didn't know what was in stored for us. Ghanaians opposed the idea of housing supposed terrorists in their country."

But did you guys get it?
"Yes we did. And we think the opposition and the public outcry at the time was understandable. Why would any nation accept persons

deemed dangerous from another that had held them prisoners, chose not to keep them in their own country, and rather transported them to another's? So, in that term I think the opposition was justifiable. So far, we think they've (Ghanaians) demonstrated good will towards us and we wouldn't abuse it anyway whatsoever. "

Is this a promise?
"Yes, it is a promise and we will never break it."
And how did you feel when you heard:
"Ghana's Parliament has ratified an agreement to allow the two ex-GITMO detainees to stay in the country?"
"I will like my brother say it (amid smiles). He cried. But it was all tears of joy. We were so elated, that's all I can say."
The Minister of Foreign Affairs and Regional Integration Shirley Ayorkor Botchway on Tuesday August 1 2017, informed Parliament that, her ministry and other stakeholders would work on an "exit plan" by the time your two-year stay in Ghana expires January 6, 2018?

What do you think?

"Allahamdulilahi,' we'll keep our trust in God."
The Foreign Minister had also stressed that: "There will be no further obligation" to keep the two – Mahmud Umar Muhammad Bin Atef and Khalid Muhammad Salih Al-Dhuby – "unless the two governments agree otherwise and in accordance with due process."
The ratification followed a Supreme Court order after it ruled that their stay in the West African country is unconstitutional without parliamentary backing.

Background

Mahmud Umar Muhammad Bin Atef and Khalid Muhammad Salih Al-Dhuby of Yemeni origin were among 17 detainees transferred from the prison camp in Cuba by the United States.
The decision to host the detainees in Ghana provoked a firestorm of controversy and outrage among Ghanaians, with many expressing fear

that the move would undermine Ghana's internal security and expose the country to attacks from religious extremists.

A seven-member Supreme Court panel presided over by Chief Justice Sophia Akuffo by six to one (6 -1) majority decision Thursday June 22, 2017 said the two are illegally in the country since the then government allowed them into the country without prior approval by Parliament.

Ghana's Road Traffic Problem: Can it be fixed?

Ever run into dead-stop-bumper-to-bumper cars in any of our cities' roads?

Or have you wondered why the roads aren't built big or bigger just like those abroad say in the United States or China?

And is it true that building bigger roads create traffic?

A commuter recently made this observation: "I'm not an expert yet whilst sitting in the traffic I observed there was enough room for the traffic problem to be solved. I think it's robbing the nation of business time."

Gladys Prempeh had been caught up in Accra's heavy traffic—a city whose vehicular and human population are increasingly jostling for space on a daily basis. But where in the city did this happen? It was on the John Atta Mills High Street near Kwame Nkrumah Mausoleum and not far from the historic Christianborg Castle. Strangely, she observed, the pedestrians' walkway was bigger than the actual pavement. That's right!

So, I'm appealing to the authorities in Ghana i.e. the roads and highway ministry and government to consider this humble appeal:

"How much space do our legs need to walk in a straight line when there's enough room for an orderly crowd to walk?" Gladys asked.

Without a doubt commuting during rush hours in Accra, Ghana, Lagos or Ibadan, Nigeria or Johannesburg, South Africa can be more than insane. The build-up starts right from one's point of departure and it bleeds all along to the destination point, for example if you live close by a freeway linking the major highway or arteries. Ironically, none of the cities afore named found itself in FORBES' March 2016 World's most heavy traffic cities.

Yes, they couldn't and didn't match the heavy weights. They were conspicuously missing in the world top ten rankings. But isn't that good news for us? That means our traffic situation or problem hasn't perhaps reached the cascading levels yet. It means we can do something about it. That means it's better late than never. And if we stitch it in time we might as well save nine. We won't find ourselves in the precipice.

So, this is just to give you a fair idea of what's trending elsewhere regarding traffic congestion:

Here's TomTom's (one of Forbes' contributors) list of the 10 global cities where the commutes are most brutal or worst. Also it includes estimates an average motorist spends sitting in traffic; for example, if congestion causes commuters to spend 30 minutes getting to or from the office, compared to 20 minutes for the same trip taken during times of free-moving traffic, then the daily delay amounts to 50%.

Mexico City tops the list with 59% extra travel time (morning peak 97%; evening peak 94%). She's followed by Bangkok: 57% extra travel time (morning peak 85%; evening peak 114%) and then Istanbul: 50% extra travel time (morning peak 62%; evening peak 94%).

Brazil city Rio de Janeiro: 47% extra travel time (morning peak 66%; evening peak 79%).

While Moscow: 44% extra travel time (morning peak 71%; evening peak 91%). The Eastern European city is followed by a sister city– Bucharest: 43% extra travel time (morning peak 83%; evening peak 87%). Central American city Salvador: 43% extra travel time (morning peak 67%; evening peak 74%).

And the rest are Recife: 43% extra travel time (morning peak 72%; evening peak 75%). Chengdu: 41% extra travel time (morning peak 73%; evening peak 81%) and Los Angeles: crowns the list with 41% extra travel time (morning peak 60%; evening peak 81%. Jim Gorzelany was one of the contributors too.

Can Ghana fix its traffic problem?

Ghana built its premier highway or motorway in the early 1960's. And that stretch connects the nation's capital Accra and the Habour City-Tema both in the Greater Accra region. How many lanes two or three, I stand to be corrected?

Several decades after that ambitious project by Ghana's first president Kwame Nkrumah most of the country's trunk roads had been mostly single lanes until 2008 when the motorway extension also known as N1 was constructed. Is it true that the bigger the road the better?

By many standards that's true. And I think most of us can attest to that. Over the years we've seen the Tema Motorway play that distinct role and none of the roads constructed decades after its birth can compare. So of course Ghana can fix its road traffic problem but there are several factors other than building bigger roads, over heads and what have you. Nonetheless, building multiple lanes has more advantage than single lanes.

So could that be a factor?

Yes and no. Yes, if a country fails to build dual carriages, flyovers or double-deckers or expand its road networks the effect could be brutal. When you have double or multiple lanes the roads can accommodate many vehicles. But you see, that isn't a full-proof case or panacea to traffic problem. Because cities like Los Angles has all that yet they're reeling in traffic congestion as shown above.

I should remind myself that correlation does not mean causation. I used to wonder and still haven't stopped wondering why our engineers couldn't build more lanes. Maybe that could transform them all into double-decker highways with cars zooming on the upper and lower levels.

But road experts think otherwise. One expert posits that: "If there's anything that traffic engineers have discovered in the last few decades it's that you can't build your way out of congestion. It's the roads themselves that cause traffic."

Does that make sense?

In 2009, two economists—Matthew Turner of the University of Toronto, Canada and Gilles Duranton of the University of Pennsylvania, USA—decided to compare the number of new roads and highways built in different U.S. cities between 1980 and 2000, and the total number of miles driven in those cities over the same period.

"We found that there's this perfect one-to-one relationship," said Turner.

If a city had increased its road capacity by 10 percent between 1980 and 1990, then the amount of driving in that city went up by 10 percent. If the amount of roads in the same city then went up by 11 percent between 1990 and 2000, the total number of miles driven also went up by 11 percent. It's like the two figures were moving in perfect lockstep, changing at the same exact rate."

According to the social scientists: "The answer has to do with what roads allow people to do: move around. As it turns out, we humans love moving around. And if you expand people's ability to travel, they will do it more, living farther away from where they work and therefore being forced to drive into town. Making driving easier also means that people take more trips in the car than they otherwise would. Finally, businesses that rely on roads will swoop into cities with many of them, bringing trucking and shipments. The problem is that all these things together erode any extra capacity you've built into your street network, meaning traffic levels stay pretty much constant. As long as driving on the roads remains easy and cheap, people have an almost unlimited desire to use them," they contended.

How do we deal with congestion on our roads?

According to studies congestion pricing has been tried successfully in places like London, Stockholm, and Singapore. Other cities are starting to look at it as a solution. Legislators in New York rejected a plan for congestion pricing in New York City in 2008 and San Francisco periodically toys with introducing the idea in downtown. 'Nobody wants to pay for something that was previously free, even if it would be in their best interests to do so.'

Duranton said that if congestion pricing is a non-starter, a more rational approach to parking could be a good secondary step in easing congestion. Parking in most cities is far cheaper than it should be, and it's too often free.

"Because it's free, people will misuse it and it will be full all the time," said Duranton. Drivers searching for parking contribute significantly to road congestion. "There are some estimates that say in the central part of cities up to 30 percent of driving is people just cruising around for parking," Duranton said.

Polls, Predictions & Prophecies

Are Ghanaians Becoming Allergic to them?

Polls are like blankets you can't go without them during cold seasons. They give allergies when you throw them on and you may likely catch pneumonia or severe cold if you decide to go without them says this writer.

This appears to be the dilemma facing Ghanaian voters and political parties in this election season. No doubt it's a season carefully shaped by the stakeholders of the game including those who claim they've the ears and the eyes of biblical prophets Samuel and Elijah. Already they know who's winning, who's won and who God has already chosen as the next president of Ghana.

In the meantime, the airwaves, cyber space or the Internet and the tabloids have all been saturated with wild polls, wild predictions and wild prophecies. Interestingly, they're all happening with less than 10 days to the December 7, general elections amid tension and rumors of rigging.

Lately, you may have observed that these polls and prophecies have been received with mixed feelings and misgivings. They're considered bad, bias and unscientific if they don't favor a particular party or an individual. On the other hand they're described as accurate, scientific and good if the odds favor the individual or the party. In a nutshell, nobody likes to taste defeat everyone wants to be a winner.

So are Ghanaians getting allergic to these polls or are fed up with them?

Could be, it seems they've been stung by the bees giving them funny feelings. The symptoms are however, different from the usual sneezing, wheezing, itchy eyes and the nasal congestion which could be caused by food poisoning, weed smoking or taking say penicillin injection.

It appears they've had enough from the prophets, the pundits and the clerics and probably enough of the 'Bitter Pill' from Pollster Ben Ephson. But as I earlier indicated they can't do without them. Mr. Ephson who is also the editor for 'The Daily Dispatch newspaper has been doing this random exercise for some time now.

Nonetheless, his latest poll had been rubbished by the NDC parliamentary candidate for Weija-Gbawe; Obuobia Darko-Opoku. The candidate was unhappy and had vehemently refused to buy into the poll conducted by the pollster in her constituency, which suggested that she will lose the December election.

"I'm not a pollster, the basics I know about polls show that it have scientific data to back it. Where is Mr. Ephson's statistics/data to buttress his claim? I do not doubt his credentials, but such comment can easily be made by any ordinary person on the street."

She dared Mr. Ephson to conduct a 'proper opinion poll' in Weija-Gbawe constituency, adding 'he'll realise my popularity rating is far higher than even the incumbent MP Rosemond Abrah because I am on the candidate who has touched base with the people."

I remain focused and not be swayed by anyone to distract my campaign with a few weeks to the election. The people of Weija-Gbawe are the best judge."

Indeed nothing seems different. Everything pollsters, pundits and prophets are doing today had been done before (in the previous elections). Aside the 1992 general elections, the 2000, 2004, 2008 and the 2012 elections didn't go down history as tension-free or without allegations of fraud, rigging and pockets of violence. We probably witnessed them all. But in the midst of all that Ghana has maintained its status as a peaceful nation.

Let me quickly point out that there was voter apathy in the 1992 parliamentary election. Many chose to stay home rather than exercise their franchise. This followed the opposition claim that the presidential election which was held separately on the 3rd of November was fraudulent and therefore boycotted it.

It was the first since the 1979 election (13 years on) and was held on the 29th of December. Voter turnout was merely 28 per cent. And the NDC won the most seats in parliament about 185 out of the 200 seats.

TV'3 anchor and news caster Mr. Abu Issa Monnie says: "Polls on elections nowadays are becoming like pundits' opinion on a football game. Until the referee blows the final whistle we may only remain hopeful."

That's right. The burden rests on the match commissioner, he calls the shot.

And I must say voters are increasingly becoming wiser during every election season. The majority have learned to keep their cards close to their chests. It fits into the old maxim that says 'once bitten twice shy'. This is typical in battleground areas and also parties' strongholds, where intimidations and threats often rear their ugly heads.

Thing is why put your card on the table, if you aren't sure who you're dealing with or not sure that could invite trouble for you?

Fact is not many people, (particularly independent and swing voters) today fancy to disclose or tell who their preferred candidate is. One's vote must remain secret all the time. However, politicians have painstakingly tried to bastardise that 'sacred' act.

I'm reminded of a story of an Island in the Far East that planned to ban bikinis. The skimpy, sexy western dress was deemed indecent by the indigenes hence the need to ban it. Consequently, the people had to vote on whether to wear the western outfit or it must be banned totally. Poll after polls suggested the majority of the Islanders wanted the dress banned and had nothing to do with it.

But it turned out more than two thirds of the populace actually liked the dress but they never openly expressed their interest. In short, they overwhelmingly voted for it instead of opposing.

This among other factors explains why most scientific polls are getting it all wrong today. Brexit was a typical example. We saw that in the just ended US presidential election where the majority of the polls gave Democratic presidential nominee Hillary Clinton a double digit lead over her main contender Republican candidate Donald J Trump. But in the end Mr. Trump won the election.

And it seems France is following suit. Scientifically conducted polls randomly select the voters interviewed. Randomness is the factor that permits a few hundred people to speak for all the voters within a statistical margin of error. In other words, you are as likely as any other voter in the district to be asked to participate in the poll.

So this is my message to all the stakeholders in this big game, please always remember polls are mere projections. A few numbers of people are usually selected to speak for the general masses and they don't represent the final outcome…Just a tip of the iceberg.

What Would Jesus Do?

'Don't Come to my Church Unless You've the Money'

Are you feeling a bit groggy, let down or drowned in debt? Is your love or marriage life on life support and needs resuscitation or you want to travel abroad? Have you been seeing pastors, consulting prophets and visiting seers for a breakthrough lately?

Then throw on your Battakari or Fugu. Fasten your boot straps, take no bread, take no water, and pocket no CD's, (because the angels will pat you down if you dare). Also pack baggage and luggage and make a move to Down South. We're going. The Lord knows where we are going. So hurry, don't hesitate my sister/brother.

If you are in Africa or traveling from any of the African nations the journey would be shorter, faster but I must warn you it might not be smooth—depending on which flight you're taking. Don't eat any cookies while onboard and don't lie to the pastor that you'd 'dry fasting.' The message is single and simple— you drink deep or you taste not.

And in case you just got onboard you're forewarned not to carry any currencies considered weak and of no value. Yes, you heard me. No Zimbabwean dollar, no Egyptian pound and no Nigerian naira. Why the smile? You think you're exempted right? The Ghanaian cedi is banned. The Indian rupee is embargoed. Even the Zambian Kwacha which as of January 1 2013 was the strongest in Africa won't be tolerated whilst in SA.

If you're coming from Europe, North America, Asia, or any of the groups that adopted some aspects of Anglo-Saxon culture and language kindly book your flight (s)as quickly as possible .You're also hereby reminded not to forget to find a wheel barrow to haul in wads of euros, dollars and pound sterling. For your information, your host wants currencies that are water-resistant and depreciating-proof.

Well don't mistake this person for President Trump.

Remember Mr. Trump issued the executive order banning entry for 90 days by citizens from Iraq, Syria, Iran, Libya, Somalia and Yemen. This person welcomes all of them regardless. This person needs the petrol dollars. This person doesn't mind where the visitor or the traveler is coming from as long as the person has the pounds, euros and dollars, preferably the US dollar.

What would Jesus do?

He warned us to be wary of false prophets and teachers. He advised us to be as wise as the serpent. Yet, Man has ignored all the advices, all the warning signs and all the things the Lord said. Thing is, if I even told you, there are lions in my house so do not enter you'd still enter anyway.

If I told you I can increase your genitalia you'd believe me isn't it?

Ice cubes will definitely melt when you take them out from the freezer right?

And if I told you that as they melt all your problems would melt away, you'd believe me?

So who would you blame the owner of the lions or the trespasser?

I might be fined for keeping lions in my house because they aren't domestic animals. But I guess you would also not be spared for acting folly. What do they say ignorance is no excuse of the law.

Some of us are like the people of biblical Nineveh—always looking for signs and wonders. Some people hold the belief that pastors and prophets would receive stiffer or tougher punishment than believers. Well I don't know about that. And I don't think anybody has an idea or know how the Lord would deal with us when he comes back.

The message is so clear: Beware of dogs or lions.

Are you still upbeat? Are you ready for the journey? Are you sure?

I love South Africa. I love Jo'burg and I love Madiba may his soul continue to rest in peace. Pretoria and perhaps Robin Island is one place I would like to visit if I happened to be in that beautiful country. Yes, I love SA but I don't think I'm taking this trip. This trip looks tricky.

There's an invitation by a lady pastor via a video on social media. I believe many of you might've seen the clip. Call her the miracle woman. She uses ice cubes or frozen water to meltdown all human problems—debts or financial, marriage, joblessness, sickness or health problems. The lady is selling the frozen water for $100, or 100 rand South Africa money. And she begins the invitation with this:

"Greetings in the name of the Almighty Lord, I am Pastor Tenge Wei of the Church of Believers with the lot of extra cash. And I have come to share with you the miracle that Lord Almighty has chosen to give me the power of. '

Today, I will share with you, how you can wash all your problems away, how you can melt all your problems away for only a hundred Rand when you come to my church and get this frozen water. This water is frozen by the power of the Lord, the power the Lord has given me. All I have to do is to pray and pray for the water…and as I pray for the water….

'Sharabosh' it freezes. And then when you give the hundred pounds, dollars, rands or euros depending on which country you come from. But the Lord Almighty will not t accept any Zimbabwean dollars, Nigeria nairas, or any other Afriican currencies that money that dot have any value. But this water what happens is you take it home with you. You put it next to your bed before you go to sleep. Then you pray, you tell the Lord all your problems that you want them to melt. When you get up in the morning you'd see that the water has melted. So you are not wasting your money if you pay me $100 dollar or 100 pounds."

"There is not one person that has come to complain the water didn't melt. So the water is guaranteed to melt away and as it melts away it melts all your problems. Please don't come to my church unless you have money. ..Because we are the Church of Believers with a lot of Extra Cash: Praise be to God," she concluded.

Remember, some waited they got the bus. Some waited they missed it. They missed it because they were ill-prepared. Some didn't wait, yet they got the bus. You've to follow your instinct always. Give your heart and mind time to dialogue, give them time to confer and share, give them time to decide. And in all that trust the Lord for a breakthrough.

Let's Roll It Up

I chose it. It was a difficult task but I chose it anyway. I intended not to talk about it, because the more I did the harder it seemed to be and the scarier it became too. I craved for indulgence. I asked everyone not to worry about me. I asked them to allow me to put my heart and mind to it. I knew what I was going for. I knew it wasn't going to be easy but I still had to do it.

They all looked crestfallen wondering if I'd really thought through what I'd decided to do. But I told them not to worry…. If I succeed history would pencil my name down and if I fail in my bid it would still say the first man who ever did try to roll it up was Mr. so and so.

Did you ever try it when you thought about it?
Did it seem impossible? Was it too hard to do it?
Did you succeed or did you fail?

Let's roll it up brother let's roll it up.

Didn't they put man in the Moon?
Didn't someone make the robots and the drones?

Didn't you see her break the world record?

Marco Polo never gave up his discovery exploits neither Isaac Newton nor Copernicus. Just remember a step in the wrong direction is better than making no move. I'm all for it and I've got to roll it all up.

Are you sure you're ready to do this?

Yes Sir, I'm ever ready.

"Stop it, you can't do it," the eyes cried out. Could they be right?

Wouldn't they ridicule me if I fail? And wouldn't they say: Ah ha, we told you so?

My eyes looked disoriented. They appeared overwhelmed by the sheer size of the choice I'd made. Let's go back home and plan properly, they suggested. I' ain't taking any of that defeatist idea. Have you forgotten procrastination is the thief of time?

Time and time tide wait for no man…. I think the earlier we start the better. Let's get our hands dirty.

Let's roll it up my sister, let's roll it up

They wouldn't budge, the harder I pressed the more oppositional they became. In fact they seemed so panicked that they tried to flee even before the battle kicked off. Calm down friends—you can't do this, I told them. Do you guys want us to be groping? We need you to explore territories, to see the unseen. Don't be cowards, don't flee. Stand your grounds and let see what the future holds for us.

As matter of fact you guys are not only here to observe the activities but also to encourage the members so don't lit the fear flame. And don't put fright into your siblings. I'm not sure if you guys get it or you've probably lost it already as you stand here trembling before this Giant.

Aren't we saying what's obvious? The eyes questioned.

How can you roll up this giant, are you out of your mind?

I'm not surprise at all. I knew you guys would be oppositional. I knew you'd act lazy and be silly. But you should continue to preach to the choir while I psyche up the rest of the group for the improbable task. And while you guys are being cynical, we would buckle up our boots straps and put on our armor. I tell you what while you guys are acting coward we would get down on it and get started.

Let's roll it up my friends, let's roll it up

As I began to roll it up I noticed I'd probably bitten more than I could chew.

Did I really make this choice? Yes I did. From there and then the battle began.

It is the longest river in the world. I'm talking about the Nile River. Or is it the Amazon River (it runs 4,345) rather, which was crowned the champion in 2007. The Nile River runs 4,258 miles from the mountains of Burundi to its famed and fertile delta fan—where Egypt meets the Mediterranean Sea.

In AD 150 Ptolemy the renowned Greek Geographer living in Roman Egypt wrote that the river originated in the 'Mountains of the Moon' deep in the interior.

Centuries later, exactly in 1862 English explorer John Hanning Speke trekked from Africa's east coast to find what he considered to be the source, where the river exits Lake Victoria in present day Uganda. Geographers believe the two lengths are close enough that measuring techniques and philosophies can be quite controversial. In fact, the geographers who crowned the Amazon champion were funded in part by the Brazilian government.

So if you didn't know, the meandering Amazon covers a mere 1, 100 miles of straight-line distance while the Nile it's about 2,400 miles from its source to the outlet, according to geographers.

But did I really mean to roll up the Nile River?

No, it couldn't be the Nile. Nobody can roll up the river's bed. Where would you begin in the first place and where would you end? That notwithstanding the scripture admonishes us to have faith in all things we set our minds and hearts to do. Our Lord said it best: (to paraphrase) If you have faith you can tell the mountain to move if you have no doubt in your heart and it will move.

The metaphor 'Mountain' could be a marriage, an education, relationship, business, occupation or a financial problem. Mountain could also mean anything that seems to hinder one's progress or growth. Health struggles and fighting addiction of any kind could be termed a mountain.

It was around June 2014. I'd met Brother Christopher on I and 12th Street near Shiloh Baptist Church in Tacoma Washington. And while we were chatting his friend showed up. I'd never met him. But I must say it was a great encounter. After a brief pleasantries and introduction Brother Christopher's friend shared with us this true story. It was so moving, so touching.

"I'm sober now. Never thought I could be a freeman. I've freed myself from the grips of the dangerous drugs. And I thank God I've stopped the crack cocaine, the heroine including the methamphetamine," he said.

"Great job Jim (not his real name)" Brother Christopher praised his friend.

He continued: "See I've been able to stop even the big ones but I can't let go this little one."

"Which is the little one?" I asked.

"It's cigarette," he replied.

Thereupon I asked him if he knew why he seemed to be addicted to the cigarette smoking or find it difficult quitting. No was his answer.

Here's why: The problem lies in the name tag, I told him. You smartly and cleverly labeled all the narcotics as giants. And I'm sure you'd so because that's the way you see them. I guarantee if you'd labeled cigarette as giant you would have fought it the same way you dealt with the rest. Instead you belittled the latter giving it no premium and no urgency to fighting it or quitting.

And here you are still fighting it with kids' gloves. But I think the will is there. I can tell you have the zeal to fight it and I'm sure you can do it.

"Wow, I've never had anyone say it this way to me," he said. It really makes sense and I'll henceforth see it as a giant too."

Imagine it as the biggest or the longest river in the world. To cross it you'll need to be focused, prepare your mind and be committed to do the task of overcoming it.

Imagine it as the highest Mountain knowing too well that climbing it to the summit won't be easy but with determination, perseverance and self-will power you can overcome it.

Imagine it as the wild beast pursuing you in the wilderness. You'd run the best run or better still fight to defend yourself and with the can do spirit still pumping you can roll it up.

Heaven by Flight

If a flight to Heaven was by a visa you can guess what would happen. The confusion would start from this: Which flight would be allowed to carry the yet-to-be 'Heavenees'?

Would it be Bowing or Lufthansa, and KLM- the Royal Dutch airliner? Would it be British Airways, Emirates or Airbus the French carrier?

Which one would win the bid to lift the million or more passengers to Heaven? There would be pre-screening, double screening, multiple-screening, screening after screening yet there be commotion. Grandpa Adam would look on and giggle and ever-vivacious Eve would love the scene—people would be peopling everywhere.

There would be middle men (who would seek to cut corners) there would be brokers everywhere, and there would be queue after queues that will snake from Accra to Papua New Guinea and beyond. In fact people would stand on the seas and oceans to form queues long queues.

Thank Goodness our flight to Heaven isn't by a spacecraft. It won't be by Delta, not by Alitalia, not by Ethiopia Airline.

If a flight to Heaven was by a visa there would be queues for passports, there would be queues for photographs, there would be queues for interviews, and there would be queues for tickets. The language at the consular would change. The fee for the visa would be unbearable for the piss-poor-soul. Visas would run out often as a result of artificial shortage created by officials at the High Commission and the fees would jump higher and higher.

Embassy officials would be bossy and bossiness would be the order of the day. There would be lions and bears to keep the consular gate yet people would troop in for visas whether they would get one or not. There would be human and vehicular traffic, there would be super chaos and there would be absolute chaos.

There would be tribal war, racial war, class war and there would be faith war. There would be gender war. There would be sexism, racism, cronyism, cannibalism and there would be hatred, jealousy, envy, animosity, barbarity and you know we already have all of them and there would be no Heaven. And Heaven would cease to be.

But there would be a safe Haven or a sanctuary. And guess what would happen… if they succeeded in vandalising Heaven what do you think would happen to a safe Haven?

Earth was made Heaven initially for Mankind. Angels envied us. Satan hates us because God loves us you already know that. Death had no place, sickness, madness, depression and disease was not part of us. Man had everything and anything. There was peace and tranquility, there was love and there was compassion until Man DECIDED!

Remember Heaven and Haven aren't the same and can never be. The latter is a place of safety or refuge. It could be a sanctuary or an asylum. Merriam-Webster dictionary defines the former as the expanse of space that seems to be over the earth like a dome firmament. Heaven is also a place or condition of utmost happiness—something that is very pleasant or enjoyable, Heaven in Christianity is the location of the throne of God and the Holy angels.

Is it not pleasant to watch the beauty of the sky, the allure of the ocean, the splendor of the flora and fauna, the tranquil of the creeks and the uniqueness of all the creatures?

So welcome each day and count it a blessing because you're already in Heaven in disguise. That's why you don't pay any bills for the sunlight or the moonlight. The stars glitter to tell you—you are unique and awesome, the air flies around to give you that healthy ambiance.

You are the reason the birds sing, you're the reason the rivers have not ceased to flow, you're the reason the mountains stand high and the Mighty Ocean restrains his rage.

Pray my sister and pray my brother. Pray for strength, pray that your legs don't give up on you, pray that your eyes would continue to see the light of day, pray that you can walk and talk, pray you can hear, pray you can eat because you still have your teeth, pray you can stand and sit ,I beseech you to pray. Thank God and be grateful that you are able to make it to your bed every day, every night at any time without any body assisting you. Pray that our body parts don't stage a coup.

What would happen if this happens?

If the eye can sneeze and the nose can cough and the head decides not to wear the cap anymore. What would happen? If the legs refuse to walk and object to run on errands, if the feet refuse to wear shoes no more. If the hands refuse to work—choose not to write or type. What would happen if that happens?

If the stomach can talk and decides to make any demands of his choosing. If he chooses to eat snakes, worms, herbs anything just anything, what would happen? If he chooses to go on a hunger strike or decides to swallow pebbles and stones. What would happen to his siblings?

If the mouth remains mum, refuses to talk and the voice shuts down its vocal cable. If the neck decides to decouple herself from the head and the teeth gets angry with the tongue what would happen?

If the tongue loses her sense of taste and decides to arm herself what would happen? Mind you he is already as sharp as a knife. So what would happen if he goes for guns and bullets? If the mind decides to break down and the heart says he's tired of thumping what would happen if that happens.

Gordon Offin-Amaniampong

Journey to Manhyia

Condolences to Otumfuo & Asanteman

Is the Queen Really Dead?

They say kings and queens 'Don't Die' they travel –that's a belief shared by Akans in Ghana.

Where do they go then? Yours truly examines

My first visit to the Manhyia Palace (the official seat of Asantehene) in 1983 never was. I felt disappointed. Bolga Naba III Martin Adongo Abilba, who ruled from the 14th of July 1972 to October 2013, had visited our residence at Patase estate a suburb of Kumasi in the Ashanti region. The Bolga King (in the Upper East Region) was visiting his friend the Asantehene— Otumfuo Opoku Ware II.

And when he dropped the news that he planned to go there (Manhyia Palace) with us I was so thrilled.

I was so filled with joy. I waited and kept waiting till I felt I'd been waiting in vain. I don't really know what happened, but hours later my aunt Theresa Essel (now deceased) told me the visit had become abortive.

Evidently, I wasn't happy at all. It meant I'd nothing to brag about.... I had planned to tell my friends when school reopened—about how Manhyia looked like, about how majestic the king looked when he pulled on his traditional Kente cloth—names like 'Adinkra', 'Dwenasa, 'Apremo', 'Nsoroma', 'Babadua' etc. had occupied my whole mind.

I'd planned to tell them about the beautiful relics I saw, the handshakes and the broad smiles I received from the king, the queen and the elders. I'd also planned to tell them about the executioners (Adumfuo/ Abrafo), the courtiers, and the trumpeters, the drummers— about the different colorful umbrellas I saw—big and small, bowl-shaped and curved in. That I saw a gigantic Fontonfrom drum that measured six feet high and about 100 widths in diameter.

Remember where there's will there's way. Going to the Manhyia Palace this time was more than easy. I made a whistle stop in Accra. I surprised my good friend Kwamina Miaful Dadzie when I showed up at his door. Perplexed, he asked me: *"How did you make it here Katakyie?"*

I flew on the broad wings of the Eagle, I told him.

There was no protocol.to be observed. No hustles and no sweats. The Manhyia Gate was wide opened for my arrival. They knew I was coming. The walls had informed them that Nana Akwasi Atokora Adwokwaa Offin-Amaniampong was coming to pay the Queen Mother (Asantehemaa) his last respect. To say fare thee well 'Abrewatia.' To tell her we still love her and she will forever be loved. To say goodbye good old Grandma and to tell her she'll be immortalized.

Kumasi is still mourning. Asanteman is grieving. All the women I saw had dyed their hairs—symbol for grief, pain and sorrow. Krobea Asante Kotoko Asantehene– Otumfuo Osei Tutu II wasn't in his beautiful regalia. Yes, it's time to either go red or go black. That's the dress code (Kobene ne Birisie). He was flanked by a high-powered array of paramount as well as divisional chiefs across the empire.

The Bantamahene, Baffour Owusu Amankwatia VI and Asafohene Acheamfuo Kwame Akowua, Nkonson and Kutimso divisions were all in attendance.

The inner circle of the dais stood the ceremonial macebearers who flaunted the high ornamental staff of **metals** before Otumfuo as retinue of linguists gathered themselves at the fringes. The trumpeters horned like peacocks. On the far right side to the king was a motionless lanky middle aged-man, whitewashed from head to toe. I asked the king: *Who's this man?*

"That's Komfo Aku the chief fetish priest," he told me.

He was clutched to his magic wand (bodua). His whole frame was festooned with mystical trappings, charms and amulets. And who else did I see– the fearsome Adumhene Kwaku Mensah (aka Diawuo). Back in the day if you lived in Dunkwa-on-Offin or Kumasi, the sounds of 'Mmentia'– trumpets made you cringe. I dreaded that name, so much as a kid no wonder I saw him here.

Eerie memory isn't it?

The paradox is that he trembled when he saw me this time ('Man pass man'). I've got more powers than him. In the writer's creative mind everything is possible. I can go to hell taunt Lucifer and come back unscathed. I can dine and wine with King Jesus. I can create my own characters; raise an army of lions to devour him (Diawuo) instantly. I can fly high to the sky and dive deep to the depth of the mighty ocean all in a matter of sec.

Anyway, Kwaku Mensah had the eyes of hyena tattooed on his forehead. And his torso bedecked with charms as well. The Adumhene also had a piece of traditional cloth called 'danta' which barely covered his manhood provoking many eyes at the Manhyia.

So where do they (kings and queens) go hereafter?

To understand this let's peer back into the yester years—basically look at how the Akans and most ethnic groups in Ghana perceive life and death. In his book titled: 'The Finish Line' this author wrote; "Life was simplified; it was glorified and was personified.

In mythology, life was portrayed as War, a Mirror, an Egg, a Shadow, etc."

Through drama, poetry and storytelling, I learned that life is like a chameleon that changes time and again. It is like a giant species that sets out on an endless journey. It is like a rainbow, it shows up beautifully in the horizon but soon it disappears. And like a beautiful flower or a butterfly it fades away in a fleeting. It is depicted as a naked light in the stormy weather."

The question is who can defy death or escape the yawning jaws of undying death (Bamua Wuo)?

Every king or queen travels to the village when s/he is invited by the Maker: The Man who sanctions life and death. Indeed, when breath flies away the body knoweth not where he goeth. It's a trip often shrouded in secrecy. Their passing is veiled. And the public only gets to know about such transitions sometimes weeks or months some may even morph into years.

On Monday November 14, 2016, the womb that bore the sixteenth occupant of the Asante Golden Stool trudged this mystery path. Asantehemaa Nana Afia Kobi Serwaa Ampem II made her final journey to the village. She was as old as a shock of corn—racking up 109 years.

According to local media reports Otumfuo Osei Tutu II the Asantehene broke the sad news to the Kumasi Traditional Council (KTC) at a meeting. Thereafter Manhyia issued a statement confirming that 'she passed away peacefully at her palace on Monday 14th November, 2016."

The statement also paid a glowing tribute to the 'Obaahemaa' saying: "She has been a pillar of strength and source of wisdom behind the transformational reign of his Majesty Otumfuo Osei Tutu II, Asantehene."

Nana Afia Kobi Serwaa Ampem who reigned as Asantehemaa for 39 years was enstooled in 1977 as the 13th queen mother of the Asante kingdom (which dates back in 1695) after the late Nana Ama Serwaa Nyarko II who reigned from 1945 to 1977.

"Time isn't precious at all, because it is an illusion. What you perceive as precious is not time but the one point that is out of time: the Now. That is precious indeed. The more you are focused on time—past and future—the more you miss the Now, the most precious thing there is"—Eckhart Tolle

Truth is we all pursue time. We focus on the past years and we also look beyond. No doubt this generation pursues time like a tsetse fly chasing a tortoise or a turtle.

But I trust the good old Grandma chose the best time. Obaahemaa will have great time with her Maker. And she'll also spend good time together with her brothers, sisters and the forebears in the ancestral world. It's a world many dread but it's a world one can't pass it on or pass it over. You've got to taste it anyhow.

Damirifa Due Otumfuo,
Damirifa Due Asanteman,
Damirifa Due Adehyeman mma,

Me'ma mo due ne amanehunu.
Nanteyie Obaahemaa, Kwansobrebre!!!

What happens when the Traffic Lights don't work?

The traffic lights at Highway 509 and S. Taylor Way were not working, when I reached the intersection on Monday morning. I didn't see the red lights, I didn't sight the greenlights and I didn't see the yellow lights. I was supposed to make a turn on the left at the crossing. But there was an obstruction.

My first reaction was to make a quick move but I paused. Instinct told me to exercise caution. All of a sudden I'd found myself in a state of confusion and a gridlock.

The orderliness that one often sees at the joint had disappeared. It'd been sacrificed on the altar of negligence. The scene had become chaotic and there was stampede. Motorists were honking everywhere— honking at one another and honking at each other. Insults were flying in the air like missiles. And there was a brawl.

"Insanity' was how a guy on a bike described the scene.

It was like a war zone. Many onlookers stood by to catch a glimpse of the melee.

Nothing seemed to move. Everything appeared to have grounded to a halt. As the minutes ticked the insanity grew stronger and bigger. I had been stuck in my lane. And I'd been gauging the tempo of the traffic in the hope that there would be a way out.

Closely behind me was a pick-up truck driven by a young man probably in his late twenties. From my rear view mirror I could tell the guy was losing his cool or he'd already lost it.

Sure, there was no way for me to maneuver because apart from what gawked me in the face there was also a double engine freight train pulling more than one hundred coaches– crawling like a tortoise on my far left near the intersection. The guy had seen all that but that wouldn't stop him from tooting his horn.

What was he up to or what was he thinking?

Did he want me to grow wings and fly or he thought I was the reason the lights weren't working?

Indeed when traffic lights don't work tempers flare and life goes bonkers. He was raging like fire—screaming his lungs out, revving his engine to emphasise his impatience. If you really want to test a man's patience or character put him at a dysfunction intersection or in a traffic jam. Also if you're dating a gal or guy and you are unsure of what you're bargaining for put the suitor at a malfunction traffic light. His reaction will give you a fair idea of what you've been romanticising.

Character is veiled but like pregnancy its obscurity cannot travel far—it has a time limit.

You would think everyone would be patient and take it slow and be careful when the lights are not working. But don't be fooled. The language there is gibberish. Expect drama galore if someone in the traffic congestion is late especially for his first date. He would blame any mishaps on the malfunctioning of the lights. Not his fault, it's the traffic lights they are to blame.

Of course that seems to be where the problem begins. The lights serve as triggers when they don't work. But they probably might not be the cause of one's rage or nasty behaviour. In most cases it's been found that individuals that indulge in such unruly conduct may be dealing with problems that are remote and may have no correlation with/to the immediate incident.

They could be related to marital or relationships, drugs, alcohol, occupational hazards, insecurity and many more.

It's like hitting a wrong button of some weird machine. The sound would freak you out and you wouldn't even know where the switch off button is located. Beside if one is running late for work, or an interview, a meeting, a party or catching a flight at the airport and he gets caught up either in a jammed traffic or in an intersection the likelihood of witnessing a road rage or chaotic scene is fifty-fifty.

In such instances it would take a person of a proven patience to endure the traffic drill. Fact is even a guy with a modicum of patience would wait, if he is running late for an interview or some important function. On the contrary those with volcanic tempers would erupt at the least provocation or no provocation at all. They wear their anger on the sleeves and they're the reason most accidents occur on our roads.

They might drink and drive or be under the influence of some substance but their sense of judgement, character and patience could help avoid many killings or accidents on our roads. If one makes good judgement by choosing not to drink and drive a soul is saved as soon as that decision is made.

Traffic police can help the situation too. Having them at such vantage points with their lights flickering could deter recalcitrant motorists. I've even seen some individuals (as volunteers) directing traffic when the lights don't work and where danger is deemed imminent.

Caution must be given all the attention it deserves when the lights don't work or when we're caught up in a traffic jam. It should be seen as a watchword and not a bet card to be toyed with. If we are able to do this, be guaranteed many lives would be saved.

Keep in mind it's better to be late at work when circumstances are direr than to be referred to as late so and so as a result of a rush or making a bad decision. Sad thing is when that precious life is wasted it can never be brought back. Therefore, save your soul if you can. Save your life if the accident is avoidable. Do not put the noose around your neck if it's not meant for you.

Remember if you rush you'll crash and if you crash you'll rust.

As I was saying, the guy behind me had an attitude. He was fuming with anger, swearing and cussing. He put his gear into reverse, backed up a little bit. Back to the drive gear and drove passed me. But he wasn't going anywhere farther than 20 metres.

From left to right, north to south cars slammed and rammed at one another as though there had been a volcanic eruption. Some of the cars had been crashed beyond recognition. Sirens of ambulances were heard from afar heading towards the direction of the chaotic scene. The paramedics were stunned by the degree of horror they witnessed.

And the young man I saw in my rear view mirror moments ago, the young man that honked incessantly at me, the energetic young man who probably was racing to go to work had had his journey cut short. He couldn't make it at/to his destination. He'd died young!

Was his death inevitable?

Was he destined to walk that path? Or was it negligence and impatience?

The in-dwelt-being (The Spirit) wails whenever the body that carries him makes a folly decision.

HATE SPEECH: How BNI Doused the Blaze

Bureau of National Investigations (BNI) earned my biggest applause when the operatives raided a radio station in the northern part of Ghana for airing hate speech. But how does the Bureau's proactive action relate to the story below:

A man and his son lived up on a hill near Think– a backcountry town notoriously known for setting up wild fires. The distance between the two neighbours was approximately two miles. Two rivers separate them. On Sunday June 2, 2000, the town as usual set another fire. But this one was different. Its flames had soared in just two minutes, proving too stubborn to be doused.

It seemed the end of Think was inevitable. Residents looked more than terrified. Fear had engulfed the town. The fire had shown its desire to ravage. And the aged were seen hobbling on the ground like airplanes. In the midst of the flames the people cried for help. *Where's help the residents wondered.* Their neighbours on Hilltop had warned Think several times not to play with fire but they ignored the warnings.

How did they deal with the situation?

At times we pretend we don't know what's going on around us. We act like the proverbial ostrich, sink our heads in the sand while our whole frame is exposed to the pleasing eye of the enemy. Ironically, even in that posture we still think we're covered and protected. We tend to gloss over that which could put our lives in danger. Perhaps, if we'd paid heed to the warnings from the get go we could have prevented the mishap.

Hate has weight but many people don't realise that. The rampant fires at Think were borne out of hate. The small town had harboured hate for years. Its people never got along. There was family feud. There was religious feud and there was tribal feud. Residents were seen always at each other's throat trying to settle scores.

How BNI Doused the Blaze

It was a father and son's timely intervention that saved Think from burning into ashes. And BNI last Friday acted in that similar fashion to douse a potential fire that was brewing in the northern part of Ghana. Media analysts believe but for the BNI's proactive action perhaps the story would have been different.

Must we be concern why not? We've seen it happened all around us. And it's all around the globe. I'm pretty sure we haven't forgotten the Rwanda story (a radio station was alleged to have aired hate speech) which triggered the genocide in the nations of the Great Lakes region. Don't forget trailblazers blaze while traitors daze. They're always looking for conflicts and rifts.

The media in Ghana reported that the security operatives raided a radio station in the Northern region and held its workers for several hours over hate speech. According to the reports the agents stormed Zaa radio, a station frequently accused of promoting hate speech and 'fanning' religious discord, when some senior scholars of the Ambariyya community on the regular Friday segment attacked and insulted leader of the Masjid Bayan Sunni sect, Shaeik Ibrahim Baasha.

"The scholars on the live broadcast show, speaker after speakers, raged against Sheik Bayan and levelled at him wild allegations including being envy and responsible for the prolonged ailment of their Supreme father, Sheik Seidu," one of the reports stated.

The tape recorded in fierce rage, deep vindictiveness and full of belligerent rhetoric was calling true Muslims to converge at a ground near the Tamale Kaladan Park to listen to a ministry broadcast and sermon where treachery, hypocrisy and rascality would be exhibited in words, the reports said.

It is also reported that the short audio received over a dozen shares in the first minute of its broadcast on WhatsApp and other social media tools and left the city of 'majority Sunni believers tensed and frail.'

Online dictionary defines hate speech as one which attacks a person or group on the basis of attributes such as race, religion or faith ethnic origin, sexual orientation, gender or disability. The term or phrase vary in meaning in different countries by law.. Some countries describe hate as speech, gesture or conduct, writing or display which is forbidden because it incites violence or prejudicial action against or by a protected group or individual on the basis of their membership of the group, or because it disparages or intimidates a protected group or individuals on the basis of their membership of the group.

The International Convenant on Civil and Political Rights (CCPR) states that 'any advocacy of national, racial or religious hatred that constitutes incitement to discrimination, hostility or violence shall be prohibited by law.

Ghana's 1992 Constitution Act 2003 section 12(2) under the criminal code states: "Every person in Ghana whatever his race, place of origin, political opinion, colour religion creed or gender shall be entitled to the fundamental human rights and freedom of the individual contained in the chapter but subject to respect of the rights and freedoms of others and for public interest."

Following the raid the BNI interrogated authorities of the station and some controversial staff including host of the disputed Friday Show. The operatives also seized a recording of the sermon while some armed personnel were left behind to watch over the station after arson threats were heard.

The latest incident isn't the station's first. Zaa radio, the reports said is known to security services in the region. In 2012, it was attacked in a suspected reprisal after violent clashes between the Ahli-Sunna and Tijanniya sects at another radio station over 'varied interpretations of a sura in the Holy Quran'.

Meanwhile the Northern Regional Minister and Chairman of the Security Council Salifu Saeed has appealed for calm in Tamale. His appeal came a day after the BNI raid. The minister said he was saddened by the development in the region.

"It saddens my heart to see how some people are blocking away developments of the region by always attempting to resolve grievances through violent attacks and destabilizing security. To make hate speech and create or spark personal disputes a subject of an Islamic sermon is needless," he said.

MINORITY NDC BINS BNI

The Minority NDC in Ghana's Parliament has literally thrown the state security agency the BNI into the dust-bin. They're disappointed in the intelligence body on its findings about the 'Contaminated Fuel' saga, amid accusation of complicity.

I dare ask: Was it not the Minority group that called for the investigation?

How quickly did Mr. Smarty become MR. Wimpy and what's the rationale behind the latest fuse? Does the Minority NDC really have a case?

Yours truly examines the enigma

TROUBLING is my word of the day. And I'm using it here as an adjective— to describe the way I feel about the ongoing 'Contaminated Fuel' story. About how I feel we've let honesty and integrity out of the eastern window at the expense of partisanship and money. Truth be told, the minority knows it'd have done the same thing or did it when the NDC was in power. The paradox is that they saw no wrong at the time. Needless to remind them (both heavyweights) of this beautiful line from the scripture: "Whosoever digs a pit will fall into it and a stone will come back on him who starts it rolling," Proverbs 26::27.

I've said it before and I will say it again: It isn't about the NDC and it isn't the NPP it's about Ghana. So let's be mindful about whatever we do today. The irony is the NPP would have done the same thing or possibly double down what its counterparts are doing now. And they would probably accuse the NDC of being corrupt and perhaps call the BNI's findings as travesty. Indeed this is an old chestnut in Ghana's political history.

However, one cannot merge into the highway without asking these distressing questions: When would this political nonsense end? Someone jokingly told me till the Parousia—the second coming of our Lord.

How could it be stopped? Maybe not until we've a new brigade of 'saints' in the helm of affairs albeit born by these same politicians. Don't get me wrong I know there're good ones amongst them but it appears whenever they (the good ones) push the right button the weasels press the wrong one. So, it has more or less become an endless cycle but where does it stop? It stops at the Flagstaff House but it would require a concerted effort. All of us must see corruption as a bad practice and not something to be glamorised.

Again it's troubling to see how politicians sometimes don't seem to get it when it's simply as it is. How as a people we fail to understand the stubborn fact that no condition is permanent and how we've suddenly failed or seemed to have lost it in the highway to our destination—a' Prosperous Ghana'.

If the headline is true: 'BNI Clears Alfred Obeng Boateng, BOST Managing Director' then my question is: What's causing this much noise again?

Have we as a people lost trust in the institutions we entrusted to work for us? Or we are just crying foul because like mobsters there must be justification for our madcap behaviour? Is it because the verdict didn't go our way? Must the BNI always find individuals and corporations guilty of an alleged wrong doing? And wouldn't our actions seek to undermine the state institutions in that regard if we continue to harass them?

I looked up the phrase 'cleared of charges' online. It means escape without penalty or escape punishment. Other synonyms include: find not guilty, get away with, go scot-free, receive no guilty verdict, and walk.

And here's where the partisanship begins. For example if you support the BOST MD Mr. Boateng you might now understand why the NDC minority is griping and are dissatisfied about the BNI's findings. And if you belong to the other side you'd cheekily ask this question: Why is the minority fighting over spilt milk?

But does being cleared of charges of allegation totally mean being exonerated of all wrong doing? Can't someone file a civil suit against BOST and its directors including the MD? That remains to be observed.

And this is how the story goes; The Bureau of National Investigations (BNI) and the National Security have cleared the Managing Director of the Bulk Oil Storage and Transportation (BOST) Company Limited, Alfred Obeng Boateng, of any wrongdoing in the sale of 5 million litres of contaminated fuel, a document sighted by Kasapafmonline.com has revealed.

This follows investigations conducted by the two state security agencies into the controversial sale of the contaminated fuel to Movenpiina Company Limited.

According to the Accra-based radio station it 'intercepted 'the report that literally said you're free to go. Here are some aspects of the facts as captured in the said report:

- The product contamination occurred on January 18, 2017 and the MD for BOST assumed office on January 23, 2017 and cannot be held responsible for it.
- As a competent MD, he interdicted the officers involved and set up a six-member committee chaired by the Head of Internal Audit Department, Mr. Edmund Aquah on February 8, 2017 to find out the causes of the contamination.
- The MD has received a draft copy of the committee's report waiting for the final report on July 7, 2017.

- A laboratory test from TOR and technical recommendation made by the General Manager, Fred Ayarkwa indicated that out of the options available, selling the product for industrial purposes such as asphalt processing, texture and cement manufacturing was the best. This option was recommended to the MD because TOR is not refining currently and the laboratory result clearly stated that treating it would not give the required quality of AGO (Diesel).
- Among the fifteen companies that expressed interest, Movenpiina price was the highest. Its initial price was GHS 0.90 per liter as the highest followed by Nation Links Oil which quoted GHS 0.80 per liter. Despite these quotations, BOST pushed Movenpiina to pay GHS1.30 per liter which is the highest BOST has ever sold contamination products. The highest that was sold under the previous administration headed by Kwame Awuah Darko was GHS 1.00 per liter.

The report in part further stated that per the company law, a company can transact business before incorporation which is referred to as pre-incorporation activities which is subject to ratification by the Board of Directors of the company.

It was also established that the private office of the BOST MD is at the Airport Residential Area whilst Movenpiina registered address is at East Legon with its operational office located at Awudomi. The telephone numbers of the company, according to the report, is different from that of the BOST MD.

It noted that Mr. Alfred Obeng Boateng is neither a Director nor a shareholder of Movenpiina according to documents at the Registrar General's Department, hence, "could not see any link between BOST MD and Movenpiina. Further findings of the security agencies also revealed that the National Petroleum Authority (NPA) has never licensed a single company or entity dealing in waste petroleum product in Ghana.

The report further revealed that between 2014 and 2016 under NDC, BOST sold contaminated products to more than 50 companies at the full glare of NPA officials but no red flag was ever raised. It said the new management followed the same convention and practice and has therefore not erred.

Per the latest status of the findings the report is expected to be submitted to the Minister of Energy Boakye Agyarko and upon receipt he would address the media to set the records straight, yours truly has learned.

As the BNI report glides to the energy minister's office (he must have had it by now) the minority on the other hand yesterday organised a press conference in Accra for the media to know its next line of action.

"We are being told that the Bureau of National Investigations (BNI), otherwise known as the BNI, is acting in a manner that we don't only smell but we can sense a cover-up in respect of the matter of the selling of the contaminated oil by BOST which matter borders on fraud, corruption and abuse of office," Minority Leader Haruna Iddrisu said.

Mr. Iddrisu said the request by the BNI for dissolution of an investigative committee set up by the Ministry of Energy following their report amounts to only what he described as a 'gargantuan cover-up'.

"The BNI is sowing seeds of corruption in the country" and "preventing sunshine on matters that are of public interest. The mere selling of contaminated oil matter to motorists and to the extent that the National Petroleum Authority (NPA) was not aware and Movenpiina Company Limited was unlicensed at the time also raises major issues."

In the meantime the minority has called on BNI to make public what they investigated. And I tend to support their call. I think the energy ministry must go ahead with its investigation. The outcome of which could be compared with the BNI's report. And I am hopeful a clearance from the ministry would put the case to rest. But anything short of that would recalibrate the tempo.

The Fallout of Contaminated Fuel: Government Contracts

How political party contributions are influencing government contract s in Ghana. Must contracts be given to whom you know or to the party that has the technical know-how and the money? What's the way forward?

Last week the Ghanaian pubic woke up to find their traditional media inundated with the 'Contaminated Fuel' story. The spectacle was much the same with the Social Media. It was followed by public outcry and the familiar blame game. The NDC Minority in Parliament had called for an immediate investigation into the alleged sale of the contaminated oil to Movenpiina Energy by Alfred Obeng Boakye the MD for Bulk Oil Storage Transport (BOST). The minority group also called for the MD's interdiction.

In less than 48 hours after the Minority's press conference the Minister of Energy Boakye Agarko set up an eight-member committee to investigate into the circumstances that precipitated the sale of the dirtied oil. And like dominos, one reaction led to another and another. The acting Chief Executive Officer of the National Petroleum Authority (NPA) Alhassan Tampilu dropped the hint that Movenpiina and Zup Oil the two companies that purchased the over 5 million litres of contaminated fuel would likely face sanctions. Beyond that NPA legal team will pursue the companies and investigations will be carried out.

It's understood both companies are not licensed to undertake any commercial activity in the downstream petroleum industry. This presupposes that their activities infringe on section 11 of the NPA Act 691, 2005. But why did they do it? Did the BOST Boss know about their status at the time?

"There's a standard sanctions which are known to everybody in the industry. For every trivial activity that they engage in they pay GHc 10, 500 approximately US$5, 000," Mr. Tampuli said.

Since the big story broke out sides had been taken amid lamentation and aspersion. My own write-up on the subject was somehow critiqued. I was reminded that during the NDC administration contaminated fuel was transacted therefore the latest case isn't a big deal. Well let's remind ourselves that what's wrong is wrong. And there's no need to double down what's deemed corruptible. Remember, it isn't about the NPP or the NDC it's about Ghana and its people. It's about the average Ghanaian who has been left impoverished, disadvantaged and underprivileged in spite of the country's huge mineral resources.

And I think while we are debating the debate and looking into the current subject, I suggest all previous transactions made by BOST retrospectively (since Ghana lifted its first oil) must be open for onward investigations.

Indeed, the latest contaminated fuel is a subject that touches political nerves especially the minority NDC and the majority NPP. And as journalists, analysts, bloggers and experts weigh into the issue; party supporters, surrogates as well as foot soldiers haven't been left out in the ongoing debate.

A leading member of OccupyGhana, a pressure group Sydney Casely-Hayford has charged Parliament to haul before it the governing board of BOST to answer some questions among them: Why BOST sold contaminated fuel to some companies without National Petroleum Authority (NPA) licence.

But perhaps what stuck with me most in the wake of the controversial story was the submission made by Kennedy Agyapong Member of Parliament (MP) for Assin North in the Central region during a radio interview. Mr. Agyapong spoke passionately about the subject and one could sense the palpable emotions in his tone as he made his case known to the public. He alleged there's huge collusion and fraud in the past sales of contaminated fuels. It's believed about 38 companies in 2015 purchased contaminated oil from BOST under similar circumstances.

"All the fuels said to be contaminated in the past are done deliberately and I have documents to prove that,' he claimed.

Who should get what as part of party contributions?

Much of Mr. Agyapong's submission focused on the sacrifices and contributions some of the party members had made towards the growth of the party. The apparent sideling of the party's chief contributors by the leadership seemed to be a grave concern for the Assin North legislator. He bemoaned the practice and warned that the NPP risk losing power in 2020, if the leadership didn't change their attitude.

Without a doubt, I get his argument: "Hwan na enhuhu na obi enkeka."

How can you cut the hand that feeds the mouth? Why would you give contracts to individuals who are supposedly NDC card bearers and leave those whose finances and contributions helped put NPP at the top rung of the ladder? And I think that would amount to what one might view as spite in the face if it turns out they (the contributors) perhaps have the requisite qualification but are not considered.

It's against this backdrop that I think the country must relook its political party campaign financing system.

What's the way forward?

In the 2008 United States presidential election fundraising increased significantly compared to the levels achieved in the previous presidential elections, according Federal Election Commission (FEC). President Barack Obama then democratic candidate raised 778, 642, and 962 and spent $760, 370,195. His republican counterpart Senator John McCain also raised 383, 913, and 384. And out of that amount he spent $358,008,447. Most of Obama's contributions came from the grassroots.

Unfortunately our system is allergic to transparency. Everything is done in secrecy and no one knows who is funding who, how much he's contributing and what's the source of the financier's contributions? I even doubt whether the Electoral Commission—the nation's electoral body has knowledge of how much for example the two major political parties the NPP and NDC raised in the 2016 presidential election. This and other factors have conspired against our quest to have a corruption free government over the years.

Political party funding are the methods that a political party uses to raise money for campaign and routine activities. This is internationally known as political finance. But it is called campaign finance in the United States.

No political party in the world can survive without funding. Much as vehicles need fuel to function so do political parties need funding to be able to operate effectively. In Ghana and elsewhere political parties are funded by contributions from party members and individual supporters (via membership fees/ dues/ subscriptions and or small donations. Also organizations, which share their political views, make contributions too. But the role of money in politics in recent times has possibly become the biggest threat to democracy.

Many governments today have become corrupt because most of their political campaigns had been funded through drug monies, and huge corporations that indulge in money laundering etc. In fact when it comes to corruption in political campaign funding one cannot even exempt the United States, arguably the best democracy in the world. And as we (Africa and for that matter Ghana) continue to monetize our political campaigns let's not forget that we're equally breeding another brat—corruption.

It's a huge challenge that confronts both matured and burgeoning democracies and it's my hope that there will come a time that sanity will prevail in our political campaigns and monetization will not become a yardstick or political barometer.

BOOTY SHARING: A Bleeding Economy

Ghana is bleeding from the nose daily, while politicians continue to pillage her and even think Ghanaians have a 'weak mind'.

One wonders where they get their monies from.

"Back off Mr. Journalist, this isn't your business," I was told.

Really, whose is it then?

The work of a journalist seems taboo to corridors of power. He's often branded perfidious and an enemy to the oligarchs (the rich few that wield power). Cocooned in their ill-gotten wealth they wish tomorrow never comes and there's never a power-shift, oblivious of the fact that the sun shines but not every day.

Well it's my duty to hold the executive, the judiciary and the legislature accountable. That they stay the course as trustees and remain answerable to the people. I'm the fourth estate of the realm and I'm duty-bound to serve as a watchdog.

Didn't you know that my pen is mightier than the 'Sharp Teeth Babies'?

If you still don't understand why I'm here and what I'm here for. Mission is straight forward. It's to inform, educate and entertain the people.

What are you angst about?

I'm worried about the spectacle— politicians (government officials) carrying bundles of money displayed in public and doled out to prospective voters as though they're magicians. The frequency and the urgency at which this monetisation thing is being executed amid the nerve that goes with it gives me shivers every day.

So if you think that's okay then don't waste my precious time. Can't or don't you see how bad the economy is—bleeding profusely by the day?

Tell me, how does it sit with you to see politicians dole out wads of monies almost every day, especially during electioneering period to people in the streets? How much is the salary of a cabinet minister, or a minister of state or a legislator/parliamentarian?

By the way my checks revealed their monthly salaries are in the region of GHc 8,000 to 10,000 (approximately US$ 5,000).

What's the market value of a 2016 Range Rover/Land Rover Sport, the V6/V8 debuts? The price range is between $64, 950 to $111,350. And please do me a favour find out from the estate developers: What's an estimated value of a three and four-bedroom house?

You know what, never mind all the hustles. Just save yourself the time and energy to find out the locations of these plush homes fitted with Jacuzzis, saunas and mega swimming pools. But find out how many of them have their children or wards in schools, colleges and universities here in Ghana and abroad. And you may find out many of the so and so they're sponsoring outside either for studies, business or otherwise.

Again, find out how many of them own petrol/gas filling stations across the country: How many of them have swine, poultry, and fish, citrus and cattle farms? How did they also acquire these assets—assets like outboard motors, articulated or semi-trucks, fuel tankers, and lands from Axim to Zabzugutatale? Furthermore, find out how they acquired the yachts and the pontoons, the pubs and the bars, the timber and the mining concessions?

Finally, find out if they'd declared all these assets to the state.

I bet you'd like this too: Do you know why inflation is jumping like kids on trampoline? Have you asked the Member of Parliament (MP) in your constituency why your area lacks portable water, proper sanitation and stable power and not the flip-flop power? Find out why 'Dumsor' is still with us even though a minister had to resign over its stubborn existence.

How come teachers, judges and nurses are agitating for salary increments?

I thought I was done with the laundry list but not yet.

Find out why NHIS is in comatose? Why you cannot afford to put food on the kitchen table as required? Find out what's wrong with our politicians? I beseech you to find out why they are looting our country and plundering her into darkness.

Do yourself a great service. Rather than asking me to back off from what I'm professionally trained to do: Stop being a panhandler, stop being a bootlicker, stop being a fair-weather friend, because you're part of the reason politicians continue to be who they are. Are they magicians or Father Christmas/Santa? They've to be one, if indeed they owe all that.

But why must Ghana bleed?

Ghana is endowed with minerals such as gold, manganese, bauxite, diamond etc. In April 2011 the country lifted its first crude oil of 992,259 barrels representing $112million from the Jubilee Fields at Cape Three Point in the western region. She's now known globally as an oil-producing nation.

Besides, Ghana has cocoa, timber, and cashew and she exports other agricultural products. Nonetheless, it's found herself in a big economic cesspool over the last five or eight years. She'd had to run to the IMF and other Bretton wood institutions to borrow (amid the sorrow) to survive the economic turbulence yet she's still wobbling down the turf.

The country's inflation has stayed in double-digits since this administration took the reins of power. Yes, we've seen infrastructural development like roads, hospitals and schools and the recently-commissioned beautiful Kwame Nkrumah Interchange in Circle, Accra. Yet the average Ghanaian is feeling the pinch. The average Ghanaian is hurting inside. It's like pulling a hair with a tweezer from the nose. Yikes!

Now, need I remind you of what President Mahama said eight years ago when he served as the vice president in the Mills-administration, 2008?

"If you vote for someone because of schools, hospitals, roads and interchanges, you have a weak mind because it is government's responsibility," Mr. Mahama said.

A 'Weak Mind,' you know what that means right?

On line Oxford Dictionary defines a weak mind or weak-minded person as one lacking determination, emotional strength or intellectual capacity. Merriam-Webster Learner's dictionary defines a weak-minded person as one having or showing a lack of mental firmness. Also, the phrase a weak mind has synonyms such as foolish, simple, feeble-minded, witless, mindless, brainless, stupid and idiotic.

At the time (during the '08 campaign season) Mr. Mahama even ridiculed the opposition New Patriotic Party (NPP) for providing social amenities and other viable infrastructural development. And this is what he said: "For the NPP to tell us they have constructed roads, hospitals, schools and other projects is an exercise in mediocrity. Every government does these."

Wasn't he (the Prez.) right about that? Yes perhaps, he was.

If so, why the pomp and the hype about the projects his administration has executed? Why did the president put his foot into his own mouth? I thought the NDC already knew that it's every government's responsibility to provide its people such projects. So why all the Dubai this and Dubai that?

Don't the people of Ghana deserve better after all the wanton loots and opulence displayed by these oligarchs?

The Ghana Revenue Authority

Indeed there has to be a way to stop or minimize this canker.

A lecturer at the Central University of Ghana, Kobina Feyinka says, perhaps the Ghana Revenue Authority (GRA) and the Registrar General's Department could be of help in solving the problem. He said the authority which is the government of Ghana agency is responsible for overall oversight of the entire taxation agency in Ghana.

GRA was established in 2009 as a merger of the Internal Revenue Service (IRS), Customs Excise and Preventive Service (CEPS), Value Added Tax Service (VATS\ and the Revenue Agencies Governing Board (RAGB) Secretariat.

He said it won't be easy to eradicate this from the system. "This will be a daunting exercise but we need to start from somewhere. I know with modicum effort it can be done, the leakage is too much. So let's first push the agenda and see if they will buy into it,' he suggested.

Meanwhile, I'm compelled by popular request to serve readers on modernghana.com and ghanawe.com websites on Friday November 18, my September 12 article titled: *'Was it Mother of all Lectures?'* It was a lecture delivered by the NPP vice presidential candidate Dr.

Mahamudu Bawumia, 'The State of Ghana's Economy—A Foundation of Concrete or Straw?

I urged members of the ruling NDC to come out to challenge Dr. Bawumia's claims that Ghana's economy was in shambles but nobody after two months of that profound public lecture has taken the bait.

Mugabe's Diary: How it ended up in my Ghetto

"In Africa the only warning they take seriously is Low Battery"— Robert Mugabe

I first learned it was kept in Santa's grotto. I'd asked the white-bearded man to lend me the maverick's diary but he refused to do so. Why would he lend out something he considered a trove? He wouldn't trade it for anything because of the name associated with it, Robert Mugabe.

You know mosquitoes don't like to be at water fronts. The breeze makes them uncomfortable plus they feel edgy. They're tiny and the wind is too strong for their wings. Yet it's a fertile ground for breeding.

There's gulf between them and comfort. If their eggs happened to be laid near the beach they're hatched within 24 to 48 hours and carried miles away by the unfriendly waft. They're dispersed like seeds of wheat and could land on anybody's closet, desk or anywhere at the weather's choosing.

Of course the world knows Robert Mugabe as President of Zimbabwe. The world knows him as a dictator, power-drunk and a stubborn cat. The world knows Mr. Mugabe as one of the longest-serving leaders in Africa who has ruled the southern African nation for more than three decades.

Indeed, Mr. Mugabe who will turn 93 years old on Tuesday February 21 2017 is perhaps not going anywhere until death invites him. That I can guarantee. And none of that surprises me, they're no longer newsworthy.

But lately, Zimbabwe's first gentleman has found himself plying into other professions. He's become a poet, motivational speaker, and an activist. Uncle Bob has become a marriage counselor, witch doctor, hair stylist, high priest, match commissioner (or a referee), sex therapist, a masseur, chef, carpenter, bus conductor, football coach you name it.

Truly, he's become Jack of all trades... The irony is that unlike the proverbial Jack Mr. Mugabe has mastered all the trades above mentioned and he's still venturing into other disciplines deemed tough and rugged. So, how did the world not know that the Zimbabwe powerful man is versatile and not a stubborn cat or an autocrat?

How did the world not know that he's not only a president but also a plumber? How did the world not know that he's a mediator (when it comes to relationships) and not a dictator?

I'm still wondering and pondering how did all that go unnoticed?

Yes, the world didn't know!

My architect told me this: When Judas is around no one takes responsibility for a crime. After all he's a known betrayer and a good kisser. He takes responsibility for no rains, no shelter, and no food. When Judas is around he's blamed for all manner of crimes be it murder, robbery, perjury, arson, treason, terrorism etc.

When Judas is around all statements are attributed to him—spoken or unspoken, written or unwritten. All sort of quotes and weird sayings end up in his big basket. The quotes are dispersed across the world just like seeds of wheat. They're transmitted or forwarded on the back of social media (WhatsApp is the biggest carrier).

The quotes are hashed and rehashed, tweaked and re-tweaked, forwarded and re-forwarded. The cycle goes on unabated. And who do they give credit to? It's none other than President Robert Mugabe of Zimbabwe. It appears he's the manufacturer of most of these side-splitting quotes. Evidently, he's not the author of any of these quotes, yet they're attributed to him.

Here are a few examples: The first quote (a rhetorical question) cast the Zimbabwean president as an activist and a motivational speaker:

"How do you convince the upcoming generation that education is the key to success when we are surrounded by poor graduates and rich criminals?"

"Don't call your girlfriend an angel because there are no females among the angels." That presents Mugabe as a Priest.

"Stop praying to God to bless your relationship rather, pray to him to bless all your boyfriends. That way you'd have a backup, if the first relationship fails." That's Mugabe the counselor or adviser.

The following quote casts him as hair stylist. "African women would be afraid to go to Brazil for the World Cup because they might meet the owner of their artificial hair.'

"Sometimes you look back at girls you spent monies on and you go like ugh. You wished you'd rather sent them to your mum. There you realise witchcraft is real." That's Robert Mugabe as witch doctor.

And I bet you would like this: "When they move from Europe to Africa they're viewed as voyages of discovery. When we move from Africa to Europe, we're called illegal immigrants."

There are also short sayings believed to have come from the eccentric leader.

A group of Africans in Europe or America are called refugees.

A group of Europeans and Americans in Africa are called tourists.

A group of Africans in the bush are called poachers while a group of Europeans in the bush are referred to as hunters.

Black people working in a foreign country are known as foreigners. White people working in a foreign country are called expatriates. And he winds up with this: "This world has failed Africans."

At times Mr. Mugabe uses sarcasm to put his supposed messages across. I've two here to share with you: "Africans have no time to rest, even after dying they have to work as ancestors."

"Though sometimes democracy is good, it should never be left at the whim of the people. People have an unquenchable affinity for wild options. They were once asked by Pontius Pilate: Do you want Jesus or Barabbas? And all said Barabbas. Now it's Trump."

Okay I've been reminded to add a third: "Donald Trump is winning in the US presidential election–and this is all Barack Obama's fault for not seeking a third term like a true African leader."

"Excuse me, where did you get all those quotes from and who said that I Robert Mugabe, a Kutama native is responsible for them?'

Sir, they're all over the cyber space, spreading like mosquitoes—breeding by the day and putting smiles on faces. Great thing is I think whether you're the source of these quotes or not the world is having a good laugh. Everyone seems to be enjoying them.

"Where did you say you're from?"

I'm from Ghana your Excellency.

"O Ghana that's where I met my first wife Sally. I taught at St Mary's Secondary at Apowa in Takoradi. Yes I was a teacher there."

Really, I didn't know that. Awesome!

Any fond memories and did you like it there?

"Of course, I did. Ghana is a lively place and the people are beautiful and friendly. Back then your first President Dr. Kwame Nkrumah had plans to make the city one of the most beautiful places in Africa. And from nowhere that small boy emerged. What's his name?"

I think you're talking about Afrifa.

"That's right. Thank you. Where is he now?

See…small boys are young. He allowed the westerners to use him to achieve what they badly wanted. That's one of the reasons why, I am not ceding power to any of my kinsmen. I don't trust them and they cannot be trusted. They would betray you and betray the nation."

Mr. Mugabe I cannot let you go without asking you this question. It seems the whole world wants to know when you are leaving office. What's your plan?

"Well, did I hear you mentioned it somewhere in your piece? I think you've divulged my unspoken wish. I'm staying put. Till death they say…"

The Two 'Angels': NDC & NPP

Where are they taking Ghanaians to?

A look into the unknown journey:

I wish I can take a journey into the minds of these two political parties. And I wish all the firecracker mouths thereof were pushed over and left to rot. Surely there are good people in both sides of the political divide. But for some reason the leadership in both parties have remained mum and allowed the brats to continue with their despicable acts.

When the tempest gets high peace and safety take cover lest they'd bear its brunt. Lately, I've been gauging the political temperature of our beloved Ghana and it appears we are taking things for granted. We seem to think that our peace is solidly encrypted and it would be impossible for anyone to decode it or wreak havoc upon us.

I touch wood. But I dare say we aren't as solid as a rock and therefore we shouldn't be smug or better still behave like the well-known ostrich. It might look pretty for some of you from where you perch. But not everyone feels the same way. Not everyone is comfortable with the way the big bus is being driven. I hope you aren't acting like the bird that told the climbing plant: "I can't be bothered."

Well, little did he know that even from that elevation on the borough of the tree he wasn't safe: How did he not know that an angry gun discriminates not?

xxxxxxx

It seems the force behind this rising temperature is politics. And I put the blame squarely on the two major political parties—the ruling NDC and the majority opposition NPP. They're the prime movers. Both parties have a large following across the country and their actions or inactions, covert or overt operations can have significant impact on us either in negative or positive way.

Is this a new phenomenon? No, we've been witnessing this trend every four years (amid tension growing like a mountain) since the inception of the Fourth Republic. Good thing is we've some stakeholders and institutions that haven't gone to sleep like the lazy koala (which sleeps for 18-22 hrs. a day) or the sloth.

Over the years and now, the National Peace Council, civil society groups, the Christian Council, traditional rulers and other religious bodies, celebrities, and eminent individuals such as Busumuru Kofi Annan (former UN Secretary General) have been working so hard to ensure that we don't lose this precious child. This child we so adore and admire.

Sure, Goodness knows where we'd have been if the peace message hadn't been preached. Perhaps, but for their interventions over the years we could have had our paths littered with grief and sorrow or had a descent into the quagmire our neighbouring countries had experienced in the past.

Again, as I aforesaid it is all politicians fault. They're responsible for stoking the fire and riling up their teaming supporters, foot-soldiers, macho men and the likes. Their proclivity for raising the political tempo has been criticised time and again, yet they do it: 'A' to satisfy their political egos and 'B' consolidate power, which often they fear to lose.

Truth is our forebears had been known to be peace-loving and it is our turn to ensure that we keep the tradition going—to uphold, to protect and to safeguard this peace. Sometimes the writings look big on the wall yet they cause no harm and sometimes the writings might look small but they can be deadly, which is why we must not be complacent or else we would be fooled by the fools.

Consider this: How could an activity dubbed 'A Health or Victory Walk' of which the president was billed to take part turned into violent?

The Sunday November 13, 'Nima-Clash' between supporters of the NDC and the NPP at the residence of Nana Akufo Addo, the flagbearer of the Elephant in the 2016 elections mirrors the small letterings. I doubt if anybody saw it coming, unless it was masterminded by evil hands: The hands that are enemies to peace and safety.

I didn't even know whose report was authentic. It seemed everything got warped up in the wake of the clash. Supporters of the two 'Angels' flooded two of the WhatsApp platforms I share with them. NDC supporters blamed the NPP and vice versa. It was more than likely that everyone had jaundiced eyes. I figured out.

So now you see how violence develops when caution is ignored. I've no interest in doing postmortem or giving accounts as to what occurred over the weekend. The question is: How do we ensure that this unfortunate incident doesn't recur?

I said evil hands, it reminds me of 'Kumepreko' the mega demo organized by the opposition parties in 1995 that sought to resist the introduction of Value Added Tax (VAT) which had been pegged at 15 percent by the NDC government. During that peaceful procession violence erupted. Supporters of the ruling government 'strayed' (it was deliberate) into the approved route earmarked for the opposition group.

As a reporter then writing for now-defunct 'The Ghanaian Periscope', we intercepted a letter from the police at the MTTU in Accra Central which had asked the marchers of the government side to disrupt the opposition's procession. Be reminded the said notice had been given to the police at the eleventh hour by the evil hands. In the process a young boy was gunned down. Guns were drawn everywhere as the unarmed marchers had to run for their lives. Lives they weren't sure if they could save in the face of the chaotic scene.

So we can blame politicians for these troubles but the police and certain institutions are also to be blamed. The police in many times had been found culpable for wrongdoing, aiding and abetting these worrisome acts. And whenever the public loses its trust in the law enforcement agencies the upshot is ugly.

In the case of the 'Nima-Clash' one would ask the following questions:

Did the police approve the NPP presidential nominee's area as the route for the victory walk?

I thought the NDC have labeled him (Nana Akufo Addo) as a 'violent' person. So who walks into a lion's den?

How would a handful of men step out from their comfort zone (residence) to attack an irate mob (in their hundreds) is that logical?

Have the marchers been using this route prior to this incident, if no why now?

A Professor of Communication Studies at Montgomery College in Maryland believes the Sunday morning incident could have been avoided if precautionary measures had been taken. Prof. Ekow Akyeampong who spoke with this writer on phone on Monday night said: "You don't throw dice when tensions are high especially with a few weeks to go for the general elections. I think it would have been logical for them to avoid that route until the elections are over."

He suggested the America's example is the way to go: "Trump Tower is a popular tourist spot. In the weeks leading up to the election Trump Tower was closed to the public."

Indeed I still maintain that caution was ignored big time. The writings were visible on the wall yet they chose to racketeer the wheels of the wagon in the hope that it couldn't get back on the road.

The wagon is back on track looking more energised than ever. He'd this message for his detractors: "We'll resist Mahama and his army," said Nana Akufo Addo.

Meanwhile the NPP has condemned the attacks that occurred at the residence of the party's presidential candidate at Nima in Accra and also called on the ruling NDC to do the same. The National Peace Council has towed similar line.

"It must be condemned. It is condemnable to pelt the residence of a prominent individual with stones said Professor Emmanuel Asante chairman of National Peace Council. In a related development the Ghana Police Service says it will beef up security presence at the residence of the NPP's flagbearer.

I must say my soul sobs and my heart bleeds when I see people toy with peace. My ears tingle and my eyes well up when I witness a crowd go bananas, burn and loot. My knees wobble and my whole frame quiver when I see carnage or anything that resembles madness. And still lost in my little world I ask myself: Who does that?

Why does peace seem repulsive to some people?

Aren't we lucky to have this air of tranquil blowing across our shores?

The Messenger

Good night and good luck America!

I bring you good tidings—'Virtuous Woman'.

I commend you for a good job done. You fought a good fight. You showed resilience and you lived with it. You gave your all to break the glass ceiling and I promise you'll get good result. Good things come to good people as good people earn good stuff. Woman, your food was good and everyone in the hood asked for more.

I 'ain't saying goodbye until the die is cast.

Good morning America, good to see you brimming with good smiles. Good to know you're ready to do your good deeds. I met the 'Good Samaritan' on my way to the Cape of Good Hope. He was in his good self and he asked me what was good. I told him the Good and the Virtuous Woman was having a good good run. Woman you've always been good to me…And I' ain't saying goodbye until the die is cast.

Good afternoon America, you know what time is it. Don't wait till dusk. Don't fret because it's wet. Make it a duty today to do what's good, for one good turn deserves another. And what's good for the goose is also good for the gander. Don't forget to cast your net wider, you'll surely catch a good fish. Time isn't on your side so don't wait, for the hour is here. Don't listen to the crook head down to the water and cast your net.

I 'ain't saying goodbye until the die is cast.

Good evening America. I bet you never thought this day would come. I doubt if you'd a wind of its advent. I'm unsure if you ever dreamt to see, to witness, and to give account of this good day as good people from all walks of life gather together in anticipation of what to come. Good is Good. Good isn't a liar. And when Good says he'd triumph over evil you've to believe him. Just dare him to do his good things.

Remember, I 'ain't saying goodbye until the die is cast.

What's up America? Are you catching the euphoria??

Can you see the good feeling in the atmosphere?

Can you hear the trumpets blowing?

My house is full. I've my good friends, good neighbors and the good people in the neighborhood here to visit. Are the people ready for the good news?

Stay tuned woman. Stay tuned America. Stay tuned good people for before midnight or twilight tomorrow you'll witness something historic, something epic and of course something euphoric.

Thank goodness we didn't waste our Votes!!!

A Triumph and not a Disaster': Is this Rhetoric?

CHATHAM HOUSE an iconic venue at the Royal Institute of International Affairs probably hosted its biggest guest ahead of the 2016 general elections last week in London. Something big was cooking, which had pulled many dignitaries there. But a bespectacled lady who stood behind a lectern looking poised to deliver a speech to a diverse crowd from across the capital was the centre of attraction.

The lady is perhaps the most vilified or criticized person and possibly the most hated individual in this political season. She's seen as a friend to one political party and a foe to another. Her job requires good judgement, good temperament and a cool head. It also requires her to be unbiased and independent even though she's her own political leanings. Integrity is also an essential requirement.

The guest was none other than the chairperson of Ghana's Electoral Commission (EC), Mrs. Charlotte Osei. Yes, Charlotte was in Chatham House and she produced her signature menu. She addressed international stakeholders about Ghana's 2016 elections, under the headline: "Ghana's 2016 Elections Process and Priorities of the Electoral Commission."

Perhaps you couldn't make it to the venue to see the EC Boss catalogued her plans for the nation in the upcoming general elections. You must've also missed her on the television screens and the sprawling radio stations across the metropolis.

Maybe, you saw her via the social media platforms or you chanced upon a group of persons who were busy involved in a gossip around the corner——where the source of the news often lives abroad, where facts and figures are indiscriminately distorted or otherwise butchered. In Ghanaian parlance: They say they say always they say— but you'd neither see nor meet who said what, when and where.

By the way, that's not a big deal I missed the Chatham House program myself. I missed her body language. And I missed the Q&A, if the forum did allow that segment. Nonetheless, I'm fortunate to have this powerful medium to examine what transpired at the venue. And I think the rest would be determined by the turf come December 7.

So, if you missed all of the above, this is another slice of the same pie.

And here's how Mrs. Osei did it— putting her best foot forward. She pitched from the get go, touting Ghana's electoral system as strong and more transparent than most electoral systems across the world, a feature she boasted, makes it impossible (I don't know about that —difficult probably will be acceptable) for anyone to rig.

"Ghana's electoral system is strong and more transparent than most electoral systems globally which makes it impossible for anyone to rig," she said.

No doubt her grand plan was to clear doubts about the EC's credibility to hold free, fair and a more transparent elections, assuring Ghanaians that per its track record the electoral body would pass the test and there was no cause for alarm. Mrs. Osei also underscored that she means good and nothing evil for the country.

"The priority of the electoral commission and my priority and I hope the priority of all Ghanaians is to see peaceful and undisputed elections on December 7,"she stated.

Critics of the EC say the electoral body doesn't understand the very laws the commission drafted. Mr. Casely-Hayford member of OccupyGhana has mocked the EC saying: "The Electoral Commission that actually drafted the Constitutional Instrument, CI 94 don't even understand what they wrote and how they were going to use it to be able to streamline and bring some sanity into the presidential and parliamentary nominations."

He claimed: "The commission is losing cases because they have totally misunderstood what they were trying to achieve."

But the EC Boss has maintained that her outfit would do everything within its power to ensure that there's triumph and not disaster in the December 7 general polls.

Her proclamation to conduct a free, fair and transparent election has also attracted criticism from a section of the populace. The critics think it's just rhetoric to water down the backlash the commission had been facing in recent times, especially in the wake of the disqualification of 12 presidential aspirants.

For example, someone posted this comment on Ghanaweb.com after the chairperson had delivered the Chatham House speech.

"Preaching virtues whilst practising vice... It's not about sweet speeches. It's all about the realities on the ground... The EC boss should put personal interest aside, to me she has something fishy with the NDC guys and the earlier she retracts her steps towards rigging the better ..."

Another wrote: "...Did you change the voters register? Are you aware that some foreigners registered with national health insurance cards? Are you aware Ghanaians don't really trust you based on your selective favouritism? You're trying to rig the election for John Mahama..."

The rest of the comment has no space here.

Indeed the question about trust and other uncertainties tend to fuel all these allegations. There has been allegation also that Mrs. Osei is an NDC card bearer and would rig the elections for the ruling party. Whether that's true or not, I think these are serious issues the EC Boss would have to deal with from now until the elections are over.

The question is: *How do you convince the voting public that you are Paul but not Saul?*

Again, to do that the EC chairperson set a beautiful template and laid bare the six successful elections Ghana had had since 1992 and also gave the assurance that the 7th election would be a success story. She painted her outfit as a viable and a more credible institution and used comparison as a vital tool to make her case, thereby comparing and contrasting Ghana's political history with her neighbors in the ECOWAS sub region.

And I believe she'd Ghana's closest neighbor to the west— the Ivory Coast including, Liberia, Sierra Leone and tiny Togo in mind.

"So not only has Ghana managed to buck its own trends since 1992, it has also defied the trends of regional politics. In the same period of time that we held our six elections and consolidated our democracy in Ghana, our neighbours in ECOWAS, have suffered 14 coups, three civil wars, a dozen regional insurgencies and countless foreign interventions. And that sort of instability of course breeds its own problems—lawlessness, terrorism, human trafficking, drugs and arms smuggling, Mrs. Osei told the gathering.

Comparison is a rhetorical or a literary device in which a writer compares and contrasts two people, places things or ideas. Politicians like it too. Here the EC chairperson compared places. Most of our neighbors had seen wars, coups and acts of terrorism as she alluded to. The distinction therefore, was more than palpable.

Which one would you prefer a country in chaos or a stable and a democratic one?

The essence of the comparison also sought to portray and project Ghana's status as a nation basking in peace and glory. In other words, we were second to none in the sub region in terms of our democratic credentials, economic stability, peace and security.

She dismissed claims that the EC is subject to political interference, noting that it has instituted a suite of specific legal measures to ensure the December polls are as transparent as possible."

But to prevent that from happening, she said the commission has made the great efforts, to build a more active presence online with new media, by creating a large following on both Facebook and Twitter and intend to hold briefings for the media and the public until the final results are declared on election day.

Additionally, she believed her outfit's good work would come to naught if the media wasn't advised to desist from declaring elections as that could cause a disturbing scene. "The greatest challenges facing Ghana's election is the potential for the media to call the election results ahead of the EC, which may tend to create confusion in the minds of the voting public."

I couldn't agree with her more on that. And I'd humbly suggest that (if this hasn't taken place already) all media houses, print and electronic should avail themselves to some sort of educational training ahead of the polls. The media is not supposed to call or declare election results. The media project elections and they are not finality. The media houses that broadcast in Akan and other Ghanaian languages must be mindful of using the right terminology to avoid confusion and commotion.

Election results declaration is the sole responsibility of the EC. As the fourth estate, our core functions are—to educate, inform and entertain the public. They haven't changed. That said I should commend Joy FM, an Accra-based radio station for a good job done in the 2012 election. The station made projections and not declarations.

Next to be cautioned were the political players of the game. And I hope the likes of Sir John, Asiedu Nketiah (aka General Mosquito) Koku Anyidoho, and Kennedy Agyepong got the message right. Mrs. Osei noted it wasn't a healthy practice for them to whip up sentiments by their incendiary remarks: "Our political stakeholders are it seems master of raising the political temperature every election year, stressing we've a legacy to protect and very real challenge to it this December."

So how exactly are we going to ensure that this election is a 'triumph and not a disaster?'

In furtherance to the above, the EC Boss catalogued a number of measures put in place to achieve that: "I believe that EC's previous successes were undoubtedly powered by its core staff with support of the tens of thousands of the temporary election officers. A significant majority of these core staff are still at post and as part of our efforts to improve on the electoral outcome, we further developed their capacity," she stated.

"Not only that, we have increased the educational qualification of the temporary officers we would be using for the elections. We have also improved the quality of their training to ensure they deliver better. And of course they will have the same experienced team supervising this year's elections.

Our commission has been responsible for the successful conduct of the previous elections which have made Ghana earn the solid reputation as a stable and mature democracy and an example for the rest of the continent, if not the world.

Despite their depth knowledge and their wide range of skills in managing elections, we are not allowing ourselves to become complacent. As a result, all our staff have received more training this year, in fact much more than in any other year."

Charlotte called on international stakeholders to begin to hold African politicians to a higher level of scrutiny discourse during African elections. This, she believed, would promote free, fair and transparent elections on the continent.

My Mistakes My Flaws

How do they shape or define me?

If I diligently crossed all my t's and meticulously dotted all my i's, what would be left for proof readers and sub editors. If ifs and ands were pots and pans there would be no works for tinker's hands. Of course, if I'd the binocular eyes of the owl or the intrepid eyes of the eagle, I could see the tiny ant crawling underneath the Earth's belly.

Regrettably, I don't have them because I'm human and I've limitations. But my limitations are also my strength. And my strength overwhelmingly defines who I am. They truly define me. And they make me to be me.

Indeed in every profession, there are bound to be mistakes—some of them minor, some of them major and some of them cataclysmic. What I did on Wednesday falls under the latter's category in my own description. Cataclysmic because it's the biggest bullet (as we used to say back in college) I've ever fired in my careership.

I wrote this: "Does anybody has the video/audio of the Ghanaian women trapped in Saudi Arabia?" Yes I wrote that. I was looking for some information so this message wouldn't sit aloof. I forwarded it to three WhatsApp platforms. Moments after, I noticed what I'd done. What went through my mind at the time is your best guess.

On two of the platforms, I prompted members about the mistake. Probably, some of them noticed it but didn't mind. Probably some did not, or they did but overlooked it. Possibly to some that was nothing all they cared about was the nugget. And possibly some did notice it and tickled themselves. Nonetheless, nobody said anything to me.

How could he do that? How couldn't I, my friend.

Don't get it all twisted, I know that the **infinitive have** is always used with do, does and did. On the other hand, **has** is only used with third person singular. So the above statement: "Does anybody...?" You use the infinitive verb **have**. But it was bound to happen and it happened for a reason.

These are few examples I like to share: Does he swim? Yes he swims. Another example John has the ball. Does he have it?

I'm not a paragon of the English Language. I make mistakes all the time. Some are typographical mistakes; some are due to android's predictive act. Sometimes we aren't ourselves. Something wasn't right! I noticed that earlier in the day. My pressure was soaring. How high? It was high.

Sometimes the chaffs find themselves in the midst of the refined grains. They slip through the cracks. And even in big establishments such as The Financial Times, The New York Times, The Guardian or The Washington Post these glitches and hitches occur.

But they're there, some for a reason: A reason sometimes we've no knowledge of and cannot control. Be reminded: "Out of bad came something good and out of the rotten came something sweet." Also out of the 'unclean' our Lord was born just remember that. Jesus died for a reason. He'd power to disappear or cause his crucifiers to sink to the bottomless pit. Yet, he succumbed to death so that you and I would have salvation. The greatest news is: He conquered death!

I'm my own editor, my own proof reader and my own sub editor. I write under intense pressure. I steal time to write my write-ups while at work. My day is normally packed with action. I look over my shoulders to get things done –often at a breakneck speed. I felt I was breaking down. I was dog-tired.

'*Slow down buddy, take a rest today and recalibrate yourself*,' the little voice whispered into my ears. Simply put, retreat and reload. I thought that was a smart idea. Indeed the soul was willing but the flesh was super tired!

I've good people who yearn for my early breakfast. I've readers itching to have my brunch, lunch and supper depending on which part of the planet they live. Thursday found me in great shape. I felt so refreshed so rejuvenated. I was still in bed at 7:00 O'clock in the morning (Pacific Time). I'd the urge to grab my phone and checked what was trending. Sooner than later I came across this on Ghana TC Radio chartroom:

"Missing my morning read! Where is my motivational thought-provoking Gordon?" Gonza queried.

And I responded: 'I'm sorry I couldn't serve you breakfast this morning my brother Gonza and all fellas on this august platform. God willing I will be back...'

What does the scripture say? "My sheep hear my voice, and I know them, and they follow me," John 10:27 (KJV).

I feel indebted to my numerous readers on, Facebook, Ghanaweb.com, modernghana.com, choice FM platform, GT Radio chartroom (via WhatsApp) etc. Folks you're the reason I keep fighting like a bison almost every day or week by week. You're the reason my adrenalin gets pumped up to do more and more. Indeed, you're the reason even when I'm tired I crave to push myself through the cracks and get my head above the chilling waters. That's the profound satisfaction I get each day I read your inspiring comments.

English dictionary defines the word perseverance as: Persistence in doing something despite difficulty or delay in achieving success. For example medicine is a field which requires dedication and perseverance. .

Perseverance's twin sister is endurance: Online dictionary defines endurance as: the fact or power of enduring an unpleasant or difficult process or situation without giving away.

Have you ever felt or come close to the limit of these two powerful words?

Or do you have what it takes to withstand wear and tear?

In 2007 around December I'd cortisone shot at 'Good Sam'. A Samaritan nurse who was with us in the theatre room seemed shocked. And early 2008 I'd two more shots. "This is your last shot you cannot take anymore, "the doctor told me.

In all three shots, I refused to have them numb my body or provide anesthesia to me. Anesthetic is a drug that produces a complete or partial loss of feeling. Or it is temporary induced state with one or more of analgesia (relief from or prevention of pain) paralysis (muscles relaxation).

Later the nurse asked me after my physician Doctor Derick had drilled the long needle inside my low back: *"How could you do that without a flinch?"*

It's endurance you've to prepare the mind for it, I told her. We all break down sometimes. Sometimes we fall. The wise fall, the rich fall, the poor fall, the great fall. Have you forgotten Samson fell? Who else comes to mind quickly? Oh, King David and his son Solomon –the wisest king.

Its human nature, we're weak and meek. But at the same time we're wonderfully and fearfully made to endure, to persevere, to be tenacious and to be bold. Therefore, don't let your mistakes hold you back or tear you apart, because not everyone sees your mistake as a failure. As matter of fact more than the majority often appreciates what you do and what you bring to the fore.

So, remember what defines you is your ability to horn your talent, to get back on your commanding legs when you hit the rock bottom or when you think you've had the biggest fall—the cataclysmic. Talent is innate everyone has it. It's shaped by our mistakes, by our flaws and by our blunders. It's shaped by correctness and success.

Why is Presidential Transition Bill important?

To say you've never seen it happen. It means you aren't that old. But history has it all in her reservoir. Presidential transitions also known as presidential interregnum across the world vary and they carry their own baggage. It is done by countries that practice democracy —be it the Westminster type in the United Kingdom or the presidential system in the United States of America (USA).

The first and the second Republics of Nkrumah and Busia administrations practised the British system. Prime Minster Busia's was between 1969 until January 13, 1972 when the National Redemption Council (NRC) led by General Acheampong toppled the government.

On his part, Dr. Nkrumah served as Ghana's first prime minister and president when the country gained independence from the British in 1957, until he was also deposed in February 24, 1966 by a military junta – the National Liberation Council (NLC) led by Brigadier Afrifa, Lieutenant colonel Emmanuel Kwasi Kotoka and co.

That happened to be the country's first political upheaval.

Barely a year later, some senior and junior officers from Ho rece regiment notably, captains Osei Poku, Arthur and Yeboah staged a counter coup that overthrew the then military administration. Kotoka was killed in that mutiny.

Ghana changed from the Westminster also known as the parliamentary system when it became republic on the 1st of July 1960. After strings of coup d'état between 1972 -1979 the country had the chance to return to civilian regime, but that was short-lived.

Bottom line the third republic under President Hilla Liman's administration (People's National Party–PNC) saw no presidential transition.

In fact the PNC administration lasted less than three years (from September 24, 1979 to December 1, 1981). That regime was overthrown by the Provisional National Defence Council (PNDC) spearheaded by then flight lieutenant Jerry John Rawlings.

It's worth noting that that was also Rawlings' third revolt. He'd the Armed Forces Revolutionary Council (AFRC) in June 4, 1979 which took power from General Akufo military regime, prior to that there was an uprising staged on the 31st of May in 1979.

And since the third and fourth republics (the fourth republic dates back 1992) the country has maintained the American system. So, I think it would be apt to cite a few examples from the US' presidential transitions as we delve into the above subject.

Meanwhile, I should point out that presidential transition is a process governments in our part of the world dread most. They hate it. It's like a bitter pill for them— difficult to swallow, even though they might've completed their term of office.

I will briefly talk about three US presidential transitions. And the first will be the 1860-1861 transition from the administration of James

Buchannan to the terms of Abraham Lincoln. That transition is seen as the most notable one by historians and political pundits.

Between the election on November 6, 1860 and inauguration on March 4, 1861, seven states seceded and conflict between secessionists and federal force began leading to the American civil war between the northern and southern states.

Reports mentioned, the end of the administration of Herbert Hoover, before the inauguration of Franklin Roosevelt (November 8, 1932-March 4, 1933 as a difficult transition period. Roosevelt refused Hoover's request to come up with a joint program to stop the downward spiral and calm investors, claiming it would tie his hands.

It had since been relatively smooth. However the most recent was the transition between Bill Clinton and George W. Bush. History has it that theirs was marred by accusations of damage, theft, vandalism and pranks. The General Accounting office estimated the cost of those pranks at $13,000 to $14,000.

Of course Ghana's democracy is just a fledgling one, but that doesn't mean doing so isn't prudent. Presidential transition is like a relay race. In athletics the two standard relays are the 4x 400-metre relay and the 4x 200-metre relay. The athletes or members of a team pass the baton (s) onto someone or a group of persons.

Basically it's all about taking responsibility for the new task ahead. As already noted Ghana's presidential transition like developed democracies hit the bumps in its first and the ones that followed had not passed the test. That means we're still at the learning curve: Still trying to put things at their right perspective.

In 2001 the transition process was characterised by what then Electoral Commissioner or Chairman Dr. Kwadwo Afari Gyan described as 'rancor' and 'acrimony' between then outgoing National Democratic Congress (NDC) administration and incoming New Patriotic Party (NPP).

The former EC chairman called for a proper presidential transition process to ensure a smooth handing over. He argued that this will prevent the spite that characterises transition to a party other than the then governing party.

In fact the NDC under the fourth republic had President Rawlings completed his two terms from 1992-2000. And that transition was between him and President Kufour of the NPP. Mr. Rawlings at the time didn't or couldn't hide his strong aversion to Mr. Kufuor. To put it lightly it was awful. Thank God we made it here!

The January 2009 presidential transition was successful given the fact that it was the country's second democratic transfer of power between opposing parties. NPP Kufuor handed over power to NDC Mills. It was symbolic, but there were problems. In short, it wasn't a smooth process.

It was against this backdrop that on Wednesday Parliament passed the presidential transitional bill. The bill is a legislation that will make the transfer of political power from one party to the other seamless after a major election in Ghana. The bill seeks to amend the presidential transition Act. 2012 (Act 845) to address the flaws in the Act.

Local media reports say no opposition was raised to the bill during deliberations. Among other remedies, it will help cure critical challenges in the past transition processes and administration problems in the transition process.

The Stone Wall: Can Africa Rise like the Ducklings?

Yesterday was great everything went well. Nothing hindered our progress. We probably were able to meet all our targets and satisfy all our heart desires. Some of us probably hit the jackpot, some won multiple awards for outstanding performance in our respective careers, and some bought themselves the latest automobiles, jets and yachts, while others moved into their new homes and new offices. And there were some that gained admission into Ivy schools and colleges and many more.

Sounds uplifting right? Think about those who got everything wrong. Nothing worked in their favour. In fact they messed up from the get go and felt tossed out even before the race was declared over. Tried as they did, nothing seemed workable. They'd found the course impenetrable and felt disoriented.

How about those who couldn't travel beyond yesterday to welcome today?

Also consider those who stumbled and fell in every step on their way. Those who never gave up when it appeared they'd reached the dead end of the road?? Yes, consider those little ducklings that never gave up the battle. They were resolute, they showed resilience in their fight and they believed in themselves despite the enormity of the challenges they faced. They never gave up until the mission was accomplished.

They were 12. They were young possibly a few weeks old. But they weren't alone treading the unknown. Their mother duck stood by like a good Shepherd. She looked emotionally stricken. Her babies were stuck at the bottom of a three-tier stair. I could see each one of them trying to reach the top. The exercise seemed intense and the participants looked determined. It looked like a drama scene and the actors were all for it. They'd created an enthralling scene– something for the eyes to behold and the minds to digest. Certainly the audience who happened to be around couldn't hide their emotions as the ducklings fell over and over again in their attempts to climb. It was like a melee.

Were they able to scale over what appeared improbable?

The look on their mother's face suggested time was running out and perhaps night was drawing nigh. They probably were out there looking for bread and butter but the enemy could also stray on their pathway. Maybe they were going to meet another family somewhere in the neighbourhood. So, of course time was of the essence.

Mother duck seemed distraught but she never took her eyes off her ducklings. From the top she watched the young ones. All 12 had found themselves at the foreground of the stairs. They jockeyed from one side to another gauging which side they could better leapfrog. After a long struggle one of them managed to find herself on step two. And the struggle continued. That move however, would motivate the rest of her siblings to give of their best.

Following that success, it didn't matter anymore as to how many times one fell or stumbled. They knew it was doable. Yes they can, if their sister had done it. As the majority kept tumbling down the duckling on the second step had made it to the top. Her Mom's face lit with indescribable joy.

'Great good girl, you've made it congratulations'.

And the minutes ticked. Mother duck cooed and cooed as the young hurdled the stairs one by one till there was none left behind. The calls were distressing. It showed a loving mom wandering around amid expectation that her babies could pass the test and they did through perseverance and die-hard mentality.

If you ever saw that video of the ducklings and their mom which was posted on the social media, sometime last week, I can guarantee you'd never give up on your dream (s) regardless. The Bible says a nation without vision will perish. And it's applicable to us as humans or individuals.

Mother ducks are very caring and protective of their young but may sometime abandon some of their ducklings if they're physically stuck in an area they cannot get out. Well this one didn't neglect her off springs. She'd faith in her babies and stood by them till the end of their struggle.

And until ducks are fully feathered around 7-9 weeks old they have trouble regulating their body temperature and more so overcoming such challenges some of us saw in that short video.

I may be branded as being nationalistic or being as ambitious as Lucifer. But is it a crime to say Africa can rise? Yes she can. Africa's destiny rests in her own hands and if she believes in herself and put her mind and heart to it she can make it to the moon and even beyond. Indeed she can rise like her siblings —Antarctica, Europe, Asia, Australia/Oceania North America and South America.

To quote Dr. Arikana Chihombori Quao Ambassador of the Africa Union to the United States: "Africa must as possible speak with voice and not as fragmented individual states, when we continue to negotiate not only with the United States but also other trade partners..."

African leaders must learn to relinquish power and avoid perpetuating themselves on the political thrones. Africa can rise if its leaders will stop looting, stop bribing and taking bribes, stop pilfering and smuggling state properties, stop siphoning state funds and create job opportunities. The leadership must give its peoples the opportunities like good education, good health facilities, good roads, good housing, and good social amenities and many more.

Be reminded, Africa had made it there before but time and bad conditions, they say do not favour beauty. She was once at the top. Once she saw the heavens and kissed her. Once she'd her siblings served her as she's doing it today for them. What went wrong is history and history is his own judge and not me.

Africa will get there, Africa can get there and Africa will rise. The road isn't smooth. And the impediments are numerous. However, we can get there if we put our act together. And let's remind ourselves that there will be no room for whiners, there will be no room for weasels and there will be no room for traitors and detractors. Also the puppets and the poodles will have no place there. Indeed Africa can regain her lost glory.

Great Expectations after Education

Is education still the key to success and have our politicians changed the padlock?

He heard the ding dong, ran to the door. It was Uncle Johnson the postmaster, he comes twice every day to deliver mails to the Andersons. He'd to beat a bleeding traffic on the Accra-Tema motorway also known as the N1 to make it to their residence at Hatso about 5:30 in the evening.

There was a priority mail that needed a signature. And the sight of it lit the face of Maibey the third son of the Andersons. But that mail didn't come close to his expectation. In a fleeting his beautiful smile would disappear and his whole frame swaddled with disappointment.

Once again his hopes had been dashed, shattered like a glass tossed from a thirty-floor building. The 24-year-old university graduate had been hunting for jobs almost three years after graduation. He'd more than 200 applications spread across the country and had attended about 50 interviews but still not landed on a job.

And it appeared each passing day dropped a bombshell!

Earlier in the day at midday Uncle Johnson dropped utility bills—water and electricity. No one in the household bothered to open it, let alone check how much they owed the power company–GRIDCO.

Why? They'd been out of power for two months. Actually, the area they lived had been christened 'Dumsorland, 'don't mistake it for Deutschland. The water problem was perhaps worse. When they'd it, it dripped like the fowl's urine.

Life was too tough for the family. Mr. Johnson's wife Mrs. Johnson was a hairdresser. Imagine. Just imagine in 'Dumsorland' when power comes it doesn't stay for six hours and it doesn't return for weeks when it goes away.

Even at the ministries (the bastion of government infrastructures) where Mr. Johnson worked as a principal secretary they couldn't avoid the drudgery of Dumsor. The menace was all over flaunting her shady shaky frame—closing down small businesses and the big ones peppered.

"Glad to see you Uncle. Anything for me?" asked Maibey.

"Not really, but I think I've got a bunch of newspapers .The rest I will call them junk mails." replied Uncle Johnson.

"Oh my gosh!"

"What's going on with this system?

If you're unemployed the excuse is that because you have no education. If you have education they say you should've studied computer science or business administration or land economy and the list goes on. If you'd computer science or either one you're told they're looking for someone with five years' experience and if you beat that hurdle they'd tell you we need guys with master's degree and all the highest degrees.

The Johnsons shared similar story. They'd two university graduates (adults, unemployed) still living with their parents. Akwasi and Kukua often told their friends jokingly that they worked at the Ministry of Works and Housing—meaning they're 'stayed-home' guys.

It was this kind of lifestyle after college education coupled with the sheer display of opulence by politicians in our part of the world that made Maibey to utter the following statement during a family gathering, courtesy of social media.

"When we were growing up, they used to tell us that education is the key to success, now we have that key, only to find out that the politicians have changed the padlock,"

Sounds paradox? But Maibey was right the guys have changed the padlock.

To get it unlocked I think one has to join the symphony orchestra group i.e. the nepotism and the cronyism club. It is basically, who you know and not what qualification one has.

See, Maibey loved sarcasm and he knew when and how to use them. He cracked everyone up. But his statement was pregnant with nuggets. As they continued to chit chat he saw some politicians flitting around like silly pigeons.

Some had their errand boys carried umbrellas over their heads in the midst of downpour. There were some distributing monies to registered voters. There were also some that decided to braid hairs in a way of buying votes. And there were still some who chose to become chefs in a spell of moment. Cooking banku, pounding fufu and dancing to tunes they've never known nor heard from Adam.

Indeed, this is what we call 'Politricks.'

US state of New Hampshire has something that probably people in Big Apple (New York City) envy. The state is well-known for its retail politics. And people in the Granite state during political campaign seasons get to see politicians across the nation jockey the length and breadth of the state kissing the kids, visiting homes, handshaking, some making kids to mention the unmentionables and so on and so forth.

It's a tradition New Hampshirites wouldn't trade for anything and for that matter wouldn't share with anybody.

Today, it seems politicians in Ghana have put that in a high gear, rivalling New Hampshire for this traditional ethos.

Gordon's Hodgepodge

Is Education still the key to Success?

Maibey and many believe it is this new brigade of politicians that have choked hold our educational system. It is suffering from asphyxia or asphyxiation.

No doubt, education is the key to success because it opens doors for people of all backgrounds and it expands the human mind with knowledge. The vast amount of knowledge gained through education prepares individuals to solve problems, teach others, function at higher level and implement transformational ideas. Without education, one's chance for securing a good job and ascending to a higher economic and social status are often limited.

In Toni CadeBambara's short story, "The Lesson', the single unifying fact is exploring life outside of your own realm of knowledge is the key to success. This has proven to be true when Miss Moore took the children of her class to see a way of life they have never known to exist.

Miss Moore taught the group of children the basic principles and values of life each day as well as the other characteristics of an education…When the children returned to their destination; they tasted the first display of how exploring life outside one's own realm of knowledge is the key success.

Education gives people tools, skills and knowledge needed to survive. So my plea to our politicians and I mean all of our politicians, let's not line our pockets with the state's funds to deny our children's children their birth right. And please don't change the padlock.

Clique Bug Bites Guardiola too

Two coaches beaten by two former clubs as their woes continue to deepen by the week:

It seems the bug that bit Mourihno has bitten Manchester City's manager Pep Guardiola. Reality has caught up with the former Barcelona and Bayern Munich coach. His demeanor after Sunday's match against

Southampton accentuated the spell that's possibly following them—as both lost 4-0 to their former clubs within a week.

Five matches with no wins obviously, convey a message that's perhaps as dreadful as the canny hidden blood-sucking bug. And the bug is subtly eating up the image and flamboyance of the celebrated coach who is credited with 14 trophies in his coaching career.

Indeed, three draws, two losses and no wins in five successive matches send wrong signal.

On September 28, City drew 3-3 with Celtic in the Uefa championship league, lost 2-0 to Tottenham (in October 2nd) and tied 1-1 with Everton on Saturday October 5. But perhaps the loss that came on Saturday October 15, (4-0 to Barca) dealt a heavy blow to the City's manager and as though that wasn't enough Guardiola couldn't redeem himself, yesterday as his side again drew 1-1 in the match against the Saints.

This is the second time in Guardiola's managerial career that he'd suffered such losses, according to BBC sports.

But this could just be a tip of the iceberg. Or it could be interpreted as the beginning of the wrath to come. And I guess no one has warned the charismatic coach to flee from the ire that awaits him at the City's gates.

I think Guardiola should be reminded that he's in England, not in Spain and not in Germany. And if he didn't know that he should ask Mourihno—a living testimony.

So far, the City manager has demonstrated that he's a stick in the mud—not ready to change his tactics, not ready to bring onboard the horses that helped pulled the wagon from the woods and certainly not ready to listen to an outsider. This scenario puts City supporters on pins and needles oblivious to the way forward.

Are they (Man City) backpedaling?

Looks like it. They're behaving like a nose dive jet.

Nonetheless, Man City are still on top of the league table, not as comfortable as they found themselves three weeks back. They lead Arsene Wenger's side (Arsenal) only by a goal difference and two over Liverpool . All three teams have 20 points apiece.

Guardiola took charge in June after former Italian manager Manuel Pellegrini exited Etihad estate. And he'd agreed to a three-year contract with the blues. City started well. They played like a team that was all for it—winning 10 straight games. Like Chelsea did during Mourihno's comeback era in 2015. They seemed unstoppable and appeared unmatched by their peers.

But what went wrong?

It's the clique bug and not until the two managers address this problem they would join the Black Stars of the 80's, 90's and the early or mid-2000's. At the time, Ghana had the best of the best but still produced the worst results in the nation's football history.

They say Guardiola likes to do things his own way. Well, here's my six pence advice: Sometimes the rules don't work or aren't applicable everywhere. In cases like that change is required. The need to tweak things and accommodate others is more than welcome. That doesn't make one a weakling. It rather creates a win-win situation.

In the meantime, all eyes are watching closely to see how things would pan out going forward. And I would like to repeat that this is England. At the City's gates intense anger is shaping up. Patience is losing traction…And if this continues he could face the resentment that the 'Special One' suffered at the Stanford Bridge.

However, the upcoming fixtures seem to tilt in City's favour albeit dicey. The Etihad men have five away matches (out of seven) against Manchester United, West Brom, Crystal Palace, Burnley and German club Monchengladbach. They will entertain Messi side and Middleborough at home.

This is Guardiola's track record: At Barcelona he sidelined Brazilian duo–Ronaldinho and Deco. And five-time African footballer of the year Samuel Eto'o and Zlatan Ibrahimović would later suffer similar fate. It's also on record Guardiola sanctioned Yaya Toure's 24 million pound departure to city.

The pattern would follow him to Germany. At Bayern Munich it was the veteran doctor Hans Muller-Wohlfahrt and the like of Mario Mandzukic, Xherdan Shaqiri, Dante and eventually Bastian Schweinsteiger that would face Guardiola's sharp teeth.

And the beat goes on. Since he took the reins of City several big names have gone missing in his selected eleven and substitute side. England goal keeper Joe Hart was axed off even before the league began, whereas Yahaya Toure,' City captain and Belgian international Vincent Kompany, Sergio Aguero are out of the perking order.

About three weeks ago I told a good friend of mine, who is Manchester United ardent supporter that despite Pep Guardiola's early superb performance at the EPL, the renowned manager would see a big dip in not too distant future.

In fact I predicted the blip might occur even before end of the first half of the league .And here we are!

But is there an antidote?

My suggestion, bring back the 'heroes'. They might not be in their best form but their inclusion would end the apathy and division in the team. They wield power and influence, plus they've got the experience. They can help make the team and can break it too.

The question is: *What the heck are the likes of Toure, Aguero, and Bastian Schweinsteiger doing at the bench?*

The German international signed a three-year 200,000 pound- a-week contract with United last summer. But all he does is wear a United shirt. In fact, I haven't even sighted him at the bench since his arrival at the Old Trafford.

Mourihno and Guardiola appear to be playing same cards and the results are troubling to put it lightly. Remember, I mentioned the cliques in my previous article about Ghana's national team the Black Stars: And I'm afraid that's probably the bug that has bitten the two coaches.

The Black Stars had two most powerful players—Abedi Pele (captain) and Tony Yeboah aka Yegoala (who once captained Frankfurt, German club) '.Rumor had it that the two weren't in good terms and they'd cliques in the team. Though both denied the allegation, there was a shred of truth in that rumor or perception.

Gordon's Hodgepodge

Bottom line you can't win a football match with a divided team, with no clear understanding and purposefulness. Be reminded the cliques always play to the tune of their idols.

EC to Print Ballot Papers Abroad

Why? Are there no companies in Ghana?

Sounds like a familiar verse in the Book of Exodus: "And they said unto Moses, because there were no graves in Egypt, has thou taken us away to die in the wilderness? Wherefore has thou dealt thus with us to carry us forth out of Egypt?" Exodus 14:11(KJV).

Palpable fear had gripped biblical Israelites en-route to the Promised Land but they realised their enemies (the Egyptians) were closing in on them, hence the above statement.

On Thursday the Electoral Commission (EC) revealed its plans to print the 2016 election ballot papers abroad at an Accra High court presided over by Justice Eric Kyei Baffour. The revelation came up when the court sat to hear the motion for an abridgment of time by the EC following a suit filed against it by Dr. Paa Kwesi Nduom presidential nominee of the Progressive People's Party (PPP), who wa s disqualified for failing to meet the electoral requirements.

The news didn't go down well with some of the people at the courtroom, particularly the policy director for the PPP Mr. Kofi Asamoah Siaw. He couldn't mask his anger and frustration about the posture of the electoral body. He quickly criticised the EC, wondering if the commission had the nation at heart.

"Are they no companies in Ghana to print ballot papers?" he asked.

"Why would the EC want to move out of the country to print ballot papers for an election here in Ghana, when there are companies that could do the job? This is against our policy to create jobs for Ghanaians."

Are foreigners the only alternative to what we need? What we are worried about as a party is the credibility of the process and the unfortunate decision by the EC to print the papers abroad. When will the printed ballots arrive?' he questioned.

And I couldn't agree with Mr. Siaw more on that. It seems as a nation we're allergic to 'made-in Ghana' goods. It seems we're averse to anything locally-made. And anything grown or manufactured in Ghana is deemed inferior. Meanwhile, some or most of the goods we import from People's Republic of China for example are just 'painte-ma-mento.'

Indeed, it seems domestication is out of the eastern corridor and the craze for western or oriental merchandise has seemingly become unstoppable and adaptable to us as a people. Isn't that true tell me? We grow rice here, yet our markets, stalls, stores and malls are flooded with China rice.

How do you expect the Small Medium Enterprise (SME's) to grow?

What's wrong with us as a people?

In apropos, King Solomon was right. Nothing under the sun is new. They've all happened before. They just metamorphose either in shape or size, time and location, this writer believes.

So now we all know that it wasn't just an empty threat by the embattled PPP nominee, if one thought so. Dr. Paa Kwesi Nduom has raised the threat level to a court suit. And it seems he's fighting tooth and nail to get his status legitimized. That's a battle he's fighting now.

The suit has Dr. Nduom as the exparte applicant with Madam Charlotte Osei the EC chairperson as the first Respondent and EC as the 2nd Respondent .The EC filed for an abridgment of case for interlocutory injunction filed by PPP restraining it from proceeding with balloting for position presidential candidates for the Dec 7th elections.

The plaintiff is also seeking a further order directed against the 1st Respondent in her capacity as Returning Officer for Presidential elections to grant the applicant the opportunity to amend and alter the one anomaly found in his nomination papers as well as amended or altered to enable him contest as a presidential candidate for the December 7, 2016 election.

The court was of the view that time was of the essence and had further instructed lawyers for EC and PPP to file their statement of case by

Monday October 24. They are also expected to appear before the court so that a date can be given for the ruling.

Mr. Siaw said they expected the process to be fair but in their case that didn't happen, hence their decision to resort to court. According to him their lawyers are capable enough to prosecute their case. And was hopeful everything would hold its sway.

The faster the case moves the better: "I want the case to travel as fast as possible because we don't want to jeopardise the electoral process," he hinted.

Does anybody remember this?

In 2012, Dr. Nduom then presidential nominee for the PPP issued this fiat: "Do not think that you're the only parties that can recruit or have macho men. We can also raise an army of lions." He was referring to the two major political parties who'd or still have the likes of 'Azoka Boys.'

I didn't see the lions on our streets though. But on a more serious note I think he meant, anything NDC/NPP can do his party—PPP can do it, perhaps worse. *Truth be told who can stand an army of roaring lions?*

Meanwhile the court has stated emphatically that it would at all times be guided by the timeline as far as election 2016 was concerned. It has therefore ordered the parties to file their case by Monday, adding they should return the following day to make viva voca (oral submission) after which a date will be set for the judgement of the court).

What led to the disqualification?

On Monday October 10, the EC knocked down 12 presidential nominees bidding to serve at the Flagstaff House—the seat of government in the 2016 December 7 poll.

The move happened to be the first major storm that had ever hit Ghana's political landscape –jolting political ambitions of the 12 candidates. Among them former first Lady Nana Konadu Agyeman-Rawlings, NDP, Dr. Edward Mahama, PNC, and Dr. Paa Kwesi Nduom, PPP have all been disqualified by the Electoral Commission(EC) to contest in the forthcoming presidential election.

But this is what led to the disqualification— fraudulent signatures, absence of required number of signatures and improper filing of nomination forms.

The Identity:
How a stonebreaker got his breakthrough

In a tiny town down the valley across the volleyball pitch situated an old house. Its wooden door had a gaping hole that could invite a bird the size of a parrot. The door had curvatured nail to lock it. Roofed with bamboo, built with mud and whitewashed with clay, it had a single wooden window that barely allowed ventilation.

The owner of the house had lived there for many many years. Town folks chose to call him Mr. Stone. He mined stones for a living. He woke up every day with the sound of the early birds that flew by his home— always quacking. They were geese, a family of about fifty.

Mr. Stone found them very interesting. He found out probably the geese were the only birds that have three collective nouns: First they're called a gaggle when they're on the ground. A skein when in flight and when flying close together they're called a plump.

He was also intrigued by the expression: "What's good for the goose is good for the gander." In other words, what's good for a man is equally good for a woman. Or better still, what a man can have or do a woman can also have it or do it.

Day by day he broke the stones. But he didn't just break them; he made sure every stone his eyes set on was broken. Why?

He was mining stones and he never knew which one could carry the hidden treasure. A diamond was buried deep somewhere. Somewhere down the belly of Mother Earth or near his vicinity.

Like a writer you've no idea which of your literary works would fetch you a million bucks tomorrow. Same goes with a sculptor, a lawyer, an estate developer, or a singer. Fact is not all of a singer's albums climb the billboard chart. Yet, even those that fail to make it to the top surprisingly sometimes rake in more money than the expected ones.

I'm reminded of the author of 'Things Fall Apart" Chinua Achebe. It's understood he got the manuscript of this famous book initially rejected by his publishers. But years later, it turned out to be the cornerstone.

It's applicable to all professions—teaching, policing, nursing, fishing, farming, building, cooking, hairdressing, fighting fire and many more. You have to make it all count. You're the chief executive of your life business, the decision maker of your daily activities and the sailor of your life boat.

You'd sink if you scull it anyhow. Always remember what makes you a good sailor is when you're able to weather the red tide or the terrible storm. So, always remember there are pitfalls and downfalls. It isn't always smooth. If someone told you, it's all smooth, all rosy ... he's nothing but a mischief. He's a liar, I told you to avoid them. Avoid a back stabber too. And who else did I tell you to avoid?

An idiot!

Yes, avoid them all... They've got nothing good to offer you, just remember that.

Therefore, never leave any stone unturned or reject a stone when quarrying. The Bible says it best: "Jesus saith unto them. Did ye never read in the scriptures: The stone which the builders rejected, the same is become the head of the corner," Matthew 21: 42 (KJV).

With passage of time the geese decided to transit at Mr. Stone's property. He'd them occasionally stopped by to say hello! And as a gesture he fed them well. It made his job much easier as it became interesting by the day. Also he never felt bored anymore.

As they visited one afternoon, Mr. Stone noticed something strange about his friends. They'd gathered at a place farther down the valley opposite his house. It was the east side. That side remarkably hosted some huge stones. And for years he'd refused to venture that terrain, but therein laid his fortune.

Altogether the geese quaked, quaked and quaked. They'd noticed something —a hidden treasure if you like. Their cacophonic noise made him think twice. He decided to go down the east side and deal with his fright. And 'Eureka' he found the diamond.

xxxxxxxxxxxxxxxxxx

This piece you've just read crossed my mind while preparing 'Banku' (a famous Ghanaian dish) on Wednesday afternoon October 2016. Earlier I almost had my stew burned!

I felt pressured by the messenger who delivered this piece. He'd no time to waste. I didn't know how many packages (in terms pages) he'd for me. I didn't know how much they weighed (in terms of content –paragraphing and all that) and I didn't know if I could get all the packages sorted out thus meeting my deadline (because I'd a lot of stuff coming up).

He insisted: "I've got two options for you. You either take the package right now or you lose it probably forever."

"I'm ready, I'm your obedient servant," I told the messenger.

"OK, go ahead and use me." And glad I did.

So, always remember you are not just a number. You're a true member of the world.

You're a global citizen, a royal among royals. You're a true champion among champions.

Always remember billions still live here, but out of many you're countered: Not just countered but you have your name cast on the unbreakable stone. There's a messenger reaching out be ready to accept his call.

Always remember you are not just a child of God but a chosen and a loved one of the Master Designer. You're loved always. You're always blessed. You're favoured always. And you're saved by his blood.

Always remember the world belongs to you because it's owned by your father in heaven. He owns it all and has it all. Therefore, if you will, he has a will with your name etched on a huge stone. Fear not, for no spears form against you can pierce through your body. Fret not because they're just pronouncing empty threats. And flight not my brother/sister because the light in you is like shards of a glass it will cut through the fright. That's your 'Identity.

Fate Decider: Sin City Holds Final Debate

Think you've seen the weirdest yet.

The hour comes not until adrenalin gets going and forefingers point to heavens. Until you see the heart races like a cheetah and observe an unusual mood swing— threatening to consume the venue slated for October 19 matchup better hold your thoughts, says author of 'The Finish Line.'

Possibly, we haven't seen the last of the huffing and the puffing from Mr. Trump yet.

BUT this is it! This is the third and final debate. This is the make or break stage And we'll perhaps see the worst, the best, the crudest and the last US 2016 presidential debate of the Democratic nominee Hillary Clinton and Republican candidate Donald Trump at University of Nevada in Las Vegas.

The debate comes on the back of wacky revelations about the candidates' past deeds.

Already the topics for the debate have been selected and will focus on immigration, the Supreme Court, debt, entitlements, economy and fitness to be president. It's hoped that barring any new developments the topics would remain unchanged.

Fox News host and moderator Chris Wallace selected the topics. Mr. Wallace was chosen by the bipartisan Commission on Presidential Debates to moderate the Las Vegas's showdown.

I can speculate that for now if any of the contenders hasn't found his/her bearing yet, this is the last chance for them to figure out and probably ask the question; *what do I do to outdo my opponent?*

And indeed what a place to decide such fate—Sin City!

On my record card I have Mrs. Clinton one win as against a nil for Mr. Trump that is if I declare the second debate as a drawn match or tie. But it seems Mrs. Clinton won the round two too. So it's two wins for Hillary. This puts her in a pole position. It also sets her on attack and defensive mode. But above all, she must stay focused throughout the debate. So far, it looks like it's hers to lose.

She leads Trump by double-digit in national polls and latest polls reveal support for Trump has plummeted after a series of sexual assault accusations. On the contrary voters have rallied behind Hillary after impressive performance in the two debates.

In the meantime Mrs. Clinton has turned her attention on traditionally right-leaning states.

Reports have it that in three battle ground states—Nevada, North Carolina and Ohio the race is in dead heat and the candidates are working at a breakneck speed to have a fair share or win those areas. According to CNN/ORC polls in the three states Hillary inches ahead of Donald in North Carolina and Nevada, but she continues to trail the republican nominee in Ohio—'one of the biggest electoral vote prize on the map'.

The polls were taken October 10-15 as accusations of sexual assault against Trump began to blaze.

Other polls show Mrs. Clinton is making great inroads. According to forecasting site FiveThirtyEight.com if presidential election were held today Hillary would coast to victory. And latest projections say her chances of winning the White House are 90 per cent compared to 10 per cent for Republican nominee Trump.

In campaigns of such magnitude one has to consider the people behind the scenes—the strategists and the surrogates and the advisers. Their tactics and advices serve as stimulant to shape the chances of the candidate. President Obama's chief adviser or strategist in 2012 election David Axelrod was a real gem in that terms.

So who are behind the candidates?

Mrs. Clinton has her husband former president Bill Clinton, sitting President Barack Obama, vice President Joe Biden, Bernie Sanders, and Elizabeth Warren. These are all great speakers and they're crisscrossing the length and breadth of the country to help her win the election.

Remember who said this famous line: "when they go low we go high...?'

That punch line was delivered by first lady Michelle Obama (at the DNC's convention) and she's viewed as Hillary's chief surrogate trekking the battle grounds and delivering punches meant to deal with Mr. Trump's sexism comments.

On the hand, according to New York Times Trump campaign's surrogate operation has relied heavily on a small cadre of supporters and cable news pundits. In June Mr. Trump hired Kevin Kellens to oversee the surrogates who defend him. New Jersey Governor Chris Christie, former and New York mayor, Rudy Giuliani are among his strategists.

Mr. Trump also has Breitbart News executive Steve Bannon as the chief executive and promoted pollster Kellyanne Conway to the role of campaign manager. This followed the resignation of Paul Manafort Mr. Trump's former campaign manager and chief strategist. He resigned in August this year after weeks of slipping poll numbers of the republican candidate.

With exactly three weeks to the election caution must be the watchword. Candidates must tread cautiously on the slippery slope turf, for there's nothing in the middle of the road except dead armadillo. *Have we seen the last of the creepy revelations yet*?

I can't tell from where I sit. But I wish both candidates Goodluck and Goodnight!

The Bells @ 6/7: What a timely intervention

Is there one you can count on?

Do it and do it again. Don't stop it because you'll never know when the bells will chime. You'll never know which side you'd find yourself. It could either be the safe zone or the unsafe side. But just when you thought it's all over, there comes someone with the plumb line to save the situation.

A God-sent rescuer is on the way running to tidy up things. When grace is coming she comes unfettered. So does favour too. They might seem miniscule to some people; however you can't downplay their significance in Man's day to day activities.

If you believe in Karma you'd understand what I'm talking about. But I hope you'd get it by and by if you aren't a believer in this act of reciprocity. It's a vibe, it's a feeling and it's an aura that radiates like the powerful sun.

xxxxxxxxxxxxxxx

I'd have been marked absent if there were a roll-call say in a class. Thank Goodness the 'time keeper' had good judgement and saved the situation. She stopped the approaching mishap that was probably minutes away. Linda figured out something must be wrong. She realised something wasn't right.

What's keeping him late today?

She possibly asked that question before she called me. But Linda knew tardiness wasn't my portion of doing things. I'm always on time, always there to be counted. And if I were a little behind time or shade late I would give her a call. But not today, I'd been ditched. I'd show up but not at six!

A few months ago a twenty-something year-old Ghanaian lady was found dead in her apartment in Worcester Massachusetts USA. Her decomposed body according to reports was discovered weeks after she passed on. Where were her workmates?

Did she have friends? And where were the neighbours?

Strange it took that long!

Elsewhere in the UK in 2009, I witnessed similar incident in Cardiff City, when a young man's fetid body was hauled out of his window across my residence. Residents said they hadn't seen him for days. That begs the question. Strangely no one checked on him until his odor invited the police.

Indeed true friends check on each other or one another from time to time in spite of their busy schedules. Life abroad is hectic and it seems one is always on the move. Busy bees, busy all day busy all night, trying to make ends meet.

What else would you expect after a 16-hour shift, 40-straight push-ups at 12:30 in the mornin' and writing 1 of 5 pages article (that translates into 1,479 words) in between those frenetic hours?

You'd of course be exhausted. Yet the body refused to surrender. I couldn't sleep till about 2am still listening to BBC news in the hope that it would lull me into sleep. At that moment I knew nature will steal my pride. She'll rob me of my long protected pride, the pride I've jealously guarded.

Hours before (during my lunch break) I'd called a few friends of mine. I'd called Brother Richard, Joseph, Billy, Jonathan, Michele and Uncle Bob. I'd also texted my Octogenarian friend —Frank Manlore to wish him good night and good luck. Frank and I have been doing this for months now.

I mentioned Uncle Bob: He's one of my good good friends. Good Old Bob lives in Gig Harbor I don't get the time to see him often since he retired from his work place here in Tacoma. I visited him last month.

He thanked me for the call and I thanked him for his time. It's karma.

Ghanaian highlife musician Akwasi Ampofo Agyei (alias Mr. A.A.A) of blessed memory put it this way: "Wo'ye papa a woye fa, wo'ye bone nso' a wo'ye fa."

Dear reader I implore you to observe sleep if you aren't familiar with death. They look alike. They must be bed-fellows I guess. I found myself in a huge class lecturing, answering questions etc... And boy, the students kept me busy!

Nonetheless I enjoyed their company and they told me: "Come back Sir Gordon. It was nice to have you here." Some of the students still tailed me as I was preparing to step out from the auditorium.

Linda's call would suddenly end my odyssey into the dreamland. . I was supposed to do shift change at six, which is why she called. I'd been saved by the bell!

But I felt relieved better than the days before. I'd clocked four out of an eight-hour normal sleep. That wasn't bad at all especially for me. I don't get it much from my crazy days. Days wrought by intensity.

"Be careful the road is slippery drive safe here," Linda told me.

Thank you my friend you made it count when it mattered most. That was the bell at six!

Why didn't you set an alarm?

I've never used an alarm. I am used to waking myself up. I get up consciously. But believe me, when you're into deep sleep alarm bells can't change the equation. I'm talking from experience. In September last year I nearly killed myself. I wasn't drank and I wasn't on any drugs. I don't do them anyway.

It was simply sleep deprivation. After five near misses of deadly accidents I finally rammed into someone's car less than a mile to my destination. I talked to myself. I called my name time and again to stay awake— telling myself of an impending danger... I dodged a train (the Link) I avoided sliding into the Puyallup River (River Rd.)

All this happened in an about 25 minutes' drive (not even an hour). And it was a week before the grand opening of the Washington State Fair in September 2015.

Perhaps the only thing I didn't do was to stop at a lay by and catch some sleep. But I was rushing home to save my other job. Hard to believe I still couldn't save it!

At seven -something my phone rang. It identified the caller as Tozia. Apparently he'd noticed something that snuck my hawkish eyes. *What's up Bro?*

"Hey I saw you wished Juliet a happy birthday and didn't acknowledge Mary," he said.

Wow I better do that quickly. 'How could I...Happy birthday Mary!!!

Ladies I hope you both have a great one today and the years ahead,' I later wrote. Mary and Juliet are my friends on Ghana TC Radio Chatroom. Thank you Tozia you made it count when it mattered most. And that was the bell at seven!!

You see how karma works? We'll need somebody. I need you, you need me and everybody needs somebody.

Gordon's Hodgepodge

Is president Mahama flogging a dead horse?

I remember former president Jerry John Rawlings struggling to say Bosnia Herzegovina on national television (GTV) during the early or mid '90's. That war was fought between 1992 and 1995. After fruitless attempt to say the Baltic name right, Mr. Rawlings gave up. But he gave up with a statement that has since stuck with me: "Language is not ours," he said.

My childhood football club Accra Hearts of Oak has this unyielding motto: 'Never say die until the bones are rotten." It's a stubborn motto that makes (or should I say made) the players stubborn, the coach stubborn, the management stubborn, the chapters stubborn and the club's supporters stubborn. Needless to say today, we don't find ourselves at the pinnacle as we used to back in the day.

The reason, I suppose the stubbornness has waned and the glint has found himself in/with the underdogs—Wa All Stars, Berekum Chelsea, Ashanti Goldfields FC etc. Our arch rivals the Porcupine Warriors—Kumasi Asante Kotoko are in the same boat with us.

I cried whenever, we lost a game!

Isn't that something?

Truth is when we serve honourably in any capacity anywhere we're always honoured and even when the undying death snips our lives we're immortalised and our souls live on.

Didn't Nigeria's Buhari come back?

And didn't the US state of Arkansas re-elect former president Bill Clinton as governor after a sore defeat?

I couldn't do with this write up without citing one of the 40 greatest quotes from Winston Churchill. The former British prime minister said this: "I may be drunk, Miss but in the morning I will be sober and you will still be ugly."

A Tory hater, Bessie Braddock (born Elizabeth Margaret Bamber a Labour MP had called the premier a drunk to which Churchill responded you are ugly.

Well, it appears one Ghanaian registered voter's statement parallels what the greatest world leader of the 20th century said over 7 decades ago. More so, it seems the voter isn't speaking for himself alone but for many registered voters in Ghana who aren't satisfied with the performance of the Mahama-led administration.

Bismarck Richardson (his pseudonym) a scrap dealer resident in Accra– Ghana's capital city made these remarks during a chat-up on WhatsApp: "Once we were blind. Once we were fools and once we let our guards down. And they took advantage of us..."

But today, I can assure you we're wiser and wide awake. We'll take their money, we'll take their rice, we'll take their outboard motors and laptops, we'll take their roofing sheets/cements, we'll take everything they'll bring to us, and will never vote for them. And there we'll see who'll have the last laugh. "

The voter said multi-party democracy is only good for Ghana if those given the mandate to rule would give their all and not be selfish or greedy. He noted: "Politicians are liars and not what they say is what they do. Too long they took us for a ride and it's about time we paid them back. We've resolved to do this."

Ah...Haven't we heard this before, one may ask?

What makes Bismarck's statement different from the previous ones?

Or is there a movement unknown to us that's driving this audacious pronouncement?

And does the statement lend any credence to the footage we saw on our TV screens and on social media platforms worldwide?

Earlier last week President Mahama was booed during his campaign tour in the Greater Accra region—a province he won in the last election (2012).

Where specifically did he go?

He was at Kokompe— a scrap dealing enclave in the Okaikoi South Constituency. The footage revealed an unhappy crowd racing towards the president's convoy amid shouts of— 'we're done with you', we're not voting for you,' and the popular one 'boys abre' meaning the youth are tired'.

At Ablekuma North constituency also in the Greater Accra region while speaking at a rally Mr. Mahama said something that rarely rears its head until crisis erupts like volcano. And he'd his chief critics in mind– the opposition NPP, stressing that if the NPP won't credit him for his 'good works' God sees that.

That sounds like someone who's losing traction. And I might not be wrong to state that probably the duck that laid the golden eggs is hibernating now.

Before a gathering the president made this humbling statement: "I am human, I'm not God. I'm not saying I have done so much, but I have done what I can and if others say they have not noticed what I have done, God who is in heaven is my witness and he sees the good works NDC has done."

There you go... What did Churchill say?

"It is no use saying, 'We are doing our best." You have got to succeed in doing what is necessary.'

Without a doubt, the president's statement calls for scrutiny. And I think a few questions would help us understand what he implied by this—: 'I'm not saying I have done so much, but I have done what I can... let's stop right there!

Question: How much is so much?

And did that much satisfy the critical mass?

Does the average Ghanaian feels, that much is good enough to put food on the kitchen table?

An Economic Think Tank, IMANI Ghana has released what it terms 'IMANIFesto Program'. It's a framework that assesses political parties manifestos using a coding system comprised of quantitative indicators. It is a final report on the implementation of the 540 promises in the 2012 NDC manifesto titled: 'Advancing the Better Ghana Agenda.'

In summary, IMANI's out-based assessment of NDC's manifesto promises yielded an overall result of 52.% indicating that about 53.% of the promises by the ruling NDC in 2012 have been achieved. The report explains that based on the institution's designated scale, 52% is interpreted as Fair performance.

President of IMANI Ghana Franklin Cudjoe says per this assessment the Mahama-led administration didn't perform poorly in terms of keeping its promises. "But at the same time, the NDC government under president Mahama did not excel in keeping its promises to Ghanaians," he said.

According to the report about 47 per cent of the promises the party made to Ghanaians during the 2012 election have not been fulfilled.

So would the president's claim: 'I did what I can...,' warrant or justify his reelection?

For example if the nation hired a football coach (A) to win the coveted All Africa Nations Cup (a trophy which has denied Ghana for decades) and (B) qualify the national men's football team to the World Cup Games but failed to deliver:

Would that coach be rehired because we participated in the competition?

And this is what Churchill meant by 'doing what is necessary'...i.e achieving the result.

All that Ghanaians are asking for is— bring back the trophy home and take us to the World Cup.

Another interesting quote from the president is this one: "God who is in heaven is my witness and he sees the good works NDC has done."

Well, we won't know that until the elections are held on December 7, and thank God we're inching closer there. But I can bet on two things here — there will be a victor and there will be a villain. Of which I'm reminded of this popular axiom: 'the voice of the people is the voice of God'.

If the people re-elect the president that means God who sits high in the heavens has indeed seen his 'good works'. However, a loss would mean rejection and non-performance.

Thing is it becomes incredulous, the idea that whenever it's election time politics or politicks finds a way to lubricate its squeaky gears— churning out lies, empty promises, quoting biblical verses known and unknown and so on and so forth.

Basically, the idea is to make them look good and perhaps appear saintly.

No doubt it's a crucial time and the smarter and cleverer one is the better...

So, who else could be identified as the president's critics apart from the opposition NPP?

Well, they could be the likes of Bismarck who have made up their minds not to vote for the Umbrella in the December 7, elections. And that's troubling news —an indication that the Greater Accra region could go all-blue, all-white and all-red (NPP colours).

Suffice to say the sturdy horse that pulled the wagon is possibly dead. *If so why flog it?*

I should point out that the president's earlier remarks humanises him. It underscores his infallibility as mortal being .That I think was humbling coming from the first gentleman of the land. It contrasts the usual bravado class of our politicians. I can however not guarantee whether this emotive appeal was pulled up because of the season we find ourselves.

The Trojan Horse Is Back: Did the Greeks loan it out?

Please… don't ask me how it got here and why of all places they chose Ghana,–the gold-rich West African nation. Observers are worried and political pundits are already reading so much into the surreal episode that happened recently.

This is probably a 'subterfuge' at its highest and politics in its embers, says this writer. I've never seen this before, goats on the rampage!

They might've been sent from above or elsewhere in the Planetiers.

But where did they come from?

What's their modus operandi?

And how does this mimic the legendary Trojan horse?

It's simply this: He who calls for a battle and doesn't know what he's in for and how the battle will be fought could be labeled a dud or a loser: Because wars aren't like throwing a dice.

xxxxxxxxxxxx

A renowned journalist in Accra Ghana had one on one interview with the country's president John Dramani Mahama at the Flagstaff House.

GOA: "Your Excellency, I must say I'm deeply humbled to meet with you:

To begin with, did you hear your main contender —Nana Akufo Addo described himself as the biblical David?"

JDM: "Yes I did."

GOA: So, does that make you the Goliath in the impending presidential election?"

JDM: "Well, you and I know who won that battle. If I say I am Goliath it means I'll taste defeat.

And I 'ain't ready for that. So, I'm also David the second."

GOA: "You think so?"

JDM: "Yes, I do. Remember they say…what you ask for is what you get."

GOA: "And how's everything going on for you?"

JDM: "It's been rough and tough. But I think I've a good chance to win again. I will win and win."

GOA: "You sounded like Donald Trump the Republican presidential nominee."

JDM: "Hahaha… Trump 'paa'?"

GOA: Anyway Sir, I think it's a great day to go down the hill?"

JDM: "You mean going to the casino at the Mall?"

GOA: "No Sir.'

JDM: "What is it?'

GOA: "To do your usual campaign rounds."

JDM: "Not today. I'm taking a break."

GOA: "No, Sir you don't need a break."

JDM: "Why not I think I need it?"'

GOA: 'The earlier you go the better, because the tuff doesn't look good. The goats are on a warpath– chewing and tearing every poster of yours in the city.' They're bleating at every street corner and it appears their action could spark a new revolution."

JDM: "What are they, life or dead goats?"

GOA: 'Life goats with beards and horns. And their bleating can be heard far from Bole. "

JDM: "You're kidding me. You mean goats too don't like me?' Ugh! Then I'm finished. What kind of game is this, is it conventional or spiritual warfare?"

GOA: "Perhaps both?' Remember, 'A' can cause 'B' and 'B can cause 'A'. Or both can be triggered by any causative agents. It could be 'C', 'D' or XYZ."''

JDM: "What do I do then?"

GOA: "The solution or answer rest in the bosom of the voters. They'll decide your fate and anybody who's seeking to become the first gentleman of our great nation."

JDM: "Walahi, that doesn't sound right!

GOA: "Why not?"

JDM: "Have you forgotten what voters in Nigeria did to Goodluck Jonathan. Luck eluded Goodluck. They thumbed him down. And I'm afraid Ghanaians might do the unexpected come December. See, I'm not the problem. It's all 'Dumsor's fault. The shambolic economy is another. Jobs and unemployment are huge factors. Corruption is driving me crazy too. I can't sleep and I can't look in the eyes of Ghanaians. I don't like the name they've given me."

GOA: "What's the name?'

JDM: "Bohyehene. Am I really... And do I look like one?"

The two laughed hysterically, ending the interview at the Flagstaff House.

The people of Troy or the Trojans carried a huge wooden horse (made by the enemy) into their city as their victory trophy. They were fighting the Greeks, who'd pretended to flee the battle. Unbeknown to them that what they transported into the heart of their city was worse than a boubou trap.

The canny Greeks had carved a wooden horse and hid a combative force of men inside it. The horse was kept in Troy and they (the Greeks) pretended sailing away. History has it that this subterfuge act followed a 'fruitless 10-year siege'. And when the Trojans went to bed in the night the Greeks crept out from their hideout and captured the Troy city.

The bloody war had been won by the Greeks—employing one of the world's best war stratagems.

Politics is like battles. And the players have all manner of strategies to employ in order to win elections.

If you asked President John Mahama who's your political arch rival or opponent he will say Nana Akufo Addo the NPP presidential nominee for 2016. In the same vein the leader of the Elephant Party sees Mr. Mahama (who is seeking reelection) as his number one contender.

Politics as we're aware always has its weird side: The side that seeks to cannibalise those who don't belong to our party and the side that demonises opponents or caricatures them. But it has its good and humor side too, which I've just done.

It's this side that makes democracy perhaps the best system of government—free speech, right to freedom and liberty, human rights, voting rights, rights to movement and association, religion etc. Can't get it better than this!

To all my people I say we cannot afford to trade democracy for autocracy or dictatorship. We cannot afford to divide ourselves in the name of politics. So, let's stand together, work together and build together.

Why We Are Who We Are

What Are Retired Public Servants Doing in Gov't Bungalows?

'Is this a Pimper's Paradise?'

You'd think they'd vacate the government bungalows after their tenure or end of service. But that isn't the case in my homeland Ghana as such bungalows are now accommodating ex- officials' girlfriends, mothers, fathers, sisters, brothers, nephews and nieces, cousins and friends. Retired public servants and their cronies have been occupying government's residences months, some of them years after the completion of their services, according to Ministry of Works & Housing.

This isn't a new phenomenon, I can emphatically say. And I'm even inclined to believe it possibly pervades across the continent.

Samuel Atta Akyea the sector minister who made this known said there are a number of retired public servants and other unauthorized persons occupying government bungalows. He seemed upset about the situation and has therefore warned the trespassers to vacate the residences as soon as possible or face the full rigors of the law.

Mr. Atta Akyea has also cautioned public sector workers living legitimately in state properties but not paying rent to do so or face possible ejection as well. His deputy Freda Prempeh who also spoke on the issue said:

"There are about five or six categories of people who have decided to do their own thing with government properties. One is people who have been on retirement for so many years – sometimes about five to six years – and are still living in government properties and are not paying anything to government. The other category, are those on retirement but have in turn given the apartment out to their nieces, their nephews, their friends and colleagues."

Some too have even left the apartment and abandoned it and nobody is even living there and there are some people living in government bungalows that we don't even have their data in the office. Those that we have their names on our data base, their data are not on that of the Controller and Accountant General so they don't pay anything to the government."

Indeed, we are who we are. And I guess the inescapable question is:

Would this eviction ever happen?

Mind you some of them as the deputy minister alluded to have lived in these state properties for nearly a decade. Didn't the previous administrations notice them and how come they weren't evicted? Wouldn't for example the MINISTER of POWER (MoP) as usual come and plead on their behalf?

Can the new cat chase the mouse out of the house?

It appears Mrs. Freda Prempeh has the touch of the Midas (with a happy ending though):

"A week ago, I wrote letters to some of the occupants, and people trooped to the office and to the Bank of Ghana to pay their rent and I raised GHS85, 000 because I gave them 24hours that if you don't pay your rent, I will evict you."

According to her the exercise to evict the squatters isn't a nine day wonder. "We are coming out with the police next week (referring to this week). If you've not paid your rent, if you are not authorised to live in a government bungalow make sure that you pack out."

Now consider the resources that would go into this exercise i.e. the personnel or man power, the vehicles, the fuel, the logistics and many more. Why do we always have to let the beard grow to the knee?

We fancy comparisons. We like to compare our democracy to that of the US or the UK. And we do so in areas such as tourism, sports, and politics you name it. But have we for a sec considered the lifestyles of the following persons?

Former US vice president Joe Biden commuted from his home state Delaware to Washington DC via Amtrak throughout his senate career. It's understood he did that virtually every working day for35 years before he became the nation's No.2 most prominent figure. But it was more than commuting to and fro, I learned. Mr. Biden also engaged the people on the train in conversations daily earning him the name 'Talkative Joe'.

In March 2011, the Amtrak station in Wilmington, Del was named after him as a long –time passenger and rail advocate.

Have we also considered emulating the shining example of Uruguay president, Jose Mojica?

The media says the 78-year-old man is the world's poorest president. BUT is he? "No I am not a poor person… poor people are those who always want more and more…those who never have enough of anything…those are the poor because they're in a never –ending cycle."

Mr. Mojica's immediate bodyguard Manuela is a three-legged dog. He opted to stay in his farm at backcountry of the nation's capital. A dusty rural road leads to his tiny farm house. Yes, he's shunned the luxurious house provided by the state for its leaders and opted to stay in the farmhouse with his wife a senator.

"I choose this austere life style. I choose not to have too much belongings so that I have time to live how I want," he says. And did I mention he's also giving 90 per cent of his salary every month to charity? His assets I guess you want to know too: Two vehicles—a tractor and a WV Beatle 1978, small amount of property and his farm house. *Cest fini!*

Several months ago I saw two striking images: The first one was a man on a bike on his way going to work. As he rode through the city's main streets scores waved and he waved back. He was dressed up to the nines (suit and tie). That man was Mark Rutte Prime Minister of the Netherlands. Ironically, the image next to Mr. Rutte's was a convoy of cars supposedly taken an African president (name withheld) to go for a haircut. You may say that's a joke. Well, I get that!

BUT when did you see an African president on commercial transport say *Tro-tro, Matatu,* on a motor bike, or bicycle?

What did Mr. Cameron say?

David Cameron former UK Prime Minister is quoted as saying: "If the amount of money stolen from Nigeria in the last 30 years was stolen from the UK the UK would cease to exist."

Mr. Kwamina Miaful Dadzie posted this comment on WhatsApp:

"…Very sad that often those who loot our nations already have enough for themselves, but still covet after others' possession," his comment followed my article titled: 'Mam-hunt For Mr. Greed.' published on moderngahana.com and the social media on August 4 2017..

In 2011 Forbes an American business magazine published the name of some African leaders who had stolen billions from their people:

Africa's Richest Dictators who were they?

First is former Nigerian military leader Sani Abacha. Upon his death in 1998 the Nigerian government uncovered over US$3 billion dollars linked to the dictator.. After a series of negotiations between the government and the Abacha family, Abacha's first son Mohammed eventually returned U$1.2 billion to the Nigerian government in 2002.

Next is Mobutu Sese Seko the former president of the DR Congo. Over his 30 years reign as a ruler of the central African nation the dictator amassed wealth estimated between US$1 billion and US$ 5billion. Next is Nigeria's former military leader Ibrahim Badamasi Babaginda, now 76 years old is believed to have laundered close to US$12 billion earned from an oil windfall during the 1992 Gulf War.

Elsewhere in east Africa, Kenya's former president Daniel Arap Moi who ruled the east-African nation from 1978 to 2002 also followed the footsteps of the lootees. During his 28 years rule Mr. Moi managed to loot nearly a billion dollars from his people. And was it not him again who sold the lions and the giraffes to the *Muzungus* for a token?

He stole lands and earned so many assets some of which are held by his children's name in Australia according to Kroll Associates, a corporate investigation and risk consultancy company that uncovered the rot.

Next is Hosni Mubarak Egypt's former president. He ruled the north-African nation for 30 good years. And guess what he too ridiculously looted an estimated US$ 70 billion. Forbes editors however think the figure is exaggerated. But the fact remains that he looted his people.

And how could I forget good old Equatorial Guinea's President Teodom Obiang. In 2006 FORBES estimated his fortune at US$600 million. And there are many more we probably don't know.

Thing is, not everyone would get the opportunity to serve his/her nation in capacities as public office holders. But it's unquestionably an honour to be given such mandate to represent the people and serve them well. A leader must be selfless not selfish, a leader must be kind not mean, a leader must be humble not arrogant. These qualities among others must be the guiding principles. They shouldn't lord themselves over the people who elected them.

A leader must learn not to be smug, sniffy, snippy and snooty. A good leader must inspire, motivate his or her people to engage with the nation's vision and not teach them how to loot, how to launder, and how to pilfer.

GHANA PUBLIC LIBRARIES: Are They Dead or Alive?

Does Ghana Have a National Library?
It's a travesty to deny any generation the right to quality education, information etcetera, says author Gordon Offin-Amaniampong

xxxxxxxxxx

Ghana hasn't done badly when it comes to her vision and goal to: 'establish, equip, manage and maintain public libraries in the country. At least she's the University of Ghana's Balme Library (established in 1959) to brag about, which is regarded as the best library in West Africa. More so, between 1909 up to date she's been able to establish public libraries in all of the nation's regional capitals.

There are more than 62 public libraries currently doted around the West-African nation, the size of Oregon State in the US. The Supreme Court Library is deemed to be the oldest, opened in 1909 and Achimota School Library, Accra comes second established in 1927.

But is that enough?

No, I don't think so. It isn't worth bragging about one asset, when you've nearly 100 of your assets neglected and left to rot. How about this: What shall it profit a Man to have 10 children and leave them all to go wayward? Would that make him/her a good or great parent?

Truth be told the structures on the ground belie the beautiful ideas and objectives set out in her books. In fact, Ghana's plan to make the country a literary and enlightened one, provide materials and other educational aids to support formal and informal education as well as develop the manpower needs of the nation would come to naught if pragmatic and robust measures aren't put in place to revitalise these libraries that are fast deteriorating.

It must be emphasised that Ghana could have done better (if not even establish more public libraries, at least maintain the few) over the years given her status as low middle income nation in the sub region. In my view, the pure neglect of these public libraries is an indictment on the nation. It reminds me of this popular saying about our forests: When the last tree dies, the last man dies. Well, guess what would happen to our generation and the ones that will follow us...they'd be bereft with knowledge because there would be no public libraries.

A former Education Minister under Kufour administration Ameyaw-Akumfi made the following remark; "Libraries in the country had completely been run down through years of neglect.

A society without a library where tourists can easily have access to information on its history and culture is a society which is not ready to inform others of its heritage."

History of Ghana public libraries

By 1928 there had begun what came to be known at the time as the public library movement in Ghana. And it was championed by then Anglican Lord Bishop of Accra Right Reverend John Aglionby. He opened his own library of some 6,000 volumes at the Bishop's House in Accra for members of the Parish.

Almost two decades later precisely 1946, the public library service began in Accra under the name of Aglionby Library in honour of the Bishop for his revolutionary efforts. Subsequent upon that groundbreaking effort the Gold Coast Library Ordinance 1949 was re-enacted in 1970 under the title Ghana Library Board Act (No. 327, 1970).

Following a series of bills initiated by GLA an Act was passed in 2008 by the Parliament of Ghana to establish the Ghana National Library Service. It superseded the Ghana Library Board Act of 1970. And based on the new local government system which placed much more emphasis on decentralization, the said Act empowered metropolitan, municipal and district assemblies to establish their own libraries.

It was expected that the Act would create an environment for the improved operation of then Board, and accelerate the development of libraries in Ghana.

But as earlier noted the ground still doesn't look good. It betrays Ghana's quest to reposition herself as tourists' destination in the sub region. From time immemorial the problems had been inadequate provision of resources such as finance, manpower and library materials. In view of the poor funding, very little has been coming in the form of new books. Aside that low salaries have also affected the recruitment of new staff and the retention of older ones.

In 1986 the PNDC government initiated a plan to turn things around. The Ministry of Education which spearheaded the initiative set up a Community Libraries Project with the aim of improving the standard of education of pupils in the country.

For example, Accra with a population of nearly 3 million has only six community libraries. These libraries are expected to serve the various communities, not only the school children. Sad to say that very little has been done to maintain them over the decades. This is partly due to our lack of maintenance culture, rendering facilities and services in these libraries in a deplorable state.

Does Ghana have a national library?

Mrs. Gladys Prempeh a Ghanaian now resident in the United Kingdom asked a Librarian the above question when she visited home this summer (2017) with her two sons. And the response was/is: No Ghana doesn't have a National Library. However, many Ghanaians think the Ghana Library Board (GLB) building sited near Bank of Ghana or the Supreme Court is a National Library. No it isn't and it doesn't meet or qualify such status. That library is called the Accra Central Library. It was established in 1956.

The GLB which was founded in 1950 is believed to be the first Ghana library service in sub-Sharan Africa. The Board was established by the 1949 Gold Coast Ordinance and it assumed responsibility for the Aglionby Library which had been started by John Aglionby—the

Anglican bishop of Accra and the British Council's mobile library for other public library services in Africa.

In 2003 then NPP government planned to build a national library in Accra to accommodate what it called 'rare literary and cultural materials'. The said library was supposed to be directly under the Presidency. Then Education Minister Prof Ameyaw Akumfi tasked GLB to work out the modalities for the implementation of the project. And in collaboration with the Carnegie Institute of the United States of America the two carried out the project and gave Padmore Library a face-lift. So in many respects the George Padmore Library which is under the GLA performs some of the functions of a National library.

There'd since been attempts to get that plan actualised but to no avail. The Ghana Library Association (GLA) at its 50th anniversary celebrations in 2012 highlighted some key topics such as: Libraries key to national development, libraries access to knowledge and of course the illusive national library the case of Ghana building a strong library association.

How Are Libraries Doing Around the World?

Across the world activities by public libraries haven't been remarkable. This is evident by the survey below.

'North American library growth is unimpressive', wrote Jonathon Sturgeon senior of The Baffler. His article was about the Annual Library Budget Survey, a global study that queries 686 senior librarians about their budget spending predictions for the year. It was published in 2016 by the Publishers Communication Group (PCG), a consultancy wing of Ingenta, the self-described "largest supplier of technology and related services for the publishing industry."

The survey found uneven growth expectations for libraries worldwide.

For North American libraries, the survey was more cautious than optimistic, with librarians in the U.S., Canada, and Mexico expecting only a 1% increase in budget spending. In other developed or "mature markets," the report says, growth expectations were negative. In Europe, for example, budgets are expected to fall by 0.1%.

According to the report in less developed markets, signs pointed to higher expectations for library growth. In the Middle East and Africa, senior librarians were anticipating growth of up to 4.2%. And in Asia experts predicted 2.8% increase in budgets.

The Charlotte Virus: A germ that won't die today

All things being equal we will live to see other general elections—presidential or parliamentary. But I've got a message for those political activists or party surrogates and members who're smiling today like a bride at a wedding ceremony to stand firm and not downplay what the Charlotte virus could cause them tomorrow.

They must be reminded that the virus will be back in subsequent elections and it could unleash a deadly blow or attack anyone if the same criteria are still operable. It's also a message for those who say they wished it happened to either party A or B.

"I wanted Akufo Addo out," says the general secretary of the National Democratic Congress (NDC) Asiedu Nketiah.

He told 'Okay FM' an Accra-based radio station (in the wake of the tsunami) that: "Akufo Addo is our party's main contender in the December 7 polls and his disqualification would have come to us as good news."

Well, this isn't a tit for tat game. This isn't malarkey. This is an issue that has lives tied to its umbilical cord. So, if you didn't get the message right please read my lines over again. I urge you to read them carefully and arm yourselves to the teeth because it could get worse or nastier tomorrow.

Can you imagine if this virus had attacked any of the major parties— either the Elephant or the Umbrella?

Just imagine if jailing the 'Montie Trio' (by the Supreme Court) could knock cabinet ministers off their feet/seats to seek the immediate release of the people who claimed responsibility for their ignoble actions. Then guess what would happen if a sitting president is disqualified to seek reelection by a constitutional body—the Electoral Commission (EC).

Last Monday, the EC knocked down 12 or so presidential nominees bidding to serve at the Flagstaff House—the seat of government in the 2016 December 7 poll.

The move is the first major storm that has ever hit Ghana's political landscape –jolting political ambitions of the 12 candidates. Among them former first Lady Nana Konadu Agyeman-Rawlings, NDP, Dr. Edward Mahama, PNC, and Dr. Paa Kwesi Nduom, PPP have all been disqualified by the Electoral Commission(EC) to contest in the forthcoming presidential election.

Indeed I received the news with mixed feelings. One of the nominees is my best friend. But I think cronyism, nepotism, mediocrity—none has a place in this all important national exercise. You can't expect the best from the EC and at the same time want the body to bend the rules when it has its criteria set out in the blue print.

Invariably games have rules likewise politics and the rules must rule and be binding.

If you know how to play with the primates you should know how to babble.

US president Barack Obama in the 2008 democratic primaries said this: 'I play by the rules." This was when Hillary Clinton (then her arch rival) started to lose her overwhelming lead in super delegates. Everything was tumbling–the Democratic Party officials whose votes Hillary was counting on to help her close the gap with Obama were defecting.

Bottom line, she wanted the DNC (Democratic National Commission) to bend the rules on her behalf but that never happened.

Truly, I think candidates —Edward Mahama and Paa Kwesi Nduom are two fantastic gentlemen. And so are the other presidential nominees. I can't vouch for Madam Akua Donkor though… Over the past decades the two in particular, have demonstrated their preparedness and avowed interest to serve as well as help deepen democracy in Ghana.

However, we should bear in mind that what happened to these candidates could have happened to any of the major parties. Perhaps it was an honest mistake or error that caused their disqualification.

I'm however, curious... Is this the first time this had happened to these candidates apart from former First Lady Agyeman Rawlings?

Or it had happened before but they got away with it?

That said I support their move to seek redress or go to court. After all that's the beauty of democracy. You can't oppress dissention and you cannot gag freedom of speech and expression.

But I hope the major parties are following the development closely. I hope they take a cue from this and be mindful they aren't bigger than Ghana. So far, I haven't heard about any riots or acts of vandalism from the affected nominees' supporters and that's a healthy development and they need to be commended.

Kudos also to the Commissioner Madam Charlotte Osei and her distinguish panel members. I think you've raised the bar and even though many see the action as unthinkable and uncalled for it would remain an indelible mark in the minds of the citizenry.

I still wonder if the commission would be able to crack the whip next time the lot falls on any of the major parties. What would happen?

How would they react?

Would they take to the streets armed with clubs and machetes?

Would they accept such move in good faith and not threaten to rape and kill?

Would they undermine the commission to bend the rules?

I can't bring the curtain down without this reminder: Read my lines because we'll cross the bridge on Offin River one day.

Chinese Miners Mine In School Zone

Was It Ignorance Or Impudence?

Boldness could best describe the way they're operating illegally in Ghana. Covertly or overtly they've demonstrated to the world that their activities aren't dying today. Maybe tomorrow but what if tomorrow doesn't come? They've downed the trees, poisoned the waters, killed the flora and fauna, raped the vegetation and even dared the authorities. Operators of illegal mining also known as Galamsey have vowed to continue their exploits despite government's six-month moratorium.

And if you haven't gotten the news yet, reports from Ghana say the Tarkwa police in the Western region yesterday arrested 10 Chinese nationals allegedly mining in front of a Senior High School in the mining town—the oldest in Ghana.

Isn't that a brazen act? It really speaks volumes. The question is: Was it a sign of disrespect to their host nation? Well it remains to be observed whether the Akufo-Addo government would be able to end the menace as the president has made it one of his signature pledges.

What else might've driven these guys to purportedly mine in a school zone could it be ignorance? I wondered. As the old saying goes, if you do not know about something you do not worry about it'. But it's also been said that this statement or term is often used falsely to justify apathy on a given subject.

So, I still tried to think aloud and even tried to play the devil's advocate. Could this not be an exaggeration? Did the reports try to cause an unnecessary fear and anxiety? Or maybe just maybe Ghanaians are tired of the influx of Chinese into their country?

Indeed one cannot lose sight of that fact the Chinese aren't solely to blame for the Galamsey activities in Ghana. It's believed majority of them have been fronting for Ghanaians. From opinion leaders to Assembly Members, chiefs, the rich and powerful in society have hands in the unholy operation. This in part, explains why governments have been finding it difficult to stop illegal mining in the country.

According to reports the 10 were caught in the act at a site at Efua Nta Kamponase opposite the Tarkwa Senior High School. They were arrested on Wednesday afternoon following a tip-off by a group called Volunteers Against Illegal Mining, whose members have been employed under the Ministry for Lands and Natural Resources.

Mr. Benito Owusu Bio a deputy Minister for Lands and Natural Resources who happened to be at a national stakeholders forum at

UMET University of Mines and Technology at Tarkwa had to leave the meeting to see to the situation, the reports said.

Denial

Some of the Chinese since their arrest have denied ever engaging in illegal mining.

One of the suspects had refuted claims of being involved in the act, suggesting he was a tourist and had been in the country for only the past two months. But that claim couldn't stand the test of time. Upon several interrogations the reports added, the suspect was unable to tell which tourist sites he had visited since his arrival. However, another Chinese confirmed being involved in the illegal act but said they had been contracted by one Ghanaian Alhaji whose full name they failed to mention.

Meanwhile the sector minister has said the suspects will be transferred to Accra for the law to take its course.

Indeed we may have failed yesterday in our fight against Galamsey. But we don't have to fail today in our collective fight against their activities. Yes, the president Akufo-Addo has vowed to pursue this fight to the end of his tenure but he alone cannot make it happen. I believe we must all put our act together to stop Galamsey. Yesterday belongs to the past and that must serve as a road map for our forward march.

Be reminded the environmental impact of their activities is unparalleled. Galamsey depletes environmental resources such as water; soil, landscape, vegetation, the ecosystem among others. We cannot afford to lose all that. So let's save the environment today for our children's children tomorrow.

At its peak around 2015 there were an estimated 50,000 foreign workers, mainly Chinese who engaged in illegal mining in the gold-rich West African nation—the second largest gold producer after South Africa.

The Devil still exists because he's many:
It sounds absurd right? But please hold your thoughts, don't crucify me yet as they did to Jesus Christ. Be gentle with me. Be considerate. And what's the last one, I nearly forgot it? Be tolerant.

I tell you, there's nothing so humbling like giving ears to the people you don't even agree with or see eye to eye.

Fact is you don't have to know me or like me to disagree or agree with me on an issue. We don't have to belong to same sect, same party, same parents, same faith or same team to help build what is ours. What we all have stake in it. *Did you get that?*

Simply put, if the price is right say it is right. And if the price is bad call it as it is.

So let me first state my point and thereafter you can draw your own conclusions:

If Confucius had told you he could turn the world upside down, it would have sparked confusion right? No doubt about that.

Glad he didn't say that. But Confucius is dead or he died. Mohammed the prophet of the Muslims is dead or he died and Jesus also died but he resurrected.

Let's fast forward it, many great men and women of our generation and two centuries back or more are all dead or have died. And humanity—rich or poor, young or old, male or female, Hindu or Buddhist is still dying and will continue to die.

xxxxxxxxxxxxxx

And now here we are…

A man goes to the highest court of the Jews— the Sanhedrin in Jerusalem, with a case many view as controversial and ridiculous. Dressed in all white he holds a scroll and a Bible in both hands looking so livid. His eyes fixed to the ceiling as though there're beams to count. He wouldn't talk to anybody until the judge calls him.

But who's touched the wrong nerve of the strange man?

He's suing none other than the Most High, God the Almighty.

What's his case?

Why has God allowed Satan or the Devil to torment the children he loves?

And he quotes John 3:16 "For God so loves the world..." to buttress his case.

The judge looks at the man pulls his glasses to the tip of his nose. Too close to the roof of his mouth and shakes his head as if to say—'Really?' He stares at the man more and finally beckons him to step forward.

'Why has it taken God so long to kill Satan?" asks the man.

At this time he draws more eyes to himself as whispers fill the courtroom like zombies creeping out from the sepulchers.

"Order," shouts the court clerk.

And the judge speaks:

"Aren't you glad that you're here today?"

"Yes I am, my Lord," says the man.

The judge continues: "We are all not right. We are all not perfect. Evil dwells in us. We commit sin(s) every day that's evil and that's the devil when he becomes an adult. We lie, we commit adultery, we fornicate, we kill and steal from people, we back bite our own friends, you name it. That's all evil."

Yet, God is still merciful. Yes he's still forgiving.

He didn't kill you when you lied. He didn't cause brimstone to fall upon you when you raped that beautiful soul neither did he allow the hungry lion to grind you when you robbed the widow across you.

He spared your life when you took your brother's life.

If I called you a 'devil' after that heinous crime would you expect God to kill you instantly/?

Remember Donald called Hillary the 'devil' at the second US presidential debate in October 9, 2016.

Did you expect God to kill her because someone cried wolf, when actually there wasn't wolf?

I bet, wicked as you are you won't even ask for repentance. But you'll pray this way: 'I must never get caught.' You'll pray that there will be more victims, more to reap from where you've never sown and more to kill and maim."

And who else was called the 'devil' at the UN's General Assembly about a decade ago?

Was it Mahmoud Ahmadinejad? No it wasn't him (the former Iranian president).

It was Hugo Chavez (former Venezuelan president now deceased) who taunted former US president George W. Bush: "The devil is here..." he mocked.

Here's how I put it, evil embedded if uncontrolled would grow to become the devil.

Better put, the evil in you is like chi Wawa, today it's barking but tomorrow it will be howling like a wolf. So, you're the reason the devil still exists. You're the reason there are many devils.

Think about it for a second. Weren't you in church yesterday when your head pastor screamed: "I bound Satan in the name of Jesus?" I step on him and I cast him in the bottomless pit."

Yet today the devil is here. But thank God the Most High, the most compassionate, the most loving and the most gracious we're still alive and even though tomorrow we'll be dead or die we understand that we're born to live and born to die.

Always remember many devils exist not because God doesn't care or love us but because we've chosen or allowed them to live in/with us.

Was there a Winner?

Sunday Night 2nd US Presidential Debate

I had it as a split-match even though Hillary Clinton appeared to be slightly ahead of her opponent Donald Trump with regard to issues. Besides, she looked presidential more composed and addressed every question posed to her either from the audience or the moderators without deviating.

That was conspicuously missing on the part of the Republican candidate. His supporters would argue that's Trump's style. The GOP candidate from the get-go resorted to heckles and failed to answer substantive questions. Such deviations would cause the moderators to remind him a few times. But even with prompts he still went off tangent.

Nonetheless, I think Mr. Trump had his way when questions about Clinton's emails and Birtherism came up. Looking 'young and restless' he made faces amidst interruptions.

The Sunday night presidential debate is the second coming on the heels of 'Trump's 2005 vulgar video/tape, which became a major issue during the night. Trump tried hard to take cover but Clinton held his tail and wouldn't let go, making sure that her opponent was punch-drunk.

I must add the debate perhaps had all the flavors. It was nasty. It was ugly. It was action-packed laced with uncut, unadulterated and uncensored questions from the audience. At one point Mr. Trump called Mrs. Clinton a 'Devil.'

A Politico writer Bren Schreckinker described it as the nastiest debate ever. And reporter Shane GoldMacher says it is the ugliest debate ever,

The punchline though to me was a questioner who'd asked the candidates to tell the country and their audience what good thing each of them had to say about the other. And they were both gracious despite the initial feisty air that grabbed the stage.

There was no handshake. No pleasantries. First to take the bait was Hillary. She showed admiration for Trump's children and said she was proud of them. Mr. Trump saw that as a compliment and thanked Mrs. Clinton. He said Clinton was a 'fighter' and she never 'quit'.

'Make America 'Grope' Again': Borrowed!

Words speak eloquently but images tell it better. They cause jaws to drop, eyes to pop and nose to shake. Take it or leave it images are like magic. And if you're still in doubt just sprint into the loo, look yourself in the mirror and ask the Man in that object:

Who am I? And if still unsure listen to yourself as you speak.

Better still, you can pinch your face (Yeah, it hurts worse there) and look closely the image again. What you see is nothing different from the true likeness of you.

That's how you look, that's who you are and that's what you're made of—beautifully and fearfully crafted. How cool is that!

How do I do that Sir Gordon?

Stop being naughty my friend, you just did it.

Knew ye not that....the secret to wisdom dwells in the Holy Book?

Anyway, please permit me to quickly put on record, that the above phrase in parenthesis isn't mine. I borrowed it from an anonymous author courtesy of mighty Facebook. I borrowed it because I find it so beguiling...

The phrase speaks volume. But perhaps what adds flavor or value to it is the word—'Grope' sandwiched between America— the world's super power and 'Again' which simply means recurrence of something.

I'm pretty sure the author didn't mean– taking America back to recession or the era when the nation witnessed its longest and deepest economic crisis –'The Great Depression' in the 1930's. At the time, literally Americans groped in darkness with their hands searching for an exit door or an escape route. But grope as in fondling someone for sexual pleasure against their will.

On July 25, 2016 under the article "Another Convention Underway' I wrote: "United States will see one of its crudest presidential campaigns ever in her political history." And indeed that's already developing. And it could be nastier in tomorrow's debate.

How did we get here?

It's a leaked video tape recorded in 2005. Republican presidential nominee Donald Trump is seen in that clip making vulgar remarks concerning women. The words could be described as disgusting prompting Trump's wife Melania Trump to condemn her husband's comments as: 'Unacceptable and offensive:"

Meanwhile Trump's chief surrogate former New York mayor, Rudy Giuliani says: "There's nothing that's going to make him drop out"

He was reacting to growing calls by many republican members—among them three of the GPO's former presidential candidates for Mr. Trump to pull out of the race.

But Mr. Giuliani parried that away saying: "That's wishful thinking. Trump is in it to win it."

Since the resurrection of that video Mr. Trump had apologised. But his opponents believe he wasn't remorseful. In part this is what he said:

"I've never said I'm a perfect person, nor pretended to be someone that I'm not. I've said and done things I regret, and the words released today on this are more than a decade-old video are one of them. Anyone who knows me knows these words don't reflect who I am."

But Trump being Trump, he changed gears right away and took a swipe at the Clintons.

"Let's be honest, we're living in the real world. This is nothing more than a distraction from the important issues we're facing today. We're losing our jobs, we are less safe than we were eight years ago."

I really don't know which eight years Mr. Trump is talking about. But I guess he meant George W, Bush's presidency.

"Bill Clinton has actually abused women, and Hillary has bullied, attacked, shamed and intimidated his victims," Trump said.

Indeed the chips have fallen and everything appears ugly.

So I kid you not dear reader. If the latest video about Mr. Trump doesn't sink the 'Trump Ship' with the mantra: "Make America Great Again' then I don't know what else could torpedo it.

In the meantime news mongers are mongering. The cable news networks, the social media, the blogosphere, the radio stations all of them have graced themselves with the news in the last 48 hours or so.

In my world, ubiquitous Eyes saw it first, always hungry to feed his unsatisfied needs. And from thereon he fed the mind what he'd chanced upon. It was like a treasure trove. They understand the rules of the game— it is simply 'pass it on'. Always pass it on.

So the strange news didn't end there. It became a telepathic movement. It moved from A to B from B to C and like a snowball it continued to cascade. Meticulous Mind known for his attention to detail— carefully spent time to download the fat dossier .At this point the couriers were ever ready. It was marked: 'Forward Download Dossier,' to recipient by name Noble Heart.

Interestingly they all had something to digest. Something gargantuan!

O' politics how crude you are. How elusive your ways can be...

Don't you have a merciful heart? Why do you do the things you do?

You elevate the lowly and cause them to fall from grace to grass. It sounds bizarre, it looks bizarre and it seems bizarre to me but tomorrow the swords will be crossed again.

The Raw Brawl: How the Rhinoceros (Rhinos) & the Lions tell our story

The dust from the desert is lifted high, thick enough to hide a victim or foe.

In the midst of it a lion is tossed midair. He seems to be in trouble.

Who cares about his fate?

There's a backup troop. Another lion stands by poised to attack his prey (the rhinos).

It's two against one. . It's dubbed the 'raw brawl'. It couldn't get nastier and the contenders couldn't let loose their guards. It could be any one's game. It could favour the far right.

And it could go to the leftists' way. Or it could be a tossup.

The cage guys had perhaps bitten more than they could chew. They've asked for a fight and they've got it. No one knows how it got here. No one knows what caused the brawl.

But even from afar one could smell the rawness of its nature. Life is tortured. The vultures would be here if the unfortunate happens.

The rhinos' thick protective skin which measures 1.5 cm has a gaping bloody wound on the left side of the thigh. But the wounded rhino is determined to take the fight to the wire. Fight till he sees the last drop of his blood.

Couldn't they have settled the issue amicably?

Perhaps, both parties could have left as winners..

But why couldn't they do that?

Paradoxically that isn't the case here. The hungry lions feel they must eat to live regardless. "Well, it can't be me today. Over my dead body," says the wounded rhinos.

Perhaps, all of us had been into this situation before.

In life you don't give up when your enemy pursues you

So are you hurting? Or do you feel worried and weary?

I can guarantee– You Are Not Alone!

We live our lives like a naked light in the storm. We all carry wound of a sort. We'll have scars.

It could be an emotional wound, a psychological wound or a physical one. Could be a wound that resulted from the loss of a loved one, loss of property, loss of relationship and loss of a lucrative job or it could be a financial loss.

It could be a chronic wound or a fresh wound. You know it better than everybody. The pain must be too strong to bear. It hurts too badly that at times you feel like— 'no I can't take it anymore.'

Well, you're the reason I shared the Rhinos and the Lions photo at the foreground on my Facebook page. You're the reason I wrote this piece. This piece cannot take away your pain.

This piece seeks to encourage you to remain focused and stay strong regardless of your wound.

But if you believe, it can give you an inner healing.

Certainly you can't give up, because if you give up you can't live up. Therefore, try and press pass your pain. Face it squarely like the Rhino. Face it with every ounce of your strength. Face it like you've lost your mind.

When I saw King Bright's photo yesterday I was struck by that element of perseverance. The image says it. It tells the whole story. And beneath that photo Bright wrote: "No matter how it hurts don't let the enemy win. May God give you the strength and the capacity to overcome your enemies."

Is AGOA helping African Countries?

Can't get it wrong, in the fight for survival only the fittest or strongest survive. And I think the sages are right. The writings on the wall are palpable as the yawning gap speaks for itself. From time immemorial, trade between African countries and the west or other blocs has been one not without misgivings or mixed feelings in terms of deficit .Yet, African nations haven't stopped it as they continue to engage their western partners in trade.

Why? The reason, African countries simply cannot do away with them. Perhaps certain things have to be done right and done well to ensure that the continent doesn't continue to hemorrhage and leave its peoples perpetually impoverished.

Exactly 14 days from today as I put pen to paper a high-powered business delegation from the United States led by US Trade Representative Ambassador Robert Lighthizer is heading to Lomé the capital city of tiny Togo (in West Africa) for a two-today summit commencing the 8th of August to the 10th.

The delegation will include senior officials from the U.S. Departments of State, Agriculture, Commerce, Labor, Transportation, Treasury, and the U.S. Agency for International Development, the U.S. Trade and Development Agency, as well as the Millennium Challenge Corporation, the Overseas Private Investment Corporation, and the **U.S.** African Development Fund. Members of Congress and their staff from both parties are also invited to attend the Forum.

According to the US Trade website, the Forum will also bring together senior government officials from the U S and 38 Sub-Saharan African AGOA-eligible countries to discuss ways to boost economic cooperation and trade between the US and Africa. The African Union and regional economic communities will also participate.

This year's Forum is themed: "The United States and Africa: Partnering for Prosperity through Trade." The 2017 Forum will explore how countries can continue to maximize the benefits of AGOA in a rapidly changing economic landscape, and highlight the important role played by women, civil society, and the private sector in promoting trade and generating prosperity.

Dr. Arikana Chihombori Quao Ambassador of the African Union to the United States told Ghana Tourist Coach Media in an interview that not all countries of the sub-Sahara Africa are qualified to participate in AGOA even though the organisation had been in existence 17 years now.

"Currently only 39 Africa countries are eligible to participate in AGOA. But I am hopeful we can increase the number to include all the countries in the sub region."

She revealed that out of the 39 or 38, just about 9 countries are truly benefitting and utilizing AGOA to the significant extent that they should. According to the Ambassador the remaining countries really needed to pick up the pace and continue to encourage the African citizens to benefit from the AGOA programme, which allows companies that are doing businesses through it to bring in products in and around Africa duty-free.

So my question then is what happened to the majority 30?

Her response: "Africa must as possible speak with one voice, when we continue to negotiate not only with the United States but other trade partners as fragmented individual states the success rate of AGOA will not be as effective. Furthermore, we need to start looking at the possibility of AGOA not being good in the past year 2025. And that we need to look into the discussion as to what do in the post AGOA period."

2025 is around the corner and therefore discussions for post AGOA should start today. AGOA is moving forward, we've had successes; we have had significant increase in trade between the United States and Africa. However, AGOA should have been much more successful than it's been. We're hoping that the remaining 8 years of AGOA, more and more African countries are going to take advantage of what AGOA has to offer."

Post AGOA however, she emphasised, 'Africa has got to begin to look at speaking with one voice, negotiating as far as trade not only with United States but also other African countries as well. There was an issue discussed of possibility of free trade areas and this should be approached in a continental viewpoint, failing that maybe regional which will be more appropriate instead of the individual Afriican countries negotiating individually."

This year's forum which is to be co-sponsored by the United States and Togo will also welcome representatives from the private sector, civil society, and the U.S.-sponsored African Women's Entrepreneurship Program (AWEP) will participate in Forum activities August 8-9. The Ministerial plenaries will follow on August 9-10, bringing together senior government officials from the United States and the 38 African beneficiary countries.

Trade disparity

As I aforementioned trade between African countries and its partners hasn't been all that favourable in the past and now. Trade data reveals for example that West African country Benin has exported almost nothing to the US since it joined membership 17 years ago. In contrast, the data shows the tiny nation has imported at least $600 million worth of US goods. That's a classic example of the fittest shall survive game. What's wrong with Benin? Are their goods not good enough to enter the US market?

Even countries that are understood to have significantly had a fair share of the deal are doing so per their petroleum and mineral producers. According to the data 99 per cent of Angola's exports from AGOA have been energy-related. The trend isn't different (but perhaps more than that of Angola) from other countries such as Nigeria, DR Congo and Botswana. So it turns out any other country with oil portfolio has experienced same.

And it's been established that over 80 per cent of all exports under AGOA fall under the energy and mineral sector.

Nonetheless the programme has chalked some successes. Statistics suggest a positive balance of trade for AGOA participant countries. In 2008, the United States exported $17,125,389 in goods to then 41 AGOA countries, and the U.S. imported $81,426,951 for a balance of $64,301,562 in favor of the AGOA countries.

AGOA was originally signed in 2000 and it was renewed for another 10 years up to 2025 by the United States Congress at the just-ended forum held d in Washington DC. The AGOA law, which enhances market access to the United States for qualifying sub-Saharan African countries, has been the cornerstone of the U.S. government's trade policy with sub-Saharan Africa since 2000. Also the law mandates that each year a special Forum be convened to discuss issues related to the implementation of the law and issues of economic cooperation and trade in general.

Eligibility

The legislation authorized the President of the United States to determine which sub-Saharan African countries would be eligible for AGOA on an annual basis. The eligibility criteria were to improve labor rights and movement toward a market-based economy. Each year, the President evaluates the sub-Saharan African countries and determines which countries should remain eligible.

I should point out countries' inclusion has swayed over the years with changes in the local political environment. For instance in December 2009, Guinea, Madagascar, and Niger were all removed from the list of eligible countries. However, by October 2011, eligibility was restored to Guinea and Niger, and by June 2014, to Madagascar as well. Around 2015 Burundi was cautioned that it would lose its AGOA eligibility status. And she did lose her inclusion by the 1st of January 2016. My checks revealed that the landlocked African nation remains suspended. In fact Burundi was suspended for its continued crackdown on opposition members. South Africa was the second country that faced suspension after Burundi.

The Forum is held in Washington every other year, and in an AGOA eligible African country in the other years. So far, the Forum has been held four times in Washington, and once each in Mauritius, Senegal, Ghana, Kenya (2009), Zambia (2011), Ethiopia (2013) and Gabon (2015).

Bagbin's Bag Had Political 'Bullets': Did he cross the Red line?

If I were Alban Bagbin the majority leader of Ghana's parliament I would have used the crocs in the Great Paga Lake instead of the driver and a driver's mate analogy or metaphor he pulled out condescendingly from his bag.

The quintessential strange reptiles have attracted peoples and tourists from far and near to the ancient town— a symbolism I believe the good people of the north identify or cherish so much.

Indeed, when it comes to news/messages 'nearness' or 'proximity' matters in the field of journalism and for that matter in communication profession, I was taught.

Mr. Bagbin made the analogy at Nandom in the Upper West region over the weekend at the NDC campaign launch, where he charged the electorate to vote massively for President John Mahama.

Spotting what looked like a red Fedora or Panama hat and right hand grasping a microphone with red head Mr. Bagbin said the scramble for the northern votes is 'between a driver and a driver's mate'—the former being president John Mahama of the ruling NDC and the latter Dr. Muhammadu Bawumia the vice presidential nominee of the opposition New Patriotic Party (NPP).

He argued it was always better to vote for the driver who would be the main 'architect' in bringing 'sustainable' development to the region.

Sounding professorial he said: "We have a driver. Somebody is driving the whole vehicle of Ghana that is H.E. John Mahama. We have another brother of us who is a driver's mate in another vehicle. Now do you want the driver to be in charge or the driver's mate? Which one do you want?' he quizzed.

His reference to Dr. Bawumia as a 'brother' is commendable. It shows maturity and respect. However, that can't be said about his likening him (Dr. Bawumia) as a driver's mate. Not only that but also it goes to show the condescending and stereotypical view of the majority leader towards the less fortunate ones in our society.

According to him the driver's mate lacks the developmental acumen and capacity to bring development to the north.

Has Bagbin forgotten the head porters in our cities who toil day and night to make ends meet? Or is he suggesting that their contributions to the economy don't count?

And that's why I think he crossed the red line.

Crossing the red line often has some social or political ramifications. But lucky him this isn't the United States, where 'political correctness or incorrectness reign supreme!

'To cross the red line' is a phrase used worldwide to mean a figurative point of no return or line the sand, or 'a limit past which safety can no longer be guaranteed, according to online dictionary.

Of course, seeking reelection in a parliament which is gradually phasing out the 'old guards' (i.e. parliamentarians that have held onto their seats for decades) with young bloods and new faces could be a tedious one.

Former Member of Parliament (MP) for Ningo Prampram in the Greater Accra region, Enoch Tei Mensah perhaps understands this better than everyone—after staying in parliament for nearly two decades a freshman annexed his seat.

And as many fight to maintain their seats or get into the august house for the first time different tactics, crude tactics, wrong tactics and tactics of all tactics are being employed. They are using weapons such as figures of speech some of them inappropriate and uncalled for.

What does it mean to be a mate?

In British English, you could say "See you then, mate' without implying anything sexual, it is just an informal form of address between men, or boys. It is also informally used to mean friend, as in 'I was with a mate.' In plumber's mate, mate means assistant.

The latter could be used for a driver's mate. Fact is, some driver's mate (s) is/are mechanics and also knows how to drive professionally. And same goes for some drivers too. There are drivers who know how to retrofit a car and there are some who are technically inept.

So why should Mr. Bagbin use driver's mate as a derogatory term? If I may ask:

How many people have the crocs killed over the past three decades?

Perhaps none, which reminds me of the expression 'the devil you know is better than the angel...' Northerners know their crocs. They sit on them, bathe with them and play with them. But can they gamble their lives with a drunk driver?

I think they would rather choose to journey with a driver's mate with less or no experience than a reckless and drunken driver.

Imagine when it's late in the night and the driver is sleepy or tired. Who will save the situation?

Imagine a drunk-driver with a busload of passengers. What would happen to those precious lives?

Imagine a driver who's no knowledge of the car he's driving. He doesn't know the calibrator isn't working. Doesn't know there's a failing brake. Doesn't know the car needs oil change and doesn't even know his fuel is tanking. Imagine that driver in that bleak situation. The headlights are off yet he's driving. All the four tyres of the car are flat yet he's driving.

Imagine passengers dictating to the driver. Why because he's lost touch with reality. Yet, he's asking for another mandate. Who does that?

I think we are finally at the lay-by.

Mayhem Looms at Manhean

Can EPA and others stop it?

Around June 1997 a queen mother from one of the Ashanti region towns paid a courtesy call on Nana Akwasi Agyeman (aka kumkom) then Mayor of Kumasi (the Ashanti Regional capital) at his residence near Dekyemso. I was investigating the maverick over allegations that he was using KMA's earthmoving machines to do his private business among other things. The interview had barely commenced when the beautiful middle-aged woman arrived.

Her mission: KMA Task Force had destroyed or pulled down a petro filling station she'd put up in one of the suburbs in Kumasi. The petrol station had been built on a site already earmarked for road construction. She'd touched a wrong nerve unbeknownst to her.

The KMA Boss turned around as though he'd a message for me. And it was simply this: "You see how Kumasi people behave. This is a queen mother. You call yourself a queen mother, when you encroach lands …you should know better. Yet you chose to do the wrong thing and now you're here to plead with me," he charged.

His eyes still fixated on the woman, seething with anger.

"How can I condone wrong doing?" he asked the woman.

And as if that wasn't enough he asked the queen mother to leave his residence immediately.

"See, when I destroyed stores and stalls at Asafo market," he narrated. 'I was characterised as a 'wicked man'. My own uncle Otumfuo Opoku Ware II called me and said: *Akwasi everyone is talking ill about you. Would you halt this exercise...* But I couldn't be bothered."

That was then two decades ago. Roughly two or three weeks ago, the police in Tarkwa, western region arrested a group of Chinse nationals that were allegedly mining in a school zone (Tarkwa Senior High Secondary School, formerly Tarsco).

May I ask: Can you do this in China, Russia or in the United States?

I don't know what's become of that case. But I hope the laws will deal with them, if it's proven to be true to serve as a deterrent to others. And just as one thought, the act of indiscipline and lawlessness must be put on breaks elsewhere in the Greater Accra region a certain petrol station operator has done the unthinkable.

Reports from the local media say owners and parents of pupils of Obek Preparatory and Young Royals Academy Schools at Manhean near Ablekuma in the Ga West Municipality of the Greater Accra Region are battling with the owner of a fuel station that's building the facility near the school.

The location of the fuel station, which is currently under construction, according to them, poses grave danger to both pupils of the two schools and also residents around.

Can EPA and others stop the project?

The Environmental Protection Agency, (EPA Ghana) is an agency of Ministry of Environment, Science Technology and Innovation, established by EPA Act 490 (1994). The agency is dedicated to improving, conserving and promoting the country's environment and striving for environmentally sustainable development with sound, efficient resource management taking into account social and equity issues. It oversees the implementation of the National Environment Policy EPA Ghana's mission is to manage, protect and enhance the country's environment and seek common solutions to global environmental problems. In recent times the agency has been flooded with fire outbreaks most of them resulting from illegal siting of petrol stations.

According to the school all efforts to stop the owner of the under construction filling station had yielded no positive result. And it portends to be a long battle.

In the meantime the authorities of the school and parents have petitioned the Environmental Protection Agency (EPA), National Petroleum Authority (NPA) and the Ghana National Fire Service (GNFS) requesting for the immediate stoppage of the pump station. They're also calling on the government to stop the project immediately.

And did you know that living close to a petrol station can be a health hazard beside fire outbreaks risks?

Health experts have warned that living near a petrol station is 'bad for your health.' They say the air in the immediate vicinity of garages is often polluted with airborne particles from evaporated fuel and therefore harmful to local residents.

Scientists from the University of Murcia in Spain who studied the effects of contamination at petrol stations have stated that: "Dangerous airborne organic compounds can travel as far as 100m from petrol stations."

Also, they found that 'dangerous airborne pollutants from garages could contaminate buildings as far as 100m away. The scientists said a 'minimum' distance of 50 metres should therefore be maintained between petrol stations and housing, and 100 metres for 'especially vulnerable' facilities such as hospitals, health centres, schools and old people's homes.'

Crackdowns

Not long ago there were calls to remove filling stations from residential areas. It was basically due to the rampant fire outbreak at a Liquefied Petroleum Gas Station at Dansoman Estates in Accra that claimed one life and injured some people has shocked many people. Currently most people who live close to gas and petrol stations live in fear that sooner or later they could suffer the same fate.

Studies have shown that EPA rules are often not followed either by the city authorities or those who are responsible for allocating plots of land to petrol station owners.

The study also named Abeka-Lapaz. There, eight fuel and nine gas stations were found sited close to houses, restaurants, super markets, schools and churches. The situation wasn't different in places such as Osu, Kaneshie, Mallam and Odorkor... Fuel and gas stations had been sited near the Osu Police Station.

The Greater Accra Region is not the only region that seems to have fallen foul of the law. At Kumasi specifically near the Kwame Nkrumah University of Science and Technology junction and Asafo, there are eight fuel stations which are all located close to houses and businesses. As a means of solving this problem The Environmental Protection Agency (EPA) has decided to remove all Liquefied Petroleum Gas (LPG) stations in residential areas that fail to meet the guidelines for the establishment of such businesses by the end of next year.

It's understood EPA has taken steps to deal with problems posed by illegally sited LPG Gas stations. And I think this must be extended to cover all illegally sited petrol stations as well. There is also the need for the formation of a high powered committee made up of civil society actors, technocrats and men from the Ghana Fire Service to study the processes leading to the granting of permits to all gas stations in Accra and other parts of the country, the study reveals.

"Let's not allow the situation to remain as it is currently otherwise thousands of lives and property in residential areas of the country will be under threat of possible fire outbreaks resulting in distraction and death. We must all abide by rules and regulations in the construction of gas and fuel stations in residential areas of Ghana."

So, somehow it seems in our part of the world it's a taboo to enforce the laws or do what's right. The reason, you could lose power in the next general elections. There's often a threat issued by the law breakers or nonconformists. Thing is if they could warn the president saying we won't vote for you in 2020, if you stop illegal mining. But the president had called their bluff. You've got to give the president credit. Our leaders rarely do that. Interestingly, many of our politicians and public office holders have fallen flat on this sword.

Basically, you succumb to pressure and allow indiscipline to take its course. Here's another example, it's a common sight— squatters and hawkers swarm the streets of Accra and other big cities day in day out. Yet you cannot ask them to leave. Why? It's a taboo. You cannot stop or evict them else they'd lose their livelihood. Yes, it's a taboo as I've already indicated to crack down on illegal miners, when they're brazenly destroying the ecosystems. Mind you if we give up they'll take us for a ride. Let's say no to indiscipline.

CHRAJ's verdict on 'Ford Gift Case'

Did the Commission for Human Rights and Administrative Justice fail to do a good job?

Right, we're back it. And it portends to be a vicious cycle.

In 2003, when institutions in Nigeria failed to work and corruption held its sway, the Financial Action Task Force (FATF) pressurized the West African nation to establish its own Economic and Financial Crimes Commission (EFCC) to combat money laundering— also known as 419 in that country.

Nigeria had been named among 23 most corrupt nations in the world.

And one man was tasked to purge the system. Renowned anti-corruption chief Mallam Nuhu Ribadu became the Commission's first executive chairman.

"With no money and no office, in four years I built that institution into one of the most successful and formidable anti-corruption agency not just in Africa but the world", says Ribadu.

xxxxxxxxxxxxxx

Indeed where there's will there's way. But more importantly it takes commitment, self-discipline, self-will power, honesty and integrity to make institutions workable, irrespective of their geographical locations. Besides, it doesn't matter how strong and how financially/or logistically well-resourced the institutions might be, if they lack these key elements, they can't be result-oriented.

Above all, agencies, commissions, bodies whatever you may call them must be independent and impartial. Therefore, under no circumstances must they be undermined or coerced by the powers that be to suit their quirks.

Fact is you cannot train a bulldog to be wild but tend to stop it from harming a kinsman who comes to rob, kill and destroy. That's not what they're known for.

Bulldogs owe their name to the fact that they were once used to guard, control and bait bulls.

What's my point here?

Simply, institutions must be built to mirror these strong animals. And I think it will be apt to say, any country without a strong legal and institutional framework is fit to be labeled a 'toothless bulldog'

Don't get me wrong. I'm not suggesting CHRAJ is a toothless bulldog but as someone made an allusion, it lacked the courage and mettle to deal with the Ford gift story. Plus, perception has engendered growing mistrust in institutions across the nation— fueling the recent public outcry.

Not long ago the nation's apex court (Supreme Court) received loads of criticism when it jailed three media men on the grounds of contempt. In the wake of that ruling, cabinet ministers signed petitions seeking the release of the 'Montie Trio'.

The CHRAJ's ruling on Thursday the 30th of September concerning president Mahama's Ford gift saga looks like fire in a garbage dump. The embers may appear dead at the periphery but beneath the seemingly cool site lies hellfire, says this writer.

And it doesn't surprise me that already there had been wide-ranging reactions from civil society groups, individuals, and political parties as well as a statement issued by the president's own lawyer following the outcome.

Mr. Emil Short a former commissioner of CHRAJ thinks the 'controversial issue' isn't over yet.

And here's why: "How did the president come to know this gentleman in the first place?" he asked.

"From what I heard about the initial evidence, the introduction was made by this Burkinabe to the vice president for one single purpose. The purpose was so that he could win contracts because he tried for so long but was not winning a contract. That was the purpose of the introduction. And that purpose should be a matter for serious examination."

Mr. Short continued: "Definitely from what I see at the moment, there are more questions than answers and I don't think we are anywhere nearing closure to such a controversial issue."

The eminent international lawyer asked the following questions:

"Was the president called?

And was he asked pertinent questions?

More Reactions

Another CHRAJ member, former chief investigator, Prof Ken Atafuah has also waded into the issue. According to him once the commission found president Mahama guilty breaching the gift policy, it ought to have been 'braver and courageous' in finding him guilty of breaching the conflict of interest law.

"I cannot comprehend how the commission was able to conclude that he didn't breach Article 284 of the constitution,' he noted.

Article 284 (chapter 24) of the 1992 constitution of Ghana states, " A public officer shall not put himself in a position where his personal interest conflicts or is likely to conflict with the performance of the functions of his office."

These reactions followed the commission's claim that it had successfully accomplished its mission. It described the nearly four-month investigations as 'extensive' adding president Mahama only violated the gift policy regime for public officers.

Meanwhile, the ruling had been hailed by the president's attorney Tony Lithur, saying it was an act of vindication for his client. In a statement he commended CHRAJ for tackling all the issues arising out from complaints against the president.

"The thoroughness of the investigations conducted by CHRAJ and the manner in which it has tackled all the issues arising from the complaints are commendable," he said.

Mr. Lithur was hopeful this would finally nail the body in the coffin. But that seems to be a far cry. The ghost of the deceased's saga appears to be coming back with wild horns amid allegations that the president is somewhat being protected by the commission.

So is CHRAJ protecting the president?

Sydney Casely-Hayford, a member of OccupyGhana believes CHRAJ is protecting the president against suits in relation to the Ford gift saga.

According to him CHRAJ had done 'a poor job and this {report} was a 'whitewash' to try and block anything that anyone comes up with to try and sue him further and it is not good enough."

Furthermore, the commission had been slammed by the Communications director of the NPP Nana Akomea. He pointed out that the investigation done by the commission in president Mahama's acceptance of Ford gift vehicle was 'carelessly' and 'unprofessionally' done.

"This work CHRAJ has done is shoddy and will go down in history as one of the shoddiest work done by any public investigator."

In October 2012, a Burkinabe contractor, Mr. Djibril Kanazoe who'd won three contracts awarded by the government of Ghana disclosed during an interview with a Joy FM's (an Accra-based radio station) investigator Manasseh Awuni that he gave Ghana's president John Mahama a Ford Expedition vehicle valued at $100,000.

So, at this point closure or not closure we live to see where the pendulum will swing.

Social Media & Wild rumours: Where would this trend end?

As they increasingly drip into politics, entertainment, sports chieftaincy and other areas the enigma grows.

There are some videos/messages you see or read that break you down—you become emotional. There are some that inspire and move you to do extraordinary things. There are wow videos. And there are others that seek to split your sides or crack your ribs or make you have belly laughs.

That's right you laugh till you drop flat on the ground!

The New Media is doing all of the above now—taking them to levels that make one wonders, what's going to happen next. Question as to who's doing what and how it's going to be done often remains problematic.

In short users have to deal with it anyhow. And do you think that's hyperbolic?

Wait till you get swooned or someone gets the last laugh of you.

Fact is you absolutely have no clue, what you're going to see/read the moment you switch your cell phone back on. It could be a prank message about the death of a loved one or a video made up to create panic and fear.

In recent times, we've read such news regarding the deaths of Her Majesty the Queen of England, boxing legend Mike Tyson, African billionaire Aliko Dangote and Ghana's football maestro Abedi Ayew Pele and many more.

Suffice to say every hour generates something new, something eerie and sometimes one is bombarded with 'Pasco' videos. 'Pasco' is a term secondary school students in Ghana used back in the day. And it simply refers to past examination question (s).

Better translation something that's outlived its usefulness or of no significance.

Indeed what users see/read every day on Facebook, Twitter, and WhatsApp platforms are mind-blowing. Ordinary people are doing extraordinary things with their smart phones in every habitable place (s) on the planet— fusing humor into areas such as politics, entertainment, sports, relationships, religion etc.

Where does this trend take us to?

I have no idea. It's a mixed bag. Sometimes the goods are good and other times they come in bad tastes. There are absolutely no gatekeepers in this field. Someone wrote: "If you can't watch them just ignore or delete them and stop whining."

Over the past week or so my eyes had seen a lot and I have had my ears full.

I saw two clips posted on WhatsApp. Both videos had gone viral on social media. The first footage probably ten seconds had two main characters—Man and Snake.

And the other one had a man who appeared like a preacher or teacher feasting his audience' ears with miracles and prophecy stories— admonishing Christians to be wary of latter day Prophets. And I must tell you I loved both videos to pieces.

They grabbed my attention; they tickled me from head to toe. And in the end I asked myself:

Is this not what life is all about?

Try and put a smile on your face, because when you smile the indwelt being gets excited.

It makes the day's activity hold its sway and everything around you attracts that positive vibe. That's my thought. I'm still beaming with smiles as I write…

Anyway, this is how the scene unfolds in video one, which I intend to dwell on: The man looks like a farmer heading home or going to farm. From the scene one can tell it's a —typical backcountry setting, yet there's a camera to capture what transpires.

I told you, you never know who's doing what and where the message/video is going to come from.

As the farmer walks down the craggy dirt road, the second character (Snake) is snaking its way from the scrubland. They're destined to cross path, but none has any idea—who, where, what, when, why and how that's going to happen. Suddenly that moment brings itself.

And the laughter begins...

Instantaneously the man falls to the ground upon sighting the snake. It looks like a cobra. Cobras are naturally dangerous. That might've scared the crap out of him—spewing his heart into his mouth. In fright he drops a bucket of water rendering the ground slippery as he wobbles helplessly.

The cobra doesn't get it easy too. The weight on him seems too heavy to bear, as he struggles to free himself from an imminent danger. Who can stand Man, the one fearfully and wonderfully made by the Most High?

A close look reveals, the man grabs the cobra lifts him high and the squirmy, slimy, sleazy guy falls like a meteor from the sky—from one end of the battleground to the other side of the road near the bush. The man he encountered runs away without looking back.

Happy ending no one is killed. All they left behind was hilarity!

So, the new media is capable of doing many things. And I pray people behind these rib-cracking videos will do more to inspire our politicians. It's my hope also that they would minimize if possible curtail these wild rumors which tend to put society on edge.

Preferable videos such as 'the Generous Duck' feeding the red fish would tremendously help.

How cool would it be if politics were devoid of insults, hatred, lies, fear, earth-shattering statements and clashes?

Of course social media have by far done more good for politicians than harm in the 21st century politics. The new media have put many politicians at the top rung of the political ladder.

Many of them today are tweeting, face-booking. They're on WhatsApp and other networks engaging millions outside their geographical locations.

Some have successfully launched their campaigns to run public offices on these platforms.

Take 2016 democrat presidential nominee for example: When Hillary Clinton joined Twitter in 2013, major news outlets immediately rushed to publish stories about her Twitter account. The Guardian, the Washington Post, the New York Times and Huffington Post treated the whole twitter story as breaking news.

Reporters Emma Axelrod and Amalia Perez believed; "\By joining Twitter, Clinton bolstered its legitimacy as a serious platform for political discourse."

Clinton's Twitter biography modestly declares that she is a "Wife, mom, lawyer, women and kids advocate, FLOAR, FLOTUS, US Senator, SecState, author, dog owner, hair icon,, pantsuit aficionado, glass ceiling cracker, TBD..."

In short Clinton used Twitter to brand herself as humorous person as an appeal to young voters.

But it's pretty hard to trust the players in this game. The irony is that they sit with their political opponents at pubs and taverns to quaff.

And thereafter mount on political platforms and spew hatred that tend to rile up their supporters to resort to clashes and skirmishes. They spread hatred, throw insults as if they're hurling stones at birds and peddle lies that are potentially deadly to cause division and acrimony.

Can Trump win?

Yours truly examines the political jigsaw:

Or what the writer calls the 'Trump Three-Tier-Trap."

I get this question a lot. The latest was yesterday: "I hear people saying that experts predict Trump win. How likely is it, your opinion?"

A political observer based in Accra, Ghana Mr. Kwamina Dadzie posed the question.

What do they say? When America sneezes the whole world catches cold.

That suggests it isn't only people here in the states that are worried about Mr. Trump's presidency or want to know the outcome of the US presidential election, but even those who live beyond our borders.

Indeed it dates back last year September during the Republican primaries. At the time as a political beast I thought former Florida Governor Jebb Bush was going to be the Grand Old Party's (GOP) nominee.

I got it wrong. My prediction failed. And one by one the controversial businessman now turned politician 'pistol-whipped' all the republican candidates that took part in the 'gladiator' politics—be them the Establishment, the Political Apprentices, the Conservative liberals, the Libertarians or the Tea Partiers–Mr. Trump trounced them all.

On the democratic side I betted on former secretary of state and First lady Hilary Clinton and I got it right. I anticipated a final matchup between her and Jebb Bush but as earlier pointed out it was a long shot. The rest is what we're dealing with now...

It's now the Clash of the Ignominious Two' a title journalist Ike Idan Biney formerly of Ghana Broadcasting Corporation (GBC), said it would have been 'more apt than what u opted for.' He was making reference to the title- the 'Clash of the Titans' for the first 2016 presidential debate between Clinton and Trump, which came off on Monday September 26.

Fact is not many people gave Mr. Trump a dog chance from the onset. Not many people considered the business mogul as someone who'd or has the political mettle to jostle with the heavyweights. His celebrity status cast doubt about his ability to contest and debate the likes of Chris Christie, John Kasich or neuro surgeon Ben Carson or Rand Paul.

Trump's story reminds me of the birth of the Carpenter's son in biblical Israel.

"Can anything good come from Nazareth?'

'That question came from Nathaniel who would later become one of Jesus' followers.

Philip simply answered him: "Come and see."

Today, he's proved many political pundits wrong– Donald John Trump is here.

And the $99 billion-question is: *Can he win the 2016 presidential poll?*

It appears what he says is what the critical mass wants to hear. If his support is pivoted in the Republican base, I dare say that cannot move or carry him to the White House. In contrast if that Trump mania is rooted in the general populace then those experts' predictions can pass.

Thing is the republican candidate has made some weirdest and most wacky statements since he began his bid to the White House. Trump's campaign earth-moving remarks range from his decision to ban all Moslems from entering the US, accusing Mexicans of being rapists and criminals to calling blacks as lazy folks. But Trump is still here.

Not only that, he ridiculed the infirmity, attacked women in the media and corporate world plus he doubted or challenged the heroism of Arizona Senator John McCain. Still Trump is here!

Trump's journey here has been fueled by what I describe as the 'Three-Tier-Trap'.

The traps consist of Fear, Lies and his signature message—making America 'Great Again'.

This philosophy mirrors McCarthyism which during the cold war period in the 1950's then Republican U.S Senator from the state of Wisconsin Joseph Raymond "Joe" McCarthy made some subversive claims that oiled cold war tensions at the time. He averred that there were large numbers of communists, Soviet spies and sympathisers inside the United States.

Evidently, his failure to validate his claims caused him to be censured by the United States senate. Following that false claim similar anti-communist activities that reared their heads in the fifties were labeled McCarthyism—a term which was coined as a result of McCarthy's unsubstantiated comment.

After his 1950 speech, Mr. McCarthy was reported to have made additional accusations of communist infiltration into certain state institutions, viz the state department, the administration of the President Harry S. Truman, the Voice of America, and United States Army.

Roughly a decade later, another republican candidate and a businessman, Barry Morris Goldwater, who was a five-term United States senator from the state of Arizona and nominee for president in the 1964 election, grabbed the headlines.

Mr. Goldwater is credited to have ignited the resurgence of the American conservative political movement in the 1960's.

At the time the GOP had built what came to be known as the legacy of the New Deal. But the firebrand politician bulldozed his conservative ideology through— sidestepping the New Deal Coalition. He managed to win then republican primaries per his ability to mobilise a large conservative constituency.

In the final analysis, Goldwater lost the 1964 presidential election to incumbent Democrat Lyndon B. Johnson by one of the largest landslides in America's political history.

Does that remind you of Mr. Trump's campaign style?

Americans like their leaders or presidents to be tough. Candidates that seem to have this character trait are more likely to be elected than their opponents who played the underdog role.

This was seen during the 1976 debate between incumbent Gerald Ford and then low-key Georgia Governor Jimmy Carter. Ford famously remarked: "There is no Soviet domination of Eastern Europe." The moderator Max Frankel of the New York Times responded sceptically, "I'm sorry what? ...did I understand you to say, sir that the Russians are not using Europe as their own sphere of influence in occupying most of the countries there and making sure with their troops that it's a communist zone?'

Did Ford back down his statement? No, he doubled down. Perhaps he made it worse.

According to the Times Mr. Ford refused to back down his original assertion insisting that 'Poland, Romania and Yugoslavia are free from Soviet interference."

That answer would become Ford's nemesis and troubled him for the rest of the campaigns and arguably cost him the election.

Talking about toughness, Ronald Reagan possibly won his bid to the White House at the expense of then 51-year-old incumbent democratic Jimmy Carter. Reagan was seen by many as a tougher candidate compared to Carter.

Throughout the republican primaries and debates Mr. Trump made Immigration, ISIS, Iran, Iraq, China and Russia as his tramp card. He's been strong critic of the NAFTA trade deal which Mrs. Clinton is believed to have been a signatory.

And during one of the Republican primary debates the candidate was asked about how he would end the war on ISIS. Here is what he said: "I would just bomb those suckers. " The way to go is to launch a bombing campaign on ISIS. According to him he would blow up the pipes. I'd blow up the refineries, every single inch there would be nothing left."

Peddling lies

Alas 'birtherism' has gone to bed. This was one of the traps Trump employed to denigrate the presidency and the person of the 44th president of America—Barack Obama. Until recently following his tacit admission the GOP nominee had maintained that the president was born in Kenya, his father's home country.

Also he lied during the first presidential debate about receiving endorsement from the ICE authority. That statement turned out to be false. Nobody at the department has ever endorsed him. Still Trump is here. He lied about meeting with Russian president Vladimir Putin that is also a lie. And the list goes on...

In spite of all that his support base has been growing significantly. After the GOP convention he'd a five-point lead over Clinton. But that lead was beclouded by nearly 16 points in national polls after the democratic convention in Pennsylvania last July.

Surprisingly, the chameleon has bounced back. Most polls across the nation showed the two are head to head. However, RealClearPolitics latest poll conducted on Wednesday September 28 put Clinton at 42– four points lead over Trump's 38.

Is Trump a Real Deal?

At the Trump Tower in New York City a big banner carried the slogan: "Make America Great Again." This was Donald J. Trump when he announced his candidacy for president of the United States election for the 2016, on June 16, 2015.

Since then he has cast himself as an entrepreneur and one outside the establishment —and that appear to be working. At least the numbers show for now and barring any serious political blunders in the few months ahead, many pundits would begin to rewrite their reports.

But I still maintain that Hillary would be the eventual winner. That I think has already started. One debate is down two more to go. Is not clear whether Trump will avail himself to mock exercises for the subsequent debates, which he earlier shunned. He blamed his poor performance at the last debate on his microphone.

Trump has also failed to win the establishment to his side and not being able to smoke peace pipe with Senator Ted Cruz, who he called the 'Lying Ted.'

His arch rival Hillary had done the opposite. She'd successfully won Vermont Senator Bernie Sanders to her camp. And the two campaigned together yesterday. . This attempt is to win the hearts and minds of Sanders' supporters. And it's seen by many political strategists as a prudent move. What probably count most in this election is for candidates making sure they stay focused, avoiding blunders and broadening base. The deciding votes are Independents, women and Immigration.

Even ducks don't discriminate: A surreal lesson for politicians to learn

At times our tanks run out. Yes, we find our energies sapped. And we wonder what to do, where to go get it and how to do it even when we chanced upon it. The lead gets twisted and the body doesn't seem to be in proper alignment. Bottom line, they zag they don't zig as expected.

It takes time, it takes energy, and it takes resources.

But you know very well that even before we get there—that's the finish line we get confronted with these questions:

Question as to whether it would come out in good or great shape?
Whether our audience would like it or not?
And whether it would create the desired impact?

Nonetheless, we still do it any way and anyhow... That's the beauty of this noble profession.

Invariably, you release the mind: The mind that spots red bandana head gear with a muffler around its neck like a prophet gone astray—wandering in the wilderness in the hope of getting something motivating, something exhilarating, a must-read something.

Glad I found one—something different. It was four days in fall September 26, 2016.

It was also a day that one would say the blogosphere and the traditional media arena, especially in the United States was saturated with the much-hyped first 2016 US presidential debate.

Needless to point out that the summer fête was over too. But Washington State, where I'm domiciled still had the sun radiating its authoritative rays. It was about half past midday on Monday Pacific Time –courtesy of Facebook someone had posted roughly one minute video of a generous duck and a group of red fish.

I really don't know how many of you saw that footage. But I can tell those who did see it had their minds appraised. If this isn't surreal what else qualify, a duck feeding other animals?

Be reminded they weren't even feathered birds, nothing close to her likeness.

xxxxxxxx

The lowly duck and her newly-fangled friends had found themselves in a pond or pool: The shoal had gathered around what seemed to be a mat floating in the waters, while the duck perched on the said object. Where there's honey there are bees and where there's money there are human beings, says this writer.

See, I didn't say what you thought...

That mat had food on it attracting the little ones to swarm around it. But there was a problem. They couldn't reach the food on the mat. And in the midst of plenty the lucky duck had a thought. She decided to do what's become increasingly hard for contemporary politicians, particularly those in developing democracies to do.

The duck showed matchless leadership trait and compassion. In several turns she served the shoal or school. It turned left and dropped some food to the guys in the water; it turned right and did the same thing—making sure everyone had something to eat; making sure no one was left out. She was really busy at it. It was breathtaking!

And it would soon capture the writer's mind: The mind that had been wandering in the wilds.

That episode would set the mind thinking and wondering the more. Trying helplessly to find answers to these mindboggling questions:

What at all is wrong with Mankind?

What's led us to become so greedy and so selfish?

Why do we breed hatred and not love?

Why do we discriminate and not eliminate these societal ills?

If the aquatic birds can feed a hungry 'multitude', why can't politicians do it when they find themselves in leadership positions?

Indeed I know why, I know the answers. I know what makes them behave that way.

How quickly did they forget the hand that feeds the mouth?

They tend to forget about the people who gave them the mandate to rule.

They pick and choose…They choose and select where to distribute the wealth. They choose times and seasons (rallies, campaigns, conventions etc.) to share the loot and hoot at the masses.

They know who the booty must go to. They know who gets what and why they must get it.

I call them the 'selected few'. I call them bootlickers. I call them leechers.

The few who make the most noise, the few who've sworn hell to cause mayhem should their masters lose power.

But seriously, I think whatever motivated this generous act from the aquatic bird has to be instilled in our politicians and humanity in general. It's better late than never so let's do it because we can do it.

xxxxxxxx

EVERYONE IS GIFTED:
Everyone is gifted. Everyone has something special and unique embedded. Something inside us that's so strong, so powerful and so willing to do the Lord's will. So let's give ourselves a push and let's not beat down ourselves. Rather let's strive to keep our heads up... if and when we falter along the life road. Above all always remember to avoid the following persons: Avoid a backstabber, avoid a liar and avoid an idiot.

Why Being Too Pessimistic?

And how long are you going to dwell in the kingdom of pessimism?

It's normal to have doubts, or be sceptic or pessimistic as humans but to burry oneself in pessimism is nothing but cancerous.

I thought some spectators would know by now that the big game is over and it was time to go home. That isn't the case. Almost two months after the crunch matchup they've remained defiant and wouldn't leave the stadium. They're still brooding over their team's loss. Still licking old wounds, what for I don't know.

They're already prophesying doom for the winning team.

Who does that a real patriot?

The fast lane is for speeding cars /vehicles so why use it if you know your car cannot keep up with the pace. Best thing to do is to change lane. Alternatively, turn to the curb if you cannot move on and do some soul searching.

If you haven't gotten the clue yet, stay with me, you'd understand it better by and by.

Don't think I'm naïve or ignorant. I know how defeat or failure tastes like. I have been there before. Nobody wants to fail but you've to remember that in any competition two things are certain—victory and defeat. Therefore, you must learn to accept any outcome.

Don't blame everybody for your failure. You blamed the referee, you blamed the pitch, and you blamed the other group that cheered their team to victory but never blamed your head coach and the players. The hard truth is, you and your team refused to play by the rules—thought it was all nonsense and immaterial.

Maybe you're the problem or the reason why we are not moving forward. Maybe you're pulling the object while we are pushing it. Maybe you are the reason we are having a bad weather. Therefore I implore you to do some self-inventory. I should think that would help. And don't hesitate to contact your doctor if the symptom still persists.

Better still seek redemption because God has answers to all problems.

When Jonah faced the odds he asked the sailors to cast him into the sea. There was a monstrous storm which made sailing difficult. He figured out God had caused the sea to be rough. So, maybe your attitude contributed to your team's loss. Do something about it instead of blaming ABCD.

Trump's victory in the last November US presidential election sparked unrest in some parts of the United States. In Portland Oregon anti-Trump protests stretched into nearly a week. Angry mob took to the streets —burning and looting property. Stores were looted and torched, cars were vandalised and some streets were blocked.

Their action got law enforcement agents busy– ensuring that things didn't get out of control but it did in some areas as we witnessed chaotic scenes in the streets. Seattle in Washington State witnessed a couple of protests after his victory.

They weren't happy and perhaps still not happy about the election of the soon-to-be-sworn-in Republican candidate Donald John Trump. On Friday 20 January 2017 the maverick will be inducted into office for his first term as the 45th president of the US. And whether you like him or not he's our president.

You probably didn't vote for him. I didn't.

And you probably never wished he was elected. But you aren't God. You don't hold the key to ones' destiny or fate. God knows best and he opposes when we propose. Mr. Trump is our President.

Democrats have won the state of Oregon since 2000. But Oregonians had voted almost exclusively Republican from its founding until 1984, except 1868, 1912 and 1984 and the four elections won by Franklin Roosevelt during the Great Depression and World War II.

God has his plan for everyone. And what is still your beef?

On December 7, 2016 voters in Ghana elected Mr. Akufo-Addo as president. The people were unhappy about the state of Ghana's economy and the way government officials carried themselves. They are familiar with the problems confronting the nation. And they know the change they voted for wouldn't happen overnight. Even a third grader needs not be told.

Like Abiba, she wakes up in the morning often with no breakfast. She sees her mom and dad quarrel over 'chop money'. She sees the anger and the frustrations in their face–the continued struggle and hustle a mother of four has to endure every single day. Dad's inability to get his 1984 Volvo car back on the road drives her crazy. But she's learned to put up with that—standing in long queue for 'Trotro' after school.

Nobody needs to tell her about what's going on. She doesn't need the finance minister to explain it in big English—'Macro and Micro Economy in stagnation. *What's that?*

Abiba and her siblings are driven away from class often for non-payments of school fees. She's lived with the problems. The continued power outages and pitch darkness that goes for weeks, the water problem in their area. She knows it all. The little one understands that life is too tough for the family and many Ghanaians.

But she sees her parents work around the clock. And so she's hopeful, things will get better. She's optimistic there's light at the end of the tunnel and therefore the problems she and the family are facing today will be a thing of the past. She doesn't pray the worse should happen to her parents. Or something calamitous must occur.

Instead she wishes them well, prays they return home with monies and goodies. She prays her dad will get his car fixed; mom will be able to fix them hot grits in the morning and their school fees get paid by them. That's the wish of Abiba.

Sometimes she becomes a bit sceptical and wonders:

Who will feed me and my siblings if they (our parents) don't come back home?

Or what would happen if they return with no food, no money?

Who would take care of them?

Nonetheless, young Abiba has ever remained faithful and hopeful. And she has never prayed evil should happen. Her best wishes have always reflected on the results—that in the midst of the hardship the family is still alive.

Since Mr. Akufo-Addo was sworn-in on Saturday January 7, 2017 as the fifth president of the Fourth Republic there are some people who haven't come to terms with that reality yet. And they haven't also hidden their dislike for this president. Must the president be liked by all or everyone?

The answer is absolutely no. Is it wrong for them to ask for good governance, accountability, tax /tariff reduction, quality education, uninterrupted utility services etc.? I don't have any problem with such demands. The problem I have with them is their lust after pessimism.

I worry about their prayers that things get worse and nothing works for good. One may ask: Do they really love Ghana and are they patriots?

Why are they still licking old wounds almost two months after the December 7 polls?

I'm referring to these guys who perhaps didn't expend a dime or pesewa in financing the NDC party yet they seem to be the ones mourning hard like doves. Can someone cry more than the child who has lost the mother or parents?

Why are some people behaving like the proverbial 'Kramo Bone'?

Does the Muslim cleric think that he will survive the shipwreck as that has been his prayer and wish every day?

Come out from the woods you hermit. Think positive, be optimistic and spurn pessimism.

The Unnecessary Pressure

A young man was travelling to the city to look for a white-colour job after his university education. Jojo woke up in the morning hours before his departure to find his grandma, grandpa, aunties, uncles, nephews and nieces, friends, cousins —all waiting at the forecourt of their residence to bid him safe journey and offer a piece of advice.

Also there, were Jojo's girlfriends, classmates, teammates, and friends from the church. The head pastor of the church Mr. Akamenko was there to pray for him. The head teacher of Jojo's elementary school –Adeapena Roman Catholic School, Mr. Diabene (his Godfather and role model) was there and the villages' watchdog group, which he served as a member had also come to say fare well.

At the lorry station he was met with yet another batch of people— almost everybody in the village was there. His six siblings tailed him (the youngest Aku carried Jojo's tiny luggage) as he strolled to the station. The fresh graduate looked terrified. The expectation appeared way too high for him.

"Mom what's going on?" he turned to his mother and wondered.

"Fret not son, you'll be fine. This is how we do it here. But you can make it work better, if you play smart and be clever," his mother told him.

Indeed it's a mundane practice. You're advised to be law-abiding, avoid bad friendship or company, don't indulge in drugs and don't womanise (if you're woman beware of men -Akos) and so on and so forth, they'd tell you.

The advices often don't come alone. For example they would say: "Kwadwo mma wo wirenfrii, me mpaboa nooo."

In translation: Kwadwo don't forget the shoes you promised me.

The irony is that Jojo hasn't even arrived in the city yet. He hasn't found a job yet. Jojo was like Bongo Man in Tema—Ghana's port city. Everything seemed new when he finally set foot in the capital. He was yet to taste the hustle and bustle life in the big city. He found Accra to be populous, more vibrant faster than he thought, far bigger than he imagined—a city that never goes to bed.

City life was livelier, he discovered. But he couldn't keep pace with it.

Life in cities can be unfriendly and tough but perhaps none of them considered that. None considered the worst case scenarios. Monies don't grow in trees and white-colour jobs are difficult to find or come by.

While sitting in the car his girlfriends also stole the least chance to pass on their love letters.

"Hey Jo, you know I will die for you. You're my world, and I don't mind dying for you," one of the letter s read.

The request lists could fill an 18-ton barrel. Jojo's ears were full to the brim. His eyes were popping. The pressure had been building from Ahodwo his tiny town and it would follow him to Accra the capital city where he later secured a job as a post master.

Such is the pressure our MP's Ministers, Mayors, DCE's and public officials face very four (4) years. And I should think theirs is sickening. The pressure mounts from Suhum to Bole, Axim, Fawomanyor, Bibiani, Gyinni, and Asempa Asa to Accra.

The foot soldiers are demanding their pound of flesh. If you fail to yield to their demand they would seize the public toilet(s) in the locale and collect the monies. Or they'd issue a threat saying, we won't vote for you next time around. The pastors who predicted your victory would never let your cell phones go to sleep. And the chiefs, and the people, and the friends and the loved ones would knock on your office doors time and again.

Where is the money coming from?

Please tell them you're just a trustee. "I'm forbidden to thrust my long hands into the national kitty and I will face the full rigors of the law if I do so."

The distance between the Flagstaff House (the seat of government) and the ministries isn't far, yet what goes on in this enclave often times sneak the lenses of the chief executive –the President. What goes on in the ministries, departments and agencies seem to be alien to the Commander In Chief the man who appointed them.

There's a buffet between the appointees and the appointer. And the middlemen often don't speak or tell the truth. They're fair-weather friends. It's always good. Everything looks great ('Obiaa se eye').
Really?'
Well I'm told there's an Eagle in the citadel who has promised the good people of Ghana that he will keep their purse safe and make them rich again. That remains to be observed going forward. Nonetheless, it can be done if we all change our old ways of doing things. Things that tend to stifle our growth, things that make our cities unsanitary, things that have the potential to kill our hopes, dreams and aspirations.

If we can act as watchdogs in our respective outfits, departments and ministries corruption would flee even before the Eagle mounts a fact-finding tour.

Remember there used to be ministers in this area not long ago, who served under the first gentleman of our nation from January 7 2013 to January 7 2017. They're gone now, new faces are here and they'll also go. Power belongs to the people, they decide, they elect and they have the mandate. Therefore let's always remember that we are accountable to them and would remain answerable to these people.

What the Heck?

What the heck are the eyebrows doing at the roof of my eyes?

When we live in our own bubbles we tend to ask such silly question. We feel awkwardness, loss of pride and fear stares us. We feel we are at the wrong side of everything and nothing seems to be right. We talk as though we own the world and the creator is just a spectator. We even question his judgement concerning creation—about how he made things this way and not that way.

We wish we were born into a certain race or class— white or black or brown or yellow. Born rich, and born a superman. Yes we wish we were born perfect without any blemish— angelic face. Sounds absurd right? You think I'm just making things up. That's exactly how some people feel every day. They hate themselves. They are never happy and never feel appreciative of who they are.

Indeed your eyebrows aren't as big as an umbrella. And they aren't as thin as a thin-thread. They are what they are. You may not like them but the creator made them so for a reason. After all, what purpose would they have served if they were made so—tiny or big?

They're like a vehicle's wiper you will never know its importance until the rains set in. Or like the tail of a cow tiny it might seem yet that's the major weapon she uses to drive away flies or insects. Always remember nobody does it better than he that created the universe and all the things therein. And don't forget he always does things his way. He doesn't need our approval.

What the heck?

Truly the eyebrows may seem insignificant but their roles cannot be modulated. Their main function is conjectured expression. They're also to prevent sweat, water and other debris from falling down into the eye socket. As already pointed out they are important to human communication and facial expression. Today it's uncommon for people to change their eyebrows by means of hair addition, removal and makeups.

Imagine if everything were made the same,–same size same kind, same shape, same weight same height and what have you. Imagine if we were all born rich or poor. Or we were all born ugly. There are times we need the wise to help us make the right decisions or do the right things and there other times we bypass the wise and fall on the folly.

Yes you know that. You're aware the fool isn't held in high esteem in our societies. The fool is mocked and he's often despised. But when situations get gory we beseech him.

So why can't we show gratitude to whatever someone does for us? Rather than measure the size or weight. Or ask how much does it worth? I can tell you this –nothing too small is too little and nothing too little is too small. Show appreciation. Say thank you. Give thanks to the Lord for the blue sky, yellow Moon and the golden Sun. Smile like River Nile. Let your smiles cross borders. Infect someone with your megabyte smile. Be the cause of his happiness and joy. Tell him or her (Brother) *you look awesome today.*

Hard to believe though it seems we have lost our appetite for appreciation. In other words our sense of gratitude appears s to have gone to sleep or swallowed by ingratitude. We taunt people with big ears and we do same to those who have tiny ones. If your mouth is big you're called names—like a pig. And if it's small you'd be labeled.

I'm tempted to believe that as a people, we build a better and stronger society whenever we show appreciation to the kindness, service and the love we get. This motivates us to reciprocate the gesture. Therefore let's not overlook the functions one plays. Let's see each other's role as crucial and invaluable.

The cornerstone story is a classic example. "The stone which the builders refused is become the head corner stone," Psalm 118:22 (KJV). Indeed the cornerstone isn't as big as the foundation stone, yet the role it plays is perhaps more critical than the latter. It is evident that the builder cannot do without it... There would be defect in the super structure.

Also consider how your whole body reacts when you accidently cut your pinky finger. The mind becomes restless. And the heart consoles the victim constantly. The cooperation of the body parts never ceases to amaze me. They show empathy and sympathises with one another when one is hurt.

Trust the brain to come out with quick solution. The brain would be checking on the pinky finger .back and forth. Must I get some band aide on it? Or must I go to the clinic and have a tetanus injection? *What do I do?* Until a solution is found and the wound is healed the whole body would remain uncomfortable.

Do you still say: What the heck?

Change Is Here:
Are we ready to make it work?

At the last town hall meeting I penciled down your sentiments and concerns. I paid attention to the details and made sure I carried my reporter's notepad with me. I heard you loud and clear. And I must say you couldn't articulate the issues better. All the concerns you expressed are of national interest. They touched nerves. And I view them as pressing issues that need urgent care.

Yes, I heard your calls for change and I witnessed your votes for change. Now change is here it is time to marry her or make her your significant other. A bond with change will definitely engender marked growth. It would help Ghana put on her most beautiful garment. It would make her shine once again and begin to lead as she used to.

However, change has come with a certain mentality—a new set of rules: Rules that many of you would feel reluctant to yield to. The reason is we are used to doing things our own way. And not until we wean ourselves of such negative attitudes we would be changing governments and administrations every four or eight years but with no meaningful impact.

Change is difficult to put up with either positive or negative. Change is something that sweeps us from our comfort zones. She would ask you to do things her own way. Change would ask you to adapt her style. Change can be controlling and annoying.

Would you leave Sodom and Gomorrah if change wants to redevelop the place?

Would you stop littering, loitering and hawking in the streets if change offered you an alternative?

Would you treat public work as your own?

Are you ready to eschew tardiness, care free attitude at public offices and schools?

If you found someone dipping his long hand into the national kitty would you report?

Would you be a whistleblower if you suspected your boss is siphoning state funds?

Would you report a neighbour if he illegally tapped power or electricity?

I trust your calls for change were sincere. I believe you called for a positive change: A change for better economy, a change for a cleaner environment(better still proper sanitation), a change for quality education, health services and housing, a change to purge corruption, a change to end 'Dumsor' and many more.

Are you ready to work with change, given all the discomfort she brings?

Would you take not, neither receive bribe from anyone?

Well in my world everything happens because I make them happen. Things happen because you hope for them and you have faith that they will happen. Sometimes you may have to wait for a long period of time like good old Father Abraham. Or be like Biblical Joseph who was thrown into a pit by his brothers, imprisoned for no criminal offence but later became Prime Minister in a foreign land–Egypt.

Sometimes change can ask you to do things that may seem odd. The walls of Jericho didn't fall because they planted dynamite in them. The people had to have faith and believed in what God had instructed them to do. They were asked to walk around the wall for seven days and blow their trumpets on the seventh day. It's all God's mega plan. Indeed he that waits on him without swaying like bamboo in a storm stands to gain.

So let's blow our trumpets by changing our same old negative practices. Let's make joyful noise with the vuvuzelas. Tell your friend to tell his friend's friend. Ring the change bell. It would sound better if you start it from your end.

See, when I told my audience that I had invited former presidents John Rawlings, John Kufuor and John Mahama to officially meet with President Akufo-Addo most of them didn't believe it would ever happen. How is that possible? One of them said to me.

Some of them thought I was joking. How could you bring three super giants to this venue?

Ladies and Gentlemen, I'm happy to let you know that three of our nation's former heads of state are joining us here this morning to discuss matters of national interest. All the three Presidents are currently in the Green Room enjoying some 'kokoo and massa'. We are also blessed to have another proud son of Ghana, Busumuru Kofi Annan (former UN Secretary General) who will act as a special observer at the same time bring his immense diplomatic experience to bear on this civil discourse.

I have got just one question for all three due to time factor:

What would you change Sirs, if you had the chance to comeback?

I think former President Rawlings would like to start.

"You know I constructed the Kanda Highway during my tenure. And I think at the time I had the political capital even to change Nima that's relocate them. You know residents in Nima were paid off to be resettled in Madina during Osagyefos time. But they refused to move. And I think today it's one of the biggest slums we have in our city. I see that as an indictment on my two administrations—military and civilian regimes."

Honourable Busumuru I noticed you wanted to say something. "Yeah, just wondering Mr. Rawlings why didn't you do it? What hindered your desire to do so?'"

"Kofi I regret, I couldn't do it especially during the revolution time because it would have been easier. There wouldn't have been any resistance whatsoever. It was all doable. What can I say I think I failed in that regard?"

Next is President Kufuor: "I strongly believe that we can make our cities' streets appear cleaner— devoid of chaos, hawking, loitering and littering if we allow the city councils to work per their by-laws without putting unnecessary pressure on them. First of all, I think all the mayors appointed to oversee our cities probably have what it takes to get them look good or better. But political expedience has denied us that chance to do what's right and fitting. I feel bad to say my administration couldn't solve the problem."

And you President Mahama: "They say opportunity once lost can never be regained. I blame myself today for not heeding the advice of my attorney Tony Lithur. I should have also listened to former Majority Leader Alban Bagbin. I think the two gentlemen had the soothsayer's eye. My administration built the Circle Interchange; we built the Legon Medical Centre, we built the Accra Regional hospital (at Ridge) and many more. But we failed to listen to the cry of the masses."

The average Ghanaian was suffering, the economy was bleeding but my aides told me we were winning and everything was fine. We were in comfortable lead... So if I had another opportunity my government would be a listening government."

Thank you all Sirs!

I will let Mr. Kofi Annan bring his closing remarks.

"I will entreat to you all to think Ghana first. Always remember we have one Ghana. And if we plan well, do things well, and change our attitudes the change we hope for will manifest. To you President Akufo-Addo, you have three former presidents to consult and seek counsel. Listen to the people and let honesty and accountability work. Rome wasn't built in a day we can do it if we make change work."

GHANA IS SIXTY

How would you like to be celebrated on this memorable occasion AMA?

If my children would listen to me, I will plead with them to do me this favour. I hate corruption, they know. I detest it, unfortunately not all of my children turned out good. Every neighbourhood has its brat, remember. And whenever I hear people say apple doesn't fall far from the tree, I get upset. The reason, some of my children fell or have fallen far from the tree. I didn't raise them to become looters or lootees God knows that and he's my witness.

They no better but I think it's an alien disease or a syndrome they've acquired —through peer pressure and self-indulgence.

We are many, I know. I know I have lots of children. Sixty years ago we were a little over 6 million (6.041.000)today that number has more than quadrupled, coupled with peoples or nationals from far and near (Africa, America, Asia, Australia and Europe) who are trooping in almost by the day in search of greener pastures.

Why, because we've found 'Black Gold'?

Indeed having many doesn't mean having maniacs. Some of them have developed long hands artificially that are capable of reaching any pockets and coffers. But I can tell you they didn't inherit it from me neither from their father. They just don't get it. 'Thou shalt not steal 'simply means rubbish to them. Of course that language is alien too. And anything alien is alien.

There are some with covetous eyes. They are so jealous so envious and so mischievous. They are greedy and stubborn. They are never satisfied with their booty and loot. They don't love the nation and never have her at heart. They are selfish and impish. They've no regrets of pillaging her.

But who gets called? It's me– Ama Ghana. I get labeled and ridiculed by the west as a corrupt nation. A nation endowed with oil, gold, bauxite, manganese, tin, cocoa, cashew, timber and many more why must my children be impoverished?

Why must my people be terrorised by hunger and killed by disease?

Why must they find themselves in the jaws of poverty?

So here's my answer to your question:

I would like to be celebrated as a corrupt-free nation. A nation that takes care of its people and not the one that steals from them to pay Paul outside. Celebrate me as beautiful, kind, hardworking and a courageous woman. Celebrate me as a virtuous woman, because my candle never goes off, my children must never go hungry in the midst of plenty. I challenge you, you leaders of today and tomorrow to use the resources wisely and take care of my people. This is how I would like to be celebrated.

Who doesn't want to be serenaded? I like pomp. I like to see my people make merry and dance. But that shouldn't be a nine day wonder. That shouldn't be only for the rich few or the aristocrats. That culture of opulence by the wealthy few must cease. Let my people rejoice in their sweat and toil .Let them be happy everyday happy every time. They must be happy in the morning, happy in the afternoon and happy in the evening and be happy year after year.

Today means a lot to me. And I am glad I'm 60 years old. I thank God for everything and how far he's brought us. I thank God for my children. Some of my friends and neighbours who joined us to celebrate this memorable anniversary were taken aback. "So soon?' one of them queried.

"Time flies, I remember when I was here in those early days of your independence Ama," said President Robert Mugabe of Zimbabwe.

On this occasion, countrymen and women, my heart grieves for the loss of my departed illustrious sons and daughters. Their voices echo deep into the walls of this proud nation. Their tears flow like rivers from the high mountain of Afadjato. They aren't happy about the state of the nation's economy.

After independence we'd a good start. I knew where we were going. We'd the prime minister of Singapore Lee Kwan Yew visited our nation. Apparently, our giant strides had caught attention from the outside world—China, South Korea including Malaysia envied our robust move. But that audacity would soon dissipate into oblivion.

Our GDP stood neck to neck with Singapore and probably same with South Korea at the time. However, as at December 2015 our GDP was worth 37.54 billion US dollars (which represents 0.06 per cent) of the world economy while Singapore's and Malaysia's stood at 297.74 billion US dollars and 296.28 billion US dollars respectively.

Paradoxically, these nations today have turned their economies around. They're manufacturing and exporting while we continue to import and depend largely on raw materials such as cocoa, timber and minerals.

Historian Walter Rodney offered some reason for this slow growth or bad performance: Rodney argues that 'by removing Africa's most valuable human resource, the slave trade robbed the continent of unknown invention and innovation and production."

Again Rodney contends that the slave trade fueled a process of underdevelopment, whereby African societies came to rely on the export resources which were crucial to their own economic growth. This practice in the long run excluded local development of those resources, he argues.

Even though the continent's woes could partly be blamed on what Rodney posited, leaders of these countries and their peoples are responsible for the bulk of the problems bedeviling them. Therefore one cannot use that as a yardstick to make a case for Africa's and for that matter Ghana's economic slow growth after independence. Ghana's first President Kwame Nkrumah had an ambitious plan to put the nation at a plinth. His plan to move Ghana after independence from a primarily agricultural economy to a mixed-agricultural-industrial one catapulted her. We were flying. Kwame told me, 'Mama forward ever backward never.'

But the brats aided by the west jolted our forward march.

From, our heroes to heroines of the past, Kwegyir Aggrey, Paa Grant, Yaa Asantewaa, Theodosia Salome Okoh, Ephraim Amu, Kuntu Blankson to Sir Aku Korsa, and all of them, I could hear their voices billow below the tombstones.

I could hear the voices of the Big Six. My son Kwame Nkrumah wept so bitterly. "Mama I told you so," he said to me. Joseph Boakye Danquah, Emmanuel Obetsebi Lamptey, Ebenezer Ako Agyei, Edward Akufo-Addo and William Ofori-Atta (Paa Willie) all together condemned the coup d'états that resurrected those days. They chastised all former military leaders. They blamed them for our woes and as a mother I couldn't agree with them more.

I spoke with my son Fiifi Atta Mills. He was as usual the man of peace. I spoke with Hilla Limann another proud son of our dear nation. I told everyone I still love them. Afrifa, Kotoka, Ankrah, Acheampong, Akuffo, Ollenu, Busia all came through with their phone calls later.

And all of them were optimistic about the new direction of the country. They believe our number one problem is corruption. Surprisingly it was my son Kutu Acheampong who said that.

So I wish you all God blessings as we mark this 60th anniversary of our great nation.

God bless our homeland Ghana.

Bribing Critics with Taxpayers' Money

How 'Babies with sharp teeth' tried it but woefully failed to silence one of their known critics in town. With tails in between their legs they sheepishly walked out from the house of the outgoing Moderator of Presbyterian Church of Ghana, Reverend Professor Emmanuel Martey.

They would have become 'dog food', if the outspoken reverend had canines or German shepherds at his residence.

BUT who let the 'Disciples' out?

How much of the taxpayers' money had already gone down the drain?

And why can't politicians stay in their lane?

Yours truly examines:

I could hear their paymasters command: "Go forth ye 'little saints', look for the critics of the administration and bribe them to keep their mouths shut."

It's simply an orchestrated mission ably commissioned by the paymasters. It's a mission to kill dissention, to undermine free speech, to silence the messenger and consequently get the message embargoed. Unfortunately it's the taxpayers' money that bleeds by the day.

Like biblical Saul heading to Damascus to cause mayhem, 'Babies with sharp teeth' are gallivanting around (in our cities, towns and villages) with fat envelopes that can kill fatling cows. Amid promises of giving mansions with swimming pools, Mercedes Benz, Cadillac and land cruisers.–only God knows how many critics they'd bribed so far.

Thankfully they couldn't kickback the likes of professor Martey—the nonconformist clergyman, who is a known critic of the governing NDC. He made this known at a press conference in Accra yesterday. Blending humor with serious talks he cracked up a team of journalists who'd gathered to hear the news from the horse's own mouth.

Reverend Martey said, he can't be cowed and would continue to speak on national issues. Readers will recall that most recently prof. Martey was sharply criticised by the members of the NDC after he allegedly promised that the Presbyterian Church would help Nana Akufo Addo build Ghana if he wins the 2016 presidential poll.

He underscored: "The clergy and the religious organisations, when they speak, they shake foundation. And it's only the church that will address the canker going on. And they want to silent all credible voices."

Putting red meat on dry bones Prof. Martey revealed that some politicians attempted to bribe him with huge sums of money to prevent him from making what they see as 'negative comments' on national issues. Even though he didn't name names the innuendoes were decisively aimed at those he described as 'babies with sharp teeth'.

Reggae legend Bob Marley said: "Who the cap fit let him wear it."

He went on to say: "Politicians have tried all means to muzzle me, to get me but they can't. They come with bribes, fat envelopes. They came to my house with $100.000 not cedis and also with promises that if you keep quiet we will give you a house at Trassaco Valley (an affluent suburb in Accra) with swimming pool. We will give you four-wheel drive. These people were lucky I didn't have big dogs in my house, else I'd have released the dogs to bite them. I will speak today I will speak tomorrow. "

Wrapping up, he said he flinches sometimes: when he sees the tax that he'd paid. "Then when my money goes, you babies with sharp teeth you're stealing the money and you don't want us to talk. We'll talk today we'll talk tomorrow."

Is this how the trustees are spending our tax money?

Are we progressing or retrogressing?

Do you feel comfortable to have some people use your balls as a stepping stone?

Can you smile like a monk at a prize-giving ceremony?

Are you satisfied with the state of condition in the nation?

Well, the reverend had spoken. You heard him loud and clear. And I thank God we've the Otabils, the Amidus, the Anas', the Marteys and their likes. Admittedly, it's a herculean task, but I implore you today to think far. Think about your future. Think about your children's children. Think outside the box.

See, nothing irritates more than when the taxpayers' money is being misappropriated by trustees and governments that promised the citizenry that it will provide them with basic social amenities such as portable water, electricity, proper sanitation, schools, clinics and roads.

Yet they turn around and renege on their promises. Ironically, they reward you when you praise them and they reward you when you keep mute over issues of national interest.

Ghana's Presidential Convoys

Has someone cast an evil spell on them?

If it were a curse one would suggest the presidency must make use of a spiritual bath—that will include preparation of purifying herbs combined with a simple candle-spell, which could possibly break the jinx. Or it's just a superstitious belief?

Anyway, this used to be a common practice amongst peoples across the world centuries ago.

In fact I'm informed this ritual is still being practised in modern Ghana and elsewhere.

Biblical Israel on countless times was asked to use hyssop to purify herself. And prophet Jeremiah sarcastically charged Jehoiakim king of Judah to undergo such purification.

Greek Philosopher Aristotle said this: "We are what we repeatedly do."

How does that sound in your ears?

Does it make them tingle?

Research has shown that our actions form our habits and our habits create our lives. And as this writer reports this is evidenced by the rate at which the country is wrought by motor accidents. Ghana's road traffic accidents record over a period of 10 years claimed a total of 20, 503 lives and recorded 63,384 injuries.

In fact if this startling report doesn't make you cringe how about this: Road crashes were responsible for at least six deaths a day and over 2,000 deaths in a year with majority of the victims being between the ages of 15 and 55 years says Mr. Daniel H. Wuaku Greater regional manager of the National Road Safety Commission (NRSC).

So the problem is like Adamic thread it runs through the rank and file. The whole populace is at risk.

On Saturday August 27, I learned with shock that Ghana's vice president Kwesi Arthur-Amissah's convoy was involved in an accident. He escaped death by a hair's breadth, after his car summersaulted several times, according to local media reports.

The veep was said to be traveling to the central part of the country (Dominase in the central region) to celebrate an historic festival called 'Akwambo' by the Fantes in Ghana.

The accident which occurred on the Winneba-Cape Coast highway (69.0 kilometres from Accra) is one of the several if not many misfortunes that had plagued Ghana's presidential convoys over the past two decades.

It also follows another one which occurred in July. The Bawku sector Commander of the Ghana Immigration Service (GIS) Mr. Roy Brew had been involved in an accident on president Mahama's convoy in the Upper east region.

Two journalists were among the people who sustained various degrees of injury in the weekend accident at Gomoa Adam. And two cars were believed to have caused it. Reports say a pick-up truck heading towards Accra from Mankesim area refused to heed the signal of the police motorcade to stop and veered into the lane of the veep's convoy.

According to the reports the vice president's vehicle managed to swerve the pick-up truck but an unregistered Daewoo saloon car which had also defied the motorcade's signal crashed the second vehicle which followed the veep's car.

Since the inception of the fourth republic (in 1992) presidential convoys have been hit by this menace.

And here is how they all happened:

Former president Jerry John Rawlings was involved in an accident months before he left office. About five of his security personnel perished. It was alleged his convoy traveling on the Accra-Tema motorway was crossed by a tro-tro (a commercial vehicle) driver. The driver died!

On November 17, 2007, President John Kufuor nearly met his tragic death as he was commuting from his airport residential area to the castle Osu, then seat of government. His attacker one Osei who rammed into the president's car tested positive for excess alcohol that morning.

The president's car tumbled several times. His driver sustained serious injuries. But it took passersby to rescue the president. The motorcade and the other security vehicles were long gone they were nowhere near the scene to rescue the troubled president.

His Vice president Aliu Mahama would months later survive a fatal motor accident but not his five body guards. Yes, all the five able-bodied men died. He was still in his car when the accident occurred. There were fatal injuries too.

In August, 2015 a presidential press corps was involved in a fatal accident— a Ghanaian Times reporter Samuel Nuamah died. According to peace FM, they were returning from Ho to Accra where President John Mahama had attended the annual convention of the EP Church.

And about 20 journalists were said to be onboard in that van (a ford bus which was not part of the presidential convoy)

And there was another one in April 15, this year— a land cruiser vehicle travelling with the presidential convoy crashed in an accident— four persons were seriously injured. It's believed the president was returning to Accra from the eastern region after his 'Accounting to People tour'.

NDC Seeds Freed!

Was the president pressurised?

And did political analysts and pundits expect this?

It's like death and tax payment. They're certain to happen says this writer. It appeared subtle but the direction of the storm suggested the release was likely. So in effect it came not as a surprise. But as many have opined it was senseless and needless clemency exercised by the president.

xxxxxxxx

Alas the seeds of the NDC have been freed. From Nsawam to Akuse prisons they're back home as freed men with the promise to recalibrate their notable fireworks which in the first place landed them in the penitentiary a month ago.

"We will continue to 'open fire' but 'never again' to go astray, a spokesperson of the "Montie Trio, Salifu Maase aka 'Mugabe' said on Friday at the forecourt of the Montie FM station in Accra.

The three media men who were freed at the behest of a presidential pardon had threatened to kill judges in the country and rape the Chief Justice during a discussion programme that pertained to the electoral register on the 29th of June this year.

Barely a month later the Supreme Court on July 27, gave the three—Godwin Ako Gunn, Alistair Nelson and Salifu Masse four months jail term. In addition to that each of them was fined 10,000Ghc. And the amount was duly paid.

A lot had happened in the wake of the furor. They ranged from petition by cabinet ministers of the ruling government to picketing by party supporters, intemperate remarks from die-hard party surrogates to admonitions and calls for circumspection.

There actually was a write up by legal luminary Tony Lithur the president's lawyer for the 2012 election petition, which sought to appeal to party members to maintain cool heads. The NDC legal expert and political strategist couldn't hide his frustration and the urgency to calm the troubling waters.

"My very humble view is not to resort to executive intervention by the grant of pardon. Let us step back for a moment. What will be the effect or at least, the perception of the grant of pardon?" he quizzed.

He's also called on members of the ruling party to: "Choose moderate language and still show respect to the judiciary. After all when it came to the crunch in 2013 it is this same body that held the balance. Let that body not see NDC as the enemy."

But as we see today his appeal came to naught. It fell on deaf ears.

Indeed an apple destined to rot will rot either preserved or refrigerated, says this writer.

So was the president pressurised?

"He was not 'capricious." He was not whimsical."

And how many times did I hear those words or phrase, at least four times.

This was a question Ghana's minister of communications Dr. Omane Boamah struggled to answer when reacting to a series of questions bordering on the release of the three contemnors on Joy FM 'Super Morning Show' programme a few days ago. .

But not once neither twice Dr. Boamah repeated the above phrase to refute any assertion that the president was compelled to grant the pardon.

President Mahama invoked article 72 in consultation with members of Council of State to grant the 'Montie Trio' remission.

So now What?

I should think issues are better understood when one plays the dualism role of being a taker at one point and a giver in another in the same scenario. Invariably, the oppressor takes delight in his exploits, whereas the oppressed or the one at the receiving end bears the brunt. And until the game is reversed the aggressor would never appreciate the trauma the oppressed endures.

For instance, if my loved one killed someone and was sentenced into prison, say 20 years for a punishment he tacitly admits he deserves: Would I be okay with the sentencing?

No I wouldn't be, that selfish element entrenched in me would want to see his/her freedom restored.

Wouldn't my kinsmen say I had been railroaded?

Wouldn't they say it was the victim's fault?

Wouldn't they say there was miscarriage of justice and that I should be set free and walk as a freed man? Wouldn't they say the judiciary was high-handed?

And wouldn't they say I showed remorse and I apologised profusely, thus I must be pardoned?

It is very obvious my children would want my immediate release; my friends would do the same and if I'm a celebrity that would even spark public uproar. You can guarantee to see my numerous fans protest on the streets with placards—carrying all manner of inscriptions.

Petitions would be signed on my behalf bringing pressure to bear upon the power that be, if I belong to the ruling class or flirt with them. Wouldn't I have the powerful do the bidding for my release? And if I had a bond set at $1million wouldn't I have them pay it for me?

I would have them visit me at the prison time and again. The airwaves and the tabloids would be inundated with my famous and infamous sentencing as my party faithfuls would trek there to and fro.

So, let the whole world say— It Is Well. Indeed it is well with us and it is well them. But it's a wakeup call to the judiciary, the adjudicating arm of government: The branch that settles disputes without fear or favour. I wonder though if it can do so now per what happened yesterday. I wonder if it wouldn't give verdict based on fear.

Hopeful & Doubtful: The saga of two brothers

A man had two boys. They lived together for several years without names. Their father decided not to give them names until they were old enough to know right from wrong. Then one day he called the boys and said: "Sons the time is right. It's time to give you names but most significantly to make one monumental choice. Remember what you choose is what you get and what you do from hereon is what you'd become," he told them.

One of the boys was named Hopeful and the other Doubtful. They had wisdom and power to choose. Hopeful chose wisdom and his brother Doubtful took power. Both grew with good aura surrounding them. They were well-bred and well fed. They lacked nothing in their father's house.

Almost a decade later Hopeful decided to leave all the trappings— the good foods, free accommodation, free ride and the hustle-free life behind. Hopeful decided to start life on his own. He travelled miles away from his beloved household.

His brother Doubtful would also leave nearly two decades after Hopeful's departure.

With expectation so high, Hopeful hit the ground running. His desire to conquer and explore new frontiers was burning. He set his goals and plans. And he remained as ambitious as Lucifer, defying all odds that came his way. Life was tough from the beginning and they never stopped but he succeeded.

"I doubt my ability to step out from my comfort zone. I doubt if I will be able to overcome all this,' said Doubtful. He'd power to do stuff but he always remained uncertain and unsure as to what to do and how to do it. He kept dithering and wavering in doubt: Always blowing hot and cold air on issues.

But before they embarked on their respective improbable journeys– this was an advice their father gave them:

When you hear people say there's corruption here and corruption there:

Ask them are you corrupt?

Obviously the response you'll get is no.

So who are those engaged in corruption? Do we know them or do we know ourselves?

Is it too hard to find them and too tough to bring them to face justice?

Or we are acting like the proverbial ostrich?

Every need has got ego to feed. And everyone pretends to be sacrosanct when it comes to dealing with corruption. How can we deal with the problem if we've no knowledge of its source or cause?

Or is it because all of us have been corrupted?

Without a doubt we can slaughter corruption if we begin to point the accusing finger to ourselves rather than someone else.

As you trudge along the life highway you'll hit the thuds and the humps. Every signal on the way, it's there for a purpose. They're there for your safety and every road user (s). Road rage isn't caused by the road itself. It's caused by the people who use the road and they do so for lack of understanding.

People are people and will remain as such. They talk they gossip they whine and they gripe. They will tell you—nothing works down here. Everything is bad and everybody's corrupt.

They'll tell you about the giants. About how powerful that man is. They'll fill your ears with the story of the untouchables and how everybody in town fears them. About how they tried it and failed miserably. When they say things can't be done here. Tell them my father taught me better than that. And everything is doable.

Be reminded positivity is what it takes to make things work. Conversely, negativity kills passion and it beclouds hope and optimism.

Don't let the world scare you. Do when you can and if you can. Don't blame everyone for your woes. And never say nobody can do it if you cannot. Do your best and leave the rest. Before long there will be a new crop of generation which can pass the test that you failed.

Some generation didn't grow up with cellular-phones drive less cars, drones etc. Today we have all of them. The next generation will be doing more sophisticated things. Mars will be inhabited not by celestial bodies but by Homo sapiens.

Indeed the world is yet to see her best, if we put doubts behind us and be hopeful and be optimistic.

I've no doubt that you will soar to the sky and even beyond it. I've no doubt that you can do the undoable and surmount the unsurmountable.

Never heard about this saying in our native Ghana? Buy power to save your mom if it is out for sale. However, if one has power and is doubtful, the element of power cannot realise its potency. In fact its influence cannot be felt, if it lacks wisdom. And all these elements must be backed by hope.

Power and Wisdom are good. He who chooses wisdom and doubt is bound to fail. He who chooses power and doubt is equally bound to fail. He who chooses hope and wisdom is likely to succeed. And he who chooses power and hope is likely to succeed too. Never choose doubtfulness. Doubtfulness is sickness and not smartness.

'Tragedy' in Cape Coast!

Or was it comedy?

Man gets his head spin 360 degrees at ICU as massive crowd disappears into thin air.

Find out what happened to him and the crowd. Did he survive the terrible theatrical accident?

And what really caused the crowd's disappearance? There's drama in the offing, writes yours truly.

Two surgeons go to the Intensive Care Unit (ICU) of the Cape Cast government hospital. A gentleman has been rushed in there—nearly butchered to death. His condition described as 'critical' by doctors.

Nurses as well as ward assistants could be seen busily attending to the patient.

Patient's middle name—D-r-a-m-a-n-i. First and last names forgotten!

One of the surgeons holds a booklet (speech) which supposedly has all the information he needs to make things right or the surgery go successful. And he's a microphone too. His counterpart clutches a notepad, pen and tape recorder. I guess he's a camera too.

Both have a mission to accomplish. The surgeon with the microphone is using the 'platform' as his launching pad. If you like call it 'Agenda 2016.' The other surgeon comes in as an observer, analyser, a messenger and reporter. He works for the biggest newspaper in the country: A 90-page daily broadsheet.

His byline is like a life line. Very crucial at this occasion!

A reporter's byline traditionally sits between the headline and the text of the story. . It can also be placed on the top of the article and sometimes at the bottom, particularly with magazines. It was tragedy for this pen-pusher—his byline was placed on the top of the story.

"The National Democratic Congress (NDC) launched its 2016 election campaign in style yesterday with President John **Dramatic** Mahama predicting that although the elections would be tough, he was confident that the NDC would triumph."

A senior journalist and an executive member of Ghana Institute of Ghana Institute of Journalism North America (GIJANA) blame the terrible mistake on what he describes as 'predictive spelling'. It's all: "The dangers of relying on auto correct and predictive spelling,' he says.

"How did this slip through. Were the proof readers and night editor sleeping?" another wonders.

Dramatic indeed!

When tragedy crosses path with comedy their audience are held spellbound. A seemingly mammoth crowd could be whittled down next to nothing. And empty seats in auditorium or stadium get occupied by phantoms, says this author and poet.

"All manner of thing shall be well when the tongues of flame are in-folded into the crowned knot of fire and the fire and the rose are one," T.S Eliot, Little Gidding.

In tragedy, according to John Morreall heroes tend to approach problems and situations in a fairly straight-forward manner. Life can be understood in simple binaries—good/bad, just/unjust, beautiful/ugly.

He notes that in comedy comic heroes tend to be messier, full of diversity and unexpected twists and turns. It is often more difficult to classify experience.

Indeed, what happened in Cape Coast, formerly capital of the Gold Coast was drama at its peak. The drums rolled. Dramani spoke and there was dramatic turn of events. The palpable scene at the stadium where the NDC had launched its 2016 election campaign was electric.

But that thick crowd would soon peter out!

Every corner of the stadium that the lenses of the camera panned—empty seats displayed their nakedness. The president's speech had dramatically lost its steam and my good old friend Jojo lost his mojo drastically. Some journalists believe that huge crowd perhaps went to the stadium because of highlife maestro Amakye Dede aka 'Iron Boy.'

Yes, the crowd-puller pulled the crowd in and after his electrifying show he pulled the crowd out. It can simply be called 'Pulled-in-Pulled-out'.

From there on, everything changed dramatically, former president Jerry John Rawlings founder of the ruling party perhaps delivered his shortest speech ever. He didn't fill the audience ears with his signature 'Boom' speeches.

He would later joke about it, that it was the First Lady Mrs. Mahama who restrained him.

The Speech That Stirred the Sixth March Waters

"Ridicule, ridicule let the whole world ridicule her," say the mockers.
    What's her crime? "She's unfit to be in the House of the nobles."
    But is she not a nobler herself?

Is she not a champion? She dared the devil, dared the status quo and stood for the voiceless in her constituency.

And you think she's the only one in our Parliament House who isn't vocal or doesn't have command over the Queen's Language? I bet there are many in that enviable Chamber. To borrow writer Rhian K Hunter's phrase there are 'squeamish ones.'

Thanks to the Brits our colonial masters who bequeathed us this beautiful language. Our laws and regulations, our rules and values, our norms, our cultures, our ethos, our heritage, our mores and our customs have all been caste in this borrowed language. Our Parliament House is English-biased. Now the chicken has come home to roost.

Didn't we foresee this happening? Didn't we know that someday we would be handicapped? Didn't we know we would leave behind the likes of Ohemaa Yaa Asantewaa? Do you dream speaking your local language or you dream speaking in English?

The Peoples Republic of China, use the Mandarin as a spoken/written language to teach in schools, colleges and in universities. The Malaysians use the Malay, the Arabians use the Arabic, the French use the French language and of course the English use the English language. If Yaa Asantewaa was here today she would receive a portion of this mockery pie because the great warrior wasn't educated. The only language she'd command over and could speak eloquently was the local dialect. Like someone alluded to in one of the WhatsApp platforms– English has never be an easy language for most Ghanaians.

That's right. We have studied the English language from Kindergarten up to the university level but we are still not familiar with all the vocabularies. No wonder some of us still refer to 'Kontomire' as cocoyam leaves and not Taro leaves. In fact most of us (including myself) didn't know the English name 'for Beduru' or Kwahu Nsusoa' as Turkey Berries until a benevolent posted that on WhatsApp platform sometime last year and reposted it the past week. Of course the last one is 'Dadesen'.

Did you know Mr. & Mrs. Asomasi? Did you know that we all got the name of this popular cooking pot wrong? For centuries we proudly referred to 'Dadesen' as 'Iron Pot'. And did you know that the right name is cauldron and not— excuse me, 'Iron Pot'?

No wonder we are butchering this borrowed language day by day. And no wonder the woman who stood tall among her peers and made it all the way to the Parliament House is today being mocked because she couldn't express herself well in English. I have delayed her name on purpose because this isn't about her. This is about our system. Our educational system is skewed towards the western culture. And let me be clear here, there's nothing wrong sharing and learning other peoples' cultures. However, it's an indictment for one to disown and frown upon his/her culture and to think that the foreign one is better and superior to his. No wonder this woman was arraigned before the 'Sanhedrin' a notable media house and there her woes deepened. But I know the story would have been different had she appeared on say Peace FM an Akan speaking radio station.

Didn't we see that coming?

Her critics say she's unqualified to rub shoulders with the honourables in the august House (mostly men) –where the Queen's English is used as an official language. They say she's uncut for her new job where the aristocrats juggle with jargons and semantics flit as if they're fireballs. But is she not the one who killed the giants at the Akwatia battle grounds?

Ms. Mercy Ama Sey the Member of Parliament (MP) for Akwatia Constituency in the Eastern region grabbed the headlines negatively on MARCH 6 2017. The fresh woman in Ghana's 7th Parliament in the Fourth Republic who defeated the incumbent National Democratic Congress (NDC) MP Mr. Baba Jamal in the 2016 parliamentary election and annexed the seat for the New Patriotic Party (NPP) is trending everywhere as though she'd committed murder.

Need I remind you of/about the fierce battle that ensued at Akwatia? The fall of Baba Jamal wasn't by the barrel of the gun or by the bullet. It was by the ballot box. It was by the thumb.

This is the same woman. This is the woman who was mocked by her opponent. Mr. Jamal described her as a 'hairdresser' yet she polled 21,433 votes as against Mr. Jamal's 15, 905. In the final analysis, Baba lost the seat to that underdog. Yes, the former deputy minister of employment and social welfare fell to the untested and unyielding 'hairdresser'.

Yet three months on, the underdog has become a laughing stock—subjected to public ridicule.

She defeated the minister including those with doctorate and master degrees that contested for the Akwatia seat. That presupposes, she is more than what her critics and opponents project her to be. She's got it. Yet she's being mocked because she isn't fluent in her delivery. Is this the way we measure smartness or intelligence?

I now know why the bird is in the cage. I understand why the crooks are still milking us. Indeed our national kitty didn't get empty for nothing. And until we learn to give everyone a chance to test the so-called unchartered waters, politicians who rattle the Queen's English would continue to bamboozle us.

Pugilist professor Azumah Nelson earned the professorial title not because he could speak fluent English. But because he was unmatched in the boxing ring. In fact the boxing living legend could barely speak English when he began punching in the early 90's. Nonetheless, with his corrupted or broken English he earned all the enviable titles. Today, Mr. Nelson flows very well with the English Language.

Another great man that readily comes to mind is the leader of Kristo Asafo Mission of Ghana, Apostle Kwadwo Sarfo Katanka. His Kantanka automobile Company limited is an achievement not only for himself but for the entire nation. The likes of these champions are many in the system doing Mother Ghana Proud.

Are we for real as a people?

Well, let me inform you alacrity isn't the same as mediocrity. Some people can rattle but they cannot write, some are good at writing but cannot rattle, while some are good at both writing and speaking. It could be that our honourable MP isn't endowed with speaking in public. So must that disqualify her as a citizen to contribute her quota to the nation?

Yes, she is a woman but a proud woman. She's a hairstylist by profession and she's now a legislator. She's on the Committee of Social Welfare & Employment at Ghana's Parliament House. How cool is that!

I think the race has just begun, so let's give her the chance to go with the flow. She encapsulated that in an interview last Wednesday when she appeared on Joy News AM show on the occasion of International Women's Day in Accra: ""April, by April I will flow"

That was her response to this question posed by the host of the AM show Mamavi: "When would we see you actively participating on the floor of Parliament?"

Apparently, she was there because of her 6th March Speech'. The speech many believe she underperformed and sought to demean the status quo.

BUT Madam Sey was the people's choice. The people of Akwatia believed in Ama and they trust she can deliver that's why they elected her. The scripture says by their fruits we will know them. I'm tempted to think that our country risks losing people of her caliber. People who are competent and capable of delivering results but cannot rattle English in public. I am afraid those people will remain as cocoons in their shells and wouldn't come out to lend a hand for fear of being mocked or ridiculed.

I'm reminded that in the 1960's Nkrumah's government didn't have loads of educated people. Rather, he tarped into the hardworking, the committed, the ready-to-serve and the can-do-spirit Ghanaians to prosecute the CPP's ambitious projects.

No wonder that period witnessed massive infrastructural development never before in the country's history. The 1960's was touted as Ghana's industrial revolution era. The Tema-Motorway, the Akosombo Dam (the biggest man-made lake in the world), the Adomi Bridge, the Tema Habour and Tema Township and many more were built in that period.

And one of the uneducated fellows the first president included in his government was legendary DC Kwakye. It is understood he was a minister without portfolio or a District Commissioner during Nkrumah's regime in the 1960's. I'm told Mr. Kwakye was a stack illiterate. He had no education and couldn't read or write English Language. At functions he spoke corrupted English or pidgin: "I can't division myself into two," is attributed to him.

But in most instances he used Twi (the local Ghanaian Language) to convey his messages. He represented the president in many times– commissioning projects and jobs initiated and completed by the then CPP government.

Question is: Why did President Nkrumah use this man? It's because he saw something in him. He saw the can-do-spirt in him. He saw in him the selfless attitude and above all, his determination to give his all for Mother Ghana.

'Salamu' (Greetings) Malawi

I think we need to talk. Seriously!

A man sold all his golden eggs to a merchant for a chicken feed, till he'd none to sell. He even accepted schnapps and other drinks for some of the eggs. And as he was drunk to stupor he didn't realise he'd depleted his stock.

Evidently his reflexes had taken the better of him. Then reality set in, but it was too late to redeem the huge losses. Had I known they say: is always at last! But it all balls down to the choices and decisions we make in our day to day lives. Good or bad choice (s) comes with its consequences.

Individuals and societies all over the world had once made mistakes or followed blindly. As a people we're born into a social milieu that has values, norms, traditions, cultures, mores, ethos, rituals and certain practices. There are good cultures and there are bad ones.

So which one are you choosing?

Is it the culture that turns against its own people or the one that sees each member in the society as equal and not a second class citizen?

Which one, is it the culture that deprives its children the pursuit of happiness or the one that grants them their immutable rights?

The news about 'hyenas' running amok in villages, towns and cities in Malawi and sleeping with underage girls continues to spark social media uproar. Personally, I felt so distraught when I read the news item two days ago. I couldn't help myself but asked this question:

Is culture made for man or man for culture?

Hard to believe there are a million or so 'hyenas' in Malawi that sleep with young girls as a form of initiation into womanhood. There are some who brag about being paid by the parents of these innocent girls to have sex with them. And there are still more who've ducked low— counting their numbers by the day.

Again, it's all in the name of culture if you didn't get that: The culture handed down to us by our forebears many centuries ago.

Question: Are there no brave men and women in Malawi, that 'hyenas' are still devouring our young girls?

'Je hakuna watu jasiri na wanawake nchini Malawi, kwamba fisi bado ni ulaji wasichana wadogo wetu?'

Or we simply don't care about the wellbeing of these future leaders whose precious lives are being mined by the hyenas?

Au sisi tu hawajali ustawi wa haya baadaye ambao thamani maisha ni kuma kuchimbwa na fisi?

And if there's anyone amongst you still applauding the government for the arrest of Eric Aniva (the hyena whose confession of the act generated social media outrage: I tell you what- ——that isn't enough. It's just a drop in a bucket. It's a slap in the face of mothers, sisters, daughters and nieces across the country. And it's an indictment to us all as a people– regardless of class, gender, creed or faith.

Does anyone have an idea the number of our young girls that have been subjected into this inhumane situation every year by these men? I bet the number s could be staggering and blow your mind. Just consider the impudence associated with such cultural practice and the time period.

So, how does the arrest of one 'hyena 'make us forget the continuous suffering and the horrible acts meted out to our young girls?

Can you hold your head up as a president or a leader serving in any capacity, while this ritual continues?

I think it's about time we talked the talk. It's about time we let go our cultural strongholds. We've been carrying them for ages like headlocks with no meaningful progress in our lives. The world is marching on, but it appears we're caught up in these mundane cultural practices. Too much water has passed under the bridge and too little has been done to right the wrongs.

And be guaranteed my sister Malawi you aren't in this cultural disease alone. My own country Ghana had been dealing with practices such as Trokosi, Female Genital Mutilation (FGM) etc. Trokosi is a ritual servitude practised in Togo, Benin and Ghana, where traditional religious shrines take human beings usually young virgin girls in payment for services or religious atonement.

Thankfully in Ghana today cultural practices such as FGM and Trokosi have been minimised if not totally banned among the people in northern Ghana and Ewes in the southeast, a tribe that runs across three countries. And I dare say that any culture (s) inimical to society must be outlawed and its ghost exorcised.

Fact is cultures and certain practices all over the world have or had once had their dark sides. Consider the slave trade. It took countries like the Great Britain and the United States centuries to abolish slavery. In Britain it was English politician William Wilberforce who championed a movement to abolish slave trade in 1807.

Between the years 1861 to 1865, the America civil war was fought. The union faced secessionists in eleven southern states known as the Confederate States of America. Eventually, the union won the war which also saw the end of slave trade in the states.

Still societies continue to deal with issues such as Albinism or achromasia, sexism, Semitism, racism and some cultural practices that are dangerous to human progress.

Thing is what makes wrong right is when wrong is perpetuated by evil and selfish people and eventually that idea is accepted by the majority. And remember thoughts or ideas are groomed, be they virtue or vice, good or evil. It's usually an idea that might be mooted by an individual like Adolf Hitler.

The asinine war of Hitler started around 1925. In his own words Hitler said:

"Make the lie big, make it simple, keep saying it and eventually they will believe it."

In effect that's how our forebears handed our cultures to us. For example it was some idiots' idea: Which simply said– let the people keep observing the culture, make it an annual or daily ritual, say it's punishable by death to refuse to bring your virgin girl to the shrine for atonement and by and by they will embrace it and believe it.

The time to tame the hyenas is now. They're many and they're deep-rooted but with concerted effort we can do it. It can be outlawed and its ghost exorcised.

The Trojan Horse Is Back: Did the Greeks loan it out?

Please… don't ask me how it got here and why of all places they chose Ghana,–the gold-rich West African nation. Observers are worried and political pundits are already reading so much into the surreal episode that happened recently.

This is probably a 'subterfuge' at its highest and politics in its embers, says this author. I've never seen this before, goats on the rampage?

They might've been sent from above or elsewhere in the Planetiers. But where did they come from?

What's their modus operandi?

And how does this mimic the legendary Trojan horse?

It's simply this: He who calls for a battle and doesn't know what he's in for and how the battle will be fought could be labeled a dud or loser: Because wars aren't like throwing a dice.

xxxxxxxxxxxx

A renowned journalist in Accra Ghana had one on one interview with the country's president John Dramani Mahama at the Flagstaff House on Friday August 11, 2016.

GOA: "Your Excellency, it's a great day to go down the hill?"

JDM: "You mean going to the casino at the Mall?"

GOA: "No Sir.'

JDM: "What is it?'

GOA: "To do your usual campaign rounds."

JDM: "Not today. I'm taking a break."

GOA: "No, Sir you don't need a break."

JDM: "Why not I think I need it?"'

GOA: 'The earlier you go the better, because the tuff doesn't look good. The goats are on a warpath– chewing and tearing every poster of yours in the city.' They're bleating at every street corner and it appears their action could spark a new revolution."

JDM: "What are they, life or dead goats?"

GOA: 'Life goats with beards and horns. And their bleating can be heard far from Bole. "

JDM: "You're kidding me. You mean goats too don't like me?' Ugh! Then I'm finished. What kind of game is this, is it conventional or spiritual warfare?"

GOA: "Perhaps both?' Remember, 'A' can cause 'B' and 'B can cause 'A'. Or both can be triggered by any causative agents. It could be 'C', 'D' or XYZ."

JDM: "What do I do then?"

GOA: "The solution or answer rest in the bosom of the voters. They'll decide your fate and anybody who's seeking to become the first gentleman of our great nation."

JDM: "Walahi, that doesn't sound right!

GOA: "Why not?"

JDM: "Have you forgotten what voters in Nigeria did to Goodluck Jonathan. Luck eluded Goodluck. They thumbed him down. And I'm afraid Ghanaians might do the unexpected come December. See, I'm not the problem. It's all 'Dumsor's fault. The shambolic economy is another. Jobs and unemployment, corruption is driving me crazy too.

I can't sleep and I can't look in the eyes of Ghanaians. I don't like the name they've given me."

GOA: "What's the name?'

JDM: "Bohyehene. Am I really... And do I look like one?"

The two laughed hysterically, ending the interview at the Flagstaff House.

The people of Troy or the Trojans carried a huge wooden horse (made by the enemy) into their city as their victory trophy. They were fighting the Greeks, who'd pretended to flee the battle. Unbeknown to them that what they transported into the heart of their city was worse than a boubou trap.

The canny Greeks had carved a wooden horse and hid a combative force of men inside it. The horse was kept in Troy and the y (Greeks) pretended sailing away. History has it that this subterfuge act followed a 'fruitless 10-year siege. And when the Trojans went to bed in the night the Greeks crept out from their hideout and captured the Troy city.

The bloody war had been won by the Greeks—employing one of the world's best war stratagems.

Politics is like battles. And the players have all manner of strategies to employ in order to win elections.

If you asked President John Mahama who's your political arch rival or opponent he will say Nana Akufo Addo the NPP presidential nominee for 2016. In the same vein the leader of the Elephant Party sees Mr. Mahama (who is seeking reelection) as his number one contender.

Politics as we're aware always has its weird side: The side that seeks to cannibalise those who don't belong to our party and the side that demonises opponents or caricatures them. But it has its good and humour side too, which I've just done.

It's this side that makes democracy the best system of government—free speech, right to freedom and liberty, human rights, voting rights, rights to movement and association, religion etc. Can't get it better than this!

To all my people I say we cannot afford to trade democracy for autocracy or dictatorship. We cannot afford to divide ourselves in the name of politics. So, lets' stand together, work together and build together.

Bent but not broken:
'Akyea na ammuye'

There are times our forward march gets jolted. We get stuck in our track. But it's ok. We have to accept it that way. It's ok to fall and it's ok to fail. However, it's not ok to give up your dreams and aspirations. It's not ok to beat yourself down because you failed or because you were defeated.

Why?

You are not in this alone. There are millions falling and failing every day. You're not the first to fail and you won't be the last to fall. Be reminded millions had fallen before you and millions would fall after you.

Therefore, when you fall, pick yourself up and move on. When you retreat do not surrender, rather reload and get back to face your challenges. They're in our lives for a reason. The challenges are there to make us a better people, to bring the best from within us and see us through our life path.

Until that happens you will never know what you are worth, what you can do and cannot do and how far you can go to make things work for the good of Mankind. Until you face the storm and overcome it you are not worth to be called a veteran captain or a seasoned warrior. Until you fall and rise from the ashes you are not worth to be knighted.

The phrase or statement: "what gets measured gets managed" is famously attributed to Peter F. Drucker. Drucker a writer and self-described ecologist in his quest to look into what comfort zone means asked himself the following questions:

What if you can measure your comfort zone? Would this encourage more people to face their challenges and live more exciting lives?

As a people we face challenges and problems every single day, be they occupational, marital, social, educational etc. But what makes us strong and a better people is the passion and the love we deploy in dealing with these challenges.

So back to Drucker's first question: Can you measure your comfort zone? I find this question very intriguing yet moving. The stubborn fact is we all aspire to have a place we can call as such—'comfort zone'. A cozy one if you like.

A place where we can build our tiny empires or kingdoms, be our own demi-gods, manage our own problems, do our own silly stuff, engage in idle talks and probably wish we stay there forever. Virtually no change whatsoever right?

Well that sounds incredibly awesome isn't it?

However, the real business will never get done. I believe monotony would creep in and we would perhaps become lethargic. So the question is: Would this kind of situation or scenario encourage more people to face their own challenges and live more exciting lives?

The Black Stars of Ghana (the Men's football team) have been winless for 35 years. They've been chasing the coveted trophy for 35 years. The last time they won the African Cup was 1982 that's 35 years ago. Thirty-five years in trophy drought!

The stars failed to make it to the grand finale the third time in a row in the just-ended tourney staged in Gabon (2017).

They became the lions' food. .The indomitable lions of Cameroon beat them two goals to nothing. It's their second defeat in nine years (AFCON 2008 hosted by Ghana) in the hands of the Lions. They succumbed. They failed. They finished fourth—lost the third place match one nil to neighbouring Burkina Faso. Bottom line they failed to win the AFCON 2017 Cup.

Already pressure has been mounting on the national coach– Avram Grant to quit. The Israeli contract will end in a few weeks but my people have no time to wait. No time to keep him. There's even strong indication that the former Chelsea Football Club manager will leave his post by end of February.

"I am very much aware that my contract comes to an end in a few weeks and I'm looking forward to speaking to the authorities who brought me here," Mr. Grant said at a press briefing.

A nation thirsty for glory once again waited in vain as disappointment rained hard on them. Hopes dashed. And the Stars went home without even a Bronze.

"It's obviously a big disappointment to us all but sometimes that is how football is," Grant explained.

But what went wrong? How long must we wait? What must we do?

Perhaps all is not lost yet. It's bent but not broken. It's rotten but not dead. A seed must rot before it can germinate to produce the required produce. The fangs of a snake may be short but they're deadly. And I'm hopeful when the time is ripe the Stars will bite.

"We missed some chances in the competition but I think Ghana has a bright future. We conceded four goals in the competition and three of them were set-pieces. We need to look at the details," the national coach submitted.

Last Friday the management of Police Hospital in Accra announced that it was closing down some parts of the facility to the public. I believe many were not happy when they heard 'shut down.' But it was all meant for good.

They'd noticed some defects which required quick fix, hence the closure. The exercise was to allow maintenance works or carry out an intended fumigation at selected units and departments. The targeted units included the Pediatric and Out-Patient departments, Radiology, Dental and Chemist units.

Quartermaster store and general administration were named as affected areas. By Monday February 6, all the affected areas according to the management would be reopened to the public. And they possibly kept their word.

A stich in time saves nine. You always suffer the greater or pay more if you allow things to get ragged. Probably our team has reached that stage. Probably it's management problem. They probably are in layers and would require a complete overhaul or just a quick fix.

I read somewhere that our team B is better than team A. My brother, just wait for the pig to grow, then you can measure its snout.

I'm not one of the 1.1 million football coaches in Ghana. But I can understand their frustration. And I wish I have the antidote. I don't have answers to the problems. I don't know why we've failed to bring home a kill though we carry guns to the bush biennially (ye wo atuo nanso yenkum nam).

So as we vigorously pursue or search for ways and means to turn things around, there's the need to put all hands on the deck to make it happen. The quest to end the trophy drought must not go under our radar screen. It's my earnest conviction that if we can help get the little things done we surely will be able to get the bigger things done as well.

Tony Lithur has littered (graced) the political path with wit.

His write-up concerning the sentencing of three contemnors (media men) is currently trending on social media platforms. The NDC legal expert and political strategist couldn't hide his frustration and the urgency to calm the troubling waters.

"My very humble view is not to resort to executive intervention by the grant of pardon. Let us step back for a moment. What will be the effect or at least, the perception of the grant of pardon?" he quizzed.

He's also called on members of the ruling party to: "Choose moderate language and still show respect to the judiciary. After all when it came to the crunch in 2013 it is this same body that held the balance. Let that body not see NDC as the enemy."

But how many rivers did we have to cross to get here?

When I wrote my article on the supreme court's jailing of the Montie Trio' last week, I was as sure as hell that someone somewhere might see the light or come out of the cloak to say –enough is enough. There better be a 'Saint' amongst them to ring the bell.

A severely injured judiciary is like an over-pruned fig. It may take longer to fruit for the first time, research has shown. In the case of the judiciary it would likely take years to redeem its bruised image, if it's undermined in any way whatsoever, observes this writer.

BUT finally, we've heard the bell rung from the NDC's corner. Suffice to say it's better late than never. Someone with hardballs has called for a ceasefire. The intervention has been hailed by many, especially those on social media platforms.

And with that I say blessed are those who have eyes to see and ears to hear...

It doesn't happen often in our part of the world. Party surrogates or supporters tend to follow the status quo. The chief does no wrong as long as he reigns and the breads of the subjects are buttered daily. Indeed it's uncommon to see party faithfuls take off party's biased-garments and jaundiced-spectacles to call spade a spade.

For a while it appeared no one cared about the injuries that were being meted out to the Judiciary, the third arm of government. And calls for decorum and circumspection were ignored.

Besides it seemed they're buying time, testing the waters to see if they could break the camel's back that's bring pressure to bear on the presidency to use its executive powers as enshrined in Article 72 of the constitution to overturn the Supreme Court's ruling on July 27, and release the three men.

In order to get the president invoke article 72 as afore stated government appointees committed themselves to signing a petition that sought to call on President Mahama to pardon the jailed media personnel.

Yes, this is how far we'd to travel amidst the display of anger and resentment towards the judiciary.

Thankfully, there appear to be an end to the furor that greeted the court's verdict. And I'm glad Mr. Lithur has done this. I trust his passionate appeal to NDC members to maintain cool heads would hold: "We should avoid the deepening perception that we are against the judiciary in such fundamental way that translates into threat of physical harm. Let's accept its verdict while we take formal steps to take a second bite at the cherry."

While appealing to his party members to exercise restraint he also empathised with them, stressing he very much understands their anger and disgust at the Supreme Court's ruling. "There's opportunity to apply for a review for what is worth," he gave the assurance.

Perhaps Lithur's whole exercise would have come to naught if he'd failed to hit the nail right on the head. He'd his eyes set on the December elections. "Let's pause for moment and reflect on the immense pressure we are bringing to bear on the person who will lead the party into the next election to take a step that may harm the party's chances," he cautioned.

"Tete Wobika-Tete Wobi kyere"

Truth be told, history has something to say. History has a lot to teach.

Lots of stuff sometimes he finds it beautifully painful to tell and pretty ugly to share.

But does he have a choice?

That's his only choice—to say, to teach and to share!

So, where were you when we rolled up the river bed to plant the corn?

Where were you when we crossed the River Rubicon?

When we broke our backbones to build the rail lines where were you?

Where were you when we sang the Lord's song in the strange land?

When we used stones as pillows in the midst of our sorrows where were you?

Did you hear the women wail? Did you hear the children weep?

And did you hear the men mourn like doves?

Where were you?

They rolled him a red carpet. But he chose not to walk on. Poured him champagne and Jonny Walker, he went for water instead.

Even the buzzing sound of the trombones, the tubas and the baritone horns couldn't make him dance.

The drummers played him the cymbals and other percussion instruments: Still he neither danced nor pranced. Historically, he recalled, trumpet –like instruments had been used as signaling devices in battles or hunting– dating back to at least 1500BC. Battles his forebears shed their precious blood. Battles that maimed, killed and decimated populations.

Those battles always made him feel like a walking dead man.

Yes history is right. Trumpets began to be used as musical instrument only in the late 14th or early 15th century.

Suddenly, there was virtual hushed. And all eyes were fixated on him. All ears ready to hear him.

His golden tulip lip seemed about ready. He stood steady and was as sturdy as the northern star.

"I've got something to say. I've got something to teach. And I've got something to share," he said.

"My name is History. I tell my own story. I tell their history. I tell her story. And I tell his-story."

'Pampaso' was the venue. Unafraid he stood on the dais. It was August 1844. And this unknown hero would make his case. Perhaps tell it as it is. He was unshakable by fright as the mammoth crowd pressed their way forward to catch a glimpse of him. He felt unbound by his surroundings and untroubled by the presence of his detractors.

The summer heat was on (Ogyakrom was recording triple digits), that made him sweat as though he'd eaten jalapeno-made sauce.

Unquestionably, he didn't want to appear unknown and be labeled as unpatriotic.

Alas! His untold story is yet to be told and the unspoken words of his unfinished job. The job no one had ever done it well, except the man whose name is synonymous with the noun Job.

Uncertain about what his ancestors bequeathed to him. It seemed unfamiliar, uncharacteristic of him to live and die unknown and unrecognisable. But he was unsure if his audience would understand his uncut, uncensored and unedited story.

It was an uphill task. Still he appeared unmoved. And it looked as if the unfathomable sequence of events that he was yet to unveil might not be able to redeem the seemingly irredeemable people.

"Is it unmentionable?" He asked.

"Woe betide any race that forgets its mores. Any race that thinks tradition has no place in modernity. Any race that has no idea about its roots… It's unpardonable. "

Folks what happened to your values? What happened to your cultures?

What happened to the customs and norms I handed to you?

What happened to the arts and ethos?

Have you thrown all of them away? Have you traded them for next to nothing?

In apropos, who cares about me, me and my unyielding self?

Who cares about me and my untold story?

Who cares about me and my unfinished blessings–blessings bestowed upon me by the One and only king, the one who loves me unconditionally?

I see you aren't happy. But what is it that makes you unhappy?

I see you aren't satisfied. What is it that makes you unsatisfied?

And I see you aren't grateful. What is it that makes you ungrateful?

Indeed Man's wants are insatiable. We're ungracious like graves —always asking for more!

Don't forget, the name is Capricorn and not unicorn. And the river at Dunkwa, Ghana isn't Rubicon it is Offin River. But the two have something in common— both waters are coloured red by mud deposits. Offin has Gold.

Julius Caesar crossed the shallow river Rubicon in 49 B.C. On the contrary, the kings and warriors that tried to cross the Offin River perished. They got drowned; hence the appellation 'Amene-ampong' later corrupted to Amaniampong.

Paradox

Where does the Train get her strength…would someone tell me?
Isn't her load too heavy and too much?
Why must she alone carry such heavy load?
Doesn't she need a break?
How much is her reward?

Why isn't she angry at her driver?
And why does the train driver give her wry look all the time?
Hey Mr. driver, look yourself in the mirror and tell me if you like the image you see.
Why assume all is well with her, and she doesn't sweat or she isn't hurting?
Don't you know the sheep sweats but it's masked by its fleece?
Why are you fuming with anger?
Seething with rage, rampaging everything you see...
Don't you know that look on your face hurts other's feelings?
Well, I know a hungry mouth is an angry man. And a closed mouth never eats.
Whatsoever caused the train to puff must've been something heavier than the lady.
I've no idea what she's carrying but I sense she's over-burdened, exhausted and shattered.
I can tell she's been doing this for ages. I can see her legs wobbling on the rail.
O'er the mountain, down the valley and across the bridges she pushes herself through the two thin lines. Like a mother duck and her ducklings in a straight line.
...She pulls along close to 150 cars or coaches on these tiny steel lines.
She grimaces, she puffs and she huffs.
From afar I scream my lungs out.
Hey Mr. Train driver don't you know the lady's tired?
Can't you feel her ordeal?
Can't you see her troubles?
Why do you make her suffer?
Why do you take delight in one's plight?
"Diapers suffer too," he tells me.
Have you seen the tower yonder?
Do you have any idea how many floors it has?
The base or the foundation has 175 floors sitting on her.
Have you seen the steel bird with the wings?
Do you know how many passengers she carries each day?

And do know how many times and miles she flies?
How about the big bowl that sits on the mighty ocean—she carries the planes, the cars, the trucks even the trains and many more.
You may say life is unfair.
Have you forgotten God does his things anyhow and he's the only one who holds the plumb line?
Remember, there's a reason: why you're born short not tall, born big not small, born poor not rich, born strong not weak and born You and not ME!

Supreme Court's Ruling on 'Montie Trio

Can we learn from biblical Solomon's wise ruling concerning the two women with two babies—one dead and the other alive?

Or can we agree to disagree and move on as a people without nick-picking and resorting to politicisation and needless threats?

In the Old Testament specifically 1 Kings Chapter 3:25-27, the Israel king, Solomon issued a command: "Get me a sword and divide the living child in two and give half to the one and half to the other."

The move followed the standoff between the two women (arch rivals). None was ready to give up on the living child. None saw eye to eye with the other. Nonetheless, the woman who lodged the complaint eventually beseeched the king not to kill the living child.

"Oh my Lord, give her the living child, and by no means kill him," remarked the woman who birthed the living child. But the other said, "He shall be neither mine nor yours, divide him."

Upon hearing that Solomon said: "Give the first woman the living child, and by no means kill him. She is his mother." And the whole Israel hailed the king's judgement.

On Tuesday August 2, a deputy minister of education, Samuel Okudzeto Ablakwa issued a statement on the jailing of these three men by the Supreme Court. And in that report I read a paragraph which I've described as so moving and so revealing. In part, the minister admonished all and sundry (Ghanaians) to be circumspect in our dealings, particularly in matters bordering on national issues.

"This is not about equalization, it is about adopting a principled stance in the national interest. It is about purifying the democratic process to ensure that it is issue driven and ideas based, nothing more." Mr. Ablakwa was reacting to pressure group—Occupy Ghana which has condemned government appointees for signing a petition that seeks to call on President Mahama to pardon the jailed media personnel.

"Even if the president holds a different view and opts not to invoke Article 72, why should that warrant sanctions on ministers?" he asked.

But as yours truly writes it remains to be observed—going forward and even now, whether we as a people can agree to disagree without demonising others and threatening to kill them because for instance a verdict isn't in our favour. And whether as proponents of 'good stuff' we can or will practice what we preach.

When two opposing sides (call them extremists) present sound argument s and the premise of their views support the conclusions, there's one place to seek redress, regardless of how appealing their arguments might seem. Invariably, the necessity to finding a neutral ground for a fair arbitration becomes more than imperative and compelling.

It's a place where citizens of the land have put their weight and trust into. And it's a place where my side, your side and the third side of the facts (presented by the pros & cons) are thoroughly and impartially looked into. The devil they say is in the detail and it's that place that disputes are resolved.

That place is where men and women wear wigs and robe gowns—not for vogue or cosmetic antics. Indeed it's euphemistic to say the Judiciary is unflappable. Its good track record of jurisprudence enables the bench to wiggle through the arguments; evidential proofs and give final verdict. Often they vote to make such monumental decisions.

Evidently, the noble men and women in this honourable place aren't infallible. They're humans suffice to say that sometimes they err. And we all do. Journalists make mistakes, teachers do, doctors and nurses make mistakes, pastors and seers do, police officers err and scientists and philosophers do too.

Nonetheless, the pedigree of these personalities (referring to the judiciary) and their knack for producing fairness and balanced judgement can't be underplayed by any stretch of imagination.

Since the sentencing of the three men for contempt on July 27, there appear to be a deep -seated division between the two big parties in Ghana, the NDC and NPP. Pressure groups have joined the fray. Civil societies as well as eminent men and women have also waded in.

The trio- Alistair Nelson, Godwin Ako Gumnn and Salifu Maase alias Mugabe, who work for an Accra-based FM station called 'Montie' had also threatened the lives of judges and rape the chief justice Her Ladyship Mrs. Georgina Wood.

Have we forgotten that this court has done it before?

Remember the landmark election dispute in 2012?

It cracked the whip. It jailed three or two 'stubborn guys' Mr. Kenneth Kuranchie editor of 'The Searchlight newspaper and co. As a journalist and one who upholds free speech, I wasn't enthused about the outcome. But, we must be mindful that our freedoms end where others noses begin.

So why can't we see eye to eye when there's misunderstanding or agree to disagree without politicising it or taking polarized stance ?

Must we always be winners?

Can't we accept defeat and see it as a way of preparing us for a major breakthrough tomorrow?

As earlier underscored, in the wake of this development members of the ruling and the biggest opposition parties have taken uncompromising stance. The leadership of the NDC have described the sentence as 'harsh' and have joined the importunate calls by many for president Mahama to use his executive powers as enshrined in Article 72 of the constitution to overturn the court's ruling and release the three men.

On the contrary, a legislator and lawyer of the opposing side Mrs. Ursula Ekufu Member of Parliament (MP) for Ablekuma West has averred that Article 72 is for exceptional circumstances and not to free persons who threatened to rape and kill judges.

She's accordingly cautioned president Mahama against 'undermining' the authority of the judiciary by heeding to the call of party members.

In a piece shared on a social media platform: 'Exclusion from Remission' legal practitioner Kwame Akufo says the following category of prisoners are excluded from remission system. They include- lifers, condemn prisoners, debtor prisoners and of course contempt of court prisoners."

He argues that per the above, contempt sentences don't merit 'our remission system so they're using the executive powers to curtail the sentence."

Meanwhile, a former president of Ghana Bar Association (GBA) Mr. Samuel Okudzeto has slammed critics in the NDC, saying his comment that president would be planning his own funeral if he grants pardon to the three persons has been clearly misunderstood.

He had warned the president against pardoning the jailed men noting that Mahama's compliance to the pardon calls will mark his own funeral.

And as expected his comment drew sharp response from the NDC, describing it as 'baseless' and a 'threat 'on the life of president Mahama. Yes, we nick-pick like kids!

Godwin Edudzi Tamakloe one of the lawyers for the contemnors has hinted that it seemed the president may pay heed to their calls, citing information he'd gathered from some quarters.

The current developments call for sober reflection says a political analyst. He opines that controversies like the 'Montie Trio' saga could drive the nation into a political quagmire if care isn't taken.

Are we there yet and can we avoid any future mishaps?

We're snowballing and it's a matter of time. How much time or how close are we?

Just guess whose hands you're chewing today. Thankfully it's the gorillas'…but it could soon be yours.

Imagine a country where a judge issues a warrant for the arrest of a criminal and the culprit refuses to comply?

Imagine a country where filling stations refuse to effect prices mandated by the regulator?

Imagine a country where the apex court's ruling is viewed as bogus and untenable?

Without a doubt there would be total anarchy. And we're certainly not ready to go down that path. Therefore, let's agree to disagree without resorting to threats, insults, acid attacks, verbal attacks and so on and so forth.

Why are my people going rogue?

Sometimes we don't get it, but we think we've got it all wrapped up. We think we've it all. We think we've seen it all and think we possibly know it all.

Give them justice they'll say no. Deny them justice and they'll be up in arms. Need I remind you folks, of what happened in the book of Exodus chapter 31, when Moses returned from Mount Horeb or Sinai to find his people indulging in syncretism?

They've made themselves a Golden Calf to worship. Long-bearded man, Aaron sanctioned that!

He couldn't resist the pressure from the stubborn Israelites. Indeed justice bewails when it comes under the brutal force of disgruntled folks— who want justice to suit their whims and caprices by hook or crook means. By any means necessary. They'll protest, they'll sign mercy books, they'll riot and some will even go bonk thus reaching a point of exhaustion in an attempt to shift the goal posts.

Friends, I implore you to take this mind walk with me, if you don't mind. And let's see how this narrative plays out. It's a father and son involved in a game of fame.

xxxxxxxxxxxxxxxxxxxxxxxxxxxxxxxxxxxxxxxxxxxxxxxxxxxxx

"Come let's play this game together son," says the father.
"Are you ready for it?"
"Papa what's the name of the game?"

As anxious and ever-ambitious as Lucifer the young man asks.
"You see what I've in my hand?"
His father shows him a glittery object that seems like a diamond.
"Yes Papa."
"Ok, I'll hide this object in one of the seven rooms in the house. And it's your task to look for it. Here are the rooms that you've to search for the hidden treasure—the living room, the bedroom, the dining room, the study room, the bathroom, the showroom and the boardroom.
You get reward each time you're able to locate the treasure.
Now here's the big catch…if you get it all without a hitch the reward will be doubled. And I reserve the right even to multiply it by any number of my choosing.
The man moves from one room to another fist clinched anytime he emerges from a room.
"Game on, time to begin the search," he instructs his son.
The young man is able to locate the object each time the father hides it. He quickly masters the game to the admiration of his Dad. Hard to believe as his rewards increase the young man starts to boast. And his ego begins to grow horns.
'See how awesome I'm. See how wonderful I'm. And see how powerful I've become," he tells his siblings, friends and the whole wide world.
His father calls him to order:
"Son why boasts thyself?'
Why do you say there's going to be a rainstorm when you know not?
Why predict blizzards when you have no knowledge of their course?
Why declare someone dead or say she's three months to live when you've no control over life and death?
Son, you must heed my advice. I'm the Builder and you're the labourer. Your labour is ineffective if I don't bless it." It turns out the young man isn't ready for guidance.
So the father invites him to the boardroom, after making his tour to each room as required by the game. He furtively places the object under his foot and asks his son to begin the search. The whole wide world is watching. Siblings and friends have gathered—fingers crossed. As he

searches from room to room he bites his nails and scratches his head constantly. And the hours cascade. Still he can't locate the treasure.

Finally he turns to his dad and says: "I've given up Papa. I can't search any longer."

How quickly did he forget that the game in the boardroom isn't like the one in the bedroom? "Always remember son, that the boardroom game is played with brains and smartness," he admonishes.

Positive Mindset

There's hope folks, all isn't lost. There's hope for everybody, even in 'Dumsor' era there's hope.

We used to make fire by rubbing stones together. We used to walk miles away to buy salt. We trekked the craggy ground day and night. We stepped on snakes and trod on scorpions once awhile. And we encountered the Bigfoot sometimes, still we lived!

There's hope for everybody.

We used to fight to survive by the day. We used to crawl on our bellies to get our prey. We used to kill the tigers, the hyenas with bows and arrows. We used to eat them raw with blood dripping down our thick beards. We used to live in caves. See how far we've come!

There's hope for everybody.

We were hewers of woods and drawers of water. No education, no means of transportation, no nothing! We were like daydreamers. Yet, our forebears never gave up their dreams. They kept their hopes high, they dreamt to see the silver lining.

There's hope for everybody.

Our survivability hinged on our ability to fight, to battle, to struggle and wrestle with any foe (s) that threatened our safety. Thank God today, education abounds, science and technology are soldiering on, humanity is creating unity among peoples of different race even in the wake of hate speeches, doom and gloom prophesies!

There's hope for everybody.

We never used the smart phones, never used the I-pads and never used the Internet. We never used the computers; we never used the cameras. The radios and the television sets. All were alien to us. We woke up to the sound of the rooster. We could read the weather by the movement of the clouds. Rain or shine we could tell.

There's hope for everybody!

When Hope went to Cape of Good Hope he taught the natives how to cope even in bad times. He taught them to fight the good fight. And he taught them to fight like Indian dog soldiers—who never ran away from battles. They tied themselves to stakes/trees and stood their ground to fight till the last drop of their blood.

There's hope for everybody.

Indeed there's hope for you and there's hope for me.

If yesterday seemed bad for you, be hopeful you'll be glad tomorrow, if not today. We can make it work if the desire is there. If we stay a little longer things will get better.

Jack & Jill: How the weakling killed the giant

A young dabbling duck named Jill was swimming alone in a pond. The short-legged webbed-feet aquatic animal was having fun in the summer sunny weather. A passerby (a woman) with her dog called Jack made a stopover by the pond.

Jack began to bark at Jill. He kept jumping and jumping. He stomped its paws on the ground, exhibiting his knack for carnage and desire to get into the water. He'd built long reputation for terrorising the waterfowls in the neighbourhood.

Jill sensed danger but she knew her terrain well.

Soon the poppy was let loose. And without delay it made his intension clear. He closed in on the young duck. The duck ducked a little low to size up her enemy. She came back up and positioned herself strategically. As if to say: "Bring it on buddy, I'm ready."

Jack took the challenge. And the owner looked on!

Dabbling duck took her opponent into a marathon race, going round and round and round. Still determined to catch his prey, Jack kept pursuing Jill. Amid the merry go round. They swung to the left, turned to the right and right to left, encircling in the water. The woman looked on pleasingly, in the hope that Jack will kill Jill.

The race went on for minutes. Jill showed no signs of fatigue but his foe, Jack appeared very weary and drowsy.

The poppy had run out of steam. He'd reached his wit end and was at the edge of dying.

Seeing Jack drowning, the owner jumped into the pond to make a last-minute attempt to save her adorable pet but it was too late, it happened too quick as he'd drunk too much water– much enough to end the race. And all too soon the die was cast.

What's the significance of this story?

More often than not lack of good judgement has put humanity in danger. It's been a bane that's thwarted mankind's laudable plans. Most of us have invited trouble home when trouble is staying put in its trouble throne. We bite more than we can chew and choose battles we've no knowledge of.

Goliath underestimated David. Joseph's brothers belittled him. King Nebuchadnezzar misjudged and underrated the power of Daniel's God—Jehovah Nissi. And Mike Tyson had no idea what Evander Holyfield had under his sleeves.

Did you weigh yourself before you jumped into the race?

Did you do so because you thought your opponent is weak?

Your opponent might appear weak. But you've got to be mindful that appearances can be deceptive. She must be strong, perhaps stronger than you thought of her.

Are you familiar with the terrain of your enemy?

If you answered no, then think twice before you jump into the fray.

If you can't mend the tattered shoe see the cobbler. He's not a medical doctor as you are but he's a doctor of ragged shoes.

If you can't mow your lawn hire a landscaper. He's good at it.

There are carpenters who build homes and there are those that build ships. BUT their functions vary!

Why stab an elephant with a needle when you've an assault rifle?

Why chase a fly in the forest when there are moose and bulls?

Why cry when you can fly like a bird, swim like a fish and gallop like a horse or run like a hare?

If you can't spell it go tell it to the wordsmith. If you can't smith it go give it to the goldsmith. Don't ask me why anvils are shaped as they are and why blacksmiths tap the anvil after a few strikes.

'The Magic City'

Cleveland is a magic city. The Ohio capital has produced two big headlines in two days. First is Michmelaniaism a newly buzzword coined by this author.

Dovetailing the controversial news is the official coronation of Mr. Donald J Trump as the Republican presidential nominee on Tuesday night. Mr. Trump clinched the nomination after earning the threshold mark of 1,237 delegates required to seal the deal.

This comes as a relief for the tough-talking GOP candidate. It also puts the pandemonium that preceded the coronation in his rearview mirror—looking forward to face off his political opponent Hillary Rodham Clinton.

So can Trump's investiture put to rest the controversy that surrounds his wife's alleged plagiarising lines from Michelle Obama's 2008 speech?

As this writer points out, you've got to play it smart and be clever when in Cleveland because what happens there spills like an oil from a wrecked ship. It transcends boundaries, flows into traditional media channels and goes viral on social media platforms.

Melania Trump's Monday night convention speech is understood to be rivaling her husband's coronation as the Republican presidential nominee for 2016. The news is still trending on mainstream media such as, CNN, BBC and MSNBC juxtaposing the speeches delivered by the two ladies. On social media where the news first broke it is believed Michmelaniaism is trouncing Trump's inauguration.

Melania has been accused of squelching lines from Michelle Obama's 2008 speech at the Democratic National Convention. David

Litt ex-Obama speech writer has described the act as 'brazen and outrageous'.

In contrast the Trump campaign sees nothing wrong with the similarities between the two speeches. Campaign chairman Paul Manafort took a swipe at presumptive Democratic nominee—Hillary Clinton.

"It's just another example as far as we're concerned, that when Hillary is threatened by a female, the first thing she does is try to destroy the person," Manafort said.

Nevertheless, as earlier mentioned Cleveland's first-born baby has been christened!

She's called Michmelania. Mich is a short form of Michelle a French baby or feminine of Michael, meaning gift from God. The name Melania is a Greek baby. In Greek the meaning of the name is: Dark, which is from the root melas.

Indeed, what woke me up from my sleep early morning on Tuesday seemed like a Mack Truck that has lost its bearing and rammed into a ramshackle building: But no it wasn't a semi-truck, I'd dreamt doodling something on a piece of paper that appeared like a new buzzword.

I feared I might jock someone else's catchphrase so I googled the meaning of plagiarism and my newly-coined word michmelaniaism. And this is what I found.

First, plagiarism is the practice of taking someone else's work or ideas and passing them off as one's own, according to online dictionary. Michmelaniaism on the other hand is an act of lifting some part of one's literary work without crediting the source or the author.

See, I credited my source. When Shirley (Rudolph McCallum) shared my write-up a few weeks back she gave me the credit. "I hate it when people bite my literary work," Shirley said.

Are we still minding our business?

Ghana's former president professor John Atta Mills of blessed memory once re-echoed this popular Akan or Fante phrase: "Di wo fie Asem," literally meaning—mind your own business. His comment followed the civil war that erupted in the Ivory Coast— Ghana's neighbour to the west.

Conflict in the former French colony began in 2002. And even though fighting ended by 2004 the country remained split in two, with a Muslim-held north and a government held Christian south. The United Nations deployed peacekeepers into the region and the French also sent soldiers to help contain and maintain the relative peace.

However, after the country's election in October 2010 the skirmish re-ignited in February 2011 over the impasse on the election results. In the wake of the renewed fighting there were calls for Ghana to intervene or send troops to help stem the tide in the region.

But president Mills avoided the gamble. He told Ghanaians to mind their own business. He feared the reprisals and the repercussions.

Consequently, the fighting crescendoed and there were influx of refugees into Ghana. Women and children had to flee the once peaceful country. Ironically some of the fighters also sought refuge in our soil.

The actions of the factions were spooky and the name of the game as usual is politics. It's universally known to be dirty, quirky and sneer. It's like a gun when loaded it takes flight (thus loaded to cause mayhem) it knows no stop until it finds its target.

It could be you, it could be me. It could be your mother or father. It could be your daughter or son, uncle or aunt, friends and loved ones. It could be anyone, it could be anybody.

Anytime I hear politicians and political activists make incendiary remarks my blood turn cold. Anytime traditional rulers and opinion leaders spew war words I begin to freeze. And anytime the very elites or the aristocrats bark like dogs I quiver.

Why not?

"Efie ne fie," there's no place like home. Where there's peace there's growth, there's progress, there's life. Conflicts drive investors away but peace and stability woo investors home.

Where would we go should conflict break out?

We are a nation sandwiched by Francophones. To the east is tiny Togo, bordered by Burkina Faso up north and of course Ivory Coast our western neighbours. And even beyond these countries there's still another layer of French-speaking neighbours. Think about it!

Would there be a safe haven for us should we plunge ourselves into darkness and fall to the throes of gloom?

Kofi Nimo knows the criminals in his neighbourhood: He knows the hideouts of the goons and the terrorists. He knows where the serial killer (s) is hiding, yet he's remained tight-lipped. It's considered 'Haram' or forbidden to give out your neighbour. Don't snitch!

When do we mind our own business?

Is it when we feel we are at our comfort zones and nothing untoward could happen to us?

Or when we think the beard that's caught fire isn't ours?

Would we be safe when the sailing boat sink?

Remember we are all in it together. A burning bush spreads it doesn't stay at one spot.

Yup, it's Kofi again rollicking in a russet chair smoking cigar. At the balcony of his plush home he spots column of smoke from a neighbour's house. That's Komla Gadzekpor's house. There's nobody in that residence. He cranes his neck to check if it's real.

Indeed, his neighbour's home has caught fire and is burning ferociously. But the aristocrat wouldn't budge. "I can't be bothered," he says to himself.

Unbeknown to him that the fire in his neighbour's house could spread into the neighbourhood and catch up with him sooner than later.

As the fire mauls Komla's home Kofi darts into his living room and make a phone call not to 911 but to his wife telling her about how their neighbour's residence is being gutted. They showed no sympathy. They laughed!

"Let it burn," remarks Kofi's wife.

But who does that, watches his neighbour's house burn to ashes?

What's the reason?

The two are at loggerheads. Kofi belongs to the opposition party and his adversary (former friend) Komla flirts with the ruling party. They used to be good friends. They went to pubs together, dinned together and had vacations together until the duo found themselves deep in the political cesspool.

Politics is gradually tearing society apart. Friends are becoming foes, pitting one tribe against the other. "It never used to be like this," an old woman tells me. "The players are now politicising everything."

So the old cliché: 'mind your own business' goes on...

The people of Fawomanyor, (not the one near Dunkwa-on-Offin in the upper Denkyira district in Central region of Ghana) have had two chiefs ruled them for decades. They aren't happy at the way their community is run. And they claim they're fed up with the two dictators.

"We want change," they cry every time. Yet, with little 'Kolikoli' from their oppressors they end up in the same whole like a crab trapped in a barrel.

Are my people ready this time round or it is mind your own business as usual?

Citizens of Sikaman are you ready for a change?

Change smells like an onion. It tastes like sugar but it can be bittersweet for the actors in the game: Be it politics, sports, entertainment, business etc. The feeling is like a soothing song that puts even the sadist beast to sleep.

Clinton Clinches Dems Nomination

The stakes couldn't be high for a mother, grandmother, a wife, a senator and a former Secretary of state delivering a final speech after none other than President Barack Obama—the master orator. But as this writer notes Hillary Clinton also needed to sharpen her claws and knuckles and go after her Republican opponent Donald Trump.

Already the Bloombergs' uppercuts and jabs from the Bidens and the Kaines and the scintillating speech by Michelle Obama had dealt enough blow to Mr. Trump and also set the venue in euphoric mood. According to political pundits what happened on Wednesday night was just a tip of the iceberg. "We might get more from the business man cum politician," says a pundit.

Former New York mayor Michael Bloomberg who literally set Wells Fargo Centre ablaze by attacking Mr. Trump laid the foundation for more attacks in the hours that followed.

Indeed before the fully-packed crowd, Hillary Clinton did what was required of her.

And I think I got it. I understood her. It seemed monotonous to me initially but the message resonated as she was coasting to the end of her 55-minute speech that climaxed a four-day long Democratic National Convention (DNC) in Philadelphia.

Hillary officially accepted the nomination as Democratic presidential candidate—an historic moment that makes her the first woman to become presidential nominee for a major party in the US and the first, former First Lady to have done so.

She casts herself as a candidate who gets it, who understands the people and who believes in togetherness. Throughout her speech she hammered home the WE narrative or passage– a thread that was conspicuously missing in Trump's speech at the Republican convention last week.

"We will rise to the challenge, just as we always have. We will not build a wall. Instead we will build an economy where everyone who wants a good job can get one. And we'll build a path to citizenship for millions of immigrants who are already contributing to our economy. We will not ban a religion. We will work with all Americans and our allies to fight and defeat terrorism," Mrs. Clinton underscored.

It would be apt to say she went for her opponent's Achilles heels. That means anywhere Trump has messed up, she tidied it up. Minority, immigrants, middle class, independent, the LGBT, police and the fire fighters, mothers whose sons and daughters had been killed by police or through gun violence etc. These voters, would be crucial in the coming election, hence her appeal.

In sharp contrast, Trump touts himself as the man with the magic wand, the only person who has solution to America's problems. And his mantra: "I will make America great again," was subjected to ridicule by Hillary last night.

With her cloves off and knuckles throbbing like a giant drum, Hillary charged: "He's forgetting every last one of us. Americans don't say: "I alone can fix it," quoting Republican candidate Donald Trump. "We say, we'll fix it together."

.."Don't let anyone tell you that our country is weak. We're not. Don't let anyone tell you we don't have what it takes. We do. And most of all, don't believe anyone who says. "I alone can fix it. Yes those were actually Donald Trump's words in Cleveland."

Sounding cool and collected Clinton made this suggestion: "They should set off alarm bells for all of us."

She also took a swipe at Trump's ambitious plan saying: "Trump also talks a big game about putting America first. Well please explain what part of America First leads him to?" She rhetorically asked.

Make Trump neck ties in China not in Colorado. Trump suits in Mexico not in Michigan. Trump furniture in Turkey not in Ohio. Trump picture frame in India not in Wisconsin."

It will be recalled that during the republican primaries Mr. Trump told the party's establishment to shut up and leave it all for him to handle. He took on two former Republican presidential candidates—Arizona Senator John McCain and Mitt Romney of Utah. He questioned the former's heroism as a war veteran in Vietnam and lampooned the latter's inability to win elections. The Bushes weren't spared.

And last but not least Mr. Trump has failed to resolve the seemingly feud between him and Ted Cruz, a move that could cost him at the presidential election. Cruz's supporters are still unhappy about the way Trump treated their candidate. And they may tend to support Hillary instead of their own Republican candidate.

On the contrary Hilary has demonstrated that there's the need to bring on board all democrats and non-democrats. The bell of unity, inclusivity, collectivity and diversity rang through her speech.

Last night her boundless gratitude to Vermont Senator Bernie Sanders who fought tooth and nail with her during the democratic primaries couldn't have come at a better time. Her countenance spoke volume and her tone was effervescent.

"And I want to thank Bernie Sanders," she said. Here the former democratic contender's name was mentioned more than four times in her speech.

At one point she repeats the senator's first name: "Bernie Bernie, your campaign inspired millions of Americans, particularly the young people who threw their hearts and souls into our primary." Yes Sanders won 12 million votes during the Democratic primaries, according to RealClearPolitics.

Clinton went on to say: "You've put economic and social justice issues front and center where they belong. And to all of your supporters here and around the country: I want you to know, I've heard you. Your cause is our cause. Our country needs your ideas, energy, and passion."

With these contrasts among other factors I expert Clinton's poll numbers after convention to improve markedly. She might gain five points or even more than Trump.

Philadelphia like the city of Cleveland has played its part of receiving thousands of people who thronged the convention grounds to make history—America's first woman hoisting a major party's flag. And come November a new chapter would be written in the nation's political history. It's now up to the major players to cross the swords, throw the jabs, debate the debates and win the hearts and minds of the people. Every vote counts. Every issue matters in this presidential election and every gaffe or goof could cause a candidate's chances of becoming America's 45th president.

THE BURNING POT: What Is In It?

When the weather is good air travel is smooth. It's arguably the fastest means of transportation. Its safety was once unquestionable until we'd the bad guys come onboard with their nails, pins and needles, crockpots, and all kinds of offensive weapon. Since then, we sometimes travel with our hearts in our mouths. Not to mention the pat downs and all the hustle one has to go through during air travel nowadays. We quiver and shiver. Our feeble legs seldom give away on us when we spot for example, a long bearded individual with Arabian face travelling with us.

The reason, we don't know whether the guy sitting next to us has a deadly device under his pant or trousers. The irony however, is sometimes it's not even the one wearing the Aaronic beard that might start the onslaught. Rather it's the unassuming individual. Thus everyone becomes a potential bomber. But must we live in this kind of paranoia state?

Kofi says Ama is a thief. Ama is corrupt. Ama has embezzled XYZ millions of dollars being state's funds. And the accused (Ama) also turns around, she accuses Kofi of taking bribes, defrauding and extorting monies from people. She says Kofi is doing the same thing or something more grievous than what she's been accused of.

Sounds complicated isn't it?

Well, when we plunge ourselves in a sea of mistrust or get obsessed with distrust and fear we often lose great stuff, something unquantifiable. It's like throwing the bad water with the baby. That notwithstanding sometimes our expression of apprehension is also justifiable. After all why ignore caution if it could prove deadly?

So, I 've got this special message for all passengers travelling to Gatwick or Timbuktu, Bobo- Diolasso, Taiwan or Tai-two, Birmingham or Amsterdam, Dusseldorf or Seattle this week Please, take note of this special message. This report is very important. And it isn't about the weather. It's also not about our air traffic control systems. I can assure you everything about our airplane is good. No kidding!

But we've a problem. I often say this: It is not the Church, not the Mosque and not the Synagogue. It's rather about the people in the buildings that are the problem. Yes, I know I am right.

There was overcast in the early morning but as you can see visibility is good. What do you see my people? It's beautiful blue sky... So there will be no problem flying to anywhere under the sun. Indeed our crew members were readying to take you to your destinations but something unusual happened. In fact what we heard this morning from our pilot and her co-pilot has left us all openmouthed. We're completely dumbfounded.

The co-pilot alleges she suspects the pilot has a bomb in her brief case. Management immediately summoned the pilot for questioning. Prior to her invitation she (the pilot) had also gone public to counter accuse her right hand officer of planning to detonate a device to bring the airplane down. In view of this latest development, which management sees as disturbing, we like to inform you all passengers that Flight# 072817GH which is scheduled to fly from Accra to Timbuktu has been cancelled till further notice.

Beside the two officers has been asked to step aside as we launch special investigation into the allegations. They should also not contact any staff that works for our company, failure to adhere to this non-contact order would result severe sanction which will include expulsion plus fine.

This is a serious allegation and we intend to give it all the attention it deserves. Meanwhile, let me make this point clear, if you think this call is 'premature,' do not hesitate to meet me immediately at the Palm wine Junction. And mind you, don't let me step out of the room before you start to whine and gripe.

So, here's my question: Did everyone get it right but I got it wrong?

Was everything straight and smooth but I saw it rough and crooked?

Why did everyone say it's good but I said it's bad? Did everyone see it as white but I saw it as black? Where were they when the chips were falling? Were they guilty but I found them innocent? Or were they innocent but I found them guilty?

Where is right? Where is wrong? And how can we establish the truth before we treat everything as a rumor? Does a rumor have a leg or head?

How did they get away with all their loot and nobody noticed them?

Did the eyes see and never winked? And did the ears hear and never bothered?

If you think it's cool, jump into the pool the crocks are waiting on the rocks.

Where do you start when you're faced with a convoluted case? And where do you stand when the stance is of no importance?

Smooth paths don't always end the way they began. They may have bumps and rumps but we don't cut short our journeys until we reach our destination. Don't go to the Intensive Care Unit (ICU) when you have a headache. OPD (Out Patient Department) is the right place to go. And unless advised by a doctor or physician, do not treat it as 'Certificate of Urgency.' No it doesn't qualify that status. In parliament it's called due process.

Another Convention Underway!

The Race to the White House is shaping up as Dems convention opens on Monday.

This writer points out that the United States will see one of its crudest presidential campaigns ever in her political history, albeit momentous to elect either its first woman president or its first maverick prez who tells it as it is…

It took Philadelphia the city of Pennsylvania nearly 70 years to get its pride back as the host of the 2016 Democratic National Convention (DNC) that kicked off on Monday July 25. Wells Fargo Center is the venue for the august gathering.

The last convention held here was in the year 2000, that was Republican National Convention and the last time Philly hosted the DNC convention was in 1948. Cleveland, Columbus, Birmingham, New York City and Phoenix were among the finalists that contested for the slot.

The Dems' convention comes one week after the Grand Old Party (GOP) held its own in Cleveland, Ohio. All didn't go well for the Republicans. Senator Ted Cruz gave a powerful speech but fell short to endorse the party's presidential nominee Donald Trump.

Cruz's failure to endorse Trump didn't come as a surprise to me. The 'Lying' Ted as he was referred to by the newly-crowned Republican presidential nominee had it rough and tough during the campaign with the brusque politician.

Also coming as a blow to the Republican presidential candidate is the announcement by Michael Bloomberg that he will endorse Hillary Clinton instead of Donald Trump. The former New York mayor is reported to be dismayed by Trump.

The GOP convention was characterised by glitches. There was picketing and there was the buzzword Michmelaniaism.

Nevertheless, those setbacks couldn't rob the shine from the mammoth gathering. As latest polls show Donald Trump comes out of his convention ahead of Hillary Clinton in the race for the white house, topping her 44% to 39% in a four-way matchup including Gary Johnson (9%).

It must be pointed out that candidates usually boost their numbers after conventions. This happened in 2000 between Al Gore and George W. Bush. Both candidates boosted their numbers by identical 8 points. And so Hillary could bounce back into lead after DNC's convention.

That said in relation to hiccups, the Democrats haven't had a smooth take off either. Just days before the Dems' convention, WikiLeaks an international non-profit journalistic organisation that publishes secret information, news leaks and classified media from anonymous sources released what seemed like a disturbing report about the party's committee plot against Vermont Senator Bernie Sanders.

The leak was also timely as it followed hours or a day after Hillary Clinton announced her presumptive vice president nominee Tim Kaine of Virginia.

Indeed that could be described as a jolt to the party's forward march to lock horns with the GOP.

Ms. Debbie Wassermann Schultz says she will resign as democratic national committee chairwoman at the end of the convention following WikiLeaks' revelation that the committee plotted against senator Sanders.

In a statement issued over the weekend, Sunday Wassermann said: "The best way' to accomplish the goals of the party was for her, "to step down as Party Chair,' after the DNC's convention from Monday to Friday.

Speakers at the Convention

Meanwhile, six heavy-weights are billed to speak at the convention. They include President Barack Obama, former president Bill Clinton, Chelsea Clinton (daughter of the Clintons), vice president Joe Biden, first lady Michelle Obama and good old Bernie Sanders (the Vermont Senator).

Mrs. Obama a headliner speaks tonight. It isn't clear if she will joke about the stolen lines from her speech by Melania Trump at the GOP's national convention held in Cleveland a week ago.

There are expected to be 4, 769 delegates to the Democrat National Convention. A candidate needs a majority of delegate votes to win the presidential nomination, which in this case is a minimum of 2, 383 votes. And it looks palpable that Mrs. Clinton will become the first woman presidential nominee for a major party.

Protests

As witnessed in the GOP convention a number of demonstrations are expected to take place near and around Wells Fargo Center —the venue. By May 19, 2016 five organised group of Sanders' supporters had applied for permits from the Philadelphia Police Department.

A joint rally between the Poor People's Economic Human Rights Campaign and the Green Party of the United States was denied a protest permit but both groups had stated unambiguously that they will go ahead with their protest regardless.

Super Delegates Reform

On July 24, the DNC Rules Committee voted overwhelmingly, 158-6, to adopt a super delegate reform package. The new rules were the result of a compromise between the Clinton and the Sanders campaign. Sanders had pressed for the complete elimination of super delegates.

Under the reform package in future Democratic National Conventions about two-thirds of super delegates would be bound to the results of state primaries and caucuses. And the remaining one-third senators, governors and US reps—would remain unbound and free to support the candidate of their choice.

Togetherness

So who gets what?

For Hillary to win the race for the White House she will need to get her party united than ever. Hence its third and fourth night themes: "Working together" and "Stronger Together" on Wednesday/Thursday respectively—Headliners Obama, Biden, Chelsea and Hillary will take the platform.

Her counterpart Donald will also need Cruz's supporters. Above all, independent, swing, libertarian voters plus issues of immigration, security and the economy will be the determining factor.

> **"Hell is empty and all the devils are here."**
> –The Tempest, William Shakespeare

BUT who let the devils out?

Nigeria is in the news again for wrong reason: Africa's most populous nation fights three battles. Battle number one is corruption. Battle number two is corruption and battle number three is corruption. Corruption has become a global canker but the menace is ruining the oil-rich west-African nation. It's shredding the moral fabric of the people and it's about time an all-prong attack was waged against the disease.

Where in the world does a police officer kill a law-abiding citizen for refusing to give/pay bribe?

Why should a nursing mother be murdered in cold blood, simply because her husband had refused to pay a $10 bribe to a law-enforcement officer?

I thought the police are to enforce peace and protect the citizenry?

And I will like to know whether this killer is still on the streets of Nigeria?

Indeed violence pursues peace ruthlessly and not until peace finds refuge in the Lord's bosom, humanity's crave for happiness will be an illusion.

On Monday the 4th of July, courtesy of PBS Hour News I saw some horrific images. I felt chills down my spine, filled with sorrow as if I'd someone drilled chisel into my head. Goose pimples swathed my whole body and my pressure soared.

I managed to hold back my tears as a man tells his harrowing story. I couldn't fathom what my very ears heard and couldn't piece my thoughts together. I was lost…I felt so for a moment.

According to PBS it all happened last month. A trigger-happy cop had squeezed two bullets into the head of a man returning from church with his wife and three children. The police officer had asked for a bribe (a thing so common in Nigeria) from the man.

And as his demand couldn't be met he resorted to shooting the man twice and eventually killing the man's wife.

The man had been downed by two gun shots. Blood gushed out as the wife and the little kids looked on helplessly.

Their father and husband writhed in pain on the ground.

"I now went down held my head and blood gushed out," says the wounded man.

But the worst was yet to bare its teeth. Evil is restless and violence is on warpath.

"Suddenly I heard my children shouting mommy's dying, mommy's dying. I quickly stood up and went back to see my wife and the blood was just pumping out."

She'd been killed by the police officer. A mother nursing their new born had been murdered in cold blood.

"She cherished me so much. She loved me so much. When I held her I discovered two bullets went through one side of the head and exited the opposite. My friend has died and left me. My wife that is assisting me is gone…"

The Burkina Bribe Gate: Are Ghanaians raising the political barometer too high?

Must they mind their own business and leave the presidency alone?

Let's see how loyalty/cronyism, gifts and bribes play out in Ghana's socio-political milieu. And could there be an impeachment if investigations establish culpability?

The dust settles not in Ghana (of course it never did in the Gold Coast), particularly in the political arena, as the tempest soars above the sky. Until the wind folds her wings the atmosphere will continue to be saturated with her residues. It has developed several angles; among them a terse message straddling the cyber space– that seeks to admonish men and women of the inky fraternity to be wary of what is to come.

That message is authored by Mr. Kojo Oppong Nkrumah an NPP aspiring member of parliament for Ofoase constituency in the eastern region.

In mid last week the former 'Super Morning Show' host of Joy FM, a privately-owned radio station in Accra appeared to have been troubled by an alleged bribe given to the first gentleman of Republic of Ghana, President John Mahama by a Burkinabe contractor.

Following the development the former radio broadcaster wrote this:

"Dear friends in the media, if you receive one of the Flagstaff House fat envelopes, tonight I am asking you to stay away from the #mahamaford story (Burkinabribegate) in your line of work tomorrow, please even if you have to take the money to pay your ECG bill (Electricity Company of Ghana), just don't let him buy you. Save Ghana, spread the word. Be bold to tell the truth. Posterity will judge you."

Kojo's message reminds me of the famous speech delivered by a former Roman politician Marcus Antonius (in William Shakespeare literature book-Julius Caesar), popularly known in English as Mark Anthony. He was Caesar's staunch supporter (also known as the Populares) and served as one of his generals during the conquest of Gual in the civil war.

Even though Caesar was a dictator his cronies perhaps never raised an eyebrow. This would trigger conspiracy leading to his assassination on the Ides of March in 44BC. His supporters crossed swords with the Optimates spearheaded by Pompey.

But Caesar's assassins got a traitor from his own camp and like the Biblical Judas Iscariot; Junius Brutus aided and abetted the slain of the powerful man.

English writer William Shakespeare writes that following Caesar's tragic death Mark Anthony (himself a dictator) asked his countrymen in Rome to lend him their ears: "Friends Romans and countrymen lend me your ears. For I have come to bury Caesar not to praise him..."

Anthony's bust in Vatican City still evokes memories of that famed speech delivered after the assassination of Julius Caesar. Indeed, in politics loyalty is pivotal and then you can pack the bus with cronies, buddies and fair-weather friends, which ultimately also come at a cost.

Loyalty/Cronyism

Loyalty is devotion and faithfulness to a cause, country, group or a person. To be able to consolidate power one needs to surround himself with a person or group of persons who are loyal to the cause and the leader. Nonetheless these persons must transcend sycophancy and must take off their jaundiced spectacles.

Cronyism on the other hand is the practice of partiality/bias in awarding jobs and other advantages to friends or trusted colleagues, especially in politics. They used to say 'Job for the Boys' and certainly it was for the boys not the guys with technical know-how.

Did anyone listen to Mr. Kofi Adams NDC National Youth Organiser on Joy FM's 'Super Morning Show last week with Nyira?

If you're Populares you'd give him a standing ovation just like Mark Anthony praised his slain boss, lashing out at Brutus for characterising Caesar as ambitious. And if you belong to the opposite camp (the Optimates) you'd probably scorn and rubbish his entire submission.

Why? Because it is what it is... As political animals some of us have been wired to behave that way—follow the majority even if they're heading down the cliff. But most importantly, the reason is that he's on the other side of the political divide. This is what is killing us as a people. We can't call spade a spade.

Gifts and Bribe

Gift is a thing given willingly to someone without payment in return as to show favour towards someone. It can be a present from person to person, a group or organisation to a person. In short the act of giving must be free will and not have any strings attached.

In contrast bribe or bribery is a practice meant to persuade someone to act in one's favour–typically legally or dishonestly by a gift of money or other inducement. Not too long ago ace investigator Anas Aremeyaw Anas in his undercover escapade busted a group of high court judges in Ghana who received monies, cows and goats as way of favoritism to their bribe givers.

So what do people give out?

They come in assortments. Between 2009 –2012 President Obama received 274 gifts from foreign countries and their leaders. These gifts are reviewed by the Protocol Unit of the State Department, surfing through each and every one of the gifts.

In March 2015, Governor John Duncan of the British Virgin Islands gave a bag of salt to the Queen of England. This was in keeping with tradition of giving a 1lb bag of salt to the British Monarch every year as rent for sparsely populated salt Island in the Caribbean archipelago.

In 2014 Saudi Royal Family gave more than $1 million in jewelry to First Lady Michelle Obama, while the president received swords, a dagger, and a robe of shear white fabric.

And guess what Mexican president Enrique Pena Nieto gifted Prince Andrew –a cigarette box, even though the British royal doesn't smoke.

It's also worthy of note that some presidents in their good judgements have refused some gifts when for instance the present smacks fishy. Ghana's first President Dr. Kwame Nkrumah said thanks to Agricultural Development Corporation (ADC) for buying a yacht for him, but he turned down the offer.

Others couldn't resist the mouth-watering gifts and they either resigned from office or faced impeachment. And it appears that's exactly where president Mahama finds himself. There's nothing wrong receiving gifts or hampers from people or companies. But when there's conflict of interest in the giving or gift it leaves much to be desired.

Does the Flagstaff House or the state have a unit or agency of this kind that peruse all gifts meant for the presidency or the president himself?

I shudder to say that our institutions have failed us. The pressure from society is too heavy and too much for them to bear. Everybody wants favour (usually money) from the minister of state, legislator, senator, mayor or the district chief executive. This explains why corruption is so prevalent in our society.

It takes two to tango.

Impeachment

Impeachment is a process in which an official is accused of unlawful activity—the outcome of which depending on the country may include the removal of that official from office as well as criminal or civil punishment.

Some group of people has suggested that president Mahama must be impeached if investigations establish any culpability on his part. I doubt if that would ever happen. None of the nation's presidents or heads of state has ever faced impeachment.

In the United States Andrew Johnson and Bill Clinton are the only two presidents to have been successfully impeached by the congress. In the case of Ghana parliament has the sole power of impeaching. However, as already pointed out that's unlikely to happen.

Social Media: Odomfo Kumfo'

It was like a huge fire ball that perhaps reached millions across the globe within an hour.

Many including myself who saw it expressed shock, sympathy and dismay. That fire was on the wheels of social media—the vehicle that probably now travels faster than the North American XB-70 Valkyrie.

Have you ever heard the expression "fire is a good servant but a bad master?"

Well, social media now rivals fire with that title. Social Media has been a revolutionary tool in the 21st century. Its ability to create, share, or exchange information, career interests, ideas, and pictures/videos in virtual communities and make news go viral is unmatched.

But the same good servant has been used by swindlers or mischief-makers to cheat, to loot and to create panic and pranks.

Over the weekend a video surfaced that showed two men had been electrocuted, while working on power lines in Accra Ghana. The less than two minutes video suggested, both men were staff of Electricity Company of Ghana (ECG).

This is how an informant captured it on one of the social media platforms: "ECG lost two workers today at Madina (a suburb of Accra). Viewer discretion is advised. Very serious…."

This followed the usual hue and cry, the blame game, the gotcha moments and the outpouring of sympathies to the alleged fallen 'heroes'.

"Sorry these men perished. May their souls Rest in Peace."

"Very sad..." wrote another.

"Sad…oh Africa when oooo when…?"

"I doubt if they'd any proper safety gears..?"

"It doesn't look like they did."

"The power was turned on unexpectedly which shouldn't have happened."

"This doesn't add up. How can power be turned on if they knew their men were on the line?

What protocols does ECG operate on?"

And the civil discourse went on and on.

However, in less than 72 hours ECG, issued a press statement advising the general public to disregard the video.

"Ignore the video which might have occurred in some other country," William Boateng General Manager (PR) of Electricity Company of Ghana (ECG) stated.

Mr. Boateng said ECG rejects reports that two of its technicians have been electrocuted, while on assignment. He added, no accident had occurred on its network anywhere in its operational area.

So where did this incident happen? Who's behind this prank? And what's the motive?

Well, whether it did happen in Ghana or not. I have a brief story to share. It's Gary Norrland's story. It all happened in May 13, 2013. It was just a typical day at work, Garry wrote. He and his co-workers were discussing weekend plans as they worked near overhead power lines.

In the process he accidentally propped back and came into contact with 12,500 volts of electricity. The accident was horrible. Mr. Norland suffered life-changing burns that required a 4-month hospital stay and more than 50 surgeries.

After his recovery Gary decided to do presentations—spreading his message of safety to all and sundry: "If you get injured, it's an impact that's going to affect everybody."

Here are a few safety tips to prevent any future mishaps, according to Mr. Norland.

First, look up and around you. Always be aware of the location of power lines, particularly when using long tools like ladders, pool skinners and pruning poles. Also keep equipment and your body at least 10 feet from power lines.

Third be careful when working on or around your roof. That includes installing or cleaning gutters, installing rooftop antennas and satellite dishes or doing repair work. Never climb trees near power lines. Never trim trees near power lines. And finally, always follow safety procedures, no matter how boring and mundane they seem.

In the United States June is observed as 'National Safety Month' and it is aimed at preventing accidents relating to fire. National Fire Protection Association (NEPA's) statistics indicate that 30 per cent of all home fires and 38 per cent of home fire deaths occur during December, January and February (holiday season).

Gordon Offin-Amaniampong

'Black Is Beautiful':
But do we really appreciate it?

Until peoples of darker hue (both Africans and Diasporas) appreciate who we are and uphold our dignity the well-known phrase, 'Black is Beautiful 'believed to have been first coined by John Stewart Rock, an African-American abolitionist of the United States will be meaningless.

In fact the black race will not only lose its pride and self-esteem but also continue to live under mental servitude.

On Wednesday May 11, the chatroom of Ghana Institute of Journalism Alumni in North America (GIJANA) was seemingly set ablaze as members took turns to express their views concerning the latest trending issue——bleach or skin lightening.

Barima Isaac Kamoko, alias Bukom Banku (a Ghanaian boxer and a bronze winner of the all Africa games held in South Africa in 1999) has got the association of the inky fraternity talking.

Or did he pee at their backyard to put it loosely?

It seemed many were appalled by the fashion. But more so, by a video of the boxer that sought to denigrate blackness. Some attributed the trend to illiteracy and ignorance. Others believed it was low self-esteem coupled with the glamorisation of fair skin texture.

For instance there's this common saying that it's easier to see a light-skinned lady in a darkroom compared to her dark-skinned peer. Light skin ladies illuminate or glamorise darkroom, so they say. Hence, dark-skinned women prefer light-skinned men and vice versa.

The chairperson of GIJANA Madam Alberta Brew is of the view that in order to deal with the problem there is the need to look into our cultures and vocabularies.

She writes: "We call our children" 'me broni' (white) to make them feel special. We say 'kokoo kum akyer' (light skin textures mask ugliness) and then we blame people when they bleach…perhaps the remedy lies in the vocabulary."

She argues that people are aware of the dangers of bleaching. And those who indulge in the practice cut across demographics, status and professions. Nonetheless, they choose to do so because it is trending.

"Most people who bleach are aware of the consequences. I have seen teachers and doctors who bleach. It could also be an addiction or low self-esteem. What can we say?" she rhetorically asks.

Would the latest discussions cause people to change the thinking about skin lightening?

It remains to be observed going forward but I doubt.

Bleaching is the use of chemicals or creams to reduce a pigment called melanin in the skin. In other words it is an attempt to lighten the tone of the skin or to bring about a more even and uniform complexion on people who may have uneven skin tones.

It is believed that many commercial skin beaching products contain chemicals that are harmful to human health.

So why do people bleach?

It must be noted that not all people use lighteners to change their skin texture. Most Caucasians who use lighteners do so to treat skin problems such as freckles, age spots, acne scars or discolouration related to hormones.

On the contrary among the black population the majority who resort to bleaching do so because of low self-esteem and the craze to be. Question is: Can a rat be a mole?

Remember a disguised rat appearing like a mole will be betrayed by its 'ratish' tail.

Since millennia the black man has been struggling to fit in. To appreciate his skin texture, acknowledge that black is strong, black is powerful, black is unique and black never crack.

Where is this momentum that our forebears built?

Where is the enthusiasm?

In my third book: 'The Finish Line' I posed the question: Doesn't the potter have the right to do whatever he wants to do with his pottery? The potter representing God reserves the right to do whatever he desires or wishes. As a craftsman he uses the clay to make his pottery. He shapes the pottery on a porter's wheel and bakes them in a kiln.

Small, large and big the porter spends diligent time to make them all. So why the sweat, why wonder that you were born black and not white or dark-skinned and not light-skinned?

South African author Stephen Bantu Biko an anti-apartheid activist in his book: "Black Consciousness Movement' aimed to dispel the stigma of materialised racism and the belief that blackness was inferior. This was a conscious effort by the activist to help black people everywhere to shed inferiority complex.

In the 1960's a cultural movement was born in the United States of America. It was simply called 'Black is Beautiful' and it aims to dispel the notion in many cultures that black people's natural features such as skin colour, facial features and hair are inherently ugly.

Today black pride is waning. And I can say emphatically that our values, standards have gone down low. I doubt if blacks themselves believe the phrase that caught fire in the early 60's. Whether blacks themselves believe black is beautiful. And whether blacks themselves practice what we preach.

I have personally been called a monkey in the states. This was back in 2008, while working with Walmart.

"Hey mum look at a monkey," a little black boy told his mother. And to my surprise the ebony young woman laughed hysterically.

From Accra to Rio de Janeiro, Kingstown to Cleveland the momentum has regressed. And only God knows where the speeding bus will stop. Though the current generation has held on to 'black' not all see it as beautiful, hence the upsurge of bleaching creams.

Research indicates that the idea of 'blackness' being ugly is highly damaging particularly to the psyche of African Americans, manifesting itself as internalized racism.

Paradoxically, this idea made its way into black communities themselves and led to practices such as paper bag parties, social events which discriminated against dark-skinned African-Americans by only admitting lighter-skinned individuals.

And to date we are still fighting, struggling to find our identity. Appreciate our skin texture and uphold our dignity. Let's be proud of who we are, be proud of our blackness. The eagle can fly it cannot swim, the fish can swim it cannot fly. Bats aren't feathered animals yet they can fly. In whatever state you find yourself it is unique and not oblique. Are you smarter than the master designer?

What would you do if you had your own way?

He wished he was never born. He prayed his life was taken away. For close to a decade the peasant farmer from Nyira a tiny town in the central part of Ghana lived a miserable life. Depression had consumed him as he felt totally disoriented with the turn of events.

He never stopped knocking on death's door. But in the midst of all this he kept faith in God.

Mr. J.J Turkson had a tough battle in his hands. He was losing almost all his close allies and best friends in life. About 10 of them had within the last ten years reached the point one would describe as 'living dead'. His legs and hands had given up on him. He could barely hear a sound without a hearing device. His sense of smell was long gone.

There was also a nagging pain on his neck. And the thought of losing his loyal friends gave him constant headache and the heart ache that followed was unimaginable. His nose had been attacked by cancer. But beyond that Mr. Turkson had locked horns with a cancerous disease to the brain.

The human brain is the body's command midpoint. It receives and sends signals to other organs through the nervous system. It is also responsible for our thoughts, feelings, and memory storage (like the computer). He couldn't piece his thoughts together any longer.

No teeth to chew bones, and no hair to comb. Mr. Turkson was like Mr. Ray, the veteran US Navy officer, I once chanced upon several years ago. Today, Ray has his low back, knees, neck, both ankles and hips replaced with metals.

He calls himself 'a remade person'.

Mr. Turkson was born a strong man with a towering frame. He exuded so much power and energy. He took good care of himself but as he advanced in years certain parts of the body began to lose their guards. He'd been unlucky. His whole life had had a nose dive.

Nonetheless one of his friends was still thumping and pumping blood throughout the body .His heart continued to beat every day until one hush afternoon when the sun failed to rise. And the dark clouds took the center stage…The farmer gave his last breath.

Our body is just like that of a car, an airplane or a building. Every part of a car plays an invaluable role. From the tyres to the engine, headlights to windscreen, brake and gear, alternator to the gas tank they are all important as they collectively help set the automobile in motion.

However, when the engine is shut off the car becomes immobile or inactive.

If Mr. Turkson had his own way he would have averted all the agonies he'd to endure.

And if Man had his own way there wouldn't be death on earth. There would be neither sorrow nor sadness if Man had the power to conquer the monster. There would be neither sickness nor poverty. There would be pure joy, peace and harmony, if Man had his own way.

Many would fight tooth and nail to bring back to life their loved ones, if Man had the wherewithal to do so. They would bring back friends and all those they'd painfully lost—either naturally or tragically.

But the dearth of strength, the dearth of power, the dearth of energy and the lack of invincibility make the whole battle a lost one. We're mortal beings and we're fragile.

This explains why even before the undying death knocks on our doors we've to fight relentlessly to stay in good shape. The battle to maintain the human body—the physical structure of Man, which includes the bones, flesh and organs.

Can you imagine a car plying in darkness without headlights or a tower without strong pillars or an airplane without a compass?

Be thankful that you're alive and kicking today. It's nothing but his Grace!

When a Fool Speaks

Jaws dropped. Their brows furrowed. And anger filled the setting.

The queens and the princesses in the jungle have met—behind closed doors.

What are they talking about?

Have their husbands gone wild?

No, it's a different ball game. Something ugly is rearing its head.

Is it really true that daughters are like mothers?
That they resemble their mothers?
And that they love their mothers?
Don't jump the gun. Wait till the chickens come home. What happened in the jungle couldn't sneak the lenses of the cameras and the cell phones. Alas the folly has spoken!

xxxxxxxxxxxxx

Everyone knows her. Everyone knows she's got a stocky body. Everybody knows she's flat snout, small eyes and large ears. She's never been ashamed of her looks and character traits. They say she's dirty, they say she's greedy and they say she's ugly. But none of the name calling makes her cringe.

Indeed, she'd remained unbreakable and immune to insults and insinuations until her own daughter launched verbal attacks on her– swearing and cursing.

"Look at her and look at me. We don't look anything alike. She's ugly. I'm beautiful. I'm not connected to her," the young swine told her mom.

Present at the meeting, were the lioness, the tigress, the leopardess and all the married/single moms in the animal kingdom.

The scene was getting giddy and nasty. The piggy dirty swine was throwing punches from all fronts. Her mom felt humiliated. She couldn't take them anymore. It seemed she'd been riding on a rollercoaster.

Mother pig felt dizzy. She staggered and nearly fell to the ground. Finally she broke down in tears. Still the dirty greedy piggy continued to swear at her.

"You're ugly, you're nothing but nasty."

"Hey, you better belt up," cried the lioness.

"How dare you speak like that to your mom? Mind you, being rude to your mom isn't cool. We don't play games here. And if you think you're superior to or better than folks here you're at liberty to leave and join the other race."

"What makes you think that you're better than your mom?"

"She's always in the sludge and her sparse bristly hair is ugly. My colour is different and I don't get myself dirty as she does," replied the piglet.

The lioness was gradually losing her cool. Her patience was thinning. And her colleagues like the tiger and the leopard couldn't hide their fury. What they were witnessing appeared unfamiliar to them. In the animal kingdom respect is demanded and not merited. Kiddies deemed naughty get flogged. Often times they vanish into thin air.

A daughter disowning her own mom! How did we get here?

Meanwhile, the empress and the queens of the jungle have unanimously condemned the behaviour of the young swine. The lioness said the piggy was the 'dumbest beast' she'd ever come across in her life. The tigress called it the 'crudest' and the Leopardess described it as the 'creepiest' she'd ever witnessed.

Folks the chickens have come home to roost. Therefore, look no further.

Flashbacks

Every dark mark I see....

Every buck that I spend at the mart

And every Mack Truck that comes my way, reminds me of Jack Black.

That blacksmith, in that black Maybach has gotten me stuck in my tracks.

I can't figure out if there's a way out. I can't read in between the lines.

But I can tell when an ugly duckling starts to quack.

It quacks around the clock. Quack, quack, quack...

Everything smacks quaky. And every time I tell myself I'm ready, Jack Black has something to say.

Something that holds me back... It is either this or that.

It's always that thing!

Back in the day everything was fine.

Jack used to give me breakfast in bed. Follow it up with brunch and lunch.

Dinner was always Jack's signature dish/meal.

My bowl never goes empty. And my stomach never growls– always full.

When it comes to steak fixing… No one does it like Jack.

Today that big bowl is denied with everything.

But what went wrong?

How come he no longer appreciates anything that I do?

Anything that I say is misread. And anything that I suggest is misjudged.

Is this the real way to go?

I never knew love has different colours.

I never thought we would ever walk this road.

Or ever come this far and ever find myself in this cesspool.

Should I say yes or should I say no?

Say no to this quack relationship: This relation that sucks like flashbacks.

Things to Say

Did it sting like a bee?

How did you feel?

If your ear didn't tingle then it isn't a bee.

Old Jomo has lost his mojo. He couldn't stand the heat he couldn't take the blow.

Mind you, you've got to be you and let me be me.

Short cuts I'm told are dangerous. Short moves can be risky.

And risky stuff ain't kiddy stuff.

How much did they rob from Peter to pay Paul?

No, ain't talking about biblical Paul.

I'm talking to you— Paul.

Look before you leap and never try to be like a bee.

Where were you when Rome was built?

Romeo died for Juliet and St. Valentine was executed for his stance for Christian marriage.

Apollonia is rising high, apes are riding as if they're on steroids and the world is shrinking so fast.

They say what goes around comes around. But what happens in between the round trip?

Did it sound like a bell? If didn't ring, then it isn't a bell.

And if it didn't beep then it isn't a cellular phone.

Birds fly, bats fly and butterflies fly.

What happened to the creeping mammals?

Have they ceased to creep when man continues to weep?

Where did the rivers go? Did they seek refuge deep down the mountains feet?

And where too did the sun go? Was it eclipsed by the clouds?

What happened to the Moon? Was she abducted by the aliens on Venus?

I can't see my little little twinkling stars. Have they stopped to glitter?

Or have they been taken hostage?

Can't wait! Just looking forward to the day when the stallions cannot run.

I'm looking forward to the day when champions will succumb to minnows and scorpions will have no venom left in them.

Gee!

What's going on, red meat crying?

She wants the lion to eat her?

That doesn't sound right.

Is it already twilight?

Oh no, the lion says no to red meat. The hungry lion has declined an offer.

The scavenger vulture has turned down carcass.

And the greedy stomach no more yearns for food.

Every day is a blessing day as long as the eye can blink its intrepid lenses and the ear can hear. Be grateful and count your blessings one by one. Be grateful that you still have a waggle tongue, body and soul.

The Garbage

And the poet asked the poet: Has man lost it?
Does he get it? Or he's simply not in touch with reality?
O' how quickly did he forget that he's still being recycled?
Are you ready to be called garbage?

I hope I can cope, answered the poet. Well, they may say you're crazy to be acting silly.

Remember they stoned Stephen. Hanged Peter upside down and crucified Jesus Christ!

The blind saw. Saul became Paul. The deaf heard. The lost was found. The demon-possessed was exorcised. The poor, who was once poured out like water, was redeemed. The lowly was elevated. The boisterous storm was calmed. The meek and weak became strong. And the outcast was welcomed home.

Pharaoh's heart was hardened. The fool remained foolish and the wicked perished on his sword. He prescribed meds for the sick and not for the healthy. By faith many were healed. Thousands pursued him for healing.

We're still a wretch. Still being molded and always being recycled.

Look across the street. Tell me what you see, the poet instructed.

I had to squint so hard to make the garbage line up with reality. From a distance it looked like a moving mountain. That's right! The humongous garbage was been ferried by a huge boat. Scrappy and trashy but someone needed it badly.

Tons of trash all meant to be recycled. All of them once used, reused and overused by humans—you and me. A recycling plant factory situated at Taylor Way near port of Tacoma was taken care of the unwanted.

When clothes and shoes are deemed tattered or worn out they're thrown away. It's like the salt of the earth, when it loses its taste it is good for nothing....

When plastic bottles, bags, rubbers are used and overused they're no longer needed or wanted. Instead they're trashed or tossed into garbage bins. Needless to say they've outlived their usefulness.

Who likes it stretched to its elastic limit, broken and irretrievable or rotten and forgotten?

Certainly nobody wants it worn-out or tatty. Everybody wants it fresh and beautiful, tasty and flashy, garish and stylish.

But, have you been described as the lost, the black sheep, the outcast, the downtrodden or the good-for-nothing yet? Or do you feel used, overused and abused?

The poet says you're still useful. Still loved by many and loved by the One who beautifully and wonderfully made you.

Be reminded you only get to be recycled until you're labeled and trashed. He came for the wretch.

Be blessed!

The Plot

A Hunter crawls on his belly like a roach. He sneaks and lurks around. He employs anything qualified to be called precision and everything deemed canny to get his game. His target nibbles on a leafy plant in the thicket, totally oblivious of its fate.

It won't be too late the trigger will ring. Late last night he missed his prey, but not today. They say joy comes in the morning...His new date will in no time have something sumptuous to eat.

Hate him or like him the hunter has no mercy for his game– sick or healthy, young or old, small or big, a she or a he.

"Yikes!" he cries.

What's amiss?

He's been bitten by an ant soldier.

"Better be quiet and lick the wound. Very painful," he mouths it.

Young antelope senses danger. Head goes up. Nose points to the heavens and ears cocked up– censoring the atmosphere and the terrain. Indeed danger looms but his greedy belly still growls. The hungry beast must eat.

Downhill his predator is poised, ready to pull the trigger. His fore finger comfortably rests on the trigger. The prey loiters around. And the hunter closes in on him.

"Today bi today," he swears in Pidgin English.

"Thursday night was blight," he recalls. But right where he finds himself the end of his target seems nigh.

'Kapayaaa!' rings the gun. The prey falls helplessly. And the hunter jubilates.

This is how Satan operates every day. When we fall he's elated. When we falter he's all happy. When we're shamed he's famed. Satan takes delight in our tragedies. Like the hunter he lurks around. He stalks us, spies on us, preys on us, wishes our downfalls and prays we don't succeed.

But God forbid!

The Bible refers to him as the prince of the earth. But see how low he goes to get his targets. He crawls on his belly on the ground like a snake, acting sneaky and being sleazy.

Sometimes we sense danger like the poor antelope but we ignore the signals. Things that ears see, eyes cannot see. And things that eyes hear ears cannot hear. Therefore, let's behave like the Thursday lucky antelope. The hunter missed her because she was tactful, careful and acted swiftly to avoid danger.

Making right choices or decisions can save us from loads of trouble and temptation. Following our instincts can help absolve us from many mishaps. Also, self-control, self-will power and being prayerful can help us maneuver our predator (s).

Matter of fact, it isn't that easy, especially for us humans. Our desires sometimes drive us to nut. But we must always remember we serve a living God who guides and protects us regardless. Let's be mindful, we build in vain, unless the Builder builds.

Be blessed always!

Darling Rainier

O' Rainier where did thou get your beauty, borrowed or bought?

You're uniquely beautiful. You're so natural. You're a real woman of substance.

Even in the midst of dark clouds you shine and outshine your peers. You shine like the sturdy northern star, dazzling everywhere you overlook. You mesmerised me this afternoon. You made me feel like a fool –stood watching you like a bull led to the poolside.

From a distance I watched you as though I've never seen you or known you. I stood hypnotised. Eyes relished on your stunning prominence and my whole mind engrossed on your beauty.

I don't know what kind of shoes you slid your feet in. You peaked so high in the sky rising beyond the clouds cutting through their thick layers. You rose through them yet you couldn't be enveloped.

O' Mount Rainier when you shine reindeer go gay. They frolic your beauty and play around like little kids stomping on trampolines.

O' how I wish you could rain on me. How I wish you could visit me same time tomorrow and perhaps every day. You've always stood tall but you looked incredibly beautiful today. You're as white as snow and your golden tulip lip glows everywhere.

May you forever wear your silver hair my darling!

Hey You!

Turn to the next page. If you can't make it, meet me at the backstage of Pantages.

I've got a message for you. Did you see all the guys who came with the vintage cars?

They all have issues. And did you know the manager at the Heritage Bank has a problem too?

Why the rage?

Why?

Think you're the only one with a baggage?

Or the only one trapped in a cage? Or the only one caught up in wreckage?

See, it's needless to get so enraged as if that would assuage your troubles.

So what is it?

Is it about age? Or it is lack of courage?

Tell me. Is it about the spillage or it's the damage?
Is the leakage too much? Or it's your baggage that's too heavy to carry?
Be reminded marriage of the two could result huge damage.
Knew ye not that everything has its advantages and disadvantages?
And don't you remember the old adage—once damaged can't be savaged?
Cheer up! Don't be discouraged. Be encouraged.
Don't let your troubles take you hostage, for it would dent your image.
They may seem intractable but be assured you can manage.
Get over it and envisage the coming of the Ancient of Age.
Change is coming. Change is on its way. So get back on stage play your part and forget about your baggage.
Forget about the rage. Forget about the cage and forget about the disadvantages. It's time to turn a new page. It's time to get the leverage.

Coward

Did they die before the brawl began?
Or they were cowed by the fighters before the fight?
Can't liken them to cobwebs, they're nobody but cowards.
Fight or don't fight
Try or don't try
Fly or don't fly
Do or don't do it
Run or don't run
Play or don't play
You tame the game or the game tames you
The Thames River takes every **** but real gamers go for the kill
A walk and talk aren't the same. You walk the talk
And don't talk the talk
Be cold or be hot
If not, give up and zip up
Drink deep or taste not

A crab shell is like a crack head
Crack not if you can't beat the beast
An angry beast is the crudest beast.
A treat at a beach is like a feast on yeast
And a fool's path ends in the cesspool.
If you think I didn't make myself right sit tight and wait for Mr. Right.

The Carpenter

Papa Carpenter never stopped to amaze his town folks. He was a man with small frame. Yet, he didn't rest at all. He was always on the move. It came as no surprise to him when some folks nicknamed him Mr. 'workaholic'.

He was very industrious, but little did he know, that being hardworking was a crime in his own town.

One evening Papa Carpenter returned home and found out the whole area of his residence had been cordoned off. There was little or no space left not blocked. He stood still visibly shaking and wondered who might've done that to him.

His whole frame bore surprise and disbelief. And for a moment he questioned:

"Is this my house?"

He pinched himself thinking he was daydreaming.

"I hope I'm not lost. I hope this is my own house. But what's going on?" He queried.

He soon came to terms with reality.

He wasn't daydreaming: "Yeah, it's my home. I'm not lost. I'm at the right place."

The sight of graffiti on the walls placards strewn on the driveway and threats on his life scared him to death. Papa Carpenter sensed danger approaching. But who was responsible for all that.

As he inched closer he sighted a note scrawled in red ink also posted on his door.

"You've been summoned to appear before the 'Odikro' chief of the town," the notice read.

Reason, he'd been disturbing his neighbours ever since he relocated to the area.

Besides, he hadn't heeded to calls from the public to stop his nuisance.

If found guilty in part, the note stated" "You'd be banished from this town."

The next day, he hurried to the chief's palace where almost everyone in the town had trooped in to hear the outcome of the case.

There were shouts and chants of 'banish him. We don't want him here."

The 'Ahenfie Police' called for order as Papa Carpenter reached for a microphone to state his case.

"Your Lordship, I work very hard to earn a living. I work so hard to get my day going. I am not a lazy bone. What many here don't appreciate is that, perhaps I work harder than everybody here gathered to get my daily bread.

That I must say doesn't come easy. I do it through perseverance. I routinely and repeatedly bang my small head against a wall every day to get my food. Is this a crime my Lord?"

How many of you here would make it if you wobbled from the top of a scaffold and had a big fall?

Which one amongst you would be able to bang his head routinely and constantly against a bronze wall?

As you all can see, I am not tall. But I'm always seen on heights. How do I get there?

It's by dint of hard work. That's me. Yes, my accusers are right. I make noise all day and all night long banging my head against bronze walls, chiseling, nailing and hammering. But I've never been taken ill. No pills and I pay no bills for medication.

There are farmers among us they make noise, there are also those who quarry stones, they make noise, there are cobblers or shoe shine boys, they make noise and there are miners operating with bulldozers, chainsaw operators they all make noise.

So why do I stand accused? If I won't be credited for what I do must I be banished for being a workaholic?

Anyway, before I retire to my seat, I will like to ask the public including those who want me banished:

Would you be the same you, if you routinely and repeatedly bang your heads against a wall?

If you took your eyes of the ball driving on a freeway would you survive?

And where do you think you'd end up if you did what I do?"

I'm a woodpecker and I will continue to do what I do. "Case quashed," says the judge!

Hello!

It was a reciprocal call. It came about half hour after she missed mine. She's good at that, always making sure all missed calls are returned. I was enjoying the usual quietness in my Belle Terrace apartment. A buzzing phone cried like a hungry baby in the bedroom. I better hurry lest I miss it.

Phone calls are like treasure troves, especially if you live by yourself far from home. I'm referring to those from loved ones and good friends. That was my cousin Gifty (Adwoa) based in Amsterdam, Holland. It was late summer 2015. Fall was warming up at the bench, readying to take the centre stage. And as usual Adwoa was also bubbling with smiles.

What's up Coz? I asked.

"Nothing much just returning your call," She replied.

In the middle of our telephony conversation Adwoa remembered an old hit song titled: 'Anyen'. It's highlife music maestro A.B Crentsil's smash song which rocked Ghana's airwaves in the mid 80's. That album also spawned a lot of controversy, she recollected.

Growing up Adwoa had heard the name witch known as 'Bayie' or Bayifo' in Akan Twi language in Ghana. Among the Fanti's in central region it is called "Anyen.' She'd also witnessed brawls, insults and accusations flit around like bullets, piercing through concrete walls and creating manholes.

So, after all, she'd something to share. Something she hadn't been able to digest. Something she couldn't wrap her mind around it for decades. The question of who is a witch or wizard remained an enigma to her.

But, was I ready for a jab that quite afternoon— enjoying my summer blues?

In Ghanaian cultural milieu witches and wizards or warlocks (as the males are referred to) feature in myths and folktales. They're considered evil, deceitful and treacherous. They're the reason accidents happen and anything considered misfortune.

For this reason and others those deemed to have witchcraft powers are often stigmatised and ostracized. It is also believed that if not evil by nature, witches may be possessed by demons or bad spirits determined to harm people.

Is it paradox?

There seems to be a cultural shift if you like. Back in the day it was usually the wrinkle-faced old woman that bore the brunt of the abuse and insults. Everyone blamed her for everything. Nowadays that thought appear to include everybody—young, old, male, female, lettered or unlettered, able or disable.

"So back to my question," Adwoa reminded me.

Online Merriam-Webster dictionary defines witch as someone that is credited with usually malignant supernatural power, especially: a woman practising wildly black witchcraft often with the aid of a devil. It explains that an ugly old woman and a charming or alluring girl or woman meets the criteria.

Adwoa needed some practical answers not the mythical and the mundane belief that every old lady is a witch.

So I decided to take her through the following questions:

What do you focus on when you pray?

Is it good or evil?

Do you pray your friend, neighbour or someone dies prematurely or something untoward happens to them?

Do you wish disaster happens or someone loses his/her job, property, loved one or become homeless?

Do you wish your child become a drunk, promiscuous, a nonentity? Are you jealous of your siblings, friends or loved ones? Are you selfish and where does that lead you to? And do you have covetous eyes?

She responded negative to all the questions above. And that somehow simplified things. Truth is people with malignant super natural power do the exact opposite. Witches and wizards operate on a mindset that tends to romanticise anything evil, anything bad, anything sad. They thrive on anything that can lead to disaster, destruction, death and devastation.

They know no stop until they see anything gory, anything grotesque anything gruesome and anything grisly. Indeed, anything bloody gives them satisfaction and pleasure!

Take for instance a person who has jealousy demon embedded within. He shows or feels envy of someone or their achievements and advantages.

Thing about people with these demons is that they ensure you lose what you possess and even want you dead. Their whole mind is configured on negativity, regression, calamity and wickedness.

Be reminded unhealthy rivalry could lead to that. And wherever good is evil finds his way there…so be careful, be focused and be alert.

Shalom!

What's your Moment?

We all have moments in our lives. There are moments of happiness. And there are moments of sadness. There are eureka moments. And there are moments that everything literally gets screwed up.

Both moments arouse some kind of craziness in our behaviours, whether it is promotion in our jobs or failure to get the promotion, success in exams or failure in the exams, first weddings in marriages or breakup in relationships, a trip into space or being told you can't make the trip, special date with a superstar, or jilted at the last minute.

It could be a new invention, or failure to have a breakthrough in the whole undertaking or study.

In Syracuse, the ancient Greece city, celebrated mathematician Archimedes was understood to have jumped out of his bathtub and hit the street butt-naked, running and shouting: eureka meaning 'I have found it.

That moment happened after the physician stepped into a bath and observed that the water level had risen. He momentarily noticed that the volume of water displaced must be equal to the volume of the part of his body he'd submerged into the bathtub.

It was that moment that purportedly drove Archimedes to the streets of Syracuse like a lunatic.

Indeed everyone gets little crazy sometimes depending on the circumstances or the moment one finds himself. When the joy moment shows up we scream words and phrases like Wow!

This is it! Got it! And of course Eureka!

And there are moments we scream Ouch, which means things have gone the wrong way. And we've got to start it all over again. They're the moments heads start to spin. They're the moments one can describe as eye-popping.

Sometimes you have to wear the shirt inside out if things don't work the opposite way. Perhaps the flipside would work better and produce the Eureka moment. A coin has two sides and each side tells its own story. Just as every moment has its downside or upside.

Moments tend not to count if the results aren't significant or don't carry much weight. Such moments fade out quickly. No one remembers them. They're easily forgotten. Still, consider each side you find yourself as a stepping stone and just move on.

Imagine if all humans had same looks, same height and same weight.

Imagine if raindrops came down like stones and snowflakes were pearls.

Imagine if mountains had no roots and the oceans had no sand on their shores.

Imagine if pillows can talk and beds can speak out the pressure they bear every day and every night.

When we wear they tear and when they tear we fear we might run out butt-naked.

Just watch out your moment when it comes...take it slow in the snow.

Remember joy comes in the morning and your silver lining moment is at the corner.

World of Abstracts: What are they?

This piece isn't a summary of a research article or thesis. This piece focuses on the very things humanity craves for or fights against every single day. The following are a few examples of abstracts: Love, peace, joy, happiness, faith, hope, trust, wisdom, courage, comfort, mercy, blessings, goodness, kindness, favour, strength, power, salvation, security, hatred, anger, poverty, disease etc.

I've many a time asked myself these questions:

Why do people desire things that aren't tangible?

How do they use them when they get them?

Who gets what?

Why do some people have more than others?

And what would happen if they were to be sold in the malls and the stores?

I do what he wants me to do. I say what he wants me to say. And I write what he wants me to write. I try not to sound like a pontiff. I try not to change other people's mind. I try not to ask them to act like me or sound like me. I strive to be myself, hold myself together and push myself through.

I fiercely resist the temptation to be arrogant. I know where it leads to. Arrogance produces ignorance. Ignorance procreates hatred and hatred wrestles with love every single day.

These are all abstracts. We don't see them, they aren't tangible but they exude power. They can make and unmake, break and un-break, build and destroy. Power itself is an abstract. Absolute power they say corrupts absolutely. Whether virtue or vice, positive or negative, good or evil they all carry power per their usage.

I strive to do my best. And if my best isn't enough I know where to go to. Not the super malls or the mega stores. If for example, wisdom or love were to be sold in the malls many of us would go home empty-handed. Many perhaps would go home with broken noses and twisted jaws, yet with nothing to show off.

The wicked would probably kill to have it all. The greed would loot and shoot. The selfish would selfishly take it all without sharing. And then we would have poverty, sickness, enmity, anger, hunger, sadness, bitterness and all the vices you can name.

There's only one BIG BANK in the world— The Holy Book or the Bible. It has everything I need. It's the reservoir of knowledge. I ask for his thought. I ask for his wisdom. I ask for his guidance. I ask for his protection. I ask for his favour and goodness and many more.

I may sound like a preacher, a teacher or a pastor, yes I've been told. I humbly say I'm none of the noble ones. I'm a low profile man. I'm a caged mind always hungry to be released into the world. I am born a messenger to carry the sword and spread the word. The world needs the word. I'm a pen pusher. I push the powerful weapon. The pen is said to be mightier than the sword because it carries the word.

We all need the word. Everyone needs the word. Early this week a good friend told a good friend:

"May the ink in your pen never run dry."

I felt humbled moment I read this moving line. It came from my good good friend, Evelyn Kyei Mensah. I must say I was deeply touched. I felt my inner man jumped in excitement. He then whispered into my ear: "This is the fuel you need for an ultimate takeoff."

Thank you Eve!

To this end, this is my # message to you good people:

If your child does well in the school's exams praise him/her. Say thank you to your partner (husband or wife) if s/he gifts you something precious or a token. It could be a good meal he fixed for dinner or the leisure walk to the beautiful park in the vicinity or the latest movie you went out together to see.

I tell you the spirit needs that. It serves as fuel for its growth!

A thank you card or a written note expressing appreciation to your child's teacher, the family doctor, the night nurse, the firefighter, the neighbour across you and the police officer would make the world smile like the sun.

Above all this, in all our endeavours let's praise our God. Let's give him all the praises he deserves. Let's glorify his majestic name. Let's pay him the utmost reverence. Let our praises hit the moon. Let's serenade him with harmonic songs. Let's say Hallelujah to his glorious name because he's Holy One and holy he'll forever be!!!

Mama's Advice

Did your Mama tell you this?

Don't bitch, don't snitch. Be there for your brother be there for your neighbour. When your sisters get into trouble man-up and be there for them. Don't forget, what the right hand does. He takes care of the left hand and the left reciprocates the gesture.

Teeth are like lions, they like red meat but they've always spared their closest neighbour (the tongue) which lives in the same den with them. It's a taboo if you like Haram and its strict observance is cherished by them: It simply says: Thou shalt not eat your neighbour.

And since creation they've obeyed the status quo just as the Pharisees have done with the mundane Mosaic Law.

Snitching is an invitation or a recipe for trouble. It breeds animosity and has the potential to resurrect old wounds. Remember trouble finds those who pursue him. Should I repeat myself? Mama says... trouble, trouble those who trouble trouble.

Also, note you can run but you can't hide. No matter how high the tide might be they'll pursue you. And they'll bewitch you for bitching and snitching on them.

Suffice to say that it would be good to be out-bitched and out-snitched because there's no reward, being either of the two. Instead, try to out-pitch your peers and compatriots. That's a great mark for the greats and the giants.

Be a saver or a frugal for a stitch in time saves nine. The more you stich the better and richer you become—stich, stich and re-stich if need be. If you put more irons in the fire you'd continue to smith. Save to pave your life pathway and always keep your eyes on the road.

Beware of the bumps and the rumps, particularly the ditches. Matter of fact, if you drink don't drive and if you drive don't drink. Watch the posted speed limits. Observe all traffic and road signs, they're life's roadmaps. They can lead you to your destination or lead you into your incarceration or death.

And be reminded life without hitches and glitches isn't worth it. Therefore, when you ran or bump into them don't fret too much. Don't be angst about them. For a hitch or glitch can be a blessing in disguise. Nonetheless, try your best to avoid them because not all that glitters is gold. Be aware if is not bless then it's a mess.

Why Accra continues to wet her bed. Or why it is what it is: A City prone to Floods

Yours truly examines the situation.

If you made Mr. Kofi Annan, former UN Secretary General the mayor of Accra, things might stay the same. If you brought UFO's (Unidentified Flying Humanoid), Aliens to manage the millennium city the value might not change.

The reason, Accra's problem is more than convoluted. It's in diapers and it stinks to the core.

What do they say? "A fish rots from head down."

When an organisation or state fails, it is the leadership that is the root cause. Nonetheless, indiscipline, lawlessness, mundane Ghanaian attitude, poor urban planning, lack of sustainable sewage infrastructure, engineering defects, poorly-maintained roads and the city authorities' lack of foresight, the Odaw River, the Korle Lagoon and the wanton littering have all conspired against Accra.

But where does the buck stop? It comes down to the trustees— the leadership that has been the mandate to steer the affairs of the nation.

Accra has a twin sister—Tema, which is located 25 kilometres (16 mi) east of the capital city. They can be called identical twins. Both cities have same or similar low-lying topography. Both are in the same enclave —the Greater Accra Region.

This is a common strand that the two share. But beneath the façade lies a troubling site for the nation's capital city. Accra is now facing catch 22 situation. It has her back thrust to a wall overwhelmed by perennial floods.

But how come Tema is faring better than her twin sister with regard to floods?

In June last year, nearly 150 lives were lost in that natural disaster. Promises were made, sods were cut, houses/structures were flattened, gutters were desilted and Odaw as well as Korle were dredged. Still there hasn't been any significant improvement.

And this has activated calls for heads to roll.

There is a section of the populace that believes the Accra mayor is responsible for all the mess. Hence, he must be given the sack. Question is-who will appoint the next mayor—the same government or the people? What's the guarantee that the new mayor won't be controlled by the puppet master?

The masses think it is the government. And the government blames the people for indiscipline, carelessness, lawlessness and the cycle continues.

Indeed what's wrong here is all of the above and it would only take a concerted effort by all and sundry to save our city.

Must Accra fire her mayor or desilt Odaw River? Must she dredge the Korle lagoon or construct storm drains? Must she deal with indiscipline and lawlessness on the streets or bulldoze houses and structures sited in/on waterways? Must she go back to the drawing board i.e. start it all over?

Perhaps the solutions lie in an arm's length (not farfetched) and all the aforementioned forms part of it. Nevertheless, Accra doesn't have the men to call the shots. It had possibly produced a couple of productive mayors, decades back. However, they'd never had the latitude or what I call the political capital to prosecute viable and sustainable projects.

Its former mayors Messrs Nat Nunoo Amarteifio and Agyiri Blanckson had once told me how they wanted to make things work. But when it came to the crunch they couldn't live up to expectation. In one of my encounters with them at separate interviews, I recall daring the mayors to call the bluff of their bosses and do what was right for the nation.

They couldn't call the shot. They didn't have the balls.

Remember the famous or infamous recent statement made by Mr. Koku Anyidohu NDC deputy General Secretary? To put it in a blunt vocabulary he pivoted.

"No individual minister will walk us into opposition. It won't happen, it can't happen," he told finance minister, Seth Terkper.

In Ghana, technocrats are sidelined and mediocrats are put in charge. They're the ones who wield power and not the guys who do the actual projects. And that explains why things never get done.

Even the layman on the city's street knows what's amiss. The ordinary guy knows why we're where we are, who we are and why we seem to be clueless or careless about what's going on.

How on earth must a country with great minds and great human resources suffer each year, wrestle with Mother nature and act like the vulture.

Over the years, governments had come and gone. Parties had flaunted their colours on uncompleted (half-baked) projects. Mayor after mayors had left their footprints on the streets of Accra. There'd been measures, there'd been policies– old and new but all to no avail. Accra is still Accra. Its value at Nkrumah Circle and the surroundings hasn't changed. It's rather worsening year after year.

Can government replicate the Tema model in Accra?

It's doable but that government must put country first. It must damn any political consequences— fear of losing power to the opposition party and it must be people-centred. That government must be selfless and not selfish or line its pockets with state funds. That government must allow its mayors to work freely and not be summoned before the presidency for unwarranted interrogation. That government must see beyond party colours/lines and entrust the work into a more capable hand.

Here's how Tema got started:

In 1952 government identified a small fishing village Torman (it was later corrupted to Tema) as the site for an extra modern seaport for the new Ghana. It acquired 166 square kilometres (64 sq. mi) of land north of the harbour and entrusted it to the Tema Development Corporation (TDC).

The new Town that was subsequently built on the site was planned as an industrial and residential complex. The villagers were evicted to make way for the project and migrated to a new fishing ground around three kilometres away. Tema grew into the industrial hub of Ghana with a carefully constructed road layout featuring landscaping and street lights.

It boasted, modern recreational centres and other social amenities rare among African cities at the time. Tema is like the biblical city built on a hill. When rains fall it stands on its commanding feet. BUT the one sited in sand crumbles.

Accra is just like the city built in sand. The city has expanded with no regard to zoning, giving a sprawled attribute. Accra has a total area of 173km2 (67 sq. mi).

It used to have one major slum, Nima. Residents in that district were paid off by then Nkrumah administration to be relocated at today Madina. That resettlement never happened, obviously the visionary was gone. And the governments that followed didn't see it as prudent to continue.

With passage of time Nima grew in size and it now has a thick beard. Accra can boast of notorious Sodom and Gomorrah, Bukom, Maamobi etc. The sprouting of these towns hasn't helped the city's proper planning befitting it as a modern city.

Until 1994 following the Konkomba-Nanumba war there was no place like Sodom and Gomorrah in Accra's central business district. What do we see now? It looks crystal clear Sodom like Nima has come to stay too. But I strongly support government's plan to relocate its residents.

Sodom can be turned into a city within city per its strategic location. And it will serve as tourists' attraction with high rise buildings overlooking the Korle lagoon. This means the Conti project must come alive if it's dead.

Roughly five years back, Ghana signed a memorandum of understanding with US group, Conti Engineering in Washington DC for the construction of storm drains, water retention reservoirs, desilting of the Odaw River and the Korle Lagoon.

I must add the desilting of Odaw River must go beyond Alajo. And all settlements upstream along the river's bank must be bulldozed to allow free runoff. The affected residents must also be properly compensated.

The object of the project was to tackle the perennial flooding in the capital.

Parliament in its wisdom I gathered went ahead and approved the integrated project which was estimated at $600 million.

In the aftermath of 2014 floods, president Mahama directed the finance ministry to as matter of urgency release the funds. But that direction appeared to have fallen on deaf ears. Evidently, the ministry has failed to release the said funds for the project's implementation.

Certainly, the harbour city doesn't have an Angel as a mayor. The city's managers are neither from Mars nor Jupiter. It took a visionary Osagyefo Dr. Kwame Nkrumah to have that dream realised. And it's doable if we put our hearts and minds to it as a people.

Tactics, Gimmicks and Politricks

There are some people in the NPP who don't have sympathy for the party's problems. There are some who pray and fast every day the party never sees daylight. There are others who keep stoking the fire fanning the flame of confusion and commotion. And there are still others who wish the Elephant's woes deepen by the day.

In a nutshell, they want the party to lose the 2016 general elections. But who does that and for what reason (s)?

Who points the left finger to his father's house or wishes the mother dead?

Would a patriot betray his own country for how much to lose his kinsmen?

This is the reality on the ground. This is the dilemma the NPP faces. And indeed if bad luck comes like cake, perhaps Ghana's biggest opposition group the New Patriotic Party (NPP) has had it all. From cynicism, backbiting, badmouthing, mudslinging, campaign smearing, raids at the party's head office in Accra, to suspension of its national executives for alleged indiscipline.

Without a doubt, in a game of politics you have to play it smart and be clever, otherwise you'd be tamed by the game. The governing NDC propagandists must be applauded. They've softly and subtly played their tactics well. And so far it appears their grand plan is working.

The term swift-boating is an American neologism used pejoratively to describe an unfair or untrue political attack. It also means a sharp attack by political opponents that is dishonest, personal and prejudicial.

In the 2004 US presidential election then Democratic candidate John Kerry appeared coasting to victory but he was soon stopped in his tracks. The patriotism and good name of the war hero was impugned. Mr. Kerry lost the election to the incumbent George W. Bush, which saw his re-election.

In politics integrity matters and if your opponent can dent that character trait then you're in for trouble. Barry Goldwater lost the 1964 US presidential election due to a political ad dubbed 'Daisy Girl' ran by Democratic candidate Lyndon B. Johnson who framed Goldwater as a warmonger.

This is one of the many strategies the NDC has mapped out to outsmart, outrun and outdo Akufo-Addo, the NPP presidential candidate. In 2008 and 2012, he was painted arrogant, snooty, drug addict, divisive and a man of no integrity.

Did it work maybe yes or maybe not?

And as the political clock tick closer to the 2016 general polls his opponents are rolling out other tactical cards and gimmicks—throwing anything and everything at him. The latest was the arrest of three South

African ex-police officers who were said to be providing security detail for the flagbearer and his running mate.

It must be pointed out, this isn't the first time. In 1999 former Italian Prime Minister Berlusconi's party Forsa delegation that visited Ghana at the behest of the NPP had its communication officer detained at the Ghana Police headquarters.

They have now framed the NPP candidate as a violent person. That's the new card being played. But how is this different from the previous schemes? They're now using NPP's own members to dig the trenches, do the dirty jobs and break the front of the party.

Who would doubt a claim by Offin-Amaniampong that the Offin River is at Dunkwa-on-Offin and it flows into River Pra?

What if the same person stood on a different platform and announced that the Offin River flows into the Paga Lake?

Last week, Dr. Nyaho-Tamakloe a founding member of the NPP (now suspended) told host of GH Today Kafui Dey: "I parted ways with my very good friend Kufour because of Akufo-Addo. The party was taking a decision on who to lead the party after Adu Boahen and at the time, I felt that Akufo-Addo was the best person to lead us and Kufour didn't take it lightly."

Then same person turns around on same platform and says this: "I have known Nana Addo for 50 years and he has no message."

He continues: "Kufour is a gentleman and he's calm and cool. And these are the type of leadership that this country needs. This country doesn't need an extremist: to me Kufour, Mahama and late Limann are on the same level and these are the type of leaders this country needs."

So who is the extremist here? And if you aren't calm who are you?

You see the fallacy of inconsistency there?

Since when did the legal luminary lose all his good credentials?

Mr. Akufo-Addo served as Minister of Justice and Attorney General under Kufuor's administration. That's how we build a family. We don't divide it. We don't betray our own kinsmen. Akufo-Addo spent his own money building constituency offices across the country. He didn't betray Mr. Kufuor he helped him to win power twice.

In the meantime Mr. Akufo-Addo has reacted to the new buzz word: Violent!

He knows where it could lead to. He knows what damage it could cause and he understands the consequence thereof if not given the attention it deserves. In his reaction he said:

"If I was truly a violent person, in 2012 I could perhaps have caused an inferno to engulf the nation in the aftermath of the disputed election results of 2012, and the close nature of the Supreme Court's election petition verdict. I love Ghana more than myself, and that is why nothing of that sort happened."

In a related development, the Editor-in-Chief of Crusading Guide newspaper, Abdul Malik Kweku Baako speaking on Joy FM's News File programme over the weekend said this about the NPP presidential candidate:

"I don't know why people have refused to see that in terms of integrity, Nana Addo is indestructible. You may not like him for one or two reasons and that is natural. He himself doesn't expect everybody to like him. But like him or not, in terms of his political and professional career, his integrity is indestructible."

You see how dirty politics is. It's Politricks. And I now understand why Hon. Kennedy Agyapong barks like the Chihuahuas or the Rottweilers.

Until the suspension of some of its bigwigs i.e. the party's national chairman, general secretary, 2nd national vice chairman and other founding members, closed-door meetings sneaked out like horses let out of their stables gallivanting.

Remember the supposed secret peace meeting that took place at the residence of former president Kufour?

A close friend and a lecturer at the University of Ghana told me: "They didn't go to Kufuor's house in a convoy. They went there from different locations, in different cars and in different times, yet before the end of the said meeting everything was on air.

But how did we get here?

Many factors contributed to that. The famous or infamous Osafo Marfo's leaked tape, opening of different financial accounts, acid attacks (that killed the northern regional chairman), and raids at the party's head office were/are among the reasons why we're here.

And indeed, they caused the Rottweilers to bark the more.

The Alan disease which once tormented the NPP presidential candidate and was deemed incurable is no longer a threat. He joined Nana Addo in his 'Rise and Build' nation tour. More so, Mr. Kyeremanteng himself had asked his followers to rally behind Mr. Akufo-Addo yet some of them have refused to pledge their unflinching support.

This is perhaps the group that maintains that Akufo-Addo can never be president. And the NDC propagandists have latched onto that assertion trumpeting it every time everywhere.

Rivaling, this 'disgruntled group' is the Ashanti and Akim card. I don't seem to get it at times. However, if the rank and file behaves like the proverbial ostrich and fail to hold the bull by the horn that issue can cause a deeper crack in the party.

So, these are some of the internal problems confronting the NPP currently. But I think overall given the tsunami that hit the party several months ago, the leadership haven't done badly. That said, they shouldn't rest on their oars because the real game has now begun.

Facing John the 4th at round two could be termed as a thriller in Manila. The incumbency card would be flaunted and JD will masterly tout about his youthfulness.

Former House Speaker of the United States Nancy Pelosi says:

"Dumb politicians are not the problem. The problem is the dumb people that keep voting for them."

Head of the Geography Department University of Ghana Dr. George Owusu says democracy is about accountability and responsibility. Ideally the ruled or the people who elect the rulers must have the political mandate to make a better decision at any giving time with respect to how they exercise their voting rights or franchise.

"It's also incumbent on the government to ensure that they deliver and provide the people the necessary social infrastructure development. This is governments' responsibility and under no circumstances should it be seen like they're doing the electorate favour," he pointed out.

Across Europe and the western world many governments have failed to renew their mandate. The reason, they couldn't deliver. But this isn't the case in Africa, the Middle East and Asia. Unfortunately there's this group that have devised a strategy of winning power anyhow.

Dr. Owusu who's also an associate professor of the Institute of the Statistical, Social and Economic Research (ISSER) noted that the group have hijacked the people's right and used their own crude tactics—wait when election is near, buy the votes which are supposed to be secret and throw the red meat at them. And like gullible they'll come running.

That seems to be the new order especially in Africa and for that matter Ghana. And the upshot has churned out a new brigade of politicians. Technocrats have lost the bid to 'mediocrats'. And democracy has become 'moneycracy'. This kind of democracy is inimical to our fledgling democracy and it makes the institution unattractive.

It stifles political pluralism and disempowers opposition parties, he underscored.

It's all Alright

Take a deep breathe. There you go...

Yep, it's Alright.

It's Alright. I mean it's A-l-r-i-g h t!

If it's loose we will make it tight. And if it's tight we will make it loose.

How much did they loot from our booth? And who's responsible for all the loot?

Light flickering like stars headlight beaming everywhere, taillight blinking elsewhere and flashlight flashing anywhere.

Everything zagging nothing zigging...

Boot-to-knee clad in all-red they marched into our hoods like tigers from the woods.

Boot for boot, pound for pound. It was an eye for an eye and a tooth for a tooth.

We were unmatched per their might; they were able to loot from our neighbourhoods.

Sometimes we cry wolf. We cry wolf 'cos we think we've been wolved and tigered.

Or targeted?

It's alright. Just remember it's alright.

Who cares to take a peep at your sleepy eyes?

Or your eyeballs that sit so deep in the sockets?

When eye blinks it blinks at a diamond ring: A sparkling diamond: A glittering gem. It speaks to the heart and the heart communicates with the mind. They're bedfellows. They follow their instinct. They're partners in crime. Time is their enemy.

It's Alright. I mean it's alright.

We stood ready to fight.... Fight to fright the looters but even in their flight they still kept their booty tight. The sages are right: No pain no gain. No power no 'Flower'. Koforidua Flowers will forever flourish. Thing is if it sounds right, it feels right. If it feels right it tastes right. If it tastes right it smells right and if it smells right…It's alright.

Follow when they hallow. If they don't hallow they'll hoot if they don't hoot they'll loot, if they don't loot they'll shoot. Just remember they're born to hoot born to loot and born to shoot but it's alright. Don't rush to double your trouble, for if you rush you'll crash and if you crash you'll rust.

Solution Water: Is it Ghana's New Black Gold?

Where in the world does the sun rise in the west?

Certainly not in our world, and I don't know if it does so in the other planets.

Would someone tell me? Is it on Jupiter or Pluto?

Apple tree bears apple fruits and not oranges. And dogs don't cry they bark. Indeed Jesus changed water into wine at a wedding when the gathering had run out of drink. Miracles had happened before our time. They happened in Abrahamic time, they happened during the exilic time, they did in the Apostolic Age and they'll continue to happen before apocalypse.

However, the scripture has cautioned us to be wary of false prophets. It says:" For false messiahs and false prophets will appear and perform great signs and wonders to deceive, if possible even the elect," Matthew 24:24.

When people throw caution to the wind they take a great risk. But it could even be riskier if they're led by a self-styled prophet, who hoodwinks his followers to believe that he holds the key to prosperity.

Many have perished for lack of knowledge and many more would walk that slippery slope road because this generation lusts after miracles and wonders. They globetrot– seeking miracles in their marriages, education, businesses, travels, wealth, sickness, litigation. I mean anything under the sun that you can think of.

How is this possible? That liquid dubbed: 'Solution Water' can stabilise one's estranged relationship, put millions of monies into one's accounts, make banks write off debts owed them by clients, cause someone abroad to remit as though he's suffering from diarrhea in giving.

Is that magic or fetishism?

Currently trending on WhatsApp is a short video put together by a Ghanaian lady based in the UK. Looking livid and appalled by what she calls 'this silly advert'; Ohemaa moved into full gear grinding the nuggets in the video.

She charged the government of Ghana to start regulating 'all these kind of adverts' because they're deceitful and don't do any good for the citizenry.

"I lay the blame on today Christians because all we need is pray for me, pray for me, quick anointing and breakthroughs."

She stressed that such practice doesn't get them to anywhere except that they allow themselves to be led astray by so-called anointed Men of God.

"What's the difference between this and going to the fetish priest?" she rhetorically asked.

"The result is from lazy Christians. I say this with vim that any Church that sells for example, solution water, handkerchiefs, holy water, and wrist band anointed oil is fake. We're so ready for quick miracles."

So what went wrong my people? Where in the Bible did Jesus or any of his Apostles sell Grace for money? Have we so soon forgotten that salvation is free and it doesn't cost a dime?

Can someone ask his/her pastor this: Why did Jesus die for us?

Is solution water, handkerchief, wrist band, holy water worth more than the blood of Jesus?

And must some Christians be told where the dog died?

I couldn't agree with you more Ohemaa. "It doesn't get any better.' We want everything in the fast lane. The third rail is slow and the middle gets choked—bumper to-bumper. So just take your hard earned money and run to a so-called pastor and all your problems in the world would disappear.

I would like to add to the call made by my sister Ohemaa, government must come tough and stop people, organisations etc. that churn out adverts like these. The Solution Water advert is believed to be airing on national TV and radio stations in Ghana.

It must be emphasised, this pray for me practice isn't peculiar to Ghana it's all over Africa and elsewhere including the United States. People don't want to pray. It's as usual cast your burden unto your pastor....

What happened in November 18, 1978 in northwest Guyana should serve as a great lesson for humanity across the world, particularly Christians. 'Jonestown Massacre' as it came to be known saw over 900 people killed as a result of cyanide poisoning. And it remained the most deadly single none-natural disaster in the US history until September 11, 2011

Jim Jones Founder and leader of The Peoples Temple poisoned the minds of his followers. They had ears but they couldn't hear. They had eyes but they couldn't see. They ignored all red lights and tell-tell signs.

In April, 1993 cult leader David Koresh led the Branch Davidians in a deadly 51-day stand-off against the FBI.

When the plot thickens a situation becomes more complex and difficult. Impulsivity seems to have its way. Common sense goes to sleep. And only God knows the outcome. Be careful, be blessed and be alert!

Gordon Offin-Amaniampong

Check the Box

It's checking time folks! And it's check, check, check, that's the way we do it. Here in uphill, Chapel Hill box checking is like chess game. So make sure you check all the boxes. Check every box, tick or check. Double check if in doubt, Remember also to check me out next time you get down the road.

If you're planning to go to downtown Chapel Hill, don't flick your bike down the hill. Try to trek down the backcountry road too. It's a highway that takes you uphill to Chapel Hill. Church Hill lives here. Sheer beauty surrounds her, a little town known for her generosity and diversity.

May I ask who is Church Hill?

He's the mayor of the town. But many here see him as the emperor. Perhaps master of all that he surveys.

Thank God I'm here. I'm here to check the boxes like many have done. Yes you've to check the boxes. Here in Chapel Hill checking the box is like taking a daily pill to cure chronic illness. Church Hill is ruthless when it comes to that. It doesn't get better than checking page after pages.

Line by line underscores the necessity to keep checking as you flip through the pages. I've seen the goose. I've seen the swan and I've seen the duck. And they're all checking at a breakneck speed. The crow is here so as the seagull.

They all live here. They live together as one people supposedly. But beneath the façade lies a deep scar: A scar that scares the people here. It makes them cringe every day. It denies them their sense of belonging. They say their hearts bleed each time they're asked to check the box.

Why?

Well, without the box checking it's hard to tell who is who and where one hails from.

Is it a bad idea Kofi?

I guess so.

Well pray that guy doesn't win, because if he wins you'll be sorry. That guy that stomps everywhere has threatened to deport every immigrant here in Chapel Hill. It will no longer be fill in the gap or check, check, check. It will be mass deportation so says the guy that currently holds the trump card for the GOP.

The question is: Who will remain here? Because we're all immigrants: We're all in a New Foundland.

The seagulls, the crows, the geese, the ducks and the likes immigrated from somewhere: You're either from the southern hemisphere, North Pole or Far East. Until then I can assure you the checking syndrome will be like a pill for everyone in Chapel Hill. Don't fret Bro!

What do they say in the Ghanaian parlance: "Whee ne Kotere yem.' Literally translated there's no fire in lizard's belly. In other words: It's a dumb squib.

Wasn't Noah ridiculed?

Think about it. If you thought your adversary would applaud you for a good job done, forget it. Forget it and start to live your life like the small ant. The tiny weakling takes time to gather his foods. Step by step, in a painstaking manner he does it so diligently that when the worse season comes he lacks nothing.

But they that scorn him gnash their teeth in no time.

Noah's Ark would cost a fortune, perhaps break world record, if it were found and auctioned today. But, you would agree with me that Noah was seen by his town folks as one beside himself or one suffering from hallucination.

Noah didn't budge. He ignored his people and did what God had asked to him to do. Do what you can do. For doers reap what they've sown. If you don't sow you don't harvest. You're born to crawl before you can walk. Walking begets running and if you believe in yourself you can fly.

Remember they that have wings fly. And they that have teeth break bones...

If you'd forgotten how irritable teething is like, I urge you to go ask a three or five-year-old kid. Teething is associated with irritability, swollen gums and soreness. Also note, every breakthrough comes with pain just like teething. Your situation may seem never-ending....

But every Egypt brings forth a 'Promised Land!

Think you're Samson or stronger than Samson, the Nazarene?

I'm pretty sure his story also resonates. Think about it, because every Samson has his Delilah.

Moses was timid. But God killed his timidity. He empowered him and the one-time coward led hundreds of thousands Israelites out of Egypt.

Most of us get our dreams killed even before they're born. We're often haunted by fear. The fear that things might fail and we will get ridiculed or scorned. Ignore the Ahitophels in your life. Remember Ahitophel was one of David's most trusted advisers. But he took a leading role in the revolt of David's son Absalom. His defection dealt a severe blow to David.

They use their tongues to kill the goose that lays the golden eggs. Do not pay heed to them. Keep doing your stuff. Do it anyway. Do it to your satisfaction. Do it as if you're crazy. Just do IT!

Take note, soothing words heal broken hearts, but fire cracker mouths rip them apart. Some mouths shoot like trumpets. Their words are like swords that pierce through the walls of the hearts. When tongues fly words like darts they kill more than guns. Our fingers aren't equal. Some fingers are dexterous on the keyboards, while some are good at pulling the triggers.

When Love Goes Rogue

When love goes rogue things begin to fall apart. But it probably shreds into pieces when it robes Halloween Costume. One sees his/her partner as a monster ('Kakaimotobi'). And lovers suddenly become haters.

Sooner honey loses its sweet taste. It turns sour. Romance suffers paralysis and words no longer have the power to persuade. They don't appeal any longer. Smiles, kisses, hugs, caresses are dwarfed by seething anger. And the usual sweet words such as: darling, sweetheart, honey, beau, babe, sweetie pie, my soulmate, my sunshine disappear.

Vows mean nothing and body tattoos quickly vanish.

All turns cold and everything tends to go crazy.

When love goes rogue it's like Michael Jackson's Thriller album which features stars in Halloween costumes. Doors go creaking, dogs howl and the thunder roars like a hungry lion— all signifying fear, fright, horror and a looming danger.

The 14-minute video released in 1982 ties together a narrative featuring actress Ola Ray. Hand in hand Ola and Michael find themselves in a bush where the pop singer is seen proposing to the actress. Ola appears to be mesmerized as she giggles irrepressibly. But a few minutes later her newly-fangled love becomes a nightmarish adventure.

Scared to death, heart in mouth and knees wobbling like a straw in a gusty wind Ola starts to run for her life and the monsters pursue her vigorously. The evil foreboding sound drowns the sound of every creature on earth.

Nonetheless love finds its natural course minutes later. The two are back together, swinging together and dancing their shoes off. And the rest of the video is the success story of the great album.

Like 'Thriller' love or relationship has her monster (s):

When knots are tied vows are made: 'For better for worse and till death do us part chimes like a bell. Some tattoo their loved ones' names on their body. And some others drink blood to seal the new bond. This is a solemn statement and it carries weight. Yet, when the unknown happens love breaks her vow.

In relationships scary things occur. Some are so dangerous, some are sickening, some are distasteful and some can cause one to take a flight to save one's poor soul. They're usually bad habits that drive other supporting factors like courage, trust, faith, understanding away.

More often than not money seems to be the major factor that breaks the backbone of relationships. It increasingly seems to be the driving force—breaking homes and shredding them into pieces. Aside that infidelity, falsehood, joblessness, battery, financial insolvency could torpedo the 'loveship' from sailing to safely.

Is there a perfect relationship?

There's absolutely no relationship without 'Halloween Costume.' In other words there isn't a perfect relationship anywhere whatsoever. To make it work the players involved must act in good faith, be selfless, be understanding, be compassionate, be respectful, be caring, be tolerant and be loving.

That takes me back to the Thriller album success story.

"Thriller' thrilled millions around the world in the early 1980's. The hit album was Michael Jackson's seventh and final single by Epic Records. It got great reviews and topped many billboard charts globally.

It was Jackson's final single, but it wasn't single-handedly done by the pop icon. Behind the great album were equally great personalities—Rod Temperton composed the song and it was produced by legend Quincy Jones.

Love is said to be the greatest of all, but love alone can't steer the giant ship to safety. Love alone can't stand, it needs other supporting pillars. The likes of Quincy Jones and Rod Tempertons can help smoothen the rough edges and turn things around.

When challenges and problems howl like dogs at us, roar like thunder and squeak like doors the temptation to take a flight is sometimes huge depending on the magnitude of the problem. Those who have been in bad relationships would tell you it's perhaps scarier than Michael Jackson's Thriller. The scars are probably deeper than what the eye sees.

Love, relationship or marriage grows when it's built upon trust, rooted in understanding, consolidated on faith, crowned with peace, capped by joy, seasoned with respect, selflessness, dedication and above all entrusted into the hands of God because of its sacredness.

Thriller won a record-breaking eight Grammy Awards in 1984. The video is a little longer than 14 minutes multiply that by at least 5 that comes up to 70. That would be a life-long relationship. Isn't it? That's my wish for you... May your love, your marriage or relationship glow and go beyond 70 years!

The Caged Mind

If I change my mind, on my way to Jericho, please remind me to look behind me. If I lose my mind and reach out for a skirt instead of a shirt please remind me, don't rebuke me. If my reflexes get the better of me please treat me gently, treat me like a loved one. Treat me like your best friend. Treat me like you'd treat yourself.

If I stumble and fall please help me get back on my feet, don't pass me by like the priest. Be my Samaritan, be my guardian Angel. If I fail twice even thrice give me another chance to prove myself. Chances are that I may be tomorrow's hero. Don't count me out. Don't write me off. Don't belittle my ability...

Be mindful to be kind to all those you find caught up in the crosswind and the crossroads. For mankind's life is like a whirlwind pacing to eternity. So remind me, if I rescind my decision to lend a helping hand. Or fail to catch up. Don't be unkind to me.

And if I still can't find my way out, maybe stuck in the box, just remember life is like a purblind eye—can't see beyond, can't see far. It's simply shortsighted. Who knows tomorrow?

Absolutely no one...

Ama Ghana:
What's going on with you?

'O thou weak, senseless and backboneless one, where art thy pride and why have thou forsaken thy own kindred? Have thou so soon become like a wounded lion running away from her whelps leaving them to fend for themselves?

You seem not yourself. You seem so weary as though misery has covered you again with her crimson garment. Have you suddenly become a proudless puppet to the regime of the strong or are you doing this to accommodate and help a fellow in trouble?

Where is your Bakari/Fugu, the warlike dress that frights the enemy? Where is your embroidery kente cloth?

Uncharacteristically, your home appears to be overtaken by the very people your forebears wrestled power from over five decades ago (March 6, 1957).

They didn't drive them away that obviously wouldn't have been a wise thing to begin with. Rather they co-existed and shared cultures and other mores. Indeed they ensured that their immutable rights, our cultures and values as well as customs stand tall all the time.

That the Adowa, Kete, Kpalongo, Asafo, Boboobo and the Azonto dances stay intact. That Dipo, Bragro, Odwira, Hogbetsotso, Aboakyere, Kundum and other festivals continue to wear their golden velvet clothes. That our foods such as fufu, tuo zaafi, banku, kelewele, mpotopoto, awiesu, nkyewie, apreprensa, Ga kome ke shito and many more aren't jettisoned or swallowed by the pizzas and the spaghettis.

That the bikinis, the G-strings, belly buttons, the tattoos and the likes don't override our waist-to-knee-skirts, tapiojoes, sakora, pin-pinis, you name it. And that all taboos will be observed.

When your siblings were under servitude you helped pulled them out from the shadows of darkness. Listen Ama, you're too strong to bow to pressures from afar: And too sacred to resort to infidelity. As a touch bearer or trailblazer, nations across Africa from east to west, north to south looked up to you. "Independence of Ghana would be meaningless unless it's linked up to the total liberation of the whole continent of Africa", Osagyefo Dr. Kwame Nkrumah said this on the day of Ghana's independence in 1957.

That was you Ama—the selfless and the unflappable Ghana that championed the cause of African emancipation. Always remember you're from 'Adehyemanmu'—the land of the Osagyefos, Gbewaas, Anokyes, Asantewaas, the Tutus, the Aggreys the Obirimankomas and the Busumurus.

Let's not boast ourselves. Let's not toast the peace we have like wine in glossy glass. Let's not flip it like pancake. Let's safeguard it and let's protect and defend our proud nation. Who can take the prey from the claws or talons of the eagle?

I bet no one. However, if we lose guard we would lose our prey. And if we stay alert we will always have our game. There would be something to look up to and posterity would be proud of us.

Stand up Ama. Get up Ohemaa!

You're so beautiful, so rich, and so kind. Get up and shake your gyrating back. You still exude power. An ideal woman that possesses the 'killing' characteristics.

Hey Mr. Gout!

Like clouds gathering momentum to unleash a heavy downpour, the pain had pitched. Its pause and temperature emphasised abnormality. His face bore discomfort and misery. He was tottering, reeling in pain. He looked pathetic!

What in the world was going on?

"Sir, are you okay?" an orderly or a nurse asked.

What kind of question is that?

Doesn't action speak for itself?

The hunter's wife doesn't know sometimes her husband also get beaten by bees. Sometimes he encounters the Bigfoot, howled at by chayote or gets chased by the hyenas. Bottom-line the hunter often doesn't tell it all.

"Barima nsu.' It's odd for a man to cry. Culturally that's how Ghanaian men are brought up. I guess the lady who took his temperature and pause was expecting him to be crying 'maa-maaa', given his pain level. It was ten over ten. It was nothing less perhaps something more.

"So the question was are you okay?"

Nope. Still bundled up by pain, stuck in the waiting room...waiting for a doctor. If you've been here before you know it takes ages. It's like waiting in line to use the public loo. It feels like releasing the 'passengers' right there one time. At some point you tell yourself come what may... Meaning you don't care being messy. Are you thinking right?

Are you oblivious of the aftermath embarrassment that would greet you?

Your expectation swirls every time you hear a knock on the door from outside. That must be the doctor you conjecture. Got beaten to it again, same lady, same question, same response. Stay as brief as possible. Can't be chatty when sitting on sharps!

Finally, doctor shows up.

"What's going on Sir?"

I've this sharp pain right on the sole of my left big toe.

"Is it located right on the joint area?

Yes, Ma'am. It's like I have a broken bone.

"It must be gout," she says.

Follows it up with quick examination, cause of pain confirmed as— Gout.

I say what?

She explains: "It's a form of arthritis characterised by severe pain, redness and tenderness in joints. After an acute gout attack, your doctor may prescribe a low daily dose of colchicine to prevent future attacks. Corticosteroid medications, such as the drug prednisone may control gout inflammation and pain."

Relief alas!

So without much ado, I issue my fiat:

Get out Mr. Gout, out from my house. Step out before you get drowned in your own tears. I can tell you've run out of clout. No steam anymore to tout yourself as the chief scout. The good old days have deserted you.

I felt depressed yesterday. Today you're under pressure, swallowed by dark clouds. From afar, I can hear you shouting, running helter skelter.

Oh how quickly did you lose your swanked clout?

Today everybody flouts your command. Your stout stature has failed to intimidate them. Certainly, no one fears you anymore. In fact nothing more of yours scares them any longer. They know you. They know you to strike from any angle of your choosing—sprouting like mushrooms from every joint of the human frame. And shouting like a wounded German shepherd.

Is there any secret about you that they don't know of now?

Are your venoms shrouded in secrecy or your deeds so subtle to beat the marauding eyes of the cameras?

And are you ready to take up their challenge?

Perhaps in the developing world you still command some clout. The reason, they still treat you as a boil. So you get pampered for weeks and even months, while you torture them.

Back in the day I recall, the giants bowed. They kowtowed to your foreboding pressure. My own eyes couldn't measure what they witnessed when the giants fell to their knees like biblical Goliath. The pain was too strong, too much for them to bear.

One of them told me: "Hey, stay away from the pink seasonings," it was Vonnie's advice.

That tickled me. Actually, I substitute them for salt because of my BP. Too much alcohol can result gout (I seldom take alcohol), the doctor told me in January 2016, when I hobbled to her office, red-eyed. My left big toe had swollen throbbing like the giant 'Fontonfrom drum. The pain was 10 over 10, not kidding you. It was an excruciating pain.

Seafood especially lobsters can also cause gout. Without a doubt sometimes I wonder if the tales told about you aren't just myths. For example, the question about—which one hurts more than the other Debt or Gout —'Eka ene Kaka'?

Old Cloak

Behold you cold-hearted man. Be bold and take off your old cloak. Soak it and wash it in hyssop. Rinse it and dry it in coal fire. You bloated your ego and let it floated on the streets of Obojo. I bet none of us would live today, if we were as ugly as a toad.

Obojo! Obojo where art thy pride and thy strength? You heartless and shameless man, you tortured and maimed strangers and you shamelessly slain your own people.

You've long carried yourself as the biggest toad in the puddle, a bully that scolds everyone either young or old. Hear me now! Take time off your busy schedule and submit yourself to the wind of change that's knocking on your door.

The poor are sick and tired of you as tomorrow looks bleak for the weak. On cold ground we slept and used stones as pillows. Anytime the thunder roars we cringe. Even your sneeze makes us take cover.

How long are you going to stop this and how many times must we cry our eyes out?

We've had our ears full so let them go to bed. Allow them to sleep because they've been overdosed with toxic tidings. Ears we beseech thee to close your doors. Close them tight such that there would be void to fill.

Big Mouth, close that window and belt up. Speak no more; we beseech thee to cry no more. Remain silent. Be silent as cold creek. We've conditioned our bellies not to growl anymore and the eyes not to shed tears.

Ages have walked by and history has been rewritten many times. But you're still stuck in your track. You haven't changed your old ways. They're same old stuff, same old disposition. Mother Earth has seized to be the giant that millions took months to connect. Stones have flown from east to west, birds are exploring new frontiers every passing day and dogs are even donning clothes.

Aren't you tired yet?

Aren't you tired of your same old scolding?

And didn't you hear the creeks weep?

Yes they wept. And their anger grew and blew minds away, because your deeds drew their tears. Tears that helped drown our fears. Under duress you made us washed our old clothes in the cold creeks. We were grilled and drilled. We dried our clothes on dry lines scotched by the scotching sun. Breezed by the sea breeze and their crease disappeared.

Aren't you tired of stoking the fire to dismember the very fabric of humanity?

Remember if mountains had scaffolds, we'd have millions climb to the top, spread their wings like birds and fly away. They will ring the bells to trumpet their feat. They'll stomp the ground and raise their thumbs. Because they've had their feet shackled for too long.

We had tomorrow borrowed to us at a cost none could bear. We teared up every day and grudgingly geared up to face the folly's wrath. How dare you sell our gold?

You sold them for million folds, told us we're too old to be stakeholders. But hold on, we've got a message for you. Next time you fold your arms hold your cheeks and mold your plans.

Conqueror

When life goes zigzag remember the Zebras. They move in groups as a way to confuse their predators. Remember you've got something that your enemies don't have. Remember, you're like the Zebras their distinctive black and white striped coats help them to confuse the predators.

If you don't know you cannot be domesticated even though you're known to be social.

When life goes zigzag remember Zimbabwe the landlocked South African nation.—sandwiched in between the Zambezi and Limpopo Rivers. The rivers will crest and overflow their banks. Yet, you'll survive. You won't be marooned by the waters. Zambezi shall crest fall and Limpopo shall return to base.

Zimbabwe, Zimbabwe you'll face stigmatisation. Your inflation will skyrocket you'll be blacklisted and labeled as a rogue nation. You'll be partitioned several times but you'll be able to stand the test of time. You'll be painted with a tainted brush. But remember when you fall you shall rise.

When life goes zigzag remember the worms—they have no legs, have no hands, have no eyes, yet they survive.

Remember Zaire when life goes zigzag you will be called DR. Congo but your character will be the same, your people will remain the same, your culture will be the same.

When life goes zigzag remember the days when you stood on ground zero. You never thought you'll make it here, never thought you'll be a hero and conqueror.

When life goes zigzag don't zag you must zig. Don't give up don't run away, don't backslide and don't let your enemies tear you down. Instead pursue your enemies. Chase them as they run to pit their tent on mount Zion. Fight them, fight the Jebusites defeat them and name the fortress the city of David.

Remember just remember, you're a conqueror.

Wisdom Bus

A Bus christened Wisdom had been running empty for nearly 24 hours. It prowled and plied every part of the city. It stopped at every bus stop and honked at every person on its way to and fro — to come on board. Every bus terminal had people and every corner the bus turned, there still were people waiting to be bused.

Interestingly nobody made an attempt to do so. They all ignored the wisdom bus. At twilight, the bus made its final round to all the terminals, in the hope that the people would join it. But every stop everywhere and everybody at every point rejected the bus.

Still it never stopped and continued its bustle.

What were they waiting for?

Elsewhere in the city pandemonium had broken out. It was dark. It was pitch dark. And it was time for evil to take the centre stage. Some were crying, some were weeping, some were yelling and some howled for help. Lo and behold help was long gone. Help was nowhere.

It was also time for the wisdom bus to head to the garage still empty. And it went empty!

The Bus the people rejected...

When wisdom exits the eastern door and logic is no longer logical then something is wrong. When laws become dogs' food and rationality is no longer rational, then something is wrong. When right becomes wrong and wrong becomes right there's neither right nor wrong.

However folly begins to rule. And when the ruled refuse to be ruled and the ruler continues to rule then all is l.ost...

Darkness

Darkness is like Hitler's mind its plans are unknown and activities unpredictable. His hands are long. He steals, he destroys and he kills. Long before he was born life was long. Wealth and health lived untroubled. Peace, joy and happiness walked saintly. And love reigned like an emperor.

Aggrieved and envious he waged war against mankind. His path littered with misery and pain. Misery knew him not yet he found him. Daylight is his enemy but plight his friend. During twilight he wears his pride and displays his prize. He's a sworn foe for mercy.

His desire for evil–doing is like a drunken monster howling in the woods. Pride is his bed and sorrow is his pillow. His elbows are like arrows that shoot to kill. If you hear him hallo try not to billow.

From Gitmo to Limbo

The tale of Sikaman—the nation that bites more than she can chew... Ayekoo king Jomo you've done the unthinkable again! And I'm pretty sure your good people would give you a big round of applause for throwing them under the speeding locomotive.

Folklore has it that for many years the lion feared the Reindeer for what he perceived to be reindeers' tough horns until a traitor revealed to the beast, they were just antlers. Antlers are extensions of the skull grown by members of the deer family– not as strong as horns. In a nutshell they're weak.

Weak medium-sized animals such as the antelopes often get mauled by the carnivorous—the powerful beasts.

Naturally the weak live in fear. Always on the run with their tails in between thighs— always pursued by their enemies. The weak is timid and is cowed. Being a weakling means living under the mercy of the world or other benefactors.

In real life, this scenario plays out time after time. The powerful nations swallow the weak ones. The weak or 'third world' nations as they're being labeled have little or no say when it comes to making tough decisions. They are like a toothless bulldog.

Problem is if you're weak and poor you rarely can resist temptation such as accepting toxic waste or contraband goods—even aware that they're hazardous and have the potential to killing your people.

Per their characteristic weak nations have puppet leaders, they're selfish and they lick boots.

So, who let the tigers out and where did they go?

The tigers have already landed in Ghana; the gold-rich nation in West Africa. The tiny country the size of Oregon in the United States just came out from the jaws of darkness that eclipsed her for more than two years. And not in the widest dream did the people see this coming—accepting what many perceive as contraband goods (two Gitmo detainees) on their soil.

The two Yemeni nationals are former Al Qaeda operatives.

At Gitmo where they were kept citizens had resisted their release from the zoo let alone allow them to co-mingle with its people. Owners of the endangered species had kept the two wild beasts for 14 years in Gitmo and it was about time they let them out not in their own country because of the high risk they might pose to the society.

Two years ago, Gitmo citizens were up in arms against their government even resisting plans to have prisoners from Gitmo tried in mainland Gitmo courts (America courts).

Were there no graves in Egypt? Were there no zoos elsewhere in the west?

Were there no other friends and allies such as Ghana in the Middle East?

Where did we go wrong king Jomo? Why are you stooping too low?

What are the benefits and how much? Are the benefits worth more than the lives of the ruled –the people who gave you the mandate to rule?

The action has already generated a heightened debate across the nation's capital and cities elsewhere. I was monitoring Joy FM, an Accra based radio station around midnight here Pacific Time in the states and I learned from the host Kojo Yankson that all attempts by him to get comments from government officials had been unsuccessful.

What are friends for one may ask? A friend in need is a friend indeed. It's prudent and morally sound to support one when need be. This is against the backdrop that the government's decision to accept the two Gitmo guys was informed by the above route. However, I think the good people of Ghana deserve to know why this decision was taken and in whose interest.

Is Ghana doing this gesture so to speak because her friend (the United States) has his hands full and can't take any more? But that is even beside the point in that citizens in the US have stated unambiguously, 'no detainees of Gitmo should set foot on American soil'.

Here's the catch, if the one who purchased the tigers and have the resource to keep them say the animals are harmful, dangerous, deadly, lethal and can no longer hold them even in the fortified Gitmo enclave how much more you— the 'weakling'. Isn't this ridiculous?

Fox News chief investigative correspondent Catherine Heridge says, the whole deal smacks something else and she believes countries such as Ghana did so not because of their love for the United States. The weakling obviously has no say.

"These countries are not taking them out of the goodness of their hearts they're taking them because they've been promised something..." she said.

Till further notice, I rest my case and pray that nothing untoward should happen in the next two years period. I'm also certain, the US will provide security and logistics to ensure that her friend, Ghana will continue to enjoy the peace and stability in the sub-region as well as her well-known hospitality to all peoples including Gitmo gurus!

Earthen Computers in 21st Century Ghana

How did that happen?

Outdated and weird as it may sound or seem pupils of a certain junior high school in Ghana West Africa are trying hard to realise their dream goals with some strange Information and Communications Technology

(ICT) tools. They've created something out of nothing and their innovative art works have gone viral on the social media.

So are these pupils shutting the stable door when the horses are already gone?

Dr. Stanley J. Pritchett president of Morris Brown College, USA says: 'Merely having access to a box-or an information box – does not necessarily mean that you have improved or that you're more literate, or that you're better able to solve problems in the community."

And here's my fuss, if those that have access to computers and other ICT tools cannot brag about their acquired skills, cannot brag that they can solve problems and cannot brag that they're literate: How then did the pupils of this Junior High School (JHS) in the Volta region end up with improvised laptop computers, cellphones, extension cords and headsets made from earthen?

Is it because the school is tucked deep somewhere in the backcountry or in the hinterlands?

Did the school miss the supplies (if there ever were any) because the community has no influential people to lobby the government at the time?

Are there other schools in the region and for that matter Ghana in general that are without computers? Sure there are many schools and I'm tempted to believe, they're in the cities too. If so why did this particular school choose to go this way?

Was it done merely to seek world attention, to ridicule the country or they did that to show the world their plight?

Their story reminds me of author Geoffrey Chaucer's great line: 'If gold rust what then will iron do?" Indeed, if those who have access to these gadgets and are using them cannot tout themselves as literate how much more the ones that have no laptop computers, no headsets, no tablets but are merely using improvised devices?

How did it happen?

Necessity they say is the mother of invention. And I think it's appropriate to say that they (pupils of the school in question) were compelled to do so when the need for those improvised ICT tools became imperative. The will was there and so they found the way to help them pursue their goals regardless of its seemingly backwardness. The creative gadgets are to facilitate studies in their school. But ridiculous as the story might seem it does not undercut the motivational spirit of the pupils.

Thomas Ahiabor the school's ICT teacher told a local TV outlet that the school had resorted to making use of these earthen tools because they lacked them. According to him the conditions at the school don't bode well for ICT training or learning. There are no teaching aids to facilitate learning, emphasising that it makes teaching of the subject challenging.

Mr. Ahiabor told the media: "I asked them to look at this (referring to the only laptop he has) my original one and concentrate on and make it once. And I can say that I'm finding it too difficult to handle the ICT using one laptop from class one (primary or elementary) to JHS.'

The question one would probably ask is:

Can these pupils compete with their compatriots in other 'fortunate' schools which have access to the right tools? How would they perform in their final BECE exams in IT? I shudder to say I don't have answers, but it remains to be observed in the years to come.

UN agency for education UNESCO" believes that education is human right for all throughout life and that access must be matched by quality." In fact UESCO charges governments across the world to make provision for access.

Article 26 (1) of the UN UDHR says: "Everyone has the right to education. Education shall be free, at least in the elementary and fundamental stages. Elementary education shall be compulsory. Technical and professional education shall be made generally available and high education shall be equally accessible to all on the basis of merit."

The rate at which ICT is transforming lives and causing digital divide has become a great concern to world leaders. *But where does the difference lie?*

Someone wrote that 'the difference is between those who have access to and the opportunity, capability to use ICT and those who have not.' Exactly, that's the challenge confronting many Junior High Schools in Ghana today, including the one in Volta region that has become the centre of attraction.

You know Man can be unjust sometimes, man can be anti-social, man can be selfish and man can be uncaring. Need I remind you?

There probably was enough room in Noah's Ark that could have saved thousands of lives yet, according to the biblical story many people perished because of their unbelief in the wake of the epic floods. It's understood that Noah was scorned, mocked and ridiculed by the people and they thought he was beside himself.

There probably were lot of laptop computers and other ICT tools ahead of Ghana's 2016 general elections. I bet there were many laptop computers that found their way into wrong hands instead of getting to right recipient. And do you've any idea how many items that were distributed or given out during the last general elections as a means to solicit votes? Not to mention the cash and the outboard motors, the roofing sheets, the Mackerels and other goodies. Yet some pupils in some parts of the country at the time and today are studying under trees, some are using clay to make computers and there are still some that are at homes because they can't either afford or don't have access.

I can tell you there were probably enough computers that could have been given to many schools across the country. But they were handed out during the December general elections to woo voters while pupils of some schools needed them badly to facilitate learning in their respective schools.

THE BIG FISH:
Where and When Is Our Catch?

Sometimes we don't have to launch out into the deep and cast our nets or let them down into the water for a catch. But at times we do need to do that in order to get our prey. Regardless, we pray all the time that we're able to meet our set targets. We pray and ever remain hopeful that our good thoughts and goals wouldn't go unfulfilled. And we pray that even when we fall double or triple times we will be able to get back on our feeble feet and our little hands wouldn't rest till they're called to eternity.

I'd relieved my co-worker at 4pm (Pacific Time, 7pm ET) on Wednesday August 30. After the brief, John Bacon fished a cell phone out of his breast pocket amid smiles. I thought he was going to show me a photograph of his 1979 1200 FXS lowrider—Harley Davidson motor bike. But it was something different. He'd something to share. He'd caught two fish in the Puyallup River on Monday 28 August 2017.

Both were salmon. One was pink the other was silver. The latter (silver) weighed about 8 pounds and approximately 24 inches long while the former (pink) weighed roughly 6 pounds and about 18 inches long, John told me.

And it was the story of the Silver Salmon that triggered this write-up. It was that story of that silver slippery aquatic creature that stuck with me. Yes, it was that story that might be viewed by many as inconsequential.

Ever remember the encounter Jesus had with Simon and his brothers?

The account is that Simon and his brothers (John, James and Andrew) had toiled hour after hour yet they caught nothing in Lake Gennesaret. They were tired. They wanted to give up. They'd thrown in the towel. They saw the mission as fruitless. And perhaps it was time to go back home empty handed. Then unexpectedly Jesus appeared.

He already knew their situation. The look on their faces emphasised worry and frustration. Shortly after speaking to them he told Simon: "Put out into deep water and let down the nets for a catch."

I could imagine the face Simon made before he acquiesced to the Lord's command.

"Master," Simon replied 'we worked hard all last night and didn't catch a thing. But if you say so, I'll let the nets down again," (Luke 5:5).

Verse six (6) of the scripture reads: "And when they had done this, they caught a great multitude of fish, and their net was breaking..."

But the great part of the narrative is that Simon and his brothers from thereon stopped catching ordinary fish. They became fishers of men as they followed Jesus in his ministry.

When and where is our catch?

You'll never know where and when you'd stand tall among the many to be counted. To be seen as a trailblazer, a champion or a winner. When and where you'll feel the glory and not feel sorry about what you've been able to accomplish. You'll never know when and where you'd have your bread fully buttered.

Indeed John Bacon had no idea what was in stored for him when he went down to fish in the Puyallup River in Tacoma Washington last Monday. John does fishing as his hobby and it seems his life is synonymous with the limbless guys with gills and fins living wholly in water.

Some days he makes a catch somedays he catches nothing. But the past Monday was unlike the others. It seemed like a miracle to John or it was just sheer coincidence. According to John it was a typical day for him. The Sun was hitting hard so he decided to go down there and do what he loves to do.

"I'd earlier failed to make any catch for about an hour. But what followed a few minutes after I'd thrown in my line left me in perplexity. I felt smack bogged," he told me.

"Suddenly I felt the fish on the end of the line. My hook had hooked the eye of the swivel of the sinker of another line. I knew I had caught a fish. I pulled it and still I couldn't see the fish but I saw the sinker and finally there it was the big one."

He said he felt so happy for the catch because it came on unexpected. John is planning to have some good soup with his silver and pink salmon. "I will give half of the big fish to my mom and share the remainder with my neighbour—an 80-something year-old woman," he told me.

And did you know this wasn't John's first, catching a fish in such strange manner. "Several years ago I caught a 30-inch fish that weighed over 10 pounds," he said.

So now you know sometimes we don't have to worry much for what we can do and can't do. Experts in fishing will tell you perhaps to make a good catch you'll need to observe the following techniques to the letter, which include: hand gathering, angling, and netting spearing, trapping. The irony is that sometimes you can observe all of the techniques above and yet make no catch.

I'm sure Simon and his brothers might've observed the fundamental drills about fishing. But they'd laboured in vain for hours until things came to the crunch. Until they encountered Jesus the techniques didn't matter and they didn't count. And there was a reason for that. Possibly it had been purposed to happen or probably some causative agent engineered its occurrence.

So just remember today that you can catch your fish sometimes unexpectedly. Someone will come and bless you when you have no clue– who he's, where he's coming from and when the catch is going to happen. Remember, it could be a catch at your job, a catch in your education, a catch in your marriage or relationship, a catch in your finances and many more. Remember, John's hook didn't hook the fish. It rather hooked another hook deep in the water. That presupposes that someone might've caught that fish but missed it in the process. You can conclude therefore that it wasn't meant for him, it was rather meant for John.

It was like when they tossed Jonah out from the boat into the sea. There was a waiting big fish believed to be a whale. Bottom line, always remain focused and keep your head up.

DVLA Consults Oracle in Sogakope or is it Credibility Doctor?

Even a First Grader knows what's wrong with (DVLA) (Driver and Vehicle Licensing Authority). The authority is suffering from credibility crisis. But its leadership says otherwise.

Can the public trust the organisation to deliver following its soul revival mission in Sogakope?

Is it true that DVLA has turned a new leaf?

On Friday 25 August, 2017 DVLA, the licensing authority in Ghana left Accra for Sogakope in the Volta Region to look critically into its (destiny) track record. Is it good or is it bad?

Kwasi Agyeman Busia the Chief Executive of the Driver and Vehicle Licensing Authority says the time has come to efficiently work together to meet the satisfaction of clients where services would be delivered to them on time.

"Corruption and unnecessary delays, which the Authority is known for, is gradually giving way to optimised service delivery towards building a respectable public institution of trust," he gave the assurance.

Mr. Busia said this at a four-day strategic review conference in Sogakope on the theme, "Accelerating Growth through People, Processes and Technology".

The DVLA Boss said the Authority was rebranding its image and activities to meet the growing expectation of the public, stressing that the intention of DVLA was to reposition itself and uplift its public image by 'resealing leakages' and 'protecting the security of its operations' to the admiration of the public.

Indeed one government institution that was or is seen as most corrupt in Ghana is DVLA. The organisation over a decade had gained the reputation for, cut corners, shady deals, delays, fake ID's etc. In fact there came a time that the general public didn't want to hear the name—DVLA. Simply there was nothing good about it anymore as it'd lost its moral standing.

The authority had not only lost the goodwill but it'd also lost the good faith Ghanaians had hitherto reposed in them. Trust was gone and respect had waned too. Too much rot was going on and it seemed they were too slow to act. What was left perhaps was nothing less than shame and low esteem.

Evidently, DVLA ceased to be the authority that could take care of its clientele. It also ceased to project itself as a reputable organisation that could put its house in order or curb corruption. Thus each passing day she saw her image sorely sinking.

In the past it seemed all attempts to redeem its image had failed. And they failed because the authority had probably only chosen to white-wash the tomb rather than overhaul the system. I don't know now, but DVLA had staff who'd been dealing with middle-men known as 'Goro Boys.'

So it came as no surprise when it embarked on the journey to Sogakope one and half weeks ago ostensibly to rebuild its sunken image. And I think it's a step in the right direction and I commend the management and staff for doing so.

In 2015 then former chief executive and others were cited in a huge scandal believed to be the biggest in the organisation's history. Dr. Justice Megaship the CEO had signed a contract sum of US$3.6 million with a US company Foto-X. The original contract which was signed between the two in 2006 was to procure project vehicles, train DVLA staff and refurbish all DVLA offices in the country ended in 2012.

Strangely, the price was shot up from US$3.6 million to $9.9million triggering public outcry. And even though the highly-publicised alleged scandal turned out to be unfounded the authority, is struggling to redeem its sunken image.

Shake-up

As things appeared murkier almost by the day the need to downsize DVLA's workforce became imperative. Around May this year, 2017 there was summary dismissal of more than 100 of its workers. The affected employees most of them administrative staff was employed within September 2016 by the former management under the Mahama administration.

It must be pointed out that government had underscored its intension to devise a mechanism that would flush out middle men who sometimes issue fake licenses at the various DVLA centres across the country. And I'm inclined to believe that if the exercise is carried through it will go a long way to help the authority's rebranding project.

He said the Authority is rebranding its image and activities to meet the growing expectation of the public. The Chief Executive said it is the intention of DVLA to reposition itself and uplift its public image by resealing leakages and protecting the security of its operations to the admiration of the public.

During his presentation on the strategic vision of the Authority Mr. Busia disclosed that DVLA had plans to construct new offices in Weija and Oda and a move to collaborate with the Environmental Protection Agency to implement emission system at all private vehicle testing stations to check smoke emission. According to him the Authority is also strategising its activities to wean itself off government subvention. He therefore called for support from the staff to work hard to meet its expectation.

The Board Chairman, Mr. Frank Davies said, the Board has confidence in the Chief Executive and management and is optimistic that with the support of the staff they would put the Authority on a higher foundation.

Mr. Davis alluded that it was unfortunate, the name of the Authority had been in the news for some unacceptable reasons, ranging from customer frustrations to clients being offered 'unauthorized service's by 'unauthorized persons'. Such phenomenon, he believed, dents the image and integrity of the Authority and also leads to massive revenue losses.

He said: "There's the dawn of a new DVLA that's responsive to customer needs and satisfaction has come and urged the staff to collaborate in the discharge of their work."

Meanwhile, Mr. Samuel Lodonu, the Volta Regional Manager of the Authority, said it is time the Authority reviewed some of its processes, which appear bureaucratic and allowed 'goro boys' to operate. According to him, it is time the Authority switched to full automation to aid and facilitate secure, reliable and real time service delivery to its cherished clients.

"I think this is the opportune time for the Authority to take a second look at some of its processes since it is obvious that some of the requirement and procedures for some of the activities push our prospective clients to the 'goro boys' when the clients become frustrated," he said.

So they're back from Sogakope with their boots perhaps full of pride amid optimism. They say action speaks louder than words. Would DVLA live up to expectation? Would it from now on support its words with action? Would the workers demonstrate integrity and loyalty to the general public (its customers)? And would they communicate honestly to the public without peddling falsehoods?

EXTON CUBIC GROUP EXITED

Did the owners know their days were numbered?

If you're a stranger in Jerusalem, then you wouldn't know that there exist mundane Mosaic laws.

Eleventh-hour contract deals often don't turn out well. We've seen such drama play out many times in many parts of the world. The reason, they tend to be mired with problems such as conflict of interest, companies/individuals not meeting terms of reference or requirements or not following due process. But they usually occur when governments from different political parties take the wheels of power.

Problem is, many forget that such contracts aren't ironclad. In other words they aren't chiseled on concrete slabs and for that matter they can be canceled or abrogated by new administrations through enactments at any time. I think former president Kufuor signed one of such contracts in 2008 at the dying embers of his tenure. However, that contract had a safe berth. It must be the Ghana Telecom (GT) contract which was sold to British telecommunication giant Vodafone at a cost of US $900 million (454 million pounds) for a 70 per cent stake in the telephony company.

On Monday 4 September, 2017 John Peter Amewu, Minister of Lands and Natural Resources, announced at a news conference in Accra that Exton Cubic Group Limited —a mining company owned by businessman Ibrahim Mahama a junior brother of former president John Mahama could not meet all the legal requirements to prospect for bauxite at Nyinahini in the Tano Offin Forest Reserve in the Ashanti region; and therefore the 'lease cannot hold'.

The Monday's announcement therefore, cancels the earlier directive for the company to move to the Nyinahin forest for the mining of bauxite.

Mr. Amewu said the NPP administration was acting in accordance with Section 87 of Act 703 of the Minerals and Mining Act, 2007 to cancel the multi-billion bauxite concession granted Mr. Ibrahim Mahama.

"The failure to obtain an Environmental Permit, Operational Permit, as well as the various statutory infractions, leading to the purported grant of the three Mining Leases to the company, render the purported leases invalid and of no effect," he told the press.

Bruce Pardy a law professor at Queen's University Kingston Ontario Canada wrote: "Government contracts are contracts. In the normal course of events, their terms may be canceled, the Crown held liable for the breach. However, government contracts are not ironclad agreements they appear to be because governments may change or cancel them by enacting legislation."

His statement was contained in a Fraser Research Bulletin, under the topic: Cancelling Contracts: The Power of Governments to Unilaterally Alter Agreements'.

As I aforementioned this isn't peculiar to Ghana. In August this year (2017), the Trump administration cancelled a contract solicitation that would have handed the management of the Federal government US$1.2 trillion portfolio of education loans to a single company. The cancellation, according to Washington Post sparked complaints from industry stakeholders.

Speaking at a press conference Mr. Amewu, who had earlier been accused of allowing Ibrahim's company into the Nyinahin Forest Reserve in the Atwima Mponua District of the Ashanti Region to start exploratory activities, said "Exton Cubic was supposed to provide an Exploration Operating Permit for the year 2017, an Exploration Operating Plan to the Minerals Commission but none of the above was fulfilled."

Did the owners know their days were numbered?

There appeared to be a silver lining from the onset so I doubt if they got a wind of what was to come.. The Lands minister had openly said that the company had permits and satisfied all requirements. And on that basis he granted Exton Cubic the permission to carry on its activities in the designated forests. But that was short-lived. This would trigger seizure of the company's equipment, war of words and threatening of lawsuits. Nonetheless, the cancellation looked inevitable.

"The absence of publication in the Gazette of a notice of the pendency of the company's applications and service of the notice on the various entities specified in the law is contrary to both Section 13(2) of Act 703 and Regulation 177 of L.I 2176," he noted.

The minister said the three mining leases included Kyekyewere (56.64 sq.km), Mpasaso (22.46 sq.km) and Kyirayaso (32.68 sq.km), adding that his attention was drawn to an attempt by the company to enter the concession on August 20 and therefore he decided to investigate that information.

Upon the investigation he said, it was established that Exton Cubic Group Limited had not complied with the mandatory laid-down procedures required to enter the concession. At this point the last option on the table was abrogation.

Commenting on the issue, Prof. Frimpong Boateng, Minister of Environment, Science, Technology and Innovation, pointed out that it's every governments priority to promote local industries.

"Every government wants to promote indigenous Ghanaian businesses .The laws are laws. This is not a political thing. This government works with the law and infractions are infractions. Nobody can say that this is a political witch-hunt. The minister mentioned a lot of infractions... so you can go through and you will know that we are not after any individuals. I will be the last person, and I am sure the president will be the last person to hunt Ghanaian business people," prof. Boateng submitted.

Meanwhile a staunch critic of Ibrahim Mahama Mr. Kennedy Agyepong MP for Assin North has urged the NPP government to tamper justice with mercy, suggesting government should allocate a portion of the bauxite concession to embattled company, Exton Cubic Ltd to mine.

"Government should meet them [Exton Cubic] half way because they've also invested, we're all Ghanaians. I think 56.64cubic metres for only one company is also too much. Let's give some of the concession to Ibrahim and spread the rest among others who have the capacity to mine the bauxite so that the proceeds stay here in Ghana for the country to develop."

The NPP MP made the plea while speaking with Adom FM a local radio station based in Tema.

So in case you're still wondering as to what's going on, I tell you what: let cool heads prevail. This is just a new normal so don't fret much. Contracts get cancelled if and when they're deemed shady or smack fishy. I'm pretty sure the GT-Vodafone deal would have been annulled if the Mills administration had suspected any wrongful act regarding its sale.

Also I think it's important for the general public particularly those in the other side of the political divide to understand that some of these events are inevitable. And I should add that if we really want our democracy to grow and be like the Americans and the Brits then we must as well welcome these political bumps (as l like to describe them) in good faith.

The ugly fact is they may not be palatable, depending on who's at the receiving end. But I believe if we're able to handle them properly when they erupt they will go a long way to deepen and strengthen our democracy. And this advice isn't for the minority NDC alone it's meant for all the political parties in Ghana. And mind you, it's imprudent to sign contracts that are deemed controversial at the eleventh-hour. So let's try to avoid them going forward.

MANNA FALLS AT GIJ

How the Lebanese Community in Ghana Reached out to GIJ Students

Manna used to fall but it didn't fall everywhere. And not every race or ethnic group received it or was a beneficiary. It had its target group—the Israelites.

On Tuesday 5 September, 2017, 'manna' literally fell at the campuses of Ghana Institute of Journalism (GIJ) my alma mater in Accra leaving students, staff and members of the academia overwhelmed. The Lebanon Ambassador to Ghana Mr. Ali H. Halabi had led a powerful delegation comprising the leadership of the Lebanese community in

Ghana to award scholarship to 20 Journalism students at the prestigious school.

The scholarship, which is an annual programme package for journalism students, was awarded to 15 undergraduates and five post-graduate students to continue their education in Levels 200, 300, 400 and the Masters Level. Here's the catch, the scholarship package covers the full tuition fees of the 15 under graduates and 75 per cent for the post-graduate students.

It was like a windfall for the beneficiaries, a gesture I believe the school would never forget and the students will live to remember. I also have no doubt in my mind that the gesture would challenge the non-beneficiary students to learn hard to become future recipients of the award.

Mr. Halabi told the gathering: at GIJ that: "The Lebanese Community in Ghana believes that promotion of freedom of speech was crucial in strengthening Ghana's growing democracy and that the media is the catalyst for social stability and economic development."

According to him the media is a 'very powerful institution' hence the need for responsible and professional journalists who would have the nation at heart.

Did you hear that?

How many years did it take our governments to remove the criminal libel law from the blueprint? You remember the 'Shitocracy' days too. I'm sure you also remember the days that the media in Ghana couldn't fully exercise their freedom of speech and expression. They were virtually 'shit-bombed', mercilessly pistol-whipped and callously iron-caged.

So, what can I say to our benefactors? Thank you so much Mr. Ambassador and the Lebanese community in Ghana. GIJ deeply appreciate your laudable gesture. And I am personally hopeful that the seed the community has sown today will have great yields tomorrow. The media as the Fourth Estate of the realm will not be a toothless bulldog and the pen will continue to wear its armor.

At the occasion the Ambassador also revealed that aside GIJ the Community has awarded similar scholarships to law students at the University of Ghana, Legon and the Kwame Nkrumah University of Science and Technology (KNUST). There are other groups in Ghana that are currently being assisted by the scholarship to complete their education, the Ambassador said. They include children of martyrs of the Ghana Armed Forces, Ghana Immigration and Police services.

Dr. Wilberforce S. Dzisah, the Rector of GIJ, congratulated the beneficiaries and expressed his utmost gratitude to the Lebanese Community for the continuous gesture. He also had an advice for the students: "I encourage you the beneficiaries to continue to learn hard to prove above the standard you've reached because the scholarship is renewable annually."

Like the orphan boy– Oliver Twist authored by Charles Dickens, Dr. Dzisah appealed to the Lebanese Community to extend the scholarship to the Public Relations students to help the brilliant but needy ones among them to also access the scholarship package.

Mr. Halabi pledged the Community's continuous support for Ghanaian students to enable them to contribute meaningfully to Ghana's development.

Timely Intervention

Speaking on behalf of the beneficiaries, Mr. Prosper Senyo, was thankful to the Community for the 'timely intervention' of providing them scholarship to continue their education at the Institute.

"We're going to work hard to excel in not just academics but to become responsible citizens touching the lives of many," he said.

Talking about timely intervention, reminds me of this biblical story. The road to Damascus was paved, it was a broad way from Jerusalem yet Saul couldn't see his way through it. Saul who would later be christened Paul had had an encounter with the spirit of God. He fell into t a sort of trance. His eyes were open yet he couldn't see for three days. Thereafter Saul's life changed forever. His past was forgotten.

His mission was to win souls and not to persecute the saints. He never let his past haunt his journey to redemption.

Today, this gesture is like the road to Damascus. My prayer is that your encounter with the Lebanese community in Ghana would change your destiny forever. You'd been left in the woods for too long. And it pleases my heart that today the men and women from the land of cedar have done you this great gesture. May this gesture act like yeast to propel you to greater heights .Don't let your past hold you back, keep your heads up because your tool is mightier than the sword.

Today your story is like these two neighbours who lived next to each other. Kojo had lost his cool. His anger had reached the moon. What was the reason for his rage? His horse had failed to make it to the next round of a competition organised by the community to see who'd the best horse in the locality. He'd struggled to understand how and why Kofi's 'horse out-performed his in the race. In fact, Kojo was so upset that he approached his neighbour after the race.

"What's the secret of your success," Kojo asked.

"I take good care of my animals," Kofi replied.

Today the media in Ghana is doing so well because of media pluralism and freedom of speech. But above all, the Criminal Libel Law has ceased to be the enemy of free speech .In 2001 Parliament unanimously voted to repeal it giving journalists the latitude to discharge their duties freely and without being intimidated.

Per this worthy gesture my expectation is that you would step out tomorrow as well-trained professional journalists– unflappable, unflustered and unruffled. Be the voice of the voiceless. Speak to the truth without fear or favour. Touch the untouchable, ruffle the feathers of the powerful and keep the Executive, the Legislature and the Judiciary on their toes.

NDC HIJACKED: Did You Know That?

But Who Are The Hijackers?

Ghana's largest opposition party the National Democratic Congress (NDC) is understood to have been intruded by what looks like blood sucking bugs or weasels. Who says so? Former President John Mahama is on record to have said that the party has been infiltrated by 'self-seeking opportunists' whose main agenda is to enrich themselves and their relatives and not the country.

"We all think about ourselves first, our families second, our parties third maybe our communities fourth and Ghana comes a fifth or even 10th," Mr. Mahama said.

Well, let's give the former president credit here, I think he deserves it. His use of the 'WE 'clause or passage to me endorses the fact or perception that he is or was a corrupt leader. He thought about himself during his presidency first, which is very typical of most African leaders. They build mansions outside their home countries say in Dubai, Paris, and Stockholm. They grab state properties left, right and centre and they launder billions of dollars if not trillions into foreign bank accounts.

You can also cite a number of contracts (some of them have conflict of interest) including eleventh-hour contracts. Remember the one president Mahama signed for his brother—Ibrahim Mahama and company Exton Cubic Group? I suppose some friends of the president benefitted from him during his tenure as vice president and president of Republic of Ghana including the Burkinabe contractor. And where was Ghana in all this? A "fifth or even 10th," as he remarked.

But does that sound familiar?

When former president John Rawlings said the NDC has lost its moral ground and the tenets—'Probity and Accountability 'that shaped the party into its existence, he was castigated by the hawks in the party and labeled as a backstabber and traitor. Some even called for his dismissal. They said he'd brought the party into 'disrepute'. And was asked to chastise—in their own words: 'Akufo-Addo corrupt government' and leave the NDC alone'.

This is Mr. Rawlings at Ashaiman in the Greater Accra region on Saturday 10 June 2017 at the party's 25th anniversary rally in a constituency considered to be one of NDC's strongholds. The rally was NDC's first biggest gathering following the aftermath of its last defeat in the 2016 December polls.

"How many times have we not gone through this stage?" Mr. Rawlings asked. "I say if we are serious, we are genuine, we are sincere, and that unity can work. Power corrupts us too quickly, too easily. We need to re-examine ourselves. We need some serious education," he bemoaned. The former president also told the gathering to be steadfast and guard against or prevent the process of unity from being hijacked.

So, perhaps the question of the day is: Where did the bugs come from and how did they get in there? I thought NDC was insulated. When were they (the opportunists) hatched? I understood it'd no breeding grounds. And who are these infiltrators or intruders? Is it the backstabber(s) (Mr. Rawlings and I'll add Mr. Amidu—citizen vigilante) or the fair-weather friends?

Also at that rally you may recall these words blared from the loud speakers: "I've accepted all blame as a leader of the party," that was Mr. Mahama then. If you didn't quite get that, let me do better translation here. He meant, he takes responsibility for all the xyz that happened to the patty. According to him there was no need to blame the foot soldiers, no need to blame the party surrogates or those with sharp teeth for the party's huge loss in 2016.

Why the U-turn now?

At the time pundits and political analysts theorised that he (president Mahama) possibly did so to sort of reposition himself as the putative nominee for the 2020 presidential race. And now it appears there are other contenders who in his mind don't qualify to hold themselves as leaders or challenge the establishment if you like.

Today, the truth has been spoken again. And I can emphatically say Mr. Rawlings isn't the problem. He is not the cause of NDC's woes.

The bugs are in the Umbrella and I suppose all of the party's paraphernalia have been infested. They've grown wings, developed sharp teeth and are spinning the party around violently.

Any lessons learned yet?

Again at the rally the central theme was about unity, which speaker after speakers latched on. But from where I sit it doesn't appear to me that the party is united. There seem to be cracks shaping up now and then. A development I believe could hurt the party going forward if it isn't resolved quickly. As usual the fair-weather friends are stoking the fire while the praise singers—the symphony orchestra group is making the most noise. They seem to be more than the 'saints' in the party.

Sure, they missed the Accountability and Probity Bus. And sure they missed the big bus to the Flagstaff House. But how didn't they know all along that the party's been infiltrated by some blood sucking bugs? How did they not know that the party is in dire need of some therapeutic?

Do you think they would believe me if I told them there were weasels in the party? Your guess is my best bet.

Where did all this 'self-opportunists 'talk happen?

Speaking at the inauguration of the first intake of students at the NDC's ideological school, Ghana Institute of Social Democracy, Mr. Mahama said people are no longer interested in how they can work to better the lives of Ghanaians but, rather, that of their own.

"We all think about ourselves first, our families second, our parties third maybe our communities fourth and Ghana comes a fifth or even 10th."

The school was established to help train party members on the social democratic philosophy and also encourage patriotism among members. Sceptics and some section of the public believe the school seeks to only indoctrinate people by brainwashing them. But Mr. Mahama explained it would rather ensure people do not become "ideological robots." He was confident products from the system will be what he described as 'more independent minded, analytical and will be ready to serve both the country and the party.'

Mr. Mahama was also hopeful the institute would help address the problem of parochialism, disunity and back-biting in the party, as they seek to forge a united front for now and the future. He said the party missed an opportunity back in 1992 to educate its members about its own ideology, making it difficult for new members of the party to understand and appreciate its own philosophy.

"It has taken the party 25 years to come around the idea of a party school. Within that time frame, NDC activists have very little understanding of their ideological roots which has not augured well for party unity and grassroots mobilisation," the former president noted.

What Would Happen if We All -THINK GHANA FIRST?

Never seek or attempt to please mankind you would fail. Never think or assume that you're the best, lest you'd be put to rest. Never pursue a fly in the wilderness; you may end up being pursued by the wild beasts. And never say never because we're still living in a wonderland.

But remember this– always do what you can and leave what you cannot for the generations after you will start off where you left off.

What would happen if we all think Ghana first??

If we all think Ghana first Ghana will be first. And it will be first in all things because there's strength in unity and there's power and growth in oneness. Ghana will be beautiful and attractive. Our economy will be stronger, our democracy will be more vibrant and our government will be more stable. The system will work, and the citizens will not work against the clock to kill man hours.

Citizens will hold their leaders into account, governments will have listening ears. They will cease to be more powerful, it will be other way round. We will be productive, result-oriented, demand-driven and always on the move to build our motherland. We will be caring and not careless about what's around us. We will be real patriots and not lip-service nationalists. State properties will be our properties it will cease to be the proverbial 'Aban dea'. it's state-owned so I don't care. I don't mind, it can go stale or go rot. Ghanaians will buy made-in-Ghana goods rather than 'patronise in painte manento' merchandise imported from elsewhere in the Far East or anywhere across the world.

Ghana will be more peaceful'. There will be less hunger, less crime, less corruption, less diseases and perhaps less of everything that inhibits growth of any form or shape.

Of course productivity will be high, there will be more jobs, unemployment will cease to be a problem and there will be less brain-drain. Sounds like utopia isn't it? However, it's doable. Other nations have done it. They did it here on our planet– Earth, not on Mars or Jupiter or Pluto. Our children are running there, our youth are flocking there, there's mass exodus to North America, Europe, the Middle East, Oceania and the Far East. Why because there are opportunities.

Things to do

There will be more opportunities here if we think or put Ghana first. But this is what we need to do: Let's develop the habit of working hard to break deadlines. Let's make good use of our time,. Time is money. A stich in time saves nine. Time and tide wait for no man. Time lost cannot be regained. It's time for a change so let's make good use of our time.

By so doing we will be able to think Ghana, and we will be able to realise our dreams, we will be able to meet our aspirations and we will be able to build the Ghana we envisage. Time has always beaten us a people it appears. We've never managed to beat the clock. The clock beats us at state functions, meetings, workshops, assignments, ceremonies etc. A dreamer's dream is never accomplished until s/he breaks the ground and start to build.

The Book of Exodus in the Bible believed to have been authored by Moses and the entire Pentateuch make us to understand that the Staff (rod KJV) used by Moses was by his side throughout important milestones in the account. The Rod played a significant role among these milestone events during the exodus. The Bible says the staff was used to produce water from a rock, was transformed into a snake and back, and was used at the parting of the Red Sea also known as the sea od Reeds.

Problems& Solutions

They said Nkrumah couldn't build the Akosombo Dam yet he built it. They said Kufour's government would fail because they'd no money. Evidently the previous government had ransacked the national kitty yet Kufour succeeded. Nobody could build a road or highway through Nima /441 but Rawlings built the Kanda Highway. Was it not president John Mahama who built the Circle Interchange Footbridge? And Akufo-Addo will continue where they left off. Free SHS has already been rolled out and it appears more goodies are in the offing.

Where there's will there's a way! The problem we have is neither the problem nor the solution it is about our mindset. Our attitudes to adapt, our attitudes to change, our attitudes to say right is right and wrong is wrong and don't turn it inside out. That's what is confronting us.

Yes it was convenient for the AMA or KMA authorities to drive the hawkers away from the streets in January 2009 (after the '08 general elections) but it was taboo or declared a no-go-zone around January 2016 (before the 7th December elections) . And I'm sure it won't be convenient for any politicians to do so around January 2019.

Have you wondered why residents of Sodom and Gomorrah are still where they are? Or seem to comeback season after seasons?

The ugly fact, whenever the authorities seemed to have held the bull by the horn and challenged the norm you see a situation like this: If NPP taskforce evict the squatters today, an NDC taskforce will show up tomorrow to welcome them and vice versa. That explains why the Accra Business District and Kwame Nkrumah Circle Area are in the state we find them. Sanity becomes insanity and it's business as usual. It's nothing but fear of retribution—the people might not vote for them (politicians) if they dare to evict them. It might be convenient today but it may be inconvenient tomorrow and the cycle moves on. But if we think Ghana first NDC will support NPP and the parties will join in unison. That's how we build stronger nations—bipartisanship.

Remember this saying: "Don't send us to opposition..."' Koku Anyidoho NDC deputy general secretary told Seth Tekper former finance minister in the Mahama-NDC government. The minister was doing what was seen to be right but the season called for absurdity. Where are they now?

Why must it take half a decade to discuss judges' salary? And guess what as at November 2016 government negotiators hadn't reached finality. It took government five years or more than five years to implement salary reviews for lower court judges.

Remember the public purse has been dripping by the day as looters dip their long hands into the kitty. And you'd think there are no solutions or laws that check wanton looting. You probably also think there are no laws that jail or put looters behind bars and you'd think Ghana is a lawless nation. But we have all the beautiful laws. In actual fact we have one of the best constitutions in the world written by constitutional gurus. Yet public office holders, governments, rulers, parliamentarians and judges have sidelined them. Thank goodness the Auditor General's Office now has the power to do what citizens are clamoring for. Don't get me wrong that law has been sitting in the books for several years. So we've almost always had the solutions to our problems but our attitudes.

Our governments know free speech is good, they know democracy is good they know human rights are universal rights yet for years they refused to decriminalise the Criminal Libel Law Constitution.

'Yentie Obiaa' (We're not listening to anybody) is what has brought us here and not the fact that we're bereft of ideas. Do you remember how long it took the previous Mahama administration to negotiate on lower court judges' salary? And tomorrow when they hit the streets of Accra you ask for solutions. Whenever you consider or take into account repercussions solutions follow. They follow because you can see through the tunnel even though it looks deep, steep and dark.

Why did you vote for the NPP or the NDC and not for example the PPP or NDP?

Is it because it is tagged an Akan party? Is it because you've cronies in that party? Did you think about Ghana first and not your stomach, and pocket? Did you think about your girlfriend and boyfriend first and not Ghana? Was it your siblings—brothers, sisters, cousins and not Ghana?

Remember, AMA provided trash cans or bins to collect refuse some miscreants took them home. You saw them did you report to the police? You saw your brother make illegal power connection which is unlawful did you report. Be reminded problems and solutions are bedfellows. They sleep together.

Fact is we cannot run away from ourselves. And we cannot blame others all the time for our troubles... How can you steal the textbooks at your school and turn around to blame the politician in Accra. How can you allow your brat kids to vandalize state properties—water or electricity (illegal power connection) and turn around to blame the government? You act like helicopter moms protecting your kids when they indulge in armed robbery, yet you talk about crime and blame the government for doing nothing.

Traffic isn't moving, who's to blame? It's the politician. The traditional rulers are selling stool lands, town lands and community lands to illegal small-scale miners (Galamsey Operators) regardless. The water bodies are being destroyed, the lands are being degraded, the forests are being demolished, and the soils are desecrated. Yet the blame is on the politician. If we think or put Ghana first the responsibility will be a shared one. It will be you and me and everyone.

FREE SHS AND ITS SUSTAINABILITY IN FUTURE

How Sound Is the Critics Argument?

What in the world meets full-proof sustainability: Is it Denmark's or Germany's free education policy? Is it America's flamboyant social intervention welfare programme? Or is it the Great Britain's internationally-acclaimed health care system? Arguably none, yes nothing in our world. Everything humanity has ever invented or created or adopted or developed since creation has faced some challenges of a sort.

However, in the midst of the huge challenges we don't give up. We relatively take profound solace in such trials if you like and continue to pursue our dreams till they get actualised. That's why today we're working painstakingly to get Komenda Sugar Factory back on track after its botched operation in 2016. Its resuscitation is very dear to our hearts. They virtually had the cart put before the horse.

Did you think we would ever get here, had we allowed pessimism to becloud our dreams and visions? Did you think we would ever have lights, refrigerators, microwaves, computers, bows and arrows, pins and needles, pillows and gallows, pans and pens and many more in our homes, if we'd clothed ouselves in pessimism? And you think all the inventors of ships, airplanes, trains, automobiles, and robots or drones never envisaged risks, challenges and problems?

Had we allowed skepticism to wrap its long arms around us we would have no electricity in Ghana today because at the time the critics didn't see the Akosombo Dam as a viable, sustainable and feasible project. And if you care to know it doesn't take magic to do all that. No, all it takes to get these dreams realised are true visionaries with good ideas, good planning and not persons with wimpy mentality. Therefore, let's avail ourselves to constructive criticisms, let's debate the debate rather than engage in 'Gladiator Politics' (pull him down). Invariably, that would take us nowhere and no place. It only tends to breed mediocrity.

Is Free SHS sustainable?

I think the narrative of sustainability and lack of sustainability of the subject matter must be viewed within the context of all the examples catalogued above. And those who think that the programme would fail must be advised to sit back and watch the real game changers. Truth is we will not sit aloof whiles the rest of the world is running.

There is no doubt that the programme will encounter some challenges i.e a sustainable funding mechanism going forward which to me is normal. So I think if anybody or group of persons, party or organisation has any ideas to offer please make them available to the state rather than blow hot and cold on the government's flagship policy.

Indeed if we cannot even catch up with the runners we mustn't pretend we live on an Island and don't know or see what's trending around us. Maybe we can crawl. Maybe a walk will do or maybe we can run if we believe we can. The Eagle soars not because it has the most powerful wings, but it soars because it's conditioned her mind to fly high. College or higher education is an important policy for any modern country. And it has for years served as the backbone for nation's rapid growth.

How does it feel to hear or learn that over 100,000 children drop out of school each year in Ghana? This is because their parents cannot afford Senior High school Education, according to Ministry of Education (MoF).

On Monday 11, September 2017 the Minority in Parliament held a press conference in Accra to announce its position on the innovative policy. It said the Free SHS programme is not sustainable. In a statement the NDC Minority stated: "First, we have discovered that the NPP Government disingenuously refused to adjust this year's GES approved fees as has been the tradition every year. This tradition in fixing fees annually factors inflation and ensures that quality is not compromised."

"We have also discovered that contrary to its public posture that the Government does not intend to leave any child behind, the projection of the Akufo-Addo cabinet is that only 85% of SHS students will accept their placements and turn up for school. In other words, the NPP Government has made provision in its budget for only 362,781 SHS students entering first year. Therefore per current placement figures, Government has made no arrangements for 62,711 students".

But the minority's claims have been rebutted, Greater Accra Regional Minister Ishmael Ashitey says: "we will look at the mobilization of funds from the markets, everywhere, from our petroleum sector, everywhere monies are being wasted, we will bring them on board and use it. That is the dream of the president. It is leadership and a matter of choice. You can decide to use your resources to purchase cars and ride in them and someone has also decided to use the same resources to implement free SHS. Is a matter of choice."

According to him the Minority had not been consistent with their position because they keep on shifting the goal post.

"They said we could not start the policy, but we have started. Now they have turned the argument saying that it is not sustainable. It will become sustainable as we go along. They will see it."

He also deflated criticisms that the policy would put lots of pressure on the economy, stressing that enough work had been done before the implementation was launched. "It will not break the economy. If you have a very educated, learned, and advanced Human Resource, it will generate a lot into your economy and so, this forms part of the economy…We have thrown our bread onto the waters and we will use it to get more fishes,' Mr. Ashitey pointed out.

Meanwhile, African Union Commission has commended the Government of Ghana for implementing the Free Senior High School policy, indicating that it is a sure way of ensuring the growth of the country and Africa as a whole.

Ambassador Thomas Kwesi Quartey, Deputy Chairperson, African Union Commission, who gave the Commendation while speaking at an UNCTAD-organised High Level Panel Discussion in Geneva, Switzerland, said the beginning of Free SHS in Ghana would give greater impetus to the AU's agenda of having every African child in school by the end of the decade.

"We would like to have a literate and a numerate Africa. We want an Africa where illiteracy is a thing of the past. With a literate and numerate Africa, the continent would be ready now to imbibe technology, apply science and technology, and find solutions."

President Akufo Addo on Tuesday 12 September 2017 launched the government's educational flagship programme—free SHS policy. And it has so far released a total of GHc 480 million to commence the implementation of the policy.

One Man's Flaws is Another's Straw

Did Tony get it right in saying that Bawumia's Comparative Analysis had Flaws?

Your Excellency it's my singular honour to welcome you back home. You've been gone for so long just like me—serving humanity as part of your diplomatic duty in the Netherlands. Indeed Ghana appreciates your good services to its people both home and abroad. Good job good man.

When you think your ears had had enough and need some breather...guess what there comes yet other exasperating sound bites. They're sounds that rattle like beads. They're sounds that echo from the straw man's ramshackle shack. Drumming from afar louder and louder, seeking attention, raising the alarm bell and of course resorting to the proverbial blame game.

What perhaps Ghana's largest opposition party—National Democratic Congress (NDC) Communication Team didn't pay attention to or never saw it as a thorny issue back then in 2012 up to 2016 has now been revealed by Uncle Tony as something that possibly caused the party's downfall.

Ambassador Dr. Tony Aidoo says: "Dr. .Bawumia was the Achilles' heel of the NDC. Not only for the 2016 elections but he started way back in 2012. He ignored the fact that for the most part of the Kufuor administration, the eight years was virtually carried by donor financial support. All the social interventions that Kufuor implemented were donor supported."

I view Dr. Aidoo's comment as an admission that then vice presidential candidate of the NPP Dr. Bawumia was a force to reckon with and for that matter a real thorn in the flesh of the NDC. His comment also smacks an act of sour grapes.

It is true the Kufour administration received much donor support but the government didn't leave the country broke after its tenure. In 2011 Ghana was ranked the fastest economic growing country in the world, according to Economy Watch.

The statistics for 2011 economic growth indicators put Ghana at 20.146%. It was in part due to the HIPC initiative no doubt about that. But one can also not downplay the fiscal discipline the NPP government enforced. President John Mills was a good man unfortunately his good deeds weren't good enough to salvage the economy –his team failed him and disappointed Ghanaians.

xxxxx

"What I missed was the inability of the NDC communication team to bring out the facts so as to challenge the comparative analysis that Dr. Bawumia was making," the known out-spoken NDC ranking member told TV3 in his first-ever interview after he returned home from his diplomatic assignment.

Yes, Mr. Ambassador you missed that one big time. But did you suggest to the team or anyone, for example, this is what we need to do?

According to him it was important for the NDC's communication team at the time to have had people with "historical recall" and "administrative memory" to counteract, emphasising that even though Dr. Bawumia had flaws in his analysis of the economy ahead of the 2016 general elections, then ruling-NDC, failed to put up an effective communication strategy to counteract the analysis of the former Deputy Governor of the Bank of Ghana now Ghana's Vice President of Republic of Ghana.

But where was Uncle Tony when the NDC communication team was supposedly not working or didn't know what to do about Dr. Bawumia's supposed comparative analysis flaws? How far is it from Accra to Amsterdam? It's approximately five and half hours trip so he could have come down, he could have sent a tweet, he could sent a telegram, he could have also yahooed the team and he could have phoned them too.

Did Dr. Aidoo reach out to the team? Did he offer any advice to the team or tell the team what to do?

Maybe he did but the Anyidohos and the General Mosquitoes ignored him.

May I crave your indulgence Mr. Ambassador, much as I respect your opinion regarding the subject matter, wouldn't it have been better if you didn't mention what you called 'Bawumia's comparative analysis flaws.' And here's why: You will never get your opponent (Dr. Bawumia) to debate him on the issue. And that makes your argument fits into a Straw Man fallacy .You know their tactics and antics already so I am not going to dwell much on that.

However, at best it seems to be the old chestnut game. I've heard it over and over yet there hasn't been any NDC economic guru that's come out to pin point the flaws in any of his analyses on the state of Ghana's economy under the period in question. Even after his (Bawumia's) 2016 big lecture, which I described as 'Mother of All Lectures' nobody showed up.

So my question is: why now when the milk is snaking on the ground. What can you salvage from the spoilt?

Don't you think you're making the party look sorely miserable as though it's bereft of ideas?

I think there's nothing to counteract though... I've said this before and I won't shy away reiterating it here. A little bit of partisanship is good for Ghana's democracy but too much of it isn't helpful. Too much partisanship, I believe would rock our sailing boat. And everyone in the boat would suffer. Fact is if we politicise everything Ghana cannot work, the country will be like a man on a treadmill. The nation cannot move forward, there will be no development or progress.

Argument on HIPC or donor support

I think Dr. Aidoo's argument that the Kufuor administration had a lot of burden taken off his government's shoulders when Ghana's creditors wrote off 66% of the country's debt as a result of the Highly Indebted Poor Countries (HIPC) initiative is untenable.

"...At the time our national debt was about 6.8 billion dollars. In effect, our debt-to-GDP ratio certainly dropped sharply so on what grounds can Bawumia compare that an economy that was virtually carried by donor financial support was managed better than an economy that did not have those support?" Dr. Aidoo argued.

First of all why did Ghana join HIPC?

I'm of the view that if one cannot appreciate or factor into where we were before the country joined HIPC then one must as well forget the argument or the comparison analysis because there were stars when the Moon showed up. Ghana joined HIPC in March 2001 and it subsequently progressed to the decision point in February 2002. It wasn't a pleasure to join the programme. The decision was borne out of necessity.

How was Ghana's economy at the time? What was the nation's GDP ratio? Who ran the economy down? Needless to say that the economy had hit rock-bottom, the national kitty had been run empty. Who doesn't want to be pardoned with debt? Is it wrong for a patient to see a doctor for medical treatment or physical therapy after you'd physically assaulted and financially abused her?

I could also infer from his argument that perhaps it was wrong for Ghana at the time to join HPIC (or metaphorically get a face-lift for our bloodied noses and broken jaws) a condition then governing NDC bequeathed Ghana in the year 2000.

History

In February 2002, the Executive Boards of the International Monetary Fund (IMF) and the International Development Associations (IDA) agreed to support a comprehensive debt reduction package for Ghana under the enhanced Heavily Indebted Poor Countries (HIPC) Initiative at the decision point. A set of floating triggers at the time was established for Ghana to reach the completion point.

The Boards also agreed to provide Ghana with interim assistance to cover part of the debt service falling due to the IMF and IDA until Ghana reached the floating completion point. The IMF provided interim debt service relief in an amount equivalent to SDR 25.1 million in nominal terms between February 2002 and May 2004, while IDA provided interim relief amounting to US$98 million over the same period. In addition, both the AfDB and the EU/EIB provided interim relief in the amount of US$52 million and EUR4.7 million, respectively.

MAN & DISASTERS

Remembering victims in Texas, Puerto Rico, Mexico etal...

Hit me with music that's one of my craves. You may hit me with love that's the fulcrum of my life. But I pray you don't hit me with a disaster. Please don't hit me with an earthquake, landslides and floods. Please don't hit me with hurricane, tornado or volcano. Please not by a car, not by a gun, not by a tree and not by a building. I hate drowning, I hate poisoning, I hate lynching.

I know Death will come rain or shine. I know the undying Death is no respecter of Man. That everyone knows. And everyone perhaps prays and wishes s/he dies in her sleep. Perhaps everyone prays that s/he makes the no return journey in peace and not in pieces.

However, they all seem to be nothing other than wishful thinking. Yes, as humans we pray any disasters must pass us by without causing harm to us. But it appears we've no control over these disasters or catastrophes whenever they strike.

Today, to all the victims in the hurricanes and the earthquake in Mexico, I just want you to know that the world hasn't forgotten about you. We share your pain and agony. We share your loss and the trauma. Our thoughts and prayers are with you. And we will continue to pray for /with you in these hard times.

The swath of devastation across the Caribbean nations– Dominica, British Virgin Islands, America Virgin Islands, Barbuda, Anguilla, Cuba, St. Martin, Guadeloupe and Puerto Rico, no doubt gives credence to the fact that we've no control over them when they aim at us.

According to the UN's Office for the Coordination of Humanitarian Assistance (UNOCHA) 99 per cent of all buildings in Barbuda were destroyed. It adds that virtually 'the entire population of the Island (which is 100, 963 as of 2016) was evacuated to nearby Antigua.'

Isn't that mind blowing?

I heard about hurricane Jean for the first time, on my way from London, UK to the U S in September 2004. My flight had to be re-routed through Chicago to Atlanta Georgia instead of Miami Florida. Jean, the hurricane with a Hebrew name —meaning gift from God had pounded the southern state including some Caribbean nations.

Since Jean's destruction in 2004, there'd been Katrina 2005, there'd been Sandy 2012 and most recent names– like Harvey, Irma, Jose and Maria have popped up. And what did they do? They've brought an untold hardship and immeasurable damage–loss of lives and property. Of course they've never been kind to Mankind in any way whatsoever.

Often their names may sound nice and romantic but there's nothing good about their acts. They've always been devastating and always been destructive. A few hours ago as I sat down to write this piece Maria was slamming Puerto Rico— the US territory with a landscape of mountains. According to reports about 90 per cent of the population is currently without power. One headline read: 'Puerto Rico Goes Dark.' City managers believe the 3.411 (2016) million nation is totally destroyed and has to be rebuilt from the scratch. The category 5 storm is expected to cause more danger in the coming days.

When hurricane Harvey hit US state of Texas last August 2017, it also caused huge damage to its people and infrastructure. Professor Samuel Adu-Prah of Sam Houston State University – a great friend of mine was one of many Texans that faced the wrath of Harvey.

Mexico Earthquake

On Tuesday 19 September 2017 Mexico witnessed one of her deadliest natural disasters since 32 years (1985). At least 30 people, mostly children, died at a primary school which collapsed in Mexico City during the Tuesday's earthquake, according to news reports.

The 7.1 magnitude quake is reported to have killed at least 225 people in total and caused major damage across states in the centre of the country. It's feared the number would increase as I monitored RT, CNN and BBC news concurrently at 8pm Pacific Time. Rescuers are still pawing through rubbles in search for survivors. Dozens of buildings were toppled; much of the electricity supply was cut and broken gas mains sparked fires, said the reports.

The tremor struck shortly after many people had taken part in an earthquake drill, exactly 32 years after another quake killed thousands in the capital.

Mexico is prone to earthquakes and earlier this month an 8.1 magnitude tremor in the south left at least 90 people dead. Though it struck a similar region, Tuesday's earthquake does not appear to be connected with the quake on 7 September, which was at least 30 times more energetic, the BBC's Jonathan Amos writes.

It is now known that as many as 37 people - 32 children and five adults - died when Enrique Rébsamen primary school collapsed in Mexico City's southern Coapa district, Efe news agency reports, quoting local media.

According to Mexican news site Reforma, 30 bodies have been found at the school and 22 people are missing. More than 500 members of the army and navy, along with 200 police officers and volunteers, have been working at the site, Mexican newspaper Milenio says.

Mexican President Enrique Peña Nieto visited the collapsed school earlier in the day where sniffing dogs were helping to find survivors. "Some voices have been heard. In the time I have been here, I have seen how at times they have asked for total silence, solidarity to listen for the voices," he said after visiting the rescue operation.

At least 209 schools are reported to have been affected by the quake, 15 of which have suffered severe damage. The epicentre of the latest quake was near Atencingo in Puebla state, about 120km (75 miles) from Mexico City, with a depth of 51km, the US Geological Survey says. The prolonged tremor hit at 13:14 local time (18:14 GMT) on Tuesday and sent thousands of residents into the streets.

Also it is reported 15 people were killed when a church near Mexico's Popocatepetl volcano collapsed during Mass. The volcano itself had a small eruption as a result of the tremor. On Wednesday schools were closed as it had been announced by the governor of the state of Mexico Alfredo del Mazo Maza. The governor also ordered all public transport to operate services for free so that people could travel home.

No Generation

There was once a doubting Thomas during the Apostolic Age. There was a Judas famed for his betrayal of our Lord Jesus Christ. There was a liar by name Ananias. Oh and there was a Peter known for his denial of the Messiah at the eleventh hour!

Every generation breeds its apologists and adversaries. No generation is holy. No generation is perfect and no generation can do it all. Every generation strives to do its best. Yet we find the worst in our midst. There are wars and rumours of war. There's poverty, hunger and hatred, while diseases and other social ills surround us.

We're like small ants, we jockey to and fro. We labour to make ends meet.

We sweat in our hearts. Actually our hearts bleed.

If nations were beads they would be rattling. Rattle like maracas.

If mountains could move, the Earth would be trampled upon. And if hyenas were as huge as the elephants the forest would be ripped of its exotic mammals.

I've never seen or heard one mend a broken stone. And never witnessed a bird begets a mouse.

Sometimes you question. What in the world is going on?

And sometimes you exclaim- oh shoot!

Did you get something wrong?

Remember no generation is holy and no generation is perfect. We're all fallible. And we count on the infallibility of the Holy One.

In part the reason why I don't blame Grandpa Adam too much. The Old man meant well…but man is man. Our choices and wishes seem to drive us crazy sometimes.

Nothing made by man will stay the same. Imagine if gold rust what would iron do?

The scripture says heaven and earth shall pass away.

Consider Solomon's temple which was destroyed and pillaged by the Babylonians around 586 BC (2 kings 25:9). It was later rebuilt by King Darius of Babylon. It would be taken over by the Romans under King Herod. And Herod would also rebuild it. To this day The Holy Temple is being refurbished.

Evil will always be subdued despite its exploits and venom. When evil cries the world hears him louder.

Why?

Because Evil thrives on bad news—bad and sad news travel faster than good news. BUT good will forever reign. The Holy One takes time to do his things. He will do it at the right time.

The Dreaded Beard

A bearded man saw one's beard. It was a dreaded beard sported by a dreadful bearded man.

"What kind of beard are you wearing?" the bearded man asked the dreadful bearded man.

It's a beard bred in a dreaded bearded man's shed.

Are there breeds in your shed wearing dreadful beards?

You bet my shed is all bearded. And everyone drink beer, except the dreadful bearded man.

Does the dreadful bearded man dread beer?

Hahaha! Not at all…the dreadful bearded man smokes vodka and drink weed.

What do you mean, how can one smoke vodka and drink weed?

The answer is simple: To be bearded is to be dreaded and to be dreadful is to be beered!

Take it easy today and be blessed!

Hurray!

We're here. We've made it here. Here to live, here to love and be loved. We're here to work and play. Here to help one another and not to hurt. We're here to serve and be served. We're here to move on and groove on.

Indeed, we're here to care, to share and to help bear one's burden. Here to give peace a chance, here to heal our world and we're here to show kindness to one another. Being here today means you're blessed and not cursed, you're climbing and not tumbling, winner and not loser; you're an originator and not an impersonator.

Yesterday we were there. We lived there, worked there, loved there, we played there, sat there and we journeyed from there to here.

It is paradox isn't it?

Oh what a journey. A lifelong journey that seems like honey, yet its ways are so complex!

I hear billions defied the sheer human traffic that bled all the way from highway 2015 on both east and west bound and merged into super highway 2016. Similar or same activities occurred on the north and southbound, according to grapevine.

Yes, you and I and everybody alive today, stubbornly stepped into the New Year with great joy and immeasurable gratitude. Cash or no cash we're alive, problems or no problems we're here, deal or no deal we find ourselves on the billions' stage. Therefore we must be glad and rejoice. We must welcome the New Year with fervent prayer and be thankful for a new day, new week and a new month!

There were accomplished and unaccomplished missions. There were targets met and others unmet. There were failures, so were successes. We built new relationships/ friendships and solidified old ones, if they were worth it and we broke some.

There were many firsts: First graduations, first marriages, first homes, first vehicles, first jobs, first relationships, first schools/colleges, first weddings and first newly-born babies. BUT, it wasn't all joy; life showed us its complexities. We lost best moms and best dads, best sisters and best brothers, best friends and best family members. We loved them and they loved us.

That's the irony of life. Those loved ones unfortunately, couldn't make it here with us. And we'll forever miss them. So sad though that we left them behind!

But beyond that we're moving on as sons and daughters of the great One, ever determined to conquer the unconquered, finish the unfinished, meet the unmet, break the unbroken, chart the unchartered and sing for the unsung heroes and heroines.

I'm not a soothsayer but I know for sure that the task ahead like many others will be more than challenging. Our world today is dealing with one kind of ism or a bug that targets all humanity, regardless of race, age, gender, class, colour, religion, nationality, faith and what have you. This ism is like a grave or gun—so greedy. Always unsatisfied and it appears unyielding.

Terrorism is the bug I'm referring to. Centuries ago, colonialism became a global tormentor. Thankfully our forebears were able to overhaul that canker, even though there are some vestiges. Nonetheless, it's apt to mention that our beautiful world with its beautiful people still have some isms living among us. The likes of racism, sexism, schism, extremism, radicalism, hooliganism and many more have become headache for mankind.

More troubling to deal with I think is terrorism. Terrorism is the world's arch enemy, undoubtedly. Truth is none of the isms aforementioned is good, but terrorism surpasses them all. So we're here confronted by an enemy who is here to behead, dehumanise, and destroy. In fact its style of operation is not only cruel and deadly but also wicked, weird, and wacky. It is for this reason that the whole world must join hands to fight this evil.

Questions: Where would be joy and happiness, if evil triumphs goodness?

Where would be peace and love?

Can we find a safe environment to prosecute our New Year resolutions?

Are we ready to hold the bull by the horn and dehorn him?

Doubt would becloud our sense of judgements and duties. We can't work, we can't play. We can't move and groove on. We can't love and be loved. Everyone would be seen or viewed as a potential suicide bomber.

Problem is, you never know who, what, when, and how a device is going to explode. The enemies' choice of location (where) for the detonation of the device is equally disturbing—airplanes, schools, hotels, resorts, malls, recreational grounds, pubs and taverns, place of worships etc.

Why they take delight in carrying out such dastardly acts I have no answers.

But we're blessed with another promising year. New born babies have joined us. The future belongs to both the young and the old. However, the burden lies on the leadership across the world, every individual or group of persons on this vast global stage must live to fulfill his /her dream and not die young to have them curtailed.

Together we can make this happen. Together we can stop the enemy from harming us, hurting us and killing us. Caring for one another is the way to go. Sharing information is another sure way to degrade and destroy the enemy. Be your brothers/sisters keeper; watch my back and I'll watch your back for you. Come on let's do this together!

Happy New Year to you all!

My Knight

If he were a fish I would call him sailfish, because it is the fastest fish in the ocean. If he were a bird I would call him peregrine falcon—it is the bird with the greatest airspeed. If he were an animal I would call him a cheetah— it is the fastest land animal. And if he were a tree I would call him the giant sequoia—it is the largest tree in the world.

Distinctively, all the above-named animals are pacesetters or trailblazers in their respective kingdoms. They may have humble and feeble beginnings yet they're world record breakers today, and the world acknowledges that.

My knight is incredibly a prodigy and he's no doubt a prime mover and a champion in his field. He's a man whose empire sprouted from an insignificant place. Like our Lord born in the manger.

What do they say; the greatest man you ever did see was once a baby.

Sure my knight was once a College dropped out!

He is American computer programmer, internet entrepreneur and philanthropist. He is the chairman, chief executive and co-founder of the social networking website, Facebook.

If I were the Queen or King of England I would knight my knight as Sir Mark Elliot Zuckerberg. Sir Zuckerberg heads possibly one of the biggest inventions of our time—Facebook (one of the social media) that has allowed billions of people to create, share, or exchange information, career interests, ideas, and pictures/videos in virtual communities and networks.

In 2012 Facebook users worldwide reached a total of one billion. And I'm one of the billion using this media tool on the eve of the New Year 2016, to knight my knight.

Sir you truly deserve the knighthood!

Roughly a decade ago, together with his college roommates and fellow Harvard University students namely—Eduardo Saverin, Andrew McCollum, Dustin Moskovitz and Chris Hughes, Sir Zuckerberg launched facebook from his Harvard's dormitory.

Unbelievably he receives a one-dollar salary per annum as CEO of Facebook. And his personal wealth as of December 2015 is estimated to be $46 billion.

Without a doubt you're my Champion of the decade. You've created a huge platform where some users stay all-day and all-night long—chatting, gossiping, writing, sharing information, pictures and videos: A platform where a user has over ten thousand friends but none acknowledges his/her birthday: A stage where a friend is complete stranger to the friend even when they cross paths.

'Me'ma wo Ayekoo' Sir Zuckerberg, your success is just a tip of the iceberg!

"Dad what would you do if you were salt?"

A man's six-year-old daughter asked him during dinner with family members and friends. Back in the day in quintessential Ghanaian households kids never asked questions. Kids were told to shut up when parents or adults were talking. They seldom had the chance to be around their parents when family friends were visiting or shared dining tables with them.

They'd no say whatsoever in their own father's house. Their suggestions carried no weight, if they ever had one at all. And their questions didn't matter. In short, kids did kids' stuff and perhaps shelved things that could have been useful to the whole family.

Thankfully many parents today are shedding the mundane cultural practice which somewhat has churned out many timid kids/adults. That said there still are homes back home that continue to deny kids the right to express their views— good or bad.

Kids are godly. They're special. Jesus made an allusion to that effect. "Let the little children come to me and do not hinder them for the kingdom of heaven belongs to such as these," Matthew 19:14.

On Easter Sunday April 8, 2007 a little girl called Nana, caused a stir around the family's dining table in Accra Ghana. None of the parents saw this coming. There were guests in the house too. It was a question deemed as adults' and not kids...

But the little girl had her finger on the trigger. The spirit had influenced her to 'disturb' the table. Nana had picked up the salt shaker. She sprinkled a little salt on her food and then remarked: "Hmmm it takes so yummy now."

Minutes later everyone on the table asked Nana to pass it on to them. She did and then gifted her dad this: "Dad what would you do if you were salt?

All the faces around the table including her dad's wore surprise and disbelief. They'd least anticipated such a question from such little one.

Salt is condiment for food. It is the substance or the mineral that makes our foods taste good. That element is called seasoning. It adds value and flavor to the meal and makes it taste 'yummy' to borrow

Nana's word. Not only that, it also serves as a preservative stuff, makes our foods stay longer and not go bad. Even the word salary takes it origin from the Latin word salt because the Roman legions were sometimes paid in salt.

Across the world in ancient times salt had been used as source of payment. And in many contexts in the Bible salt is used metaphorically, signifying— permanence, purification, usefulness, value, wisdom etc. Fact is we as humans have all the qualities salt possesses. We have those qualities in abundance but perhaps we've failed to let those characters in us play their roles.

The reality is we risk losing our saltiness and would ultimately be good for nothing, if things stay as they are. Now back to Nana's question.

First of all, let's not kid ourselves to think that we are going to be here on (Earth) forever. We're mortal beings, we live to die. But until death comes we have time on our side to be kind, to be merciful, to be forgiving and to show love and give love. We have the opportunity to be a 'Good Samaritan' of a kind. We've the opportunity to touch lives and save lives.

That's all it takes. It's all about love. You can't gossip about me, if you love me. Love isn't hateful, love forgives, love cares and shares, love is merciful, love is peaceful, love comforts, love listens, and love feels and love acts.

Nana acted at the opportune time. Everyone on the dining table needed salt but they felt reluctant to do so, until the little girl took the mantle and showed them the light. Your act of giving must know no boundaries. Continue to do the good deeds, because you never know when the Lord is coming back.

Be the salt of the earth. Add value to lives and let your flavor be felt. Also place your service at the doors of the needy, the hungry the lost and the poor. By doing so, you'd turn lives around, shape futures and make lives meaningful and useful. Salt preserves foods, so use your God given talents to redeem souls.

Afehyiapa!

This is my hamper my humble hamper. It mimics the story of this man and many others. But it doesn't compare. It doesn't compare a friend of mine who lost his Mum this past Wednesday: My deepest condolence to you again Mr. Daniel Ato Aidoo, President Ghana Institute of Journalism Association of North America (GIJANA). And it doesn't compare the many that my eyes saw, ears heard and my heart felt this year.

So I will tell this man's story, rather than mine.

There was a man in tarps who always tucked himself in a little corner near Yakima avenue and 11th street around Hilltop, in Tacoma Washington State. He asked for alms and begged for foods. He was homeless, jobless and near to nakedness.

The weather was freaky cold outside when I chanced upon him. It'd scaled down to a single digit. Frigid! Yet he sat in that rough condition. Not too far away from his little kingdom he'd witnessed a young man gunned down by someone. Too close to him a woman and her four children had a terrible accident.

Right around him, he'd seen too much. He'd his ears full each passing day. Those who passed by to drop some change into his wobbly hands shared too much with him. They'd all been there and seen it all: Like how they lost it all but got back on their feet. Some had attempted suicides. They came too close to that, but they pulled it all back together.

Touched by their stories the homeless guy made his mind up to turn a new leaf, change his ways and put all the pieces back together. On that fateful cold day from morning to about six in the evening, he'd some change. It was two dollars fifty cents.

So, while strolling down the street he decided to go to a corner store at the vicinity and get some pop/soda. But he changed his mind right there. He bought a power ball lottery ticket and stashed it in his ragged wallet. That was a winning ticket worth $175 million.

He was back on the street, back to do same old stuff— his usual spot, at the little corner sitting on a goldmine. No clue, no hope but compelled to cope the sting weather. He'd faith to buy the ticket but perhaps he didn't believe he could be the eventual winner. Perhaps forgetfulness had stolen his mind. However destiny was spouting its long waited glory.

And month after month he was ravaged by the harsh weather. But spring was coming. Spring was on its way like a whirl wind...

Haven't you noticed all the trees around you shed their leaves during autumn/fall?

Yes they do. And then comes spring—the trees get a new look, new life with new beginning.

Man in tarps had alas found his winning ticket. His whole life has changed for the best. He's risen from the depth of poverty to the height of wealth. The distance between him and poverty is a billion miles away. He'd his four tyres grounded but they're now back on road, pumped up like never before.

Life is good, so let's stand firm when we get beaten by hardships. Let's continue to be faithful to our Maker and let's strive to be strong even when we take the hardest knock.

Never think you're the only one, head down under the water. You're not alone in the mess so don't beat yourself down too much. There are many—some in bad situation, some worse condition and still some in a worst state. However, they still smile, feel blessed that another day has found them.

We began 2015 like a wall clock. We ticked and we tocked. Tick-tock, tick-tock: The seconds moved into minutes, minutes switched into hours, hours transformed into days and days crawled into weeks, weeks into months and months morphed into years. It's an annual cycle but the events and happenings could be different.

Too many of us have unclaimed winning tickets. It's our money so let's go get it. Lots of us are sitting on gold mines. It's our gold so let's go mine it!

It's time for revelation... Whatever you stashed deep into your pockets, wallets and purses will be found. Whatever you lost in 2015, you'll get it double or quadrupled in 2016. If it's sickness you're trading it with wellness. Everything deemed negative will be positive as we're approaching the New Year.

Mema Mo nyinaa Afehyiapa'!
Merry Christmas to you all!
Joyeux Noel a vous!
Feliz Navidad a tados!
Buon Natale a tutti voi

Geseende Kersfees ann juvulle almal!
Frohe Weihnachten euch allen!

Got your Miracle (s) yet?

Miracles are not oracles. Oracles are used as channels to seek answers to mysteries. They're prophecies and forewarnings. Miracles are not spectacles. Spectacles are objects that enhance visions. They can be show offs and displays.

Miracles are not pinnacles. Pinnacles are high points of things. They're summits. You may call them mountains, zeniths, apexes etc. They've pins in their name but don't stab. Miracles are not debacles. Debacles are things considered disastrous, catastrophes and tragedies.

Miracles are not chronicles. Chronicles are records, they're histories, and they're journals. Miracles are not pickles. Pickles are plights, difficulties and they can be scrapes. Miracles are not fickle. Fickle is being indecisive. A fickle mind is like a hanging bell—always swinging. It follows the wind's direction.

Miracles are not bicycles. If they were we'd ride them. Miracles are not articles. Articles are features or write-ups. They also can be courses, trainings and apprenticeships. Miracles are not tentacles. Tentacles are feelers and limbs. Miracles are not nickels. If they were everybody would pick a nickel to buy a popsicle.

Miracles are like spikes that trigger wonders. Miracles are seals of a divine mission. They are vehicles that create sensational scenes, phenomenal results and jaw breaking outcomes. Here are few biblical miracles:

The crossing of the Red Sea, Lazarus' resurrection, the hemorrhage woman, the Blind Bartimus, the feeding of the five-thousand, the resurrection of Tabitha, the ten plagues of Egypt, the burning bush, Jonah and the whale, the man with the dropsy hand, the Shunamite woman and her son and many more.

How about our time?

Miracles are still happening. They aren't done yet and they won't be done in our generation:—the plane that landed on the Hudson River in New York (Jan 15, 2009), The Brazilian Grandma and her grandson who survived after being ran over by a car... Not a scratch was found on them. The amazing Russian woman who lived to deliver a stunning number of 69 babies, yet like Samson's mother her name is not known. Samson's father was called Manoah.

The Russian woman who lived from 1707-1782 was married to Feodor Vassilyev a peasant from Shuya. Tell me if this isn't a miracle what else would qualify?

She gave birth to sixteen pair of twins, seven sets of triplets, and four sets of quadruplets. Incredibly, 67 of her children survived infant mortality, which was prevalent at the time.

My family is a living testimony: on Monday morning June 15, God miraculously saved my children from an ominous accident on their way to school in Accra Ghana.

A heavily-loaded sand truck rammed into their car. But they all escaped unhurt. It wasn't a minibus as I'd earlier posted on my Facebook. It was a sand truck!

Some people get their miracles at home. Some receive them in the streets. Miracles walk to some individuals. Others have to chase them. From coast to coast people globetrot for miracles. It takes days for some, others get them after decades.

It took a crippled 36 years to meet his miracle. He was limited by his condition. He watched many come by day after day, week after week, and year after year to get healing in a pond.

Until he met the great one, Jesus himself: It took him three decades and six. But it did happen. He waited. He stayed put. Same spot for 36 years.

Your's is on its way!

Goodluck!

A blip from a lip can flip an ultimate result. And when it does, it breeds— shock, suspense, sadness, happiness, fame, shame, victory, defeat and many more. It was all Steve Harvey's fault. And he called it a 'horrible mistake'. His lip had done perhaps TV's biggest upset ever.

The 2015 Miss Universe host nearly reduced the size of a great pageant to that of an ant. Mr. Harvey on Sunday December 20, '15 evening mistakenly declared Miss Colombia, Ariadna Gutierrez winner, when she was the first runner-up.

Miss Ariadna couldn't wait a second: First she raised Colombia's flag, gave a hug, and received flower bouquet. Next was a clinched fist, followed by a kiss in the air, waved to a cheering crowd and then the ultimate crown. But that jubilation was short-lived. Like a knife put in butter her newly-fangled joy was shredded.

Back on stage was Steve the man with the gavel— back with the real deal- sounding apologetic:

"Ok folks ah there's....I have to apologise....the first runner is Colombia. Miss Universe 2015 is the Philippines."

I will take responsibility for this. It was my mistake....please don't hold it against the ladies."

Pia Alonzo Wurtzbach, the contestant from the Philippines had won. Her whole demeanor was custom-made. She stood very cool as they waited for the final verdict. And even after the first upset and the ultimate prize, Pia celebrated with shock and disbelief.

Like biblical Isaac she couldn't understand how quickly the event turned on her favour.

"What?" she mouthed... awestruck, as Steve came back to rewrite the report.

In the book of Genesis chapter 22 a miracle happened. There was surprise!

Abraham and his son Isaac were heading to the land of Moriah up on the mountains to offer a burnt offering (a sacrifice) to God. Isaac noticed there was nothing to be sacrificed. So he asked his dad like any inquisitive child would do:

Hey Dad Where is the lamb for the sacrifice. Where is it?

And his dad Abraham replied: "God will provide..."

The irony is that Isaac had no idea he was to be sacrificed. On his part, Abraham hanged on faith, the abstract noun. He trusted the Man who'd asked him to make the sacrifice. He knew his God wasn't a pagan god.

Up on the mountain he got his beloved son Isaac bound ready to slit his throat, but out of nowhere, there was lamb and God asked him to sacrifice it instead of Isaac.

Didn't Jacob steal his brother Esau's birth right?

Esau sold it, one would argue, but it had already been pre-destined. There are times we go: This is it!

The reason we've expended so much energy and time—burn the midnight candles and did all the sacrifices we could yet, things don't work out as expected. Or you think you've got it all wrapped up especially, when the first storm has passed you by. Let's wait till we see the red tide settles. Life is so complicated.

I don't think there was a loser in last night's mega show. Both girls are beautiful and they've got something to cheer. For Miss Philippines it would seem like the lamb in the bush, whereas Miss Colombia would see it as a stolen birth right.

Howbeit, it is what it is. There's always a lamb in the thicket, as there's always a real winner behind a first runner-up. This wasn't a marginal error in a survey. It was Steve Harvey's error and it produced the biggest drama and upset!

Little Rock

It was a crime in this mining town (with a population of about 25,000 people) to let loose one's dog to wander in the streets. Law breakers were heavily fined and if one failed to pay the penalty s/he was put behind bars. Little Rock was once known for its love for the four-legged friends.

But not anymore...such reputation was fast disappearing like a sun sinking deep in the horizon at the twilight.

"It never used to be like this back in the day, when one could jog with her dog or walk it out without any fears, "a passerby whispered.

New king means new law the town had enstooled a new king. But little did they know they'd given power to a tyrant—one who would turn their day into night and make lives miserable for them. During his installation he'd promised to be just, fair and kind to the people. Sadly, it was just a lip-service. His first one hundred days in the palace had been nothing but high-handedness.

He'd ruffled many feathers and sent quivers down the spines of many more.

Many were flogged and went to jail for the offence. No one benefitted the usual second chance. And those who disobeyed his orders were banished forever. He'd earlier threatened to ban dogs from being bred or reared in the town. And then there was a U-turn, having realised that the idea was unpopular and could backfire. Not only that but also, he feared it might cost his ascension to the imperial throne.

Consequently, He toned down his language and tweaked his statement.

"I'm not banning dogs, you can keep them." He'd set a booboo trap. They couldn't read between the lines and they soon fell for it. He was a tiger in a sheep cloth and he revealed it menacingly when he finally got power from the people.

Scores faced his wrath among them a widow. Her two bulldogs had been let loose. They'd crossed the red line. Ninja and spider had been taken captive. They wouldn't see their owner again. About half hour later the poor woman was summoned before the elders at the palace. Her fate was immediately known——the pets would be killed plus an imminent imprisonment hanged over her head, if she failed to pay the fine.

As she watched in consternation Ninja and Spider were killed. She pled for mercy since she lived on a breadline but the elders wouldn't budge. The king had asked the guards to carry her away: Away to the penitentiary.

She'd long envisioned what was to come so on her way to the palace the widow hid her only jewelry on her cloth. Should it come down to the wire she would pawn it to save her life.

"Your majesty," the widow cried. "Would his royal highness accept this from his subject (jewelry passed down four generations before me)?"

The trinkets were worth almost a million dollars!

"Hahaha, you're now talking. Hurry and bring it over," he laughed hysterically.

But that would be his last laugh. Citizens of Little Rock had had enough. It was time for a revolt. Truly, the frog croaks when the small sac in its throat can no longer hold water. The nonsense was too much. And too soon, men, women and children armed with clubs, machetes, bows and arrows would fill the town's main street on a warpath to the palace.

The king had fooled many and it was time for him to be fooled too. His reign had been derailed. His henchmen, the guards and some of the elders had fled even before the mob made their way inside the palace.

When you surround yourself with fools and the greed they've nothing to offer you except shame and destruction. Luck evaded him and he was killed.

The widow got her jewelry back. The tyrants couldn't take it away in their haste to escape the onslaught. Those incarcerated for years got their freedoms back— got lives back together and made it in a grand style. The banished returned home.

They said no more to tyrannical rule and goodbye to the evil that descended upon their once peaceful loved town. Furthermore, the ban on dogs was lifted immediately...Indeed out of bad had come something good something worth celebrating.

Little Rock was back on her feet!

I guess you all know who good leaders are:

Good leaders aren't bullies. They love their people and are tolerant. They aren't selfish. They're selfless and do not arrogate power to themselves. Good leaders don't spew hateful words. They're mindful of what to say, filter what to speak and censor themselves before they mount public daises.

Good leaders don't give empty promises. They fulfill them. They're not scaremongers they're peace makers. They're not big-headed. They are charming and loved by many.

So, don't get pawned by the greed and the haughty, look out for the red flags, check the right lists, take the right decisions and the right choices and make the right move. Listen and listen well, when in doubt cross check or double check. Don't just listen to stuff and run with it. Remember, you're making a lifelong decision– a decision that can help or hurt you tomorrow.

Hello!

Tired and wants to give up?

Don't Give Up, 'cos if you give up you can't live up.

Keep crawling if that's the only defence you have. Crawl on your feeble knees to safety, because your enemies are not tired yet. Be reminded every inch you take in your flee is crucial as they ruthlessly pursue you. Slowly but sure, crawl like a tortoise and be wise. You should never look back.

Yeah, backward never forward ever!

Keep walking…you should walk the walk– surely walk your way out of danger. When they press hard to find you—you should walk harder in their haste and duck down under the rock. And like a little bug keep mute to outfox them.

Remember it's not over until it's over!

Keep running…run as fast as Carl Lewis. Run as much as your commanding legs can run and carry you through. Indeed, your strong legs need no fuel to keep you going– all you need is sterling stamina, unbroken strength and unfettered power. Therefore, run the good run— continue to run. And as fast as they run after you, the faster you'll run away from them. If they run faster, you'll run the fastest run.

The faster you run the safer!

Keep riding...In their pursuit to track you down you'll ride high on the back of the untiring horse, whose pace is unmatched by any beast. So, be bold, be poised, be determined and keep riding...

Your pursuer is angrier!

Keep flying...fly on the wings of the wind. On the imperious wings of the flying Eagle you'll find refuge. He will soar above your enemies. Fly you to a safe haven. Fly you to paradise. Fly you to the Holy and the peaceful place. Fly you to the everlasting kingdom. A Kingdom of no worries, a kingdom devoid of troubles, hustles and bustles.

Always remember to count on Him. When the going gets rough and tough you know who to fall on— He's your forever bronze wall.

Forever and ever count on Him!

Tattoos N Looks

Don't judge the ink man for what he wears and how he looks.

Looks can be deceptive. Looks are like books' covers, they may appear unattractive outside.

But inside may have good stuff, pool of knowledge and food for the brain.

Is there one who has more tattoos on herself than a Zebra?

The majestic beast has black and white stripes that extend from every part of its body except the stomach and inner thighs. The lines look good on the Zebra and humanity admires her. Yet, we're quick to judge when we see similar lines on humans. We even frown on them.

Why?

Why are we so quick to judge people?

Is it because they've what we don't have?

Or is it, sheer jealousy?

Who made us judges upon them?

And who told you, you're the only good man left on planet EARTH Mr. Perfect?

Some like it black. Some like it black- black. Some like it white. Some like it white-white. Some like cold and some like it pro- old. Don't get your knickers in a twist for merely seeing someone's tattoos on her body. Their meanings may be different from what you might've thought.

From head to toe their portrayals may vary. Some carry them for lost beloved ones; some wear them to express affection, some tattoo for the love of it, some just do it to show off –go starkers etc.

Tattoos have been of old. Tools for tattoos have traced its existence as far back in the upper Paleolithic or the Neolithic period. Never met Otzi the Iceman but it's understood– the oldest discovery of tattooed human skin to date is found on the body of this Ink man dating to between3370 and 3100 (4th millennium) BC.

Otzi the Iceman had 61 carbon-ink tattoos, consisting of 19 groups of lines, simple dots and lines on his lower spine, left wrist, behind, the knees and the ankles.

So if you think tattoos are just 21 century craze thing, you've got it all warped. Allow all of them to grow together. It would be premature to start uprooting the ones you consider to be bad and therefore cannot weather the storm. There's reason for the season.

The Schism

Unity we stand divided we fall. I grew up with this mantra and I've imbibed every detail of its essence and philosophical implication. Unity has several symbolisms but the one that's stuck with me over the years is the broom.

The broom is commonly used to sweeping dirt and cleaning stuff.

Apart from its symbolism it also has cultural dimension. The Metis people of Canada have a broom dancing tradition. The dancing exhibition draws people from all walks of life to show off their skills. It's fun to watch.

'Jumping the broom' is a wedding tradition that originated in marriages of slaves in the United States in the 19th century.

In Africa, particularly Ghana the broom represents unity. And it appears every African child growing up is handed this wise saying: "It's much easier to break a stick fiber than the whole bunch"— a symbol which underpins the necessity for humanity to live in oneness rather than being divided.

Unity is important. Unity is indispensable. And unity is the bedrock of nations' growth and their survivability. Jesus encapsulated that in the synoptic gospels during his ministry: "Every kingdom divided against itself is brought to desolation, and every city or house divided against itself shall not stand," Matthew 12:25 (KJV).

But it seems today's world is doing the opposite. The walls between humans have increasingly become stronger than concrete walls with barbed wires built at our nations' borders. We tear down artificial walls, build and solidify human walls leaving in its trail— tribal wars, sectarian wars, ethnic wars and wars between/ among nations.

When the Berlin wall in Germany came down in 1990, the whole world celebrated it. That wall divided Berlin from 1961 to 1989 constructed by German Democratic Republic (GDR). And since its collapse the east and the west have been living together resulting –a stronger Germany in terms of economic growth.

Oh how easy it is to tear down artificial walls…our society has failed to forge unity among ourselves. As division is painstakingly sowing the seeds of hatred, enmity, selfishness, cruelty, malice, wickedness, terror, confusion, rancor, racism, sectarianism, cronyism, nepotism.

Brothers and sisters have become enemies. The common phrase now is—Friends today enemies tomorrow. No one cares about nobody. And nobody dares to care. The schism has grown horns with different colours. It has deepened so much so that fathers no longer trust their sons. Mothers hate their daughters and citizens no longer trust their governments.

In the traditional settings subjects have revolted against their kings and chiefs, while servants have turned against their masters.

Everything seems to be affected by the trending disease. Nobody seems to see eye to eye with the other.

There are social walls, cultural walls, walls of colour and walls of class. There are walls of ideology, personality walls, race walls, and faith walls. There are black and black walls, walls between Latinos and

Latina, walls in marriage, walls even in churches. May the Lord have mercy on us.

The Spider (Ananse)

Give him dirty looks and he'll shrug them off!

In fact, if labeling kills, the African folklore king—Kwaku Ananse (the Spider) would be dead by now. He's shrewd, street smart and stubborn. His idiosyncratic artwork has won him many appellations such as 'Ahuntahunu' which literally means all-knowing, 'Ahoampamgyeine' meaning ubiquitous and 'Ahuabobirim' — a name that evokes trepidation.

Ananse has universally earned his name as the webmaster and commander in chief in craftsmanship. For centuries he has featured in mythology, culture and symbolism. He also exudes command and respect, particularly in African folklore and Greek mythology.

Irrefutably, the African folktale would be a piecemeal without featuring such a doyen character. Ananse is a character who dazzles, swindles and delights many. And he does so with perseverance and impeccable patience.

I should think it'd be better to allow the great man speak for himself. So, Kwaku the ball is now in your court...

Thank you Akwasi...that's nice of you. See, some folks have gone bald (like the vulture). This is why I say– if you can't take it, better don't go get it!

Lend me your ears folks. Let's start with a question: Who speaks for the dead man?

Certainly it's his ghost. I've got it all wrapped up in my good size 'coconut'. You know what they say about me— a prankster, mischief and malice. But I'm like a dead goat. I've got a thick skin: A skin that's shock-absorbing and absurdity-proof.

Those who don't know will know it today. I've been robbed time and again. Booed time after time and tossed over and over again.

The sages are right: 'If you keep your mouth shut you'd get a warped haircut.'

I've got a woman and three children. We work in unison to keep our heritage, safeguard our security and sustain our livelihood. We work around the clock. And we have estates all around the world most of them skyscrapers.

On my thin chest I hold their names—like playing cards. I reserve the right to keep their names 'cos they're minors. Anyway, I'll only release them as my punch line, so hold your horses.

They're beautiful and cheerful. They say like Father like son. But some say they look like their mother. They say they say always they say. They never tell you the source of their story.

My template (s) has been used year in year out. Yet I get no credit for it. You heard me right, my artwork has been plagiarised countless times. I make the African kings and Queens look majestic and beautiful in their Bonwire Kent clothes.

In the Far East, China has bastardised my patent right. She's copied Ghana— the home of Kente. But Ghana has also stolen from me. And the whole world has done what everyone has done to me.

Every fatty animal mimics the piggery. The secret of creation is embedded in my artistic worlds. That's how God made me. Just like he gave to the little ant —an unsurpassed wisdom and asked mankind to go to him and learn its ways.

Textile weaving, spinning, basketry, knot-work, crocheting and net-making all originated from my secretive art work.

So, if Man thinks he knows it all, let him bury his head in shame. There are more hidden from humanity. I still have the treasure trove. Consider the terminologies—the World Wide Web and the internet, they all educe the inter-connectivity of my web.

Not a single soul here on earth can deny the fact that he or she hasn't copied my unique artwork. However, I've become a laughing stock and public ridicule.

Everybody hunts right?

But when Kwaku hunts he's labeled a crook, a trickster and a thief. I set my traps and lie in wait just like every hunter does, yet my style has been questioned and challenged. I have learnt something in this world —whatever you do they'll talk about you.

My maker told me this from creation: "Kwaku Entie Obiaa," to wit Kwaku don't listen to anybody. You've the stage so play your part. Those who don't know will know it today. My wife's name is Okonore Yaa. For ages Okonore and I have been working hard to take care of our children- Ntekuma, Tirikenekene (Humpty-Dumpty), and Nankronwhea (skimpy-leggy).

And with our powers combined we're stronger than even the famous Planetiers. Bottom-line, we aren't crooks as many suggest. We are smart, shrewd and enigmatic (SSE). I am Kwaku Ananse, my name remains unchanged.

The Crab

Who Am I?

It was dubbed the 'gathering for all' —small or big we arrived at the mall. The fearsome and the giants had taken their seats. In twos, in threes and in large groups they trooped in. Saul was there and Paul was the MC.

Paul is tall and so he towered everybody. Nobody cared about his habit of smoking as he fished into his breast pocket for Pall Mall cigarette. I was overwhelmed by the numbers that showed up.

One by one we lined up —to greet the giants at the dais.

The King was there. And the Queen was there too!

Miles away the throbbing sounds of the giant 'Fontonfrom' drums travelled. The trumpeters trumpeted and the vuvuzelas blared. The dancers pranced and the singers sang. Line by line we surged to the podium.

Paul called for calm as we pressed forward to greet the overlords. One after the other we approached the stage. Alas I'd made it. Face to face I'd made it there. I stretched forth my hand for handshakes but they wouldn't budge. None would look me in the eye. The reason, they wouldn't tell.

But Paul would even heighten their fears. With his baritone voice he'd spread the word. All along I never knew many dreaded me including the giants. Kids at the mall began to flee and their moms in their flight sought refuge at the town hall.

But Who Am I?

I have walking and swimming legs. My pincers or chelae are used to seize and subdue my prey. That's how I eat to live. Truth be told, my handshakes aren't pleasant. They seem stroppy and uninviting. But that's about me. That's who I am.

I'm like anybody gathered here. I have two eyes small though, and I have a heart just like you.

My shoulders are broad and my joints are adaptable as the caterpillars'. I've got stomach, intestines, mouth, short and long antenna—used for sensing danger.

I don't count myself out and I won't succumb to pressure 'cos I know I belong here.

Call me an amphibian.

Why?

I live both on the land and in the oceans.

Though many say they don't like me. They don't like me because they can't handle me.

My meat is laced in my bone. To eat me, I must be broken into pieces. Indeed broken with pliers and hammers, even though I'm not that big and my carapace isn't bronze. .

My handshakes are fiercely detested because my claws and pincers are as sharp as the Eagle's talon.

Now you know who I am. I'm a crab and my delicacy is in my bone. My Maker made me for a reason. His handiwork is just awesome and handsome. So, just be grateful for who YOU ARE— because even the giants fear you: plus you've got something they can never take away.

Be Blessed Always!!

MALI—The Twenty-One

Drowned by tears: Robed in sorrow...

Her streets littered with grief. Echoes of pain beat the four walls of her corridors. She'd lost 21 of her household members. 21 mauled by guns, 21 from across the world. Their missions truncated. Walls riddled with bullets. Doors slammed like tremors...Fear gripped each soul.

It was a chaotic scene. They were holidaying at an upscale hotel (Radisson Blu) in the Sahel region of West Africa. Targeted by the Enemies of Life: Oblivious of the looming danger. And in a spell of moment the enemies would strike.

They'd done it again!

In Mali's capital city, Bamako, tourists, from Turkey, India, China, Israel, Belgium and the US had come under the enemies' attacks. Armed to the teeth they massacred them. Some of them were businessmen/women, some of them were revelers and some of them were diplomats. This is how their life journey ended.

Twenty-one murdered in cold blood, 21 mauled by guns.

May their souls Rest in Peace.

Once a Tiger...

The entire forest is glum. The daily hustles have gone dead, likewise the night escapades. No one goes out, no one comes in. All activities grounded except one man. Only one man is seen jockeying to and fro.

Mighty Tiger ('Osebo' aka 'Krotwamansa' in Akan Twi) is at it— roaming and roving, looking for a prey. The red-eyed beast must eat by any means necessary.

But who's going to be at his knife's edge?

Hours of fruitless search has triggered the Tiger's ferocious rampage resulting— coughing, puffing and huffing. Luck seems to evade him today. He sprays urine and marks trees as he surges.

His weeks of going rogue (terrorising the unfortunate ones) in the animal kingdom have compelled many to seek refuge elsewhere: Elsewhere far from his range. For security reasons even those who aren't at risk flee.

The rodents have ducked very low in their holes. The monkeys have taken cover too. And the medium-sized animals, which he commonly preys upon, have travelled way beyond his territory—covering 60 to 100 kilometres (23 to 39 square miles).

The charismatic beast has become more frustrated, very hungry very angry. He roars and moans as he moves along. He takes his predatory swagger into the waters notably the rivers, the streams and the lakes, but after swimming for several hours there's no catch.

His reflexes seem to have gotten the better of him. The vulnerable animals perhaps, have learnt their lessons well. As patience runs to the eastern door, frustration takes over her imposing throne.

Man must eat! Plan B must be rolled out!

Dressed in white cloth (symbolism for repentance in the animal kingdom), he decides to go to the king—Elephant, declaring: 'Your highness, I hereby declare before you that henceforth I won't terrorise my neighbours and I won't prey on them."

"Sounds altruistic ', says the king.

"But tell me how you would cope in the days ahead?"

"Well, I hope to cope…. I pledge to stay calm and stay focused."

The king takes tiger's pronouncement at its face value. And a few hours later a big summit is convened. The seemingly great news is announced. Tiger is asked to make his decision known to the gathering. He grabs the megaphone amidst sobs.

Obviously they're nothing, but crocodile's tears:

"I Tiger alias Krotwamansa, this day do promise not to terrorise any animal or animals here in the kingdom. I pray to be law-abiding and stay calm in my reclusive place."

Hundreds hail his statement, describing it as significant. However, many remain sceptical. The elders say, if you aren't familiar with death just look at a napping person. Only time will tell.

Meanwhile, under the canopy, where the tiger family is seated the cubs and their mothers (with drawn faces) wail hysterically. They question:

How can we survive Papa?

What kind of declaration is this?

"God will provide," remarks the tiger. He looks over his shoulders, assuring the family to take heart and not be discouraged.

Soon the summit is over and every attendee leaves. The historic declaration has become the talk of the town. The deer, the antelope, the elk, the reindeer and all the medium-sized animals share the news as they head home.

Trouble trouble those who trouble trouble. And the dare devils among them would soon smell the rat. They would face the tiger's music courtesy of curiosity and inquisition. The tiger family has somehow not reneged on the great declaration made at 'Ogyakrom'.

Two days gone by without marauding. Two days starving the little ones.

But he remains focused in the hope that the Great Provider will provide.

Is there a way to spot wrong choices?

They say everyone makes mistakes regarding life choices and heads down the wrong path. The deer family is treading down that wrong path. They've made the boldest decision to visit the Tiger. And their mission is to offer felicitations and praises to the rogue.

Yes, the tiger's den has been declared a safe haven but who will dare go in there…the deers are daring, the deers are going. And danger is looming. Before they could say jack all of them have been rounded up.

The incident has gone viral. The king is troubled upon receiving the news, and the super powers—the lion, the buffalo, the hyena, the bison etc. are all dumbfounded. Immediate action must be taken to stop the carnage. Nonetheless, the powerful are well aware; they aren't dealing with an ordinary brat.

How do you deal with a rogue? Negotiate, make a treaty or lock horns with him?

That remains to be seen. In the meantime let's do sober reflection.

Let's always look before we leap. Let's mind our own business… and where our support is needed let's think twice before we act. Let's not invite troubles home if we can help prevent their occurrence. Let's be careful in our dealings with other folks, other peoples and other worlds. Let's not play smart and not be clever. Let's hope for the better.

Let's remember, once a tiger always a tiger.

The Head

The head isn't big but she carries so many loads.

In her dwells the mind (computer). Within her things get done and undone. She has so much to think about. So many things to do... Though she's not as big as the elephant, its contents perhaps weigh more than the giant in the forest.

....So why take a scorn at someone's load?
Knew ye not that everyone knows the weight of his load?

Only the carrier knows it all. And it's only him who bears it all. For he who carries it feels it as he who feels it also tastes it. Ain't no joke in joking with one's load... Don't belittle one's burden, if you have no knowledge of how much his load weighs.

Our stress levels aren't the same. Our problems vary too. Some are light weight and some are eye-popping.... But they all wear the burden shoes. Sometimes you feel like giving up, sometimes you feel like a blob, because you can't bear it any longer.

Oftentimes, the results are the same. Many times the solutions just don't fit. Ships and airplanes offload their loads at certain point in time. But the head carries her load year in year out.

It took only one Man to do all the wonderful things in the universe. Our God is great and he's a master designer.

Be blessed always!

The Fiery Soul

Inside a man lives a willing soul always fired up: A soul so willing to do the best for Mankind.

Ever ready to fulfill Man's dreams to the fullest: Always upbeat to raise Man's hopes to the highest.

Need a friend?

Don't worry; you've a true friend right inside you. The greatest companion: The companion of companions. The one who mends broken hearts and sets sullen souls on fire: The soul ever ready to lead and guide you but not to mislead you into a ditch.

When we weary He's as fiery as ever. Make a date with him. And be blessed always!

Where's Utopia?

I'm not looking for Utopia.

She must be farfetched. And I don't want to wait in vain. I'm looking for a young Morning basking in beauty and unity. A morning clad in PEACE and CALM. I look forward to seeing a quiet Afternoon brimming with the GRACE smile and crowned with MERCY.

I'm all set for an untroubled evening. An evening devoid of barbarism, hooliganism, vandalism, satanism, bloodbath, pandemonium, you name it.

I'm ever ready to meeting with a Night– marching side by side with LOVE, humility and sympathy. I look forward to welcoming a new Dawn with a new JOY. An unbridled joy, an absolute calm, a peace that flows like a river, grace that floats over my crown down to my toes, mercy that calms nerves, a sympathy that understands my fate and a love that transcends it all:

That's what I'm looking for. Not Utopia.

Wednesday couldn't make the journey. A young morning suffered violence. And violence overtook her violently. She was just eleven 11 Pacific Time. Her journey derailed. At least 14 killed more than 17 seriously wounded. More guns more dead.

San Bernardino, California becomes the second mass shooting (after Sandy hook elementary school) in the US and 355th in 2015 #ALONE.

My thoughts and prayers go to the injured and the bereaved families. May their souls Rest in Peace.

Be Blessed Always!

Beware & Share

BEWARE of what you SHARE…But why do we share?
We share because we CARE. WE don't Share to SCARE.
We share because we are AWARE of your NIGHTMARE.
We don't share to PARE. We share to ensure your WELFARE.
We share to give you a THOROUGHFARE and not to ENSNARE.
We PREPARE and DARE to SHARE. That's why we SHARE.
We don't COMPARE when we SHARE.
We DECLARE in our hearts to SHARE and DARE in our minds to SHARE.
And we will always SHARE.
Neighbour, did you know that God's Angels count every step you take?
Did you know they measure the words that come forth of your mouth?
Did you know the Angels weigh each breath you breathe?
I ask, do you've any idea how much God treasures you?
And do you know how many Angels he deploys each day and night to guard you?
Do you know Satan hates you because God loves you?
Please never stop to count your blessings each day and every night because GOD hasn't stopped loving you and pouring his amazing grace upon you.
And you'll always be loved.

Poor Man

Rains pour when the poor man's bread is thinning.
But his troubles double when they fail to rain.
The poor man's world runs on an empty tank.
And the rains ahead remain a mirage.
How'd he not figure out what was to come?
Why'd the rains fail to make his day glow?
Heavens have locked up the rains gate.
And hell has run amok.

Dawn to dusk he toils his pity soul, yet everything seems to go down below.
Slowly but sure he finds himself in the ghettoes.
All too soon his night is troubled by the mosquitoes.
And so soon his solitary state deepens his woes.
Everything beautiful seems ugly to him and anything colourful is colourless at his sight.
His binocular eyes search all around him for manna, as his empty belly roars like a lion.
His bony knees quiver when his needs become much needed.
And his anxiety peaks when the night draws nigh.
Bells chime because they're hungry.
Strangely their dinging sounds are nuisance to others.
Guns don't ring unless they're triggered and angered.
Lo and behold, the dogs are barking. And down the alley the cops are backing.
Guns drawn!
Their presence stirs his anger…. Yep, an angry man is a hungry mouth.
Step by step danger looms. Evidently nothing scary scares him any longer.
His appetite for pills knows no bound.
But down the hills his loving soul is soon stolen!

The Uncut

Can't cut the hand that feeds the mouth, if you do you'd be starved to death. Can't cut the nose that fronts the face, if you do you'd smite the face. Can't cut the butt that wears the pant, if you do you'd become a shapeless being.

Can't cut! You simply cannot cut!

Can't cut the bond that cements the family, if you do you'd become a hermit. Can't cut the line that generates the power if you do there'd be pitch darkness (Dumsor). Can't cut the shaft that brings forth the nations, if you do you'd be disobeying God's decree…

Can't cut! You simply cannot cut!

Can't cut the tree that provides the shade, if you do you'd have a barren land. Can't cut the tape that has the soundbite, if you do you'd kill its originality. Can't cut the cloth that covers the front-gate, if you do you'd become an exhibitionist.

Can't cut! You simply cannot cut!

Can't cut the barrel that stores the water, if you do there'd be thirst. Can't cut the fist that throws the punch, if you do you'd leave the ring face-disfigured. Can't cut the chain that supplies the strength, if you do you'd be a weakling.

Can't cut! You simply cannot cut!

Can't cut the line of Peace, can't cut the line of Mercy, can't cut the line of Unity, can't cut the line of Grace, can't cut the line of Salvation, and you can't cut the line of Love. Leave them all uncut, all uncensored, all unedited and all untouched.

Treat each one with respect. Extend love to one another and give everyone what's due him/her.

The Beard

It was a bee's knees. Got many open-mouthed and caused millions to wonder!

Children couldn't resist its flamboyance; women fell head over heels for it. And even men fancied it. Indeed, it was awesome!

Wondering?

... You'll soon get served.

I'm talking about the Aaronic beard. It's been relived over the centuries. Santa wears it every Yuletide and curious children mob him.

Biblical Aaron perhaps, wore the thickest and the longest beard ever on earth during the post-exilic period. His brother Moses carried it too. Likewise Grandpa Abraham, but none compared to that of Aaron.

Of course, no one ever associates Abraham with his beard. He's famously known for his covenant with God. Moses' name is synonymous with the Ten Commandments.

Aaron was a Levi, meaning he was a priest. In the book of Exodus it says: "Anoint Aaron his sons and consecrate them so they may serve me as priests," (EX 30:30). But that priesthood role didn't make him. What made Aaron popular was his distinctive attractive beard.

What is shaping your personality?

How do you want to be remembered?

The Smithsonian has one of the world's strangest artifacts at its National Museum of Natural History. That strange relic is the world's longest beard. And it belongs to Hans Langseth, a Norwegian-born American who immigrated to the United States as a young man.

In 1922 Langseth broke the Guinness Book of World Records, for wearing the longest beard. That beard measured 17 feet 6 inches long. Before his death in 1927 he made a final wish. That his beard be cut off (after his open-casket funeral) and stored for posterity.

His son complied with the dad's wish, kept the beard for years at their home in North Dakota. 'Jack' had stayed in the box for too long so, he decided to hand it over to the Smithsonian for keep. Millions today throng there to see that beard.

We all have something to show. Your little lamp could be the brightest light when it's brought out of the box. See, where one's facial hair has landed him. Little things count. Indeed they matter.

The eagle is known for its ability to soar. Usain Bolt is famous for his swiftness in the athletic discipline. Michael Jackson would ever be remembered for his iconic pop music, the Lyrebird is most distinguished for its great ability to mimic natural and artificial sounds for its environment.

Mother Teresa is remembered for founding the Missionaries of Charity- a Roman Catholic religious congregation. The snail is identified with its snail's pace mannerism; Lionel Messi for his dribbling prowess, LeBron James has made his name in the basketball game arena and my own ubiquitous Anas Aremeyaw Anas Ghana's ace investigative journalist has cut a niche for himself in the field of journalism.

We all can make it anyway. You don't have to be Oprah Winfrey. You've got to be you. And the journey starts from you. Our Creator meant well when he made you and that hasn't changed and it will never change. Be the servants who put their talents into use and got medals for being obedient.

Don't be like the one who hid his talent, for fear that he would be reprimanded by his master, if the business failed.

Remember, you wore neither mustache nor beard at birth. It's innate and you have to nurture it. Let it grow and let it glow.

What is in WAIT?

They say it pays to wait.

WAIT stands for— 'Work Approved Indefinite Triumph', according to goapedia.

Most people view WAIT as a pain in the neck. Some have likened it as bug in a cloak. The longer one's dream takes to come into fruition the more stressful s/he becomes. ….It takes a huge toll on one's self. And the upshot is often unpleasant.

Abraham, meaning father of a multitude (in Hebrew) had to wait for decades to have the promised son –Isaac. I won't bother you with the rest of the story.

The 21st century Man's life has virtually become a doorknob—we labour here we labour there. Left -right, forward-backward. We press hard pass our stress to make way for good fortunes. Yet, our lives seem to be like walking on a treadmill—absolutely going nowhere.

It seems our whole being is systematically configured, working in tandem and keeping pace with the social media mania. Our fingers are as deft as triggers, this time on keyboards. We text at home, we facebook at work, we WhatsApp in bed and we tweet at nights. We IMO, we Viber and we stay on phones for long hours!

But what at all is behind or driving this phenomenon?

It looks as though the trend has been stimulated by broken homes, occupational hazards, lack of trustworthy relationships ,friendships etc. Neighbours today don't talk to/with neighbours. Neighbours have become acquaintances.

In September this year, I said Good morning to a neighbour. His response:

"What's good about the morning?"

His attitude had hit the roof and his demeanor emphasised anger.

Hard to believe nowadays, everybody has become a stranger in his/her own manger.

Even parents have little or no time to spend with their children. They're constantly on the move, moving up and down: Trying to put food on the kitchen table, trying to make ends meet, trying to squeeze water from the rocks.

The question: - *Are we reliving the Mosaic days?*

Harder they try but harder they hit the rock bottom or fall through the cracks. Each passing day mimics the proverbial white elephant.

Try, cuts the shadow of useless and the cycle begets an endless pursuit. Pursuit of happiness appears fading fast as reality and fantasy pick a brawl in the straw.

The hysteria is deafening. You scream your lungs out as if you're sitting in an 'Extreme Scream' or in a 'Wild Cat' at the amusement park.

Gosh, when is this gonna last!

I've got a message for you: Message for those whose faiths never waver.

I challenge you as I do to myself every day to believe that the long wait will soon be over. BUT, don't just believe, do whatever you're capable of doing and do IT.

Sooner very soon, the sea of hardships that overwhelmed you will surrender. Thames shall be tamed and Mississippi will be missing in your life's pathway.

Pretty soon, you'll see the Judases—trouble, sickness, stress, pain, poverty and the likes running helter skelter.

You'll break the jaws of poverty, tear down the walls of pain and ruthlessly uproot the chains of madness, joblessness, homelessness and sickness.

From thereon, you'll see the whelps of the lioness wander in the wilderness. Be bold, stand firm and let nobody push you over. Reload your gun and turn the winless streak into winsome spree. Trade your sickness with happiness and replace the seat of pains with gains.

Alas you'll make a joyful noise saying: "My hard Work has been Approved Indefinitely and Triumph has put his indelible mark on my crown. Remember, there's always a lamb in the bush. Miracles still happen…somebody somewhere in Amsterdam- Holland (like the biblical shunamite woman) received hers over the weekend.

The Old Lady

*****An old lady had many friends. They were many!

They included: Bankers, car dealers, wine makers, dressmakers, hairdressers, cobblers, goldsmiths and a poet. Her kind deeds had travelled beyond the vintage home she dwelt— tucked deep in the slum suburb of the city. She'd no children and lived alone.

Lowly she was seen by many, but every day was a good day for her. And every birthday was like Christmas. At her 75th birthday (Diamond Jubilee), she sat in an old russet chair in front of her home. And as a treat, she gave candies or toffees to kids who passed by (her daily ritual).

Unbeknown to her, the bankers showed up and rained upon her the dollars, the pound sterling and the Euros. At the balcony draped in different colours were the Rose Royce, the Maybach, the Mercedes Benz, and the Cadillacs.

Wines flowed like water and the goldsmiths adorned her with gold and ornaments. In droves, the dressmakers, hairdressers and the cobblers poured in their gifts. She was also serenaded by the symphony orchestra group in the city.

Then followed the poet, his frail hand clutched a piece of paper shaking yet poised. He turned right to look at Paulette (that's her name). It seemed like a hill. Still, he gathered courage to deliver what he'd on the paper.

"This is what I have for you. I wrote this poem for you," he said.

I wrote this poem for you because your hands are dropsy, yet they can reach afar.

You're crippled, but many grip unto you as an anchor.

Even though you're blind, you can see beyond the horizon.

Your heart is broken, yet you've found huge space to accommodate all.
You lived in the woods and thought no one knew about you.
Make hay 'cos today you are out of the woods...
This poem is a poem for all my friends who've already celebrated their birthdays. To those who are celebrating it this month and to those who're yet to celebrate theirs this year—2015. Remember little things count and someone has good thought of you.

'Asem Se Be'

Too little done so much to do Mr. Dolittle....
But what went wrong?
What really set the clock back? How did we get here?
Are we still on the fourth gear? If so, what happened to the first gear you promised the nation?
Sikaman has no more fire in her belly. The nation that once supplied power to neighbouring Togo, Ivory Coast and its environs is now reeling in darkness. Power has gone out of her. She's been touched by Mr. Dolittle and his clueless brigade, rocking the steady boat.
Indeed, darkness has unleashed its intrepid venom upon the proud citizens of Sikaman. And the very things that once stood as sturdy as the northern star are literally falling apart. They're zagging instead of zigging. They're tumbling instead of climbing. Kitchen soups have lost their flavor. Box irons are gradually replacing electric irons. And as the minnows wail, the giants—mining companies, hospitals, universities have joined the chorus.
Seriously, thought of you, has always produced mixed feelings and misgivings.
Doubts about your capabilities to give a sustainable or an uninterrupted power to the people of 'Sikaman' have crescendoed in recent times. The situation has been overwhelming and I dare say the trust reposed in you by the people is waning fast: As fast as a speedy locomotive whose drunken driver has no regard for any mishaps.

Sikaman has been groping in darkness. Pitch darkness has swallowed her. And things are really going bad. From foods, goods to loss of lives, it seems everything isn't working any longer. The tales of Kwaku Ananse has been told repeatedly by the Man with the Hammer. And if you care to know, patience has lost her mojo.

I'm on my way to Sikaman but please drop me at the Palm Wine junction, where Messrs Do-nothing and Do-something have met. There, I have an axe to pick. Yep, I have got an axe to grind. I think we must hammer home where the truth is.

Truth be told, you've let the nation down. You asked the good people of this country to give you chance and in return you'll give them their choice. But what did they get back?

Loads of promises: Empty promises: The tale of Ananse, told in Axim in the south has journeyed all the way to Zanzugutatale in the north. And the 'value' has never changed. Instead, you've doubled down your clueless' promises.

The Boys are tired 'Boys Abre". Their legs have given up on them. The soldiers can no longer march on. Their tarp clothes and tattered boots speak volumes amid the trending catchy commercial by TIGO the cellular company: "Drop that Yam."

Are the people really ready to drop the yam into the dam?

Akosombo dam used to generate 75% of the country's energy. That is no more; the old lady perhaps has outlived her prowess as power has gone out of her too. And since somewhere in 2002, the nation's energy woes have been deepening year after year.

So what can the newly created bureau —Ministry of Power do to change the current situation, (the erratic power supply)?

What's new on the table?

Is this ministry the real deal or are we to look forward to yet another do-nothing agency?

But who is to blame. Is it ECG, GRIDCO, VRA or the Ministry of Energy?

Where does the buck stop?

Some Friends

It doesn't get better till it gets bad.
When it gets better your circle of friends get bigger.
If they're fair-weather friends you're guaranteed of moving from bad
    to worse.
And when it gets worse they'll run helter skelter—from east to west.
Farther and louder news about you will go viral.
A true friend will rather standby you and be there for you.
True friends are arguably better than siblings. But blood is thicker
    than water.
You're like a raw diamond no one notices its beauty till it gets refined
    and starts to glitter.

Time

Crawl when it's time to crawl don't walk. Walk when it's time to walk don't run. Run when it's time to run don't fly. And if you believe you can fly, don't hesitate. Put on your stubborn swagger and fly. Fly with the butterflies, fly with the birds if possible fly with the eagles. That's where you ought to be.

Going Beatitude

Blessed be the Heart that loves and despises hatred
Blessed be the Mind that chooses good over evil
Blessed be the Soul that cries when he sees others in pain
Blessed be the Head that carries/bears the burden of his neighbour
Blessed be the Eyes that see tomorrow as wonderful and peaceful
Blessed be the Ears that listen tolerantly
Blessed be the Neck that supports the head
Blessed be the Mouth that speaks for the voiceless
Blessed be the smooth Tongue and not the sharp one
Blessed be the Hand that feeds the mouth
Blessed be the belly that serves as a reservoir...

Blessed be the Legs that anchor the human body
Blessed be the Feet that tread cautiously and wisely
Blessed be the Spirit that picks up the broken and the rotten ones from the dirt
Blessed be the Man that prays for the world and its peoples
Blessed are those who celebrate you before your death
Blessed are those who care and share
Blessed are the people who don't cast evil but spread love
And may His unfinished blessings continue to rain upon EVERYONE
Be blessed!

The Stressful Beast

We all have our moments and ways of dealing with stress—the beast that burps out like yeast.

Some people eat to kill stress. Others read to kill stress. While some people breed to kill stress. To some people dancing is the antidote to killing off stress; whereas some people use writing as a weapon to kill stress. Some people listen to music to kill stress. And others sing and hum to kill stress.

Some people do exercise to kill stress. Others pray and meditate to kill stress.

One beast with at least ten ways and means of killing it.

But in which way freedom must come—don't allow stress to hold you captive. You've got to find a way to kill the stressful beast.

***The secret of beauty is in the heart. And it unveils itself when it reaches the pinnacle. ***

The Horse & the Tortoise

Is the Race for the Swift?

"Bring it on..."
But guess who's throwing up the challenge and to whom?

He's sluggish tortoise, the guy whose pace raises eyebrows. But he seems unfazed and untroubled for what could be described as an uphill task ahead. He's accepted a race competition, not with his peers like the snail or the worm, ironically.

Question is: Why would anyone dare an opponent who by all standards is rated more powerful, faster, stronger and bigger than himself?

Statistically, an adult male Aldabra tortoise weighs approximately 550 pounds. His opponent weighs close to 1,200 pounds. In view of the disparity, the sponsors christened the event a 'mis-match '.

But the slow dude maintains: 'I've got it all together my friends. I've got my mind made up and I'm determinedly pumped up. I know the battle isn't mine, the battle is the Lord's."

The tortoise is running with the horse.

Did that tickle you…sounds funny isn't it?

Records show giant tortoises move very slowly on dry land at only 0.17 mph (0.27km/h). The fastest recorded tortoise speed is 5mph.

On the contrary, the horse can run at a speed of up to around 27-40mph which is about 43.5—64-4km/h. The fastest speed of a race horse had been recorded at 43.97mph which is about 70.76 km/ph.

It's a two-day race—contestants are supposed to start it from their respective homes and end it at the town's biggest social venue the Jackson's Park, where many have gathered. Horse has the biggest following singing his praises. And from the get go the tortoise is on the run at his own pace.

His opponent, however, goes to bed. 'I know tortoise, he's slow. If l even sleep the whole day/night I will still overtake him."

By midday the following day the horse gets up and starts to gallop, brimming with joy. But it's too late: Too much water has passed under the bridge. Tortoise has already touched the finish line, amid pomp.

Hours later horse emerges—hopping, jumping and galloping, thinking his opponent is slugging. The Frenchman will say: "Tout est fini." It's all over.

And the winner is slow Tortoise!

This story isn't peculiar to my two characters. It often plays up in real life situations. In life confidence is so important. When a person is confident he's showing that he has faith in his talent, abilities and personal strength. It doesn't matter how big, how strong and how tough the task is you've got to believe in yourself.

Tortoise had confidence he believed it and he did it. In contrast his opponent was complacent. Complacency is a feeling of smug satisfaction with oneself or one's achievements, often combined with a lack of awareness of imminent trouble and shame. The horse was full of that he underrated and belittled his opponent, oblivious of the looming humiliation.

Always remember, God doesn't make you run with the horse without giving you the horsepower. Also be reminded that with confidence you're halfway through with the battle in hand and victory is at the corner.

Bigotry Outburst

It takes a brave man or a few courageous men to call a stubborn king to order. And that is what happened yesterday. Some republican candidates took turns to condemn the party's current front-runner Donald Trump, following his assertion that Muslims must be banned from entering into the United States.

This isn't Mr. Trump's first bigotry outburst—attacking blacks, Hispanics, Muslims etc. However, the latest outrageous comments have prompted the establishment to weigh in. Former vice president, Dick Cheney has described Mr. Trump's call as un-American and "went against everything we believe in."

Could this be a precursor to Republican Party's defeat in 2016?

I posed this question to Professor Felix Odartey Wellington of Cape Breton University in Canada. The communications expert thinks that whatever the business tycoon says now would have its ramifications either negative or positive.

"Trump purports to represent what he claims has hitherto been a silent majority. Therefore, his victory or defeat in the primaries and subsequently, the general election in 2016 will help us find out what the true nature of US society is," he said.

Like many worried observers I have asked myself the question: What at all does Mr. Trump want? He claims he wants to make America great once again. But is this the way to go?

I think using some imagery would perhaps bring the church home. See, dry lands crave for water, while wetlands ask for more. Man's wants are insatiable. This is legendary and it will continue to live with us. We're like Oliver Twist authored (second novel) by Charles Dickens.

"'Oliver asked for more....'

There's nothing wrong with/about asking for more.

The scripture says: "To whom much is given much is required," Luke 12:48.

For example, if you tasted a certain drink and you liked it, there's nothing wrong to ask for more from the person who gifted you in the first place. But, there's a big BUT— the obsession or the love for it is what creates the/a problem.

Imageries such as lands, earth, gates and sheep are frequently used in the Holy Bible, particularly in the Old Testament. Their depictions are deep and thoughtful in man's life journey. They help guide us navigate our way through the labyrinth road.

"Make a joyful noise unto the Lord, all ye lands," or "Shout to Jehovah, all the earth," Psalm 100:1 (KJV).

The earth or land is symbolism of peoples across the world. We are different in many ways: Different in physiological make-ups i.e. different in colours, different in mannerisms and different in shapes. Our cultures are different. We speak differently, dress differently and eat differently.

We have different religions, different faiths, different ideologies and different all that.

In the midst of all this, mankind has learnt to cohabitate. Mingle with one another regardless the boundaries that divide us. From the

Adamic Age, Stone Age, to Agrarian Age to this day and Age people are still peopling. It's an endless cycle.

Can't stop it, no you simply cannot stop it.

There once lived a king in a powerful kingdom. His mantra was: "I don't listen to any one. I do what I do and say what I want to say." A brief translation in Twi—a local language in my native Ghana: "Mentie Obiaa.'

He exuded power and was wealthy and famous. Far and near he was loved. His neighbours accorded him with much respect and recognition, until he was carried away by ego and jettisoned into the deep sea. His glory soon faded!

Ego is like a Carmel on heat. She knows no stop until she feeds her sexual gratification.

What happened?

For years, king after kings had welcomed strangers into the great empire. And they assiduously helped built the great kingdom. However, he became ungrateful and very unruly, chastising the very people whose sweats and toils built the great kingdom.

How quickly he invited enemies into his kingdom without noticing. The once loved king had become a pariah, stubborn and hateful. Even his neighbours weren't spared with his ruthless verbal attacks and maltreatments.

Soon, they found new allies, new friends and new wealthy kingdoms. And the plot began— using the nearby nations to launch their onslaughts. His kingdom eventually collapsed after years of incessant wars.

Are some people asking for more than they can chew?

Looks like it. Mr. Trump's new call for banning Muslims from entering the United States is tactically imprudent, politically unwise and socially polarising.

There are always warning signs for humanity to look up to. But we either ignore them or think they aren't meant for us. When our consciences are guided by tolerance for one another we certainly build a formidable and a more prosperous kingdom (s), no doubt about that.

Kingdoms are built by peoples across the world. They may be called strangers, aliens, immigrants, foreigners and what have you. But they're still people. People yesterday are the people today and they will be the people tomorrow.

They breathe like you do and the warm blood that runs through you, same blood runs through them. They may have long noses and big heads, they may be dark-skinned and have long legs, they may wear hijabs and carry long beards, they may look short and wear rakusu around their necks, they may wear chogou or kasaya and they may be Christians, Muslims, Buddhists, Hindus but they're all God's peoples.

God loves you and He loves them too, perhaps more.

I can't wrap up my write-up without going to the wisdom bank to cash this cheque: A cheque God handed to the biblical Israelites: "You shall neither wrong a stranger nor oppress him, for you were strangers in the land of Egypt," Exodus 22:21 (KJV).

The comeback kid

Someone described him as a pain in the neck. In the circles of his haters he is seen as an imp always trying to pull off surprises and do the unthinkable. They believe his overt or covert actions if not checked could help torpedo the smooth-sailing boat on the high seas.

To a great number of people he's a maverick, controversial, opinionated and tough-talking character.

Hate him or love him. His name is Dr. Charles Wireko Brobbey the man I know very well. He's a friend and an uncle. Nicknamed Tarzan (an archetypal feral child raised in the jungle), a character I suspect he borrowed from Edgar Rice Burroughs fictional novel 'Tarzan of the Apes' first published in 1912.

Perhaps it's this nickname that has shaped his strange persona.

His tough-talking posture swayed him to the shores of Chorkor beach about a fortnight ago. He wrote an article. Yes he wrote....an article that sought to impugn his own party's vice presidential candidate for the 2012 election (regarding the party's petition at the Supreme Court). And the mob mobbed him!

And a bounty was set over his head: He was given a cheque marked 'Suspension,' which might mutate into dismissal (if found liable) sometime in the future should the leadership stick to their guns. He spoke his mind and he might've meant well but that didn't go down well with many of the NPP party faithfuls.

Like many, I cringed when I read the publication. And I knew then it wouldn't take long for him to be caught up by the raging Sun.... Be reminded always that as an African child you don't point your left finger to your father's home. That's uncustomary. It's discourteous and unwarranted.

Again, always remember that your freedom ends where probably my nose begins. Be as it may, we're a family and we must learn how to deal with family matters such that we don't overstep our boundaries or hurt one's feelings.

That said I must commend Chuck for the apology he rendered today to Dr. Bawumia. I think he's shown maturity and demonstrated strength. He's palpably shown the other side of him as someone not invincible or insidious.

"I am sorry that my attempt to indict the woefully inadequate briefings on the innards of the electoral process by those on your side who were counterparts of the NDC General Secretary on the IPAC – may have resulted in an unintended unfair portrayal of you."

Please be assured that I have not suddenly changed my mind about your competence and capabilities. I still have a very high regard of you."

Even though he says he still stands by his controversial write-up. I think his candid apology must be taken seriously without any recourse. I'm sure the recipient referring to Dr. Bawumia would welcome Chuck's apology wholeheartedly.

I commend you Sir, because not many people are used to the word sorry. For more than three times I heard you mention it.

But what's in the word SORRY that makes many feel allergic to?

S—stands for sincerity
O—stands for openness
R—stands for remorse
R—stands for renewal
Y—stands for yes

Yes I can attest you did it. Your whole demeanor expressed that. It was sincere, genuine and remorseful. And I'm hopeful it's now time for renewal. Certainly that's the way to go. Guilt and remorse can consume us if we don't offload them. Now go and sin no more.

I wish you good luck and good day!

Time to Bite

The sleeping dogs are no longer sleeping. With wide-eyed they've been let loose and pretty soon the brats would smell the rat. Trespassers would have themselves to blame as many cautions had gone unheeded lately.

As though to say enough with the nonsense, enough with the rough tactics and enough with the intemperate language the president of the panel hearing the ongoing presidential petition in Accra on Wednesday said the bench was more than ready to enforce sanctions on any person or group of persons deemed to have breached the ethics of the profession.

The warning came after lead counsel for the petitioners Philip Addison during his cross-examination with Dr. Afari-Gyan was said to have acted unethically. The room was tensed. There were a few murmurings and one could feel the temperature at its sears.

"Please listen to me when I am talking... you have to keep quiet," a judge at the bench yelled.

Sounding cool yet spewing fiery words Justice William Atuguba warned that the court would soon crack the whip. "We will walk you out, deal with you for contempt or refer you to the disciplinary committee."

I guess counsels on both sides didn't hear me last week, when I advised them to be circumspect in their pronouncements. I wasn't surprise though because two days after my admonition the bench also hammered home the same message. But little did they know that discipline had long gone pass the eastern window.

Casualty

Who would be the first casualty with the scalpel being brandished ferociously?

Well the Supreme Court (SC) of Ghana didn't mince words. For once it unveiled its crimson teeth, stressing that it wields the power and wouldn't hesitate this time around to unleash its hefty punch on any foul-mouthed person. Mr. Atuguba told the lawyers to watch out: "Your final time has been wiped clean..."

Spokespersons of the two legal teams say, they won't cry foul if any of their members fall victim. That remains to be seen though.

But I am personally happy to read that the 'honeymoon' is over. .And those who feel they can wear their egos, anger and pride to the court house better think twice, because the once toothless bulldog now has dragon teeth.

Examination Malpractice: An old Bug yet Poisonous

When school children deemed to be future leaders are taught how to cheat in final year exams and not to refrain from such malpractices then it begs the question. It begs the question when supposedly role models such as teachers prescribe dishonesty drug for students' consumption and supervisors tend to ensure its execution.

Ashaiman near Ghana's port city of Tema in the Greater Accra region has grabbed the headlines again, barely two weeks after the nasty street riot in that municipality.

Its latest case involves exam misconduct. Teachers, invigilators or examination supervisors are thought to have aided, abetted and colluded with school pupils in the 2013 Basic Education Certificate Examination (BECE).

By and large, this calls for immediate enquiry and appropriate action. The Ghana Education Service (GES) Ministry of Education (MOE), West Africa Examinations Council (WAEC), Council of Heads and Assisted Secondary Schools (CHASS), Parents /Guardians as well as other stake holders must all join hands to fight this old bug.

On another serious note, I think we've come too far to still walk this dangerous path, which has the potential to breeding not only semi-educated graduates (half-baked cakes) but also a new brigade of corrupt aristocrats— in the years to come.

What more do we need to know, if 'Kalabuleism' in Kutu Acheampong's era and the current Judgement Debt Saga aren't enough signs to inform us as a nation that we've a putrid wound on our face that need to be cured with a great sense of urgency.

Aren't we incubating square pegs which would certainly not fit in the round holes tomorrow? Indeed it suffices to say that we're digging our own mental graves, the cost of which could more than double the infamous 'Gargantuan' freebies.

Perhaps we're looking for another buzzword and I bet we would find it, if immediate steps aren't taken to cure such cancer.

But the question is: Where did integrity go? That some examination invigilators of the 2013 BECE at Ashaiman stooped too low to be bought by high school students for a paltry sum of GHC4 its equivalence (US$2, GB1.50).

The inducement fee was to put the cats to sleep so that the mice could have a field day. And they had it. In all three centres in that locale benefited from the unholy generosity.

"Our invigilators sometimes stood on the corridors and told us to help one another but warned us to do that carefully and tactfully," a student disclosed to an Accra-based newspaper 'The Finder'.

The students had assistance from the invigilators in the Mathematics, Basic Design and Technical Skills papers. Actually it is reported, the supervisors became so dishonourably charitable that they even prompted students to re-shade their papers for the correct answer(s), if they were done wrong initially.

Why not? Their power to sting had been bought by schoolchildren for next to nothing.

According to the students after each section they graciously offered some sort of 'perks' to the invigilators.

"After each paper some of us willingly buy them yoghurt and pastries to appreciate their kindness."

Frankly, I think Ashaiman has raised the exam notoriety bar to another level. For I have heard or probably witnessed students carry foreign materials ('Apor' in local parlance) to exam halls, heard about leakages and learned about students helping themselves during exams. But never read or heard that the mice could play with the cats.

Junior High School Students buying pastries for invigilators?

That is what bothers me!

It is understood the students were asked by their teachers to pay the monies so as to seek favour from the invigilators. But where did these children get the monies from?

Possibly from the parents— this smacks dishonesty and irresponsibility. And until we address this issue holistically our fight to uproot it would go nowhere.

Charity they say begins at home, teachers alone can't take the blame, neither the invigilators nor the supervisors. But the sheer connivance of what seems to be like a 'Triangular Trade' syndicate to initiate our young children into this gross behaviour is very shameful.

Over the years examination malpractices have been a major problem facing the West Africa Examination body. Early this year it had to cancel some papers of the Senior High School Certificate Exams due to leakages.

It is worthy also to note that WAEC's knack for excellence and integrity can't be questioned.

However, there seems to be no end in sight to this menace, even though the council had been administering punitive actions such as cancellation of papers, withholding of results and sometimes banning culprits from writing future exams.

It's like a wood worm. Across the borders of all the Anglophone countries in the West African Sub-region i.e. Sierra –Leone, Liberia, the

Gambia, Ghana and Nigeria examination malpractice has eaten deep into the morale fibres of the students.

Bayelsa state in neighbouring Nigeria last year (2012) was in the news for a bad reason. It was reported to have snatched the worst malpractices record in the country's exams history. Dovetailing her, were Sokoto, Ekiti, and Imo states.

In fact Bayelsa's index record stood at 44. 99 per cent, reports Exam Ethics Marshal International.

Tracing the old bug

Indeed examination misconducts have been of old. I certainly don't know where it originated from and when it started. But I assume it must have predated the days of civilisation or learning /education.

Today, the world over, this bug has proven to be an enigma. It began its marathon race from the Primary/Elementary Schools, Junior High and Senior Secondary Schools, Colleges to the Universities.

As already noted it has roped into its drag net principals, teachers, lecturers, invigilators, exam administrators, supervisors and even parents.

This doesn't bode well for a country whose educational system in the sub-region has over the years been hailed as a radiant example. It sends a very wrong signal, because the nation is knowingly or unknowingly rewarding undeserving graduates with certificates.

The danger is that probably in not too distant future students who burn the midnight candles would feel disinterested. And instead of sticking to achieving laurels on merits they would be looking for shortcuts. Better translation 'by hook and crook means'.

And once they get poisoned by the old bug the critical mass suffers. There are already bad nuts in the system—weeding them out has been a nightmare for the nation. This is why I suggest in addition, the 'Bazooka' Approach –Citizen Vigilante, also known as the Martin Amidu Crusading Style.

But again I should think we must learn a lesson from how the judgement debt saga came about. For what would iron do if gold is said to rust?

If the watchman who is supposed to watch the land lord is sleeping at the guard post, what would happen when the trigger-happy-idiot with the assault weapon raffle enters the house?

This is clarion call to all and sundry, so let's help halt the collusion galore.

Can't blame the youth.

You know what they say: a bad workman blames his tool. "This hammer is very bad. It's never been a useful device ever since I had it. "

Guess what?

The answer isn't far from your reach. As matter of fact, it's close to your nose. And [please], if it doesn't hit, it means it doesn't fit. Better still, don't get stuck with that bad hammer, fix it or dispose it: before it causes you your job and livelihood.

Period!

Since when did it become 'Haram' or forbidden for our brothers and sisters in the showbiz industry to comment or share their opinions on national issues—energy, unemployment, education, 'Trokosi' etc.? The idea of self-government is eloquently crafted in three words in the constitution: We the people.

Mind you, it didn't say we the politicians or we the government. The emphasis is on the proud citizens of Ghana. Therefore every citizen in Ghana, young or old, rich or poor, male or female, able or disable has the right to express his or her views without fear or favour.

Indeed, I find it preposterously untenable the argument by a section of Ghanaians who think that people in the showbiz industry have no right to comment on the current erratic power situation in the country dubbed 'Dumor'. I think it's all yoked in ignorance and narcissistic tendency.

It's pointless to blame the Ghanaian youth of today and for that matter the discerning actors and actresses who feel the government they voted into power has let them down. Or not delivering. You can't demonise them let alone issue threats to them, for merely expressing their inalienable rights.

Celebrities aren't chiefs. Ghana's constitution bars traditional rulers to engage in active politics. Yet, over the years we've seen politicians with their tails up run to them like a camel on heat——seeking for their support and blessing.

Democracy is government for the people, by the people and to the people, so my fellow Ghanaians let's continue to jaw-jaw. Let's debate the debate and let's allow everyone to exercise his/her right or freedom of expression. And last but not least, let the strainer separate the chaff from the grains.

Battle for the Flagstaff House

Thought of Basra or Fallujah in Iraq raises the eyebrows. How about Misrata in Gaddafi's Libya? Both cities had to be fiercely battled for to prove a point. In Iraq a dictator was ousted and later hanged like a dog. But in Libya a reformed son (though once a rogue) lost his soul.

I have lost count of the Supreme Court's (SC) sittings or proceedings in Ghana, concerning the 2012 presidential result petition. This is due in part to the drama, the anxiety and the sheer lack of proximity. Besides, my internet service has been interrupted and my wont to the public libraries lately hasn't been that keen. Nonetheless, my appetite for that landmark case still remains unsullied.

Slowly but sure the SC is discharging its constitutional duties with much gusto. However, a number of people have raised concerns about the ongoing case. They think there have been undue delays and reckless tackling on behalf of the Bench. Instead of focusing on the crucial matter before it they argue, the eminent panel is chasing flies in the forest.

I seem to share their viewpoint, though with a little reservation. I tend to believe that if the bench overlooks those 'noisy guys'— before long they might pollute the already edgy atmosphere and plunge the nation into the depths of misery. And we're not ready for that. So, let's allow the honourable men and women in wigs do their work honourably.

For sooner than later the blacksmith would satisfactorily come out with a sparkling diamond and the buyers would equally feel satisfied. That's what the whole nation is anticipating. That's what identifies us as Ghanaians and that's what makes us the first nation of Africa.

In fact from where we sit geographically on the world map (the confluence of the Equator and the Greenwich Meridian line) says a lot about us as a people of love and God's nation.

Unquestionably free speech allows a thriving democracy but unguided or misguided tongue is as deadly as a stray bullet. We must therefore be wary not to be seen as rushing the court— for an unduly rushed ship can crash prematurely.

And to those who have fallen on the Supreme Court's scalpel I take no delight in it. I wish them Godspeed in wherever they've found themselves today. Remember weeks ago, the court warned that it was combat ready to deal decisively with any foul-mouthed citizen who trespassed. And before long that web has trapped its first victims (flies). Let's see if the web can catch the big animals too...

The Battle for the Jubilee/Flagstaff House

Unlike Basra which the Brits military took by precision guided weapons or Misrata where Gadhafi's loyalists fought with their last blood roughly two years ago, in Nkrumah's Ghana we've resolved to let democracy work regardless. We've amply demonstrated that over the last two decades. Determinedly, we're marching forward with one triumphant weapon—the power of the ballot to occupy the Flagstaff House. And in anytime that there arises an electoral dispute such as the one that hangs over our heads presently we shall fall on the judiciary.

Without a doubt, I believe Ghana's apex court would live up to that expectation and together we will rejoice in the outcome.

And oh who told you that President Mahama has been sleeping well? Let no one throw dust into your eyes. Neither John the 4th (JD as he's affectionately called) nor Nana Akufo Addo the opposition candidate have had these times/days easy. Imagine spectators going nut at the stadia, feel their heart beats and you'll know what I'm talking about.

The scenario is much akin to the 2000 US presidential result counts. As George Herbert watched George Walker battled Al Gore for the US 43rd presidential slot to the White House, the senior Bush couldn't control his heightened anxiety– he nearly broke down.

Indeed, I can authoritatively state that both men are having sleepless nights. And if anyone has doubts about this, I challenge that fellow to get close or closer to these two public figures and watch closely their temple veins as they pause vigorously each day court sits. Of course watching an event of this magnitude from either inside or outside the courtroom and even across the frontiers of Ghana sometimes makes one's blood go cold.

Even me, who sits several thousand miles away often get sneezes from that unusual allergies. Their (Nana and John) temperatures have been rising amid uncertainties and uneasiness. They say uneasy lies the head that wears the crown. This presupposes that Mr. Mahama may be feeling the heat more. But he takes solace in the fact that, once he'd been a caretaker president and point number two— won an election that perhaps has produced a much protracted court dispute in Ghana's political history.

However, the mere thought of probably vacating that house sooner or later gives him insomnia as we hear some of his supporters say; the governing NDC party won't surrender power should it lose the historic case.

The situation isn't different from the other end. What does he lose one might ask? Well, his (Nana's) case is as equally daisy if not humongous. First look at it from this lens: Nana's long political ambition that seemed to have manifested in 2008 came crashing just inches at the 'Gate of Osu Castle then seat of government.

Unfortunately, he lost in a hair's breadth to a classmate and a fellow lawyer friend, late president Evans Atta Mills. He didn't coil himself in the proverbial 'once beaten twice shy…' instead he came back to fight a battle that could be likened to that of Fallujah onslaught because the stakes were high just much as they're today.

Even though 2016 doesn't look far off but in politics is like a thousand years!

Many factors would come to the fore. Prominent among them which is an internal issue is Age. It must be noted that this concern would rear its head if he overcomes it internally. Mr. Akufo Addo will be 72 not bad per any stretch of imagination considering the likes of Robert Mugabe in Zimbabwe. But politics being politics and its usual horseplay opponents would capitalise on it.

Already speculations are rife that the young aspirants in his Elephant party have started to sprout gingerly amid the usual jostle for power.

The Alan disease which perhaps is incurable would surely resurface. Next, will be the northern card. The petitioners' star witness Dr. Mahamudu Bawumia who partnered Nana in the 2012 general elections is seen as a young blood with energy and swagger.

Rivaling, the northern card is the Ashanti and Akim factor. I don't seem to get it at times. However, if the rank and file behaves like the proverbial ostrich and fail to hold the bull by the horn that issue can cause a deep crack in the party.

Externally, there will surely be the same John from the opposing party: A nightmare for Nana Akufo Addo and his party. The incumbency card would be flaunted and JD will masterly tout about his youthfulness to garner the women and the young votes...

Now you can see why those who sit close to the furnace feel the heat more than those who watch the game from the popular stands. All this go to buttress the assertion that the fight for Flagstaff House isn't as cool as cucumber as being bandied around.

It's really getting nervy!

Kudos Koku!

They that crucify, dread to be crucified. They fear crucifixion and pray it never happens to them.

Why them. Why not their adversaries?

Apparently, they'd do everything humanly possible to resist that ominous fate, if that's the way to go.

It's common for them to execute lies, educe fear, and resort to all kind of fallacies to make them look good, while they demonise their opponents. In politics this is often the trademark. The incumbent uses this tactic against the party in opposition. And those who peddle the lies are like a speeding bullet.

On Tuesday, the National Democratic Congress (NDC) deputy general secretary, Koku Anyidoho claimed that there are some forces within the comity of nations that are scheming against the Mahama-administration in its bid to win the 2016 presidential election.

That claim at best sounds outrageous and preposterous. It challenges conventional wisdom and has the propensity to embarrass the country as well as drag its image into disrepute.

But how quickly did Koku forget that what goes around comes around?

His claim, if true suggests that the very powers he accuses today helped the NDC to win the previous elections.

How quickly did he forget that when NDC was in opposition, it loathed continuity?

Indeed I remember one of its ranking members (in 1999) remarked that the NPP would remain in opposition forever.

"Where would they get money to govern the country if they win. The national kitty is empty," the party member added.

Pianoforte is an Italian oxymoron. Piano means soft or quiet and forte means loud.

Mr. Anyidoho was so loud on an Accra-based radio station—Adom FM, claiming that the international state and non-state actors would benefit more when the largest opposition party, New Patriotic Party (NPP) which is seen as a pro-market party comes to power.

If his inferences are anything to go by it presupposes that the NDC is an anti-market party, the reason why perhaps the multinationals are ending the love affair with the ruling party.

"We must beware that certain international community are using all forms of covert and overt means to ensure the government loses favour in the eyes of the Ghanaian electorate so they have the NPP in power," Mr. Anyidoho stated.

Here are a few questions to muse on: Do Ghanaian voters need international powers to tell them that the governing NDC sucks?

Did the NDC have these powers schemed in the party's favour while in opposition?

Aren't Ghanaians well aware that the ghost of 'Dumsor' is still lurking around?

Must they be told that corruption is now robbed in cassock— panhandling in the main streets of Accra the capital city?

Is continuity good or bad? I'm just asking.

Was the NDC interested in regime change when it found herself in opposition?

Certain international actors are against the Mahama-administration. Really?

Who are they?

Seriously I view the claim that international powers are influencing Ghanaian voters as an affront to the citizenry of the great country whose forebears shed their blood to defend and uphold the very tenets of self-rule and political independence.

However, let's not forget that these powers that be are like civil servants and are ready to work with any administration that has the political capital. More often than not the issue of influence or scheming arises when parties get bankrolled by these powers and multinationals.

But where does it stop?

Are political parties willing to stop chasing these powers for grants, aids and funds?

When Otabil Sneezes knees jerk....

"Is there no longer a prophet of the Lord here whom we can inquire of?" (1Kings 22: 7),

Jehoshaphat King of Judah posed this question to his brother who was the king of Israel. In response, the Israel king said: "There is still one prophet through whom we can inquire of the Lord, but I hate him because he never prophesies anything good about me, bad always bad. He is Micaiah the son of Imlah."

The rest of the story is biblical history. But its applicability is as useful for leaders of today and tomorrow as it was in the past. I think it's about time we as a people learned to accommodate and tolerate others' views if even we don't agree with them. It's needless to unleash verbal attacks on one self for merely presenting alternative or different opinions.

And it is also about time some folks in the governing NDC realised that the 'Otabil Pill' viewed by them as a bitter pill isn't dying of now or going away soon. Indeed, there will be more Otabils and more in the likes of the Isaiahs, the Micaiahs, and the Jeremiahs, who will not succumb to pressures from the powers that be but speak to the truth.

Founder and Overseer of International Central Gospel Church (ICGC) Dr. Mensa Otabil is in the news again nearly two years (November 2014) after he compared Ghana's economy to a 'sinking ship.' That comment drove Ghana's Minister of Communications Dr. Omane Boamah from his office to the studios of Joy FM an Accra-based radio station to otherwise make his case.

That comment didn't go down well with many members of the governing NDC.

And a few days ago Dr. Otabil delivered what I describe as sublime speech at a book launch in Ghana's capital city Accra. And as usual it did touch nerves.

BUT was it sleazy? No. Was it ambiguous? No.

Was it poisonous or slanderous? No, it had none of that.

It was a message perhaps pregnant with nuggets…So loud and clear. It was neither laced with ginger nor jalapeno. Or was it?

What I can say about it is that: It was newsworthy and catchy. So it didn't take long for the mainstream and social media, the tabloids and those in the blogosphere to latch onto it. And probably in less than 24 to 48 hours like a monstrous storm it had ambled its way deep into the corridors of the officialdom—The Jubilee House, resulting red-eyed, dropped jaws and wolf crying.

Yes they cried for help, while there were no wolves. Be reminded, when Otabil sneezes knees get jerked and many catch cold. The bold survive though.

Why? Because, it's refreshing to listen to him speak. Besides, it resonates well with the people and makes them keep their guards tight. However, the ripples like gun residues often create a marked discomfort for the officialdom. It makes them become paranoia, unreasonable, cynics and high-rated apologists for their masters.

So what at all was in that speech that's gotten some members of the ruling NDC to vent their anger and frustration on the noble preacher?

Did the speaker or the preacher step on supposedly big fatty toes or ruffled cocky feathers?

If it did, then I can guarantee them, they haven't seen the best or worst of his sneeze yet. They better brace themselves and face their nemesis because it's coming like a wild fire, unstoppable, unbreakable, and untamable.

How did it all start and to whom was this message or speech meant for?

It was tailored for the Ghanaian electorate who for years had been settling for half-baked breads. To the good people who get served with lies and empty promises every four years. Get wooed by politicians during election season and get swindled by them when all is over either victory or defeat.

They don't get value for the tax they pay. They don't get good roads, no proper sanitation, no basic amenities etc.

Great case had been stated. The import was crystal clear. But it would soon be twisted by the cynics.

They hold the view that the preacher preaches doom and gloom when the NDC is in power and pronounces prosperity and booming economy when it's NPPs turn. Indeed the critics believe that the pastor's speech is meant to cause voters dissatisfaction come 2016 general election.

Really?

Let's not kid ourselves. Ghanaians are well aware that many of the promises made by this administration had gone unfulfilled. Notably, building 200, 000 houses within five years through the STX Korea deal, bridging the poverty gap between the north and the south, reducing or taming armed robbery in the country, making all political appointees declare their assets within six months into the Mahama-led government and put money into the pockets of Ghanaians to mention but a few.

Surprisingly, some of the social intervention programmes introduced by the previous administration like the school feeding programme, the national health insurance scheme need immediate resuscitation or they'd die soon.

So they think Ghanaians have lost it huh? Ghanaians don't know they are hungry? Don't know that the economy has been zagging instead of zigging? Don't know that the cycle of distributing 'bentoa', rice and cooking oil, corned beef, roofing sheets to the people only happens before and during electioneering time?

And of course they've forgotten that the ghost of 'Dumsor hasn't been exorcised yet. Don't know that the ends can't meet. Don't know that people are dying at the hospitals for lack of good facilities and so on and so forth?

Whose story would these critics believe?

Their very own former president Jerry John Rawlings and the founder of the NDC has on a number of times criticised the party's abysmal performance since its assumption into power. They say if the crocodile comes out from the waters and says it is damn cold down there you need no more validation.

In fact that speech delivered at a book launch was harmless. BUT the cynics saw it differently. It amounts to subversion and has the propensity to cause unrest in the state, that's how a section of the critics described it.

Since then they've sharpened their mouths and tongues like the butcher's scalpel butchering the good stuff— going all out to smear, ridicule and even equate the preacher to a mutineer.

It was good stuff yet viewed as bad. Harmless it was, yet seen as harmful. And I think opponents of Dr. Otabil must reposition themselves. They can't see well from where they sit. VIP or VVIP stands aren't good to capture or see eye to eye with folks who present constructive criticisms.

There appears always to be a missing link that often breeds animosity and pettiness, mediocrity and underdevelopment. The yawning gap creates insecurity and insensitivity between the haves and the have nots. And when folks like Otabil speaks he's misconstrued and tagged as NPP surrogate or a doomsday prophet.

Would the critics have welcomed the speech if they were at the popular stand?

Or if they'd found themselves at the opposite end?

Let's be pragmatic folks. Let's not become mere stomach politicians. Let's think about Ghana, think about the future of our children. Let's think about their wellbeing for they deserve a better Ghana not a Ghana that would wake up tomorrow and resort to panhandling.

The Distress Call: Ghanaians must reject Coal Power

Is Ghana Ready to face the wrath of the lose canon?

The first priority of every government must be to defend its nation and protect the citizens. It's a precedent that no government should roll it like a dice or gamble with it. For what shall it profit a nation to gain zillions of fortunes and lose its people?

Ghana's number 1 energy producer Volta River Authority (VRA) plans to build a coal plant in the first quarter of 2017, according to ESI AFRICA, Africa's power journal. The report dated 17 May 2016, says the 700MW coal plant will be sited in the coastal town of Aboano in the central region of Ghana (about 60 kilometres from Accra.

Already the proposal has triggered concerns from various bodies such as Green Peace International, Ghana Youth Environmental Movement and discerning users of Ghana Tourism Chat Radio, a US-based online network.

May I ask: Has Ghana finished tapping into hydro power, fossil fuel-crude oil natural gas plus the other renewable energies such as solar, wind, thermal, biomass, etc.?

The country is building the biggest photovoltaic (PV) and the largest solar energy plant in Africa. The Nzema project is expected to provide electricity to more than 100,000 homes. The 155 megawatt plant shall increase Ghana's electricity generating capacity by 6%. The fourth largest solar power in the world is being developed by Blue Energy, a UK-based renewable energy investment company.

So why Coal Power?

Coal is said to be one of the world's most used energy resources. It accounts for about 40% of the world's electricity. Industry experts believe, it will soon replace oil and could become the major source of primary energy.

Without a doubt the mineral has placed itself at a pole position on the global energy stage due to its abundance, affordability and wide distribution across the world.

In spite of its marked success, the business has come under attacks because of the health hazards it poses to peoples and its strains on national economies. It's understood to be the driving force behind climate change and ecological destruction.

Many studies have given credence to the fact that coal mining or power is potentially dangerous to human health. One of such studies was conducted in 2008 by West Virginia University (WVU) in the United States. The University's Institute for Health Policy Research shows that people living in coal mining communities have a 70 per cent increased risk for developing kidney disease.

They also have 64 per cent increased risk for developing chronic obstructive pulmonary disease (COPD) such as emphysema. And are 30 per cent more likely to report high blood pressure (hypertension).

The same study concluded that mortality rates are higher in coal-mining communities than in other areas of the country or region and that there are 313 deaths in West Virginia from coal-mining pollution every year. The study accounted for restricted access to healthcare, higher than average smoking rates and lower than average income levels.

Green Peace International has added its voice to the call to halt the plan to build the plant in Ghana. It says: "Coal burning leads to acid rain and smog and emits more than 60 different hazardous air pollutants such as a variety of toxic metals, organic compounds, acid gases, Sulphur, nitrogen, carbon dioxide and particulate matter."

"Let's kick against this…It is outmode and belongs to the ancient of days," Mr. Kwame Boakye alias Tozia submitted this at Ghana TC Radio chatroom.

Does Ghana have what it takes to deal with the problem s coal industry generates?

China is the chief coal producer while the United States comes in second. Other major coal producers are India and Australia, Japan, Russia and South Africa. Five countries namely, China, the US, Russia, India and Japan accounted for over 75% of worldwide coal consumption.

Currently, all the above-mentioned nations are struggling to stop hazardous air pollutants in their respective countries. The worst casualty in this plight is China.

Elsewhere in the US, Democratic frontrunner Hillary Clinton during a CNN interview last Sunday didn't mince words as to how she plans "to put a lot of coal miners and coal companies out of business."

So if the big boys are struggling to overcome the environmental hazards posed by coal, what's the guarantee that Ghana and for that matter VRA can and will be able to do so. I think VRA's assertion that it has addressed issues regarding the environment and the climate must not be taken serious.

Ben Sackey the manager of environment and social impact at VRA said the authority will: "conduct reasonable overall planning for the plant area, arrange high-nose equipment far from the area which is sensitive to noise, and reduce noise level by green-belt planting—that is planting arbor and shrubs on roadsides around the main powerhouse and nearby other sound sources required."

To help stop this project from coming into fruition, the agency responsible for the environment –Environmental Protection Agency (EPA) must act in good faith and consider the future and the wellbeing of Ghanaians. It must live above reproach and try to prevent any attempt (s) by a group or group of persons to grease the palms of its officials.

The Ghana government must also stand up against this. After all, we haven't been able to accomplish all the projects streamlined to shore up the country's energy shortfalls.

In the meantime VRA is working 'closely' with EPA to ensure that all the stringent environmental requirements are met.

The agency came under attack during the last Accra floods with regard petrol stations that that had been sited (with permit from EPA) residential areas.

The first Ghana government-sponsored public electricity began in 1914 at Sekondi-Takoradi in the western region. It was operated by then Ghana Railway Administration (now Ghana Railway Corporation). Fourteen years later in 1928, power supply was extended to the twin harbour cities.

Over three decades on, the Ghana Electricity Division brought into operation the first 161,000 volts transmission system in Ghana which was used to carry power from Tema power station. At its peak in 1965 about 75% of the power was used in the nation's capital Accra.

And by 1994 Ghana's total generating capacity had increased to about 1, 187 megawatts plus an annual production which totaled approximately 4,490 million kilowatts and the main source of supply is VRA with six 127-megawatts turbines. I'm not sure if all its six turbines are still operable now.

The Evil That Men Do...

Evil was up in arms. It unleashed its powerful venom on innocent souls three days ago in Arabia and Europe. Nearly a week and half before, another disaster struck elsewhere in the Mediterranean.

And so, I took three days off (writing on my FBP) –three days of mourning with three nations—France, Lebanon and Russia, which came under the ruthless attacks from 'Enemies of Life'.

Three days of mulling over two palpable questions: - First, have the enemies out-paced and out-smart the world's reputable intelligent agencies?

Second, are we safe in our world today?

These two questions are ominous. And I'm pretty sure many out there share my concern and perhaps fear: The fear of not knowing what's going to happen in the next moment to one's life— whether one is shopping at a mall, watching movie in a theatre, sitting in a classroom, visiting a tavern or clubbing, having a romantic date in a cozy hotel, eating in a restaurant or taking a leisurely walk in a city's main street.

It seems paradox but that's the reality on the ground.

One moment comes with joy but the other brings doom and gloom. Uncertainty and anxiety are playing crucial roles in our lives today. *Who is doing what and when?* You never know...

A friend wrote on 'Choice Squad' platform courtesy of WhatsApp:

"Air travel has become an ordeal since 9/11! As if that's not enough...apart from the great inconvenience you go through at airports, you sit in a plane and thoughts begin to flash through your mind some 'evil 'character could be pointing an RPG up your xxxx for all u know. What a life!!!"

He wondered.

In my third book—'The Finish Line' I attempted to tinker with the age old question—what is life or what does it entail? In part I wrote:

"......My intention was not to focus on Aristotle's, Pluto's and the scientific community's universal definition but to coin or postulate my own definition.

I peered back into the yester years. Life was simplified; it was glorified and was personified.

In mythology, life was portrayed as war, a mirror, an egg, and a shadow etc.

Through drama, poetry and storytelling, I learned that life is like a chameleon that changes time and again. It's like a giant species that sets out on an endless journey. It is like a rainbow it shows up beautifully in the horizon, but soon it disappears.

And like a beautiful flower or a butterfly it fades away in a fleeting. It is depicted as a naked light in the stormy weather..."

Indeed, our life is tinged with fears. Consider the tears that flowed from the streets of St Petersburg Russia on the 31st of October to Beirut Lebanon and Paris France on November 13.

At least 41 people were killed in two suicide bombings in the Lebanese capital. Islamic State (IS) the militant group (based in Syria and Iraq) claimed responsibility for the attacks. IS or ISIS had hailed the Paris attacks and said it was responsible. 129 people were killed and over 350 injured.

In the Russian disaster, the metrojet plane (Airbus A321) crashed in Egypt's Sinai Peninsula. On board were tourists returning from holidays in the country's popular Sharm el-Sheikh resort. All 224 passengers didn't survive. Again, ISIS praised the loss of precious lives...

Unlike Al Qaeda, the modus operandi adopted by the Enemies of life, ISIS and other terrorist groups are subtle and deadly. They've been using soft target tactics (STT) to unleash their wicked plots and it appears they're winning.

The Belligerence

The display of eagerness by the enemies to fight, attack and cause mayhem is beyond comprehension. ISIS, Boko Haram, Al-Shabab, AQAP (Al-Qaeda in the Arabian Peninsula) etc. are all sworn enemies of peace and mercy. Their trademark is horror and they would go all out to unleash pain upon society.

It seems the enemies are waging a relentless war against peoples they regard as 'Infidels' (a person who does not believe or accept a particular faith. In Christian use an unbeliever. ISIS in particular has gained the notoriety of beheading westerners—the US, the UK and other nationalities such as Chinese.

What has made enemies of life fearsome, particularly ISIS?

In June 2014 Reuters reported that up to 15 per cent of French people said they have a positive attitude toward the Islamic State. It is believed the share of ISIS supporters is largest among France's younger generation, according to a poll conducted in 2014.

It says twice as many French people expressed a positive reaction to ISIS militants than in Britain, where the number of favourability of ISIS stands at 7 per cent; Germany had a mere 2 per cent of the respondents who supported ISIS.

The poll was carried out in July among 1,000 people aged over 15 years (over 18 in Britain in each country. It was conducted by ICM Research for the Russian news agency Rossiya Segodya.

US Intelligence officials believe over 150 American citizens and residents have travelled or attempted to travel to Syria as foreign fighters. This is what makes ISIS fearsome...the spate of radicalisation among disgruntled youth across developing and developed world coupled with home-grown terrorists or cells make the war against the enemies dicey.

Co-ordinated Attacks on ISIS

The US-led force including the Great Britain, Saudi Arabia and other Arabian nations are already fighting the enemies. Russia joined the fray last month and she's frantically finding ways and means to seek a peaceful exit of Syria's beleaguered president— Al -Assad. There've been renewed attacks from France following the three days attack on her citizenry.

Last week the US reported that in a drone strike it had killed one of ISIS most notorious guys, Mohammed Emwazi also known as Jihadi John, a British citizen.

But the end of Jihadi John doesn't mean ISIS has been decapitated. The world has many of his likes to fight. And the war must be multipronged, dedicated and focused.

Former president George W. Bush said it best. He called the enemies 'Axis of Evil". And the rest would be told....

The Measuring Rod—*who wields it?*

My blood turns cold anytime I hear or observe words flit around like a silly pigeon. It simply means I'm allergic to incendiary remarks or verbal attacks, abusive epithets and inflammatory statements .They give me palpitations and troubling feelings. And I try to quarantine myself or avoid watching them dart around.

Unfortunately I get to observe them at least ten times in every full moon on the mainstream and the social media (twitter, Facebook, WhatsApp, etc.) platforms. Attacks on leaders in high office (presidents, prime ministers), traditional rulers (queens and kings), the clergy and the elderly across the globe seem to be the new phenomenon.

It used to be bad but I think it's worse now.

Who is to blame?

I squarely attribute it to the new media, which have given reportage or information dissemination a splint in its tortuous walk. Literally, news goes viral by just a tap on the send key.

Here in the United States, the trend is gaining momentum. It gets tenser during political campaign seasons. Thank God! We aren't there yet. But a prominent figure and a former mayor of New York, Rudy Giuliani last Wednesday took a swipe at the president. His unkind words about President Barack Obama have caught fire and it's burning ferociously across the media landscape.

Speaking at a private fundraising ceremony for Republican Wisconsin Governor Scott Walker (2016 presidential hopeful) Mr. Giuliani remarked he doesn't believe that the president 'loves America'.

"Obama doesn't love you. And he doesn't love me. He wasn't brought up the way you were brought up and I was brought up through love of this country."

And as though that wasn't enough to bring the person (Mr. Obama) and the presidency into disrepute, two days afterwards, the former high-profile mayor who served the city of New York diligently especially in the wake of the 9/11 attacks on America, has been talking on other media platforms defending his scathing remarks.

The question is, does anybody wield the right to determine as to who loves America?

I mean, who wields the measuring rod: The rod to ascertain the 'un-love' citizen in this great nation: This nation of immigrants—from every corner of the planet Earth?

Suffice to say that opinions are like noses everyone has one. And Mr. Giuliani isn't exception. But be reminded that one's freedom ends where one's nose begins. So, if one pokes his nose into another's affairs it's deemed interference.

Indeed, Article 19 of the United States constitution guarantees that everyone has the right to freedom of opinion and expression. This right includes freedom to hold opinions without interference and to seek, receive and impart information and ideas through any media and regardless of frontiers."

Freedom of speech is also the political right to communicate one's opinions and ideas.

However these rights or freedoms aren't cast or chiseled on grindstone. Governments across the world restrict speech with varied limitations, which include libel, slander, obscenity, pornography, sedition, hate speech, incitement, fighting words, classified information and many more.

Articlde19 wasn't lazy, it additionally states that the exercise of these right carries "special duties and responsibilities" and may therefore be subject to certain restrictions" when necessary" for respect of the rights or reputation of others" or for the protection of national security or of public), order or of public health or morals".

So, let's respect our leaders. Let's be circumspect in our social and political discourse and let's not offend one another's sensibilities. The scripture says, by their fruits we shall know them. The Obama tree isn't a fig tree. Without a doubt its fruits are as visible as the Niagara Falls and his love for America is unquestionable (having been elected twice by the loving people of # *USA.*

Ferguson

Emotional judgment is symptomatic thread that seemingly runs through every human being. It feels like, it seems like, it sounds like and it tastes like, we often hear eyewitnesses echo these phraseologies in the event of any mishaps. It's often mired with spin, distortion and concoction. It breeds tension and creates commotion.

Howbeit, the length of a frog is determined only after its demise.

Ferguson has lost a son, a black teenage boy, slain by a white police officer—sparking racial tension and putting the predominantly black city on edge. Never before has citizens of this great nation (the United States of America) witnessed gun-toting police officers with all military accoutrements.

The cry of Ferguson has been heard all over the world. Renowned individuals across the globe had weighed in among them the UN Boss, Ban kil-Moon. In apropos, it's apt to say tension has spiraled and perhaps nerves are breaking. . A curfew is already in place, evidently to check looters and rioters.

I pray cool heads remain as independent inquiry team works painstakingly to unravel the truth. I'm also hopeful the clarion call by The Black Panther group that all protests be stalled should be upheld. My heart goes out to the parents of Michael Brown. And I pray also for the police officer involved, Darren Wilson to be steadfast in the Lord.

All said I know Ferguson will not forget her slain son!

A Child

When I was a child I talked like a child, thought like a child and acted like a child. I dwelt in the kingdom of naivety. I used to think that Nazareth, the hometown of our Lord was in heaven. And most biblical towns and names like Abraham, Moses, Mary, Martha all dwelt in heaven.

That was me. That was my thinking!

Kids today have a different view regarding this childish thinking. They know where Nazareth is located. They're using iPads, tablets, and computers to solve problems. They're inventing big stuff. A true testament of how far we've come in the midst of terrorism, wars, poverty, hunger etc.

Indeed we are who we are because of his divine power and amazing grace.

Grandma

Over two decades ago, Grandma, in her usual storytelling past time, shared this tale with me.

And I like to share it with you too.

Once upon a time, the eye told his siblings, "I have seen it all— the people, the buildings, the machines, the beautiful flowers, plants and trees, the mighty ocean and the wild life.

I have seen everything up in the heavens and anything at the bottom of the ocean. I see the beauty every day, so are the greats and the celebs. Nothing seems new to me anymore because I've seen them all.

"How did you get there," his brother leg asks.

Have you forgotten that all of us contributed to your self-acclaimed success story, and it wasn't solely you who made it happen?

Be reminded, in our world, the watchword is unity or collective responsibility: I need you, you need me and everybody needs somebody.

Humans

If we all as humans will be pleased with what we have: Be happy about who we are, how we look, what we do and can do, prosecute our God-given talents, and appreciate one another: I think the world would be a better place to live in. Consequently, there would be less of everything considered malice or vice. There would be less envy, less poverty, less hunger, less disease, less corruption and fewer wars.

WET EYES

When you see wet eyes don't rush to judge. Don't conclude and label them as 'weeping souls.' For sometimes we shed tears not because we're broke. But we do so because our hearts are broken. We don't cry for the love of it, or for crying sake. But we cry because our tears have crested and our eyes overwhelmed us. Sometimes we howl not because we're wolves. But we howl because we want someone to reach out to us. Not for money, not for bread, not for material stuff. But because we need love, we want to be comforted. Because we need a caring companion, we need hugs and soothing words: Words that heal a sullen soul and encourage Mankind.

I KNOW

I know one thing for sure:
When I'm poured out like water into the gutter you'll reach out for me...
I know one thing for sure:
You're the ubiquitous, smart post-master
that delivers the right package at the right time. ..
I know one thing for sure:
Your grace, favour and mercies are unfailing and undone. ...
I know one thing for sure:
You're the chief chef or the vivacious barrister at the espresso, you'll feed me when I'm hungry, shelter me when I'm homeless and put clothes on my back when I'm naked. ..
I know one thing for sure
You're the chief surgeon at the Good Samaritan hospital, mending the broken hearts, sewing the broken bones and delivering the newly born babies..
I know one thing for sure:
You're the unbiased judge at the supreme court with no jaundiced eye, giving fair judgment.
I know one thing for sure:
You're pure, powerful, wonderful and awesome God.
I know one thing for sure:
You're God of the patriarch— God of Abraham, God of Isaac and God of Jacob.
I know one thing for sure:
That you're Alpha and Omega, the first and the last, Jehovah Nissi.

The River

Who can remove the River's bed beneath her?

You either mess it up or regret you dared: For she's laid it firmly straight up from the mountain and down below the mighty Ocean. She navigates her way through the rugged terrain. Unbelievably her size shrinks along the way but she never stops plodding along.

And as the terrain determines how fast, how wide and how slow the river goes. So does man's life trajectory. Keep moving on don't stop for you never know what lies ahead.

Knock knock

Just landed from the wings of the morning and I was blessed to have Grace served me a great breakfast. I suppose you'd one too.

How was your breakfast brother/sister?
What was it?
Did you have enough to eat?
And if you're yet to, what are you going to have?

Well, just to whip your appetite: Grace is a generous woman. She's so kind, so genteel and so caring. She makes sure every morning I get the right meal at the right time. And she comes running whenever I call upon her.

On the big bowl today were'–love, mercy, comfort, favour, joy, happiness and goodness. The side plate had compassion, peace, longevity prosperity, security and obedience. Above all, Grace has put by salvation, deliverance and protection at the bank for me. And she says I can withdraw them anytime of my choosing. Let your breakfast be rich and sumptuous, courtesy of Grace.

Comfort Zone

Are you in your comfort zone and prefer to remain there?

Life race we're told isn't for the swift. It's laced with mystery. When we start it and when we end it, where we start it and where we end it, how we start it and how we end it, why we start it and why we end it, how we start it and how we end it and finally what we do with it— all these are basically what define us...

Rising Sun

What did you see this morning when the rooster crowed: The rising Sun or the stormy weather?

What did you hear from across the street near your neighbourhood: The ringing guns or the singing nuns (Angels)?

What did you say when you stood on your commanding legs and yawned wider than the barge in your garage: Thank you Lord or no thanks. I can't be bothered?

What did think about yourself seeing another glorious day: A blessed one or cursed one?

Remember you're fearfully and wonderfully made, carefully woven with the Adamic thread.

There's something inside you that's so strong.

You're too special to let go your avid dreams. Too unique to think you're oblique. Indeed, you're the Rising Sun.

It's never too late to put on your confidence jacket.

Do you market yourself as a hero/victor or a wimp?

Think positive and be gratitude each day of your life.

Heroes

Heroes aren't bootlickers.
They aren't eyes-servers.
They don't pay lip service.
Heroes are fighters. They fight till the end of the battle.
They aren't quitters. Heroes don't quit, they don't run away. They don't give up they live up to see the fruits of their toils.
Heroes prevail in all their travail.
They rise in the midst of crisis.
They see failure as success....

They taste it as though it were a scone or meat pie. They feel it as if it were a soft blanket.
Heroes don't shelve their talents.
They share them.
Their counterparts (wimps) behave like weasels always displaying opportunistic streaks; Always scheming to do evil to people.
Be a hero.

Wise sayings

— The things that humans do often shock humans and beat humanity's understanding: The horror and the terror, the carnage and the mayhem, the butchery and the barbarity–clearly defy human norm and logic. Suffice to say, people with evil minds nurture evil, plant evil and they harvest evil. France, the world mourns with you and we stand by you.'

— The shoes of justice can be unpredictable. Nice and cool for the super-rich, because they control the system. It's tepid for the average rich because they can bribe their way through.
  But it's extremely hot for the piss- poor, because they've no options except to be goaded by the powers that be.

— Mountains Are Giants, yet they don't move.

— Labourers Labour for nothing …if their masters are cheaters.

— The morning smile is like the rising sun.

— Trouble waters find way to calm their nerves.

— 'Sometimes a ceasefire is as hot as coal-fire.

— Whenever you're down imagine, yourself as a football player at the bench who yearns time after time to come into the game. Players at the bench always crave to come back determinedly to justify their inclusion but above all stay in the game forever. Therefore, I implore you to stay the course and press pass the stress.

— You're just like the river that takes its source from the mountain—small from the beginning, but its ending is often big or wide. Be reminded that all the greatest men and women you know of today and even before were once unknown. '

— God's mercies, blessings and grace are like a pouring rain. Whenever it falls, every rooftop gets its share of it.

— Sometimes your portion of the meat is immaterial. It could be the side with the bile or just a bone with a morsel sitting on it. That bile may not kill you but heal you from some ailment or sickness you've been battling with for ages.

— Do what you're capable of doing. Never count yourself out of the equation, for you're more than that. Place yourself at the mid-point—that is where you belong.

— Crows are intelligent and beautiful, yet they're caricatured.

— When we kick start today, we can reach somewhere tomorrow. Then our children will continue from there to the next level possible.

— Good and evil are like stockbrokers and their products come not without strings.

— God's mercy endures forever and his goodness and kindness even follow the unbeliever.

— 'Don't yell at Satan, if you don't have fire in your belly'.

— 'Tears are shed not for fear but as panacea for relief and healing of the body and soul.'

— 'An unstable mind is like a frozen computer, haunted by an intrepid virus. It slows down its tempo, it kills its potency and it floods its quadrangular screen with pop-up ads....'

— 'It's all about love. You're loved for exactly who you are and everything around you is loved as well. Mankind is absolutely loved by the Divine Creator who makes no mistakes and creates beautifully.'

— Can a Man draw a scalpel to cut his own ear and eat it?

— Trees walk in the night, when Man goes to sleep.

— The secret of beauty is in the heart. And it unveils itself when it reaches the pinnacle.

— Good message is like good medicine. It's like good food. And it does good things to the body.'

— Happiness is in your mind. Joy dwells in your heart. And your eyes find friends on the peripheral.

— The mouse rules the house when the cat is on a sabbatical leave. Stay alert and be blessed.

— God's creation is beyond magnificent. It's perfect and serene, lovely and joyful, peaceful and purposeful. And with unbending Hope and Faith we are more than Conquerors.

— When you live don't forget to leave your footprints for tomorrow to take stock.

— Teeth are like lions, they like red meat but they've always spared their closest neighbour (the tongue) which lives in the same den with them.

— Road rage isn't caused by the road itself. It's caused by the people who used the road and they do so for lack of understanding.

— People are people and will remain as such. They talk, they gossip, they whine and they gripe.

— Violence pursues peace ruthlessly and not until peace finds refuge in the Lord's bosom humanity's crave for peace will become an illusion.

— The fangs of a snake may be short but they're deadly.

CPSIA information can be obtained
at www.ICGtesting.com
Printed in the USA
LVHW03s0827180718
584008LV00007B/32/P